THE COLLECTED STORIES OF

PHILIP K. DICK

VOLUME TWO

THE COLLECTED STORIES OF PHILIP K. DICK VOLUME TWO

First published in Great Britain in 2023 by Gollancz
an imprint of The Orion Publishing Group Ltd
Carmelite House, 50 Victoria Embankment
London EC4Y 0DZ

An Hachette UK Company

The authorised representative in the EEA is Hachette Ireland,
8 Castlecourt Centre, Dublin 15, D15 XTP3, Ireland (email: info@hbgi.ie)

3 5 7 9 10 8 6 4

A CIP catalogue record for this book is available from the British Library.

ISBN (Mass Market Paperback) 978 1 39961 125 1
ISBN (eBook) 978 1 39961 126 8

Printed in Great Britain by Clays Ltd, Elcograf, S.p.A.

www.gollancz.co.uk

CONTENTS

THE COMPLETE SHORT STORIES

VOLUME 2

THE COLLECTED STORIES OF

PHILIP K. DICK

VOLUME TWO

THE COSMIC POACHERS

'What kind of ship is it?' Captain Shure demanded, staring fixedly at the viewscreen, his hands gripping the fine adjustment.

Navigator Nelson peered over his shoulder. 'Wait a minute.' He swung the control camera over and snapped a photograph from the screen. The photograph disappeared down the message tube to the chart room. 'Keep calm. We'll get a determination from Barnes.'

'What are they doing here? What are they after? They must know the Sirius system is closed.'

'Notice the balloon sides.' Nelson traced the screen with his finger. 'It's a freighter. Look at the bulge. It's a cargo carrier.'

'And while you're looking, notice *that*.' Shure whirled the enlarger. The image of the ship bloated, expanding until it filled the screen. 'See that row of projections?'

'So?'

'Heavy guns. Countersunk. For deep-space firing. It's a freighter, but it's also armed.'

'Pirates, maybe.'

'Maybe.' Shure toyed with the communications mike. 'I'm tempted to put a call back to Terra.'

'Why?'

'This may be a scout.'

Nelson's eyes flickered. 'You think they're in the process of sounding us out? But if there are more, why don't our screens pick them up?'

'The rest may be out of range.'

'More than two light years? I have the screens up to maximum. And they're the best screens available.'

The determination popped up the tube from the chart room, skidding out on the table. Shure broke it open and scanned it rapidly. He passed it to Nelson. 'Here.'

The ship was Adharan design. First-class, from a recent freighter group. Barnes had noted in his own hand: 'But not supposed to be armed. Must have added the cannon. Not standard equipment on Adharan freighters.'

'Then it's not bait,' Shure murmured. 'We can rule that out. What's the story on Adhara? Why would an Adharan ship be in the Sirius system? Terra has closed this whole region off for years. They must know they can't trade here.'

'No one knows much about Adharans. They participated in the All-galaxy Trade Conference, but that's all.'

'What race are they?'

'Arachnid type. Typical of this area. Based on the Great Murzim Stem. They're a variant of the Murzim original. They keep mostly to themselves. Complex social structure, very rigid patterns. Organic-state grouping.'

'You mean they're insects.'

'I suppose. In the same sense we're lemurs.'

Shure turned his attention back to the viewscreen. He reduced magnification, watching intently. The screen followed the Adharan ship automatically, maintaining a direct alignment with it.

The Adharan ship was heavy and black, awkward in comparison to the sleek Terran cruiser. It bulged like a well-fed worm, its somber sides swollen almost to a full sphere. An occasional guide light blinked on and off as the ship approached the outermost planet of the Sirius system. It moved slowly, cautiously, feeling its way along. It entered the orbit of the tenth planet and began maneuvering for descent. Brake jets burst on, flashing red. The bloated worm drifted down, lowering itself toward the surface of the planet.

'They're landing,' Nelson murmured.

'That's fine. They'll be stationary. Good target for us.'

On the surface of the tenth planet the Adharan freighter lay resting, its jets dying into silence. A cloud of exhaust particles rose from it. The freighter had landed between two mountain ranges, on a barren waste of gray sand. The surface of the tenth planet was utterly barren. No life, atmosphere or water existed. The planet was mostly rock, cold gray rock, with vast shadows and pits, a corroded sickly surface, hostile and bleak.

Abruptly the Adharan ship came to life. Hatches popped open. Tiny black dots rushed from the ship. The dots increased in number, a flood of specks pouring out of the freighter, scurrying across the sand. Some of them reached the mountains and disappeared among the craters and peaks. Others gained the far side, where they were lost in the long shadows.

'I'll be damned,' Shure muttered. 'It doesn't make sense. What are they after? We've gone over these planets with a fine tooth comb. There's nothing anyone would want, down there.'

'They may have different wants, or different methods.'

Shure stiffened. 'Look. Their cars are coming back to the ship.'

The black dots had reappeared, emerging from the shadows and craters. They hurried back toward the mother worm, racing across the sand. The hatches opened. One by one the cars popped into the ship and disappeared. A few belated cars made their way to the ship and entered. The hatches clamped shut.

'What in hell could they have found?' Shure said.

Communications Officer Barnes entered the control room, craning his neck. 'Still down there? Let me have a look. I've never seen an Adharan ship.'

On the surface of the planet the Adharan ship stirred. Suddenly it shuddered, quivering from stem to stern. It rose from the surface, gaining altitude rapidly. It headed for the ninth planet. For a time it circled the ninth planet, observing the pitted, eroded surface below. Empty basins of dried-up oceans stretched out like immense pie pans.

The Adharan ship selected one of the basins and settled down to a landing, blowing clouds of exhaust up into the sky.

'The same damn thing again,' Shure murmured.

Hatches opened. Black specks leaped out onto the surface and rushed off in all directions.

Shure's jaw jutted out angrily. 'We have to find out what they're after. Look at them go! They know exactly what they're doing.' He grabbed up the communications mike. Then he dropped it. 'We can handle this alone. We won't need Terra.'

'It's armed, don't forget.'

'We'll catch it as it lands. They're stopping at each planet in order. We'll go all the way in to the fourth planet.' Shure moved rapidly, bringing the command chart into position. 'When they land on the fourth planet we'll be there waiting for them.'

'They may put up a fight.'

'Maybe. But we have to find out what they're loading–and whatever it is, it belongs to us.'

The fourth planet of the Sirius system had an atmosphere, and some water. Shure landed his cruiser in the ruins of an ancient city, long deserted.

The Adharan freighter had not appeared. Shure scanned the sky and then raised the main hatch. He and Barnes and Nelson stepped outside cautiously, armed with heavy-duty Slem rifles. Behind them the hatch slammed back in place and the cruiser took off, soaring up into the sky.

They watched it go, standing together with their rifles ready. The air was cold and thin. They could feel it blowing around their pressure suits.

Barnes turned up the temperature of his suit. 'Too cold for me.'

'Makes you realize we're still Terrans, even though we're light years from home,' Nelson said.

'Here's the outline,' Shure said. 'We can't blast them. That's out. We're after their cargo. If we blast them we'll blast the cargo along with them.'

‘What’ll we use?’

‘We’ll shoot a vapor cloud around them.’

‘A vapor cloud? But–’

‘Captain,’ Nelson said, ‘we can’t use a vapor cloud. We won’t be able to get near them until the vapor has become inert.’

‘There’s a wind. The vapor will dissipate very quickly. Anyhow, it’s all we can do. We’ll have to take the chance. As soon as the Adharan is sighted, we must be ready to open fire.’

‘What if the cloud misses?’

‘Then we’re in for a fight.’ Shure studied the sky intently. ‘I think it’s coming. Let’s go.’

They hurried to a hill of piled-up rocks, remains of columns and towers heaped in great mounds, mixed with debris and rubble.

‘This will do.’ Shure crouched down, his Slem rifle held tightly. ‘Here they come.’

The Adharan ship had appeared above them. It was preparing to land. Down it settled, its jets roaring, exhaust particles rising. With a crash it struck the ground, bouncing a little and finally coming to rest.

Shure gripped his phone. ‘Okay.’

Above them in the sky the cruiser appeared, sweeping down over the Adharan. From the cruiser a blue-white cloud shot, drilled out by pressure jets directly at the black Adharan ship. The cloud reached the parked freighter. It billowed around it, fusing into it.

The surface of the Adharan hull glowed briefly. It began to fall in, eaten away. Corroded. The Terran cruiser swept past, completing its run. It disappeared into the sky.

From the Adharan ship figures were emerging, jumping out onto the ground. The figures sprang in all directions, long-legged, leaping wildly around. Most of the figures hopped excitedly up onto their ship, dragging hoses and equipment, working frantically, disappearing into the vapor cloud.

‘They’re spraying.’

More Adharans appeared, leaping frantically up and down, onto their ship, onto the ground, some this way, others in no particular direction at all.

'Like when you step on an ant hill,' Barnes murmured.

The hull of the Adharan ship was covered with clinging Adharans, spraying desperately, trying to halt the corrosive action of the vapor. Above them the Terran cruiser reappeared, entering a second run. It grew, swelling from a dot into a tear-shaped needle, flashing in the sunlight from Sirius. The freighter's bank of guns jutted up desperately, trying to align themselves with the swiftly moving cruiser.

'Bomb close by,' Shure ordered into his phone. 'But no direct hits. I want to save the cargo.'

The cruiser's bomb racks opened. Two bombs fell, singing down in an expert arc. They straddled the inert freighter, bursting on both sides. Towering clouds of rock and debris rose up, billowing over the freighter. The black form shuddered, Adharans sliding off the hull onto the ground. The bank of guns fired a few futile blasts and the cruiser swept past and disappeared.

'They haven't got a chance,' Nelson murmured. 'They can't leave the ground until they've got their hull sprayed.'

Most of the Adharans were beginning to flee from their ship, scattering onto the ground.

'It's almost over,' Shure said. He got to his feet and stepped out from the ruins. 'Let's go.'

A white flare burst up from the Adharans showering sparks in the sky. The Adharans milled aimlessly around, confused by the attack. The cloud of vapor had virtually dissipated. The flare was the conventional signal of capitulation. The cruiser was circling again, above the freighter, waiting for orders from Shure.

'Look at them,' Barnes said. 'Insects, big as people.'

'Come on!' Shure said impatiently. 'Let's go. I'm anxious to see what's inside.'

The Adharan commander met them outside its ship. It moved toward them, apparently dazed from the attack.

Nelson and Shure and Barnes gazed at it in revulsion. 'Lord,' Barnes muttered. 'So that's what they're like.'

The Adharan stood almost five feet tall, enclosed in a black chitin shell. It stood on four slender legs, two more weaving uncertainly half-way up its body. It wore a loose belt, holding its gun and equipment. Its eyes were complex, multi-lensed. Its mouth was a narrow slit at the base of its elongated skull. It had no ears.

Behind the Adharan commander a group of crew members stood uncertainly, some of them with weapon tubes partly raised. The Adharan commander made a series of sharp clicks with its mouth, waving its antennae. The other Adharans lowered their tubes.

'How is communication with this race possible?' Barnes asked Nelson.

Shure moved forward. 'It doesn't matter. We have nothing to say to them. They know they are illegally here. It's the cargo we're interested in.'

He pushed past the Adharan commander. The group of Adharans made way for him. He entered the ship, Nelson and Barnes following after him.

The interior of the Adharan ship reeked and dripped with slime. The passages were narrow and dark, like long tunnels. The floor was slippery underfoot. A few crew members scuttled around in the darkness, their claws and antennae waving nervously. Shure flashed his light down one of the corridors.

'This way. It looks like the main passage.'

The Adharan commander followed close behind them. Shure ignored him. Outside, the cruiser had landed nearby. Nelson could see Terran soldiers standing around on the surface.

Ahead of them a metal door closed off the corridor. Shure indicated the door, making an opening motion.

'Open it.'

The Adharan commander retreated, making no move to open the door. A few more Adharans scuttled up, all of them with weapon tubes.

'They may fight yet,' Nelson said calmly.

Shure raised his Slem rifle at the door. 'I'll have to blast it.'

The Adharans clicked excitedly. None of them approached the door.

'All right,' Shure said grimly. He fired. The door dissolved, smoking into ruins. It sank down, leaving an opening wide enough to pass through. The Adharans rushed around wildly, clicking to each other. More of them left the hull and poured into the ship, flocking around the three Terrans.

'Come on,' Shure said, stepping through the gaping hole. Nelson and Barnes followed him, Slem rifles ready.

The passage led down. The air was heavy and thick, and as they walked down the passage, Adharans pressed behind them.

'Get back.' Shure spun, his rifle up. The Adharans halted. 'Stay back. Come on. Let's go.'

The Terrans turned a corner. They were in the hold. Shure advanced cautiously, moving with care. Several Adharan guards stood with drawn weapon tubes.

'Get out of the way.' Shure waved his Slem rifle. Reluctantly, the guards moved aside. 'Come on!'

The guards separated. Shure advanced.

And stopped, amazed.

Before them was the cargo of the ship. The hold was half-filled with carefully stacked orbs of milky fire, giant jewels like immense pearls. Thousands of them. As far back as they could see. Disappearing back into the recesses of the ship, endless stacks of them. All glowing with a soft radiance, an inner illumination that lit up the vast hold of the ship.

'Incredible!' Shure muttered.

'No wonder they were willing to slip in here without permission.' Barnes took a deep breath, his eyes wide. 'I think I'd do the same. Look at them!'

'Big, aren't they?' Nelson said.

They glanced at each other.

'I've never seen anything like it,' Shure said, dazed. The Adharan guards were watching them warily, their weapon tubes ready. Shure advanced toward the first row of jewels, stacked neatly with mathematical precision. 'It doesn't seem possible. Jewels piled up like–like a warehouse full of doorknobs.'

'They may have belonged to the Adharans at one time,' Nelson said thoughtfully. 'Maybe they were stolen by the city-builders of the Sirius system. Now they're getting them back.'

'Interesting,' Barnes said. 'Might explain why the Adharans found them so easily. Perhaps charts or maps existed.'

Shure grunted. 'In any case they're *ours*, now. Everything in the Sirius system belongs to Terra. It's all been signed, sealed and agreed on.'

'But if these were originally stolen from the Adharans–'

'They shouldn't have agreed to the closed-system treaties. They have their own systems. This belongs to Terra.' Shure reached up toward one of the jewels. 'I wonder how it feels.'

'Careful, Captain. It may be radioactive.'

Shure touched one of the jewels.

The Adharans grabbed him, throwing him back. Shure struggled. An Adharan caught hold of his Slem rifle and twisted it out of his hands.

Barnes fired. A group of Adharans puffed out of existence. Nelson was down on one knee, firing at the passage entrance. The passage was choked with Adharans. Some were firing back. Thin heat beams cut over Nelson's head.

'They can't get us,' Barnes gasped. 'They're afraid to fire. Because of the jewels.'

The Adharans were retreating into the passage, away from the hold. Those with weapons were being ordered back by the commander.

Shure snatched Nelson's rifle and blasted a knot of Adharans into particles. The Adharans were closing the passage. They rolled heavy emergency plates into position and welded them rapidly into place.

'Burn a hole,' Shure barked. He turned his gun on the wall of the ship. 'They're trying to seal us in here.'

Barnes turned his gun on the wall. The two Slem beams ate into the side of the ship. Abruptly the wall gave way, a circular hole falling out.

Outside the ship Terran soldiers were fighting with the Adharans. The Adharans were retreating, making their way back as best they could, firing and hopping. Some of them hopped up onto their ship. Others turned and fled, throwing their guns down. They milled about in helpless confusion, running and leaping in all directions, clicking wildly.

The parked cruiser glowed into life, its heavy guns lowering into position.

'Don't fire,' Shure ordered through his phone. 'Leave their ship alone. It isn't necessary.'

'They're finished,' Nelson gasped, jumping onto the ground. Shure and Barnes leaped after him, out of the Adharan ship onto the surface. 'They don't have a chance. They don't know how to fight.'

Shure waved a group of Terran soldiers over to him. 'Over here! Hurry up, damn it.'

Milky jewels were spilling out of the ship onto the ground, rolling and bouncing through the hole. Part of the containing struts had been blasted away. Stacks of jewels cascaded down and rolled around their feet, getting in their way.

Barnes scooped one up. It burned his gloved hand faintly, tingling his fingers. He held it to the light. The globe was opaque. Vague shapes swam in the milky fire, drifting back and forth. The globe pulsed and glowed, as if it were alive.

Nelson grinned at him. 'Really something, isn't it?'

'Lovely.' Barnes picked up another. On the hull of the ship an Adharan fired down at him futilely. 'Look at them all. There must be thousands of them.'

'We'll get one of our merchant ships here and have them loaded up,' Shure said. 'I won't feel safe until they're on their way back to Terra.'

Most of the fighting had ceased. The remaining Adharans were being rounded up by the Terran soldiers.

'What about them?' Nelson said.

Shure didn't answer. He was examining one of the jewels, turning it over and over. 'Look at it,' he murmured. 'Brings out different colors each way you hold it. Did you ever see anything like it?'

The big Terran freighter bumped to a landing. Its loading hatches dropped down. Jitney cars rumbled out, a fleet of stubby trucks. The jitney cars crossed to the Adharan ship. Ramps dropped into place, as robot scoops prepared to go to work.

'Shovel them up,' Silvanus Fry rambled, crossing over to Captain Shure. The Manager of Terran Enterprises wiped his forehead with a red handkerchief. 'Astonishing haul, Captain. Quite a find.' He put out his moist palm and they shook.

'I can't understand how we could have missed them,' Shure said. 'The Adharans walked in and picked them up. We watched them going from one planet to the next, like some sort of honey bee. I don't know why our own teams didn't find them.'

Fry shrugged. 'What does it matter?' He examined one of the jewels, tossing it up in the air and catching it. 'I imagine every woman on Terra will have one of these around her neck–or will want one of these around her neck. In six months they won't know how they ever lived without them. That's the way people are, Captain.' He put the globe into his briefcase, snapping it shut. 'I think I'll take one home to my own wife.'

The Adharan commander was brought over by a Terran soldier. He was silent, clicking nothing. The surviving Adharans had been stripped of their weapons and allowed to resume work on their ship. They had got the hull patched and most of the corrosion repaired.

'We're letting you go,' Shure said to the Adharan commander. 'We could try you as pirates and shoot you, but there wouldn't be much point in it. Better tell your government to stay out of the Sirius system from now on.'

'He can't understand you,' Barnes said mildly.

'I know. This is a formality. He gets the general idea, though.'

The Adharan commander stood silently, waiting.

'That's all.' Shure waved impatiently toward the Adharan ship. 'Go on. Take off. Clear out of here. And don't come back.'

The soldier released the Adharan. The Adharan made his way slowly back to his ship. He disappeared through the hatch. The Adharans working on the hull of the ship gathered up their equipment and followed their commander inside.

The hatches closed. The Adharan ship shuddered, as its jets roared into life. Awkwardly it lifted from the surface, rising up into the sky. It turned, heading toward outer space.

Shure watched it until it was gone.

'That's that.' He and Fry walked rapidly toward the cruiser. 'You think these jewels will attract some attention on Terra?'

'Of course. Is there any doubt?'

'No.' Shure was deep in thought. 'They got to only five of the ten planets. There should be more on the remaining inner planets. After this load gets back to Terra we can begin work on the inner planets. If the Adharans found them we should be able to.'

Fry's eyes glittered behind his glasses. 'Fine. I didn't realize there would be more.'

'There are.' Shure frowned, rubbing his jaw. 'At least, there ought to be.'

'What's wrong?'

'I can't understand why we never found them.'

Fry clapped him on the back. 'Don't worry!'

Shure nodded, still deep in thought. 'But I can't understand why we never found them ourselves. Do you think it means anything?'

The Adharan commander sat at his control screen, adjusting his communication circuits.

The Check Base on the second planet of the Adharan system came into focus. The commander raised the sound cone to his neck.

'Bad luck.'

'What occurred?'

'Terrans attacked us and seized the balance of our cargo.'

'How much was still aboard?'

'Half. We had been to only five of the planets.'

'That's unfortunate. They took the load to Terra?'

'I presume.'

Silence for a time. 'How warm is Terra?'

'Fairly warm, I understand.'

'Maybe it will work out all right. We didn't contemplate any hatching on Terra, but if–'

'I don't like the idea of Terrans having a good part of our next generation. I'm sorry we hadn't gotten farther in the distribution.'

'Don't worry. We'll petition the Mother to lay a whole new group to make up for it.'

'But what would the Terrans want with our eggs? Nothing but trouble will come, when hatching begins. I can't understand them. Terran minds are beyond comprehension. I shudder to think what it will be like when the eggs hatch.–And on a humid planet, hatching should begin fairly soon . . .'

PROGENY

Ed Doyle hurried. He caught a surface car, waved fifty credits in the robot driver's face, mopped his florid face with a red pocket-handkerchief, unfastened his collar, perspired and licked his lips and swallowed piteously all the way to the hospital.

The surface car slid up to a smooth halt before the great white-domed hospital building. Ed leaped out and bounded up the steps three at a time, pushing through the visitors and convalescent patients standing on the broad terrace. He threw his weight against the door and emerged in the lobby, astonishing the attendants and persons of importance moving about their tasks.

'Where?' Ed demanded, gazing around, his feet wide apart, his fists clenched, his chest rising and falling. His breath came hoarsely, like an animal's. Silence fell over the lobby. Everyone turned toward him, pausing in their work. 'Where?' Ed demanded again. 'Where is she? *They?*'

It was fortunate Janet had been delivered of a child on this of all days. Proxima Centauri was a long way from Terra and the service was bad. Anticipating the birth of his child, Ed had left Proxima some weeks before. He had just arrived in the city. While stowing his suitcase in the luggage tread at the station the message had been handed to him by a robot courier: *Los Angeles Central Hospital. At once.*

Ed hurried, and fast. As he hurried he couldn't help feeling pleased he had hit the day exactly right, almost to the hour. It was a good feeling. He had felt it before, during years of business dealings in the 'colonies,' the frontier, the fringe of Terran civilization where the streets were still lit by electric lights and doors opened by hand.

That was going to be hard to get used to. Ed turned toward the door behind him, feeling suddenly foolish. He had shoved it open, ignoring the eye. The door was just now closing, sliding slowly back in place. He calmed down a little, putting his handkerchief away in his coat pocket. The hospital attendants were resuming their work, picking up their activities where they had left off. One attendant, a strapping late-model robot, coasted over to Ed and halted.

The robot balanced his noteboard expertly, his photocell eyes appraising Ed's flushed features. 'May I inquire whom you are looking for, sir? Whom do you wish to find?'

'My wife.'

'Her name, sir?'

'Janet. Janet Doyle. She's just had a child.'

The robot consulted his board. 'This way, sir.' He coasted off down the passage.

Ed followed nervously. 'Is she okay? Did I get here in time?' His anxiety was returning.

'She is quite well, sir.' The robot raised his metal arm and a side door slid back. 'In here, sir.'

Janet, in a chic blue-mesh suit, was sitting before a mahogany desk, a cigarette between her fingers, her slim legs crossed, talking rapidly. On the other side of the desk a well-dressed doctor sat listening.

'Janet!' Ed said, entering the room.

'Hi, Ed.' She glanced up at him. 'You just now get in?'

'Sure. It's–it's all over? You–I mean, it's *happened?*'

Janet laughed, her even white teeth sparkling. 'Of course. Come in and sit. This is Doctor Bish.'

'Hello, Doc.' Ed sat down nervously across from them. 'Then it's all over?'

'The event has happened,' Doctor Bish said. His voice was thin and metallic. Ed realized with a sudden shock that the doctor was a robot. A top-level robot, made in humanoid form, not like the ordinary metal-limbed workers. It had fooled him–he had been away so long. Doctor Bish appeared plump and well fed, with kindly features and eyeglasses. His large fleshy hands rested on the desk, a ring on one finger. Pinstripe suit and necktie. Diamond tie clasp. Nails carefully manicured. Hair black and evenly parted.

But his voice had given him away. They never seemed to be able to get a really human sound into the voice. The compressed air and whirling disc system seemed to fall short. Otherwise, it was very convincing.

'I understand you've been situated near Proxima, Mr Doyle,' Doctor Bish said pleasantly.

Ed nodded. 'Yeah.'

'Quite a long way, isn't it? I've never been out there. I have always wanted to go. Is it true they're almost ready to push on to Sirius?'

'Look, Doc–'

'Ed, don't be impatient.' Janet stubbed out her cigarette, glancing reprovingly up at him. She hadn't changed in six months. Small blond face, red mouth, cold eyes like little blue rocks. And now, her perfect figure back again. 'They're bringing him here. It takes a few minutes. They have to wash him off and put drops in his eyes and take a wave shot of his brain.'

'*He?* Then it's a boy?'

'Of course. Don't you remember? You were with me when I had the shots. We agreed at the time. You haven't changed your mind, have you?'

'Too late to change your mind now, Mr Doyle,' Doctor Bish's toneless voice came, high-pitched and calm. 'Your wife has decided to call him Peter.'

'Peter.' Ed nodded, a little dazed. 'That's right. We did decide, didn't we? Peter.' He let the word roll around in his mind. 'Yeah. That's fine. I like it.'

The wall suddenly faded, turning from opaque to transparent. Ed spun quickly. They were looking into a brightly lit room, filled with hospital equipment and white-clad attendant robots. One of the robots was moving toward them, pushing a cart. On the cart was a container, a big metal pot.

Ed's breathing increased. He felt a wave of dizziness. He went up to the transparent wall and stood gazing at the metal pot on the cart.

Doctor Bish rose. 'Don't you want to see, too, Mrs Doyle?'

'Of course.' Janet crossed to the wall and stood beside Ed. She watched critically, her arms folded.

Doctor Bish made a signal. The attendant reached into the pot and lifted out a wire tray, gripping the handles with his magnetic clamps. On the tray, dripping through the wire, was Peter Doyle, still wet from his bath, his eyes wide with astonishment. He was pink all over, except for a fringe of hair on the top of his head, and his great blue eyes. He was little and wrinkled and toothless, like an ancient withered sage.

'Golly,' Ed said.

Doctor Bish made a second signal. The wall slid back. The attendant robot advanced into the room, holding his dripping tray out. Doctor Bish removed Peter from the tray and held him up for inspection. He turned him around and around, studying him from every angle.

'He looks fine,' he said at last.

'What was the result of the wave photo?' Janet asked.

'Result was good. Excellent tendencies indicated. Very promising. High development of the–' The doctor broke off. 'What is it, Mr Doyle?'

Ed was holding out his hands. 'Let me have him, Doc. I want to hold him.' He grinned from ear to ear. 'Let's see how heavy he is. He sure looks big.'

Doctor Bish's mouth fell open in horror. He and Janet gaped.

'Ed!' Janet exclaimed sharply. 'What's the matter with you?'

'Good heavens, Mr Doyle,' the doctor murmured.

Ed blinked. 'What?'

'If I had thought you had any such thing in mind–' Doctor Bish quickly returned Peter to the attendant. The attendant rushed Peter from the room, back to the metal pot. The cart and robot and pot hurriedly vanished, and the wall banged back in place.

Janet grabbed Ed's arm angrily. 'Good Lord, Ed! Have you lost your mind? Come on. Let's get out of here before you do something else.'

'But–'

'Come on.' Janet smiled nervously at Doctor Bish. 'We'll run along now, Doctor. Thanks so much for everything. Don't pay any attention to him. He's been out there so long, you know.'

'I understand,' Doctor Bish said smoothly. He had regained his poise. 'I trust we'll hear from you later, Mrs Doyle.'

Janet pulled Ed out into the hall. 'Ed, what's the matter with you? I've never been so embarrassed in all my life.' Two spots of red glowed in Janet's cheeks. 'I could have kicked you.'

'But what–'

'You know we aren't allowed to touch him. What do you want to do, ruin his whole life?'

'But–'

'Come on.' They hurried outside the hospital, on to the terrace. Warm sunlight streamed down on them. 'There's no telling what harm you've done. He may already be hopelessly warped. If he grows up all warped and–and neurotic and emotional, it'll be your fault.'

Suddenly Ed remembered. He sagged, his features drooping with misery. 'That's right. I forgot. Only robots can come near the children. I'm sorry, Jan. I got carried away. I hope I didn't do anything they can't fix.'

'How *could* you forget?'

'It's so different out at Prox.' Ed waved to a surface car, crestfallen and abashed. The driver drew up in front of them. 'Jan, I'm sorry as hell. I really am. I was all excited. Let's go have a cup of coffee some place and talk. I want to know what the doctor said.'

Ed had a cup of coffee and Janet sipped at a brandy frappé. The Nymphite Room was pitch black except for a vague light oozing up from the table between them. The table diffused a pale illumination that spread over everything, a ghostly radiation seemingly without source. A robot waitress moved back and forth soundlessly with a tray of drinks. Recorded music played softly in the back of the room.

'Go on,' Ed said.

'Go on?' Janet slipped her jacket off and laid it over the back of her chair. In the pale light her breasts glowed faintly. 'There's not much to tell. Everything went all right. It didn't take long. I chatted with Doctor Bish most of the time.'

'I'm glad I got here.'

'How was your trip?'

'Fine.'

'Is the service getting any better? Does it still take as long as it did?'

'About the same.'

'I can't see why you want to go all the way out there. It's so–so cut off from things. What do you find out there? Are plumbing fixtures really that much in demand?'

'They need them. Frontier area. Everyone wants the refinements.' Ed gestured vaguely. 'What did he tell you about Peter? What's he going to be like? Can he tell? I guess it's too soon.'

'He was going to tell me when you started acting the way you did. I'll call him on the vidphone when we get home. His wave pattern should be good. He comes from the best eugenic stock.'

Ed grunted. 'On your side, at least.'

'How long are you going to be here?'

'I don't know. Not long. I'll have to go back. I'd sure like to see him again, before I go.' He glanced up hopefully at his wife. 'Do you think I can?'

'I suppose.'

'How long will he have to stay there?'

'At the hospital? Not long. A few days.'

Ed hesitated. 'I didn't mean at the hospital, exactly. I mean with *them*. How long before we can have him? How long before we can bring him home?'

There was silence. Janet finished her brandy. She leaned back, lighting a cigarette. Smoke drifted across to Ed, blending with the pale light. 'Ed, I don't think you understand. You've been out there so long. A lot has happened since you were a child. New methods, new techniques. They've found so many things they didn't know. They're making progress, for the first time. They know what to do. They're developing a real methodology for dealing with children. For the growth period. Attitude development. Training.' She smiled brightly at Ed. 'I've been reading all about it.'

'How long before we get him?'

'In a few days he'll be released from the hospital. He'll go to a child guidance center. He'll be tested and studied. They'll determine his various capacities and his latent abilities. The direction his development seems to be taking.'

'And then?'

'Then he's put in the proper educational division. So he'll get the right training. Ed, you know, I think he's really going to be something! I could tell by the way Doctor Bish looked. He was studying the wave pattern charts when I came in. He had a look on his face. How can I describe it?' She searched for the word. 'Well, almost–almost a greedy look. Real excitement. They take so much interest in what they're doing. He–'

'Don't say he. Say *it*.'

'Ed, really! What's got into you?'

'Nothing.' Ed glared sullenly down. 'Go on.'

'They make sure he's trained in the right direction. All the time he's there ability tests are given. Then, when he's about nine, he'll be transferred to–'

'Nine! You mean nine *years*?'

'Of course.'

'But when do we get him?'

'Ed, I thought you knew about this. Do I have to go over the whole thing?'

'My God, Jan! We can't wait nine years!' Ed jerked himself upright. 'I never heard of such a thing. Nine years? Why, he'll be half grown up then.'

'That's the point.' Janet leaned towards him, resting her bare elbow against the table. 'As long as he's growing he has to be with them. Not with us. Afterwards, when he's finished growing, when he's no longer so plastic, then we can be with him all we want.'

'Afterwards? When he's eighteen?' Ed leaped up, pushing his chair back. 'I'm going down there and get him.'

'Sit down, Ed.' Janet gazed up calmly, one supple arm thrown lightly over the back of her chair. 'Sit down and act like an adult for a change.'

'Doesn't it matter to you? Don't you care?'

'Of course I care.' Janet shrugged. 'But it's necessary. Otherwise he won't develop correctly. It's for *his* good. Not ours. He doesn't exist for us. Do you want him to have conflicts?'

Ed moved away from the table. 'I'll see you later.'

'Where are you going?'

'Just around. I can't stand this kind of place. It bothers me. I'll see you later.' Ed pushed across the room to the door. The door opened and he found himself on the shiny noonday street. Hot sunlight beat down on him. He blinked, adjusting himself to the blinding light. People streamed around him. People and noise. He moved with them.

He was dazed. He had known, of course. It was there in the back of his mind. The new developments in child care. But it had been abstract, general. Nothing to do with him. With *his* child.

He calmed himself, as he walked along. He was getting all upset about nothing. Janet was right, of course. It was for Peter's good. Peter didn't exist for them, like a dog or cat. A pet to have around the house. He was a human being, with his own life. The training was for him, not for them. It was to develop him, his abilities, his powers. He was to be molded, realized, brought out.

Naturally, robots could do the best job. Robots could train him scientifically, according to a rational technique. Not according to emotional whim. Robots didn't get angry. Robots didn't nag and whine. They didn't spank a child or yell at him. They didn't give conflicting orders. They didn't quarrel among themselves or use the child for their own ends. And there could be no *Oedipus Complex*, with only robots around.

No complexes at all. It had been discovered long ago that neurosis could be traced to childhood training. To the way parents brought up the child. The inhibitions he was taught, the manners, the lessons, the punishments, the rewards. Neuroses, complexes, warped development, all stemmed from the subjective relationship existing between the child and the parent. If perhaps the parent could be eliminated as a factor . . .

Parents could never become objective about their children. It was always a biased, emotional projection the parent held toward the child. Inevitably, the parent's view was distorted. No parent could be a fit instructor for his child.

Robots could study the child, analyze his needs, his wants, test his abilities and interests. Robots would not try to force the child to fit a certain mold. The child would be trained along his own lines; wherever scientific study indicated his interest and need lay.

Ed came to the corner. Traffic whirred past him. He stepped absently forward.

A clang and crash. Bars dropped in front of him, stopping him. A robot safety control.

'Sir, be more careful!' the strident voice came, close by him.

'Sorry.' Ed stepped back. The control bars lifted. He waited for the lights to change. It was for Peter's own good. Robots could train him right. Later on, when he was out of growth stage, when he was not so pliant, so responsive–'It's better for him,' Ed murmured. He said it again, half aloud. Some people glanced at him and he colored. Of course it was better for him. No doubt about it.

Eighteen. He couldn't be with his son until he was eighteen. Practically grown up.

The lights changed. Deep in thought, Ed crossed the street with the other pedestrians, keeping carefully inside the safety lane. It was best for Peter. But eighteen years was a long time.

'A hell of a long time,' Ed murmured, frowning. 'Too damn long a time.'

*

Doctor 2g-Y Bish carefully studied the man standing in front of him. His relays and memory banks clicked, narrowing down the image identification, flashing a variety of comparison possibilities past the scanner.

'I recall you, sir,' Doctor Bish said at last. 'You're the man from Proxima. From the colonies. Doyle, Edward Doyle. Let's see. It was some time ago. It must have been–'

'Nine years ago,' Ed Doyle said grimly. 'Exactly nine years ago, practically to the day.'

Doctor Bish folded his hands. 'Sit down, Mr Doyle. What can I do for you? How is Mrs Doyle? Very engaging wife, as I recall. We had a delightful conversation during her delivery. How–'

'Doctor Bish, do you know where my son is?'

Doctor Bish considered, tapping his fingers on the desk top, the polished mahogany surface. He closed his eyes slightly, gazing off into the distance. 'Yes. Yes, I know where your son is, Mr Doyle.'

Ed Doyle relaxed. 'Fine.' He nodded, letting his breath out in relief.

'I know exactly where your son is. I placed him in the Los Angeles Biological Research Station about a year ago. He's undergoing specialized training there. Your son, Mr Doyle, has shown exceptional ability. He is, shall I say, one of the few, the very few we have found with real possibilities.'

'Can I see him?'

'See him? How do you mean?'

Doyle controlled himself with an effort. 'I think the term is clear.'

Doctor Bish rubbed his chin. His photocell brain whirred, operating at maximum velocity. Switches routed power surges, building up loads and leaping gaps rapidly, as he contemplated the man before him. 'You wish to *view* him? That's one meaning of the term. Or do you wish to talk to him? Sometimes the term is used to cover a more direct contact. It's a loose word.'

'I want to talk to him.'

'I see.' Bish slowly drew some forms from the dispenser on his desk. 'There are a few routine papers that have to be filled out first, of course. Just how long did you want to speak to him?'

Ed Doyle gazed steadily into Doctor Bish's bland face. 'I want to talk to him several hours. *Alone.*'

'Alone?'

'No robots around.'

Doctor Bish said nothing. He stroked the papers he held, creasing the edges with his nail. 'Mr Doyle,' he said carefully, 'I wonder if you're in a proper emotional state to visit your son. You have recently come in from the colonies?'

'I left Proxima three weeks ago.'

'Then you have just arrived here in Los Angeles?'

'That's right.'

'And you've come to see your son? Or have you other business?'

'I came for my son.'

'Mr Doyle, Peter is at a very critical stage. He has just recently been transferred to the Biology Station for his higher training. Up to now his training has been general. What we call the non-differentiated stage. Recently he has entered a new period. Within the last six months Peter has begun advanced work along his specific line, that of organic chemistry. He will–'

'What does Peter think about it?'

Bish frowned. 'I don't understand, sir.'

'How does *he* feel? Is it what he wants?'

'Mr Doyle, your son has the possibility of becoming one of the world's finest bio-chemists. In all the time we have worked with human beings, in their training and development, we have never come across a more alert and integrated faculty for the assimilation of data, construction of theory, formulation of material, than that which your son possesses. All tests indicate he will rapidly rise to the top of his chosen field. He is still only a child, Mr Doyle, but it is the children who must be trained.'

Doyle stood up. 'Tell me where I can find him. I'll talk to him for two hours and then the rest is up to him.'

'The rest?'

Doyle clamped his jaw shut. He shoved his hands in his pockets. His face was flushed and set, grim with determination. In the nine years he had grown much heavier, more stocky and florid. His thinning hair had turned iron-gray. His clothes were dumpy and unpressed. He looked stubborn.

Doctor Bish sighed. 'All right, Mr Doyle. Here are your papers. The law allows you to observe your boy whenever you make proper application. Since he is out of his non-differentiated stage, you may also speak to him for a period of ninety minutes.'

'Alone?'

'You can take him away from the Station grounds for that length of time.' Doctor Bish pushed the papers over to Doyle. 'Fill these out, and I'll have Peter brought here.'

He looked up steadily at the man standing before him.

'I hope you'll remember that any emotional experience at this crucial stage may do much to inhibit his development. He has chosen his field, Mr Doyle. He must be permitted to grow along his selected lines, unhindered by situational blocks. Peter has been in contact with our technical staff throughout his entire training period. He is not accustomed to contact with other human beings. So please be careful.'

Doyle said nothing. He grabbed up the papers and plucked out his fountain pen.

He hardly recognized his son when the two robot attendants brought him out of the massive concrete Station building and deposited him a few yards from Ed's parked surface car.

Ed pushed the door open. 'Pete!' His heart was thumping heavily, painfully. He watched his son come toward the car, frowning in the bright sunlight. It was late afternoon, about four. A faint breeze blew across the parking lot, rustling a few papers and bits of debris.

Peter stood slim and straight. His eyes were large, deep brown, like Ed's. His hair was light, almost blond. More like Janet's. He had Ed's jaw, though, the firm line, clean and well chiseled. Ed grinned at him. Nine years it had been. Nine years since the robot attendant had lifted the rack up from the conveyor pot to show him the little wrinkled baby, red as a boiled lobster.

Peter had grown. He was not a baby any longer. He was a young boy, straight and proud, with firm features and wide, clear eyes.

'Pete,' Ed said. 'How the hell are you?'

The boy stopped by the door of the car. He gazed at Ed calmly. His eyes flickered, taking in the car, the robot driver, the heavy-set man in the rumpled tweed suit grinning nervously at him.

'Get in. Get inside.' Ed moved over. 'Come on. We have places to go.'

The boy was looking at him again. Suddenly Ed was conscious of his baggy suit, his unshined shoes, his gray stubbled chin. He flushed, yanking out his red pocket-handkerchief and mopping his forehead uneasily. 'I just got off the ship, Pete. From Proxima. I haven't had time to change. I'm a little dusty. Long trip.'

Peter nodded. '4.3 light years, isn't it?'

'Takes three weeks. Get in. Don't you want to get in?'

Peter slid in beside him. Ed slammed the door.

'Let's go.' The car started up. 'Drive–' Ed peered out the window. 'Drive up there. By the hill. Out of town.' He turned to Pete. 'I hate big cities. I can't get used to them.'

'There are no large cities in the colonies, are there?' Pete murmured. 'You're unused to urban living.'

Ed settled back. His heart had begun to slow down to its normal beat. 'No, as a matter of fact it's the other way around, Pete.'

'How do you mean?'

'I went to Prox *because* I couldn't stand cities.'

Peter said nothing. The surface car was climbing, going up a steel highway into the hills. The Station, huge and impressive, spread out like a heap of cement bricks directly below them. A few cars moved along the road, but not many. Most transportation was by air, now. Surface cars had begun to disappear.

The road leveled off. They moved along the ridge of the hills. Trees and bushes rose on both sides of them. 'It's nice up here,' Ed said.

'Yes.'

'How–how have you been? I haven't seen you for a long time. Just once. Just after you were born.'

'I know. Your visit is listed in the records.'

'You been getting along all right?'

'Yes. Quite well.'

'They treating you all right?'

'Of course.'

After a while Ed leaned forward. 'Stop here,' he said to the robot driver.

The car slowed down, pulling over to the side of the road. 'Sir, there is nothing–'

'This is fine. Let us out. We'll walk from here.'

The car stopped. The door slid reluctantly open. Ed stepped quickly out of the car, on to the pavement. Peter got out slowly after him, puzzled. 'Where are we?'

'No place.' Ed slammed the door. 'Go on back to town,' he said to the driver. 'We won't need you.'

The car drove off. Ed walked to the side of the road. Peter came after him. The hill dropped away, falling down to the beginnings of the city below. A vast panorama stretched out, the great metropolis in the late afternoon sun. Ed took a deep breath, throwing his arms out. He took off his coat and tossed it over his shoulder.

'Come on.' He started down the hillside. 'Here we go.'

'Where?'

'For a walk. Let's get off this damn road.'

They climbed down the side of the hill, walking carefully, holding on to the grass and roots jutting out from the soil. Finally they came to a level place by a big sycamore tree. Ed threw himself down on the ground, grunting and wiping sweat from his neck.

'Here. Let's sit here.'

Peter sat down carefully, a little way off. Ed's blue shirt was stained with sweat. He unfastened his tie and loosened his collar. Presently he searched through his coat pockets. He brought out his pipe and tobacco.

Peter watched him fill the pipe and light it with a big sulphur match. 'What's that?' he murmured.

'This? My pipe.' Ed grinned, sucking at the pipe. 'Haven't you ever seen a pipe?'

'No.'

'This is a good pipe. I got this when I first went out to Proxima. That was a long time ago, Pete. It was twenty-five years ago. I was just nineteen, then. Only about twice as old as you.'

He put his tobacco away and leaned back, his heavy face serious, preoccupied.

'Just nineteen. I went out there as a plumber. Repair and sales, when I could make a sale. Terran Plumbing. One of those big ads you used to see. Unlimited opportunities. Virgin lands. Make a million. Gold in the streets.' Ed laughed.

'How did you make out?'

'Not bad. Not bad at all. I own my own line, now, you know. I service the whole Proxima system. We do repairing, maintenance, building, construction. I've got six hundred people working for me. It took a long time. It didn't come easy.'

'No.'

'Hungry?'

Peter turned. 'What?'

'Are you hungry?' Ed pulled a brown paper parcel from his coat and unwrapped it. 'I still have a couple of sandwiches from the trip. When I come in from Prox I bring some food along with me. I don't like to buy in the diner. They skin you.' He held out the parcel. 'Want one?'

'No thank you.'

Ed took a sandwich and began to eat. He ate nervously, glancing at his son. Peter sat silently, a short distance off, staring ahead without expression. His smooth handsome face was blank.

'Everything all right?' Ed said.

'Yes.'

'You're not cold, are you?'

'No.'

'You don't want to catch cold.'

A squirrel crossed in front of them, hurrying toward the sycamore tree. Ed threw it a piece of his sandwich. The squirrel ran off a way, then came back slowly. It scolded at them, standing up on its hind feet, its great gray tail flowing out behind it.

Ed laughed. 'Look at him. Ever see a squirrel before?'

'I don't think so.'

The squirrel ran off with the piece of sandwich. It disappeared among the brush and bushes.

'Squirrels don't exist out around Prox,' Ed said.

'No.'

'It's good to come back to Terra once in a while. See some of the old things. They're going, though.'

'Going?'

'Away. Destroyed. Terra is always changing.' Ed waved around at the hillside. 'This will be gone, some day. They'll cut down the trees. Then they'll level it. Some day they'll carve the whole range up and carry it off. Use it for fill, some place along the coast.'

'That's beyond our scope,' Peter said.

'What?'

'I don't receive that type of material. I think Doctor Bish told you. I'm working with bio-chemistry.'

'I know,' Ed murmured. 'Say, how the hell did you ever get mixed up with that stuff? Bio-chemistry?'

'The tests showed that my abilities lie along those lines.'

'You enjoy what you're doing?'

'What a strange thing to ask. Of course I enjoy what I'm doing. It's the work I'm fitted for.'

'It seems funny as hell to me, starting a nine-year-old kid off on something like that.'

'Why?'

'My God, Pete. When I was nine I was bumming around town. In school sometimes, outside mostly, wandering here and there. Playing. Reading. Sneaking into the rocket launching yards all the time.' He considered. 'Doing all sorts of things. When I was sixteen I hopped over to Mars. I stayed there a while. Worked as a hasher. I went on to Ganymede. Ganymede was all sewed up tight. Nothing doing there. From Ganymede I went out to Prox. Got a work-away all the way out. Big freighter.'

'You stayed at Proxima?'

'I sure did. I found what I wanted. Nice place, out there. Now we're starting on to Sirius, you know.' Ed's chest swelled. 'I've got an outlet in the Sirius system. Little retail and service place.'

'Sirius is 8.8 light years from Sol.'

'It's a long way. Seven weeks from here. Rough grind. Meteor swarms. Keeps things hot all the way out.'

'I can imagine.'

'You know what I thought I might do?' Ed turned toward his son, his face alive with hope and enthusiasm. 'I've been thinking it over. I thought maybe I'd go out there. To Sirius. It's a fine little place we have. I drew up the plans myself. Special design to fit with the characteristics of the system.'

Peter nodded.

'Pete–'

'Yes?'

'Do you think maybe you'd be interested? Like to hop out to Sirius and take a look? It's a good place. Four clean planets. Never touched. Lots of room. Miles and miles of room. Cliffs and mountains. Oceans. Nobody around. Just a few colonists, families, some construction. Wide, level plains.'

'How do you mean, interested?'

'In going all the way out.' Ed's face was pale. His mouth twitched nervously. 'I thought maybe you'd like to come along and see how things are. It's a lot like Prox was, twenty-five years ago. It's good and clean out there. No cities.'

Peter smiled.

'Why are you smiling?'

'No reason.' Peter stood up abruptly. 'If we have to walk back to the Station we'd better start. Don't you think? It's getting late.'

'Sure.' Ed struggled to his feet. 'Sure, but–'

'When are you going to be back in the Sol system again?'

'Back?' Ed followed after his son. Peter climbed up the hill toward the road. 'Slow down, will you?'

Peter slowed down. Ed caught up with him.

'I don't know when I'll be back. I don't come here very often. No ties. Not since Jan and I separated. As a matter of fact I came here this time to–'

'This way.' Peter started down the road.

Ed hurried along beside him, fastening his tie and putting his coat on, gasping for breath. 'Peter, what do you say? You want to hop out to Sirius with me? Take a look? It's a nice place out there. We could work together. The two of us. If you want.'

'But I already have my work.'

'That stuff? That damn chemistry stuff?'

Peter smiled again.

Ed scowled, his face dark red. 'Why are you smiling?' he demanded. His son did not answer. 'What's the matter? What's so damn funny?'

'Nothing,' Peter said. 'Don't become excited. We have a long walk down.' He increased his pace slightly, his supple body swinging in long, even strides. 'It's getting late. We have to hurry.'

Doctor Bish examined his wristwatch, pushing back his pin-striped coat sleeve. 'I'm glad you're back.'

'He sent the surface car away,' Peter murmured. 'We had to walk down the hill on foot.'

It was dark outside. The Station lights were coming on automatically, along the rows of buildings and laboratories.

Doctor Bish rose from his desk. 'Sign this, Peter. Bottom of this form.'

Peter signed. 'What is it?'

'Certifies you saw him in accord with the provisions of the law. We didn't try to obstruct you in any way.'

Peter handed the paper back. Bish filed it away with the others. Peter moved toward the door of the doctor's office. 'I'll go. Down to the cafeteria for dinner.'

'You haven't eaten?'

'No.'

Doctor Bish folded his arms, studying the boy. 'Well?' he said. 'What do you think of him? This is the first time you've seen your father. It must have been strange for you. You've been around us so much, in all your training and work.'

'It was–unusual.'

'Did you gain any impressions? Was there anything you particularly noticed.'

'He was very emotional. There was a distinct bias through everything he said and did. A distortion present, virtually uniform.'

'Anything else?'

Peter hesitated, lingering at the door. He broke into a smile. 'One other thing.'

'What was it?'

'I noticed–' Peter laughed. 'I noticed a distinct odor about him. A constant pungent smell, all the time I was with him.'

'I'm afraid that's true of all of them,' Doctor Bish said. 'Certain skin glands. Waste products thrown off from the blood. You'll get used to it, after you've been around them more.'

'Do I have to be around them?'

'They're your own race. How else can you work with them? Your whole training is designed with that in mind. When we've taught you all we can, then you will–'

'It reminded me of something. The pungent odor. I kept thinking about it, all the time I was with him. Trying to place it.'

'Can you identify it now?'

Peter reflected. He thought hard, concentrating deeply. His small face wrinkled up. Doctor Bish waited patiently by his desk, arms folded. The automatic heating system clicked on for the night, warming the room with a soft glow that drifted gently around them.

'I know!' Peter exclaimed suddenly.

'What was it?'

'The animals in the biology lab. It was the same smell. The same smell as the experimental animals.'

They glanced at each other, the robot doctor and the promising young boy. Both of them smiled, a secret, private smile. A smile of complete understanding.

'I believe I know what you mean,' Doctor Bish said. 'In fact, I know *exactly* what you mean.'

SOME KINDS OF LIFE

'Joan, for heaven's sake!'

Joan Clarke caught the irritation in her husband's voice, even through the wall-speaker. She left her chair by the vidscreen and hurried into the bedroom. Bob was rooting furiously around in the closet, pulling down coats and suits and tossing them on the bed. His face was flushed with exasperation.

'What are you looking for?'

'My uniform. Where is it? Isn't it here?'

'Of course. Let me look.'

Bob got sullenly out of the way. Joan pushed past him and clicked on the automatic sorter. Suits bobbed by in quick succession, parading for her inspection.

It was early morning, about nine o'clock. The sky was bright blue. Not a single cloud was visible. A warm spring day, late in April. The ground outside the house was damp and black from the rains of the day before. Green shoots were already beginning to poke their way up through the steaming earth. The sidewalk was dark with moisture. Wide lawns glittered in the sparkling sunlight.

'Here it is.' Joan turned off the sorter. The uniform dropped into her arms and she carried it over to her husband. 'Now next time don't get so upset.'

'Thanks.' Bob grinned, embarrassed. He patted the coat. 'But look, it's all creased. I thought you were going to have the darn thing cleaned.'

'It'll be all right.' Joan started up the bed-maker. The bed-maker smoothed out the sheets and blankets, folding them in place. The spread settled carefully around the pillows. 'After you've had it on awhile it'll look just lovely. Bob, you're the fussiest man I know.'

'Sorry, honey,' Bob murmured.

'What's wrong?' Joan came up to him and put her hand on his broad shoulder. 'Are you worried about something?'

'No.'

'Tell me.'

Bob began to unfasten his uniform. 'It's nothing important. I didn't want to bother you. Erickson called me at work yesterday to tell me my group is up again. Seems they're calling two groups at once now. I thought I wouldn't get jerked out for another six months.'

'Oh, Bob! Why didn't you *tell* me?'

'Erickson and I talked a long time. "For God's sake!" I told him. "I was just up." "I know that, Bob," he said, "I'm sorry as hell about it but there's nothing I can do. We're all in the same boat. Anyhow, it won't last long. Might as well get it over with. It's the Martian situation. They're all hot and bothered about it." That's what he said. He was nice about it. Erickson's a pretty good guy for a Sector Organizer.'

'When–when do you have to go?'

Bob looked at his watch. 'I have to get down to the field by noon. Gives me three hours.'

'When will you be back?'

'Oh, I should be back in a couple days–if everything goes all right. You know how these things are. It varies. Remember last October when I was gone a whole week? But that's unusual. They rotate the groups so fast now you're practically back before you start.'

Tommy came strolling in from the kitchen. 'What's up, Dad?' He noticed the uniform. 'Say, your group up again?'

'That's right.'

Tommy grinned from ear to ear, a delighted teenage grin. 'You going to get in on the Martian business? I was following it over the vidscreen. Those Martians look like a bunch of dry weeds tied together in a bundle. You guys sure ought to be able to blow *them* apart.'

Bob laughed, whacking his son on the back. 'You tell 'em, Tommy.'

'I sure wish I was coming.'

Bob's expression changed. His eyes became hard like gray flint. 'No, you don't, kid. Don't say that.'

There was an uncomfortable silence.

'I didn't mean anything,' Tommy muttered.

Bob laughed easily. 'Forget it. Now all of you clear out so I can change.'

Joan and Tommy left the room. The door slid shut. Bob dressed swiftly, tossing his robe and pajamas on the bed and pulling his dark green uniform around him. He laced his boots up and then opened the door.

Joan had got his suitcase from the hall closet. 'You'll want this, won't you?' she asked.

'Thanks.' Bob picked up the suitcase. 'Let's go out to the car.' Tommy was already absorbed at the vidscreen, beginning his schoolwork for the day. A biology lesson moved slowly across the screen.

Bob and Joan walked down the front steps and along the path to their surface car, parked at the edge of the road. The door opened as they approached. Bob threw his suitcase inside and sat down behind the wheel.

'Why do we have to fight the Martians?' Joan asked suddenly. 'Tell me, Bob. Tell me why.'

Bob lit a cigarette. He let the gray smoke drift around the cabin of the car. 'Why? You know as well as I do.' He reached out a big hand and thumped the handsome control board of the car. 'Because of this.'

'What do you mean?'

'The control mechanism needs rexeroid. And the only rexeroid deposits in the whole system are on Mars. If we lose Mars we lose this.' He ran his hand over the gleaming control board. 'And if we lose this how are we going to get around? Answer me that.'

'Can't we go back to manual steering?'

'We could ten years ago. But ten years ago we were driving less than a hundred miles per hour. No human being could steer at the speeds these days. We couldn't go back to manual steering without slowing down our pace.'

'Can't we do that?'

Bob laughed. 'Sweetheart, it's ninety miles from here to town. You really think I could keep my job if I had to drive the whole way at thirty-five miles an hour? I'd be on the road all my life.'

Joan was silent.

'You see, we must have the darn stuff–the rexeroid. It makes our control equipment possible. We depend on it. We need it. We must keep mining operations going on Mars. We can't afford to let the Martians get the rexeroid deposits away from us. See?'

'I see. And last year it was kryon ore from Venus. We had to have that. So you went and fought on Venus.'

'Darling, the walls of our houses wouldn't maintain an even temperature without kryon. Kryon is the only non-living substance in the system that adjusts itself to temperature changes. Why, we'd–we'd all have to go back to floor furnaces again. Like my grandfather had.'

'And the year before it was lonolite from Pluto.'

'Lonolite is the only substance known that can be used in constructing the memory banks of the calculators. It's the only metal with true retentive ability. Without lonolite we'd lose all our big computing machines. And you know how far we'd get without them.'

'All right.'

'Sweetheart, you know I don't *want* to go. But I have to. We all have to.' Bob waved toward the house. 'Do you want to give that up? You want to go back to the old days?'

'No.' Joan moved away from the car. 'All right, Bob. I'll see you in a day or two then?'

'I hope so. This trouble should be over soon. Most of the New

York groups are being called. The Berlin and Oslo groups are already there. It shouldn't take long.'

'Good luck.'

'Thanks.' Bob closed the door. The motor started up automatically. 'Say goodbye to Tommy for me.'

The car drove off, gaining speed, the automatic control board guiding it expertly into the main stream of traffic flowing down the highway. Joan watched until the car blended with the endless tide of flashing metal hulls, racing across the countryside in a bright ribbon toward the distant city. Then she went slowly back inside the house.

Bob never came back from Mars, so in a manner of speaking, Tommy became the man of the house. Joan got a release from school for him and after a while he began work as a lab technician at the Government Research Project a few miles down the road.

Bryan Erickson, the Sector Organizer, stopped one evening to see how they were getting along. 'Nice little place you have here,' Erickson said, wandering around.

Tommy swelled with pride. 'Sure is, isn't it? Sit down and make yourself comfortable.'

'Thanks.' Erickson peered into the kitchen. The kitchen was in the process of putting out a meal for the evening dinner. 'Quite a kitchen.'

Tommy came up beside him. 'See that unit there on top of the stove?'

'What's it do?'

'It's a selector on the kitchen. It sets up a new combination every day. We don't have to figure out what to eat.'

'Amazing.' Erickson glanced at Tommy. 'You seem to be doing all right.'

Joan looked up from the vidscreen. 'As well as could be expected.' Her voice was toneless, flat.

Erickson grunted. He walked back into the living room. 'Well, I guess I'll be running along.'

'What did you come for?' Joan asked.

'Nothing in particular, Mrs Clarke.' Erickson hesitated by the door, a big man, red-faced, in his late thirties. 'Oh, there was one thing.'

'What is it?' Her voice was emotionless.

'Tom, have you made out your Sector Unit card?'

'My Sector Unit card!'

'According to law you're supposed to be registered as part of this sector—*my* sector.' He reached in his pocket. 'I have a few blank cards with me.'

'Gee!' Tommy said, a little frightened. 'So soon? I thought it wasn't until I got to be eighteen.'

'They've changed the ruling. We took quite a beating on Mars. Some of the sectors can't fill their quotas. Have to dig deeper from now on.' Erickson grinned good-naturedly. 'This is a good sector, you know. We have a lot of fun drilling and trying out the new equipment. I finally got Washington to consign us a whole squadron of the new double-jet small fighters. Each man in my sector gets the use of a fighter.'

Tommy's eyes lit up. 'Really?'

'In fact the user gets to bring the fighter home over the weekend. You can park it on your lawn.'

'No kidding?' Tommy sat down at the desk. He filled the Unit card out happily.

'Yes, we have a pretty good time,' Erickson murmured.

'Between wars,' Joan said quietly.

'What's that, Mrs Clarke?'

'Nothing.'

Erickson accepted the filled-out card. He put it away in his wallet. 'By the way,' he said.

Tommy and Joan turned toward him.

'I guess you've been seeing the gleco-war on the vidscreen. I guess you know all about that.'

'The gleco-war?'

'We get all our gleco from Callisto. It's made from the hides of some kind of animal. Well, there's been a little trouble with the natives. They claim–'

'What is a gleco?' Joan said tightly.

'That's the stuff that makes your front door open for you only. It's sensitive to your pressure pattern. Gleco is made from these animals.'

There was silence, the kind you can cut with a knife.

'I guess I'll be going.' Erickson moved toward the door. 'We'll see you the next training session, Tom. Right?' He opened the door.

'Right,' Tommy murmured.

'Goodnight.' Erickson left, closing the door after him.

'But I *have* to go!' Tommy exclaimed.

'Why?'

'The whole sector is going. It's required.'

Joan stared out the window. 'It isn't right.'

'But if I don't go we'll lose Callisto. And if we lose Callisto . . .'

'I know. Then we'll have to go back to carrying door keys. Like our grandfathers did.'

'That's right.' Tommy stuck out his chest, turning from side to side. 'How do I look?'

Joan said nothing.

'How do I look? Do I look all right?'

Tommy looked fine in his deep green uniform. He was slim and straight, much better looking than Bob. Bob had been gaining weight. His hair had been thinning. Tommy's hair was thick and black. His cheeks were flushed with excitement, his blue eyes flashing. He pulled his helmet in place, snapping the strap.

'Okay?' he demanded.

Joan nodded. 'Fine.'

'Kiss me goodbye. I'm off to Callisto. I'll be back in a couple of days.'

'Goodbye.'

'You don't sound very happy.'

'I'm not,' Joan said. 'I'm not very happy.'

Tommy came back from Callisto all right but during the trektone-war on Europa something went wrong with his double-jet small fighter and the Sector Unit came back without him.

'Trektone,' Bryan Erickson explained, 'is used in vidscreen tubes. It's very important, Joan.'

'I see.'

'You know what the vidscreen means. Our whole education and information come over it. The kids learn from it. They get their schooling. And in the evening we use the pleasure-channels for entertainment. You don't want us to have to go back to–'

'No, no–of course not. I'm sorry.' Joan waved a signal and the coffee table slid into the living room, bearing a pot of steaming coffee. 'Cream? Sugar?'

'Just sugar, thanks.' Erickson took his cup and sat silently on the couch, sipping and stirring. The house was quiet. It was late evening, about eleven o'clock. The shades were down. The vid-screen played softly in the corner. Outside the house the world was dark and unmoving except for a faint wind stirring among the cedar trees at the end of the grounds.

'Any news from the various fronts?' Joan asked after a while, leaning back and smoothing down her skirt.

'The fronts?' Erickson considered. 'Well, some new developments in the iderium-war.'

'Where is that?'

'Neptune. We get our iderium from Neptune.'

'What is iderium used for?' Joan's voice was thin and remote as if she were a long way off. Her face had a pinched look, a kind of strained whiteness. As if a mask had settled into place and remained, a mask through which she looked from a great distance.

'All the newspaper machines require iderium,' Erickson explained. 'Iderium lining makes it possible for them to detect events as they occur and flash them over the vidscreen. Without iderium we'd have to go back to reporting news and writing it up by hand. That would introduce the personal bias. Slanted news. The iderium news machines are impartial.'

Joan nodded. 'Any other news?'

'Not much more. They say some trouble might be going to break out on Mercury.'

'What do we get from Mercury?'

'That's where our ambroline comes from. We use ambroline in all kinds of selector units. In your kitchen–the selector you have in there. The meal selector that sets up the food combinations. That's an ambroline unit.'

Joan gazed vacantly into her coffee cup. 'The natives on Mercury–they're attacking us?'

'There's been some riots, agitation, that sort of thing. Some Sector Units have been called out already. The Paris unit and the Moscow unit. Big units, I believe.'

After a time Joan said, 'You know, Bryan, I can tell you came here with something on your mind.'

'Oh, no. Why do you say that?'

'I can tell. What is it?'

Erickson flushed, his good-natured face red. 'You're pretty acute, Joan. As a matter of fact I did come for something.'

'What is it?'

Erickson reached into his coat and brought out a folded mimeographed paper. He passed it to Joan. 'It isn't my idea, understand. I'm just a cog in a big machine.' He chewed his lip nervously. 'It's because of the heavy losses in the trektone-war. They need to close ranks. They're up against it, so I hear.'

'What does all this mean?' Joan passed the paper back. 'I can't make out all this legal wording.'

'Well, it means women are going to be admitted into Sector Units in the–in the absence of male members of the family.'

'Oh. I see.'

Erickson got up quickly, relieved that his duty had been done. 'I guess I'll have to run along now. I wanted to bring this over and show it to you. They're handing them out all along the line.' He stuck the paper away in his coat again. He looked very tired.

'It doesn't leave very many people, does it?'

'How do you mean?'

'Men first. Then children. Now women. It seems to take in everybody, just about.'

'Kind of does, I guess. Well, there must be a reason. We have to hold these fronts. The stuff must be kept coming in. We've got to have it.'

'I suppose so.' Joan rose slowly. 'I'll see you later on, Bryan.'

'Yes, I should be around later in the week. I'll see you then.'

Bryan Erickson came back just as the nymphite-war was breaking out on Saturn. He grinned apologetically at Mrs Clarke as she let him in.

'Sorry to bother you so early in the morning,' Erickson said. 'I'm in a big rush, running around all over the sector.'

'What is it?' Joan closed the door after him. He was in his Organizer's uniform, pale green with silver bands across his shoulders. Joan was still in her dressing robe.

'Nice and warm in here,' Erickson said, warming his hands against the wall. Outside, the day was bright and cold. It was November. Snow lay over everything, a cold blanket of white. A few stark trees jutted up, their branches barren and frozen. Far off along the highway the bright ribbon of surface cars had diminished to a trickle. There were few people going to the city, anymore. Most surface cars were in storage.

'I guess you know about the trouble on Saturn,' Erickson murmured. 'You've heard.'

'I saw some shots, I think. Over the vidscreen.'

'Quite a ruckus. Those Saturn natives are sure big. My golly, they must be fifty feet high.'

Joan nodded absently, rubbing her eyes. 'It's a shame we need anything from Saturn. Have you had breakfast, Bryan?'

'Oh, yes, thanks–I've eaten.' Erickson turned his back to the wall. 'Sure is good to get in out of the cold. You certainly keep your house nice and neat. I wish my wife kept our place this neat.'

Joan crossed to the windows and let up the shades. 'What do we use from Saturn?'

'It would have to be nymphite, of all things. Anything else we could give up. But not nymphite.'

'What is nymphite used for?'

'All aptitude-testing equipment. Without nymphite we wouldn't be able to tell who was fit for what occupation, including President of the World Council.'

'I see.'

'With nymphite testers we can determine what each person is good for and what kind of work he should be doing. Nymphite is the basic tool of modern society. With it we classify and grade ourselves. If anything should happen to the supply . . .'

'And it all comes from Saturn?'

'I'm afraid so. Now the natives are rioting, trying to take over the nymphite mines. It's going to be a tough struggle. They're big. The government is having to call up everyone it can get.'

Suddenly Joan gasped. 'Everyone?' Her hand flew to her mouth. 'Even women?'

'I'm afraid so. Sorry, Joan. You know it isn't my idea. Nobody wants to do it. But if we're going to save all these things we have–'

'But whom will that leave?'

Erickson did not answer. He was sitting down at the desk, making out a card. He passed it to her. Joan took it automatically. 'Your unit card.'

'But who will be left?' Joan asked again. 'Can't you tell me? Will anyone be left?'

The rocketship from Orion landed with a great crashing roar. Exhaust valves poured out clouds of waste material, as the jet compressors cooled into silence.

There was no sound for a time. Then the hatch was unscrewed carefully and swung inward. Cautiously N'tgari-3 stepped out, waving an atmosphere-testing cone ahead of him.

'Results?' his companion queried, his thoughts crossing to N'tgari-3.

'Too thin to breathe. For us. But enough for some kinds of life.' N'tgari-3 gazed around him, across the hills and plains, off in the distance. 'Certainly is quiet.'

'Not a sound. Or any sign of life.' His companion emerged. 'What's that over there?'

'Where?' N'tgari-3 asked.

'Over that way.' Luci'n-6 pointed with his polar antenna. 'See?'

'Looks like some kind of building units. Some sort of mass structures.'

The two Orionians raised their launch to hatch-level and slid it out onto the ground. With N'tgari-3 at the wheel they set off across the plain toward the raised spot visible on the horizon. Plants grew on all sides, some tall and sturdy, some fragile and small with multi-colored blossoms.

'Plenty of immobile forms,' Luci'n-6 observed.

They passed through a field of gray-orange plants, thousands of stalks growing uniformly, endless plants all exactly alike.

'They look as if they were artificially sowed,' N'tgari-3 murmured.

'Slow the launch down. We're coming to some sort of structure.'

N'tgari-3 slowed down the launch almost to a stop. The two Orionians leaned out the port, gazing in interest.

A lovely structure rose up, surrounded by plants of all kinds, tall plants, carpets of low plants, beds of plants with astonishing blossoms. The structure itself was neat and attractive, obviously the artifact of an advanced culture.

N'tgari-3 leaped out of the launch. 'Maybe we're about to encounter the legendary Beings from Terra.' He hurried across the carpet of plants, a long uniform ground-covering, up to the front porch of the structure.

Luci'n-6 followed him. They examined the door. 'How does it open?' Luci'n-6 asked.

They burned a neat hole in the lock and the door slid back. Lights came on automatically. The house was warm, heated by the walls.

'How–how developed! How very advanced.'

They wandered from room to room, gazing around them at the vidscreen, at the elaborate kitchen, at the furniture in the bedroom, at the drapes, the chairs, the bed.

'But where are the Terrans?' N'tgari-3 said at last.

'They'll be right back.'

N'tgari-3 paced back and forth. 'This gives me an odd feeling. I can't put my antenna on it. A sort of uncomfortable feeling.' He hesitated. 'It isn't possible they're *not* coming back, is it?'

'Why not?'

Luci'n-6 began to fiddle with the vidscreen. 'Hardly likely. We'll wait for them. They'll be back.'

N'tgari-3 peered out the window nervously. 'I don't see them. But they *must* be around. They couldn't just walk off and leave all this behind. Where would they go? Why?'

'They'll be back.' Luci'n-6 got some static on the vidscreen. 'This isn't very impressive.'

'I have a feeling they won't.'

'If the Terrans don't return,' Luci'n-6 said thoughtfully, fooling with the vidscreen controls, 'it will be one of the greatest puzzles known to archaeology.'

'I'll keep watching for them,' N'tgari-3 said impassively.

MARTIANS COME IN CLOUDS

Ted Barnes came in all grim-faced and trembling. He threw his coat and newspaper over the chair. 'Another cloud,' he muttered. 'A whole cloud of them! One was up on Johnson's roof. They were getting it down with a long pole of some kind.'

Lena came and took his coat to the closet. 'I'm certainly glad you hurried right on home.'

'I get the shakes when I see one of them.' Ted threw himself down on the couch, groping in his pockets for cigarettes. 'Honest to God it really gets me.'

He lit up, blowing smoke around him in a gray mist. His hands were beginning to quiet down. He wiped sweat from his upper lip and loosened his necktie. 'What's for dinner?'

'Ham.' Lena bent over to kiss him.

'How come? Some sort of occasion?'

'No.' Lena moved back toward the kitchen door. 'It's that canned Dutch ham your mother gave us. I thought it was about time we opened it.'

Ted watched her disappear into the kitchen, slim and attractive in her bright print apron. He sighed, relaxing and leaning back. The quiet living room, Lena in the kitchen, the television set playing to itself in the corner, made him feel a little better.

He unlaced his shoes and kicked them off. The whole incident had taken only a few minutes but it had seemed much longer. An eternity–standing rooted to the sidewalk, staring up at Johnson's roof. The crowd of shouting men. The long pole. And . . .

. . . and *it*, draped over the peak of the roof, the shapeless gray bundle evading the end of that pole. Creeping this way and that, trying to keep from being dislodged.

Ted shuddered. His stomach turned over. He had stood fixed to the spot, gazing up, unable to look away. Finally some fellow running past had stepped on his foot, breaking the spell and freeing him. He had hurried on, getting away as fast as he could, relieved and shaken. Lord . . . !

The back door slammed. Jimmy wandered into the living room, his hands in his pockets. 'Hi, Dad.' He stopped by the bathroom door, looking across at his father. 'What's the matter? You're all funny-looking.'

'Jimmy, come over here.' Ted stubbed out his cigarette. 'I want to talk to you.'

'I have to go wash for dinner.'

'Come here and sit down. Dinner can wait.'

Jimmy came over and slid up onto the couch. 'What's the matter? What is it?'

Ted studied his son. Round little face, tousled hair hanging down in his eyes. Smudge of dirt on one cheek. Jimmy was eleven. Was this a good time to tell him? Ted set his jaw grimly. Now was as good a time as any–while it was strong in his mind.

'Jimmy, there was a Martian up on Johnson's roof. I saw it on the way home from the bus depot.'

Jimmy's eyes grew round. 'A buggie?'

'They were getting it with a pole. A cloud of them's around. They come in clouds every few years.' His hands were beginning to shake again. He lit another cigarette. 'Every two or three years. Not as often as they used to. They drift down from Mars in clouds, hundreds of them. All over the world–like leaves.' He shuddered. 'Like a lot of dry leaves blowing down.'

'Gosh!' Jimmy said. He got off the couch onto his feet. 'Is it still there?'

'No, they were getting it down. Listen.' Ted leaned toward the boy. 'Listen to me–I'm telling you this so you'll stay away from them.

If you see one of them you turn around and run as fast as you can. You hear? Don't go near it–stay away. Don't . . .'

He hesitated. 'Don't pay any attention to it. You just turn around and run. Get somebody, stop the first man you see and tell him, then come on home. Do you understand?'

Jimmy nodded.

'You know what they look like. They showed you pictures at school. You must have–'

Lena came to the kitchen door. 'Dinner's ready. Jimmy, aren't you washed?'

'I stopped him,' Ted said, getting up from the couch. 'I wanted to have a talk with him.'

'You mind what your father tells you,' Lena said. 'About the buggies–remember what he says or he'll give you the biggest whipping you ever heard of.'

Jimmy ran to the bathroom. 'I'll get washed.' He disappeared, slamming the door behind him.

Ted caught Lena's gaze. 'I hope they get them taken care of soon. I hate even to be outside.'

'They should. I heard on television they're more organized than last time.' Lena counted mentally. 'This is the fifth time they've come. The fifth cloud. It seems to be tapering off. Not as often, any more. The first was in nineteen hundred and fifty-eight. The next in fifty-nine. I wonder where it'll end.'

Jimmy hurried out of the bathroom. 'Let's eat!'

'Okay,' Ted said. 'Let's eat.'

It was a bright afternoon with the sun shining down everywhere. Jimmy Barnes rushed out of the school yard, through the gate and onto the sidewalk. His heart was hammering excitedly. He crossed over to Maple Street and then onto Cedar, running the whole way.

A couple of people were still poking around on Johnson's lawn–a policeman and a few curious men. There was a big ruined place in the center of the lawn, a sort of tear where the grass had been ripped back. The flowers all around the house had been trampled flat. But there was no sign whatsoever of the buggie.

While he was watching Mike Edwards came over and punched him on the arm. 'What say, Barnes.'

'Hi. Did you see it?'

'The buggie? No.'

'My Dad saw it, coming home from work.'

'Bull!'

'No, he really did. He said they were getting it down with a pole.'

Ralf Drake rode up on his bike. 'Where is it? Is it gone?'

'They already tore it up,' Mike said. 'Barnes says his old man saw it, coming home last night.'

'He said they were poking it down with a pole. It was trying to hang onto the roof.'

'They're all dried-up and withered,' Mike said, 'like something that's been hanging out in the garage.'

'How do you know?' Ralf said.

'I saw one once.'

'Yeah. I'll bet.'

They walked along the sidewalk, Ralf wheeling his bike, discussing the matter loudly. They turned down Vermont Street and crossed the big vacant lot.

'The TV announcer said most of them are already rounded up,' Ralf said. 'There weren't very many this time.'

Jimmy kicked a rock. 'I'd sure like to see one before they get them all.'

'I'd sure like to *get* one,' Mike said.

Ralf sneered. 'If you ever saw one you'd run so fast you wouldn't stop until the sun set.'

'Oh, yeah?'

'You'd run like a fool.'

'The heck I would. I'd knock the ol' buggie down with a rock.'

'And carry him home in a tin can?'

Mike chased Ralf around, out into the street and up to the corner. The argument continued endlessly all the way across town and over to the other side of the railroad tracks. They walked past the ink works and the Western Lumber Company loading platforms. The sun sank low in the sky. It was getting to be evening. A cold wind came up, blowing through the palm trees at the end of the Hartly Construction Company lot.

'See you,' Ralf said. He hopped on his bike, riding off. Mike and Jimmy walked back toward town together. At Cedar Street they separated.

'If you see a buggie give me a call,' Mike said.

'Sure thing.' Jimmy walked on up Cedar Street, his hands in his pockets. The sun had set. The evening air was chill. Darkness was descending.

He walked slowly, his eyes on the ground. The streetlights came on. A few cars moved along the street. Behind curtained windows he saw bright flashes of yellow, warm kitchens and living rooms. A television set brayed out, rumbling into the gloom. He passed along the brick wall of the Pomeroy Estate. The wall turned into an iron fence. Above the fence great silent evergreens rose dark and unmoving in the evening twilight.

For a moment Jimmy stopped, kneeling down to tie his shoe. A cold wind blew around him, making the evergreens sway slightly. Far off a train sounded a dismal wail echoing through the gloom. He thought about dinner, Dad with his shoes off, reading the newspapers. His mother in the kitchen–the TV set murmuring to itself in the corner–the warm, bright living room.

Jimmy stood up. Above him in the evergreens something moved. He glanced up, suddenly rigid. Among the dark branches something rested, swaying with the wind. He gaped, rooted to the spot.

A buggie. Waiting and watching, crouched silently up in the tree.

It was *old*. He knew that at once. There was a dryness about it, an odor of age and dust. An ancient gray shape, silent and unmoving, wrapped around the trunk and branches of the evergreen. A mass of cobwebs, dusty strands and webs of gray wrapped and trailing across the tree. A nebulous wispy presence that made the hackles of his neck rise.

The shape began to move but so slowly he might not have noticed. It was sliding around the trunk, feeling its way carefully, a little at a time. As if it were sightless, blind. Feeling its way inch by inch, an unseeing gray ball of cobwebs and dust.

Jimmy moved back from the fence. It was completely dark. The sky was black above him. A few stars glittered distantly, bits of remote fire. Far down the street a bus rumbled, turning a corner.

A buggie–clinging to the tree above him. Jimmy struggled, pulling himself away. His heart was thumping painfully, choking him. He could hardly breathe. His vision blurred, fading and receding. The buggie was only a little way from him, only a few yards above his head.

Help–he had to get help. Men with poles to push the buggie down–people–right away. He closed his eyes and pushed away from the fence. He seemed to be in a vast tide, a rushing ocean dragging at him, surging over his body, holding him where he was. He could not break away. He was caught. He strained, pushing against it. One step . . . another step . . . a third–

And then he heard it.

Or rather *felt* it. There was no sound. It was like a drumming, a kind of murmuring like the sea, inside his head. The drumming lapped against his mind, beating gently around him. He halted. The murmuring was soft, rhythmic. But insistent–urgent. It began to separate, gaining form–form and substance. It flowed, breaking up into distinct sensations, images, scenes.

Scenes–of another world, *its* world. The buggie was talking to him, telling him about its world, spinning out scene after scene with anxious haste.

'Get away,' Jimmy muttered thickly.

But the scenes still came, urgently, insistently, lapping at his mind.

Plains–a vast desert without limit or end. Dark red, cracked and scored with ravines. A far line of blunted hills, dust-covered, corroded. A great basin off to the right, an endless empty piepan with white-crusted salt riming it, a bitter ash where water had once lapped.

'Get away!' Jimmy muttered again, moving a step back.

The scenes grew. Dead sky, particles of sand, whipped along, carried endlessly. Sheets of sand, vast billowing clouds of sand and dust, blowing endlessly across the cracked surface of the planet. A few scrawny plants growing by rocks. In the shadows of the mountains great spiders with old webs, dust-covered, spun centuries ago. Dead spiders, lodged in cracks.

A scene expanded. Some sort of artificial pipe, jutting up from the red-baked ground. A vent–underground quarters. The view changed. He was seeing below, down into the core of the planet–layer after layer of crumpled rock. A withered wrinkled planet without fire or life or moisture of any kind. Its skin cracking, its pulp drying out and blowing up in clouds of dust. Far down in the core a tank of some sort–a chamber sunk in the heart of the planet.

He was inside the tank. Buggies were everywhere, sliding and moving around. Machines, construction of different kinds, buildings, plants in rows, generators, homes, rooms of complex equipment.

Sections of the tank were closed off–bolted shut. Rusty, metal doors–machinery sinking into decay–valves closed, pipes rusting away–dials cracked and broken. Lines clogged–teeth missing from gears–more and more sections closed. Fewer buggies–fewer and fewer . . .

The scene changed. Earth, seen from a long way off–a distant green sphere, turning slowly, cloud-covered. Broad oceans, blue water miles deep–moist atmosphere. The buggies drifting through empty reaches of space, drifting slowly toward Earth, year after year. Drifting endlessly in the dark wastes with agonizing slowness.

Now Earth expanded. The scene was almost familiar. An ocean surface, miles of foaming water, a few gulls above, a distant shore line. The ocean, Earth's ocean. Clouds wandering above in the sky.

On the surface of the water flat spheres drifted, huge metal discs. Floating units, artificially built, several hundred feet around. Buggies rested silently on the discs, absorbing water and minerals from the ocean under them.

The buggie was trying to tell him something, something about itself. Discs on the water–the buggies wanted to use the water, to live on the water, on the surface of the ocean. Big surface discs, covered with buggies–it wanted him to know that, to see the discs, the water discs.

The buggies would live on the water, not on the land. Only the water–they wanted his permission. They wanted to use the water. That was what it was trying to tell him–that they wanted to use the surface of the water between the continents. Now the buggie was asking, imploring. It wanted to know. It wanted him to say, to answer, to give his permission. It was waiting to hear, waiting and hoping–imploring . . .

The scenes faded, winking out of his mind. Jimmy stumbled back, falling against the curb. He leaped up again, wiping damp grass from his hands. He was standing in the gutter. He could still see the buggie resting among the branches of the evergreen. It was almost invisible. He could scarcely make it out.

The drumming had receded, left his mind. The buggie had withdrawn.

Jimmy turned and fled. He ran across the street and down the other side, sobbing for breath. He came to the corner and turned up Douglas Street. At the bus-stop stood a heavy-set man with a lunchbucket under his arm.

Jimmy ran up to the man. 'A buggie. In the tree.' He gasped for breath. 'In the big tree.'

The man grunted. 'Run along, kid.'

'A buggie!' Jimmy's voice rose in panic, shrill and insistent. 'A buggie up in the tree!'

Two men loomed up out of the darkness. 'What? A buggie?'

'Where?'

More people appeared. 'Where is it?'

Jimmy pointed, gesturing. 'Pomeroy Estate. The tree. By the fence.' He waved, gasping.

A cop appeared. 'What's going on?'

'The kid's found a buggie. Somebody get a pole.'

'Show me where it is,' the cop said, grabbing hold of Jimmy's arm. 'Come on.'

Jimmy led them back down the street, to the brick wall. He hung back, away from the fence. 'Up there.'

'Which tree?'

'That one–I think.'

A flashlight flicked on, picking its way among the evergreens. In the Pomeroy house lights came on. The front door opened.

'What's going on there?' Mr Pomeroy's voice echoed angrily.

'Got a buggie. Keep back.'

Mr Pomeroy's doors slammed quickly shut.

'*There* it is!' Jimmy pointed up. '*That* tree.' His heart almost stopped beating. 'There. Up *there*!'

'Where?'

'I see it.' The cop moved back, his pistol out.

'You can't shoot it. Bullets go right through.'

'Somebody get a pole.'

'Too high for a pole.'

'Get a torch.'

'Somebody bring a torch!'

Two men ran off. Cars were stopping. A police car slid to a halt, its siren whirring into silence. Doors opened, men came running over. A searchlight flashed on, dazzling them. It found the buggie and locked into place.

The buggie rested unmoving, hugging the branch of the evergreen. In the blinding light it looked like some giant cocoon clinging uncertainly to its place. The buggie began to move hesitantly, creeping around the trunk. Its wisps reached out, feeling for support.

'A torch, damn it! Get a torch here!'

A man came with a blazing board ripped from a fence. They poured gasoline over newspapers heaped in a ring around the base of the tree. The bottom branches began to burn, feebly at first, then more brightly.

'Get more gas!'

A man in a white uniform came lugging a tank of gasoline. He threw the tankful of gas onto the tree. Flames blazed up, rising rapidly. The branches charred and crackled, burning furiously.

Far above them the buggie began to stir. It climbed uncertainly to a higher branch, pulling itself up. The flames licked closer. The buggie increased its pace. It undulated, dragging itself onto the next branch above. Higher and higher it climbed.

'Look at it go.'

'It won't get away. It's almost at the top.'

More gasoline was brought. The flames leaped higher. A crowd had collected around the fence. The police kept them back.

'There it goes.' The light moved to keep the buggie visible.

'It's at the top.'

The buggie had reached the top of the tree. It rested, holding onto the branch, swaying back and forth. Flames leaped from branch to branch, closer and closer to it. The buggie felt hesitantly around, blindly, seeking support. It reached, feeling with its wisps. A spurt of fire touched it.

The buggie crackled, smoke rising from it.

'It's burning!' An excited murmur swept through the crowd. 'It's finished.'

The buggie was on fire. It moved clumsily, trying to get away. Suddenly it dropped, falling to the branch below. For a second it hung on the branch, crackling and smoking. Then the branch gave way with a rending crackle.

The buggie fell to the ground, among the newspapers and gasoline.

The crowd roared. They seethed toward the tree, flowing and milling forward.

'*Step* on it!'

'*Get* it!'

'*Step* on the damn thing!'

Boots stamped again and again, feet rising and falling, grinding the buggie into the ground. A man fell, pulling himself away, his glasses hanging from one ear. Knots of struggling people fought with each other, pressing inward, trying to reach the tree. A flaming branch fell. Some of the crowd retreated.

'I *got* it!'

'Get *back*!'

More branches fell, crashing down. The crowd broke up, streaming back, laughing and pushing.

Jimmy felt the cop's hand on his arm, big fingers digging in. 'That's the end, boy. It's all over.'

'They get it?'

'They sure did. What's your name?'

'My name?' Jimmy started to tell the cop his name but just then some scuffling broke out between two men and the cop hurried over.

Jimmy stood for a moment, watching. The night was cold. A frigid wind blew around him, chilling him through his clothing. He thought suddenly of dinner and his father stretched out on the couch, reading the newspaper. His mother in the kitchen fixing dinner. The warmth, the friendly yellow homey warmth.

He turned and made his way through the people to the edge of the street. Behind him the charred stalk of the tree rose black and smoking into the night. A few glowing remains were being stamped out around its base. The buggie was gone, it was over, there was nothing more to see.

Jimmy hurried home as if the buggie were chasing him.

'What do you say to that?' Ted Barnes demanded, sitting with his legs crossed, his chair back from the table. The cafeteria was full of noise and the smell of food. People pushed their trays along on the racks in front of them, gathering dishes from the dispensers.

'Your kid really did that?' Bob Walters said, across from him, with open curiosity.

'You sure you're not stringing us along?' Frank Hendricks said, lowering his newspaper for a moment.

'It's the truth. The one they got over at the Pomeroy Estate–I'm talking about that one. It was a real son-of-a-gun.'

'That's right,' Jack Green admitted. 'The paper says some kid spotted it first and brought the police.'

'That was my kid,' Ted said, his chest swelling. 'What do you guys think about that?'

'Was he scared?' Bob Walters wanted to know.

'Hell no!' Ted Barnes replied strongly.

'I'll bet he was.' Frank Hendricks was from Missouri.

'He sure wasn't. He got the cops and brought them to the place–last night. We were sitting around the dinner table, wondering where the hell he was. I was getting a little worried.' Ted Barnes was still the proud parent.

Jack Green got to his feet, looking at his watch. 'Time to get back to the office.'

Frank and Bob got up also. 'See you later, Ted.'

Green thumped Ted on the back. 'Some kid you got, Barnes–chip off the old block.'

Ted grinned. 'He wasn't a bit afraid.' He watched them go out of the cafeteria onto the busy noonday street. After a moment he gulped down the rest of his coffee and wiped his chin, standing slowly up. 'Not a damn bit afraid–not one damn bit.'

He paid for his lunch and pushed his way outside onto the street, his chest still swelled up. He grinned at people passing by as he walked back to the office, all aglow with reflected glory.

'Not a bit afraid,' he murmured, full of pride, a deep glowing pride. 'Not one damn bit!'

THE COMMUTER

The little fellow was tired. He pushed his way slowly through the throng of people, across the lobby of the station, to the ticket window. He waited his turn impatiently, fatigue showing in his drooping shoulders, his sagging brown coat.

'Next,' Ed Jacobson, the ticket seller, rasped.

The little fellow tossed a five-dollar bill on the counter. 'Give me a new commute book. Used up the old one.' He peered past Jacobson at the wall clock. 'Lord, is it really that late?'

Jacobson accepted the five dollars. 'OK, mister. One commute book. Where to?'

'Macon Heights,' the little fellow stated.

'Macon Heights.' Jacobson consulted his board. 'Macon Heights. There isn't any such place.'

The little man's face hardened in suspicion. 'You trying to be funny?'

'Mister, there isn't any Macon Heights. I can't sell you a ticket unless there is such a place.'

'What do you mean? I live there!'

'I don't care. I've been selling tickets for six years and there is no such place.'

The little man's eyes popped with astonishment. 'But I have a home there. I go there every night. I–'

'Here.' Jacobson pushed him the chart board. 'You find it.'

The little man pulled the board over to one side. He studied it frantically, his finger trembling as he went down the list of towns.

'Find it?' Jacobson demanded, resting his arms on the counter. 'It's not there, is it?'

The little man shook his head, dazed. 'I don't understand. It doesn't make sense. Something must be wrong. There certainly must be–'

Suddenly he vanished. The board fell to the cement floor. The little fellow was gone–winked out of existence.

'Holy Caesar's Ghost,' Jacobson gasped. His mouth opened and closed. There was only the board lying on the cement floor.

The little man had ceased to exist.

'What then?' Bob Paine asked.

'I went around and picked up the board.'

'He was really gone?'

'He was gone, all right.' Jacobson mopped his forehead. 'I wish you had been around. Like a light he went out. Completely. No sound. No motion.'

Paine lit a cigarette, leaning back in his chair. 'Had you ever seen him before?'

'No.'

'What time of day was it?'

'Just about now. About five.' Jacobson moved toward the ticket window. 'Here comes a bunch of people.'

'Macon Heights.' Paine turned the pages of the State city guide. 'No listing in any of the books. If he reappears I want to talk to him. Get him inside the office.'

'Sure. I don't want to have nothing to do with him. It isn't natural.' Jacobson turned to the window. 'Yes, lady.'

'Two round-trip tickets to Lewisburg.'

Paine stubbed his cigarette out and lit another. 'I keep feeling I've heard the name before.' He got up and wandered over to the wall map. 'But it isn't listed.'

'There is no listing because there is no such place,' Jacobson said. 'You think I could stand here daily, selling one ticket after another, and not know?' He turned back to his window. 'Yes, sir.'

'I'd like a commute book to Macon Heights,' the little fellow said, glancing nervously at the clock on the wall. 'And hurry it up.'

Jacobson closed his eyes. He hung on tight. When he opened his eyes again the little fellow was still there. Small wrinkled face. Thinning hair. Glasses. Tired, slumped coat.

Jacobson turned and moved across the office to Paine. 'He's back.' Jacobson swallowed, his face pale. 'It's him again.'

Paine's eyes flickered. 'Bring him right in.'

Jacobson nodded and returned to the window. 'Mister,' he said, 'could you please come inside?' He indicated the door. 'The Vice-President would like to see you for a moment.'

The little man's face darkened. 'What's up? The train's about to take off.' Grumbling under his breath, he pushed the door open and entered the office. 'This sort of thing has never happened before. It's certainly getting hard to purchase a commute book. If I miss the train I'm going to hold your company–'

'Sit down,' Paine said, indicating the chair across from his desk. 'You're the gentleman who wants a commute book to Macon Heights?'

'Is there something strange about that? What's the matter with all of you? Why can't you sell me a commute book like you always do?'

'Like–like we *always* do?'

The little man held himself in check with great effort. 'Last December my wife and I moved out to Macon Heights. I've been riding your train ten times a week, twice a day, for six months. Every month I buy a new commute book.'

Paine leaned toward him. 'Exactly which one of our trains do you take, Mr–'

'Critchet. Ernest Critchet. The B train. Don't you know your own schedules?'

'The B train?' Paine consulted a B train chart, running his pencil along it. No Macon Heights was listed. 'How long is the trip? How long does it take?'

'Exactly forty-nine minutes.' Critchet looked up at the wall clock. 'If I ever get on it.'

Paine calculated mentally. Forty-nine minutes. About thirty miles from the city. He got up and crossed to the big wall map.

'What's wrong?' Critchet asked with marked suspicion.

Paine drew a thirty-mile circle on the map. The circle crossed a number of towns, but none of them was Macon Heights. And on the B line there was nothing at all.

'What sort of place is Macon Heights?' Paine asked. 'How many people, would you say?'

'I don't know. Five thousand, maybe. I spend most of my time in the city. I'm a bookkeeper over at Bradshaw Insurance.'

'Is Macon Heights a fairly new place?'

'It's modern enough. We have a little two-bedroom house, a couple years old.' Critchet stirred restlessly. 'How about a commute book?'

'I'm afraid,' Paine said slowly, 'I can't sell you a commute book.'

'What? Why not?'

'We don't have any service to Macon Heights.'

Critchet leaped up. 'What do you mean?'

'There's no such place. Look at the map yourself.'

Critchet gaped, his face working. Then he turned angrily to the wall map, glaring at it intently.

'This is a curious situation, Mr Critchet,' Paine murmured. 'It isn't on the map, and the State city directory doesn't list it. We have no schedule that includes it. There are no commute books made up for it. We don't–'

He broke off. Critchet had vanished. One moment he was there, studying the wall map. The next moment he was gone. Vanished. Puffed out.

'Jacobson!' Paine barked. 'He's gone!'

Jacobson's eyes grew large. Sweat stood out on his forehead. 'So he is,' he murmured.

Paine was deep in thought, gazing at the empty spot Ernest Critchet had occupied. 'Something's going on,' he muttered.

'Something damn strange.' Abruptly he grabbed his overcoat and headed for the door.

'Don't leave me alone!' Jacobson begged.

'If you need me I'll be at Laura's apartment. The number's some place in my desk.'

'This is no time for games with girls.'

Paine pushed open the door to the lobby. 'I doubt,' he said grimly, 'if this is a game.'

Paine climbed the stairs to Laura Nichols' apartment two at a time. He leaned on the buzzer until the door opened.

'Bob!' Laura blinked in surprise. 'To what do I owe this–'

Paine pushed past her, inside the apartment. 'Hope I'm not interrupting anything.'

'No, but–'

'Big doings. I'm going to need some help. Can I count on you?'

'On me?' Laura closed the door after him. Her attractively furnished apartment lay in half shadow. At the end of the deep green couch a single table lamp burned. The heavy drapes were pulled. The phonograph was on low in the corner.

'Maybe I'm going crazy.' Paine threw himself down on the luxuriant green couch. 'That's what I want to find out.'

'How can I help?' Laura came languidly over, her arms folded, a cigarette between her lips. She shook her long hair back out of her eyes. 'Just what did you have in mind?'

Paine grinned at the girl appreciatively. 'You'll be surprised. I want you to go downtown tomorrow morning bright and early and–'

'Tomorrow morning! I have a job, remember? And the office starts a whole new string of reports this week.'

'The hell with that. Take the morning off. Go downtown to the main library. If you can't get the information there, go over to the county courthouse and start looking through the back tax records. Keep looking until you find it.'

'It? Find what?'

Paine lit a cigarette thoughtfully. 'Mention of a place called Macon Heights. I know I've heard the name before. Years ago. Got the picture? Go through the old atlases. Old newspapers in the reading room. Old magazines. Reports. City proposals. Propositions before the State legislature.'

Laura sat down slowly on the arm of the couch. 'Are you kidding?'

'No.'

'How far back?'

'Maybe ten years–if necessary.'

'Good Lord! I might have to–'

'Stay there until you find it.' Paine got up abruptly. 'I'll see you later.'

'You're leaving. You're not taking me out to dinner?'

'Sorry.' Paine moved toward the door. 'I'll be busy. Real busy.'

'Doing what?'

'Visiting Macon Heights.'

Outside the train endless fields stretched off, broken by an occasional farm building. Bleak telephone poles jutted up toward the evening sky.

Paine glanced at his wristwatch. Not far, now. The train passed through a small town. A couple of gas stations, roadside stands, television store. It stopped at the station, brakes grinding. Lewisburg. A few commuters got off, men in overcoats with evening papers. The doors slammed and the train started up.

Paine settled back against his seat, deep in thought. Critchet had vanished while looking at the wall map. He had vanished the first time when Jacobson showed him the chart board . . . When he had been shown there was no such place as Macon Heights. Was there some sort of clue there? The whole thing was unreal, dreamlike.

Paine peered out. He was almost there–if there were such a place. Outside the train the brown fields stretched off endlessly. Hills and level fields. Telephone poles. Cars racing along the State highway, tiny black specks hurrying through the twilight.

But no sign of Macon Heights.

The train roared on its way. Paine consulted his watch. Fifty-one minutes had passed. And he had seen nothing. Nothing but fields.

He walked up the car and sat down beside the conductor, a white-haired old gentleman. 'Ever hear of a place called Macon Heights?' Paine asked.

'No, sir.'

Paine showed his identification. 'You're sure you never heard of any place by that name?'

'Positive, Mr Paine.'

'How long have you been on this run?'

'Eleven years, Mr Paine.'

Paine rode on until the next stop, Jacksonville. He got off and transferred to a B train heading back to the city. The sun had set. The sky was almost black. Dimly, he could make out the scenery out there beyond the window.

He tensed, holding his breath. One minute to go. Forty seconds. Was there anything? Level fields. Bleak telephone poles. A barren, wasted landscape between towns.

Between? The train rushed on, hurtling through the gloom. Paine gazed out fixedly. Was there something out there? Something beside the fields?

Above the fields a long mass of translucent smoke lay stretched out. A homogeneous mass, extended for almost a mile. What was it? Smoke from the engine? But the engine was diesel. From a truck along the highway? A brush fire? None of the fields looked burned.

Suddenly the train began to slow. Paine was instantly alert. The train was stopping, coming to a halt. The brakes screeched, the cars lurched from side to side. Then silence.

Across the aisle a tall man in a light coat got to his feet, put his hat on, and moved rapidly toward the door. He leaped down from the train, onto the ground. Paine watched him, fascinated. The man walked rapidly away from the train across the dark fields. He moved with purpose, heading toward the bank of gray haze.

The man rose. He was walking a foot off the ground. He turned to the right. He rose again, now–three feet off the ground. For a moment he walked parallel to the ground, still heading away from the train. Then he vanished into the bank of haze. He was gone.

Paine hurried up the aisle. But already the train had begun gathering speed. The ground moved past outside. Paine located the conductor, leaning against the wall of the car, a pudding-faced youth.

'Listen,' Paine grated. 'What was that stop!'

'Beg pardon, sir?'

'That stop! Where the hell were we?'

'We always stop there.' Slowly, the conductor reached into his coat and brought out a handful of schedules. He sorted through them and passed one to Paine. 'The B always stops at Macon Heights. Didn't you know that?'

'No!'

'It's on the schedule.' The youth raised his pulp magazine again. 'Always stops there. Always has. Always will.'

Paine tore the schedule open. It was true. Macon Heights was listed between Jacksonville and Lewisburg. Exactly thirty miles from the city.

The cloud of gray haze. The vast cloud, gaining form rapidly. As if something were coming into existence. As a matter of fact, something *was* coming into existence.

Macon Heights!

He caught Laura at her apartment the next morning. She was sitting at the coffee table in a pale pink sweater and dark slacks. Before her was a pile of notes, a pencil and eraser, and a malted milk.

'How did you make out?' Paine demanded.

'Fine. I got your information.'

'What's the story?'

'There was quite a bit of material.' She patted the sheaf of notes. 'I summed up the major parts for you.'

'Let's have the summation.'

'Seven years ago this August the county board of supervisors voted on three new suburban housing tracts to be set up outside the city. Macon Heights was one of them. There was a big debate. Most of the city merchants opposed the new tracts. Said they would draw too much retail business away from the city.'

'Go on.'

'There was a long fight. Finally two of the three tracts were approved. Waterville and Cedar Groves. But not Macon Heights.'

'I see,' Paine murmured thoughtfully.

'Macon Heights was defeated. A compromise; two tracts instead of three. The two tracts were built up right away. You know. We passed through Waterville one afternoon. Nice little place.'

'But no Macon Heights.'

'No. Macon Heights was given up.'

Paine rubbed his jaw. 'That's the story, then.'

'That's the story. Do you realize I lose a whole half-day's pay because of this? You *have* to take me out, tonight. Maybe I should get another fellow. I'm beginning to think you're not such a good bet.'

Paine nodded absently. 'Seven years ago.' All at once a thought came to him. 'The vote! How close was the vote on Macon Heights?'

Laura consulted her notes. 'The project was defeated by a single vote.'

'A single vote. Seven years ago.' Paine moved out into the hall. 'Thanks, honey. Things are beginning to make sense. Lots of sense!'

He caught a cab out front. The cab raced him across the city, toward the train station. Outside, signs and streets flashed by. People and stores and cars.

His hunch had been correct. He *had* heard the name before. Seven years ago. A bitter county debate on a proposed suburban tract. Two towns approved; one defeated and forgotten.

But now the forgotten town was coming into existence–seven years later. The town and an undetermined slice of reality along with it. *Why?* Had something changed in the past? Had an alteration occurred in some past continuum?

That seemed like the explanation. The vote had been close. Macon Heights had *almost* been approved. Maybe certain parts of the past were unstable. Maybe that particular period, seven years ago, had been critical. Maybe it had never completely 'jelled.' An odd thought: the past changing, after it had already happened.

Suddenly Paine's eyes focused. He sat up quickly. Across the street was a store sign, halfway along the block. Over a small, inconspicuous establishment. As the cab moved forward Paine peered to see.

BRADSHAW INSURANCE

[OR]

NOTARY PUBLIC

He pondered. Critchet's place of business. Did it also come and go? Had it always been there? Something about it made him uneasy.

'Hurry it up,' Paine ordered the driver. 'Let's get going.'

When the train slowed down at Macon Heights, Paine got quickly to his feet and made his way up the aisle to the door. The grinding wheels jerked to a halt and Paine leaped down onto the hot gravel siding. He looked around him.

In the afternoon sunlight, Macon Heights glittered and sparkled, its even rows of houses stretching out in all directions. In the center of the town the marquee of a theater rose up.

A theater, even. Paine headed across the track toward the town. Beyond the train station was a parking lot. He stepped up onto the lot and crossed it, following a path past a filling station and onto a sidewalk.

He came out on the main street of the town. A double row of stores stretched out ahead of him. A hardware store. Two drugstores. A dime store. A modern department store.

Paine walked along, hands in his pockets, gazing around him at Macon Heights. An apartment building stuck up, tall and fat. A janitor was washing down the front steps. Everything looked new and modern. The houses, the stores, the pavement and sidewalks.

The parking meters. A brown-uniformed cop was giving a car a ticket. Trees, growing at intervals. Neatly clipped and pruned.

He passed a big supermarket. Out in front was a bin of fruit, oranges and grapes. He picked a grape and bit into it.

The grape was real, all right. A big black concord grape, sweet and ripe. Yet twenty-four hours ago there had been nothing here but a barren field.

Paine entered one of the drugstores. He leafed through some magazines and then sat down at the counter. He ordered a cup of coffee from the red-cheeked little waitress.

'This is a nice town,' Paine said, as she brought the coffee.

'Yes, isn't it?'

Paine hesitated. 'How–how long have you been working here?'

'Three months.'

'Three months?' Paine studied the buxom little blonde. 'You live here in Macon Heights?'

'Oh, yes.'

'How long?'

'A couple years, I guess.' She moved away to wait on a young soldier who had taken a stool down the counter.

Paine sat drinking his coffee and smoking, idly watching the people passing by outside. Ordinary people. Men and women, mostly women. Some had grocery bags and little wire carts. Automobiles drove slowly back and forth. A sleepy little suburban town. Modern, upper middle-class. A quality town. No slums here. Small, attractive houses. Stores with sloping glass fronts and neon signs.

Some high school kids burst into the drugstore, laughing and bumping into each other. Two girls in bright sweaters sat down next to Paine and ordered lime drinks. They chatted gaily, bits of their conversation drifting to him.

He gazed at them, pondering moodily. They were real, all right. Lipstick and red fingernails. Sweaters and armloads of school books. Hundreds of high school kids, crowding eagerly into the drugstore.

Paine rubbed his forehead wearily. It didn't seem possible. Maybe he was out of his mind. The town was *real*. Completely real. It must have always existed. A whole town couldn't rise up out of nothing; out of a cloud of gray haze. Five thousand people, houses and streets and stores.

Stores. Bradshaw Insurance.

Stabbing realization chilled him. Suddenly he understood. It was spreading. Beyond Macon Heights. Into the city. The city was changing, too. Bradshaw Insurance. Critchet's place of business.

Macon Heights couldn't exist without warping the city. They interlocked. The five thousand people came from the city. Their jobs. Their lives. The city was involved.

But how much? How much was the city changing?

Paine threw a quarter on the counter and hurried out of the drugstore, toward the train station. He had to get back to the city. Laura, the change. Was she still there? Was his *own* life safe?

Fear gripped him. Laura, all his possessions, his plans, hopes and dreams. Suddenly Macon Heights was unimportant. His own world was in jeopardy. Only one thing mattered now. He had to make sure of it; make sure his own life was still here. Untouched by the spreading circle of change that was lapping out from Macon Heights.

'Where to, buddy?' the cabdriver asked, as Paine came rushing out of the train station.

Paine gave him the address of the apartment. The cab roared out into traffic. Paine settled back nervously. Outside the window the streets and office buildings flashed past. White-collar workers were already beginning to get off work, swelling out onto the sidewalks to stand in clumps at each corner.

How much had changed? He concentrated on a row of buildings. The big department store. Had that always been there? The little boot-black shop next to it. He had never noticed that before.

NORRIS HOME FURNISHINGS

He didn't remember *that*. But how could he be sure? He felt confused. How could he tell?

The cab let him off in front of the apartment house. Paine stood for a moment, looking around him. Down at the end of the block the owner of the Italian delicatessen was out putting up the awning. Had he ever noticed a delicatessen there before?

He could not remember.

What had happened to the big meat market across the street? There was nothing but neat little houses; older houses that looked like they'd been there plenty long. Had a meat market ever been there? The houses *looked* solid.

In the next block the striped pole of a barbershop glittered. Had there always been a barbershop there?

Maybe it had always been there. Maybe, and maybe not. Everything was shifting. New things were coming into existence, others going away. The past was altering, and memory was tied to the past. How could he trust his memory? How could he be sure?

Terror gripped him. Laura. His world . . .

Paine raced up the front steps and pushed open the door of the apartment house. He hurried up the carpeted stairs to the second floor. The door of the apartment was unlocked. He pushed it open and entered, his heart in his mouth, praying silently.

The living room was dark and silent. The shades were half pulled. He glanced around wildly. The light blue couch, magazines on its arms. The low blond-oak table. The television set. But the room was empty.

'Laura!' he gasped.

Laura hurried from the kitchen, eyes wide with alarm. 'Bob! what are you doing home? Is anything the matter?'

Paine relaxed, sagging with relief. 'Hello, honey.' He kissed her, holding her tight against him. She was warm and substantial; completely real. 'No, nothing's wrong. Everything's fine.'

'Are you sure?'

'I'm sure.' Paine took off his coat shakily and dropped it over the back of the couch. He wandered around the room, examining things, his confidence returning. His familiar blue couch, cigarette burns on its arms. His ragged footstool. His desk where he did his work at night. His fishing rods leaning up against the wall behind the bookcase.

The big television set he had purchased only last month; that was safe, too.

Everything, all he owned, was untouched. Safe. Unharmed.

'Dinner won't be ready for half an hour,' Laura murmured anxiously, unfastening her apron. 'I didn't expect you home so early. I've just been sitting around all day. I did clean the stove. Some salesman left a sample of a new cleanser.'

'That's OK.' He examined a favorite Renoir print on the wall. 'Take your time. It's good to see all these things again. I–'

From the bedroom a crying sound came. Laura turned quickly. 'I guess we woke up Jimmy.'

'Jimmy?'

Laura laughed. 'Darling, don't you remember your own son?'

'Of course,' Paine murmured, annoyed. He followed Laura slowly into the bedroom. 'Just for a minute everything seemed strange.' He rubbed his forehead, frowning. 'Strange and unfamiliar. Sort of out of focus.'

They stood by the crib, gazing down at the baby. Jimmy glared back up at his mother and dad.

'It must have been the sun,' Laura said. 'It's so terribly hot outside.'

'That must be it. I'm OK now.' Paine reached down and poked at the baby. He put his arm around his wife, hugging her to him. 'It must have been the sun,' he said. He looked down into her eyes and smiled.

THE WORLD SHE WANTED

Half-dozing, Larry Brewster contemplated the litter of cigarette-butts, empty beer-bottles, and twisted match-folders heaped on the table before him. He reached out and adjusted one beer-bottle—thereby achieving just the right effect.

In the back of the Wind-Up the small dixieland jazz combo played noisily. The harsh jazz-sound mixed with the murmur of voices, the semi-darkness, the clink of glasses at the bar. Larry Brewster sighed in happy contentment. 'This,' he stated, 'is Nirvana.' He nodded his head slowly, agreeing with the words uttered. 'Or at least the seventh level of zen-buddhist heaven.'

'There aren't seven levels in the zen-buddhist heaven,' a competent female voice corrected, from directly above him.

'That's a fact,' Larry admitted, reflecting on the matter. 'I was speaking metaphorically, not literally.'

'You should be more careful; you should mean exactly what you say.'

'And say exactly what you mean?' Larry peered up. 'Have I had the pleasure of knowing you, young lady?'

The slender, golden-haired girl dropped into the seat across the table from Larry, her eyes sharp and bright in the half-gloom of the bar. She smiled at him, white teeth sparkling. 'No,' she said. 'We've never met; our time has just now arrived.'

'Our—our time?' Larry drew himself up slowly, pulling his lanky frame together. There was something in the girl's bright, competent face that vaguely alarmed him, penetrating his alcoholic haze.

Her smile was too calm, too assured. 'Just exactly what do you mean?' Larry murmured. 'What's this all about?'

The girl slipped out of her coat, revealing full, rounded breasts and supple figure. 'I'll have a martini,' she said. 'And by the way–my name is Allison Holmes.'

'Larry Brewster.' Larry studied the girl intently. 'What did you say you wanted?'

'A martini. Dry.' Allison smiled coolly across at him. 'And get one for yourself, why don't you?'

Larry grunted under his breath. He signalled to the waiter. 'A dry martini, Max.'

'Okay, Mr Brewster.'

A few minutes later Max returned and set a martini glass on the table. When he had gone, Larry leaned toward the blonde-haired girl. 'Now, Miss Holmes–'

'None for you?'

'None for me.' Larry watched her sip her drink. Her hands were small and dainty. She wasn't bad-looking, but he didn't like the self-satisfied calmness in her eyes. 'What's this business about our time having come? Let me in on it.'

'It's very simple. I saw you sitting here and I knew you were the one. In spite of the messy table.' She wrinkled her nose at the litter of bottles and match-folders. 'Why don't you have them clear it off?'

'Because I enjoy it. You knew I was the *one*? Which one?' Larry was getting interested. 'Go on.'

'Larry, this is a very important moment in my life.' Allison gazed around her. 'Who would think I'd find you in a place like this? But that's the way it's always been for me. This is only one link of a great chain going back–well, as far back as I can remember.'

'What chain is that?'

Allison laughed. 'Poor Larry. You don't understand.' She leaned toward him, her lovely eyes dancing. 'You see, Larry, I know something no one else knows–no one else in this world. Something I learned when I was a little girl. Something–'

'Wait a minute. What do you mean by "this world"? You mean

there are nicer worlds than this? Better worlds? Like in Plato? This world is only a–'

'Certainly not!' Allison frowned. 'This is the best world, Larry. The best of all possible worlds.'

'Oh. Herbert Spencer.'

'The best of all possible worlds–for me.' She smiled at him, a cold, secret smile.

'Why for you?'

There was something almost predatory in the girl's finely-chiseled face as she answered. 'Because,' she said calmly, 'this is *my* world.'

Larry raised an eyebrow. 'Your world?' Then he grinned good-naturedly. 'Sure it is, baby; it belongs to all of us.' He waved expansively around at the room. 'Your world, my world, the banjo player's world–'

'No.' Allison shook her head firmly. 'No, Larry. My world; it belongs to me. Everything and everybody. All mine.' She moved her chair around until she was close by him. He could smell her perfume, warm and sweet and tantalizing. 'Don't you understand? This is mine. All these things–they're here for me; for my happiness.'

Larry edged away a little. 'Oh? You know, as a philosophical tenet that's a bit hard to maintain. I'll admit Descartes said the world is known to us only through our senses, and our senses reflect our own–'

Allison laid her small hand on his arm. 'I don't mean that. You see, Larry, there are *many* worlds. All kinds of worlds. Millions and millions. As many worlds as there are people. Each person has his own world, Larry, his own private world. A world that exists for him, for his happiness.' She lowered her gaze modestly. 'This happens to be *my* world.'

Larry considered. 'Very interesting, but what about other people? Me, for example.'

'You exist for my happiness, of course; that's what I'm talking about.' The pressure of her small hand increased. 'As soon as I saw you, I knew you were the one. I've been thinking about this for several days now. It's time *he* came along. The man for me. The man intended for me to marry–so my happiness can be complete.'

'Hey!' Larry exclaimed, drawing back.

'What's wrong?'

'What about *me*?' Larry demanded. 'That's not fair! Doesn't *my* happiness count?'

'Yes . . . but not here, not in this world.' She gestured vaguely. 'You have a world someplace else, a world of your own; in this world you're merely a part of my life. You're not completely real. I'm the only one in this world who's *completely* real. All the rest of you are here for me. You're just–just *partly* real.'

'I see.' Larry sat back slowly, rubbing his jaw. 'Then I sort of exist in a lot of different worlds. A little bit here, a little bit there, according to where I'm needed. Like now, for instance, in this world. I've been wandering around for twenty-five years, just so I could turn up when you needed me.'

'That's right,' Allison's eyes danced merrily; 'you have the idea.' Suddenly she glanced at her wristwatch. 'It's getting late. We better go.'

'Go?'

Allison stood up quickly, picking up her tiny purse and pulling her coat around her. 'I want to do so many things with you, Larry! So many places to see! So much to do!' She took hold of his arm. 'Come on. Hurry up.'

Larry rose slowly. 'Say, listen–'

'We're going to have lots of fun.' Allison steered him toward the door. 'Let's see . . . What would be nice . . .'

Larry halted angrily. 'The check! I can't just walk out.' He fumbled in his pocket. 'I owe about–'

'No check; not tonight. This is my special night.' Allison spun toward Max, cleaning up the vacated table. 'Isn't that right?'

The old waiter looked up slowly. 'What's that, Miss?'

'No check tonight.'

Max shook his head. 'No check tonight, Miss. The boss's birthday; drinks on the house.'

Larry gaped. 'What?'

'Come on.' Allison tugged at him, pulling him through the heavy plush doors, out onto the cold, dark New York sidewalk. 'Come on, Larry–we have so much to do!'

Larry murmured, 'I still don't know where that cab came from.'

The cab drove off, racing away down the street. Larry looked around. Where were they? The dark streets were silent and deserted.

'First,' Allison Holmes said, 'I want a corsage. Larry, don't you think you should present your fiancée with a corsage? I want to go in looking nice.'

'A corsage? At this time of night?' Larry gestured at the dark, silent streets. 'Are you kidding?'

Allison pondered, then she crossed the street, abruptly; Larry followed after her. Allison came up to a closed-up flower shop, its sign off, door locked. She rapped with a coin on the plate glass window.

'Have you gone crazy?' Larry cried. 'There's nobody in there, this time of night!'

In the back of the flower shop somebody stirred. An old man came slowly toward the window, removing his glasses and putting them in his pocket. He bent down and unlocked the door. 'What is it, lady?'

'I want a corsage, the best you have.' Allison pushed into the shop, gazing around at the flowers in awe.

'Forget it, buddy,' Larry murmured; 'don't pay any attention to her. She's–'

'That's all right.' The old man sighed. 'I was going over my income tax; I can use a break. There should be some already made up. I'll open the refrigerator.'

Five minutes later they were out on the street again, Allison gazing ecstatically down at the great orchid pinned to her coat. 'It's beautiful, Larry!' she whispered. She squeezed his arm, gazing up in his face. 'Thanks a lot; now, let's go.'

'Where? Maybe you found an old guy sweating over his tax

returns at one o'clock in the morning, but I defy you to find anything else in this god-forsaken graveyard.'

Allison looked around. 'Let's see . . . Over this way. This big old house over here. I wouldn't be a bit surprised–' She tugged Larry down the sidewalk, her high heels clattering in the night silence.

'All right,' Larry murmured, grinning a little. 'I'll go along with you; this ought to be interesting.'

No light showed in the great square house; all the shades were down. Allison hurried down the walk, feeling her way through the darkness, up onto the porch of the house.

'Hey!' Larry exclaimed, suddenly alarmed. Allison had taken hold of the doorknob; she pushed the door open.

A burst of light struck them, light and sound. The murmur of voices. Past a heavy curtain people moved, an immense room of people. Men and women in evening dress, bending over long tables and counters.

'Oh, oh,' Larry muttered. 'Now you've got us into it; this is no place for us.'

Three tough-looking gorillas came strolling over, their hands in their pockets. 'Okay, mister; let's go.'

Larry started out. 'That's fine by me. I'm an easy-going person.'

'Nonsense.' Allison caught hold of his arm, her eyes glittering with excitement. 'I always wanted to visit a gambling-place. Look at all the tables! What are they doing? What's that over there?'

'For Lord's sake,' Larry gasped desperately. 'Let's get out of here. These people don't know us.'

'You bet we don't,' one of the three hulking bruisers rasped. He nodded to his companions. 'Here we go.' They grabbed hold of Larry and propelled him toward the door.

Allison blinked. 'What are you doing to him? You stop that!' She concentrated, her lips moving. 'Let me–let me talk to *Connie*.'

The three bruisers froze. They turned toward her slowly. 'To *who*? Who did you say, lady?'

Allison smiled up at them. 'To Connie–I think. Isn't that what

I said? Connie. Where is he?' She looked around. 'Is that him over there?'

A small dapper man at one of the tables turned resentfully at his name, his face twisting with annoyance.

'Let it go, lady,' one of the bruisers said quickly. 'Don't bother Connie; he don't like to be bothered.' He closed the door, pushing Larry and Allison past the curtain, into the big room. 'You go and play. Enjoy yourselves; have a good time.'

Larry looked down at the girl beside him. He shook his head weakly. 'I could sure use a drink–a stiff one.'

'All right,' Allison said happily, her eyes fastened on the roulette table. 'You go have your drink. I'm going to start playing!'

After a couple of good stiff scotch-and-waters, Larry slid off the stool and wandered away from the bar, over toward the roulette table in the center of the room.

A big crowd had collected around the table. Larry closed his eyes, steadying himself; he knew already. After he had gathered his strength he pushed his way through the people and up to the table.

'What does this one mean?' Allison was asking the croupier, holding up a blue chip. In front of her was an immense stack of chips–all colors. Everyone was murmuring and talking and looking at her.

Larry made his way over to her. 'How are you getting along? Lost your dowry yet?'

'Not yet. According to this man, I'm ahead.'

'He should know,' Larry sighed wearily; 'he's in the business.'

'Do you want to play, too?' Allison asked, accepting an armload of chips. 'You can have these. I've got more.'

'I see that. But–no, thanks; it's out of my line. Come on.' Larry led her away from the table. 'I think the time has come for you and me to have a little chat. Over in the corner where it's quiet.'

'A chat?'

'I got to thinking about it; this thing has gone far enough.'

Allison trailed after him. Larry strode over to the side of the room. In a huge fireplace, a roaring fire blazed. Larry threw himself down in a deep chair, pointing to the chair next to it. 'Sit,' Larry said.

Allison sat down, crossing her legs and smoothing down her skirt. She leaned back, sighing. 'Isn't this nice? The fire and everything? Just what I always imagined.' She closed her eyes dreamily.

Larry took his cigarettes out and lit up slowly, deep in thought. 'Now look here, Miss Holmes–'

'Allison. After all, we're going to be married.'

'Allison, then. Look here, Allison, this whole thing is absurd. While I was at the bar I got to thinking it over. It isn't right, this crazy theory of yours.'

'Why not?' Her voice was sleepy, far-off.

Larry gestured angrily. 'I'll tell you why not. You claim I'm only *partly* real. Isn't that right? You're the only one who's completely real.'

Allison nodded. 'That's right.'

'But look! I don't know about all these other people–' Larry waved at them deprecatingly. 'Maybe you're right about them. Maybe they *are* only phantoms. But not me! You can't say I'm just a phantom.' He banged his fist against the arm of the chair. 'See? You call that just partly real?'

'The chair's only partly real, too.'

Larry groaned. 'Damn it, I've been in this world twenty-five years, and I just met you a few hours ago. Am I supposed to believe I'm not really alive? Not really–not really me? That I'm only a sort of–a hunk of scenery in your world? Part of the fixtures?'

'Larry, darling. You *have* your own world. We each have our own world. But this one happens to be mine, and you're in it for me.' Allison opened her large blue eyes. 'In your real world I may exist a little for you, too. All our worlds overlap, darling; don't you see? You exist for me in my world. Probably I exist for you in yours.' She smiled. 'The Great Designer has to be economical–like all good artists. Many of the worlds are similar, almost the same. But each of them belongs to only one person.'

'And this one is yours.' Larry let his breath out with a sigh. 'Okay, baby. You have your mind made up; I'll play along with you–for a while, at least. I'll string along.' He contemplated the girl leaning back in the deep chair next to him. 'You know, you're not bad-looking, not bad at all.'

'Thank you.'

'Yeah, I'll bite. For a while, at least. Maybe we *are* meant for each other. But you've got to calm down a little; you try your luck too hard. If you're going to be around me, you better take it a little easier.'

'What do you mean, Larry?'

'All this. This place. What if the cops come? Gambling. Running around.' Larry gazed off into the distance. 'No, this isn't right. This isn't the kind of life I've got pictured. You know what I see in my mind's eye?' Larry's face lit up with wistful pleasure. 'I see a little house, baby. Out in the country. Way out. The farm country. Flat fields. Maybe Kansas. Colorado. A little cabin. With a well. And cows.'

Allison frowned. 'Oh?'

'And you know what else? Me, out in the back. Farming. Or–or feeding the chickens. Ever fed chickens?' Larry shook his head happily. 'A lot of fun, baby. And squirrels. Ever walk in the park and feed squirrels? Gray squirrels, big long tails? Tails as long as the squirrels.'

Allison yawned. Abruptly she got to her feet, picking up her purse. 'I think it's time we ran along.'

Larry got up slowly. 'Yeah, I guess it is.'

'Tomorrow is going to be a busy day. I want to get started early.' Allison made her way through the people, toward the door. 'First of all, I think we should begin looking for–'

Larry stopped her. 'Your chips.'

'What?'

'Your chips. Turn them in.'

'What for?'

'For money–I think they call it now.'

'Oh, bother.' Allison turned to a heavy-set man sitting at the black-jack table. 'Here!' She dumped the chips in the man's lap. 'You take them. All right, Larry. Let's go!'

The cab pulled up in front of Larry's apartment. 'Is this where you live?' Allison asked, gazing up at the building. 'It's not very modern, is it?'

'No.' Larry pushed the door open. 'And the plumbing isn't very good, either. But what the hell.'

'Larry?' Allison stopped him as he started to get out.

'Yes?'

'You won't forget about tomorrow, will you?'

'Tomorrow?'

'We have so much to do. I want you to be up bright and early, ready to go places. So we can get things done.'

'How about six o'clock in the evening? Is that early enough?' Larry yawned. It was late, and cold.

'Oh, no. I'll be by for you at ten A.M.'

'Ten! But my job. I go to work!'

'Not tomorrow. Tomorrow is *our* day.'

'How the hell am I going to live if I don't–'

Allison reached up, putting her slender arms around him. 'Don't worry; it'll be all right. Remember? This is my world.' She pulled him down to her, kissing him on the mouth. Her lips were sweet and cool. She held onto him tightly, her eyes closed.

Larry broke away. 'All right, already.' He straightened his tie, standing up on the pavement.

'Tomorrow, then. And don't worry about your old job. Goodbye, Larry darling.' Allison slammed the door. The cab drove off down the dark street. Larry gazed after it, still dazed. Finally he shrugged and turned toward the apartment house.

Inside, on the table in the hall, was a letter for him. He scooped it up, opening it as he climbed the stairs. The letter was from his office, Bray Insurance Company. The annual vacation schedule for the staff, listing the two weeks doled out to each employee. He didn't even have to find his name to know when *his* began.

'*Don't worry*,' Allison had said.

Larry grinned ruefully, stuffing the letter in his coat pocket. He unlocked his apartment door. Ten o'clock did she say? Well, at least he would have a good night's sleep.

The day was warm and bright. Larry Brewster sat out on the front steps of the apartment building, smoking and thinking while he waited for Allison.

She was doing all right; no doubt about that. A hell of a lot of things seemed to fall like ripe plums into her lap. No wonder she thought it was her world . . . She was getting the breaks, all right. But some people were like that. Lucky. Walked into fortune every time; won on quiz shows; found money in the gutter; bet on the right horse. It happened.

Her world? Larry grinned. Apparently Allison really believed it. Interesting. Well, he'd string along with her a little while longer, at least; she was a nice kid.

A horn sounded, and Larry glanced up. A two-tone convertible was parked in front of him, the top down. Allison waved. 'Hi! Come on!'

Larry got up and came over. 'Where did you get this?' He opened the door and slid in slowly.

'This?' Allison started the car up. It zoomed out into traffic. 'I forget; I think someone gave it to me.'

'You forget!' He stared at her. Then he relaxed against the soft seat. 'Well? What's first on the list?'

'We're going to look at our new house.'

'Whose new house?'

'Ours. Yours and mine.'

Larry sank down into the seat. 'What! But you–'

Allison spun the car around a corner. 'You'll love it; it's nice. How big is your apartment?'

'Three rooms.'

Allison laughed merrily. 'This is eleven rooms. Two stories. Half an acre. Or so they tell me.'

'Haven't you seen it?'

'Not yet. My lawyer just called me this morning.'

'Your lawyer?'

'It's part of an estate left to me.'

Larry pulled himself together slowly. Allison, in a scarlet two-piece outfit, gazed happily at the road ahead, her small face blank and contented. 'Let me get all this straight. You've never seen it; your lawyer just called you; you get it as part of an estate.'

'That's right. Some old uncle of mine. I forget his name. I didn't expect him to leave me anything.' She turned toward Larry, beaming warmly at him. 'But this is such a special time for me. It's important that *everything* go right. My whole world . . .'

'Yeah. Your whole world. Well, I hope you like the house after you see it.'

Allison laughed. 'I will. After all, it exists for me; that's what it's there for.'

'You've got this worked out like an exact science,' Larry murmured. 'Everything that happens to you is for the best. You're pleased with everything. So it *must* be your world. Maybe you're just making the best of things–Telling yourself you really like the things that happen to you.'

'Do you think so?'

He frowned in thought as they zipped along. 'Tell me,' he said finally, 'how did you learn about these multiple worlds? Why are you so sure this one is yours?'

She smiled at him. 'I worked it out myself,' she said. 'I studied logic and philosophy, and history–and there was always something that puzzled me. Why were there so many vital changes in the fortunes of people and nations that seemed to come about providentially, just at the right moment? Why did it really seem as if my world had to be just the way it was, so that all through history, strange things happened which make it work out that way.

'I'd heard the "This Is the Best of All Possible Worlds" theory, but it didn't make sense the way I read about it. I studied the religions of mankind, and scientific speculations of the existence of a Creator–but something was lacking, something which either couldn't be accounted for, or was just overlooked.'

Larry nodded. 'Well, sure. It's easy; if this is the best of all possible worlds, then why is there so much suffering–unnecessary suffering–in it, if there's a benevolent and all-powerful Creator, as so many millions have believed, do believe, and will believe in the future, no doubt, then how do you account for the existence of evil?' He grinned at her. 'And you worked out the answer to all that, eh–just tossed it off like a martini?'

Allison sniffed. 'You don't have to put it that way . . . Well, it *is* simple and I'm not the only one who's figured it out, although obviously I'm the only one in *this* world . . .'

'Okay,' Larry broke in, 'I'll hold back objections until you've told me how you did it.'

'Thank you, darling,' she said. 'You see, you *are* understanding–even if you don't agree with me right off the bat . . . Well, that would get tiresome, I'm sure. It's much more fun if I have to work to convince you . . . Oh, don't get impatient, I'll come to the point.'

'Thank you,' he said.

'It's simple, like the egg-trick, once you know the angle. The reason why both the benevolent Creator *and* the "Best of All Possible Worlds" theory seem to bog down is because we start out with an unjustified assumption–that this is the *only* world. But suppose we try a different approach: assume a Creator of infinite power; surely, such a being would be capable of creating infinite worlds . . . or at least, so large a number of them to seem infinite to us.

'If you assume *that*, then everything else makes sense. The Creator set forces into motion; He created separate worlds for every single human being in existence; each one exists for that human being alone. He's an artist, but He uses an economy of means, so that there's much duplication of themes and events and motives throughout the worlds.'

'Oh,' Larry replied softly, 'now I begin to see what you're driving at. In some worlds, Napoleon won the battle of Waterloo–although only in his own world did *everything* work out just right for him; in this one he had to lose . . .'

'I'm not sure Napoleon ever existed in my world,' Allison said thoughtfully. 'I think he's just a name in the records, although some such person did exist in other worlds. In my world, Hitler was defeated; Roosevelt died–I'd be sorry about that, only I didn't know him, and he wasn't very real, anyway; they were both just images carried over from other people's worlds . . .'

'All right,' he said. 'And everything worked out wonderfully for you, all your life, huh? You were never really sick, or hurt, or hungry . . .'

'That's about it,' she agreed. 'I've had some hurts and frustrations, but nothing really . . . well, really crippling. And every one has been important toward getting something I really wanted, or getting to understand something important. You see, Larry, the logic is perfect; I deduced it all from the evidence. There's no other answer that will stand up.'

Larry smiled. 'What does it matter what I think? You're not going to change your mind.'

Larry gazed at the building in sick disgust. 'That's a house?' he muttered at last.

Allison's eyes danced with happiness as she looked up at the great mansion. 'What, darling? What did you say?'

The house was immense–and super-modern, like a pastry-cook's nightmare. Great columns reared up, connected by sloping beams and buttresses. The rooms were set one on top of each other like shoe-boxes, each at its own angle. The whole building was finished in some kind of bright metal shingle, a frightening butter-yellow. In the morning sun the house blazed and sparkled.

'What are–those?' Larry indicated some forlorn plants snaking up the irregular sides of the house. 'Are those supposed to be there?'

Allison blinked, frowning a little. 'What did you say, darling?

You mean the bougainvillea? That's a very exotic plant. It comes from the South Pacific.'

'What's it do? Hold the house together?'

Allison's smile vanished. She raised her eyebrow. 'Darling, are you feeling all right? Is there anything the matter?'

Larry moved back toward the car. 'Let's go back to town. I'm getting hungry for lunch.'

'All right,' Allison said, watching him oddly. 'All right, we'll go back.'

That night, after dinner, Larry seemed moody and unresponsive. 'Let's go to the Wind-Up,' he said suddenly. 'I feel like seeing something familiar, for a change.'

'What do you mean?'

Larry nodded at the expensive restaurant they had just left. 'All those fancy lights. And little people in uniforms whispering in your ear. In French.'

'If you expect to order food you should know some French,' Allison stated. Her face twisted into an angry pout. 'Larry, I'm beginning to wonder about you. The way you acted out at the house. The strange things you said.'

Larry shrugged. 'The sight of it drove me temporarily insane.'

'Well, I certainly hope you recover.'

'I'm recovering each minute.'

They came to the Wind-Up. Allison started to go inside. Larry stopped for a moment, lighting a cigarette. The good old Wind-Up; he felt better already, just standing in front of it. Warm, dark, noisy, the sound of the ragged dixieland combo in the background–

His spirits returned. The peace and contentment of a good rundown bar. He sighed, pushing the door open.

And stopped, stricken.

The Wind-Up had changed. It was well-lit. Instead of Max the waiter, there were waitresses in neat white uniforms bustling around. The place was full of well-dressed women, sipping cocktails and chatting. And in the rear was an imitation gypsy orchestra, with a long-haired churl in fake costume, torturing a violin.

Allison turned around. 'Come on!' she snapped impatiently. 'You're attracting attention, standing there in the door.'

Larry gazed for a long time at the imitation gypsy orchestra; at the bustling waitresses; the chatting ladies; the recessed neon lighting. Numbness crept over him. He sagged.

'What's the matter?' Allison caught his arm crossly. 'What's the matter with you?'

'What–what happened?' Larry waved his hand feebly at the interior. 'There been an accident?'

'Oh, this. I forgot to tell you. I spoke to Mr O'Mallery about it. Just before I met you last night.'

'Mr O'Mallery?'

'He owns this building. He's an old friend of mine. I pointed out how–how *dirty* and unattractive his little place was getting. I pointed out what a few improvements would do.'

Larry made his way outside, onto the sidewalk. He ground his cigarette out with his heel and shoved his hands in his pockets.

Allison hurried after him, her cheeks red with indignation. 'Larry! Where are you going?'

'Goodnight.'

'Goodnight?' She stared at him in astonishment. 'What do you mean?'

'I'm going.'

'Going where?'

'Out. Home. To the park. Anywhere.' Larry started off down the sidewalk, hunched over, hands in his pockets.

Allison caught up with him, stepping angrily in front of him. 'Have you gone out of your mind? Do you know what you're saying?'

'Sure. I'm leaving you; we're splitting up. Well, it was nice. See you sometime.'

The two spots in Allison's cheeks glowed like two red coals. 'Just a minute, Mr Brewster. I think you've forgotten something.' Her voice was hard and brittle.

'Forgotten something? Like what?'

'You *can't* leave; you can't walk out on me.'

Larry raised an eyebrow. 'I can't?'

'I think you better reconsider, while you still have time.'

'I don't get your drift.' Larry yawned. 'I think I'll go home to my three-room apartment and go to bed. I'm tired.' He started past her.

'Have you forgotten?' Allison snapped. 'Have you forgotten that you're not *completely real*? That you exist only as a part of my world?'

'Lord! Are you going to start *that* again?'

'Better think about it before you walk off. You exist for my benefit, Mr Brewster. This is *my* world; remember that. Maybe in your own world things are different, but this is *my* world. And in my world things do as *I* say.'

'So long,' Larry Brewster said.

'You're–you're still leaving?'

Slowly, Larry Brewster shook his head. 'No,' he said. 'No, as a matter of fact, I'm not; I've changed my mind. You're too much trouble. *You're leaving.*'

And as he spoke a ball of radiant light gently settled over Allison Holmes, engulfing her in a glowing aura of splendor. The ball of light lifted, carrying Miss Holmes up into the air, raising her effortlessly above the level of the buildings, into the evening sky.

Larry Brewster watched calmly, as the ball of light carried Miss Holmes off. He was not surprised to see her gradually fade and grow indistinct–until all at once there was nothing.

Nothing but a faint shimmer in the sky. Allison Holmes was gone.

For a long time Larry Brewster stood, deep in thought, rubbing his jaw reflectively. He would miss Allison. In some ways he had liked her; for a while, she had been fun. Well, she was off now. In this world, Allison Holmes had not been completely real. What he had known, what Larry had called 'Allison Holmes,' wasn't any more than a partial appearance of her.

Then he paused, remembering: as the ball of radiant light had carried her away, he had seen a glimpse—a glimpse past her into a different world, one which was obviously *her* world, her real world, the world she wanted. The buildings were uncomfortably familiar; he could still remember the house . . .

Then—Allison had been real, after all—existing in Larry's world, until the time came for her to be transported to hers. Would she find another Larry Brewster there—one who saw eye-to-eye with her? He shuddered at the thought.

In fact, the whole experience had been somewhat unnerving.

'I wonder why,' he murmured softly. He thought back to other unpleasant events, remembering how they had led him to greater satisfactions for their having happened—richness of experience he could not have appreciated without them. 'Ah well,' he sighed, 'it's all for the best.'

He started to walk home slowly, hands in his pockets, glancing up at the sky every now and then, as if for confirmation . . .

A SURFACE RAID

Harl left the third level, catching a tube car going North. The tube car carried him swiftly through one of the big junction bubbles and down to the fifth level. Harl caught an exciting, fugitive glimpse of people and outlets, a complex tangle of mid-period business and milling confusion.

Then the bubble was behind him and he was nearing his destination, the vast industrial fifth level, sprawling below everything else like some gigantic, soot-encrusted octopus of the night's misrule.

The gleaming tube car ejected him and continued on its way, disappearing down the tube. Harl bounded agilely into the receiving strip and slowed to a stop, still on his feet, swaying expertly back and forth.

A few minutes later he reached the entrance to his father's office. Harl raised his hand and the code door slid back. He entered, his heart thumping with excitement. The time had come.

Edward Boynton was in the planning department studying the outline for a new robot bore when he was informed that his son had entered the main office.

'I'll be right back,' Boynton said, making his way past his policy staff and up the ramp into the office.

'Hello, Dad,' Harl exclaimed, squaring his shoulders. Father and son exchanged handclasps. Then Harl sat down slowly. 'How are things?' he asked. 'I guess you expected me.'

Then Edward Boynton seated himself behind his desk. 'What do you want here?' he demanded. 'You know I'm busy.'

Harl smiled thinly across at his father. In his brown industrial-planner uniform, Edward Boynton towered above his young son, a massive man with broad shoulders and thick blond hair. His blue eyes were cold and hard as he returned the young man's level gaze.

'I happened to come into some information.' Harl glanced uneasily around the room. 'Your office isn't tapped, is it?'

'Of course not,' the elder Boynton assured him.

'No screens or ears?' Harl relaxed a little. 'I've learned that you and several others from your department are going up to the surface soon.' Harl leaned eagerly toward his father. 'Up to the surface–on a raid for saps.'

Ed Boynton's face darkened. 'Where did you hear that?' He gazed intently at his son. 'Did anyone in this department–?'

'No,' Harl said quickly. 'No one informed. I picked up the information on my own, in connection with my educational activities.'

Ed Boynton began to understand. 'I see. You were experimenting with channel taps, cutting across the confidential channels. Like they teach you to do in communications.'

'That's right. I happened to pick up a conversation between you and Robin Turner concerning the raid.'

The atmosphere in the room became easier, more friendly. Ed Boynton relaxed, settling back in his chair. 'Go on,' he urged.

'It was mere chance. I had cut across ten or twelve channels, holding each one for only a second. I was using the Youth League equipment. All at once I recognized your voice. So I stayed on and caught the whole conversation.'

'Then you heard most of it.'

Harl nodded. 'Exactly when are you going up, Dad? Have you set an exact date?'

Ed Boynton frowned. 'No,' he said, 'I haven't. But it will be sometime this week. Almost everything is arranged.'

'How many are going?' Harl asked.

'We're taking up one mother ship and about thirty eggs. All from this department.'

'Thirty eggs? Sixty or seventy men.'

'That's right.' Ed Boynton stared intently at his son. 'It won't be a big raid. Nothing compared to some of the Directorate raids of the past few years.'

'But big enough for a single department.'

Ed Boynton's eyes flickered. 'Be careful, Harl. If such loose talk should get out–'

'I know. I cut the recorder off as soon as I picked up the drift of your talk. I know what would happen if the Directorate found out a department was raiding without authorization–for its own factories.'

'Do you really know? I wonder.'

'One mother ship and thirty eggs,' Harl exclaimed, ignoring the remark. 'You'll be on the surface for about forty hours?'

'About. It depends on what luck we have.'

'How many saps are you after?'

'We need at least two dozen,' the elder Boynton replied.

'Males?'

'For the most part. A few females, but males primarily.'

'For the basic-industry factory units, I assume.' Harl straightened in his chair. 'All right, then. Now that I know more about the raid itself I can get down to business.'

He stared hard at his father.

'Business?' Boynton glanced up sharply. 'Precisely what do you mean?'

'My exact reason for coming down here.' Harl leaned across the desk toward his father, his voice clipped and intense. 'I'm going along with you on the raid. I want to go along–to get some saps for myself.'

For a moment there was an astonished silence. Then Ed Boynton laughed. 'What are you talking about? What do *you* know about saps?'

The inner door slid back, and Robin Turner came quickly into the office. He joined Boynton behind the desk.

'He can't go,' Turner said flatly. 'It would increase the risks tenfold.'

Harl glanced up. 'There *was* an ear in here, then.'

'Of course. Turner always listens in.' Ed Boynton nodded, regarding his son thoughtfully. 'Why do you want to go along?'

'That's my concern,' Harl said, his lips tightening.

Turner rasped: 'Emotional immaturity. A sub-rational adolescent craving for adventure and excitement. There's still a few like him who can't throw the old brain completely off. After two hundred years you'd think–'

'Is that it?' Boynton demanded. 'You have some non-adult desire to go up and see the surface?'

'Perhaps,' Harl admitted, flushing a little.

'You can't come,' Ed Boynton stated emphatically. 'It's far too dangerous. We're not going up there for romantic adventure. It's a job–a grim, hard, exacting job. The saps are getting wary. It's becoming more and more difficult to bring back a full load. We can't spare any of our eggs for whatever romantic foolishness–'

'I know it's getting hard,' Harl interrupted. 'You don't have to convince me that it's almost impossible to round up a whole load.' Harl looked up defiantly at Turner and his father. He chose his words carefully. 'And I know that's why the Directorate considers private raids a major crime against the State.'

Silence.

Finally, Ed Boynton sighed, a reluctant admiration in his stare. He looked his son slowly up and down. 'Okay, Harl,' he said. 'You win.'

Turner said nothing. His face was hard.

Harl got quickly to his feet. 'Then it's all settled. I'll return to my quarters and get prepared. As soon as you're ready to go, notify me at once. I'll join you at the launching stage on the first level.'

The elder Boynton shook his head. 'We're not leaving from the first level. It would be too risky.' His voice was heavy. 'There are too many Directorate guards prowling around. We have the ship down here at fifth level, in one of the warehouses.'

'Where shall I meet you, then?'

Ed Boynton stood up slowly. 'We'll notify you, Harl. It will be soon, I promise you. In a couple of periods, at the most. Be at your vocational quarters.'

'The surface is completely cool, isn't it?' Harl asked. 'There aren't any radioactive areas left?'

'It's been cool for fifty years,' his father assured him.

'Then I won't have to worry about a radiation shield,' Harl said. 'One more thing, Dad. What language will we have to use? Can we speak our regular–'

Ed Boynton shook his head. 'No. The saps never mastered any of the rational semantic systems. We'll have to revert to the old traditional forms.'

Harl's face fell. 'I don't know any of the traditional forms. They're not being taught anymore.'

Ed Boynton shrugged. 'It doesn't matter.'

'How about their defenses? What sort of weapons should I bring? Will a screen and blast rifle be sufficient?'

'Only the screen is of vital importance,' the elder Boynton said. 'When the saps see us they scatter in all directions. One look at us and off they go.'

'Fine,' Harl said. 'I'll have my screen checked over.' He moved toward the door. 'I'll go back up to the third level. I'll be expecting your signal. I'll have my equipment ready.'

'All right,' Ed Boynton said.

The two men watched the door slide shut after the youth.

'Quite a boy,' Turner muttered.

'Turning out to be something, after all,' Ed Boynton murmured. 'He'll go a long way.' He rubbed his jaw thoughtfully. 'But I wonder how he'll act up on the surface during the raid.'

Harl met with his group leader on the third level, an hour after he left his father's office.

'Then it's all settled?' Fashold asked, looking up from his report spools.

'All settled. They're going to signal me as soon as the ship is ready.'

'By the way.' Fashold put down his spools, pushing the scanner back. 'I've learned something about the saps. As a YL leader I have access to the Directorate files. I've learned something virtually no one else knows.'

'What is it?' asked Harl.

'Harl, the saps are related to us. They're a different species, but they're very closely related to us.'

'Go on,' Harl urged.

'At one time there was only the one species–the saps. Their full name is *homo sapiens*. We grew out of them, developed from them. We're biogenetic mutants. The change occurred during the Third World War, two and a half centuries ago. Up to that time there had never been any *technos*.'

'*Technos?*'

Fashold smiled. 'That's what they called us at first. When they thought of us only as a separate class, and not as a distinct race. *Technos*. That was their name for *us*. That was how they always referred to us.'

'But why? It's a strange name. Why *technos*, Fashold?'

'Because the first mutants appeared among the technocratic classes and gradually spread throughout all other educated classes. They appeared among scientists, scholars, field workers, trained groups, all the various specialized classes.'

'And the saps didn't realize–'

'They thought of us only as a class, as I've just told you. That was during the Third World War and after. It was during the Final War that we fully emerged as recognizably and profoundly different. It became evident that we weren't just another specialized offshoot of *homo sapiens*. Not just another class of men more educated than the rest, with higher intellectual capacities.'

Fashold gazed off into the distance. 'During the Final War we emerged and showed ourselves for what we really were–a superior species supplanting *homo sapiens* in the same way that *homo sapiens* had supplanted Neanderthal man.'

Harl considered what Fashold had said. 'I didn't realize we were so closely related to them. I had no idea we had emerged so lately.'

Fashold nodded. 'It was only two centuries ago, during the war that ravaged the surface of the planet. Most of us were working down in the big underground laboratories and factories under the different mountain ranges–the Urals, the Alps, and the Rockies. We were down underground, under miles of rock and dirt and clay. And on the surface *homo sapiens* slugged it out with the weapons we designed.'

'I'm beginning to understand. We designed the weapons for them to fight the war. They used our weapons without realizing–'

'We designed them and the saps used them to destroy themselves,' Fashold interjected. 'It was Nature's crucible, the elimination of one species and the emergence of another. We gave them the weapons and they destroyed themselves. When the war ended the surface was fused, and nothing but ash and hydroglass and radioactive clouds remained.

'We sent out scouting parties from our underground labs and found nothing but a silent, barren waste. It had been accomplished. They were gone, wiped out. And we had come to take their place.'

'Not all of them could have been wiped out,' Harl pointed out. 'There are still a lot of them up there on the surface.'

'True,' Fashold admitted. 'Some survived. Scattered remnants here and there. Gradually, as the surface cooled, they began to reform again, getting together and building little villages and huts. Yes, and even clearing some of the land–planting and growing things. But they're still remnants of a dying race now almost extinct, as the Neanderthal is extinct.'

'So nothing exists now but males and females without homes.'

'There are a few villages here and there–wherever they've managed to clear the surface. But they've descended to utter savagery, and live like animals, wearing skins and hunting with rocks and spears. They've become almost bestial remnants who offer no organized resistance when we go up to raid a few of their villages for our factories.'

'Then we–' Harl broke off abruptly as a faint bell sounded. He turned in startled apprehension, snapping on the vidphone.

His father's face formed on the screen, hard and stern. 'Okay, Harl,' he said. 'We're ready.'

'So soon? But–'

'We set the time ahead. Come down to my office.' The image on the screen dimmed and vanished.

Harl did not move.

'They must have got worried,' Fashold said, grinning. 'They were apparently afraid you'd pass the information along.'

'I'm all ready,' Harl said. He picked up his blast gun from the table. 'How do I look?'

In his silver communications uniform Harl looked splendid and impressive. He had put on heavy military boots and gloves. In one hand he gripped his blast gun. Around his waist was his screen control-belt.

'What's that?' Fashold asked, as Harl lowered black goggles over his eyes.

'These? Oh, they're for the sun.'

'Of course–The sun. I forgot.'

Harl cradled his gun, balancing it expertly. 'The sun would blind me. The goggles protect my eyes. I'll be safe up there, with my screen and gun, and these goggles.'

'I hope so.' Still grinning, Fashold thumped him on the back as he moved toward the door. 'Bring back a lot of saps. Do a good job–and don't forget to include a female!'

The mother ship moved slowly from the warehouse, and out onto the lift stage, a rotund black teardrop emerging from storage. Its port locks slid back, and ramps climbed to meet the locks. Immediately supplies and equipment were on their way up, rising into the bowels of the ship.

'Almost ready,' Turner said, his face twitching with nervousness as he gazed through the observation windows at the loading ramps outside. 'I hope nothing goes wrong. If the Directorate should find out–'

'Quit worrying!' Ed Boynton ordered. 'You picked the wrong time to let your thalamic impulses take over control.'

'Sorry.' Turner tightened his lips and moved away from the windows. The lift stage was ready to rise.

'Let's get started,' Boynton urged. 'Have you men from the department at each level?'

'Nobody but department members will be near the stage,' Turner replied.

'Where is the balance of the crew?' Boynton demanded.

'At the first level. I sent them up during the day.'

'Very well.' Boynton gave the signal, and the stage under the ship began slowly to rise, lifting them steadily toward the level above.

Harl peered out the observation windows, watching the fifth level drop below and the fourth level, the vast commercial center of the under-surface system, come into view.

'Won't be long,' Ed Boynton said, as the fourth level glided past. 'So far so good.'

'Where will we finally emerge?' Harl asked.

'In the latter stages of the war our various underground structures were connected by tunnels. That original network formed the basis of our present system. We'll emerge at one of the original entrances, located in the mountain range called "The Alps".'

'The Alps,' Harl murmured.

'Yes, in Europe. We have maps of the surface, showing locations of sap villages in that region. A whole cluster of villages lie to the North and North East in what used to be Denmark and Germany. We've never raided there before. The saps have managed to clear the slag away from several thousand acres in that region, and seem gradually to be reclaiming most of Europe.'

'But why, Dad?' Harl asked.

Ed Boynton shrugged. 'I don't know. They don't seem to have set themselves any organized objective. They show no signs at all, in fact, of emerging from their savage state. All their traditions were lost–books and records, inventions, and techniques. If you ask me–' He broke off abruptly. 'Here comes the third level. We're almost there.'

The huge mother ship roared slowly along, gliding above the surface of the planet. Harl peered out, awed by what he saw below.

Across the surface of the earth lay a crust of slag, an endless coating of blackened rock. The mineral deposit was unbroken except for occasional hills sharply jutting up, ash-covered, and with a few sparse bushes growing near their tops. Great sheets of sun-darkening ash drifted across the sky, but nothing living stirred. The surface of the earth was dead and barren, without sign of life.

'Is it all like that?' Harl asked.

Ed Boynton shook his head. 'Not all. The saps have reclaimed some of the land.' He gripped his son's arm and pointed. 'See off that way? They've done quite a bit of clearing up there.'

'Just how do they clear the slag?' Harl asked.

'It's hard,' his father replied. 'Fused, like volcanic glass–hydroglass–from the hydrogen bombs. They pick it away bit by bit, year after year. With their hands, with rocks, and with the axes made from the glass itself.'

'Why don't they develop better tools?'

Ed Boynton grinned wryly. 'You know the answer to that. *We* made most of their tools for them, their tools and weapons and inventions, for hundreds of years.'

'Here we go,' Turner said. 'We're landing.'

The ship settled down, coming to rest on the surface of the slag. For a moment the blackened rock rumbled under them. Then there was silence.

'We're down,' Turner said.

Ed Boynton studied the surface map, sending it darting through the scanner. 'We'll send out ten eggs as a starter. If we don't have much luck here we'll take the ship farther North. But we should do well. This area has never been raided before.'

'How will the eggs cover?' Turner asked.

'The eggs will fan out in a spectrum, giving each egg a separate area. Our egg will move over toward the right. If we have any success, we'll return to the ship at once. Otherwise, we'll stay out until nightfall.'

'Nightfall?' Harl asked.

Ed Boynton smiled. 'Until dark. Until this side of the planet is turned away from the sun.'

'Let's go,' Turner said impatiently.

The port locks opened. The first eggs scooted out onto the slag, their treads digging into the slippery surface. One by one they emerged from the black hull of the mother ship, tiny spheres with their backs tapering into jet tubes, and their noses blunted into control turrets. They roared off across the slag and disappeared.

'Ours, next,' Ed Boynton said.

Harl nodded and gripped his blast rifle tightly. He lowered his protection goggles over his eyes, and Turner and Boynton did the same. They entered their egg, Boynton seating himself behind the controls.

A moment later they shot out of the ship onto the smooth surface of the planet.

Harl peered out. He could see nothing but slag on all sides. Slag and drifting clouds of ash.

'It's dismal,' he murmured. 'Even with the goggles the sun burns my eyes.'

'Don't look at it then,' Ed Boynton cautioned. 'Look away from it.'

'I can't help it. It's so–so strange.'

Ed Boynton grunted and increased the egg's speed. Far ahead of them something was coming into view. He headed the egg toward it.

'What's that?' Turner asked, alarmed.

'Trees,' Boynton said, reassuringly. 'Trees growing up in a clump. It marks the end of the slag. Then there's ash for a while, and finally fields the saps have planted.'

Boynton drove the egg to the edge of the slag area. He stopped it where the slag ended and the clump of trees began, snapping off the jets and locking the treads. He and Harl and Turner got out cautiously, their guns ready.

Nothing stirred. There was only silence, and the endless surface of slag. Between drifting clouds of ash the sky was a pale robin's-egg blue, and a few moisture clouds drifted with the ash. The air smelled good. It was thin and crisp, and the sun shed a friendly warmth.

'Put your screens on,' Ed Boynton warned. As he spoke he snapped the switch at his belt and his own screen hummed, flashing on around him. Swiftly, Boynton's figure dimmed, wavering and fading. It winked out–and was gone.

Turner quickly followed suit. 'Okay,' his voice came, from a glimmering oval to Harl's right. 'You next.'

Harl turned on his screen. For an instant a strange cold fire enveloped him from head to foot, bathing him in sparks. Then his body too dimmed and vanished. The screens were functioning perfectly.

In Harl's ears a faint clicking sounded, warning him of the presence of the two others. 'I can hear you,' Harl said. 'Your screens are in my earphones.'

'Don't wander off,' Ed Boynton cautioned. 'Keep by us and listen for the clicks. It's dangerous to be separated, up here on the surface.'

Harl advanced carefully. The other two were on his right, a few yards off. They were crossing a dry yellow field overgrown with some kind of plant. The plants had long stalks that broke and crunched underfoot. Behind Harl was a trail of broken vegetation. He could clearly see the similar trails which Turner and his father were leaving.

But now it became necessary for him to separate from Turner and his father. Ahead of Harl the outline of a sap village rose up, its huts fashioned from some kind of plant fiber piled in heaps on top of wooden frames. He could see the shadowy outlines of animals tied to the huts. Trees and plants encircled the village, and he could distinguish the moving forms of people, and hear their voices.

People–saps. His heart beat quickly. With luck he might capture and bring back three or four for the Youth League. He felt suddenly confident and unafraid. Surely it would not be difficult. Planted fields, tied-up animals, rickety huts leaning and tilting–

The smell of dung commingling with the heat of the late afternoon became almost intolerable as Harl advanced. Cries, and other sounds of feverish human activity, drifted to him. The ground was flat and dry, weeds and plants grew up everywhere. He left the yellow field and came onto a narrow footpath, littered with human refuse and animal dung.

And just beyond the road was the village.

The clicks had diminished in his earphones. Now they died out completely. Harl grinned to himself. He had moved away from Turner and Boynton, and was no longer in contact with them. They had no idea where he was.

He turned to the left, circling cautiously around the edge of the village. He passed by a hut, then several in a cluster. Around him green trees and plants grew in great clumps, and directly ahead of him gleamed a narrow stream with sloping, moss-covered banks.

A dozen people were washing at the edge of the stream, the children leaping into the water and scrambling up on the bank.

Harl halted, gazing at them in astonishment. Their skins were dark, almost black. A shiny, coppery black it was–a rich bronze mixed in with the dirt-color. *Was* it dirt?

He suddenly realized that the bathers had been burned black by the constant sun. The hydrogen explosions had thinned the atmosphere, searing off most of the layer of moisture clouds and for two hundred years the sun had beat mercilessly down on them–in sharp contrast to his own race. Under-surface, there was no ultraviolet light to burn the skin, or to raise the pigment level. He and the other *technos* had lost their skin color. There was no need for it in their subterranean world.

But the bathers were incredibly dark, a rich reddish-black color. And they had nothing on at all. They were leaping and jumping eagerly about, splashing through the water and sunning themselves on the bank.

Harl watched them for a time. Children and three or four scrawny, elderly females. Would they do? He shook his head, and warily encircled the stream.

He continued on back among the huts, walking slowly and carefully, gazing alertly around with his gun held ready.

A faint breeze blew against him, rustling through the trees to his right. The sounds of the bathing children mixed with the dung smell, the wind, and the swaying of the trees.

Harl advanced cautiously. He was invisible, but he knew that he might at any moment be discovered and tracked down by his footprints or the sounds he might make. And if someone ran against him–

He stealthily darted past a hut, and emerged into an open place, a flat area of beaten earth. In the shade of the hut a dog lay sleeping with flies crawling over its lean flanks. An old woman was sitting on the porch of the rude dwelling, combing her long gray hair with a bone comb.

Harl passed by her cautiously. In the center of the open place a group of young men were standing. They were gesturing and talking together. Some were cleaning their weapons, long spears and knives of an inconceivable primitiveness. On the ground lay a dead animal, a huge beast with long, gleaming tusks and a thick hide. Blood oozed from its mouth–thick, dark blood. One of the young men turned suddenly–and kicked it with his foot.

Harl came up to the young men, and stopped. They were dressed in cloth clothing, long leg garments and shirts. Their feet were bare on top, for they wore loosely-woven vegetable-fiber sandals instead of shoes. They were clean-shaven, but their skin gleamed almost ebony black. Their sleeves were rolled up, exposing bulging, glistening muscles, dripping with sweat in the hot sun.

Harl could not understand what they were saying, but he was sure they were speaking one of the archaic traditional tongues.

He passed on. At the other side of the open place a group of old men was sitting cross-legged in a circle, weaving rough cloth on crude frames. Harl watched them in silence for a time. Their chatter drifted noisily up to him. Each old man was bent intently over his frame, his eyes glued on his work.

Beyond the row of huts some younger men and women were plowing a field, dragging the plow by ropes securely attached to their waists and shoulders.

Harl wandered on, fascinated. Everyone was engaged in some kind of activity–except the dog asleep under the hut. The young men with their spears, the old woman in front of the hut combing her hair, and weaving.

In one corner a huge woman was teaching a child what appeared to be an adding and subtracting game, using small sticks in lieu of figures. Two men were removing the hide from a small furred animal, stripping the pelt off carefully.

Harl passed a wall of hides, all hung up carefully to dry. The dull stench irritated his nostrils, making him want to sneeze. He passed a group of children pounding grain in a hollowed-out stone, beating the grain into meal. None of them looked up as he passed.

Some animals were tied together in a bunch. Some lay in the shade, big beasts with huge udders. They watched him silently.

Harl came to the edge of the village and stopped. From that point onward deserted fields stretched out. For perhaps a mile beyond the fields were trees and bushes, and beyond that the endless miles of slag.

He turned and walked back. Off to one side, sitting in the shade, a young man was chipping away at a block of hydroslag, cutting it carefully with a few rough tools. He seemed to be fashioning a weapon. Harl watched him, watched the endless, solemn blows descending again and again. The slag was hard. It was a long tedious job.

He walked on. A group of women were mending broken arrows. Their chatter followed him for a time, and he found himself wishing he could understand it. Everyone was busy, working rapidly. Dark, shiny arms rose and fell, and the chattering murmur of voices drifted back and forth.

Activity. Laughter. A child's laughter echoed suddenly through the village, and a few heads turned. Harl bent down, intently studying a man's head at close range.

A strong face he had. His twisted knotted hair was short, and his teeth were even and white. On his arms were copper bracelets, almost matching the rich bronze hue of his skin. His bare chest was marked with tattoos, etched into his flesh with brightly colored pigments.

Harl wandered back the way he had come. He passed the old woman on the porch, and paused again to observe her. She had stopped combing her hair. Now she was fixing a child's hair, braiding it skillfully back into an elaborate pattern. Harl watched her, fascinated. The pattern was intricate, complex, and the task took a long time. The old woman's faded eyes were intent on the child's hair, on the detailed work. Her withered hands flew.

Harl walked on, moving toward the stream. He passed the bathing children again. They had all climbed out on the bank and were drying themselves in the sun. So these were the *saps*. The race that was dying out–the dying race, soon to be extinct. Remnants.

But they did not appear to be a dying race. They were working hard, tirelessly chipping at the hydroslag, fixing their arrows, hunting, plowing, pounding grain, weaving, combing–

He stopped suddenly, rigid, his blast gun at his shoulder. Ahead of him, through the trees by the stream, something moved. Then he heard two voices–a man's voice and a woman's voice, raised in excited conversation.

Harl advanced cautiously. He pushed past a flowering bush, and peered into the gloom between the trees.

A man and woman were sitting at the edge of the water, in the dark shadow of the tree. The man was making bowls, shaping them out of wet clay scooped up from the water. His fingers flew, expertly, rapidly. He spun the bowls, turning them on a revolving platform between his knees.

As the man finished the bowls the woman took them and painted them with deft, vigorous strokes of a crude brush gleaming with red pigment.

The woman was beautiful. Harl gazed down at her in stunned admiration. She sat almost motionless, resting against a tree, holding each bowl securely as she painted it. Her black hair hung down to her waist, falling across her shoulders and back. Her features were finely cut, each line clear and vivid, her dark eyes immense. She studied each bowl intently, her lips moving a little and Harl noticed that her hands were small and delicately fashioned.

He walked over toward her, moving carefully. The woman did not hear him or look up. In growing wonder he realized that her coppery body was small and beautifully formed, her limbs slender and supple. She did not seem to be aware of him.

Suddenly the man spoke again. The woman glanced up, lowering the bowl to the ground. She rested a minute, cleaning her brush with a leaf. She wore rough leg garments, reaching down to her knees, and tied at her waist with a twisted flaxen rope. She wore no other garment. Her feet and shoulders were bare, and in the afternoon sun her bosom rose and fell quickly as she breathed.

The man said something else. After a moment the woman picked up another bowl and began to paint again. The two of them worked rapidly, silently, both intent on their work.

Harl studied the bowls. They were all of similar design. The man made them rapidly, building them up from coils of clay, and then snaking the coils around and around, higher and higher. He slapped water against the clay, rubbing the surface smooth and firm. Finally he laid them out in rows, to dry in the sun.

The woman selected the bowls that were dry and then painted them.

Harl watched her. He studied her a long time—the way she moved her coppery body, the intense expression on her face, the faint movement of her lips and chin. Her fingers were slender and exquisitely tapered. Her nails were long, coming finally to a point. She held each bowl carefully, turning it with expert care, painting her design with rapid strokes.

He watched her closely. She was painting the same design on each bowl, painting it again and again. A bird, and then a tree. A line that appeared to represent the ground. A cloud suspended directly above it.

What was the precise significance of that recurrent motif? Harl bent closer, peering intently. Was it really the same? He watched the skillful motion of her hands as she took bowl after bowl, starting the design again and again. The design was basically the same–but each time she made it a little different. No two bowls came out exactly the same.

He was both puzzled, and fascinated. It was the same design, but altered slightly each time. The color of the bird would be altered–or the length of its plume. Less frequently the position of the tree, or the cloud. Once she painted two tiny clouds hovering above the ground. Sometimes she put grass and the outline of hills in the background.

Suddenly the man got to his feet, wiping his hands on his cloth. He spoke to the girl and then hurried off, threading his way through the bushes until he was lost to view.

Harl glanced around excitedly. The girl went right on painting rapidly, calmly. The man had disappeared and the girl remained alone, painting quietly by herself.

Harl was caught in the grip of conflicting and almost overpowering emotions. He wanted to speak to the girl, to ask her about her painting, her design. He wanted to ask her why she changed it each time.

He wanted to sit down and talk to her. To speak to her and hear her talk to him. It was strange. He didn't understand it himself. His vision swam, twisting and blurring, and sweat dripped from his neck and stooping shoulders. The girl continued to paint. She did not look up, or suspect that he was standing directly in front of her. Harl's hand flew to his belt. He took a deep breath, hesitating. Dared he? Should he? The man would be back–

Harl pressed the stud on his belt. Around him the screen hissed, and sparked.

The girl glanced up, startled. Her eyes widened in swift horror. She screamed.

Harl stepped quickly back, gripping his gun, appalled by what he had done.

The girl scrambled to her feet, sending bowls and paints flying. She gazed at him, her eyes still wide, her mouth open. Slowly she backed away toward the bushes. Then abruptly she turned and fled, crashing through the shrubbery, screaming and shrieking.

Harl straightened in sudden fear. Quickly, he restored his screen. The village was alive with growing sound. He could hear voices raised in excited panic, and the sound of people running, crashing through the bushes–the entire village erupting in a torrent of excited activity.

Harl made his way quickly down the stream, past the bushes and out into the open.

Suddenly he stopped, his heart pounding furiously. A crowd of *saps* was hurrying toward the stream–men with spears, old women, and shrieking children. At the edge of the bushes they stopped, staring and listening, their faces frozen in a strange, intent expression. Then they were advancing into the bushes, furiously pushing the branches out of the way–*searching for him.*

Abruptly his earphones clicked.

'Harl!' Ed Boynton's voice came clear and sharp. 'Harl, lad!'

Harl jumped, then cried out in desperate gratefulness. 'Dad, I'm here.'

Ed Boynton gripped his arm, yanking him off balance. 'What's the matter with you? Where did you go? What did you do?'

'You got him?' Turner's voice broke in. 'Come on then–both of you! We have to get out of here, fast. They're scattering white powder everywhere.'

Saps were rushing around, throwing the powder into the air in great clouds. It drifted through the air, settling down over everything. It appeared to be a kind of pulverized chalk. Other saps were sprinkling oil from big jars and shouting in high-pitched excitement.

'We better get out,' Boynton agreed grimly. 'We don't want to tangle with them when they're aroused.'

Harl hesitated. 'But–'

'Come on!' his father urged, tugging at his arm. 'Let's go. We haven't a moment to lose.'

Harl gazed back. He could not see the women, but saps were running everywhere, throwing their sheets of chalk and sprinkling the oil. Saps with iron-tipped spears advanced ominously, kicking at the weeds and bushes as they circled about.

Harl allowed himself to be led by his father. His mind whirled. The woman was gone, and he was sure that he would never see her again. When he had made himself visible she had screamed, and run off.

Why? It didn't make sense. Why had she recoiled from him in blind terror? What had he done?

And what did it matter to him whether he saw her again or not? Why was she important? He did not understand. He did not understand *himself*. There was no rational explanation for what had happened. It was totally incomprehensible.

Harl followed his father and Turner back to the egg, still bewildered and wretched, still trying to understand, to grasp the meaning of what had happened between him and the woman. It did not make sense. He had gone out of his mind and then she had gone out of *her* mind. There had to be some meaning to it–if he could only grasp it.

At the egg Ed Boynton halted, glancing back. 'We were lucky to get away,' he said to Harl, shaking his head. 'When they're aroused they're like beasts. They're animals, Harl. That's what they are. Savage animals.'

'Come on,' Turner said impatiently. 'Let's get out of here–while we still can walk.'

Julie continued to shudder even after she had been carefully bathed and purified in the stream and rubbed down with oil by one of the older women.

She sat in a heap, her arms wrapped around her knees, shaking and trembling uncontrollably. Ken, her brother, stood beside her, grim-faced, his hand on her bare, coppery shoulder.

'What was it?' Julie murmured. 'What was it?' She shuddered. 'It was–horrible. It revolted me, made me ill, just to look at it.'

'What did it look like?' Ken demanded.

'It was–it was like a man. But it couldn't have been a man. It was metallic all over, from head to foot, and it had huge hands and feet. Its face was all pasty white like–like meal. It was–sickly. Hideously sickly. White and metallic, and sickly. Like some kind of root dug up out of the soil.'

Ken turned to the old man sitting behind him, who was listening intently. 'What was it?' he demanded. 'What was it, Mr Stebbins? You know about such things. What did she see?'

Mr Stebbins got slowly to his feet. 'You say it had white skin? Pasty? Like dough? And huge hands and feet?'

Julie nodded. 'And–something else.'

'What?'

'It was *blind*. It had something instead of eyes. Two black spaces. Darkness.' She shuddered and stared toward the stream.

Suddenly Mr Stebbins tensed, his jaw hardening. He nodded. 'I know,' he said. 'I know what it was.'

'What was it?'

Mr Stebbins muttered to himself, frowning. 'It's not possible. But your description–' He stared off in the distance, his brow wrinkled. 'They live underground,' he said finally, 'under the surface. They emerge from the mountains. They live in the earth, in great tunnels and chambers they have hewn out for themselves. They are not men. They look like men, but they are not. They live under the ground and dig the metal from the earth. They dig and hoard the metal. They seldom come up to the surface. They cannot look at the sun.'

'What are they called?' Julie asked.

Mr Stebbins searched his mind, thinking back through the years. Back to the old books and legends he had heard. Things that lived under the ground . . . Like men but not men . . . Things that dug tunnels, that mined metals . . . Things that were blind and had great hands and feet and pasty white skin.

'Goblins,' Mr Stebbins stated. 'What you saw was a goblin.'

Julie nodded, gazing down wide-eyed at the ground, her arms clasped around her knees. 'Yes,' she said. 'That sounds like what it was. It frightened me. I was so afraid. I turned and ran. It seemed so horrible.' She looked up at her brother, smiling a little. 'But I'm better now . . .'

Ken rubbed his big dark hands together, nodding with relief. 'Fine,' he said. 'Now we can get back to work. There's a lot to do. A lot of things to get done.'

PROJECT: EARTH

The sound echoed hollowly through the big frame house. It vibrated among the dishes in the kitchen, the gutters along the roof, thumping slowly and evenly like distant thunder. From time to time it ceased, but then it began again, booming through the quiet night, a relentless sound, brutal in its regularity. From the top floor of the big house.

In the bathroom the three children huddled around the chair, nervous and hushed, pushing against each other with curiosity.

'You sure he can't see us?' Tommy rasped.

'How could he see us? Just don't make any noise.' Dave Grant shifted on the chair, his face to the wall. 'Don't talk so loud.' He went on looking, ignoring them both.

'Let me see,' Joan whispered, nudging her brother with a sharp elbow. 'Get out of the way.'

'Shut up.' Dave pushed her back. 'I can see better now.' He turned up the light.

'I want to see,' Tommy said. He pushed Dave off the chair onto the bathroom floor. 'Come on.'

Dave withdrew sullenly. 'It's our house.'

Tommy stepped cautiously up onto the chair. He put his eye to the crack, his face against the wall. For a time he saw nothing. The crack was narrow and the light on the other side was bad. Then, gradually, he began to make out shapes, forms beyond the wall.

Edward Billings was sitting at an immense old-fashioned desk. He had stopped typing and was resting his eyes. From his vest pocket he had taken a round pocket watch. Slowly, carefully, he wound the great watch. Without his glasses his lean, withered face seemed naked and bleak, the features of some elderly bird. Then he put his glasses on again and drew his chair closer to the desk.

He began to type, working with expert fingers the towering mass of metal and parts that reared up before him. Again the ominous booming echoed through the house, resuming its insistent beat.

Mr Billings' room was dark and littered. Books and papers lay everywhere, in piles and stacks, on the desk, on the table, in heaps on the floor. The walls were covered with charts, anatomy charts, maps, astronomy charts, signs of the zodiac. By the windows rows of dust-covered chemical bottles and packages lay stacked. A stuffed bird stood on the top of the bookcase, gray and drooping. On the desk was a huge magnifying glass, Greek and Hebrew dictionaries, a postage stamp box, a bone letter opener. Against the door a curling strip of flypaper moved with the air currents rising from the gas heater.

The remains of a magic lantern lay against one wall. A black satchel with clothes piled on it. Shirts and socks and a long frock coat, faded and threadbare. Heaps of newspapers and magazines, tied with brown cord. A great black umbrella against the table, a pool of sticky water around its metal point. A glass frame of dried butterflies, pressed into yellowing cotton.

And at the desk the huge old man hunched over his ancient typewriter and heaps of notes and papers.

'Gosh,' Tommy said.

Edward Billings was working on his report. The report was open on the desk beside him, an immense book, leather-bound, bulging at its cracked seams. He was transferring material into it from his heaps of notes.

The steady thumping of the great typewriter made the things in the bathroom rattle and shake, the light fixture, the bottles and tubes in the medicine cabinet. Even the floor under the children's feet.

'He's some kind of Communist agent,' Joan said. 'He's drawing maps of the city so he can set off bombs when Moscow gives the word.'

'The heck he is,' Dave said angrily.

'Don't you see all the maps and pencils and papers? Why else would–'

'Be quiet,' Dave snapped. 'He will hear us. He is not a spy. He's too old to be a spy.'

'What is he, then?'

'I don't know. But he isn't a spy. You're sure dumb. Anyhow, spies have beards.'

'Maybe he's a criminal,' Joan said.

'I talked to him once,' Dave said. 'He was coming downstairs. He spoke to me and gave me some candy out of a bag.'

'What kind of candy was it?'

'I don't know. Hard candy. It wasn't any good.'

'What's he do?' Tommy asked, turning from the crack.

'Sits in his room all day. Typing.'

'Doesn't he work?'

Dave sneered. 'That's what he does. He writes on his report. He's an official with a company.'

'What company?'

'I forget.'

'Doesn't he ever go out?'

'He goes out on the roof.'

'On the roof?'

'He has a porch he goes out on. We fixed it. It's part of the apartment. He's got a garden. He comes downstairs and gets dirt from the backyard.'

'Shhh!' Tommy warned. 'He turned around.'

Edward Billings had got to his feet. He was covering the typewriter with a black cloth, pushing it back and gathering up the pencils and erasers. He opened the desk drawer and dropped the pencils into it.

'He's through,' Tommy said. 'He's finished working.'

The old man removed his glasses and put them away in a case.

He dabbed at his forehead wearily, loosening his collar and necktie. His neck was long and the cords stood out from yellow, wrinkled skin. His Adam's apple bobbed up and down as he sipped some water from a glass.

His eyes were blue and faded, almost without color. For a moment he gazed directly at Tommy, his hawk-like face blank. Then abruptly he left the room, going through a door.

'He's going to bed,' Tommy said.

Mr Billings returned, a towel over his arm. At the desk he stopped and laid the towel over the back of the chair. He lifted the massive report book and carried it from the desk over to the bookcase, holding it tightly with both hands. It was heavy. He laid it down and left the room again.

The report was very close. Tommy could make out the gold letters stamped into the cracked leather binding. He gazed at the letters a long time–until Joan finally pushed him away from the crack, shoving him impatiently off the chair.

Tommy stepped down and moved away, awed and fascinated by what he had seen. The great report book, the huge volume of material on which the old man worked, day after day. In the flickering light from the lamp on the desk he had easily been able to make out the gold-stamped words on the ragged leather binding.

PROJECT B: EARTH

'Let's go,' Dave said. 'He'll come in here in a couple minutes. He might catch us watching.'

'You're afraid of him,' Joan taunted.

'So are you. So is Mom. So is everybody.' He glanced at Tommy. 'You afraid of him?'

Tommy shook his head. 'I'd sure like to know what's in that book,' he murmured. 'I'd sure like to know what that old man is doing.'

The late afternoon sunlight shone down bright and cold. Edward Billings came slowly down the back steps, an empty pail in one hand, rolled-up newspapers under his arm. He paused a moment, shielding his eyes and gazing around him. Then he disappeared into the backyard, pushing through the thick wet grass.

Tommy stepped out from behind the garage. He raced silently up the steps two at a time. He entered the building, hurrying down the dark corridor.

A moment later he stood before the door of Edward Billings' apartment, his chest rising and falling, listening intently.

There was no sound.

Tommy tried the knob. It turned easily. He pushed. The door swung open and a musty cloud of warm air drifted past him out into the corridor.

He had little time. The old man would be coming back with his pail of dirt from the yard.

Tommy entered the room and crossed to the bookcase, his heart pounding excitedly. The huge report book lay among heaps of notes and bundles of clippings. He pushed the papers away, sliding them from the book. He opened it quickly, at random, the thick pages crackling and bending.

Denmark

Figures and facts. Endless facts, pages and columns, row after row. The lines of type danced before his eyes. He could make little out of them. He turned to another section.

New York

Facts about New York. He struggled to understand the column heads. The number of people. What they did. How they lived. What they earned. How they spent their time. Their beliefs. Religion. Politics. Philosophy. Morals. Their age. Health. Intelligence. Graphs and statistics, averages and evaluations.

Evaluations. Appraisals. He shook his head and turned to another section.

California

Population. Wealth. Activity of the state government. Ports and harbors. Facts, facts, facts–

Facts on everything. Everywhere. He thumbed through the

report. On every part of the world. Every city, every state, every country. Any and all possible information.

Tommy closed the report uneasily. He wandered restlessly around the room, examining the heaps of notes and papers, the bundles of clippings and charts. The old man, typing day after day. Gathering facts, facts about the whole world. The earth. A report on the earth, the earth and everything on it. All the people. Everything they did and thought, their actions, deeds, achievements, beliefs, prejudices. A great report of all the information in the whole world.

Tommy picked up the big magnifying glass from the desk. He examined the surface of the desk with it, studying the wood. After a moment he put down the glass and picked up the bone letter knife. He put down the letter knife and examined the broken magic lantern in the corner. The frame of dead butterflies. The drooping stuffed bird. The bottles of chemicals.

He left the room, going out onto the roof porch. The late afternoon sunlight flickered fitfully; the sun was going down. In the center of the porch was a wooden frame, dirt and grass heaped around it. Along the rail were big earthen jars, sacks of fertilizer, damp packages of seeds. An over-turned spray gun. A dirty trowel. Strips of carpet and a rickety chair. A sprinkling can.

Over the wood frame was a wire netting. Tommy bent down, peering through the netting. He saw plants, small plants in rows. Some moss, growing on the ground. Tangled plants, tiny and very intricate.

At one place some dried grass was heaped up in a pile. Like some sort of cocoon.

Bugs? Insects of some sort? Animals?

He took a straw and poked it through the netting at the dried grass. The grass stirred. Something was in it. There were other cocoons, several of them, here and there among the plants.

Suddenly something scuttled out of one of the cocoons, racing across the grass. It squeaked in fright. A second followed it. Pink, running quickly. A small herd of shrilling pink things, two inches high, running and dashing among the plants.

Tommy leaned closer, squinting excitedly through the netting, trying to see what they were. Hairless. Some kind of hairless animals. But tiny, tiny as grasshoppers. Baby things? His pulse raced wildly. Baby things or maybe–

A sound. He turned quickly, rigid.

Edward Billings stood at the door, gasping for breath. He set down the pail of dirt, sighing and feeling for his handkerchief in the pocket of his dark blue coat. He mopped his forehead silently, gazing at the boy standing by the frame.

'Who are you, young man?' Billings said, after a moment. 'I don't remember seeing you before.'

Tommy shook his head. 'No.'

'What are you doing here?'

'Nothing.'

'Would you like to carry this pail out onto the porch for me? It's heavier than I realized.'

Tommy stood for a moment. Then he came over and picked up the pail. He carried it out onto the roof porch and put it down by the wood frame.

'Thank you,' Billings said. 'I appreciate that.' His keen, faded-blue eyes flickered as he studied the boy, his gaunt face shrewd, yet not unkind. 'You look pretty strong to me. How old are you? About eleven?'

Tommy nodded. He moved back toward the railing. Below, two or three stories down, was the street. Mr Murphy was walking along, coming home from the office. Some kids were playing at the corner. A young woman across the street was watering her lawn, a blue sweater around her slim shoulders. He was fairly safe. If the old man tried to do anything–

'Why did you come here?' Billings asked.

Tommy said nothing. They stood looking at each other, the stooped old man, immense in his dark old-fashioned suit, the young boy in a red sweater and jeans, a beanie cap on his head, tennis shoes and freckles. Presently Tommy glanced toward the wood frame covered with netting, then up at Billings.

'That? You wanted to see that?'

'What's in there? What are they?'

'They?'

'The things. Bugs? I never saw anything like them. What are they?'

Billings walked slowly over. He bent down and unfastened the corner of the netting. 'I'll show you what they are. If you're interested.' He twisted the netting loose and pulled it back.

Tommy came over, his eyes wide.

'Well?' Billings said presently. 'You can see what they are.'

Tommy whistled softly. 'I thought maybe they were.' He straightened up slowly, his face pale. 'I thought maybe–but I wasn't sure. Little tiny men!'

'Not exactly,' Mr Billings said. He sat down heavily in the rickety chair. From his coat he took a pipe and a worn tobacco pouch. He filled the pipe slowly, shaking tobacco into it. 'Not exactly men.'

Tommy continued to gaze down into the frame. The cocoons were tiny huts, put together by the little men. Some of them had come out in the open now. They gazed up at him, standing together. Tiny pink creatures, two inches high. Naked. That was why they were pink.

'Look closer,' Billings murmured. 'Look at their heads. What do you see?'

'They're so small–'

'Go get the glass from the desk. The big magnifying glass.' He watched Tommy hurry into the study and come out quickly with the glass. 'Now tell me what you see.'

Tommy examined the figures through the glass. They seemed to be men, all right. Arms, legs–some were women. Their heads. He squinted.

And then recoiled.

'What's the matter?' Billings grunted.

'They're–they're queer.'

'Queer?' Billings smiled. 'Well, it all depends on what you're used to. They're different–from you. But they're not queer. There's nothing wrong with them. At least, I hope there's nothing wrong.'

His smile faded, and he sat sucking on his pipe, deep in silent thought.

'Did you make them?' Tommy asked.

'I?' Billings removed his pipe. 'No, not I.'

'Where did you get them?'

'They were lent to me. A trial group. In fact, *the* trial group. They're new. Very new.'

'You want–you want to sell one of them?'

Billings laughed. 'No, I don't. Sorry. I have to keep them.'

Tommy nodded, resuming his study. Through the glass he could see their heads clearly. They were not quite men. From the front of each forehead antennae sprouted, tiny wire-like projections ending in knobs. Like the vanes of insects he had seen. They were not men, but they were similar to men. Except for the antennae they seemed normal–the antennae and their extreme minuteness.

'Did they come from another planet?' Tommy asked. 'From Mars? Venus?'

'No.'

'Where, then?'

'That's a hard question to answer. The question has no meaning, not in connection with them.'

'What's the report for?'

'The report?'

'In there. The big book with all the facts. The thing you're doing.'

'I've been working on that a long time.'

'How long?'

Billings smiled. 'That can't be answered, either. It has no meaning. But a long time indeed. I'm getting near the end, though.'

'What are you going to do with it? When it's finished.'

'Turn it over to my superiors.'

'Who are they?'

'You wouldn't know them.'

'Where are they? Are they here in town?'

'Yes. And no. There's no way to answer that. Maybe someday you'll–'

'The report's about us,' Tommy said.

Billings turned his head. His keen eyes bored into Tommy. 'Oh?'

'It's about us. The report. The book.'

'How do you know?'

'I looked at it. I saw the title on the back. It's about the earth, isn't it?'

Billings nodded. 'Yes. It's about the earth.'

'You're not from here, are you? You're from someplace else. Outside the system.'

'How–how do you know that?'

Tommy grinned with superior pride. 'I can tell. I have ways.'

'How much did you see in the report?'

'Not much. What's it for? Why are you making it? What are they going to do with it?'

Billings considered a long time before he answered. At last he spoke. 'That,' he said, 'depends on *those*.' He gestured toward the wood frame. 'What they do with the report depends on how Project C works.'

'Project C?'

'The third project. There've been only two others before. They wait a long time. Each project is planned carefully. New factors are considered at great length before any decision is reached.'

'Two others?'

'Antennae for these. A complete new arrangement of the cognitive faculties. Almost no dependence on innate drives. Greater flexibility. Some decrease in over-all emotional index, but what they lose in libido energy they gain in rational control. I would expect more emphasis on individual experience, rather than dependence on traditional group learning. Less stereotyped thinking. More rapid advance in situation control.'

Billings' words made little sense. Tommy was lost. 'What were the others like?' he asked.

'The others? Project A was a long time ago. It's dim in my mind. Wings.'

'Wings.'

'They were winged, depending on mobility and possessing considerable individualistic characteristics. In the final analysis we allowed them too much self-dependence. Pride. They had concepts of pride and honor. They were fighters. Each against the others. Divided into atomized antagonistic factions and–'

'What were the rest like?'

Billings knocked his pipe against the railing. He continued, speaking more to himself than to the boy standing in front of him. 'The winged type was our first attempt at high-level organisms. Project A. After it failed we went into conference. Project B was the result. We were certain of success. We eliminated many of the excessive individualistic characteristics and substituted a group orientation process. A herd method of learning and experiencing. We hoped general control over the project would be assured. Our work with the first project convinced us that greater supervision would be necessary if we were to be successful.'

'What did the second kind look like?' Tommy asked, searching for a meaningful thread in Billings' dissertation.

'We removed the wings, as I said. The general physiognomy remained the same. Although control was maintained for a short time, this second type also fractured away from the pattern, splintering into self-determined groups beyond our supervision. There is no doubt that surviving members of the initial type A were instrumental in influencing them. We should have exterminated the initial type as soon–'

'Are there any left?'

'Of Project B? Of course.' Billings was irritated. 'You're Project B. That's why I'm down here. As soon as my report is complete the final disposition of your type can be effected. There is no doubt my recommendation will be identical with that regarding Project A. Since your Project has moved out of jurisdiction to such a degree that for all intents and purposes you are no longer functional–'

But Tommy wasn't listening. He was bent over the wood frame, peering down at the tiny figures within. Nine little people, men and women both. Nine–and no more in all the world.

Tommy began to tremble. Excitement rushed through him. A plan was dawning, bursting alive inside him. He held his face rigid, his body tense.

'I guess I'll be going.' He moved from the porch, back into the room toward the hall door.

'Going?' Billings got to his feet. 'But–'

'I have to go. It's getting late. I'll see you later.' He opened the hall door. 'Goodbye.'

'Goodbye,' Mr Billings said, surprised. 'I hope I'll see you again, young man.'

'You will,' Tommy said.

He ran home as fast as he could. He raced up the porch steps and inside the house.

'Just in time for dinner,' his mother said, from the kitchen.

Tommy halted on the stairs. 'I have to go out again.'

'No you don't! You're going to–'

'Just for a while. I'll be right back.' Tommy hurried up to his room and entered, glancing around.

The bright yellow room. Pennants on the walls. The big dresser and mirror, brush and comb, model airplanes, pictures of baseball players. The paper bag of bottle caps. The small radio with its cracked plastic cabinet. The wooden cigar boxes full of junk, odds and ends, things he had collected.

Tommy grabbed up one of the cigar boxes and dumped its contents out on the bed. He stuck the box under his jacket and headed out of the room.

'Where are you going?' his father demanded, lowering his evening newspaper and looking up.

'I'll be back.'

'Your mother said it was time for dinner. Didn't you hear her?'

'I'll be back. This is important.' Tommy pushed the front door open. Chill evening air blew in, cold and thin. 'Honest. Real important.'

'Ten minutes.' Vince Jackson looked at his wristwatch. 'No longer. Or you don't get any dinner.'

'Ten minutes.' Tommy slammed the door. He ran down the steps, out into the darkness.

A light showed, flickering under the bottom and through the keyhole of Mr Billings' room.

Tommy hesitated a moment. Then he raised his hand and knocked. For a time there was silence. Then a stirring sound. The sound of heavy footsteps.

The door opened. Mr Billings peered out into the hall.

'Hello,' Tommy said.

'You're back!' Mr Billings opened the door wide and Tommy walked quickly into the room. 'Did you forget something?'

'No.'

Billings closed the door. 'Sit down. Would you like anything? An apple? Some milk?'

'No.' Tommy wandered nervously around the room, touching things here and there, books and papers and bundles of clippings.

Billings watched the boy a moment. Then he returned to his desk, seating himself with a sigh. 'I think I'll continue with my report. I hope to finish very soon.' He tapped a pile of notes beside him. 'The last of them. Then I can leave here and present the report along with my recommendations.'

Billings bent over his immense typewriter, tapping steadily away. The relentless rumble of the ancient machine vibrated through the room. Tommy turned and stepped out of the room, onto the porch.

In the cold evening air the porch was pitch black. He halted, adjusting to the darkness. After a time he made out the sacks of fertilizer, the rickety chair. And in the center, the wood frame with its wire netting over it, heaps of dirt and grass piled around.

Tommy glanced back into the room. Billings was bent over the typewriter, absorbed in his work. He had taken off his dark blue coat and hung it over the chair. He was working in his vest, his sleeves rolled up.

Tommy squatted beside the frame. He slid the cigar box from under his jacket and laid it down, lid open. He grasped the netting and pried it back, loose from the row of nails.

From the frame a few faint apprehensive squeaks sounded. Nervous scuttlings among the dried grass.

Tommy reached down, feeling among the grass and plants. His fingers closed over something, a small thing that squirmed in fright, twisting in wild terror. He dropped it into the cigar box and sought another.

In a moment he had them all. Nine of them, all nine in the wood cigar box.

He closed the lid and slipped it back under his jacket. Quickly he left the porch, returning to the room.

Billings glanced up vaguely from his work, pen in one hand, papers in the other. 'Did you want to talk to me?' he murmured, pushing up his glasses.

Tommy shook his head. 'I have to go.'

'Already? But you just came!'

'I have to go.' Tommy opened the door to the hall. 'Goodnight.'

Billings rubbed his forehead wearily, his face lined with fatigue. 'All right, boy. Perhaps I'll see you again before I leave.' He resumed his work, tapping slowly away at the great typewriter, bent with fatigue.

Tommy shut the door behind him. He ran down the stairs, outside on the porch. Against his chest the cigar box shook and moved. Nine. All nine of them. He had them all. Now they were his. They belonged to him–and there weren't any more of them, anywhere in the world. His plan had worked perfectly.

He hurried down the street toward his own house, as fast as he could run.

He found an old cage out in the garage he had once kept white rats in. He cleaned it and carried it upstairs to his room. He spread papers on the floor of the cage and fixed a water dish and some sand.

When the cage was ready he emptied the contents of the cigar box into it.

The nine tiny figures huddled together in the center of the cage, a little bundle of pink. Tommy shut the door of the cage and fastened it tightly. He carried the cage to the dresser and then drew a chair up by it so he could watch.

The nine little people began to move around hesitantly, exploring the cage. Tommy's heart beat with rapid excitement as he watched them.

He had got them away from Mr Billings. They were his, now. And Mr Billings didn't know where he lived or even his name.

They were talking to each other. Moving their antennae rapidly, the way he had seen ants do. One of the little people came over to the side of the cage. He stood gripping the wire, peering out into the room. He was joined by another, a female. They were naked. Except for the hair on their heads they were pink and smooth.

He wondered what they ate. From the big refrigerator in the kitchen he took some cheese and some hamburger, adding crumbled up bits of bread and lettuce leaves and a little plate of milk.

They liked the milk and bread. But they left the meat alone. The lettuce leaves they used to begin the making of little huts.

Tommy was fascinated. He watched them all the next morning before school, then again at lunch time, and all afternoon until dinner.

'What you got up there?' his Dad demanded, at dinner.

'Nothing.'

'You haven't got a snake, have you?' his Mom asked apprehensively. 'If you have another snake up there, young man–'

'No.' Tommy shook his head, bolting down his meal. 'It's not a snake.'

He finished eating and ran upstairs.

The little creatures had finished fixing their huts out of the lettuce leaves. Some were inside. Others were wandering around the cage, exploring it.

Tommy seated himself before the dresser and watched. They were smart. A lot smarter than the white rats he had owned. And cleaner. They used the sand he had put there for them. They were smart–and quite tame.

After a while Tommy closed the door of the room. Holding his breath he unfastened the cage, opening one side wide. He reached in his hand and caught one of the little men. He drew him out of the cage and then opened his hand carefully.

The little man clung to his palm, peering over the edge and up at him, antennae waving wildly.

'Don't be afraid,' Tommy said.

The little man got cautiously to his feet. He walked across Tommy's palm, to his wrist. Slowly he climbed Tommy's arm, glancing over the side. He reached Tommy's shoulder and stopped, gazing up into his face.

'You're sure small,' Tommy said. He got another one from the cage and put the two of them on the bed. They walked around the bed for a long time. More had come to the open side of the cage and were staring cautiously out onto the dresser. One found Tommy's comb. He inspected it, tugging at the teeth. A second joined him. The two tiny creatures tugged at the comb, but without success.

'What do you want?' Tommy asked. After a while they gave up. They found a nickel lying on the dresser. One of them managed to turn it up on end. He rolled it. The nickel gained speed, rushing toward the edge of the dresser. The tiny men ran after it in consternation. The nickel fell over the side.

'Be careful,' Tommy warned. He didn't want anything to happen to them. He had too many plans. It would be easy to rig up things for them to do–like fleas he had seen at the circus. Little carts to pull. Swings, slides. Things they could operate. He could train them, and then charge admission.

Maybe he could take them on tour. Maybe he'd even get a write-up in the newspaper. His mind raced. All kinds of things. Endless possibilities. But he had to start out easy–and be careful.

The next day he took one to school in his pocket, inside a fruit jar. He punched holes in the lid so it could breathe.

At recess he showed it to Dave and Joan Grant. They were fascinated.

'Where did you get it?' Dave demanded.

'That's my business.'

'Want to sell it?'

'It's not *it*. It's him.'

Jean blushed. 'It doesn't have anything on. You better make it put clothes on right away.'

'Can you make clothes for them? I have eight more. Four men and four women.'

Joan was excited. 'I can–if you'll give me one of them.'

'The heck I will. They're mine.'

'Where did they come from? Who made them?'

'None of your business.'

Joan made little clothes for the four women. Little skirts and blouses. Tommy lowered the clothing into the cage. The little people moved around the heap uncertainly, not knowing what to do.

'You better show them,' Joan said.

'Show them? Nuts to you.'

'I'll dress them.' Joan took one of the tiny women from the cage and carefully dressed her in a blouse and skirt. She dropped the figure back in. 'Now let's see what happens.'

The others crowded around the dressed woman, plucking curiously at the clothing. Presently they began to divide up the remaining clothes, some taking blouses, some skirts.

Tommy laughed and laughed. 'You better make pants for the men. So they'll all be dressed.'

He took a couple of them out and let them run up and down his arms.

'Be careful,' Joan warned. 'You'll lose them. They'll get away.'

'They're tame. They won't run away. I'll show you.' Tommy put them down onto the floor. 'We have a game. Watch.'

'A game?'

'They hide and I find them.'

The figures scampered off, looking for places to hide. In a moment none were in sight. Tommy got down on his hands and knees, reaching under the dresser, among the bedcovers. A shrill squeak. He had found one.

'See? They like it.' He carried them back to the cage, one by one. The last one stayed hidden a long time. It had got into one of the dresser drawers, down in a bag of marbles, pulling the marbles over its head.

'They're clever,' Joan said. 'Wouldn't you give me even one of them?'

'No,' Tommy said emphatically. 'They're mine. I'm not letting them get away from me. I'm not giving any of them to *anybody*.'

Tommy met Joan after school the next day. She had made little trousers and shirts for the men.

'Here.' She gave them to him. They walked along the sidewalk. 'I hope they fit.'

'Thanks.' Tommy took the clothes and put them in his pocket. They cut across the vacant lot. At the end of the lot Dave Grant and some kids were sitting around in a circle, playing marbles.

'Who's winning?' Tommy said, stopping.

'I am,' Dave said, not looking up.

'Let me play.' Tommy dropped down. 'Come on.' He held out his hand. 'Give me your agate.'

Dave shook his head. 'Get away.'

Tommy punched him on the arm. 'Come on! Just one shot.' He considered. 'Tell you what–'

A shadow fell over them.

Tommy looked up. And blanched.

Edward Billings gazed down silently at the boy, leaning on his umbrella, its metal point lost in the soft ground. He said nothing. His aged face was lined and hard, his eyes like faded blue stones.

Tommy got slowly to his feet. Silence had fallen over the children. Some of them scrambled away, snatching up their marbles.

'What do you want?' Tommy demanded. His voice was dry and husky, almost inaudible.

Billings' cold eyes bored into him, two keen orbs, without warmth of any kind. 'You took them. I want them back. Right away.' His voice was hard, colorless. He held out his hand. 'Where are they?'

'What are you talking about?' Tommy muttered. He backed away. 'I don't know what you mean.'

'The Project. You stole them from my room. I want them back.'

'The heck I did. What do you mean?'

Billings turned toward Dave Grant. 'He's the one you meant, isn't he?'

Dave nodded. 'I saw them. He has them in his room. He won't let anybody near them.'

'You came and stole them. *Why?*' Billings moved toward Tommy ominously. 'Why did you take them? What do you want with them?'

'You're crazy,' Tommy murmured, but his voice trembled. Dave Grant said nothing. He looked away sheepishly. 'It's a lie,' Tommy said.

Billings grabbed him. Cold, ancient hands gripped him, digging into his shoulders. 'Give them back! I want them. I'm responsible for them.'

'Let go.' Tommy jerked loose. 'I don't have them with me.' He caught his breath. 'I mean–'

'Then you do have them. At home. In your room. Bring them here. Go and get them. All nine.'

Tommy put his hands in his pockets. Some of his courage was returning. 'I don't know,' he said. 'What'll you give me?'

Billings' eyes flashed. 'Give you?' He raised his arm threateningly. 'Why, you little–'

Tommy jumped back. 'You can't make me return them. You don't have any control over us.' He grinned boldly. 'You said so yourself. We're out of your power. I heard you say so.'

Billings' face was like granite. 'I'll take them. They're mine. They belong to me.'

'If you try to take them I'll call the cops. And my Dad'll be there. My Dad and the cops.'

Billings gripped his umbrella. He opened and shut his mouth, his face a dark, ugly red. Neither he nor Tommy spoke. The other kids gazed at the two of them wide-eyed, awed and subdued.

Suddenly a thought twisted across Billings' face. He looked down at the ground, the crude circle and the marbles. His cold eyes flickered. 'Listen to this. I will–I will play against you for them.'

'What?'

'The game. Marbles. If you win you can keep them. If I win I get them back at once. All of them.'

Tommy considered, glancing from Mr Billings down at the circle on the ground. 'If I win you won't ever try to take them? You will let me keep them–for good?'

'Yes.'

'All right.' Tommy moved away. 'It's a deal. If you win you can have them back. But if I win they belong to me. And you don't ever get them back.'

'Bring them here at once.'

'Sure. I'll go get them.'–And my agate, too, he thought to himself. 'I'll be right back.'

'I'll wait here,' Mr Billings said, his huge hands gripping the umbrella.

Tommy ran down the porch steps, two at a time.

His mother came to the door. 'You shouldn't be going out again so late. If you're not home in half an hour you don't get any dinner.'

'Half an hour,' Tommy cried, running down the dark sidewalk, his hands pressed against the bulge in his jacket. Against the wood cigar box that moved and squirmed. He ran and ran, gasping for breath.

Mr Billings was still standing by the edge of the lot, waiting silently. The sun had set. Evening was coming. The children had gone home. As Tommy stepped onto the vacant lot a chill, hostile wind moved among the weeds and grass, flapping against his pants legs.

'Did you bring them?' Mr Billings demanded.

'Sure.' Tommy halted, his chest rising and falling. He reached slowly under his jacket and brought out the heavy wood cigar box. He slipped the rubber band off it, lifting the lid a crack. 'In here.'

Mr Billings came close, breathing hoarsely. Tommy snapped the lid shut and restored the rubber band. 'We have to play.' He put the box down on the ground. 'They're mine–unless you win them back.'

Billings subsided. 'All right. Let's begin, then.'

Tommy searched his pockets. He brought out his agate, holding it carefully. In the fading light the big red-black marble gleamed, rings of sand and white. Like Jupiter. An immense, hard marble.

'Here we go,' Tommy said. He knelt down, sketching a rough circle on the ground. He emptied out a sack of marbles into the ring. 'You got any?'

'Any?'

'Marbles. What are you going to shoot with?'

'One of yours.'

'Sure.' Tommy took a marble from the ring and tossed it to him. 'Want me to shoot first?'

Billings nodded.

'Fine.' Tommy grinned. He took aim carefully, closing one eye. For a moment his body was rigid, set in an intense, hard arc. Then he shot. Marbles rattled and clinked, rolling out of the circle and into the grass and weeds beyond. He had done well. He gathered up his winnings, collecting them back in the cloth sack.

'Is it my turn?' Billings asked.

'No. My agate's still in the ring.' Tommy squatted down again. 'I get another shot.'

He shot. This time he collected three marbles. Again his agate was within the circle.

'Another shot,' Tommy said, grinning. He had almost half. He knelt and aimed, holding his breath. Twenty-four marbles remained. If he could get four more he would have won. Four more–

He shot. Two marbles left the circle. And his agate. The agate rolled out, bouncing into the weeds.

Tommy collected the two marbles and the agate. He had nineteen in all. Twenty-two remained in the ring.

'Okay,' he murmured reluctantly. 'It's your shot this time. Go ahead.'

Edward Billings knelt down stiffly, gasping and tottering. His face was gray. He turned his marble around in his hand uncertainly.

'Haven't you ever played before?' Tommy demanded. 'You don't know how to hold it, do you?'

Billings shook his head. 'No.'

'You have to get it between your first finger and your thumb.' Tommy watched the stiff old fingers fumble with the marble. Billings dropped it once and picked it quickly up again. 'Your thumb makes it go. Like this. Here, I'll show you.'

Tommy took hold of the ancient fingers and bent them around the marble. Finally he had them in place. 'Go ahead.' Tommy straightened up. 'Let's see how you do.'

The old man took a long time. He gazed at the marbles in the ring, his hand shaking. Tommy could hear his breathing, the hoarse, deep panting, in the damp evening air.

The old man glanced at the cigar box resting in the shadows. Then back at the circle. His fingers moved–

There was a flash. A blinding flash. Tommy gave a cry, wiping at his eyes. Everything spun, lashing and tilting. He stumbled and fell, sinking into the wet weeds. His head throbbed. He sat on the ground, rubbing his eyes, shaking his head, trying to see.

At last the drifting sparks cleared. He looked around him, blinking.

The circle was empty. There were no marbles in the ring. Billings had got them all.

Tommy reached out. His fingers touched something hot. He jumped. It was a fragment of glass, a glowing red fragment of molten glass. All around him, in the damp weeds and grass, fragments of glass gleamed, cooling slowly into darkness. A thousand splinters of stars, glowing and fading around him.

Edward Billings stood up slowly, rubbing his hands together.

'I'm glad that's over,' he gasped. 'I'm too old to bend down like that.'

His eyes made out the cigar box, lying on the ground.

'Now they can go back. And I can continue with my work.' He picked up the wood box, putting it under his arm. He gathered up his umbrella and shuffled away, toward the sidewalk beyond the lot.

'Goodbye,' Billings said, stopping for a moment. Tommy said nothing.

Billings hurried off down the sidewalk, the cigar box clutched tightly.

He entered his apartment, breathing rapidly. He tossed his black umbrella into the corner and sat down before the desk, laying the cigar box in front of him. For a moment he sat, breathing deeply and gazing down at the brown and white square of wood and cardboard.

He had won. He had got them back. They were his, again. And just in time. The filing date for the report was practically upon him.

Billings slid out of his coat and vest. He rolled up his sleeves, trembling a little. He had been lucky. Control over the B type was extremely limited. They were virtually out of jurisdiction. That, of course, was the problem itself. Both the A and B types had managed to escape supervision. They had rebelled, disobeying orders and therefore putting themselves outside the limit of the plan.

But these–the new type, Project C. Everything depended on them. They had left his hands, but now they were back again. Under control, as intended. Within the periphery of supervisory instruction.

Billings slid the rubber band from the box. He raised the lid, slowly and carefully.

Out they swarmed–fast. Some headed to the right, some to the left. Two columns of tiny figures racing off, head down. One reached the edge of the desk and leaped. He landed on the rug, rolling and falling. A second jumped after him, then a third.

Billings broke out of his paralysis. He grabbed frantically, wildly. Only two remained. He swiped at one and missed. The other—

He grabbed it, squeezing it tight between his clenched fingers. Its companion wheeled. It had something in its hand. A splinter. A splinter of wood, torn from the inside of the cigar box.

It ran up and stuck the end of the splinter into Billings' finger.

Billings gasped in pain. His fingers flew open. The captive tumbled out, rolling on its back. Its companion helped it up, half-dragging it to the edge of the desk. Together the two of them leaped.

Billings bent down, groping for them. They scampered rapidly, toward the door to the porch. One of them was at the lamp plug. It tugged. A second joined it and the two tiny figures pulled together. The lamp cord came out of the wall. The room plunged into darkness.

Billings found the desk drawer. He yanked it open, spilling its contents onto the floor. He found some big sulphur matches and lit one.

They were gone—out onto the porch.

Billings hurried after them. The match blew out. He lit another, shielding it with his hand.

The creatures had got to the railing. They were going over the edge, catching hold of the ivy and swinging down into the darkness.

He got to the edge too late. They were gone, all of them. All nine, over the side of the roof, into the blackness of the night.

Billings ran downstairs and out onto the back porch. He reached the ground, hurrying around the side of the house, where the ivy grew up the side.

Nothing moved. Nothing stirred. Silence. No sign of them anywhere.

They had escaped. They were gone. They had worked out a plan of escape and put it into operation. Two columns, going in opposite directions, as soon as the lid was lifted. Perfectly timed and executed.

Slowly Billings climbed the stairs to his room. He pushed the door open and stood, breathing deeply, dazed from the shock.

They were gone. Project C was already over. It had gone like the others. The same way. Rebellion and independence. Out of supervision. Beyond control. Project A had influenced Project B–and now, in the same way, the contamination had spread to C.

Billings sat down heavily at his desk. For a long time he sat immobile, silent and thoughtful, gradual comprehension coming to him. It was not his fault. It had happened before–twice before. And it would happen again. Each Project would carry the discontent to the next. It would never end, no matter how many Projects were conceived and put into operation. The rebellion and escape. The evasion of the plan.

After a time, Billings reached out and pulled his big report book to him. Slowly he opened it to the place he had left off. From the report he removed the entire last section. The summary. There was no use scrapping the current Project. One Project was as good as any other. They would all be equal–equal failures.

He had known as soon as he saw them. As soon as he had raised the lid. They had clothes on. Little suits of clothing. Like the others, a long time before.

THE TROUBLE WITH BUBBLES

Nathan Hull left his surface car and crossed the pavement on foot, sniffing the chill morning air. Robot work-trucks were starting to rumble past. A gutter slot sucked night debris greedily. A vanishing headline caught his eye momentarily:

PACIFIC TUBE COMPLETED;
ASIAN LAND MASS LINKED

He passed on away from the corner, hands in his pockets, looking for Farley's house.

Past the usual Worldcraft Store with its conspicuous motto: 'Own Your Own World!' Down a short grass-lined walk and onto a sloping tilt-front porch. Up three imitation marble stairs. Then Hull flicked his hand before the code beam and the door melted away.

The house was still. Hull found the ascent tube to the second floor and peered up. No sound. Warm air blew around him, tinged with faint smells–smells of food and people and familiar objects. Had they gone? No. It was only the third day; they'd be around someplace, maybe up on the roof terrace.

He ascended to the second floor and found it also vacant. But distant sounds drifted to his ears. A tinkle of laughter, a man's voice. A woman's–perhaps Julia's. He hoped so–hoped she were still conscious.

He tried a door at random, steeling himself. Sometimes during the third and fourth days the Contest Parties got a little rough. The door melted, but the room was empty. Couches, empty glasses, ashtrays, exhausted stimulant tubes, articles of clothing strewn everywhere–

Abruptly Julia Marlow and Max Farley appeared, arm in arm, followed by several others, pushing forward in a group, excited and red-cheeked, eyes bright, almost feverish. They entered the room and halted.

'Nat!' Julia broke away from Farley and came breathlessly up to him. 'Is it that late already?'

'Third day,' Hull said. 'Hello, Max.'

'Hello, Hull. Sit down and make yourself comfortable. Can I get you something?'

'Nothing. Can't stay. Julia–'

Farley waved a robant over, sweeping two drinks from its chest tray. 'Here, Hull. You can stay long enough for one drink.'

Bart Longstreet and a slender blonde appeared through a door. 'Hull! You here? So soon?'

'Third day. I'm picking Julia up. If she still wants to leave.'

'Don't take her away,' the slim blonde protested. She wore a *sideglance* robe, invisible out of the corner of the eye, but an opaque fountain when looked at directly. 'They're judging right now. In the lounge. Stick around. The fun's just beginning.' She winked at him with heavy blue-lidded eyes, glazed and sleep-drugged.

Hull turned to Julia. 'If you want to stay . . .'

Julia put her hand nervously on his arm, standing close to him. Not losing her fixed smile she grated in his ear: 'Nat, for God's sake, get me out of here. I can't stand it. Please!'

Hull caught her intense appeal, her eyes bright with desperation. He could feel the mute urgency quivering through her body, tense and strained. 'Okay, Julia. We'll take off. Maybe get some breakfast. When did you last eat?'

'Two days. I think. I don't know.' Her voice trembled. 'They're judging right now. God, Nat, you should have seen–'

'Can't go until the judging's over,' Farley rumbled. 'I think they're almost through. You didn't enter, Hull? No entry for you?'

'No entry.'

'Surely you're an owner–'

'Nope. Sorry.' Hull's voice was faintly ironic. 'No world of my own, Max. Can't see it.'

'You're missing something.' Max beamed dopily, rocking back on his heels. 'Quite a time–best Contest Party for weeks. And the real fun begins *after* the judging. All this is just preliminary.'

'I know.' Hull moved Julia rapidly toward the descent tube. 'We'll see you. So long, Bart. Give me a call when you're out of here.'

'Hold it!' Bart murmured suddenly, cocking his head. 'The judging's over. The winner is going to be announced.' He pushed toward the lounge, the others excitedly behind. 'You coming, Hull? Julia?'

Hull glanced at the girl. 'All right.' They followed reluctantly. 'For a minute, maybe.'

A wall of sound struck them. The lounge was a seething chaos of milling men and women.

'I won!' Lora Becker shouted in ecstasy. People pushed and shoved around her, toward the Contest table, grabbing up their entries. Their voices grew in volume, an ominous rumble of discordant sound. Robants calmly moved furniture and fixtures back out of the way, clearing the floor rapidly. An unleashed frenzy of mounting hysteria was beginning to fill the big room.

'I knew it!' Julia's fingers tightened around Hull's arm. 'Come on. Let's get out before they start.'

'Start?'

'Listen to them!' Julia's eyes flickered with fear. 'Come on, Nat! I've had enough. I can't stand any more of this.'

'I told you before you came.'

'You did, didn't you?' Julia smiled briefly, grabbing her coat from a robant. She fastened the coat rapidly around her breasts and shoulders. 'I admit it. You told me. Now let's go, for God's sake.' She turned, making her way through the surging mass of people toward the descent tube. 'Let's get out of here. We'll have breakfast. You were right. These things aren't for us.'

Lora Becker, plump and middle-aged, was making her way up onto the stand beside the judges, her entry clasped in her arms. Hull paused a moment, watching the immense woman struggle up, her chemically corrected features gray and sagging in the unwinking overhead lights. The third day–a lot of old-timers were beginning to show the effects, even through their artificial masks.

Lora reached the stand. 'Look!' she shouted, holding up her entry. The Worldcraft bubble glittered, catching the light. In spite of himself Hull had to admire the thing. If the actual world inside was as good as the exterior . . .

Lora turned on the bubble. It glowed, winking into brilliance. The roomful of people became silent, gazing up at the winning entry, the world that had taken the prize over all other comers.

Lora Becker's entry was masterful. Even Hull had to admit it. She increased the magnification, bringing the microscopic central planet into focus. A murmur of admiration swept the room.

Again Lora increased the magnification. The central planet grew, showing a pale green ocean lapping faintly at a low shoreline. A city came into view, towers and broad streets, fine ribbons of gold and steel. Above, twin suns beamed down, warming the city. Myriads of inhabitants swarmed about their activities.

'Wonderful,' Bart Longstreet said softly, coming over beside Hull. 'But the old hag has been at it sixty years. No wonder she won. She's entered every Contest I can remember.'

'It's nice,' Julia admitted in a clipped voice.

'You don't care for it?' Longstreet asked.

'I don't care for any of this!'

'She wants to go,' Hull explained, moving toward the descent tube. 'We'll see you later, Bart.'

Bart Longstreet nodded. 'I know what you mean. In many ways I agree. You mind if I–'

'Watch!' Lora Becker shouted, her face flushed. She increased the magnification to maximum focus, showing details of the minute city. 'See them? *See?*'

The inhabitants of the city came into sharp view. They hurried about their business, endless thousands of them. In cars and on foot. Across spidery spans between buildings, breathtakingly beautiful.

Lora held the Worldcraft bubble up high, breathing rapidly. She gazed around the room, her eyes bright and inflamed, glittering unhealthily. The murmurings rose, sweeping up in excitement. Numerous Worldcraft bubbles came up, chest-high, gripped in eager, impassioned hands.

Lora's mouth opened. Saliva dribbled down the creases of her sagging face. Her lips twitched. She raised her bubble up over her head, her doughy chest swelling convulsively. Suddenly her face jerked, features twisting wildly. Her thick body swayed grotesquely–and from her hands the Worldcraft bubble flew, crashing to the stand in front of her.

The bubble smashed, bursting into a thousand pieces. Metal and glass, plastic parts, gears, struts, tubes, the vital machinery of the bubble, splattered in all directions.

Pandemonium broke loose. All around the room other owners were smashing their worlds, breaking them and crushing them, stamping on them, grinding the delicate control mechanisms underfoot. Men and women in a frenzy of abandon, released by Lora Becker's signal, quivering in an orgy of Dionysian lust. Crushing and breaking their carefully constructed worlds, one after another.

'God,' Julia gasped, struggling to get away, Longstreet and Hull beside her.

Faces gleamed with sweat, eyes feverish and bright. Mouths gaped foolishly, muttering meaningless sounds. Clothes were torn, ripped off. A girl went down, sliding underfoot, her shrieks lost in the general din. Another followed, dragged down into the milling mass. Men and women struggled in a blur of abandon, cries and gasps. And on all sides the hideous sounds of smashing metal and glass, the unending noise of worlds being destroyed one after another.

Julia dragged Hull from the lounge, her face white. She shuddered, closing her eyes. 'I knew it was coming. Three days, building up to this. Smashed–they're smashing them all. All the worlds.'

Bart Longstreet made his way out after Hull and Julia. 'Lunatics.' He lit a cigarette shakily. 'What the hell gets into them? This has happened before. They start breaking, smashing their worlds up. It doesn't make sense.'

Hull reached the descent tube. 'Come along with us, Bart. We'll have breakfast–and I'll give you my theory, for what it's worth.'

'Just a second.' Bart Longstreet scooped up his Worldcraft bubble from the arms of a robant. 'My Contest entry. Don't want to lose it.'

He hurried after Julia and Hull.

'More coffee?' Hull asked, looking around.

'None for me,' Julia murmured. She settled back in her chair, sighing. 'I'm perfectly happy.'

'I'll take some.' Bart pushed his cup toward the coffee dispenser. It filled the cup and returned it. 'You've got a nice little place here, Hull.'

'Haven't you seen it before?'

'I don't get up this way. I haven't been in Canada in years.'

'Let's hear your theory,' Julia murmured.

'Go ahead,' Bart said. 'We're waiting.'

Hull was silent for a moment. He gazed moodily across the table, past the dishes, at the thing sitting on the window ledge. Bart's Contest entry, his Worldcraft bubble.

'"Own Your Own World."' Hull quoted ironically. 'Quite a slogan.'

'Packman thought it up himself,' Bart said. 'When he was young. Almost a century ago.'

'That long?'

'Packman takes treatments. A man in his position can afford them.'

'Of course.' Hull got slowly to his feet. He crossed the room and returned with the bubble. 'Mind?' he asked Bart.

'Go ahead.'

Hull adjusted the controls mounted on the bubble's surface. The interior scene flickered into focus. A miniature planet, revolving slowly. A tiny blue-white sun. He increased the magnification, bringing the planet up in size.

'Not bad,' Hull admitted presently.

'Primitive. Late Jurassic. I don't have the knack. I can't seem to get them into the mammal stage. This is my sixteenth try. I never can get any farther than this.'

The scene was a dense jungle, steaming with fetid rot. Great shapes stirred fitfully among the decaying ferns and marshes. Coiled, gleaming, reptilian bodies, smoking shapes rising up from the thick mud–

'Turn it off,' Julia murmured. 'I've seen enough of them. We viewed hundreds for the Contest.'

'I didn't have a chance.' Bart retrieved his bubble, snapping it off. 'You have to do better than the Jurassic, to win. Competition is keen. Half the people there had their bubbles into the Eocene–and at least ten into the Pliocene. Lora's entry wasn't much ahead. I counted several city-building civilizations. But hers was almost as advanced as we are.'

'Sixty years,' Julia said.

'She's been trying a long time. She's worked hard. One of those to whom it's not a game but a real passion. A way of life.'

'And then she smashes it,' Hull said thoughtfully. 'Smashes the bubble to bits. A world she's been working on for years. Guiding it through period after period. Higher and higher. Smashes it into a million pieces.'

'Why?' Julia asked. 'Why, Nat? Why do they do it? They get so far, building it up–and then they tear it all down again.'

Hull leaned back in his chair. 'It began,' he stated, 'when we failed to find life on any of the other planets. When our exploring parties came back empty-handed. Eight dead orbs–lifeless. Good for nothing. Not even lichen. Rock and sand. Endless deserts. One after the other, all the way out to Pluto.'

'It was a hard realization,' Bart said. 'Of course, that was before our time.'

'Not much before. Packman remembers it. A century ago. We waited a long time for rocket travel, flight to other planets. And then to find nothing . . .'

'Like Columbus finding the world really was flat,' Julia said. 'With an edge and a void.'

'Worse. Columbus was looking for a short route to China. They *could* have continued the long way. But when we explored the system and found nothing we were in for trouble. People had counted on new worlds, new lands in the sky. Colonization. Contact with a variety of races. Trade. Minerals and cultural products to exchange. But most of all the thrill of landing on planets with amazing life-forms.'

'And instead of that . . .'

'Nothing but dead rock and waste. Nothing that could support life–our own or any other kind. A vast disappointment set in on all levels of society.'

'And then Packman brought out the Worldcraft bubble,' Bart murmured. '"Own Your Own World." There was no place to go, outside of Terra. No other worlds to visit. You couldn't leave here and go to another world. So instead, you–'

'Instead you stayed home and put together your own world.' Hull smiled wryly. 'You know, he has a child's version out, now. A sort of preparation kit. So the child can cover the basic problems of world-building before he even has a bubble.'

'But look, Nat,' Bart said. 'The bubbles seemed like a good idea, at first. We couldn't leave Terra so we built our own worlds right here. Sub-atomic worlds, in controlled containers. We start life going on a sub-atomic world, feed it problems to make it evolve, try to raise it higher and higher. In theory there's nothing wrong with the idea. It's certainly a creative pastime. Not a merely passive viewing like television. In fact, world-building is the ultimate art form. It takes the place of all entertainments, all the passive sports as well as music and painting–'

'But something went wrong.'

'Not at first,' Bart objected. 'At first it was creative. Everybody bought a Worldcraft bubble and built his own world. Evolved life farther and farther. Molded life. Controlled it. Competed with others to see who could achieve the most advanced world.'

'And it solved another problem,' Julia added. 'The problem of leisure. With robots to work for us and robants to serve us and take care of our needs–'

'Yes, that was a problem,' Hull admitted. 'Too much leisure. Nothing to do. That, and the disappointment of finding our planet the only habitable planet in the system.

'Packman's bubbles seemed to solve both problems. But something went wrong. A change came. I noticed it right away.' Hull stubbed out his cigarette and lit another. 'The change began ten years ago–and it's been growing worse.'

'But why?' Julia demanded. 'Explain to me why everyone stopped building their worlds creatively and began to destroy.'

'Ever seen a child pull wings off a fly?'

'Certainly. But–'

'The same thing. Sadism? No, not exactly. More a sort of curiosity. Power. Why does a child break things? Power, again. We must never forget something. These world bubbles are *substitutes*. They take the place of something else, of finding genuine life on our own planets. And they're just too damn small to do that.

'These worlds are like toy boats in a bath tub. Or model rocketships you see kids playing with. They're surrogates, not the actual thing. These people who operate them–why do they want them? Because they can't explore real planets, big planets. They have a lot of energy dammed up inside them. Energy they can't express.

'And bottled-up energy sours. It becomes aggressive. People work with their little worlds for a time, building them up. But finally they reach a point where their latent hostility, their sense of being deprived, their–'

'It can be explained more easily,' Bart said calmly. 'Your theory is too elaborate.'

'How do you explain it?'

'Man's innate destructive tendencies. His natural desire to kill and spread ruin.'

'There's no such thing,' Hull said flatly. 'Man isn't an ant. He has no fixed direction to his drives. He has no instinctive "desire to destroy" any more than he has an instinctive desire to carve ivory letter-openers. He has *energy*–and the outlet it takes depends on the opportunities available.

'That's what's wrong. All of us have energy, the desire to move, act, do. But we're bottled up here, sealed off, on one planet. So we buy Worldcraft bubbles and make little worlds of our own. But microscopic worlds aren't enough. They're as satisfactory as a toy sailboat is to a man who wants to go sailing.'

Bart considered a long time, deep in thought. 'You may be right,' he admitted finally. 'It sounds reasonable. But what's your suggestion? If the other eight planets are dead–'

'Keep exploring. Beyond the system.'

'We're doing that.'

'Try to find outlets that aren't so artificial.'

Bart grinned. 'You feel this way because you never caught the hang of it.' He thumped his bubble fondly. 'I don't find it artificial.'

'But most people do,' Julia put in. 'Most people aren't satisfied. That's why we left the Contest Party.'

Bart grunted. 'It's turning sour, all right. Quite a scene, wasn't it?' He reflected, frowning. 'But the bubbles are better than nothing. What do you suggest? Give up our bubbles? What should we do instead? Just sit around and talk?'

'Nat loves to talk,' Julia murmured.

'Like all intellectuals.' Bart tapped Hull's sleeve. 'When you sit in your seat in the Directorate you're with the Intellectual and Professional class–gray stripe.'

'And you?'

'Blue stripe. Industrial. You know that.'

Hull nodded. 'That's right. You're with Terran Spaceways. The ever-hopeful company.'

'So you want us to give up our bubbles and just sit around. Quite a solution to the problem.'

'You're going to *have* to give them up.' Hull's face flushed. 'What you do after that is your affair.'

'What do you mean?'

Hull turned toward Longstreet, eyes blazing. 'I've introduced a bill in the Directorate. A bill that will outlaw Worldcraft.'

Bart's mouth fell open. 'You *what?*'

'On what grounds?' Julia asked, waking up.

'On moral grounds,' Hull stated calmly. 'And I think I can get it through.'

The Directorate hall buzzed with murmuring echoes, its vast reaches alive with moving shadows, men taking their places and preparing for the session's business.

Eldon von Stern, Directorate Floor Leader, stood with Hull off to one side behind the platform. 'Let's get this straight,' von Stern said nervously, running his fingers through his iron-gray hair. 'You intend to *speak* for this bill of yours? You want to defend it yourself?'

Hull nodded. 'That's right. Why not?'

'The analytical machines can break the bill down and present an impartial report for the members. Spellbinding has gone out of style. If you present an emotional harangue you can be certain of losing. The members won't–'

'I'll take the chance. It's too important to leave to the machines.'

Hull gazed out over the immense room that was slowly quieting. Representatives from all over the world were in their places. White-clad property owners. Blue-clad financial and industrial magnates. The red shirts of leaders from factory cooperatives and communal farms. The green-clad men and women representing the middle-class consumer group. His own gray-striped body, at the extreme right, the doctors, lawyers, scientists, educators, intellectuals and professionals of all kinds.

'I'll take the chance,' Hull repeated. 'I want to see the bill passed. It's time the issues were made clear.'

Von Stern shrugged. 'Suit yourself.' He eyed Hull curiously. 'What do you have against Worldcraft? It's too powerful a combine to buck. Packman himself is here, someplace. I'm surprised you–'

The robot chair flashed a signal. Von Stern moved away from Hull, up onto the platform.

'Are you sure you want to speak for the bill?' Julia said, standing beside Hull in the shadows. 'Maybe he's right. Let the machines analyze the bill.'

Hull was gazing out across the sea of faces, trying to locate Packman. The owner of Worldcraft was sitting out there. Forrest Packman, in his immaculate white shirt, like an ancient, withered angel. Packman preferred to sit with the property group, considering Worldcraft real estate instead of industry. Property still had the edge on prestige.

Von Stern touched Hull's arm. 'All right. Take the chair and explain your proposal.'

Hull stepped out onto the platform and seated himself in the big marble chair. The endless rows of faces before him were carefully devoid of expression.

'You've read the terms of the proposal I'm speaking for,' Hull began, his voice magnified by the speakers on each member's desk. 'I propose we should declare Worldcraft Industries a public menace and the real property the possession of the State. I can state my grounds in a few sentences.

'The theory and construction of the Worldcraft product, the sub-atomic universe system, is known to you. An infinite number of sub-atomic worlds exist, microscopic counterparts of our own spatial coordinate. Worldcraft developed, almost a century ago, a method of controlling to thirty decimals the forces and stresses involved on these micro-coordinate planes, and a fairly simplified machine which could be manipulated by any adult person.

'These machines for controlling specific areas of sub-atomic coordinates have been manufactured and sold to the general public with the slogan: "Own Your Own World." The idea is that the owner of the machine becomes literally a world owner, since the machine controls forces that govern a sub-atomic universe that is directly analogous to our own.

'By purchasing one of these Worldcraft machines, or bubbles, the person finds himself in possession of a virtual universe, to do with as he sees fit. Instruction manuals supplied by the Company show him how to control these minute worlds so that life-forms appear and rapidly evolve, giving rise to higher and higher forms until at last–assuming the owner is sufficiently skillful–he has in his personal possession a civilization of beings on a cultural par with our own.

'During the last few years we have seen the sale of these machines grow until now almost everyone possesses one or more sub-atomic worlds, complete with civilizations. And these years have also seen many of us take our private universes and grind the inhabitants and planets into dust.

'There is no law which prevents us from building up elaborate civilizations, evolved at an incredible rate of speed, and then crushing them out of existence. That is why my proposal has been presented. These minute civilizations are not dreams. They are real. They actually exist. The microscopic inhabitants are–'

A restless stir moved through the vast hall. There were murmurs and coughs. Some members had switched off their speakers. Hull hesitated. A chill touched him. The faces below were blank, cold, uninterested. He continued rapidly.

'The inhabitants are, at present, subject to the slightest whim their owner may feel. If we wish to reach down and crush their world, turn on tidal waves, earthquakes, tornados, fire, volcanic action–if we wish to destroy them utterly, there is nothing they can do.

'Our position in relation to these minute civilizations is godlike. We can, with a wave of the hand, obliterate countless millions. We can send the lightning down, level their cities, squash their tiny buildings like ant hills. We can toss them about like toys, playthings, victims of our every whim.'

Hull stopped, rigid with apprehension. Some of the members had risen and strolled out. Von Stern's face twisted with ironic amusement.

Hull continued lamely. 'I want to see Worldcraft bubbles outlawed. We owe it to these civilizations on humanitarian grounds, on moral grounds–'

He went on, finishing as best he could. When he got to his feet there was a faint ripple of applause from the gray-striped professional group. But the white-clad property owners were utterly silent. And the blue industrialists. The red shirts and the green-clad consumer representatives were silent, impassive, even a little amused.

Hull returned to the wings, cold with the stark realization of defeat. 'We've lost,' he muttered, dazed. 'I don't understand.'

Julia took his arm. 'Maybe an appeal on some other grounds . . . Maybe the machines can still–'

Bart Longstreet came out of the shadows. 'No good, Nat. Won't work.'

Hull nodded. 'I know.'

'You can't moralize Worldcraft away. That's not the solution.'

Von Stern had given the signal. The members began to cast their votes, the tabulation machines whirring to life. Hull stood staring silently out at the murmuring room, crushed and bewildered.

Suddenly a shape appeared in front of him, cutting off his view. Impatiently he moved to one side–but a rasping voice stopped him.

'Too bad, Mr Hull. Better luck next time.'

Hull stiffened. 'Packman!' he muttered. 'What do you want?'

Forrest Packman came out of the shadows, moving toward him slowly, feeling his way blindly along.

Bart Longstreet stared at the old man with unconcealed hostility. 'I'll see you later, Nat.' He turned abruptly and started off.

Julia stopped him. 'Bart, do you have to–'

'Important business. I'll be back later.' He moved off down the aisle, toward the industrial section of the hall.

Hull faced Packman. He had never seen the old man so close

before. He studied him as he advanced slowly, feeling his way along on the arm of his robant.

Forrest Packman was old–a hundred and seven years. Preserved by hormones and blood transfusions, elaborate washing and rejuvenating processes that maintained life in his ancient, withered body. His eyes, deep-sunk, peered up at Hull as he came near, shrunken hands clutching the arm of his robant, breath coming hoarse and dry.

'Hull? You don't mind if I chat with you as the voting goes on? I won't be long.' He peered blindly past Hull. 'Who left? I couldn't see–'

'Bart Longstreet. Spaceways.'

'Oh, yes. I know him. Your speech was quite interesting, Hull. It reminded me of the old days. These people don't remember how it was. Times have changed.' He stopped, letting the robant wipe his mouth and chin. 'I used to be interested in rhetoric. Some of the old masters . . .'

The old man rambled on. Hull studied him curiously. Was this frail withered old man really the power behind Worldcraft? It didn't seem possible.

'Bryan,' Packman whispered, voice dry as ashes. 'William Jennings Bryan. I never heard him, of course. But they say he was the greatest. Your speech wasn't bad. But you don't understand. I listened carefully. You have some good ideas. But what you're trying to do is absurd. You don't know enough about people. Nobody's really interested in–'

He broke off, coughing feebly, his robant gripping him with metal supports.

Hull pushed impatiently past. 'The voting is almost finished. I want to hear. If you have anything to say to me you can file a regular memo plate.'

Packman's robant stepped out, barring his way. Packman went on slowly, shakily. 'Nobody is really interested in such appeals, Hull. You made a good speech but you don't have the idea. Not yet, at least. But you talk well, better than I've heard for a long time.

These young fellows, faces all washed, running around like office boys–'

Hull strained, listening to the vote. The impassive robant body cut off his view, but over Packman's dry rasp he could hear the results. Von Stern had risen and was reading the totals, group by group.

'Four hundred against, thirty-five in favor,' von Stern stated. 'The proposal has been defeated.' He tossed the tabulation cards down and picked up his agenda. 'We'll continue with the next business.'

Behind Hull, Packman broke off suddenly, his skull-like head cocked on one side. His deep-sunk eyes glittered and the trace of a smile twitched across his lips. 'Defeated? Not even all the grays voted for you, Hull. Now maybe you'll listen to what I have to say.'

Hull turned away from the hall. The robant lowered its arm. 'It's over,' Hull said.

'Come on.' Julia moved uneasily away from Packman. 'Let's get out of here.'

'You see,' Packman continued relentlessly, 'you have potentials that could be developed into something. When I was your age I had the same idea you have. I thought if people could see the moral issues involved, they would respond. But people aren't like that. You have to be realistic, if you want to get somewhere. People . . .'

Hull scarcely heard the dry, raspy voice whispering away. Defeat. Worldcraft, the world bubbles, would continue. The Contest Parties: bored, restless men and women with too much time, drinking and dancing, comparing worlds, building up to the climax–then the orgy of breaking and smashing. Over and over. Endlessly.

'Nobody can buck Worldcraft,' Julia said. 'It's too big. We'll have to accept the bubbles as a part of our lives. As Bart says, unless we have something else to offer in their place . . .'

Bart Longstreet came rapidly out of the shadows. 'You still here?' he said to Packman.

'I lost,' Hull said. 'The vote–'

'I know. I heard it. But it doesn't matter.' Longstreet pushed past

Packman and his robant. 'Stay here. I'll join you in a second. I have to see von Stern.'

Something in Longstreet's voice made Hull look up sharply. 'What is it? What's happened?'

'Why doesn't it matter?' Julia demanded.

Longstreet stepped up on the platform and made his way to von Stern. He handed him a message plate and then retired to the shadows.

Von Stern glanced at the plate–

And stopped talking. He got to his feet slowly, the plate gripped tightly. 'I have an announcement to make.' Von Stern's voice was shaking, almost inaudible. 'A dispatch from Spaceways' check station on Proxima Centauri.'

An excited murmur rushed through the hall.

'Exploring ships in the Proxima system have contacted trading scouts from an extra-galactic civilization. An exchange of messages has already occurred. Spaceways ships are moving toward the Arcturan system with the expectation of finding–'

Shouts, a bedlam of sound. Men and women on their feet, screaming in wild joy. Von Stern stopped reading and stood, his arms folded, his gray face calm, waiting for them to quiet.

Forrest Packman stood unmoving, his withered hands pressed together, his eyes shut. His robant sent support braces around him, catching him in a shield of protecting metal.

'Well?' Longstreet shouted, pushing back to them. He glanced at the frail, withered figure held up by the robant's supports, then at Hull and Julia. 'What do you say, Hull? Let's get out of here–so we can celebrate.'

'I'll fly you home,' Hull said to Julia. He looked around for an inter-continental cruiser. 'Too bad you live so far away. Hong Kong is so damn out of the way.'

Julia caught his arm. 'You can drive me yourself. Remember? The Pacific Tube is open. We're connected with Asia, now.'

'That's right.' Hull opened the door of his surface car and Julia slid in. Hull got behind the wheel and slammed the door. 'I forgot, with all these other things on my mind. Maybe we can see each other more often. I wouldn't mind spending a few days' vacation in Hong Kong. Maybe you'll invite me.'

He sent the car out into traffic, moving with the remote-controlled beam. 'Tell me more,' Julia asked. 'I want to know all Bart said.'

'Not much more. They've known for some time that something was up. That's why he wasn't too worried about Worldcraft. He knew the bottom would fall out as soon as the announcement was made.'

'Why didn't he tell you?'

Hull grinned wryly. 'How could he? Suppose the first reports were wrong? He wanted to wait until they were sure. He knew what the results would be.' Hull gestured. 'Look.'

On both sides of the strip a tide of men and women poured out of buildings, up from the underground factories, a seething mass milling everywhere in disordered confusion, shouting and cheering, throwing things in the air, tossing paper out of windows, carrying each other on their shoulders.

'They're working it off,' Hull said. 'The way it should be. Bart says Arcturus is supposed to have seven or eight fertile planets, some of them inhabited, some just forests and oceans. The extra-galactic traders say that most systems have at least one usable planet. They visited our system a long time ago. Our early ancestors may have traded with them.'

'Then there's plenty of life in the galaxy?'

Hull laughed. 'If what they say is true. And the fact that *they* exist is proof enough.'

'No more Worldcraft.'

'No.' Hull shook his head. No more Worldcraft. Stock was already being dumped. Worthless. Probably the State would absorb the bubbles already in existence and seal them off, leaving the inhabitants free to determine their own futures.

The neurotic smashing of laboriously achieved cultures was a thing of the past. The buildings of living creatures would no longer be pushed over to amuse some god suffering from *ennui* and frustration.

Julia sighed, leaning against Hull. 'Now we can take it easy. Sure, you're invited to stay. We can take out permanent cohabitation papers if you want to–'

Hull leaned forward suddenly, his body rigid. 'Where's the Tube?' he demanded. 'The strip should be hitting it any minute.'

Julia peered ahead, frowning. 'Something's wrong. Slow down.'

Hull slowed the car. An obstruction signal was flashing ahead. Cars were stopping on all sides, shifting into emergency retard lanes.

He ground the car to a halt. Rocket cruisers were sweeping overhead, exhaust tubes shattering the evening silence. A dozen uniformed men ran across a field, directing a rumbling robot derrick.

'What the hell–' Hull muttered. A soldier stepped up to the car, swinging a communication flare.

'Turn around. We need the whole strip.'

'But–'

'What happened?' Julia asked.

'The Tube. Earthquake, someplace halfway out. Broke the Tube in ten sections.' The soldier hurried off. Construction robots rushed past in a hand cart, assembling equipment as they went.

Julia and Hull stared at each other wide-eyed. 'Good Lord,' Hull muttered. 'Ten places. And the Tube must have been full of cars.'

A Red Cross ship landed, its ports grating open. Dollies shuttled across to it, loading injured men.

Two relief workers appeared. They opened the door to Hull's car, getting in the back. 'Drive us to town.' They sank down, exhausted. 'We got to get more help. Hurry it.'

'Sure.' Hull started the car again, gained speed.

'How did it happen?' Julia asked one of the grim-faced exhausted men, who dabbed automatically at the cuts on his face and neck.

'Earthquake.'

'But why? Didn't they build it so–'

'Big quake.' The man shook his head wearily. 'Nobody expected. Total loss. Thousands of cars. Tens of thousands of people.'

The other worker grunted. 'An act of God.'

Hull stiffened suddenly. His eyes flickered.

'What is it?' Julia asked him.

'Nothing.'

'Are you sure? Is something wrong?'

Hull said nothing. He was deep in thought, his face a mask of startled, growing horror.

BREAKFAST AT TWILIGHT

'Dad?' Earl asked, hurrying out of the bathroom. 'You going to drive us to school today?'

Tim McLean poured himself a second cup of coffee. 'You kids can walk for a change. The car's in the garage.'

Judy pouted. 'It's raining.'

'No it isn't,' Virginia corrected her sister. She drew the shade back. 'It's all foggy, but it isn't raining.'

'Let me look.' Mary McLean dried her hands and came over from the sink. 'What an odd day. Is that fog? It looks more like smoke. I can't make out a thing. What did the weatherman say?'

'I couldn't get anything on the radio,' Earl said. 'Nothing but static.'

Tim stirred angrily. 'That darn thing on the blink again? Seems like I just had it fixed.' He got up and moved sleepily over to the radio. He fiddled idly with the dials. The three children hurried back and forth, getting ready for school. 'Strange,' Tim said.

'I'm going.' Earl opened the front door.

'Wait for your sisters,' Mary ordered absently.

'I'm ready,' Virginia said. 'Do I look all right?'

'You look fine,' Mary said, kissing her.

'I'll call the radio repair place from the office,' Tim said.

He broke off. Earl stood at the kitchen door, pale and silent, his eyes wide with terror.

'What is it?'

'I–I came back.'

'What is it? Are you sick?'

'I can't go to school.'

They stared at him. 'What is wrong?' Tim grabbed his son's arm. 'Why can't you go to school?'

'They–they won't let me.'

'*Who?*'

'The soldiers.' It came tumbling out with a rush. 'They're all over. Soldiers and guns. And they're coming here.'

'Coming? Coming here?' Tim echoed, dazed.

'They're coming here and they're going to–' Earl broke off, terrified. From the front porch came the sound of heavy boots. A crash. Splintering wood. Voices.

'Good Lord,' Mary gasped. 'What is it, Tim?'

Tim entered the living room, his heart laboring painfully. Three men stood inside the door. Men in gray-green uniforms, weighted with guns and complex tangles of equipment. Tubes and hoses. Meters on thick cords. Boxes and leather straps and antennas. Elaborate masks locked over their heads. Behind the masks Tim saw tired, whisker-stubbled faces, red-rimmed eyes that gazed at him in brutal displeasure.

One of the soldiers jerked up his gun, aiming at McLean's middle. Tim peered at it dumbly. *The gun.* Long and thin. Like a needle. Attached to a coil of tubes.

'What in the name of–' he began, but the soldier cut him off savagely.

'Who are you?' His voice was harsh, guttural. 'What are you doing here?' He pushed his mask aside. His skin was dirty. Cuts and pocks lined his sallow flesh. His teeth were broken and missing.

'Answer!' a second soldier demanded. 'What are you doing here?'

'Show your blue card,' the third said. 'Let's see your Sector number.' His eyes strayed to the children and Mary standing mutely at the dining room door. His mouth fell open.

'A *woman!*'

The three soldiers gazed in disbelief.

'What the hell is this?' the first demanded. 'How long has this woman been here?'

Tim found his voice. 'She's my wife. What is this? What–'

'Your *wife?*' They were incredulous.

'My wife and children. For God's sake–'

'Your wife? And you'd bring her here? You must be out of your head!'

'He's got ash sickness,' one said. He lowered his gun and strode across the living room to Mary. 'Come on, sister. You're coming with us.'

Tim lunged.

A wall of force hit him. He sprawled, clouds of darkness rolling around him. His ears sang. His head throbbed. Everything receded. Dimly, he was aware of shapes moving. Voices. The room. He concentrated.

The soldiers were herding the children back. One of them grabbed Mary by the arm. He tore her dress away, ripping it from her shoulders. 'Gee,' he snarled. 'He'd bring her here, and she's not even strung!'

'Take her along.'

'OK, Captain.' The soldier dragged Mary toward the front door. 'We'll do what we can with her.'

'The kids.' The captain waved the other soldier over with the children. 'Take them along. I don't get it. No masks. No cards. How'd this house miss getting hit? Last night was the worst in months!'

Tim struggled painfully to his feet. His mouth was bleeding. His vision blurred. He hung on tight to the wall. 'Look,' he muttered. 'For God's sake–'

The captain was staring into the kitchen. 'Is that–is that *food?*' He advanced slowly through the dining room. 'Look!'

The other soldiers came after him, Mary and the children forgotten. They stood around the table, amazed.

'Look at it!'

'Coffee.' One grabbed up the pot and drank it greedily down. He choked, black coffee dripping down his tunic. 'Hot. Jeeze. Hot coffee.'

'Cream!' Another soldier tore open the refrigerator. 'Look. Milk. Eggs. Butter. Meat.' His voice broke. 'It's full of food.'

The captain disappeared into the pantry. He came out, lugging a case of canned peas. 'Get the rest. Get it all. We'll load it in the snake.'

He dropped the case on the table with a crash. Watching Tim intently, he fumbled in his dirty tunic until he found a cigarette. He lit it slowly, not taking his eyes from Tim. 'All right,' he said. 'Let's hear what you have to say.'

Tim's mouth opened and closed. No words came. His mind was blank. Dead. He couldn't think.

'This food. Where'd you get it? And these things.' The captain waved around the kitchen. 'Dishes. Furniture. How come this house hasn't been hit? How did you survive last night's attack?'

'I–' Tim gasped.

The captain came toward him ominously. 'The woman. And the kids. All of you. What are you doing here?' His voice was hard. 'You better be able to explain, mister. You better be able to explain what you're doing here–or we'll have to burn the whole damn lot of you.'

Tim sat down at the table. He took a deep, shuddering breath, trying to focus his mind. His body ached. He rubbed blood from his mouth, conscious of a broken molar and bits of loose tooth. He got out a handkerchief and spat the bits into it. His hands were shaking.

'Come on,' the captain said.

Mary and the children slipped into the room. Judy was crying. Virginia's face was blank with shock. Earl stared wide-eyed at the soldiers, his face white.

'Tim,' Mary said, putting her hand on his arm. 'Are you all right?'

Tim nodded. 'I'm all right.'

Mary pulled her dress around her. 'Tim, they can't get away with it. Somebody'll come. The mailman. The neighbors. They can't just–'

'Shut up,' the captain snapped. His eyes flickered oddly. 'The mailman? What are you talking about?' He held out his hand. 'Let's see your yellow slip, sister.'

'Yellow slip?' Mary faltered.

The captain rubbed his jaw. 'No yellow slip. No masks. No cards.'

'They're geeps,' a soldier said.

'Maybe. And maybe not.'

'They're geeps, Captain. We better burn 'em. We can't take any chances.'

'There's something funny going on here,' the captain said. He plucked at his neck, lifting up a small box on a cord. 'I'm getting a polic here.'

'A polic?' A shiver moved through the soldiers. 'Wait, Captain. We can handle this. Don't get a polic. He'll put us on 4 and then we'll never–'

The captain spoke into the box. 'Give me Web B.'

Tim looked up at Mary. 'Listen, honey. I–'

'Shut up.' A soldier prodded him. Tim lapsed into silence.

The box squawked. 'Web B.'

'Can you spare a polic? We've run into something strange. Group of five. Man, woman, three kids. No masks, no cards, the woman not strung, dwelling completely intact. Furniture, fixtures, about two hundred pounds of food.'

The box hesitated. 'All right. Polic on the way. Stay there. Don't let them escape.'

'I won't.' The captain dropped the box back in his shirt. 'A polic will be here any minute. Meanwhile, let's get the food loaded.'

From outside came a deep thundering roar. It shook the house, rattling the dishes in the cupboard.

'Jeez,' a soldier said. 'That was close.'

'I hope the screens hold until nightfall.' The captain grabbed up the case of canned peas. 'Get the rest. We want it loaded before the polic comes.'

The two soldiers filled their arms and followed him through the house, out the front door. Their voices diminished as they strode down the path.

Tim got to his feet. 'Stay here,' he said thickly.

'What are you doing?' Mary asked nervously.

'Maybe I can get out.' He ran to the back door and unlatched it, hands shaking. He pulled the door wide and stepped out on the back porch. 'I don't see any of them. If we can only . . .'

He stopped.

Around him gray clouds blew. Gray ash, billowing as far as he could see. Dim shapes were visible. Broken shapes, silent and unmoving in the grayness.

Ruins.

Ruined buildings. Heaps of rubble. Debris everywhere. He walked slowly down the back steps. The concrete walk ended abruptly. Beyond it, slag and heaps of rubble were strewn. Nothing else. Nothing as far as the eye could see.

Nothing stirred. Nothing moved. In the gray silence there was no life. No motion. Only the clouds of drifting ash. The slag and the endless heaps.

The city was gone. The buildings were destroyed. Nothing remained. No people. No life. Jagged walls, empty and gaping. A few dark weeds growing among the debris. Tim bent down, touching a weed. Rough, thick stalk. And the slag. It was a metal slag. Melted metal. He straightened up–

'Come back inside,' a crisp voice said.

He turned numbly. A man stood on the porch, behind him, hands on his hips. A small man, hollow-cheeked. Eyes small and bright, like two black coals. He wore a uniform different from the soldiers'. His mask was pushed back, away from his face. His skin was yellow, faintly luminous, clinging to his cheekbones. A sick face, ravaged by fever and fatigue.

'Who are you?' Tim said.

'Douglas. Political Commissioner Douglas.'

'You're–you're the polic,' Tim said.

'That's right. Now come inside. I expect to hear some answers from you. I have quite a few questions.

'The first thing I want to know,' Commissioner Douglas said, 'is how this house escaped destruction.'

Tim and Mary and the children sat together on the couch, silent and unmoving, faces blank with shock.

'Well?' Douglas demanded.

Tim found his voice. 'Look,' he said. 'I don't know. I don't know anything. We woke up this morning like every other morning. We dressed and ate breakfast–'

'It was foggy out,' Virginia said. 'We looked out and saw the fog.'

'And the radio wouldn't work,' Earl said.

'The radio?' Douglas's thin face twisted. 'There haven't been any audio signals in months. Except for government purposes. This house. All of you. I don't understand. If you were geeps–'

'Geeps. What does that mean?' Mary murmured.

'Soviet general-purpose troops.'

'Then the war has begun.'

'North America was attacked two years ago,' Douglas said. 'In 1978.'

Tim sagged. '1978. Then this is 1980.' He reached suddenly into his pocket. He pulled out his wallet and tossed it to Douglas. 'Look in there.'

Douglas opened the wallet suspiciously. 'Why?'

'The library card. The parcel receipts. Look at the dates.' Tim turned to Mary. 'I'm beginning to understand now. I had an idea when I saw the ruins.'

'Are we winning?' Earl piped.

Douglas studied Tim's wallet intently. 'Very interesting. These are all old. Seven and eight years.' His eyes flickered. 'What are you trying to say? That you came from the past? That you're time travelers?'

The captain came back inside. 'The snake is all loaded, sir.'

Douglas nodded curtly. 'All right. You can take off with your patrol.'

The captain glanced at Tim. 'Will you be–'

'I'll handle them.'

The captain saluted. 'Fine, sir.' He quickly disappeared through the door. Outside, he and his men climbed aboard a long thin truck, like a pipe mounted on treads. With a faint hum the truck leaped forward.

In a moment only gray clouds and the dim outline of ruined buildings remained.

Douglas paced back and forth, examining the living room, the wallpaper, the light fixture and chairs. He picked up some magazines and thumbed through them. 'From the past. But not far in the past.'

'Seven years?'

'Could it be? I suppose. A lot of things have happened in the last few months. Time travel.' Douglas grinned ironically. 'You picked a bad spot, McLean. You should have gone farther on.'

'I didn't pick it. It just happened.'

'You must have done *something*.'

Tim shook his head. 'No. Nothing. We got up. And we were–here.'

Douglas was deep in thought. 'Here. Seven years in the future. Moved forward through time. We know nothing about time travel. No work has been done with it. There seem to be evident military possibilities.'

'How did the war begin?' Mary asked faintly.

'Begin? It didn't begin. You remember. There was war seven years ago.'

'The real war. This.'

'There wasn't any point when it became–this. We fought in Korea. We fought in China. In Germany and Yugoslavia and Iran. It spread, farther and farther. Finally the bombs were falling here. It came like the plague. The war *grew*. It didn't begin.' Abruptly he put his notebook away. 'A report on you would be suspect. They might think that I had the ash sickness.'

'What's that?' Virginia asked.

'Radioactive particles in the air. Carried to the brain. Causes insanity. Everybody has a touch of it, even with the masks.'

'I'd sure like to know who's winning,' Earl repeated. 'What was that outside? That truck. Was it rocket propelled?'

'The snake? No. Turbines. Boring snout. Cuts through the debris.'

'Seven years,' Mary said. 'So much has changed. It doesn't seem possible.'

'So much?' Douglas shrugged. 'I suppose so. I remember what I was doing seven years ago. I was still in school. Learning. I had an apartment and a car. I went out dancing. I bought a TV set. But these things were there. The twilight. This. Only I didn't know. None of us knew. But they were there.'

'You're a Political Commissioner?' Tim asked.

'I supervise the troops. Watch for political deviation. In a total war we have to keep people under constant surveillance. One Commie down in the Webs could wreck the whole business. We can't take chances.'

Tim nodded. 'Yes. It was there. The twilight. Only we didn't understand it.'

Douglas examined the books in the bookcase. 'I'll take a couple of these along. I haven't seen fiction in months. Most of it disappeared. Burned back in '77.'

'Burned?'

Douglas helped himself. 'Shakespeare. Milton. Dryden. I'll take the old stuff. It's safer. None of the Steinbeck and Dos Passos. Even a polic can get in trouble. If you stay here, you better get rid of *that*.' He tapped a volume of Dostoevski, *The Brothers Karamazov*.

'If we stay! What else can we do?'

'You want to stay?'

'No,' Mary said quietly.

Douglas shot her a quick glance. 'No, I suppose not. If you stay you'll be separated, of course. Children to the Canadian Relocation Centers. Women are situated down in the undersurface factory-labor camps. Men are automatically a part of Military.'

'Like those there who left,' Tim said.

'Unless you can qualify for the id block.'

'What's that?'

'Industrial Designing and Technology. What training have you had? Anything along scientific lines?'

'No. Accounting.'

Douglas shrugged. 'Well, you'll be given a standard test. If your IQ is high enough you could go in the Political Service. We use a lot of men.' He paused thoughtfully, his arms loaded with books. 'You better go back, McLean. You'll have trouble getting accustomed to this. I'd go back, if I could. But I can't.'

'Back?' Mary echoed. 'How?'

'The way you came.'

'We just came.'

Douglas halted at the front door. 'Last night was the worst rom attack so far. They hit this whole area.'

'Rom?'

'Robot operated missiles. The Soviets are systematically destroying continental America, mile by mile. Roms are cheap. They make them by the million and fire them off. The whole process is automatic. Robot factories turn them out and fire them at us. Last night they came over here–waves of them. This morning the patrol came in and found nothing. Except you, of course.'

Tim nodded slowly. 'I'm beginning to see.'

'The concentrated energy must have tipped some unstable time fault. Like a rock fault. We're always starting earthquakes. But a *time quake* . . . Interesting. That's what happened, I think. The release of energy, the destruction of matter, sucked your house into the future. Carried the house seven years ahead. This street, everything here, this very spot, was pulverized. Your house, seven years back, was caught in the undertow. The blast must have lashed back through time.'

'Sucked into the future,' Tim said. 'During the night. While we were asleep.'

Douglas watched him carefully. 'Tonight,' he said, 'there will be another rom attack. It should finish off what is left.' He looked at his watch. 'It is now four in the afternoon. The attack will begin in a few hours. You should be undersurface. Nothing will survive up here. I can take you down with me, if you want. But if you want to take a chance, if you want to stay here–'

'You think it might tip us back?'

'Maybe. I don't know. It's a gamble. It might tip you back to your own time, or it might not. If not–'

'If not we wouldn't have a chance of survival.'

Douglas flicked out a pocket map and spread it open on the couch. 'A patrol will remain in this area another half-hour. If you decide to come undersurface with us, go down the street this way.' He traced a line on the map. 'To this open field here. The patrol is a Political unit. They'll take you the rest of the way down. You think you can find the field?'

'I think so,' Tim said, looking at the map. His lips twisted. 'That open field used to be the grammar school my kids went to. That's where they were going when the troops stopped them. Just a little while ago.'

'Seven years ago,' Douglas corrected. He snapped the map shut and restored it to his pocket. He pulled his mask down and moved out the front door onto the porch. 'Maybe I'll see you again. Maybe not. It's your decision. You'll have to decide one way or the other. In any case–good luck.'

He turned and walked briskly from the house.

'Dad,' Earl shouted, 'are you going in the Army? Are you going to wear a mask and shoot one of those guns?' His eyes sparkled with excitement. 'Are you going to drive a *snake?*'

Tim McLean squatted down and pulled his son to him. 'You want that? *You want to stay here?* If I'm going to wear a mask and shoot one of those guns we can't go back.'

Earl looked doubtful. 'Couldn't we go back later?'

Tim shook his head. 'Afraid not. We've got to decide now, whether we're going back or not.'

'You heard Mr Douglas,' Virginia said disgustedly. 'The attack's going to start in a couple hours.'

Tim got to his feet and paced back and forth. 'If we stay in the house we'll get blown to bits. Let's face it. There's only a faint chance we'll be tipped back to our own time. A slim possibility–a long shot. Do we want to stay here with roms falling all around us, knowing any second it may be the end–hearing them come closer, hitting nearer–lying on the floor, waiting, listening–'

'Do you really want to go back?' Mary demanded.

'Of course, but the risk–'

'I'm not asking you about the risk. I'm asking you if you really want to go back. Maybe you want to stay here. Maybe Earl's right. You in a uniform and a mask, with one of those needle guns. Driving a snake.'

'With you in a factory-labor camp! And the kids in a Government Relocation Center! How do you think that would be? What do you think they'd teach them? What do you think they'd grow up like? And believe . . .'

'They'd probably teach them to be very useful.'

'Useful! To what? To themselves? To mankind? Or to the war effort . . .?'

'They'd be alive,' Mary said. 'They'd be safe. This way, if we stay in the house, wait for the attack to come–'

'Sure,' Tim grated. 'They would be alive. Probably quite healthy. Well fed. Well clothed and cared for.' He looked down at his children, his face hard. 'They'd stay alive, all right. They'd live to grow up and become adults. But what kind of adults? You heard what he said! Book burnings in '77. What'll they be taught from? What kind of ideas are left, since '77? What kind of beliefs can they get from a Government Relocation Center? What kind of values will they have?'

'There's the id block,' Mary suggested.

'Industrial Designing and Technology. For the bright ones. The clever ones with imagination. Busy slide rules and pencils. Drawing and planning and making discoveries. The girls could go into that. They could design the guns. Earl could go into the Political Service. He could make sure the guns were used. If any of the troops deviated, didn't want to shoot, Earl could report them and have them hauled off for reeducation. To have their political faith strengthened–in a world where those *with* brains design weapons and those *without* brains fire them.'

'But they'd be alive,' Mary repeated.

'You've got a strange idea of what being alive is! You call that alive? Maybe it is.' Tim shook his head wearily. 'Maybe you're right. Maybe we should go undersurface with Douglas. Stay in this world. Stay alive.'

'I didn't say that,' Mary said softly. 'Tim, I had to find out if you *really* understood why it's worth it. Worth staying in the house, taking the chance we won't be tipped back.'

'Then you want to take the chance?'

'Of course! We *have* to. We can't turn our children over to them–to the Relocation Center. To be taught how to hate and kill and destroy.' Mary smiled up wanly. 'Anyhow, they've always gone to the Jefferson School. And here, in this world, it's only an open field.'

'Are we going back?' Judy piped. She caught hold of Tim's sleeve imploringly. 'Are we going back now?'

Tim disengaged her arm. 'Very soon, honey.'

Mary opened the supply cupboards and rooted in them. 'Everything's here. What did they take?'

'The case of canned peas. Everything we had in the refrigerator. And they smashed the front door.'

'I'll bet we're beating them!' Earl shouted. He ran to the window and peered out. The sight of the rolling ash disappointed him. 'I can't see anything! Just the fog!' He turned questioningly to Tim. 'Is it always like this, here?'

'Yes,' Tim answered.

Earl's face fell. 'Just fog? Nothing else. Doesn't the sun shine ever?'

'I'll fix some coffee,' Mary said.

'Good.' Tim went into the bathroom and examined himself in the mirror. His mouth was cut, caked with dried blood. His head ached. He felt sick at his stomach.

'It doesn't seem possible,' Mary said, as they sat down at the kitchen table.

Tim sipped his coffee. 'No. It doesn't.' Where he sat he could see out the window. The clouds of ash. The dim, jagged outline of ruined buildings.

'Is the man coming back?' Judy piped. 'He was all thin and funny-looking. He isn't coming back, is he?'

Tim looked at his watch. It read ten o'clock. He reset it, moving the hands to four-fifteen. 'Douglas said it would begin at nightfall. That won't be long.'

'Then we're really staying in the house,' Mary said.

'That's right.'

'Even though there's only a little chance?'

'Even though there's only a little chance we'll get back. Are you glad?'

'I'm glad,' Mary said, her eyes bright. 'It's worth it, Tim. You know it is. Anything's worth it, any chance. *To get back*. And something else. We'll all be here together . . . We can't be–broken up. Separated.'

Tim poured himself more coffee. 'We might as well make ourselves comfortable. We have maybe three hours to wait. We might as well try to enjoy them.'

At six-thirty the first rom fell. They felt the shock, a deep rolling wave of force that lapped over the house.

Judy came running in from the dining room, face white with fear. 'Daddy! What is it?'

'Nothing. Don't worry.'

'Come on back,' Virginia called impatiently. 'It's your turn.' They were playing Monopoly.

Earl leaped to his feet. 'I want to see.' He ran excitedly to the window. 'I can see where it hit!'

Tim lifted the shade and looked out. Far off, in the distance, a white glare burned fitfully. A towering column of luminous smoke rose from it.

A second shudder vibrated through the house. A dish crashed from the shelf, into the sink.

It was almost dark outside. Except for the two spots of white Tim could make out nothing. The clouds of ash were lost in the gloom. The ash and the ragged remains of buildings.

'That was closer,' Mary said.

A third rom fell. In the living room windows burst, showering glass across the rug.

'We better get back,' Tim said.

'Where?'

'Down in the basement. Come on.' Tim unlocked the basement door and they trooped nervously downstairs.

'Food,' Mary said. 'We better bring the food that's left.'

'Good idea. You kids go on down. We'll come along in a minute.'

'I can carry something,' Earl said.

'Go on down.' The fourth rom hit, farther off than the last. 'And stay away from the window.'

'I'll move something over the window,' Earl said. 'The big piece of plywood we used for my train.'

'Good idea.' Tim and Mary returned to the kitchen. 'Food. Dishes. What else?'

'Books.' Mary looked nervously around. 'I don't know. Nothing else. Come on.'

A shattering roar drowned out her words. The kitchen window gave, showering glass over them. The dishes over the sink tumbled down in a torrent of breaking china. Tim grabbed Mary and pulled her down.

From the broken window rolling clouds of ominous gray drifted into the room. The evening air stank, a sour, rotten smell. Tim shuddered.

'Forget the food. Let's get back down.'

'But–'

'Forget it.' He grabbed her and pulled her down the basement stairs. They tumbled in a heap, Tim slamming the door after them.

'Where's the food?' Virginia demanded.

Tim wiped his forehead shakily. 'Forget it. We won't need it.'

'Help me,' Earl gasped. Tim helped him move the sheet of plywood over the window above the laundry tubs. The basement was cold and silent. The cement floor under them was faintly moist.

Two roms struck at once. Tim was hurled to the floor. The

concrete hit him and he grunted. For a moment blackness swirled around him. Then he was on his knees, groping his way up.

'Everybody all right?' he muttered.

'I'm all right,' Mary said. Judy began to whimper. Earl was feeling his way across the room.

'I'm all right,' Virginia said. 'I guess.'

The lights flickered and dimmed. Abruptly they went out. The basement was pitch-black.

'Well,' Tim said. 'There they go.'

'I have my flashlight.' Earl winked the flashlight on. 'How's that?'

'Fine,' Tim said.

More roms hit. The ground leaped under them, bucking and heaving. A wave of force shuddering the whole house.

'We better lie down,' Mary said.

'Yes. Lie down.' Tim stretched himself out awkwardly. A few bits of plaster rained down around them.

'When will it stop?' Earl asked uneasily.

'Soon,' Tim said.

'Then we'll be back?'

'Yes. We'll be back.'

The next blast hit them almost at once. Tim felt the concrete rise under him. It grew, swelling higher and higher. He was going up. He shut his eyes, holding on tight. Higher and higher he went, carried up by the ballooning concrete. Around him beams and timbers cracked. Plaster poured down. He could hear glass breaking. And a long way off, the licking crackles of fire.

'Tim,' Mary's voice came faintly.

'Yes.'

'We're not going to–to make it.'

'I don't know.'

'We're not. I can tell.'

'Maybe not.' He grunted in pain as a board struck his back, settling over him. Boards and plaster, covering him, burying him. He could smell the sour smell, the night air and ash. It drifted and rolled into the cellar, through the broken window.

'Daddy,' Judy's voice came faintly.

'What?'

'Aren't we going back?'

He opened his mouth to answer. A shattering roar cut his words off. He jerked, tossed by the blast. Everything was moving around him. A vast wind tugged at him, a hot wind, licking at him, gnawing at him. He held on tight. The wind pulled, dragging him with it. He cried out as it seared his hands and face.

'Mary–'

Then silence. Only blackness and silence.

Cars.

Cars were stopping nearby. Then voices. And the noise of footsteps. Tim stirred, pushing the boards from him. He struggled to his feet.

'Mary.' He looked around. 'We're back.'

The basement was in ruins. The walls were broken and sagging. Great gaping holes showed a green line of grass beyond. A concrete walk. The small rose garden. The white stucco house next door.

Lines of telephone poles. Roofs. Houses. The city. As it had always been. Every morning.

'We're back!' Wild joy leaped through him. *Back*. Safe. It was over. Tim pushed quickly through the debris of his ruined house. 'Mary, are you all right?'

'Here.' Mary sat up, plaster dust raining from her. She was white all over, her hair, her skin, her clothing. Her face was cut and scratched. Her dress was torn. 'Are we really back?'

'Mr McLean! You all right?'

A blue-clad policeman leaped down into the cellar. Behind him two white-clad figures jumped. A group of neighbors collected outside, peering anxiously to see.

'I'm OK,' Tim said. He helped Judy and Virginia up. 'I think we're all OK.'

'What happened?' The policeman pushed boards aside, coming over. 'A bomb? Some kind of a bomb?'

'The house is a shambles,' one of the white-clad interns said. 'You sure nobody's hurt?'

'We were down here. In the basement.'

'You all right, Tim?' Mrs Hendricks called, stepping down gingerly into the cellar.

'What happened?' Frank Foley shouted. He leaped down with a crash. 'God, Tim! What the hell were you doing?'

The two white-clad interns poked suspiciously around the ruins. 'You're lucky, mister. Damn lucky. There's nothing left upstairs.'

Foley came over beside Tim. 'Damn it, man! I *told* you to have that hot water heater looked at!'

'What?' Tim muttered.

'The hot water heater! I told you there was something wrong with the cut-off. It must've kept heating up, not turned off . . .' Foley winked nervously. 'But I won't say anything, Tim. The insurance. You can count on me.'

Tim opened his mouth. But the words didn't come. What could he say?–No, it wasn't a defective hot water heater that I forgot to have repaired. No, it wasn't a faulty connection in the stove. It wasn't any of those things. It wasn't a leaky gas line, it wasn't a plugged furnace, it wasn't a pressure cooker we forgot to turn off.

It's war. Total war. And not just war for me. For my family. For my house.

It's for your house, too. Your house and my house and all the houses. Here and in the next block, in the next town, the next state and country and continent. The whole world, like this. Shambles and ruins. Fog and dank weeds growing in the rusting slag. War for all of us. For everybody crowding down into the basement, white-faced, frightened, somehow sensing something terrible.

And when it really came, when the five years were up, there'd be no escape. No going back, tipping back into the past, away from it. When it came for them all, it would have them for eternity; there would be no one climbing back out, as he had.

Mary was watching him. The policeman, the neighbors, the

white-clad interns–all of them were watching him. Waiting for him to explain. To tell them what it was.

'Was it the hot water heater?' Mrs Hendricks asked timidly. 'That was it, wasn't it, Tim? Things like that do happen. You can't be sure . . .'

'Maybe it was home brew,' a neighbor suggested, in a feeble attempt at humor. 'Was that it?'

He couldn't tell them. They wouldn't understand, because they didn't want to understand. They didn't want to know. They needed reassurance. He could see it in their eyes. Pitiful, pathetic fear. They sensed something terrible–and they were afraid. They were searching his face, seeking his help. Words of comfort. Words to banish their fear.

'Yeah,' Tim said heavily. 'It was the hot water heater.'

'I thought so!' Foley breathed. A sigh of relief swept through them all. Murmurs, shaky laughs. Nods, grins.

'I should have got it fixed,' Tim went on. 'I should have had it looked at a long time ago. Before it got in such bad shape.' Tim looked around at the circle of anxious people, hanging on his words. 'I should have had it looked at. Before it was too late.'

A PRESENT FOR PAT

'What is it?' Patricia Blake demanded eagerly.

'What's what?' Eric Blake murmured.

'What did you bring? I *know* you brought me something!' Her bosom rose and fell excitedly under her mesh blouse. 'You brought me a present. I can tell!'

'Honey, I went to Ganymede for Terran Metals, not to find you curios. Now let me unpack my things. Bradshaw says I have to report to the office early tomorrow. He says I better report some good ore deposits.'

Pat snatched up a small box, heaped with all the other luggage the robot porter had deposited at the door. 'Is it jewelry? No, it's too big for jewelry.' She began to tear the cord from the box with her sharp fingernails.

Eric frowned uneasily. 'Don't be disappointed, honey. It's sort of strange. Not what you expect.' He watched apprehensively. 'Don't get mad at me. I'll explain all about it.'

Pat's mouth fell open. She turned pale. She dropped the box quickly on the table, eyes wide with horror. 'Good Lord! What *is* it?'

Eric twisted nervously. 'I got a good buy on it, honey. You can't usually pick one of them up. The Ganymedeans don't like to sell them, and I–'

'*What is it?*'

'It's a god,' Eric muttered. 'A minor Ganymedean deity. I got it practically at cost.'

Pat gazed down at the box with fear and growing disgust. 'That? That's a–a *god*?'

In the box was a small, motionless figure, perhaps ten inches high. It was old, terribly old. Its tiny clawlike hands were pressed against its scaly breast. Its insect face was twisted in a scowl of anger–mixed with cynical lust. Instead of legs it rested on a tangle of tentacles. The lower portion of its face dissolved in a complex beak, mandibles of some hard substance. There was an odor to it, as of manure and stale beer. It appeared to be bisexual.

Eric had thoughtfully put a little water dish and some straw in the box. He had punched air holes in the lid and crumpled up newspaper fragments.

'You mean it's an idol.' Pat regained her poise slowly. 'An *idol* of a deity.'

'No.' Eric shook his head stubbornly. 'This is a genuine deity. There's a warranty, or something.'

'Is it–dead?'

'Not at all.'

'Then why doesn't it move?'

'You have to arouse it.' The bottom of the figure's belly cupped outward in a hollow bowl. Eric tapped the bowl. 'Place an offering here and it comes to life. I'll show you.'

Pat retreated. 'No thanks.'

'Come on! It's interesting to talk to. Its name is–' He glanced at some writing on the box. 'Its name is Tinokuknoi Arevulopapo. We talked most of the way back from Ganymede. It was glad of the opportunity. And I learned quite a few things about gods.'

Eric searched his pockets and brought out the remains of a ham sandwich. He wadded up a bit of the ham and stuffed it into the protruding belly-cup of the god.

'I'm going in the other room,' Pat said.

'Stick around.' Eric caught her arm. 'It only takes a second. It begins to digest right away.'

The belly-cup quivered. The god's scaly flesh rippled. Presently the cup filled with a sluggish dark-colored substance. The ham began to dissolve.

Pat snorted in disgust. 'Doesn't it even use its mouth?'

'Not for eating. Only for talking. It's a lot different from usual life-forms.'

The tiny eye of the god was focused on them now. A single, unwinking orb of icy malevolence. The mandibles twitched.

'Greetings,' the god said.

'Hi.' Eric nudged Pat forward. 'This is my wife. Mrs Blake. Patricia.'

'How do you do,' the god grated.

Pat gave a squeal of dismay. 'It talks English.'

The god turned to Eric in disgust. 'You were right. She *is* stupid.'

Eric colored. 'Gods can do anything they want, honey. They're omnipotent.'

The god nodded. 'That is so. This is Terra, I presume.'

'Yes. How does it look?'

'As I expected. I have already heard reports. Certain reports about Terra.'

'Eric, are you sure it's safe?' Pat whispered uneasily. 'I don't like its looks. And there's something about the way it talks.' Her bosom quivered nervously.

'Don't worry, honey,' Eric said carelessly. 'It's a nice god. I checked before I left Ganymede.'

'I'm benevolent,' the god explained matter-of-factly. 'My capacity has been that of Weather Deity to the Ganymedean aborigines. I have produced rain and allied phenomena when the occasion demanded.'

'But that's all in the past,' Eric added.

'Correct. I have been a Weather Deity for ten thousand years. There is a limit to even a god's patience. I craved new surroundings.' A peculiar gleam flickered across the loathsome face. 'That is why I arranged to be sold and brought to Terra.'

'You see,' Eric said, 'the Ganymedeans didn't want to sell it. But it whipped up a thunderstorm and they sort of had to. That's partly why it was so cheap.'

'Your husband made a good purchase,' the god said. Its single eye roved around curiously. 'This is your dwelling? You eat and sleep here?'

'That's right,' Eric said. 'Pat and I both–'

The front door chimed. 'Thomas Matson stands on the threshold,' the door stated. 'He wishes admission.'

'Golly,' Eric said. 'Good old Tom. I'll go let him in.'

Pat indicated the god. 'Hadn't you better–'

'Oh, no. I want Tom to see it.' Eric stepped to the door and opened it.

'Hello,' Tom said, striding in. 'Hi, Pat. Nice day.' He and Eric shook hands. 'The Lab has been wondering when you'd get back. Old Bradshaw is leaping up and down to hear your report.' Matson's bean-pole body bent forward in sudden interest. 'Say, what's in the box?'

'That's my god,' Eric said modestly.

'Really? But God is an unscientific concept.'

'This is a different god. I didn't invent it. I bought it. On Ganymede. It's a Ganymedean Weather Deity.'

'Say something,' Pat said to the god. 'So he'll believe your owner.'

'Let's debate my existence,' the god said sneeringly. 'You take the negative. Agreed?'

Matson grinned. 'What is this, Eric? A little robot? Sort of hideous-looking.'

'Honest. It's a god. On the way it did a couple of miracles for me. Not big miracles, of course, but enough to convince me.'

'Hearsay,' Matson said. But he was interested. 'Pass a miracle, god. I'm all ears.'

'I am not a vulgar showpiece,' the god growled.

'Don't get it angry,' Eric cautioned. 'There's no limit to its powers, once aroused.'

'How does a god come into being?' Tom asked. 'Does a god create itself? If it's dependent on something prior then there must be a more ultimate order of being which–'

'Gods,' the tiny figure stated, 'are inhabitants of a higher level, a greater plane of reality. A more advanced dimension. There are a number of planes of existence. Dimensional continuums, arranged in a hierarchy. Mine is one above yours.'

'What are you doing here?'

'Occasionally beings pass from one dimensional continuum to another. When they pass from a superior continuum to an inferior–as I have done–they are worshipped as gods.'

Tom was disappointed. 'You're not a god at all. You're just a life-form of a slightly different dimensional order that's changed phase and entered our vector.'

The little figure glowered. 'You make it sound simple. Actually, such a transformation requires great cunning and is seldom done. I came here because a member of my race, a certain malodorous Nar Dolk, committed a heinous crime and escaped into this continuum. Our law obliged me to follow in hot pursuit. In the process this flotsam, this spawn of dampness, escaped and assumed some disguise or other. I continually search, but he has not yet been apprehended.' The small god broke off suddenly. 'Your curiosity is idle. It annoys me.'

Tom turned his back on the god. 'Pretty weak stuff. We do more down at the Terran Metals Lab than this character ever–'

The air cracked, ozone flashing. Tom Matson shrieked. Invisible hands lifted him bodily and propelled him to the door. The door swung open and Matson sailed down the walk, tumbling in a heap among the rose bushes, arms and legs flailing wildly.

'Help!' Matson yelled, struggling to get up.

'Oh, dear,' Pat gasped.

'Golly.' Eric shot a glance at the tiny figure. 'You did that?'

'Help him,' Pat urged, white-faced. 'I think he's hurt. He looks funny.'

Eric hurried outside and helped Matson to his feet. 'You OK? It's your own fault. I told you if you kept annoying it something might happen.'

Matson's face was ablaze with rage. 'No little pipsqueak god is going to treat me like this!' He pushed Eric aside, heading back for the house. 'I'll take it down to the Lab and pop it in a bottle of formaldehyde. I'll dissect it and skin it and hang it up on the wall. I'll have the first specimen of a god known to–'

A ball of light glowed around Matson. The ball enveloped him, settling in place around his lean body so that he looked like a filament in an incandescent light.

'What the hell!' Matson muttered. Suddenly he jerked. His body faded. He began to shrink. With a faint whoosh he diminished rapidly. Smaller and smaller he dwindled. His body shuddered, altering strangely.

The light winked out. Sitting stupidly on the walk was a small green toad.

'See?' Eric said wildly. 'I told you to keep quiet! Now look what it's done!'

The toad hopped feebly toward the house. At the porch it sagged into immobility, defeated by the steps. It uttered a pathetic, hopeless *chug*.

Pat's voice rose in a wail of anguish. 'Oh, Eric! Look what it's done! Poor Tom!'

'His own fault,' Eric said. 'He deserves it.' But he was beginning to get nervous. 'Look here,' he said to the god. 'That's not a very nice thing to do to a grown man. What'll his wife and kids think?'

'What'll Mr Bradshaw think?' Pat cried. 'He can't go to work like that!'

'True,' Eric admitted. He appealed to the god. 'I think he's learned his lesson. How about turning him back? OK?'

'You just better undo him!' Pat shrieked, clenching her small fists. 'If you don't undo him you'll have Terran Metals after you. Even a god can't stand up to Horace Bradshaw.'

'Better change him back,' Eric said.

'It'll do him good,' the god said. 'I'll leave him that way for a couple of centuries–'

'Centuries!' Pat exploded. 'Why, you little blob of slime!' She advanced ominously toward the box, shaking with wrath. 'See here! You turn him back or I'll take you out of your box and drop you into the garbage disposal unit!'

'Make her be still,' the god said to Eric.

'Calm down, Pat,' Eric implored.

'I will not calm down! Who does it think it is? A present! How *dare* you bring this moldy bit of refuse into our house? Is this your idea of a–'

Her voice ceased abruptly.

Eric turned apprehensively. Pat stood rigid, her mouth open, a word still on her lips. She did not move. She was white all over. A solid gray-white that made cold chills leap up Eric's spine. 'Good Lord,' he said.

'I turned her to stone,' the god explained. 'She made too much noise.' It yawned. 'Now, I think I'll retire. I'm a little tired, after my trip.'

'I can't believe it,' Eric Blake said. He shook his head numbly. 'My best friend a toad. My wife turned to stone.'

'It's true,' the god said. 'We deal out justice according to how people act. They both got what they deserved.'

'Can–can she hear me?'

'I suppose.'

Eric went over to the statue. 'Pat,' he begged imploringly. 'Please don't be mad. It isn't my fault.' He gripped her ice-cold shoulders. 'Don't blame me! I didn't do it.' The granite was hard and smooth under his fingers. Pat stared blankly ahead.

'Terran Metals indeed,' the god grumbled sourly. Its single eye studied Eric intently. 'Who is this Horace Bradshaw? Some local deity, perhaps?'

'Horace Bradshaw owns Terran Metals,' Eric said gloomily. He sat down and shakily lit a cigarette. 'He's about the biggest man on Terra. Terran Metals owns half the planets in the system.'

'Kingdoms of this world do not interest me,' the god said non-committally, subsiding and shutting its eye. 'I will retire now. I wish to contemplate certain matters. You may wake me later, if you wish. We can converse on theological subjects, as we did on the ship coming here.'

'Theological subjects,' Eric said bitterly. 'My wife a stone block and it wants to talk about religion.'

But the god was already withdrawn, retired into itself.

'A lot you care,' Eric muttered. Anger flickered in him. 'This is the thanks I get for taking you off Ganymede. Ruin my household and my social life. Fine god you are!'

No response.

Eric concentrated desperately. Maybe when the god awoke it would be in a better mood. Maybe he could persuade it to turn Matson and Pat back to their usual forms. Faint hope stirred. He could appeal to the god's better side. After it had rested and slept for a few hours . . .

If nobody came looking for Matson.

The toad sat disconsolately on the walk, drooping with misery. Eric leaned toward it. 'Hey, Matson!'

The toad looked slowly up.

'Don't worry, old man. I'll get it to turn you back. It's a cinch.' The toad didn't stir. 'A lead-pipe cinch,' Eric repeated nervously.

The toad drooped a little more. Eric looked at his watch. It was late afternoon, almost four. Tom's shift at Terran began in half an hour. Sweat came out on his forehead. If the god went on sleeping and didn't wake up in half an hour–

A buzz. The vidphone.

Eric's heart sank. He hurried over and clicked the screen on, steeling himself. Horace Bradshaw's sharp, dignified features faded into focus. His keen glance bored into Eric, penetrating his depths.

'Blake,' he grunted. 'Back from Ganymede, I see.'

'Yes, sir.' Eric's mind raced frantically. He moved in front of the screen, cutting off Bradshaw's view of the room. 'I'm just starting to unpack.'

'Forget that and get over here! We're waiting to hear your report.'

'Right now? Gosh, Mr Bradshaw. Give me a chance to get my things away.' He fought desperately for time. 'I'll be over tomorrow morning bright and early.'

'Is Matson there with you?'

Eric swallowed. 'Yes, sir. But–'

'Put him on. I want to talk to him.'

'He–he can't talk to you right now, sir.'

'What? Why not?'

'He's in no shape to–that is, he–'

Bradshaw snarled impatiently. 'Then bring him along with you. And he better be sober when he gets here. I'll see you at my office in ten minutes.' He broke the circuit. The screen faded abruptly.

Eric sank wearily down in a chair. His mind reeled. Ten minutes! He shook his head, stunned.

The toad hopped a little, stirring on the walk. It emitted a faint, despondent sound.

Eric got heavily to his feet. 'I guess we have to face the music,' he murmured. He bent down and picked up the toad, putting it gingerly in his coat pocket. 'I guess you heard. That was Bradshaw. We're going down to the Lab.'

The toad stirred uneasily.

'I wonder what Bradshaw is going to say when he sees you.' Eric kissed his wife's cold granite cheek. 'Good-bye, honey.' He moved numbly down the walk to the street. A moment later he hailed a robot cab and entered it. 'I have a feeling this is going to be hard to explain.' The cab zipped off down the street. 'Hard as hell to explain.'

Horace Bradshaw stared in dumbfounded amazement. He removed his steel-rimmed glasses and wiped them slowly. He fitted them back on his hard, hawklike face and peered down. The toad rested silently in the center of the immense mahogany desk.

Bradshaw pointed shakily at the toad. 'This–this is Thomas Matson?'

'Yes, sir,' Eric said.

Bradshaw blinked in wonder. 'Matson! What in the world has happened to you?'

'He's a toad,' Eric explained.

'So I see. Incredible.' Bradshaw pressed a stud on his desk. 'Send in Jennings from the Biology Lab,' he ordered. 'A toad.' He poked the toad with his pencil. 'Is that really you, Matson?'

The toad *chugged.*

'Good Lord.' Bradshaw sat back, wiping his forehead. His grim expression faded into sympathetic concern. He shook his head sadly. 'I can't believe it. Some kind of bacterial blight, I suppose. Matson was always experimenting on himself. He took his work seriously. A brave man. A good worker. He did much for Terran Metals. Too bad he had to end this way. We'll extend full pension to him, of course.'

Jennings entered the office. 'You wanted me, sir?'

'Come in.' Bradshaw beckoned him impatiently in. 'We have a problem for your department. You know Eric Blake here.'

'Hi, Blake.'

'And Thomas Matson.' Bradshaw indicated the toad. 'From the Nonferrous Lab.'

'I know Matson,' Jennings said slowly. 'That is, I know a Matson from Nonferrous. But I don't recall–that is, he was taller than this. Almost six feet.'

'This is him,' Eric said gloomily. 'He's a toad now.'

'What happened?' Jennings' scientific curiosity was aroused. 'What's the lowdown?'

'It's a long story,' Eric said evasively.

'Can't you tell it?' Jennings scrutinized the toad professionally. 'Looks like a regular type of toad. You're sure this is Tom Matson? Come clean, Blake. You must know more than you're telling!'

Bradshaw studied Eric intently. 'Yes, what *did* happen, Blake? You have a strange, shifty look. Are you responsible for this?' Bradshaw half rose from his chair, his grim face bleak. 'See here. If it's your fault one of my best men has been incapacitated for further work–'

'Take it easy,' Eric protested, his mind racing frantically. He patted the toad nervously. 'Matson is perfectly safe–as long as nobody steps on him. We can rig up some sort of protective shield and an automatic communication system that'll enable him to spell out words. He can continue his work. With a few adjustments here and there everything should speed along perfectly.'

'Answer me!' Bradshaw roared. 'Are you responsible for this? Is this *your* doing?'

Eric squirmed helplessly. 'In a way, I suppose. Not exactly. Not *directly*.' His voice wavered. 'But I guess you'd say if it hadn't been for me . . .'

Bradshaw's face set in a rigid mask of rage. 'Blake, you're fired.' He yanked a heap of forms from his desk dispenser. 'Get out of here and never come back. And get your hand off that toad. It belongs to Terran Metals.' He shoved a paper across the desk. 'Here's your paycheck. And don't bother looking for work elsewhere. I'm listing you on the inter-system blacklist. Good day.'

'But, Mr Bradshaw–'

'Don't plead.' Bradshaw waved his hand. 'Just go. Jennings, get your biology staff busy at once. This problem must be licked. I want you to rearrange this toad back to its original shape. Matson is a vital part of Terran Metals. There's work to be done, work only Matson can do. We can't have this sort of thing holding up our research.'

'Mr Bradshaw,' Eric begged desperately. 'Please listen. I want to see Tom back as he was. But there's only one way we can get him back his original shape. We–'

Bradshaw's eyes were cold with hostility. 'You still here, Blake? Must I call my guards and have you dismembered? I'm giving you one minute to be off Company land. Understand?'

Eric nodded miserably. 'I understand.' He turned and shuffled unhappily toward the door. 'So long, Jennings. So long, Tom. I'll be home if you want me, Mr Bradshaw.'

'Sorcerer,' Bradshaw snapped. 'Good riddance.'

'What would you do,' Eric asked the robot cabdriver, 'if your wife had turned to stone, your best friend were a toad, and you had lost your job?'

'Robots have no wives,' the driver said. 'They are nonsexual. Robots have no friends, either. They are incapable of emotional relationships.'

'Can robots be fired?'

'Sometimes.' The robot drew his cab up before Eric's modest six-room bungalow. 'But consider. Robots are frequently melted down and new robots made from the remains. Recall Ibsen's *Peer Gynt*, the section concerning the Button Molder. The lines clearly anticipate in symbolic form the trauma of robots to come.'

'Yeah.' The door opened and Eric got out. 'I guess we all have our problems.'

'Robots have worse problems than anybody.' The door shut and the cab zipped off, back down the hill.

Worse? Hardly. Eric entered his home slowly, the front door automatically opening for him.

'Welcome, Mr Blake,' the door greeted him.

'I suppose Pat's still here.'

'Mrs Blake is here, but she is in a cataleptic state, or some similar condition.'

'She's been turned to stone.' Eric kissed the cold lips of the statue gloomily. 'Hi, honey.'

He got some meat from the refrigerator and crumbled it into the belly-cup of the god. Presently digestive fluid rose and covered the food. In a short time the single eye of the god opened, blinked a few times, and focused on Eric.

'Have a good sleep?' Eric inquired icily.

'I wasn't asleep. My mind was turned toward matters of cosmic import. I detect a hostile quality in your voice. Has something unfavorable occurred?'

'Nothing. Nothing at all. I just lost my job, on top of everything else.'

'Lost your job? Interesting. What else do you refer to?'

Eric exploded in rage. 'You've messed up my whole life, damn you!' He jabbed at the silent, unmoving figure of his wife. 'Look! My wife! Turned to granite. And my best friend, a toad!'

Tinokuknoi Arevulopapo yawned. 'So?'

'*Why?* What did I ever do to you? Why do you treat me this way? Look at all I've done for you. I only brought you here to Terra. Fed you. Fixed you up a box with straw and water and newspapers. That's all.'

'True. You did bring me to Terra.' Again an odd gleam flickered across the god's dark face. 'All right. I'll restore your wife.'

'You will?' Pathetic joy surged through Eric. Tears came to his eyes. He was too relieved to ask any questions. 'Gosh, I sure would appreciate it!'

The god concentrated. 'Stand out of the way. It's easier to distort the molecular arrangement of a body than to restore the original configuration. I hope I can get it exactly as it was.' It made a faint motion.

Around Pat's silent figure the air stirred. The pale granite shuddered. Slowly, color seeped back into her features. She gasped sharply, her dark eyes flashing with fear. Color filled her arms, shoulders, breasts, spreading through her trim body. She cried out, tottering unsteadily. '*Eric!*'

Eric caught her, hugging her tight. 'Gosh, honey. I'm sure glad you're all right.' He crushed her against him, feeling her heart thump with terror. He kissed her soft lips again and again. 'Welcome back.'

Pat pulled abruptly away. 'That little snake. That miserable particle of waste. Wait until I get my hands on it.' She advanced toward the god, eyes blazing. 'Listen, you. What's the idea? How *dare* you!'

'See?' the god said. 'They never change.'

Eric pulled his wife back. 'You better shut up or you'll be granite again. Understand?'

Pat caught the urgent rasp in his voice. She subsided reluctantly. 'All right, Eric, I give up.'

'Listen,' Eric said to the god. 'How about Tom? How about restoring him?'

'The toad? Where is he?'

'In the Biology Lab. Jennings and his staff are working on him.'

The god considered. 'I don't like the sound of that. The Biology Lab? Where is that? How far away?'

'Terran Metals. Main Building.' Eric was impatient. 'Maybe five miles. How about it? Maybe if you restore him Bradshaw will give me my job back. You owe it to me. Set things back the way they were.'

'I can't.'

'You *can't*! Why the hell not?'

'I thought gods were omnipotent,' Pat sniffed petulantly.

'I can do anything–at short range. The Terran Metals Biology Lab is too far. Five miles is beyond my limit. I can distort molecular arrangements within a limited circle only.'

Eric was incredulous. 'What? You mean you can't turn Tom back?'

'That's the way it is. You shouldn't have taken him out of the house. Gods are subject to natural law just as you are. Our laws are different, but they are still laws.'

'I see,' Eric murmured. 'You should have said.'

'As far as your job goes, don't worry about that. Here, I'll create some gold.' The god made a motion with its scaly hands. A section of curtain flashed suddenly yellow and crashed to the floor with a metallic tinkle. 'Solid gold. That ought to keep you a few days.'

'We're no longer on the gold standard.'

'Well, whatever you need. I can do anything.'

'Except turn Tom back into a human being,' Pat said. 'Fine god you are.'

'Shut up, Pat,' Eric muttered, deep in thought.

'If there were some way I could be closer to him,' the god said cautiously. 'If he were within range . . .'

'Bradshaw will never let him go. And I can't set foot around there. The guards will tear me to bits.'

'How about some platinum?' The god made a pass and a section of the wall glowed white. 'Solid platinum. A simple change of atomic weight. Will that help?'

'No!' Eric paced back and forth. 'We've got to get that toad away from Bradshaw. If we can get him back here–'

'I have an idea,' the god said.

'What?'

'Perhaps you could get me in there. Perhaps if I could get onto the Company grounds, within range of the Biology Lab . . .'

'It's worth a try,' Pat said, putting her hand on Eric's shoulder. 'After all, Tom's your best friend. It's a shame to treat him this way. It's–it's un-Terran.'

Eric grabbed his coat. 'It's settled. I'll drive as close as I can to the Company grounds. I ought to be able to get near enough before the guards catch sight of me to–'

A crash. The front door collapsed abruptly in a heap of ash. Teams of robot police surged into the room, blastguns ready.

'All right,' Jennings said. 'That's him.' He strode quickly into the house. 'Get him. And get that thing in the box.'

'Jennings!' Eric swallowed in alarm. 'What the hell is this?'

Jennings' lip curled. 'Cut out the pretense, Blake. You're not fooling me.' He tapped a small metal case under his arm. 'The toad revealed all. So you've got a non-Terrestrial in this house, have you?' He laughed coldly. 'There's a law against bringing non-Terrans to Earth. You're under arrest, Blake. You'll probably get life.'

'Tinokuknoi Arevulopapo!' Eric Blake squeaked. 'Don't forsake me at a time like this!'

'I'm coming,' the god grunted. It heaved violently. 'How's this?'

The robot police jerked as a torrent of force erupted from the box. Abruptly they disappeared, winking out of existence. Where they had stood a horde of mechanical mice milled aimlessly, spilling frantically through the doorway, out into the yard.

Jennings' face showed astonishment and then panic. He retreated, waving his blaster menacingly. 'See here, Blake. Don't think you can scare me. We've got this house surrounded.'

A bolt of force hit him in the stomach. The bolt lifted him and shook him like a rag doll. His blaster skidded from his fingers, falling to the floor. Jennings groped for it desperately. The blaster turned into a spider and crawled rapidly off, out of his reach.

'Set him down,' Eric urged.

'All right.' The god released Jennings. He crashed to the floor, stunned and frightened. He scrambled wildly to his feet and ran from the house, down the path to the sidewalk.

'Oh dear,' Pat said.

'What is it?'

'Look.'

Pulled up in a circle around the house was a solid line of atomic cannon. Their snouts gleamed wickedly in the late afternoon sunlight. Groups of robot police stood around each cannon, waiting alertly for instructions.

Eric groaned. 'We're sunk. One blast and we're finished.'

'Do something!' Pat gasped. She prodded the box. 'Enchant them. Don't just sit there.'

'They are out of range,' the god replied. 'As I explained, my power is limited by distance.'

'You in there!' a voice came, magnified by a hundred loudspeakers. 'Come out with your hands up. Or we open fire!'

'Bradshaw,' Eric groaned. 'He's out there. We're trapped. You sure you can't do something?'

'Sorry,' the god said. 'I can put up a shield against the cannon.' It concentrated. Outside the house a dull surface formed, a globe rapidly hardening around them.

'All right,' Bradshaw's magnified voice came, muffled by the shield. 'You asked for it.'

The first shell hit. Eric found himself lying on the floor, his ears ringing, everything going around and around. Pat lay beside him, dazed and frightened. The house was a shambles. Walls, chairs, furniture, all was in ruins.

'Fine shield,' Pat gasped.

'The concussion,' the god protested. Its box lay in the corner on its side. 'The shield stops the shells, but the concussion–'

A second shell struck. A wall of pressure rolled over Eric, stunning him. He skidded, tossed by a violent wind, crashing against heaps of debris that had been his house.

'We can't last,' Pat said faintly. 'Tell them to stop, Eric. Please!'

'Your wife is right,' the god's calm voice came up, from its overturned box. 'Surrender, Eric. Give yourself up.'

'I guess I better.' Eric pulled himself up on his knees. 'But golly, I don't want to spend the rest of my life in prison. I knew I was breaking the law when I smuggled the damn thing in here, but I never thought–'

A third shell hit. Eric tumbled down, his chin smacking the floor. Plaster and rubble rained down on him, choking and blinding him. He fought his way up, grabbing hold of a jutting beam.

'Stop!' he shouted.

There was sudden silence.

'Are you willing to surrender?' the magnified voice boomed.

'Surrender,' the god murmured.

Eric's mind raced desperately. 'I–I have a deal. A compromise.' He thought fast, his brain in high gear. 'I have a proposal.'

There was a long pause. 'What's the proposal?'

Eric stepped warily through the rubble to the edge of the shield. The shield was almost gone. Only a shimmering haze remained, through which the circle of atomic cannon was visible, the cannon and the robot police.

'Matson,' Eric gasped, getting his breath. 'The toad. We'll make the following deal. We'll restore Matson to his original shape. We'll return the non-Terrestrial to Ganymede. In return, you waive prosecution and I get my job back.'

'Absurd! My labs can easily restore Matson without your help.'

'Oh yeah? Ask Matson. He'll tell you. If you don't agree, Matson will be a toad for the next two hundred years–at least!'

A long silence followed. Eric could see figures moving back and forth, conferring behind the guns.

'All right,' Bradshaw's voice came at last. 'We agree. Drop the shield and come forward. I'll send Jennings with the toad. No tricks, Blake!'

'No tricks.' Eric sagged with relief. 'Come along,' he said to the god, picking up the dented box. 'Drop the shield and let's get this over with. Those cannon make me nervous.'

The god relaxed. The shield—what was left of it—wavered and faded, blinking off.

'Here I come.' Eric advanced warily, the box in his hands. 'Where's Matson?'

Jennings came toward him. 'I have him.' His curiosity overcame his suspicion. 'This ought to be interesting. We should make a close study of all extra-dimensional life. Apparently they possess science much in advance of our own.'

Jennings squatted down, placing the small green toad carefully on the grass.

'There he is,' Eric said to the god.

'Is this close enough?' Pat asked icily.

'This is sufficient,' the god said. 'This is exactly right.' It turned its single eye on the toad and made a few brief motions with its scaly claws.

A shimmer hovered over the toad. Extra-dimensional forces were at work, fingering and plucking at the toad molecules. Abruptly the toad twitched. For a second it shuddered, an insistent vibration lapped over it. Then—

Matson ballooned into existence, the familiar bean-pole figure, towering over Eric and Jennings and Pat.

'Lord,' Matson breathed shakily. He got out his handkerchief and wiped his face. 'I'm glad that's over. Wouldn't want to go through that again.'

Jennings retreated hurriedly toward the circle of cannon. Matson turned and headed after him. Eric and his wife and god were suddenly alone in the center of the lawn.

'Hey!' Eric demanded, cold alarm plucking at him. 'What is this? What the hell's going on?'

'Sorry, Blake,' Bradshaw's voice came. 'It was essential to restore Matson. But we can't alter the law. The law is above any man, even me. You're under arrest.'

Robot police swarmed forward, grimly surrounding Eric and Pat. 'You skunk,' Eric choked, struggling feebly.

Bradshaw came out from behind the cannon, hands in his

pockets, grinning calmly. 'Sorry, Blake. You should be out of jail in ten or fifteen years, though. Your job will be waiting for you–I promise. As for this extra-dimensional being, I'm quite interested in seeing it. I've heard of such things.' He peered toward the box. 'I'm happy to take charge of it. Our labs will perform experiments and tests on it which will . . .'

Bradshaw's words died. His face turned a sickly hue. His mouth opened and closed, but no sounds came.

From the box came a swelling, frenzied buzz of rage. '*Nar Dolk*! I knew I'd find you!'

Bradshaw retreated, trembling violently. 'Why, of all persons. Tinokuknoi Arevulopapo! What are you doing on Terra?' He stumbled, half falling. 'How did you, that is, after so long, how could–'

Then Bradshaw was running, scattering robot police in all directions, rushing wildly past the atomic cannon.

'Nar Dolk!' the god screamed, swelling with fury. 'Scourge of the Seven Temples! Flotsam of Space! I knew you were on this miserable planet! Come back and take your punishment!'

The god burst upward, flashing into the air. It raced past Eric and Pat, growing as it flew. A sickening, nauseous wind, warm and damp, lapped at their faces, as the god gained speed.

Bradshaw–Nar Dolk–ran frantically. And as he ran he *changed*. Immense wings sprouted from him. Great leathery wings, beating the air in frantic haste. His body oozed and altered. Tentacles replaced his legs. Scaly claws replaced arms. Gray hide rippled as he flew up, wings flapping noisily.

Tinokuknoi Arevulopapo struck. For a brief moment the two locked together, twisting and rolling in the air, wings and claws raking and flapping.

Then Nar Dolk broke away, fluttering up. A blazing flash, a pop, and he was gone.

For a moment Tinokuknoi Arevulopapo hovered in the air. The scaly head turned, the single eye glancing back and down at Eric and Pat. It nodded briefly. Then, with a curious shimmy, it vanished.

The sky was empty except for a few feathers and the dull stench of burning scales.

Eric was the first to speak. 'Well,' he said. 'So that's why it wanted to come to Terra. I guess I was sort of exploited.' He grinned sheepishly. 'The first Terran ever to be exploited.'

Matson gawked, still peering up. 'They're gone. Both of them. Back to their own dimension, I guess.'

A robot policeman plucked at Jennings' sleeve. 'Shall we arrest anyone, sir? With Mr Bradshaw gone you are next in charge.'

Jennings glanced at Eric and Pat. 'I suppose not. The evidence has departed. It seems somewhat silly, anyhow.' He shook his head. 'Bradshaw. Imagine! And we worked for him for years. Damn strange business.'

Eric put his arm around his wife. He pulled her against him, hugging her tight. 'I'm sorry, honey,' he said softly.

'Sorry?'

'Your present. It's gone. I guess I'll have to get you something else.'

Pat laughed, pressing against him. 'That's all right. I'll let you in on a secret.'

'What?'

Pat kissed him, her lips warm against his cheek. 'As a matter of fact–I'm just as glad.'

THE HOOD MAKER

'A hood!'

'Somebody with a hood!'

Workers and shoppers hurried down the sidewalk, joining the forming crowd. A sallow-faced youth dropped his bike and raced over. The crowd grew, businessmen in gray coats, tired-faced secretaries, clerks and workmen.

'Get him!' The crowd swarmed forward. 'The old man!'

The sallow-faced youth scooped up a rock from the gutter and hurled it. The rock missed the old man, crashing against a store front.

'He's got a hood, all right!'

'Take it away!'

More rocks fell. The old man gasped in fear, trying to push past two soldiers blocking his way. A rock struck him on the back.

'What you got to hide?' The sallow-faced youth ran up in front of him. 'Why you afraid of a probe?'

'He's got something to hide!' A worker grabbed the old man's hat. Eager hands groped for the thin metal band around his head.

'Nobody's got a right to hide!'

The old man fell, sprawling to his hands and knees, umbrella rolling. A clerk caught hold of the hood and tugged. The crowd surged, struggling to get to the metal band. Suddenly the youth gave a cry. He backed off, the hood held up. 'I got it! I got it.' He ran to his bike and pedalled off rapidly, gripping the bent hood.

A robot police car pulled up to the curb, siren screaming. Robot cops leaped out, clearing the mob away.

'You hurt?' They helped the old man up.

The old man shook his head, dazed. His glasses hung from one ear. Blood and saliva streaked his face.

'All right.' The cop's metal fingers released. 'Better get off the street. Inside someplace. For your own good.'

Clearance Director Ross pushed the memo plate away. 'Another one. I'll be glad when the Anti-Immunity Bill is passed.'

Peters glanced up. 'Another?'

'Another person wearing a hood—a probe shield. That makes ten in the last forty-eight hours. They're mailing more out all the time.'

'Mailed, slipped under doors, in pockets, left at desks—countless ways of distribution.'

'If more of them notified us—'

Peters grinned crookedly. 'It's a wonder any of them do. There's a reason why hoods are sent to these people. They're not picked out at random.'

'Why are they picked?'

'They have something to hide. Why else would hoods be sent to them?'

'What about those who *do* notify us?'

'They're afraid to wear them. They pass the hoods on to us—to avoid suspicion.'

Ross reflected moodily. 'I suppose so.'

'An innocent man has no reason to conceal his thoughts. Ninety-nine per cent of the population is glad to have its mind scanned. Most people *want* to prove their loyalty. But this one per cent is guilty of something.'

Ross opened a manila folder and took out a bent metal band. He studied it intently. 'Look at it. Just a strip of some alloy. But it effectively cuts off all probes. The teeps go crazy. It buzzes them when they try to get past. Like a shock.'

'You've sent samples to the lab, of course.'

'No. I don't want any of the lab workers turning out their own hoods. We have trouble enough!'

'Who was this taken from?'

Ross stabbed a button on his desk. 'We'll find out. I'll have the teep make a report.'

The door melted and a lank sallow-faced youth came into the room. He saw the metal band in Ross's hand and smiled, a thin, alert smile. 'You wanted me?'

Ross studied the youth. Blonde hair, blue eyes. An ordinary-looking kid, maybe a college sophomore. But Ross knew better. Ernest Abbud was a telepathic mutant–a teep. One of several hundred employed by Clearance for its loyalty probes.

Before the teeps, loyalty probes had been haphazard. Oaths, examinations, wire-tappings, were not enough. The theory that each person had to prove his loyalty was fine–as a theory. In practice few people could do it. It looked as if the concept of guilty until proved innocent might have to be abandoned and the Roman law restored.

The problem, apparently insoluble, had found its answer in the Madagascar Blast of 2004. Waves of hard radiation had lapped over several thousand troops stationed in the area. Of those who lived, few produced subsequent progeny. But of the several hundred children born to the survivors of the blast, many showed neural characteristics of a radically new kind. A human mutant had come into being–for the first time in thousands of years.

The teeps appeared by accident. But they solved the most pressing problem the Free Union faced: the detection and punishment of disloyalty. The teeps were invaluable to the Government of the Free Union–and the teeps knew it.

'You got this?' Ross asked, tapping the hood.

Abbud nodded. 'Yes.'

The youth was following his thoughts, not his spoken words. Ross flushed angrily. 'What was the man like?' he demanded harshly. 'The memo plate gives no details.'

'Doctor Franklin is his name. Director of the Federal Resources Commission. Sixty-seven years of age. Here on a visit to a relative.'

'Walter Franklin! I've heard of him.' Ross stared up at Abbud. 'Then you already–'

'As soon as I removed the hood I was able to scan him.'

'Where did Franklin go after the assault?'

'Indoors. Instructed by the police.'

'They arrived?'

'After the hood had been taken, of course. It went perfectly. Franklin was spotted by another telepath, not myself. I was informed Franklin was coming my way. When he reached me I shouted that he was wearing a hood. A crowd collected and others took up the shout. The other telepath arrived and we manipulated the crowd until we were near him. I took the hood myself–and you know the rest.'

Ross was silent for a moment. 'Do you know how he got that hood? Did you scan that?'

'He received it by mail.'

'Does he–'

'He has no idea who sent it or where it came from.'

Ross frowned. 'Then he can't give us any information about them. The senders.'

'The Hood Makers,' Abbud said icily.

Ross glanced quickly up. 'What?'

'The Hood Makers. *Somebody* makes them.' Abbud's face was hard. '*Somebody* is making probe screens to keep us out.'

'And you're sure–'

'Franklin knows nothing! He arrived in the city last night. This morning his mail machine brought the hood. For a time he deliberated. Then he purchased a hat and put it on over the hood. He set out on foot toward his niece's house. We spotted him several minutes later, when he entered range.'

'There seems to be more of them, these days. More hoods being sent out. But you know that.' Ross set his jaw. 'We've got to locate the senders.'

'It'll take time. They apparently wear hoods constantly.' Abbud's face twisted. 'We have to get so damn close! Our scanning range is extremely limited. But sooner or later we'll locate one of them. Sooner or later we'll tear a hood off somebody–and find *him* . . .'

'In the last year five thousand hood-wearers have been detected,' Ross stated. 'Five thousand–and not one of them knows anything. Where the hoods come from or who makes them.'

'When there are more of us, we'll have a better chance,' Abbud said grimly. 'Right now there are too few of us. But eventually–'

'You're going to have Franklin probed, aren't you?' Peters said to Ross. 'As a matter of course.'

'I suppose so.' Ross nodded to Abbud. 'You might as well go ahead on him. Have one of your group run the regular total probe and see if there's anything of interest buried down in his non-conscious neural area. Report the results to me in the usual way.'

Abbud reached into his coat. He brought out a tape spool and tossed it down on the desk in front of Ross. 'Here you are.'

'What's this?'

'The total probe on Franklin. All levels–completely searched and recorded.'

Ross stared up at the youth. 'You–'

'We went ahead with it.' Abbud moved toward the door. 'It's a good job. Cummings did it. We found considerable disloyalty. Mostly ideological rather than overt. You'll probably want to pick him up. When he was twenty-four he found some old books and musical records. He was strongly influenced. The latter part of the tape discusses fully our evaluation of his deviation.'

The door melted and Abbud left.

Ross and Peters stared after him. Finally Ross took the tape spool and put it with the bent metal hood.

'I'll be damned,' Peters said. 'They went ahead with the probe.'

Ross nodded, deep in thought. 'Yeah. And I'm not sure I like it.'

The two men glanced at each other–and knew, as they did so, that outside the office Ernest Abbud was scanning their thoughts.

'Damn it!' Ross said futilely. 'Damn it!'

*

Walter Franklin breathed rapidly, peering around him. He wiped nervous sweat from his lined face with a trembling hand.

Down the corridor the echoing clang of Clearance agents sounded, growing louder.

He had got away from the mob—spared for a while. That was four hours ago. Now the sun had set and evening was settling over greater New York. He had managed to make his way half across the city, almost to the outskirts—and now a public alarm was out for his arrest.

Why? He had worked for the Free Union Government all his life. He had done nothing disloyal. Nothing, except open the morning mail, find the hood, deliberate about it, and finally put it on. He remembered the small instruction tag:

GREETINGS!

This probe screen is sent to you with compliments of the maker and the earnest hope that it will be of some value to you. Thank you.

Nothing else. No other information. For a long time he had pondered. Should he wear it? He had never done anything. He had nothing to hide—nothing disloyal to the Union. But the thought fascinated him. If he wore the hood his mind would be his own. Nobody could look into it. His mind would belong to him again, private, secret, to think as he wished, endless thoughts for no one else's consumption but his own.

Finally he had made up his mind and put on the hood, fitting his old Homburg over it. He had gone outside—and within ten minutes a mob was screaming and yelling around him. And now a general alarm was out for his arrest.

Franklin wracked his brain desperately. What could he do? They could bring him up before a Clearance Board. No accusation would be brought: it would be up to him to clear himself, to prove he was loyal. *Had* he ever done anything wrong? Was there something he had done he was forgetting? He had put on the hood. Maybe that was it. There was some sort of an Anti-Immunity bill up in Congress to make wearing of a probe screen a felony, but it hadn't been passed yet—

The Clearance agents were near, almost on him. He retreated down the corridor of the hotel, glancing desperately around him. A red sign glowed: EXIT. He hurried toward it and down a flight of basement stairs, out onto a dark street. It was bad to be outside, where the mobs were. He had tried to remain indoors as much as possible. But now there was no choice.

Behind him a voice shrilled loudly. Something cut past him, smoking away a section of the pavement. A Slem-ray. Franklin ran, gasping for breath, around a corner and down a side street. People glanced at him curiously as he rushed past.

He crossed a busy street and moved with a surging group of theater goers. Had the agents seen him? He peered nervously around. None in sight.

At the corner he crossed with the lights. He reached the safety zone in the center, watching a sleek Clearance car cruising toward him. Had it seen him go out to the safety zone? He left the zone, heading toward the curb on the far side. The Clearance car shot suddenly forward, gaining speed. Another appeared, coming the other way.

Franklin reached the curb.

The first car ground to a halt. Clearance agents piled out, swarming up onto the sidewalk.

He was trapped. There was no place to hide. Around him tired shoppers and office workers gazed curiously, their faces devoid of sympathy. A few grinned at him in vacant amusement. Franklin peered frantically around. No place, no door, no person–

A car pulled up in front of him, its doors sliding open. 'Get in.' A young girl leaned toward him, her pretty face urgent. 'Get in, damn it!'

He got in. The girl slammed the doors and the car picked up speed. A Clearance car swung in ahead of them, its sleek bulk blocking the street. A second Clearance car moved in behind them.

The girl leaned forward, gripping the controls. Abruptly the car lifted. It left the street, clearing the cars ahead, gaining altitude rapidly. A flash of violet lit up the sky behind them.

'Get down!' the girl snapped. Franklin sank down in his seat. The car moved in a wide arc, passing beyond the protective columns of a row of buildings. On the ground, the Clearance cars gave up and turned back.

Franklin settled back, mopping his forehead shakily. 'Thanks,' he muttered.

'Don't mention it.' The girl increased the car's speed. They were leaving the business section of the city, moving above the residential outskirts. She steered silently, intent on the sky ahead.

'Who are you?' Franklin asked.

The girl tossed something back to him. 'Put that on.'

A hood. Franklin unfastened it and slipped it awkwardly over his head. 'It's in place.'

'Otherwise they'll get us with a teep scan. We have to be careful all the time.'

'Where are we going?'

The girl turned to him, studying him with calm gray eyes, one hand resting on the wheel. 'We're going to the Hood Maker,' she said. 'The public alarm for you is top priority. If I let you off you won't last an hour.'

'But I don't understand.' Franklin shook his head, dazed. 'Why do they want me? What have I done?'

'You're being framed.' The girl brought the car around in a wide arc, wind whistling shrilly through its struts and fenders. 'Framed by the teeps. Things are happening fast. There's no time to lose.'

The little bald-headed man removed his glasses and held out his hand to Franklin, peering near-sightedly. 'I'm glad to meet you, Doctor. I've followed your work at the Board with great interest.'

'Who are you?' Franklin demanded.

The little man grinned self-consciously. 'I'm James Cutter. The Hood Maker, as the teeps call me. This is our factory.' He waved around the room. 'Take a look at it.'

Franklin gazed around him. He was in a warehouse, an ancient wooden building of the last century. Giant worm-scored beams rose up, dry and cracking. The floor was concrete. Old-fashioned fluorescent lights glinted and flickered from the roof. The walls were streaked with water stains and bulging pipes.

Franklin moved across the room, Cutter beside him. He was bewildered. Everything had happened fast. He seemed to be outside New York, in some dilapidated industrial suburb. Men were working on all sides of him, bent over stampers and molds. The air was hot. An archaic fan whirred. The warehouse echoed and vibrated with a constant din.

'This–' Franklin murmured. 'This is–'

'This is where we make the hoods. Not very impressive, is it? Later on we hope to move to new quarters. Come along and I'll show you the rest.'

Cutter pushed a side door open and they entered a small laboratory, bottles and retorts everywhere in cluttered confusion. 'We do our research in here. Pure and applied. We've learned a few things. Some we may use, some we hope won't be needed. And it keeps our refugees busy.'

'Refugees?'

Cutter pushed some equipment back and seated himself on a lab table. 'Most of the others are here for the same reason as you. Framed by the teeps. Accused of deviation. But we got to them first.'

'But why–'

'Why were you framed? Because of your position. Director of a Government Department. All these men were prominent–and all were framed by teep probes.' Cutter lit a cigarette, leaning back against the water-stained wall. 'We exist because of a discovery made ten years ago in a Government lab.' He tapped his hood. 'This alloy–opaque to probes. Discovered by accident, by one of these men. Teeps came after him instantly, but he escaped. He made a number of hoods and passed them to other workers in his field. That's how we got started.'

'How many are here?'

Cutter laughed. 'Can't tell you that. Enough to turn out hoods and keep them circulating. To people prominent in Government.

People holding positions of authority. Scientists, officials, educators–'

'Why?'

'Because we want to get them first, before the teeps. We got to you too late. A total probe report had *already* been made out on you, before the hood was even in the mail.

'The teeps are gradually getting a stranglehold over the Government. They're picking off the best men, denouncing them and getting them arrested. If a teep says a man is disloyal Clearance has to haul him in. We tried to get a hood to you in time. The report couldn't be passed on to Clearance if you were wearing a hood. But they outsmarted us. They got a mob after you and snatched the hood. As soon as it was off they served the report to Clearance.'

'So that's why they wanted it off.'

'The teeps can't file a framed report on a man whose mind is opaque to probes. Clearance isn't that stupid. The teeps have to get the hoods off. Every man wearing a hood is a man out of bounds. They've managed so far by stirring up mobs–but that's ineffectual. Now they're working on this bill in Congress. Senator Waldo's Anti-Immunity Bill. It would outlaw wearing hoods.' Cutter grinned ironically. 'If a man is innocent why shouldn't he want his mind probed? The bill makes wearing a probe shield a felony. People who receive hoods will turn them over to Clearance. There won't be a man in ten thousand who'll keep his hood, if it means prison and confiscation of property.'

'I met Waldo, once. I can't believe he understands what his bill would do. If he could be made to see–'

'Exactly! If he could be made to see. This bill has to be stopped. If it goes through we're licked. And the teeps are in. Somebody has to talk to Waldo and make him see the situation.' Cutter's eyes were bright. 'You know the man. He'll remember you.'

'What do you mean?'

'Franklin, we're sending you back again–to meet Waldo. It's our only chance to stop the bill. And it has to be stopped.'

*

The cruiser roared over the Rockies, brush and tangled forest flashing by below. 'There's a level pasture over to the right,' Cutter said. 'I'll set her down, if I can find it.'

He snapped off the jets. The roar died into silence. They were coasting above the hills.

'To the right,' Franklin said.

Cutter brought the cruiser down in a sweeping glide. 'This will put us within walking distance of Waldo's estate. We'll go the rest of the way on foot.' A shuddering growl shook them as the landing fins dug into the ground—and they were at rest.

Around them tall trees moved faintly with the wind. It was mid-morning. The air was cool and thin. They were high up, still in the mountains, on the Colorado side.

'What are the chances of our reaching him?' Franklin asked.

'Not very good.'

Franklin started. 'Why? Why not?'

Cutter pushed the cruiser door back and leaped out onto the ground. 'Come on.' He helped Franklin out and slammed the door after him. 'Waldo is guarded. He's got a wall of robots around him. That's why we've never tried before. If it weren't crucial we wouldn't be trying now.'

They left the pasture, making their way down the hill along a narrow weed-covered path. 'What are they doing it for?' Franklin asked. 'The teeps. Why do they want to get power?'

'Human nature, I suppose.'

'*Human* nature?'

'The teeps are no different from the Jacobins, the Roundheads, the Nazis, the Bolsheviks. There's always some group that wants to lead mankind—for its own good, of course.'

'Do the teeps believe that?'

'Most teeps believe they're the natural leaders of mankind. Non-telepathic humans are an inferior species. Teeps are the next step up, *homo superior*. And because they're superior, it's natural they should lead. Make all the decisions for us.'

'And you don't agree,' Franklin said.

'The teeps are different from us—but that doesn't mean they're superior. A telepathic faculty doesn't imply general superiority. The teeps aren't a superior race. They're human beings with a special ability. But that doesn't give them a right to tell us what to do. It's not a new problem.'

'Who should lead mankind, then?' Franklin asked. 'Who should be the leaders?'

'*Nobody* should lead mankind. It should lead itself.' Cutter leaned forward suddenly, body tense.

'We're almost there. Waldo's estate is directly ahead. Get ready. Everything depends on the next few minutes.'

'A few robot guards.' Cutter lowered his binoculars. 'But that's not what's worrying me. If Waldo has a teep nearby, he'll detect our hoods.'

'And we can't take them off.'

'No. The whole thing would be out, passed from teep to teep.' Cutter moved cautiously forward. 'The robots will stop us and demand identification. We'll have to count on your Director's clip.'

They left the bushes, crossing the open field toward the buildings that made up Senator Waldo's estate. They came onto a dirt road and followed it, neither of them speaking, watching the landscape ahead.

'Halt!' A robot guard appeared, streaking toward them across the field 'Identify yourselves!'

Franklin showed his clip. 'I'm Director level. We're here to see the Senator. I'm an old friend.'

Automatic relays clicked as the robot studied the identification clip. 'From the Director level?'

'That's right,' Franklin said, becoming uneasy.

'Get out of the way,' Cutter said impatiently. 'We don't have any time to waste.'

The robot withdrew uncertainly. 'Sorry to have stopped you, sir. The Senator is inside the main building. Directly ahead.'

'All right.' Cutter and Franklin advanced past the robot. Sweat stood out on Cutter's round face. 'We made it,' he murmured. 'Now let's hope there aren't any teeps inside.'

Franklin reached the porch. He stepped slowly up, Cutter behind him. At the door he halted, glancing at the smaller man. 'Shall I–'

'Go ahead.' Cutter was tense. 'Let's get right inside. It's safer.'

Franklin raised his hand. The door clicked sharply as its lens photographed him and checked his image. Franklin prayed silently. If the Clearance alarm had been sent out this far–

The door melted.

'Inside,' Cutter said quickly.

Franklin entered, looking around in the semi-darkness. He blinked, adjusting to the dim light of the hall. Somebody was coming toward him. A shape, a small shape, coming rapidly, lithely. Was it Waldo?

A lank, sallow-faced youth entered the hall, a fixed smile on his face. 'Good morning, Doctor Franklin,' he said. He raised his Slem-gun and fired.

Cutter and Ernest Abbud stared down at the oozing mass that had been Doctor Franklin. Neither of them spoke. Finally Cutter raised his hand, his face drained of color.

'Was that necessary?'

Abbud shifted, suddenly conscious of him. 'Why not?' He shrugged, the Slem-gun pointed at Cutter's stomach. 'He was an old man. He wouldn't have lasted long in the protective-custody camp.'

Cutter took out his package of cigarettes and lit up slowly, his eyes on the youth's face. He had never seen Ernest Abbud before. But he knew who he was. He watched the sallow-faced youth kick idly at the remains on the floor.

'Then Waldo is a teep,' Cutter said.

'Yes.'

'Franklin was wrong. He *does* have full understanding of his bill.'

'Of course! The Anti-Immunity Bill is an integral part of our activity.' Abbud waved the snout of the Slem-gun. 'Remove your hood. I can't scan you–and it makes me uneasy.'

Cutter hesitated. He dropped his cigarette thoughtfully to the floor and crushed it underfoot. 'What are you doing here? You usually hang out in New York. This is a long way out here.'

Abbud smiled. 'We picked up Doctor Franklin's thoughts as he entered the girl's car–before she gave him the hood. She waited too long. We got a distinct visual image of her, seen from the back seat, of course. But she turned around to give him the hood. Two hours ago Clearance picked her up. She knew a great deal–our first real contact. We were able to locate the factory and round up most of the workers.'

'Oh?' Cutter murmured.

'They're in protective custody. Their hoods are gone–and the supply stored for distribution. The stampers have been dismantled. As far as I know we have all the group. You're the last one.'

'Then does it matter if I keep my hood?'

Abbud's eyes flickered. 'Take it off. I want to scan you–Mister Hood Maker.'

Cutter grunted. 'What do you mean?'

'Several of your men gave us images of you–and details of your trip here. I came out personally, notifying Waldo through our relay system in advance. I wanted to be here myself.'

'Why?'

'It's an occasion. A great occasion.'

'What position do *you* hold?' Cutter demanded.

Abbud's sallow face turned ugly. 'Come on! Off with the hood! I could blast you now. But I want to scan you first.'

'All right. I'll take it off. You can scan me, if you want. Probe all the way down.' Cutter paused, reflecting soberly. 'It's your funeral.'

'What do you mean?'

Cutter removed his hood, tossing it onto a table by the door. 'Well? What do you see? What do I know–*that none of the others knew?*'

For a moment Abbud was silent.

Suddenly his face twitched, his mouth working. The Slem-gun swayed. Abbud staggered, a violent shudder leaping through his lank frame. He gaped at Cutter in rising horror.

'I learned it only recently,' Cutter said. 'In our lab. I didn't want to use it–but you forced me to take off my hood. I always considered the alloy my most important discovery–until this. In some ways, this is even more important. Don't you agree?'

Abbud said nothing. His face was a sickly gray. His lips moved but no sound came.

'I had a hunch–and I played it for all it was worth. I knew you telepaths were born from a single group, resulting from an accident–the Madagascar hydrogen explosion. That made me think. Most mutants, that we know of, are thrown off universally by the species that's reached the mutation stage. Not a single group in one area. The whole world, wherever the species exists.

'Damage to the germ plasma of a specific group of humans is the cause of your existence. You weren't a mutant in the sense that you represented a natural development of the evolutionary process. In no sense could it be said that homo sapiens had reached the mutation stage. So perhaps you weren't a mutant.

'I began to make studies, some biological, some merely statistical. Sociological research. We began correlating facts on you, on each member of your group we could locate. How old you were. What you were doing for a living. How many were married. Number of children. After a while I came across the facts you're scanning right now.'

Cutter leaned toward Abbud, watching the youth intently.

'You're not a true mutant, Abbud. Your group exists because of a chance explosion. You're different from us because of damage to the reproductive apparatus of your parents. You lack one specific characteristic that true mutants possess.' A faint smile twitched across Cutter's features. 'A lot of you are married. But not one birth has been reported. Not one birth! Not a single teep child! You can't reproduce, Abbud. You're *sterile*, the whole lot of you. When you die there won't be any more.

'You're not mutants. You're freaks!'

Abbud grunted hoarsely, his body trembling. 'I see this, in your mind.' He pulled himself together with an effort. 'And you've kept this secret, have you? You're the only one who knows?'

'Somebody else knows,' Cutter said.

'Who?'

'*You* know. You scanned me. And since you're a teep, all the others–'

Abbud fired, the Slem-gun digging frantically into his own middle. He dissolved, showering in a rain of fragments. Cutter moved back, his hands over his face. He closed his eyes, holding his breath.

When he looked again there was nothing.

Cutter shook his head. 'Too late, Abbud. Not fast enough. Scanning is instant–and Waldo is within range. The relay system . . . And even if they missed *you*, they can't avoid picking me up.'

A sound. Cutter turned. Clearance agents were moving rapidly into the hall, glancing down at the remains on the floor and up at Cutter.

Director Ross covered Cutter uncertainly, confused and shaken. 'What happened? Where–'

'Scan him!' Peters snapped. 'Get a teep in here quick. Bring Waldo in. Find out what happened.'

Cutter grinned ironically. 'Sure,' he said, nodding shakily. He sagged with relief. 'Scan me. I have nothing to hide. Get a teep in here for a probe–if you can find any . . .'

OF WITHERED APPLES

Something was tapping on the window. Blowing up against the pane, again and again. Carried by the wind. Tapping faintly, insistently.

Lori, sitting on the couch, pretended not to hear. She gripped her book tightly and turned a page. The tapping came again, louder and more imperative. It could not be ignored.

'Darn!' Lori said, throwing her book down on the coffee table and hurrying to the window. She grasped the heavy brass handles and lifted.

For a moment the window resisted. Then, with a protesting groan, it reluctantly rose. Cold autumn air rushed into the room. The bit of leaf ceased tapping and swirled against the woman's throat, dancing to the floor.

Lori picked the leaf up. It was old and brown. Her heart skipped a beat as she slipped the leaf into the pocket of her jeans. Against her loins the leaf cut and tingled, a little hard point piercing her smooth skin and sending exciting shivers up and down her spine. She stood at the open window a moment, sniffing the air. The air was full of the presence of trees and rocks, of great boulders and remote places. It was time–time to go again. She touched the leaf. She was *wanted.*

Quickly Lori left the big living room, hurrying through the hall into the dining room. The dining room was empty. A few chords of laughter drifted from the kitchen. Lori pushed the kitchen door open. 'Steve?'

Her husband and his father were sitting around the kitchen

table, smoking their cigars and drinking steaming black coffee. 'What is it?' Steve demanded, frowning at his young wife. 'Ed and I are in the middle of business.'

'I–I want to ask you something.'

The two men gazed at her, brown-haired Steven, his dark eyes full of the stubborn dignity of New England men, and his father, silent and withdrawn in *her* presence. Ed Patterson scarcely noticed her. He rustled through a sheaf of feed bills, his broad back turned toward her.

'What is it?' Steve demanded impatiently. 'What do you want? Can't it wait?'

'I have to go,' Lori blurted.

'Go where?'

'Outside.' Anxiety flooded over her. 'This is the last time. I promise. I won't go again, after this. Okay?' She tried to smile, but her heart was pounding too hard. 'Please let me, Steve.'

'Where does she go?' Ed rumbled.

Steve grunted in annoyance. 'Up in the hills. Some old abandoned place up there.'

Ed's gray eyes flickered. 'Abandoned farm?'

'Yes. You know it?'

'The old Rickley farm. Rickley moved away years ago. Couldn't get anything to grow, not up there. Ground's all rocks. Bad soil. A lot of clay and stones. The place is all overgrown, tumbled down.'

'What kind of farm was it?'

'Orchard. Fruit orchard. Never yielded a damn thing. Thin old trees. Waste of effort.'

Steve looked at his pocket watch. 'You'll be back in time to fix dinner?'

'Yes!' Lori moved toward the door. 'Then I can go?'

Steve's face twisted as he made up his mind. Lori waited impatiently, scarcely breathing. She had never got used to Vermont men and their slow, deliberate way. Boston people were quite different. And her group had been more the college youths, dances and talk, and late laughter.

'Why do you go up there?' Steve grumbled.

'Don't ask me, Steve. Just let me go. This is the last time.' She writhed in agony. She clenched her fists. 'Please!'

Steve looked out the window. The cold autumn wind swirled through the trees. 'All right. But it's going to snow. I don't see why you want to–'

Lori ran to get her coat from the closet. 'I'll be back to fix dinner!' she shouted joyfully. She hurried to the front porch, buttoning her coat, her heart racing. Her cheeks were flushed a deep, excited red as she closed the door behind her, her blood pounding in her veins.

Cold wind whipped against her, rumpling her hair, plucking at her body. She took a deep breath of the wind and started down the steps.

She walked rapidly onto the field, toward the bleak line of hills beyond. Except for the wind there was no sound. She patted her pocket. The dry leaf broke and dug hungrily into her.

'I'm coming . . .' she whispered, a little awed and frightened. 'I'm on my way . . .'

Higher and higher the woman climbed. She passed through a deep cleft between two rocky ridges. Huge roots from old stumps spurted out on all sides. She followed a dried-up creek bed, winding and turning.

After a time low mists began to blow about her. At the top of the ridge she halted, breathing deeply, looking back the way she had come.

A few drops of rain stirred the leaves around her. Again the wind moved through the great dead trees along the ridge. Lori turned and started on, her head down, hands in her coat pockets.

She was on a rocky field, overgrown with weeds and dead grass. After a time she came to a ruined fence, broken and rotting. She stepped over it. She passed a tumbled-down well, half filled with stones and earth.

Her heart beat quickly, fluttering with nervous excitement. She was almost there. She passed the remains of a building, sagging timbers and broken glass, a few ruined pieces of furniture strewn nearby. An old automobile tire caked and cracked. Some damp rags heaped over rusty, bent bedsprings.

And there it was–directly ahead.

Along the edge of the field was a grove of ancient trees. Lifeless trees, withered and dead, their thin, blackened stalks rising up leaflessly. Broken sticks stuck in the hard ground. Row after row of dead trees, some bent and leaning, torn loose from the rocky soil by the unending wind.

Lori crossed the field to the trees, her lungs laboring painfully. The wind surged against her without respite, whipping the foul-smelling mists into her nostrils and face. Her smooth skin was damp and shiny with the mist. She coughed and hurried on, stepping over the rocks and clods of earth, trembling with fear and anticipation.

She circled around the grove of trees, almost to the edge of the ridge. Carefully, she stepped among the sliding heaps of rocks. Then–

She stopped, rigid. Her chest rose and fell with the effort of breathing. 'I came,' she gasped.

For a long time she gazed at the withered old apple tree. She could not take her eyes from it. The sight of the ancient tree fascinated and repelled her. It was the only one alive, the only tree of all the grove still living. All the others were dead, dried-up. They had lost the struggle. But this tree still clung to life.

The tree was hard and barren. Only a few dark leaves hung from it–and some withered apples, dried and seasoned by the wind and mists. They had stayed there, on the branches, forgotten and abandoned. The ground around the tree was cracked and bleak. Stones and decayed heaps of old leaves in ragged clumps.

'I came,' Lori said again. She took the leaf from her pocket and held it cautiously out. 'This tapped at the window. I knew when I heard it.' She smiled mischievously, her red lips curling. 'It tapped and tapped, trying to get in. I ignored it. It was so–so impetuous. It annoyed me.'

The tree swayed ominously. Its gnarled branches rubbed together. Something in the sound made Lori pull away. Terror rushed through her. She hurried back along the ridge, scrambling frantically out of reach.

'Don't,' she whispered. '*Please.*'

The wind ceased. The tree became silent. For a long time Lori watched it apprehensively.

Night was coming. The sky was darkening rapidly. A burst of frigid wind struck her, half turning her around. She shuddered, bracing herself against it, pulling her long coat around her. Far below, the floor of the valley was disappearing into shadow, into the vast cloud of night.

In the darkening mists the tree was stern and menacing, more ominous than usual. A few leaves blew from it, drifting and swirling with the wind. A leaf blew past her and she tried to catch it. The leaf escaped, dancing back toward the tree. Lori followed a little way and then stopped, gasping and laughing.

'No,' she said firmly, her hands on her hips. 'I won't.'

There was silence. Suddenly the heaps of decayed leaves blew up in a furious circle around the tree. They quieted down, settling back.

'No,' Lori said. 'I'm not afraid of you. You can't hurt me.' But her heart was hammering with fear. She moved back farther away.

The tree remained silent. Its wiry branches were motionless.

Lori regained her courage. 'This is the last time I can come,' she said. 'Steve says I can't come any more. He doesn't like it.'

She waited, but the tree did not respond.

'They're sitting in the kitchen. The two of them. Smoking cigars and drinking coffee. Adding up feed bills.' She wrinkled her nose. 'That's all they ever do. Add and subtract feed bills. Figure and figure. Profit and loss. Government taxes. Depreciation on the equipment.'

The tree did not stir.

Lori shivered. A little more rain fell, big icy drops that slid down her cheeks, down the back of her neck and inside her heavy coat.

She moved closer to the tree. 'I won't be back. I won't see you again. This is the last time. I wanted to tell you . . .'

The tree moved. Its branches whipped into sudden life. Lori felt something hard and thin cut across her shoulder. Something caught her around the waist, tugging her forward.

She struggled desperately, trying to pull herself free. Suddenly the tree released her. She stumbled back, laughing and trembling with fear. 'No!' she gasped. 'You can't have me!' She hurried to the edge of the ridge. 'You'll never get me again. Understand? And I'm not afraid of you!'

She stood, waiting and watching, trembling with cold and fear. Suddenly she turned and fled, down the side of the ridge, sliding and falling on the loose stones. Blind terror gripped her. She ran on and on, down the steep slope, grabbing at roots and weeds–

Something rolled beside her shoe. Something small and hard. She bent down and picked it up.

It was a little dried apple.

Lori gazed back up the slope at the tree. The tree was almost lost in the swirling mists. It stood, jutting up against the black sky, a hard unmoving pillar.

Lori put the apple in her coat pocket and continued down the side of the hill. When she reached the floor of the valley she took the apple out of her pocket.

It was late. A deep hunger began to gnaw inside her. She thought suddenly of dinner, the warm kitchen, the white tablecloth. Steaming stew and biscuits.

As she walked she nibbled on the little apple.

Lori sat up in bed, the covers falling away from her. The house was dark and silent. A few night noises sounded faintly, far off. It was past midnight. Beside her Steven slept quietly, turned over on his side.

What had wakened her? Lori pushed her dark hair back out of her eyes, shaking her head. What–

A spasm of pain burst loose inside her. She gasped and put her hand to her stomach. For a time she wrestled silently, jaws locked, swaying back and forth.

The pain went away. Lori sank back. She cried out, a faint, thin cry. 'Steve–'

Steven stirred. He turned over a little, grunting in his sleep.

The pain came again. Harder. She fell forward on her face, writhing in agony. The pain ripped at her, tearing at her belly. She screamed, a shrill wail of fear and pain.

Steve sat up. 'For God's sake–' He rubbed his eyes and snapped on the lamp. 'What the hell–'

Lori lay on her side, gasping and moaning, her eyes staring, knotted fists pressed into her stomach. The pain twisted and seared, devouring her, eating into her.

'Lori!' Steven grated. 'What is it?'

She screamed. Again and again. Until the house rocked with echoes. She slid from the bed, onto the floor, her body writhing and jerking, her face unrecognizable.

Ed came hurrying into the room, pulling his bathrobe around him. 'What's going on?'

The two men stared helplessly down at the woman on the floor.

'Good God,' Ed said. He closed his eyes.

The day was cold and dark. Snow fell silently over the streets and houses, over the red brick county hospital building. Doctor Blair walked slowly up the gravel path to his Ford car. He slid inside and turned the ignition key. The motor leaped alive, and he let the brake out.

'I'll call you later,' Doctor Blair said. 'There are certain particulars.'

'I know,' Steve muttered. He was still dazed. His face was gray and puffy from lack of sleep.

'I left some sedatives for you. Try to get a little rest.'

'You think,' Steve asked suddenly, 'if we had called you earlier–'

'No.' Blair glanced up at him sympathetically. 'I don't. In a thing like that, there's not much chance. Not after it's burst.'

'Then it *was* appendicitis?'

Blair nodded. 'Yes.'

'If we hadn't been so damn far out,' Steve said bitterly. 'Stuck out in the country. No hospital. Nothing. Miles from town. And we didn't realize at first–'

'Well, it's over now.' The upright Ford moved forward a little. All at once a thought came to the Doctor. 'One more thing.'

'What is it?' Steve said dully.

Blair hesitated. 'Post mortems–very unfortunate. I don't think there's any reason for one in this case. I'm certain in my own mind . . . But I wanted to ask–'

'What is it?'

'Is there anything the girl might have swallowed? Did she put things in her mouth? Needles–while she was sewing? Pins, coins, anything like that? Seeds? Did she ever eat watermelon? Sometimes the appendix–'

'No.' Steve shook his head wearily. 'I don't know.'

'It was just a thought.' Doctor Blair drove slowly off down the narrow tree-lined street, leaving two dark streaks, two soiled lines that marred the packed, glistening snow.

Spring came, warm and sunny. The ground turned black and rich. Overhead the sun shone, a hot white orb, full of strength.

'Stop here,' Steve murmured.

Ed Patterson brought the car to a halt at the side of the street. He turned off the motor. The two men sat in silence, neither of them speaking.

At the end of the street children were playing. A high school boy was mowing a lawn, pushing the machine over wet grass. The street was dark in the shade of the great trees growing along each side.

'Nice,' Ed said.

Steve nodded without answering. Moodily, he watched a young girl walking by, a shopping bag under her arm. The girl climbed the stairs of a porch and disappeared into an old-fashioned yellow house.

Steve pushed the car door open. 'Come on. Let's get it over with.'

Ed lifted the wreath of flowers from the back seat and put them in his son's lap. 'You'll have to carry it. It's your job.'

'All right.' Steve grabbed the flowers and stepped out onto the pavement.

The two men walked up the street together, silent and thoughtful.

'It's been seven or eight months, now,' Steve said abruptly.

'At least.' Ed lit a cigar as they walked along, puffing clouds of gray smoke around them. 'Maybe a little more.'

'I never should have brought her up here. She lived in town all her life. She didn't know anything about the country.'

'It would have happened anyhow.'

'If we had been closer to a hospital–'

'The doctor said it wouldn't have made any difference. Even if we'd called him right away instead of waiting until morning.' They came to the corner and turned. 'And as you know–'

'Forget it,' Steve said, suddenly tense.

The sounds of the children had fallen behind them. The houses had thinned out. Their footsteps rang out against the pavement as they walked along.

'We're almost there,' Steve said.

They came to a rise. Beyond the rise was a heavy brass fence, running the length of a small field. A green field, neat and even. With carefully placed plaques of white marble criss-crossing it.

'Here we are,' Steve said tightly.

'They keep it nice.'

'Can we get in from this side?'

'We can try.' Ed started along the brass fence, looking for a gate.

Suddenly Steve halted, grunting. He stared across the field, his face white. '*Look.*'

'What is it?' Ed took off his glasses to see. 'What are you looking at?'

'I was right.' Steve's voice was low and indistinct. 'I thought there was something. Last time we were here . . . I saw . . . You see it?'

'I'm not sure. I see the tree, if that's what you mean.'

In the center of the neat green field the little apple tree rose proudly. Its bright leaves sparkled in the warm sunlight. The young tree was strong and very healthy. It swayed confidently with the wind, its supple trunk moist with sweet spring sap.

'They're *red*,' Steve said softly. 'They're already red. How the hell can they be red? It's only April. How the hell can they be red so soon?'

'I don't know,' Ed said. 'I don't know anything about apples.' A strange chill moved through him. But graveyards always made him uncomfortable. 'Maybe we ought to go.'

'Her cheeks were that color,' Steve said, his voice low. 'When she had been running. Remember?'

The two men gazed uneasily at the little apple tree, its shiny red fruit glistening in the spring sunlight, branches moving gently with the wind.

'I remember, all right,' Ed said grimly. 'Come on.' He took his son's arm insistently, the wreath of flowers forgotten. 'Come on, Steve. Let's get out of here.'

HUMAN IS

Jill Herrick's blue eyes filled with tears. She gazed at her husband in unspeakable horror. 'You're–you're hideous!' she wailed.

Lester Herrick continued working, arranging heaps of notes and graphs in precise piles.

'Hideous,' he stated, 'is a value judgment. It contains no factual information.' He sent a report tape on Centauran parasitic life whizzing through the desk scanner. 'Merely an opinion. An expression of emotion, nothing more.'

Jill stumbled back to the kitchen. Listlessly, she waved her hand to trip the stove into activity. Conveyor belts in the wall hummed to life, hurrying the food from the underground storage lockers for the evening meal.

She turned to face her husband one last time. 'Not even a *little* while?' she begged. 'Not even–'

'Not even for a month. When he comes you can tell him. If you haven't the courage, I'll do it. I can't have a child running around here. I have too much work to do. This report on Betelgeuse XI is due in ten days.' Lester dropped a spool on Fomalhautan fossil implements into the scanner. 'What's the matter with your brother? Why can't he take care of his own child?'

Jill dabbed at swollen eyes. 'Don't you understand? I *want* Gus here! I begged Frank to let him come. And now you–'

'I'll be glad when he's old enough to be turned over to the Government.' Lester's thin face twisted in annoyance. 'Damn it, Jill, isn't dinner ready yet? It's been ten minutes! What's wrong with that stove?'

'It's almost ready.' The stove showed a red signal light. The robant waiter had come out of the wall and was waiting expectantly to take the food.

Jill sat down and blew her small nose violently. In the living room, Lester worked on unperturbed. His work. His research. Day after day. Lester was getting ahead; there was no doubt of that. His lean body was bent like a coiled spring over the tape scanner, cold gray eyes taking in the information feverishly, analyzing, appraising, his conceptual faculties operating like well-greased machinery.

Jill's lips trembled in misery and resentment. Gus–little Gus. How could she tell him? Fresh tears welled up in her eyes. Never to see the chubby little fellow again. He could never come back–because his childish laughter and play bothered Lester. Interfered with his research.

The stove clicked to green. The food slid out, into the arms of the robant. Soft chimes sounded to announce dinner.

'I hear it,' Lester grated. He snapped off the scanner and got to his feet. 'I suppose he'll come while we're eating.'

'I can vid Frank and ask–'

'No. Might as well get it over with.' Lester nodded impatiently to the robant. 'All right. Put it down.' His thin lips set in an angry line. 'Damn it, don't dawdle! I want to get back to my work!'

Jill bit back the tears.

Little Gus came trailing into the house as they were finishing dinner.

Jill gave a cry of joy. 'Gussie!' She ran to sweep him up in her arms. 'I'm so glad to see you!'

'Watch out for my tiger,' Gus muttered. He dropped his little gray kitten onto the rug and it rushed off, under the couch. 'He's hiding.'

Lester's eyes flickered as he studied the little boy and the tip of gray tail extending from under the couch.

'Why do you call it a tiger? It's nothing but an alley cat.'

Gus looked hurt. He scowled. 'He's a tiger. He's got stripes.'

'Tigers are yellow and a great deal bigger. You might as well learn to classify things by their correct names.'

'Lester, please–' Jill pleaded.

'Be quiet,' her husband said crossly. 'Gus is old enough to shed childish illusions and develop a realistic orientation. What's wrong with the psych testers? Don't they straighten this sort of nonsense out?'

Gus ran and snatched up his tiger. 'You leave him alone!'

Lester contemplated the kitten. A strange, cold smile played about his lips. 'Come down to the lab some time, Gus. We'll show you lots of cats. We use them in our research. Cats, guinea pigs, rabbits–'

'Lester!' Jill gasped. 'How can you!'

Lester laughed thinly. Abruptly he broke off and returned to his desk. 'Now clear out of here. I have to finish these reports. And don't forget to tell Gus.'

Gus got excited. 'Tell me what?' His cheeks flushed. His eyes sparkled. 'What is it? Something for me? A *secret*?'

Jill's heart was like lead. She put her hand heavily on the child's shoulder. 'Come on, Gus. We'll go sit out in the garden and I'll tell you. Bring–bring your tiger.'

A click. The emergency vidsender lit up. Instantly Lester was on his feet. 'Be quiet!' He ran to the sender, breathing rapidly. 'Nobody speak!'

Jill and Gus paused at the door. A confidential message was sliding from the slot into the dish. Lester grabbed it up and broke the seal. He studied it intently.

'What is it?' Jill asked. 'Anything bad?'

'Bad?' Lester's face shone with a deep inner glow. 'No, not bad at all.' He glanced at his watch. 'Just time. Let's see, I'll need–'

'What is it?'

'I'm going on a trip. I'll be gone two or three weeks. Rexor IV is into the charted area.'

'Rexor IV? You're going there?' Jill clasped her hands eagerly. 'Oh, I've always wanted to see an old system, old ruins and cities! Lester, can I come along? Can I go with you? We never took a vacation, and you always promised–'

Lester Herrick stared at his wife in amazement. 'You?' he said. '*You* go along?' He laughed unpleasantly. 'Now hurry and get my things together. I've been waiting for this a long time.' He rubbed his hands together in satisfaction. 'You can keep the boy here until I'm back. But no longer. Rexor IV! I can hardly wait!'

'You have to make allowances,' Frank said. 'After all, he's a scientist.'

'I don't care,' Jill said. 'I'm leaving him. As soon as he gets back from Rexor IV. I've made up my mind.'

Her brother was silent, deep in thought. He stretched his feet out, onto the lawn of the little garden. 'Well, if you leave him you'll be free to marry again. You're still classed as sexually adequate, aren't you?'

Jill nodded firmly. 'You bet I am. I wouldn't have any trouble. Maybe I can find somebody who likes children.'

'You think a lot of children,' Frank perceived. 'Gus loves to go visit you. But he doesn't like Lester. Les needles him.'

'I know. This past week has been heaven, with him gone.' Jill patted her soft blonde hair, blushing prettily. 'I've had fun. Makes me feel alive again.'

'When'll he be back?'

'Any day.' Jill clenched her small fists. 'We've been married five years and every year it's worse. He's so–so inhuman. Utterly cold and ruthless. Him and his work. Day and night.'

'Les is ambitious. He wants to get to the top in his field.' Frank lit a cigarette lazily. 'A pusher. Well, maybe he'll do it. What's he in?'

'Toxicology. He works out new poisons for Military. He invented the copper sulphate skin-lime they used against Callisto.'

'It's a small field. Now take me.' Frank leaned contentedly against the wall of the house. 'There are thousands of Clearance lawyers. I could work for years and never create a ripple. I'm content just to be. I do my job. I enjoy it.'

'I wish Lester felt that way.'

'Maybe he'll change.'

'He'll *never* change,' Jill said bitterly. 'I know that, now. That's why I've made up my mind to leave him. He'll always be the same.'

Lester Herrick came back from Rexor IV a different man. Beaming happily, he deposited his anti-grav suitcase in the arms of the waiting robant. 'Thank you.'

Jill gasped speechlessly. 'Les! What–'

Lester moved his hat, bowing a little. 'Good day, my dear. You're looking lovely. Your eyes are clear and blue. Sparkling like some virgin lake, fed by mountain streams.' He sniffed. 'Do I smell a delicious repast warming on the hearth?'

'Oh, Lester.' Jill blinked uncertainly, faint hope swelling in her bosom. 'Lester, what's happened to you? You're so–so different.'

'Am I, my dear?' Lester moved about the house, touching things and sighing. 'What a dear little house. So sweet and friendly. You don't know how wonderful it is to be here. Believe me.'

'I'm afraid to believe it,' Jill said.

'Believe what?'

'That you mean all this. That you're not the way you were. The way you've always been.'

'What way is that?'

'Mean. Mean and cruel.'

'I?' Lester frowned, rubbing his lip. 'Hmm. Interesting.' He brightened. 'Well, that's all in the past. What's for dinner? I'm faint with hunger.'

Jill eyed him uncertainly as she moved into the kitchen. 'Anything you want, Lester. You know our stove covers the maximum select-list.'

'Of course.' Lester coughed rapidly. 'Well, shall we try sirloin steak, medium, smothered in onions? With mushroom sauce. And white rolls. With hot coffee. Perhaps ice cream and apple pie for dessert.'

'You never seemed to care much about food,' Jill said thoughtfully.

'Oh?'

'You always said you hoped eventually they'd make intravenous intake universally applicable.' She studied her husband intently. 'Lester, what's happened?'

'Nothing. Nothing at all.' Lester carelessly took his pipe out and lit it rapidly, somewhat awkwardly. Bits of tobacco drifted to the rug. He bent nervously down and tried to pick them up again. 'Please go about your tasks and don't mind me. Perhaps I can help you prepare–that is, can I do anything to help?'

'No,' Jill said. 'I can do it. You go ahead with your work, if you want.'

'Work?'

'Your research. In toxins.'

'Toxins!' Lester showed confusion. 'Well, for heaven's sake! Toxins. Devil take it!'

'What, dear?'

'I mean, I really feel too tired, just now. I'll work later.' Lester moved vaguely around the room. 'I think I'll just sit and enjoy being home again. Off that awful Rexor IV.'

'Was it awful?'

'Horrible.' A spasm of disgust crossed Lester's face. 'Dry and dead. Ancient. Squeezed to a pulp by wind and sun. A dreadful place, my dear.'

'I'm sorry to hear that. I always wanted to visit it.'

'Heaven forbid!' Lester cried feelingly. 'You stay right here, my dear. With me. The–the two of us.' His eyes wandered around the room. 'Two, yes. Terra is a wonderful planet. Moist and full of life.' He beamed happily. 'Just right.'

'I don't understand it,' Jill said.

'Repeat all the things you remember,' Frank said. His robot pencil poised itself alertly. 'The changes you've noticed in him. I'm curious.'

'Why?'

'No reason. Go on. You say you sensed it right away? That he was different?'

'I noticed it at once. The expression on his face. Not that hard, practical look. A sort of mellow look. Relaxed. Tolerant. A sort of calmness.'

'I see,' Frank said. 'What else?'

Jill peered nervously through the back door into the house. 'He can't hear us, can he?'

'No. He's inside playing with Gus. In the living room. They're Venusian otter-men today. Your husband built an otter slide down at his lab. I saw him unwrapping it.'

'His talk.'

'His what?'

'The way he talks. His choice of words. Words he never used before. Whole new phrases. Metaphors. I never heard him use a metaphor in all our five years together. He said metaphors were inexact. Misleading. And–'

'And what?' The pencil scratched busily.

'And they're *strange* words. Old words. Words you don't hear any more.'

'Archaic phraseology?' Frank asked tensely.

'Yes.' Jill paced back and forth across the small lawn, her hands in the pockets of her plastic shorts. 'Formal words. Like something–'

'Something out of a book?'

'Exactly! You've noticed it?'

'I noticed it.' Frank's face was grim. 'Go on.'

Jill stopped pacing. 'What's on your mind? Do you have a theory?'

'I want to know more facts.'

She reflected. 'He plays. With Gus. He plays and jokes. And he–he eats.'

'Didn't he eat before?'

'Not like he does now. Now he *loves* food. He goes in the kitchen and tries endless combinations. He and the stove get together and cook up all sorts of weird things.'

'I thought he'd put on weight.'

'He's gained ten pounds. He eats, smiles and laughs. He's constantly polite.' Jill glanced away coyly. 'He's even–romantic! He always said *that* was irrational. And he's not interested in his work. His research in toxins.'

'I see.' Frank chewed his lip. 'Anything more?'

'One thing puzzles me very much. I've noticed it again and again.'

'What is it?'

'He seems to have strange lapses of–'

A burst of laughter. Lester Herrick, eyes bright with merriment, came rushing out of the house, little Gus close behind.

'We have an announcement!' Lester cried.

'An announzelmen,' Gus echoed.

Frank folded his notes up and slid them into his coat pocket. The pencil hurried after them. He got slowly to his feet. 'What is it?'

'You make it,' Lester said, taking little Gus's hand and leading him forward.

Gus's plump face screwed up in concentration. 'I'm going to come live with you,' he stated. Anxiously he watched Jill's expression. 'Lester says I can. Can I? Can I, Aunt Jill?'

Her heart flooded with incredible joy. She glanced from Gus to Lester. 'Do you–do you really mean it?' Her voice was almost inaudible.

Lester put his arm around her, holding her close to him. 'Of course, we mean it,' he said gently. His eyes were warm and understanding. 'We wouldn't tease you, my dear.'

'No teasing!' Gus shouted excitedly. 'No more teasing!' He and Lester and Jill drew close together. 'Never again!'

Frank stood a little way off, his face grim. Jill noticed him and broke away abruptly. 'What is it?' she faltered. 'Is anything–'

'When you're quite finished,' Frank said to Lester Herrick, 'I'd like you to come with me.'

A chill clutched Jill's heart. 'What is it? Can I come, too?'

Frank shook his head. He moved toward Lester ominously. 'Come on, Herrick. Let's go. You and I are going to take a little trip.'

The three Federal Clearance Agents took up positions a few feet from Lester Herrick, vibro-tubes gripped alertly.

Clearance Director Douglas studied Herrick for a long time. 'You're sure?' he said finally.

'Absolutely,' Frank stated.

'When did he get back from Rexor IV?'

'A week ago.'

'And the change was noticeable at once?'

'His wife noticed it as soon as she saw him. There's no doubt it occurred on Rexor.' Frank paused significantly. 'And you know what that means.'

'I know.' Douglas walked slowly around the seated man, examining him from every angle.

Lester Herrick sat quietly, his coat neatly folded across his knee. He rested his hands on his ivory-topped cane, his face calm and expressionless. He wore a soft gray suit, a subdued necktie, French cuffs, and shiny black shoes. He said nothing.

'Their methods are simple and exact,' Douglas said. 'The original psychic contents are removed and stored–in some sort of suspension. The interjection of the substitute contents is instantaneous. Lester Herrick was probably poking around the Rexor city ruins, ignoring the safety precautions–shield or manual screen–and they got him.'

The seated man stirred. 'I'd like very much to communicate with Jill,' he murmured. 'She surely is becoming anxious.'

Frank turned away, face choked with revulsion. 'God. It's still pretending.'

Director Douglas restrained himself with the greatest effort. 'It's certainly an amazing thing. No physical changes. You could look at it and never know.' He moved toward the seated man, his face hard. 'Listen to me, whatever you call yourself. Can you understand what I say?'

'Of course,' Lester Herrick answered.

'Did you really think you'd get away with it? We caught the others–the ones before you. All ten of them. Even before they got here.' Douglas grinned coldly. 'Vibro-rayed them one after another.'

The color left Lester Herrick's face. Sweat came out on his forehead. He wiped it away with a silk handkerchief from his breast pocket. 'Oh?' he murmured.

'You're not fooling us. All Terra is alerted for you Rexorians. I'm surprised you got off Rexor at all. Herrick must have been extremely careless. We stopped the others aboard ship. Fried them out in deep space.'

'Herrick had a private ship,' the seated man murmured. 'He bypassed the check station going in. No record of his arrival existed. He was never checked.'

'*Fry it!*' Douglas grated. The three Clearance agents lifted their tubes, moving forward.

'No.' Frank shook his head. 'We can't. It's a bad situation.'

'What do you mean? Why can't we? We fried the others–'

'They were caught in deep space. This is Terra. Terran law, not military law, applies.' Frank waved toward the seated man. 'And it's in a human body. It comes under regular civil laws. We've got to *prove* it's not Lester Herrick–that it's a Rexorian infiltrator. It's going to be tough. But it can be done.'

'How?'

'His wife. Herrick's wife. Her testimony. Jill Herrick can assert the difference between Lester Herrick and this thing. She knows–and I think we can make it stand up in court.'

It was late afternoon. Frank drove his surface cruiser slowly along. Neither he nor Jill spoke.

'So that's it,' Jill said at last. Her face was gray. Her eyes dry and bright, without emotion. 'I knew it was too good to be true.' She tried to smile. 'It seemed so wonderful.'

'I know,' Frank said. 'It's a terrible damn thing. If only–'

'*Why?*' Jill said. 'Why did he–did it do this? Why did it take Lester's body?'

'Rexor IV is old. Dead. A dying planet. Life is dying out.'

'I remember, now. He–it said something like that. Something about Rexor. That it was glad to get away.'

'The Rexorians are an old race. The few that remain are feeble. They've been trying to migrate for centuries. But their bodies are too weak. Some tried to migrate to Venus–and died instantly. They worked out this system about a century ago.'

'But it knows so much. About us. It speaks our language.'

'Not quite. The changes you mentioned. The odd diction. You see, the Rexorians have only a vague knowledge of human beings. A sort of ideal abstraction, taken from Terran objects that have found their way to Rexor. Books mostly. Secondary data like that. The Rexorian idea of Terra is based on centuries-old Terran literature. Romantic novels from our past. Language, custom, manners from old Terran books.

'That accounts for the strange archaic quality to *it*. It had studied Terra, all right. But in an indirect and misleading way.' Frank grinned wryly. 'The Rexorians are two hundred years behind the times–which is a break for us. That's how we're able to detect them.'

'Is this sort of thing–common? Does it happen often? It seems unbelievable.' Jill rubbed her forehead wearily. 'Dreamlike. It's hard to realize that it's actually happened. I'm just beginning to understand what it means.'

'The galaxy is full of alien life forms. Parasitic and destructive entities. Terran ethics don't extend to them. We have to guard constantly against this sort of thing. Lester went in unsuspectingly–and this thing ousted him and took over his body.'

Frank glanced at his sister. Jill's face was expressionless. A stern little face, wide-eyed, but composed. She sat up straight, staring fixedly ahead, her small hands folded quietly in her lap.

'We can arrange it so you won't have to actually appear in court,' Frank went on. 'You can vid a statement and it'll be presented as evidence. I'm certain your statement will do. The Federal courts will help us all they can, but they have to have *some* evidence to go on.'

Jill was silent.

'What do you say?' Frank asked.

'What happens after the court makes its decision?'

'Then we vibro-ray it. Destroy the Rexorian mind. A Terran patrol ship on Rexor IV sends out a party to locate the–er–original contents.'

Jill gasped. She turned toward her brother in amazement. 'You mean–'

'Oh, yes. Lester is alive. In suspension, somewhere on Rexor. In one of the old city ruins. We'll have to force them to give him up. They won't want to, but they'll do it. They've done it before. Then he'll be back with you. Safe and sound. Just like before. And this horrible nightmare you've been living will be a thing of the past.'

'I see.'

'Here we are.' The cruiser pulled to a halt before the imposing Federal Clearance Building. Frank got quickly out, holding the door for his sister. Jill stepped down slowly. 'Okay?' Frank said.

'Okay.'

When they entered the building, Clearance agents led them through the check screens, down the long corridors. Jill's high heels echoed in the ominous silence.

'Quite a place,' Frank observed.

'It's unfriendly.'

'Consider it a glorified police station.' Frank halted. Before them was a guarded door. 'Here we are.'

'Wait.' Jill pulled back, her face twisting in panic. 'I–'

'We'll wait until you're ready.' Frank signaled to the Clearance agent to leave. 'I understand. It's a bad business.'

Jill stood for a moment, her head down. She took a deep breath, her small fists clenched. Her chin came up, level and steady. 'All right.'

'You ready?'

'Yes.'

Frank opened the door. 'Here we are.'

Director Douglas and the three Clearance agents turned expectantly as Jill and Frank entered. 'Good,' Douglas murmured, with relief. 'I was beginning to get worried.'

The sitting man got slowly to his feet, picking up his coat. He gripped his ivory-headed cane tightly, his hands tense. He said nothing. He watched silently as the woman entered the room, Frank behind her. 'This is Mrs Herrick,' Frank said. 'Jill, this is Clearance Director Douglas.'

'I've heard of you,' Jill said faintly.

'Then you know our work.'

'Yes. I know your work.'

'This is an unfortunate business. It's happened before. I don't know what Frank has told you–'

'He explained the situation.'

'Good.' Douglas was relieved. 'I'm glad of that. It's not easy to explain. You understand, then, what we want. The previous cases were caught in deep space. We vibro-tubed them and got the original contents back. But this time we must work through legal channels.' Douglas picked up a vidtape recorder. 'We will need your statement, Mrs Herrick. Since no physical change has occurred we'll have no direct evidence to make our case. We'll have only your testimony of character alteration to present to the court.'

He held the vidtape recorder out. Jill took it slowly.

'Your statement will undoubtedly be accepted by the court. The court will give us the release we want and then we can go ahead. If everything goes correctly we hope to be able to set up things exactly as they were before.'

Jill was gazing silently at the man standing in the corner with his coat and ivory-headed cane. 'Before?' she said. 'What do you mean?'

'Before the change.'

Jill turned toward Director Douglas. Calmly, she laid the vidtape recorder down on the table. 'What change are you talking about?'

Douglas paled. He licked his lips. All eyes in the room were on Jill. 'The change in *him*.' He pointed at the man.

'Jill!' Frank barked. 'What's the matter with you?' He came quickly toward her. 'What the hell are you doing? You know damn well what change we mean!'

'That's odd,' Jill said thoughtfully. 'I haven't noticed any change.'

Frank and Director Douglas looked at each other. 'I don't get it,' Frank muttered, dazed.

'Mrs Herrick–' Douglas began.

Jill walked over to the man standing quietly in the corner. 'Can we go now, dear?' she asked. She took his arm. 'Or is there some reason why my husband has to stay here?'

The man and woman walked silently along the dark street.

'Come on,' Jill said. 'Let's go home.'

The man glanced at her. 'It's a nice afternoon,' he said. He took a deep breath, filling his lungs. 'Spring is coming–I think. Isn't it?'

Jill nodded.

'I wasn't sure. It's a nice smell. Plants and soil and growing things.'

'Yes.'

'Are we going to walk? Is it far?'

'Not too far.'

The man gazed at her intently, a serious expression on his face. 'I am very indebted to you, my dear,' he said.

Jill nodded.

'I wish to thank you. I must admit I did not expect such a–'

Jill turned abruptly. 'What is your name? Your *real* name.'

The man's gray eyes flickered. He smiled a little, a kind, gentle smile. 'I'm afraid you would not be able to pronounce it. The sounds cannot be formed . . .'

Jill was silent as they walked along, deep in thought. The city lights were coming on all around them. Bright yellow spots in the gloom. 'What are you thinking?' the man asked.

'I was thinking perhaps I will still call you Lester,' Jill said. 'If you don't mind.'

'I don't mind,' the man said. He put his arm around her, drawing her close to him. He gazed down tenderly as they walked through the thickening darkness, between the yellow candles of light that marked the way. 'Anything you wish. Whatever will make you happy.'

ADJUSTMENT TEAM

It was bright morning. The sun shone down on the damp lawns and sidewalks, reflecting off the sparkling parked cars. The Clerk came walking hurriedly, leafing through his instructions, flipping pages and frowning. He stopped in front of the small green stucco house for a moment, and then turned up the walk, entering the back yard.

The dog was asleep inside his shed, his back turned to the world. Only his thick tail showed.

'For heaven's sake,' the Clerk exclaimed, hands on his hips. He tapped his mechanical pencil noisily against his clipboard. 'Wake up, you in there.'

The dog stirred. He came slowly out of his shed, head first, blinking and yawning in the morning sunlight. 'Oh, it's you. Already?' He yawned again.

'Big doings.' The Clerk ran his expert finger down the traffic-control sheet. 'They're adjusting Sector T137 this morning. Starting at exactly nine o'clock.' He glanced at his pocket watch. 'Three-hour alteration. Will finish by noon.'

'T137? That's not far from here.'

The Clerk's thin lips twisted with contempt. 'Indeed. You're showing astonishing perspicacity, my black-haired friend. Maybe you can divine why I'm here.'

'We overlap with T137.'

'Exactly. Elements from this Sector are involved. We must make sure they're properly placed when the adjustment begins.' The Clerk glanced toward the small green stucco house. 'Your particular task concerns the man in there. He is employed by a business establishment lying within Sector T137. It's essential that he be there before nine o'clock.'

The dog studied the house. The shades had been let up. The kitchen light was on. Beyond the lace curtains dim shapes could be seen, stirring around the table. A man and woman. They were drinking coffee.

'There they are,' the dog murmured. 'The man, you say? He's not going to be harmed, is he?'

'Of course not. But he must be at his office early. Usually he doesn't leave until after nine. Today he must leave at eight-thirty. He must be within Sector T137 before the process begins, or he won't be altered to coincide with the new adjustment.'

The dog sighed. 'That means I have to summon.'

'Correct.' The Clerk checked his instruction sheet. 'You're to summon at precisely eight-fifteen. You've got that? Eight-fifteen. No later.'

'What will an eight-fifteen summons bring?'

The Clerk flipped open his instruction book, examining the code columns. 'It will bring A Friend with a Car. To drive him to work early.' He closed the book and folded his arms, preparing to wait. 'That way he'll get to his office almost an hour ahead of time. Which is vital.'

'Vital,' the dog murmured. He lay down, half inside his shed. His eyes closed. 'Vital.'

'Wake up! This must be done exactly on time. If you summon too soon or too late–'

The dog nodded sleepily. 'I know. I'll do it right. I *always* do it right.'

Ed Fletcher poured more cream in his coffee. He sighed, leaning back in his chair. Behind him the oven hissed softly, filling the kitchen with warm fumes. The yellow overhead light beamed down.

'Another roll?' Ruth asked.

'I'm full.' Ed sipped his coffee. 'You can have it.'

'Have to go.' Ruth got to her feet, unfastening her robe. 'Time to go to work.'

'Already?'

'Sure. You lucky bum! Wish I could sit around.' Ruth moved toward the bathroom, running her fingers through her long black hair. 'When you work for the Government you start early.'

'But you get off early,' Ed pointed out. He unfolded the *Chronicle*, examining the sporting green. 'Well, have a good time today. Don't type any wrong words, any double-entendres.'

The bathroom door closed, as Ruth shed her robe and began dressing.

Ed yawned and glanced up at the clock over the sink. Plenty of time. Not even eight. He sipped more coffee and then rubbed his stubbled chin. He would have to shave. He shrugged lazily. Ten minutes, maybe.

Ruth came bustling out in her nylon slip, hurrying into the bedroom. 'I'm late.' She rushed rapidly around, getting into her blouse and skirt, her stockings, her little white shoes. Finally she bent over and kissed him. 'Good-bye, honey. I'll do the shopping tonight.'

'Good-bye.' Ed lowered his newspaper and put his arm around his wife's trim waist, hugging her affectionately. 'You smell nice. Don't flirt with the boss.'

Ruth ran out the front door, clattering down the steps. He heard the click of her heels diminish down the sidewalk.

She was gone. The house was silent. He was alone.

Ed got to his feet, pushing his chair back. He wandered lazily into the bathroom, and got his razor down. Eight-ten. He washed his face, rubbing it down with shaving cream, and began to shave. He shaved leisurely. He had plenty of time.

The Clerk bent over his round pocket watch, licking his lips nervously. Sweat stood out on his forehead. The second hand ticked on. Eight-fourteen. Almost time.

'Get ready!' the Clerk snapped. He tensed, his small body rigid. 'Ten seconds to go!'

'Time!' the Clerk cried.

Nothing happened.

The Clerk turned, eyes wide with horror. From the little shed a thick black tail showed. The dog had gone back to sleep.

'TIME!' the Clerk shrieked. He kicked wildly at the furry rump. 'In the name of God–'

The dog stirred. He thumped around hastily, backing out of the shed. 'My goodness.' Embarrassed, he made his way quickly to the fence. Standing up on his hind paws, he opened his mouth wide. 'Woof!' he summoned. He glanced apologetically at the Clerk. 'I beg your pardon. I can't understand how–'

The Clerk gazed fixedly down at his watch. Cold terror knotted his stomach. The hands showed eight-sixteen. 'You failed,' he grated. 'You failed! You miserable flea-bitten rag-bag of a wornout old mutt! You failed!'

The dog dropped and came anxiously back. 'I failed, you say? You mean the summons time was–?'

'You summoned too late.' The Clerk put his watch away slowly, a glazed expression on his face. 'You summoned too late. We won't get A Friend with a Car. There's no telling what will come instead. I'm afraid to see what eight-sixteen brings.'

'I hope he'll be in Sector T137 in time.'

'He won't,' the Clerk wailed. 'He won't be there. We've made a mistake. We've made things go wrong!'

Ed was rinsing the shaving cream from his face when the muffled sound of the dog's bark echoed through the silent house.

'Damn,' Ed muttered. 'Wake up the whole block.' He dried his face, listening. Was somebody coming?

A vibration. Then–

The doorbell rang.

Ed came out of the bathroom. Who could it be? Had Ruth forgotten something? He tossed on a white shirt and opened the front door.

A bright young man, face bland and eager, beamed happily at

him. 'Good morning, sir.' He tipped his hat. 'I'm sorry to bother you so early–'

'What do you want?'

'I'm from the Federal Life Insurance Company. I'm here to see you about–'

Ed pushed the door closed. 'Don't want any. I'm in a rush. Have to get to work.'

'Your wife said this was the only time I could catch you.' The young man picked up his briefcase, easing the door open again. 'She especially asked me to come this early. We don't usually begin our work at this time, but since she asked me, I made a special note about it.'

'OK.' Sighing wearily, Ed admitted the young man. 'You can explain your policy while I get dressed.'

The young man opened his briefcase on the couch, laying out heaps of pamphlets and illustrated folders. 'I'd like to show you some of these figures, if I may. It's of great importance to you and your family to–'

Ed found himself sitting down, going over the pamphlets. He purchased a ten-thousand-dollar policy on his own life and then eased the young man out. He looked at the clock. Practically nine-thirty!

'Damn.' He'd be late to work. He finished fastening his tie, grabbed his coat, turned off the oven and the lights, dumped the dishes in the sink, and ran out on the porch.

As he hurried toward the bus stop he was cursing inwardly. Life insurance salesmen. Why did the jerk have to come just as he was getting ready to leave?

Ed groaned. No telling what the consequences would be, getting to the office late. He wouldn't get there until almost ten. He set himself in anticipation. A sixth sense told him he was in for it. Something bad. It was the wrong day to be late.

If only the salesman hadn't come.

Ed hopped off the bus a block from his office. He began walking rapidly. The huge clock in front of Stein's Jewelry Store told him it was almost ten.

His heart sank. Old Douglas would give him hell for sure. He could see it now. Douglas puffing and blowing, red-faced, waving his thick finger at him; Miss Evans, smiling behind her typewriter; Jackie, the office boy, grinning and snickering; Earl Hendricks; Joe and Tom; Mary, dark-eyed, full bosom and long lashes. All of them, kidding him the whole rest of the day.

He came to the corner and stopped for the light. On the other side of the street rose a big white concrete building, the towering column of steel and cement, girders and glass windows–the office building. Ed flinched. Maybe he could say the elevator got stuck. Somewhere between the second and third floor.

The street light changed. Nobody else was crossing. Ed crossed alone. He hopped up on the curb on the far side–

And stopped, rigid.

The sun had winked off. One moment it was beaming down. Then it was gone. Ed looked up sharply. Gray clouds swirled above him. Huge, formless clouds. Nothing more. An ominous, thick haze that made everything waver and dim. Uneasy chills plucked at him. *What was it?*

He advanced cautiously, feeling his way through the mist. Everything was silent. No sounds–not even the traffic sounds. Ed peered frantically around, trying to see through the rolling haze. No people. No cars. No sun. Nothing.

The office building loomed up ahead, ghostly. It was an indistinct gray. He put out his hand uncertainly–

A section of the building fell away. It rained down, a torrent of particles. Like sand. Ed gaped foolishly. A cascade of gray debris, spilling around his feet. And where he had touched the building, a jagged cavity yawned–an ugly pit marring the concrete.

Dazed, he made his way to the front steps. He mounted them. The steps gave way underfoot. His feet sank down. He was wading through shifting sand, weak, rotted stuff that broke under his weight.

He got into the lobby. The lobby was dim and obscure. The overhead lights flickered feebly in the gloom. An unearthly pall hung over everything.

He spied the cigar stand. The seller leaned silently, resting on the counter, toothpick between his teeth, his face vacant. *And gray*. He was gray all over.

'Hey,' Ed croaked. 'What's going on?'

The seller did not answer. Ed reached out toward him. His hand touched the seller's gray arm–and passed right through.

'Good God,' Ed said.

The seller's arm came loose. It fell to the lobby floor, disintegrating into fragments. Bits of gray fiber. Like dust. Ed's senses reeled.

'Help!' he shouted, finding his voice.

No answer. He peered around. A few shapes stood here and there: a man reading a newspaper, two women waiting at the elevator.

Ed made his way over to the man. He reached out and touched him.

The man slowly collapsed. He settled into a heap, a loose pile of gray ash. Dust. Particles. The two women dissolved when he touched them. Silently. They made no sound as they broke apart.

Ed found the stairs. He grabbed hold of the banister and climbed. The stairs collapsed under him. He hurried faster. Behind him lay a broken path–his footprints clearly visible in the concrete. Clouds of ash blew around him as he reached the second floor.

He gazed down the silent corridor. He saw more clouds of ash. He heard no sound. There was just darkness–rolling darkness.

He climbed unsteadily to the third floor. Once, his shoe broke completely through the stair. For a sickening second he hung, poised over a yawning hole that looked down into a bottomless nothing.

Then he climbed on, and emerged in front of his own office: DOUGLAS AND BLAKE, REAL ESTATE.

The hall was dim, gloomy with clouds of ash. The overhead lights flickered fitfully. He reached for the door handle. The handle came off in his hand. He dropped it and dug his fingernails into the door. The plate glass crashed past him, breaking into bits. He tore the door open and stepped over it, into the office.

Miss Evans sat at her typewriter, fingers resting quietly on the keys. She did not move. She was gray, her hair, her skin, her clothing.

She was without color. Ed touched her. His fingers went through her shoulder, into dry flakiness.

He drew back, sickened. Miss Evans did not stir.

He moved on. He pushed against a desk. The desk collapsed into rotting dust. Earl Hendricks stood by the water cooler, a cup in his hand. He was a gray statue, unmoving. Nothing stirred. No sound. No life. The whole office was gray dust–without life or motion.

Ed found himself out in the corridor again. He shook his head, dazed. What did it mean? Was he going out of his mind? Was he–?

A sound.

Ed turned, peering into the gray mist. A creature was coming, hurrying rapidly. A man–a man in a white robe. Behind him others came. Men in white, with equipment. They were lugging complex machinery.

'Hey–' Ed gasped weakly.

The men stopped. Their mouths opened. Their eyes popped.

'Look!'

'Something's gone wrong!'

'One still charged.'

'Get the de-energizer.'

'We can't proceed until–'

The men came toward Ed, moving around him. One lugged a long hose with some sort of nozzle. A portable cart came wheeling up. Instructions were rapidly shouted.

Ed broke out of his paralysis. Fear swept over him. Panic. Something hideous was happening. He had to get out. Warn people. Get away.

He turned and ran, back down the stairs. The stairs collapsed under him. He fell half a flight, rolling in heaps of dry ash. He got to his feet and hurried on, down to the ground floor.

The lobby was lost in the clouds of gray ash. He pushed blindly through, toward the door. Behind him, the white-clad men were coming, dragging their equipment and shouting to each other, hurrying quickly after him.

He reached the sidewalk. Behind him the office building wavered and sagged, sinking to one side, torrents of ash raining down in heaps. He raced toward the corner, the men just behind him. Gray cloud swirled around him. He groped his way across the street, hands outstretched. He gained the opposite curb–

The sun winked on. Warm yellow sunlight streamed down on him. Cars honked. Traffic lights changed. On all sides men and women in bright spring clothes hurried and pushed: shoppers, a blue-clad cop, salesmen with briefcases. Stores, windows, signs . . . noisy cars moving up and down the street . . .

And overhead was the bright sun and familiar blue sky.

Ed halted, gasping for breath. He turned and looked back the way he had come. Across the street was the office building–as it had always been. Firm and distinct. Concrete and glass and steel.

He stepped back a pace and collided with a hurrying citizen. 'Hey,' the man grunted. 'Watch it.'

'Sorry.' Ed shook his head, trying to clear it. From where he stood, the office building looked like always, big and solemn and substantial, rising up imposingly on the other side of the street.

But a minute ago–

Maybe he was out of his mind. He had seen the building crumbling into dust. Building–and people. They had fallen into gray clouds of dust. And the men in white–they had chased him. Men in white robes, shouting orders, wheeling complex equipment.

He was out of his mind. There was no other explanation. Weakly, Ed turned and stumbled along the sidewalk, his mind reeling. He moved blindly, without purpose, lost in a haze of confusion and terror.

The Clerk was brought into the top-level Administrative chambers and told to wait.

He paced back and forth nervously, clasping and wringing his hands in an agony of apprehension. He took off his glasses and wiped them shakily.

Lord. All the trouble and grief. And it wasn't his fault. But he would have to take the rap. It was his responsibility to get the Summoners routed out and their instructions followed. The miserable flea-infested Summoner had gone back to sleep–and *he* would have to answer for it.

The doors opened. 'All right,' a voice murmured, preoccupied. It was a tired, care-worn voice. The Clerk trembled and entered slowly, sweat dripping down his neck into his celluloid collar.

The Old Man glanced up, laying aside his book. He studied the Clerk calmly, his faded blue eyes mild–a deep, ancient mildness that made the Clerk tremble even more. He took out his handkerchief and mopped his brow.

'I understand there was a mistake,' the Old Man murmured. 'In connection with Sector T137. Something to do with an element from an adjoining area.'

'That's right.' The Clerk's voice was faint and husky. 'Very unfortunate.'

'What exactly occurred?'

'I started out this morning with my instruction sheets. The material relating to T137 had top priority, of course. I served notice on the Summoner in my area that an eight-fifteen summons was required.'

'Did the Summoner understand the urgency?'

'Yes, sir.' The Clerk hesitated. 'But–'

'But what?'

The Clerk twisted miserably. 'While my back was turned the Summoner crawled back in his shed and went to sleep. I was occupied, checking the exact time with my watch. I called the moment–but there was no response.'

'You called at eight-fifteen exactly?'

'Yes, sir! Exactly eight-fifteen. But the Summoner was asleep. By the time I managed to arouse him it was eight-*sixteen*. He summoned, but instead of A Friend with a Car we got–A Life Insurance Salesman.' The Clerk's face screwed up with disgust. 'The Salesman kept the element there until almost nine-thirty. Therefore he was late to work instead of early.'

For a moment the Old Man was silent. 'Then the element was not within T137 when the adjustment began.'

'No. He arrived about ten o'clock.'

'During the middle of the adjustment.' The Old Man got to his feet and paced slowly back and forth, face grim, hands behind his back. His long robe flowed out behind him. 'A serious matter. During a Sector Adjustment all related elements from other Sectors must be included. Otherwise, their orientations remain out of phase. When this element entered T137 the adjustment had been in progress fifty minutes. The element encountered the Sector at its most de-energized stage. He wandered about until one of the adjustment teams met him.'

'Did they catch him?'

'Unfortunately, no. He fled, out of the Sector. Into a nearby fully energized area.'

'What–what then?'

The Old Man stopped pacing, his lined face grim. He ran a heavy hand through his long white hair. 'We do not know. We lost contact with him. We will reestablish contact soon, of course. But for the moment he is out of control.'

'What are you going to do?'

'He must be contacted and contained. He must be brought up here. There's no other solution.'

'Up *here*!'

'It is too late to de-energize him. By the time he is regained he will have told others. To wipe his mind clean would only complicate matters. Usual methods will not suffice. I must deal with this problem myself.'

'I hope he's located quickly,' the Clerk said.

'He will be. Every Watcher is alerted. Every Watcher and every Summoner.' The Old Man's eyes twinkled. 'Even the Clerks, although we hesitate to count on them.'

The Clerk flushed. 'I'll be glad when this thing is over,' he muttered.

*

Ruth came tripping down the stairs and out of the building, into the hot noonday sun. She lit a cigarette and hurried along the walk, her small bosom rising and falling as she breathed in the spring air.

'Ruth.' Ed stepped up behind her.

'Ed!' She spun, gasping in astonishment. 'What are you doing away from–?'

'Come on.' Ed grabbed her arm, pulling her along. 'Let's keep moving.'

'But what–?'

'I'll tell you later.' Ed's face was pale and grim. 'Let's go where we can talk. In private.'

'I was going down to have lunch at Louie's. We can talk there.' Ruth hurried along breathlessly. 'What is it? What's happened? You look so strange. And why aren't you at work? Did you–did you get fired?'

They crossed the street and entered a small restaurant. Men and women milled around, getting their lunch. Ed found a table in the back, secluded in a corner. 'Here.' He sat down abruptly. 'This will do.' She slid into the other chair.

Ed ordered a cup of coffee. Ruth had salad and creamed tuna on toast, coffee and peach pie. Silently, Ed watched her as she ate, his face dark and moody.

'Please tell me,' Ruth begged him.

'You really want to know?'

'Of course I want to know!' Ruth put her small hand anxiously on his. 'I'm your wife.'

'Something happened today. This morning. I was late to work. A damn insurance man came by and held me up. I was half an hour late.'

Ruth caught her breath. 'Douglas fired you.'

'No.' Ed ripped a paper napkin slowly into bits. He stuffed the bits in the half-empty water glass. 'I was worried as hell. I got off the bus and hurried down the street. I noticed it when I stepped up on the curb in front of the office.'

'Noticed what?'

Ed told her. The whole works. Everything.

When he had finished, Ruth sat back, her face white, hands trembling. 'I see,' she murmured. 'No wonder you're upset.' She drank a little cold coffee, the cup rattling against the saucer. 'What a terrible thing.'

Ed leaned intently toward his wife. 'Ruth. Do you think I'm going crazy?'

Ruth's red lips twisted. 'I don't know what to say. It's so strange . . .'

'Yeah. Strange is hardly the word for it. I poked my hands right through them. Like they were clay. Old dry clay. Dust. Dust figures.' Ed lit a cigarette from Ruth's pack. 'When I got out I looked back and there it was. The office building. Like always.'

'You were afraid Mr Douglas would bawl you out, weren't you?'

'Sure. I was afraid–and guilty.' Ed's eyes flickered. 'I know what you're thinking. I was late and I couldn't face him. So I had some sort of protective psychotic fit. Retreat from reality.' He stubbed the cigarette out savagely. 'Ruth, I've been wandering around town since. Two and a half hours. Sure, I'm afraid. I'm afraid like hell to go back.'

'Of Douglas?'

'No! The men in white.' Ed shuddered. 'God. Chasing me. With their damn hoses and–and equipment.'

Ruth was silent. Finally she looked up at her husband, her dark eyes bright. 'You have to go back, Ed.'

'Back? Why?'

'To prove something.'

'Prove what?'

'Prove it's all right.' Ruth's hand pressed against his. 'You have to, Ed. You have to go back and face it. To show yourself there's nothing to be afraid of.'

'The hell with it! After what I saw? Listen, Ruth. I saw the fabric of reality split open. I saw–*behind*. Underneath. I saw what was really there. And I don't want to go back. I don't want to see dust people again. Ever.'

Ruth's eyes were fixed intently on him. 'I'll go back with you,' she said.

'For God's sake.'

'For *your* sake. For your sanity. So you'll know.' Ruth got abruptly to her feet, pulling her coat around her. 'Come on, Ed. I'll go with you. We'll go up there together. To the office of Douglas and Blake, Real Estate. I'll even go in with you to see Mr Douglas.'

Ed got up slowly, staring hard at his wife. 'You think I blacked out. Cold feet. Couldn't face the boss.' His voice was low and strained. 'Don't you?'

Ruth was already threading her way toward the cashier. 'Come on. You'll see. It'll all be there. Just like it always was.'

'OK,' Ed said. He followed her slowly. 'We'll go back there–and see which of us is right.'

They crossed the street together, Ruth holding on tight to Ed's arm. Ahead of them was the building, the towering structure of concrete and metal and glass.

'There it is,' Ruth said. 'See?'

There it was, all right. The big building rose up, firm and solid, glittering in the early afternoon sun, its windows sparkling brightly.

Ed and Ruth stepped up onto the curb. Ed tensed himself, his body rigid. He winced as his foot touched the pavement–

But nothing happened: the street noises continued; cars, people hurrying past; a kid selling papers. There were sounds, smells, the noise of a city in the middle of the day. And overhead was the sun and the bright blue sky.

'See?' Ruth said. 'I was right.'

They walked up the front steps, into the lobby. Behind the cigar stand the seller stood, arms folded, listening to the ball game. 'Hi, Mr Fletcher,' he called to Ed. His face lit up good-naturedly. 'Who's the dame? Your wife know about this?'

Ed laughed unsteadily. They passed on toward the elevator. Four or five businessmen stood waiting. They were middle-aged men, well dressed, waiting impatiently in a bunch. 'Hey, Fletcher,' one said. 'Where you been all day? Douglas is yelling his head off.'

'Hello, Earl,' Ed muttered. He gripped Ruth's arm. 'Been a little sick.'

The elevator came. They got in. The elevator rose. 'Hi, Ed,' the elevator operator said. 'Who's the good-looking gal? Why don't you introduce her around?'

Ed grinned mechanically. 'My wife.'

The elevator let them off at the third floor. Ed and Ruth got out, heading toward the glass door of Douglas and Blake, Real Estate.

Ed halted, breathing shallowly. 'Wait.' He licked his lips. 'I–'

Ruth waited calmly as Ed wiped his forehead and neck with his handkerchief. 'All right now?'

'Yeah.' Ed moved forward. He pulled open the glass door.

Miss Evans glanced up, ceasing her typing. 'Ed Fletcher! Where on earth have you been?'

'I've been sick. Hello, Tom.'

Tom glanced up from his work. 'Hi, Ed. Say, Douglas is yelling for your scalp. Where have you been?'

'I know.' Ed turned wearily to Ruth. 'I guess I better go in and face the music.'

Ruth squeezed his arm. 'You'll be all right. I know.' She smiled, a relieved flash of white teeth and red lips. 'OK? Call me if you need me.'

'Sure.' Ed kissed her briefly on the mouth. 'Thanks, honey. Thanks a lot. I don't know what the hell went wrong with me. I guess it's over.'

'Forget it. So long.' Ruth skipped back out of the office, the door closing after her. Ed listened to her race down the hall to the elevator.

'Nice little gal,' Jackie said appreciatively.

'Yeah.' Ed nodded, straightening his necktie. He moved unhappily toward the inner office, steeling himself. Well, he had to face it. Ruth was right. But he was going to have a hell of a time explaining it to the boss. He could see Douglas now, thick red wattles, big bull roar, face distorted with rage–

Ed stopped abruptly at the entrance to the inner office. He froze rigid. The inner office–it was *changed*.

The hackles of his neck rose. Cold fear gripped him, clutching at his windpipe. The inner office was different. He turned his head slowly, taking in the sight: the desks, chairs, fixtures, file cabinets, pictures.

Changes. Little changes. Subtle. Ed closed his eyes and opened them slowly. He was alert, breathing rapidly, his pulse racing. It was changed, all right. No doubt about it.

'What's the matter, Ed?' Tom asked. The staff watched him curiously, pausing in their work.

Ed said nothing. He advanced slowly into the inner office. The office had been *gone over*. He could tell. Things had been altered. Rearranged. Nothing obvious–nothing he could put his finger on. But he could tell.

Joe Kent greeted him uneasily. 'What's the matter, Ed? You look like a wild dog. Is something–?'

Ed studied Joe. He was different. Not the same. What was it?

Joe's face. It was a little fuller. His shirt was blue-striped. Joe never wore blue stripes. Ed examined Joe's desk. He saw papers and accounts. The desk–it was too far to the right. And it was bigger. It wasn't the same desk.

The picture on the wall. It wasn't the same. It was a different picture entirely. And the things on top of the file cabinet–some were new, others were gone.

He looked back through the door. Now that he thought about it, Miss Evans' hair was different, done a different way. And it was lighter.

In here, Mary, filing her nails, over by the window–she was taller, fuller. Her purse, lying on the desk in front of her–a red purse, red knit.

'You always . . . have that purse?' Ed demanded.

Mary glanced up. 'What?'

'That purse. You always have that?'

Mary laughed. She smoothed her skirt coyly around her shapely thighs, her long lashes blinking modestly. 'Why, Mr Fletcher. What do you mean?'

Ed turned away. *He knew*. Even if she didn't. She had been

redone—changed: her purse, her clothes, her figure, everything about her. None of them knew—but him. His mind spun dizzily. They were all changed. All of them were different. They had all been remolded, recast. Subtly—but it was there.

The wastebasket. It was smaller, not the same. The window shades—white, not ivory. The wallpaper was not the same pattern. The lighting fixtures . . .

Endless, subtle changes.

Ed made his way back to the inner office. He lifted his hand and knocked on Douglas's door.

'Come in.'

Ed pushed the door open. Nathan Douglas looked up impatiently.

'Mr Douglas—' Ed began. He came into the room unsteadily—and stopped.

Douglas was not the same. Not at all. His whole office was changed: the rugs, the drapes. The desk was oak, not mahogany. And Douglas himself . . .

Douglas was younger, thinner. His hair, brown. His skin not so red. His face smoother. No wrinkles. Chin reshaped. Eyes green, not black. He was a different man. But still Douglas—a different Douglas. A different version!

'What is it?' Douglas demanded impatiently. 'Oh, it's you, Fletcher. Where were you this morning?'

Ed backed out. Fast.

He slammed the door and hurried back through the inner office. Tom and Miss Evans glanced up, startled. Ed passed them by, grabbing the hall door open.

'Hey!' Tom called. 'What—?'

Ed hurried down the hall. Terror leaped through him. He had to hurry. He had *seen*. There wasn't much time. He came to the elevator and stabbed the button.

No time.

He ran to the stairs and started down. He reached the second floor. His terror grew. It was a matter of seconds.

Seconds!

The public phone. Ed ran into the phone booth. He dragged the door shut after him. Wildly, he dropped a dime in the slot and dialed. He had to call the police. He held the receiver to his ear, his heart pounding.

Warn them. Changes. Somebody tampering with reality. Altering it. He had been right. The white-clad men . . . their equipment . . . going through the building.

'Hello!' Ed shouted hoarsely. There was no answer. No hum. Nothing.

Ed peered frantically out the door.

And he sagged, defeated. Slowly he hung up the telephone receiver.

He was no longer on the second floor. The phone booth was rising, leaving the second floor behind, carrying him up, faster and faster. It rose floor by floor, moving silently, swiftly.

The phone booth passed through the ceiling of the building and out into the bright sunlight. It gained speed. The ground fell away below. Buildings and streets were getting smaller each moment. Tiny specks hurried along, far below, cars and people, dwindling rapidly.

Clouds drifted between him and the earth. Ed shut his eyes, dizzy with fright. He held on desperately to the door handles of the phone booth.

Faster and faster the phone booth climbed. The earth was rapidly being left behind, far below.

Ed peered up wildly. *Where?* Where was he going? Where was it taking him?

He stood gripping the door handles, waiting.

The Clerk nodded curtly. 'That's him, all right. The element in question.'

Ed Fletcher looked around him. He was in a huge chamber. The edges fell away into indistinct shadows. In front of him stood a man with notes and ledgers under his arm, peering at him through steel-rimmed glasses. He was a nervous little man, sharp-eyed, with celluloid collar, blue serge suit, vest, watch chain. He wore black shiny shoes.

And beyond him–

An old man sat quietly, in an immense modern chair. He watched Fletcher calmly, his blue eyes mild and tired. A strange thrill shot through Fletcher. It was not fear. Rather it was a vibration, rattling his bones–a deep sense of awe, tinged with fascination.

'Where–what is this place?' he asked faintly. He was still dazed from his quick ascent.

'Don't ask questions!' the nervous little man snapped angrily, tapping his pencil against his ledgers. 'You're here to answer, not ask.'

The Old Man moved a little. He raised his hand. 'I will speak to the element alone,' he murmured. His voice was low. It vibrated and rumbled through the chamber. Again the wave of fascinated awe swept Ed.

'Alone?' The little fellow backed away, gathering his books and papers in his arms. 'Of course.' He glanced hostilely at Ed Fletcher. 'I'm glad he's finally in custody. All the work and trouble just for–'

He disappeared through a door. The door closed softly behind him. Ed and the Old Man were alone.

'Please sit down,' the Old Man said.

Ed found a seat. He sat down awkwardly, nervously. He got out his cigarettes and then put them away again.

'What's wrong?' the Old Man asked.

'I'm just beginning to understand.'

'Understand what?'

'That I'm dead.'

The Old Man smiled briefly. 'Dead? No, you're not dead. You're . . . visiting. An unusual event, but necessitated by circumstances.' He leaned toward Ed. 'Mr Fletcher, you have got yourself involved with something.'

'Yeah,' Ed agreed. 'I wish I knew what it was. Or how it happened.'

'It was not your fault. You were a victim of a clerical error. A mistake was made–not by you. But involving you.'

'What mistake?' Ed rubbed his forehead wearily. 'I–I got in on something. I saw *through*. I saw something I wasn't supposed to see.'

The Old Man nodded. 'That's right. You saw something you were not supposed to see–something few elements have been aware of, let alone witnessed.'

'Elements?'

'An official term. Let it pass. A mistake was made, but we hope to rectify it. It is my hope that–'

'Those people,' Ed interrupted. 'Heaps of dry ash. And gray. Like they were dead. Only it was everything: the stairs and walls and floor. No color or life.'

'That Sector had been temporarily de-energized. So the adjustment team could enter and effect changes.'

'Changes.' Ed nodded. 'That's right. When I went back later, everything was alive again. But not the same. It was all different.'

'The adjustment was complete by noon. The team finished its work and re-energized the Sector.'

'I see,' Ed muttered.

'You were supposed to have been in the Sector when the adjustment began. Because of an error you were not. You came into the Sector late–during the adjustment itself. You fled, and when you returned it was over. You saw, and you should not have seen. Instead of a witness you should have been part of the adjustment. Like the others, you should have undergone changes.'

Sweat came out on Ed Fletcher's head. He wiped it away. His stomach turned over. Weakly, he cleared his throat. 'I get the picture.' His voice was almost inaudible. A chilling premonition moved through him. 'I was supposed to be changed like the others. But I guess something went wrong.'

'Something went wrong. An error occurred. And now a serious problem exists. You have seen these things. You know a great deal. And you are not coordinated with the new configuration.'

'Gosh,' Ed muttered. 'Well, I won't tell anybody.' Cold sweat poured off him. 'You can count on that. I'm as good as changed.'

'You have already told someone,' the Old Man said coldly.

'Me?' Ed blinked. 'Who?'

'Your wife.'

Ed trembled. The color drained from his face, leaving it sickly white. 'That's right. I did.'

'Your wife knows.' The Old Man's face twisted angrily. 'A woman. Of all the things to tell–'

'I didn't know.' Ed retreated, panic leaping through him. 'But I know *now*. You can count on me. Consider me changed.'

The ancient blue eyes bored keenly into him, peering far into his depths. 'And you were going to call the police. You wanted to inform the authorities.'

'But I didn't know *who* was doing the changing.'

'Now you know. The natural process must be supplemented–adjusted here and there. Corrections must be made. We are fully licensed to make such corrections. Our adjustment teams perform vital work.'

Ed plucked up a measure of courage. 'This particular adjustment. Douglas. The office. What was it for? I'm sure it was some worthwhile purpose.'

The Old Man waved his hand. Behind him in the shadows an immense map glowed into existence. Ed caught his breath. The edges of the map faded off in obscurity. He saw an infinite web of detailed sections, a network of squares and ruled lines. Each square was marked. Some glowed with a blue light. The lights altered constantly.

'The Sector Board,' the Old Man said. He sighed wearily. 'A staggering job. Sometimes we wonder how we can go on another period. But it must be done. For the good of all. For *your* good.'

'The change. In our–our Sector.'

'Your office deals in real estate. The old Douglas was a shrewd man, but rapidly becoming infirm. His physical health was waning. In a few days Douglas will be offered a chance to purchase a large unimproved forest area in western Canada. It will require most of his assets. The older, less virile Douglas would have hesitated. It is imperative he not hesitate. He must purchase the area and clear the land at once. Only a younger man—a younger Douglas—would undertake this.

'When the land is cleared, certain anthropological remains will be discovered. They have already been placed there. Douglas will lease his land to the Canadian Government for scientific study. The remains found there will cause international excitement in learned circles.

'A chain of events will be set in motion. Men from numerous countries will come to Canada to examine the remains. Soviet, Polish, and Czech scientists will make the journey.

'The chain of events will draw these scientists together for the first time in years. National research will be temporarily forgotten in the excitement of these non-national discoveries. One of the leading Soviet scientists will make friends with a Belgian scientist. Before they depart they will agree to correspond—without the knowledge of their governments, of course.

'The circle will widen. Other scientists on both sides will be drawn in. A society will be founded. More and more educated men will transfer an increasing amount of time to this international society. Purely national research will suffer a slight but extremely critical eclipse. The war tension will somewhat wane.

'This alteration is vital. And it is dependent on the purchase and clearing of the section of wilderness in Canada. The old Douglas would not have dared take the risk. But the altered Douglas, and his altered, more youthful staff, will pursue this work with wholehearted enthusiasm. And from this, the vital chain of widening events will come about. The beneficiaries will be *you*. Our methods may seem strange and indirect. Even incomprehensible. But I assure you we know what we're doing.'

'I know that now,' Ed said.

'So you do. You know a great deal. Much too much. No element should possess such knowledge. I should perhaps call an adjustment team in here . . .'

A picture formed in Ed's mind: swirling gray clouds, gray men and women. He shuddered. 'Look,' he croaked. 'I'll do anything.

Anything at all. Only don't de-energize me.' Sweat ran down his face. 'OK?'

The Old Man pondered. 'Perhaps some alternative could be found. There is another possibility . . .'

'What?' Ed asked eagerly. 'What is it?'

The Old Man spoke slowly, thoughtfully. 'If I allow you to return, you will swear never to speak of the matter? Will you swear not to reveal to anyone the things you saw? The things you know?'

'Sure!' Ed gasped eagerly, blinding relief flooding over him. 'I swear!'

'Your wife. She must know nothing more. She must think it was only a passing psychological fit–retreat from reality.'

'She thinks that already.'

'She must continue to.'

Ed set his jaw firmly. 'I'll see that she continues to think it was a mental aberration. She'll never know what really happened.'

'You are certain you can keep the truth from her?'

'Sure,' Ed said confidently. 'I know I can.'

'All right.' The Old Man nodded slowly. 'I will send you back. But you must tell no one.' He swelled visibly. 'Remember: you will eventually come back to me–everyone does, in the end–and your fate will not be enviable.'

'I won't tell her,' Ed said, sweating. 'I promise. You have my word on that. I can handle Ruth. Don't give it a second thought.'

Ed arrived home at sunset.

He blinked, dazed from the rapid descent. For a moment he stood on the pavement, regaining his balance and catching his breath. Then he walked quickly up the path.

He pushed the door open and entered the little green stucco house.

'Ed!' Ruth came flying, face distorted with tears. She threw her arms around him, hugging him tight. 'Where the hell have you been?'

'Been?' Ed murmured. 'At the office, of course.'

Ruth pulled back abruptly. 'No, you haven't.'

Vague tendrils of alarm plucked at Ed. 'Of course I have. Where else–?'

'I called Douglas about three. He said you left. You walked out, practically as soon as I turned my back. Eddie–'

Ed patted her nervously. 'Take it easy, honey.' He began unbuttoning his coat. 'Everything's OK. Understand? Things are perfectly all right.'

Ruth sat down on the arm of the couch. She blew her nose, dabbing at her eyes. 'If you knew how much I've worried.' She put her handkerchief away and folded her arms. 'I want to know where you were.'

Uneasily, Ed hung his coat in the closet. He came over and kissed her. Her lips were ice cold. 'I'll tell you all about it. But what do you say we have something to eat? I'm starved.'

Ruth studied him intently. She got down from the arm of the couch. 'I'll change and fix dinner.'

She hurried into the bedroom and slipped off her shoes and nylons. Ed followed her. 'I didn't mean to worry you,' he said carefully. 'After you left me today I realized you were right.'

'Oh?' Ruth unfastened her blouse and skirt, arranging them over a hanger. 'Right about what?'

'About me.' He manufactured a grin and made it glow across his face. 'About . . . what happened.'

Ruth hung her slip over the hanger. She studied her husband intently as she struggled into her tight-fitting jeans. 'Go on.'

The moment had come. It was now or never. Ed Fletcher braced himself and chose his words carefully. 'I realized,' he stated, 'that the whole darn thing was in my mind. You were right, Ruth. Completely right. And I even realize what caused it.'

Ruth rolled her cotton T-shirt down and tucked it in her jeans. 'What was the cause?'

'Overwork.'

'Overwork?'

'I need a vacation. I haven't had a vacation in years. My mind isn't on the job. I've been daydreaming.' He said it firmly, but his heart was in his mouth. 'I need to get away. To the mountains. Bass fishing. Or–' He searched his mind frantically. 'Or–'

Ruth came toward him ominously. 'Ed!' she said sharply. 'Look at me!'

'What's the matter?' Panic shot through him. 'Why are you looking at me like that?'

'Where were you this afternoon?'

Ed's grin faded. 'I told you. I went for a walk. Didn't I tell you? A walk. To think things over.'

'Don't lie to me, Eddie Fletcher! I can tell when you're lying!' Fresh tears welled up in Ruth's eyes. Her breasts rose and fell excitedly under her cotton shirt. 'Admit it! You didn't go for a walk!'

Ed stammered weakly. Sweat poured off him. He sagged helplessly against the door. 'What do you mean?'

Ruth's black eyes flashed with anger. 'Come on! I want to know where you were! Tell me! I have a right to know. What really happened?'

Ed retreated in terror, his resolve melting like wax. It was going all wrong. 'Honest. I went out for a–'

'Tell me!' Ruth's sharp fingernails dug into his arm. 'I want to know where you were–and who you were with!'

Ed opened his mouth. He tried to grin, but his face failed to respond. 'I don't know what you mean.'

'You know what I mean. Who were you with? Where did you go? Tell me! I'll find out sooner or later.'

There was no way out. He was licked–and he knew it. He couldn't keep it from her. Desperately he stalled, praying for time. If he could only distract her, get her mind on something else. If she would only let up, even for a second. He could invent something–a better story. Time–he needed more time. 'Ruth, you've got to–'

Suddenly there was a sound: the bark of a dog, echoing through the dark house.

Ruth let go, cocking her head alertly. 'That was Dobbie. I think somebody's coming.'

The doorbell rang.

'You stay here. I'll be right back.' Ruth ran out of the room, to the front door. 'Darn it.' She pulled the front door open.

'Good evening!' The young man stepped quickly inside, loaded down with objects, grinning broadly at Ruth. 'I'm from the Sweep-Rite Vacuum Cleaner Company.'

Ruth scowled impatiently. 'Really, we're about to sit down at the table.'

'Oh, this will only take a moment.' The young man set down the vacuum cleaner and its attachments with a metallic crash. Rapidly, he unrolled a long illustrated banner, showing the vacuum cleaner in action. 'Now, if you'll just hold this while I plug in the cleaner–'

He bustled happily about, unplugging the TV set, plugging in the cleaner, pushing the chairs out of his way.

'I'll show you the drape scraper first.' He attached a hose and nozzle to the big gleaming tank. 'Now, if you'll just sit down I'll demonstrate each of these easy-to-use attachments.' His happy voice rose over the roar of the cleaner. 'You'll notice–'

Ed Fletcher sat down on the bed. He groped in his pocket until he found his cigarettes. Shakily he lit one and leaned back against the wall, weak with relief.

He gazed up, a look of gratitude on his face. 'Thanks,' he said softly. 'I think we'll make it–after all. Thanks a lot.'

THE IMPOSSIBLE PLANET

'She just stands there,' Norton said nervously. 'Captain, you'll have to talk to her.'

'What does she want?'

'She wants a ticket. She's stone deaf. She just stands there staring and she won't go away. It gives me the creeps.'

Captain Andrews got slowly to his feet. 'Okay. I'll talk to her. Send her in.'

'Thanks.' To the corridor Norton said, 'The Captain will talk to you. Come ahead.'

There was motion outside the control room. A flash of metal. Captain Andrews pushed his desk scanner back and stood waiting.

'In here.' Norton backed into the control room. 'This way. Right in here.'

Behind Norton came a withered little old woman. Beside her moved a gleaming robant, a towering robot servant, supporting her with its arm. The robant and the tiny old woman entered the control room slowly.

'Here's her papers.' Norton slid a folio onto the chart desk, his voice awed. 'She's three hundred and fifty years old. One of the oldest sustained. From Riga II.'

Andrews leafed slowly through the folio. In front of the desk the little woman stood silently, staring straight ahead. Her faded eyes were pale blue. Like ancient china.

'Irma Vincent Gordon,' Andrews murmured. He glanced up. 'Is that right?'

The old woman did not answer.

'She is totally deaf, sir,' the robant said.

Andrews grunted and returned to the folio. Irma Gordon was one of the original settlers of the Riga system. Origin unknown. Probably born out in space in one of the old sub-C ships. A strange feeling drifted through him. The little old creature. The centuries she had seen! The changes.

'She wants to travel?' he asked the robant.

'Yes, sir. She has come from her home to purchase a ticket.'

'Can she stand space travel?'

'She came from Riga, here to Fomalhaut IX.'

'Where does she want to go?'

'To Earth, sir,' the robant said.

'*Earth!*' Andrews' jaw dropped. He swore nervously. 'What do you mean?'

'She wishes to travel to Earth, sir.'

'You see?' Norton muttered. 'Completely crazy.'

Gripping his desk tightly, Andrews addressed the old woman. 'Madam, we can't sell you a ticket to Earth.'

'She can't hear you, sir,' the robant said.

Andrews found a piece of paper. He wrote in big letters:

CAN'T SELL YOU A TICKET TO EARTH

He held it up. The old woman's eyes moved as she studied the words. Her lips twitched. 'Why not?' she said at last. Her voice was faint and dry. Like rustling weeds.

Andrews scratched an answer.

NO SUCH PLACE

He added grimly:

MYTH—LEGEND—NEVER EXISTED

The old woman's faded eyes left the words. She gazed directly at Andrews, her face expressionless. Andrews became uneasy. Beside him, Norton sweated nervously.

'Jeez,' Norton muttered. 'Get her out of here. She'll put the hex on us.'

Andrews addressed the robant. 'Can't you make her understand. There is no such place as Earth. It's been proved a thousand times. No such primordial planet existed. All scientists agree human life arose simultaneously throughout the–'

'It is her wish to travel to Earth,' the robant said patiently. 'She is three hundred and fifty years old and they have ceased giving her sustentation treatments. She wishes to visit Earth before she dies.'

'But it's a myth!' Andrews exploded. He opened and closed his mouth, but no words came.

'How much?' the old woman said. 'How much?'

'I can't do it!' Andrews shouted. 'There isn't–'

'We have a kilo positives,' the robant said.

Andrews became suddenly quiet. 'A thousand positives.' He blanched in amazement. His jaws clamped shut, the color draining from his face.

'How much?' the old woman repeated. 'How much?'

'Will that be sufficient?' the robant asked.

For a moment Andrews swallowed silently. Abruptly he found his voice. 'Sure,' he said. 'Why not?'

'Captain!' Norton protested. 'Have you gone nuts? You know there's no such place as Earth! How the hell can we–'

'Sure, we'll take her.' Andrews buttoned his tunic slowly, hands shaking. 'We'll take her anywhere she wants to go. Tell her that. For a thousand positives we'll be glad to take her to Earth. Okay?'

'Of course,' the robant said. 'She has saved many decades for this. She will give you the kilo positives at once. She has them with her.'

'Look,' Norton said. 'You can get twenty years for this. They'll take your articles and your card and they'll–'

'Shut up.' Andrews spun the dial of the intersystem vidsender.

Under them the jets throbbed and roared. The lumbering transport had reached deep space. 'I want the main information library at Centaurus II,' he said into the speaker.

'Even for a thousand positives you can't do it. Nobody can do it. They tried to find Earth for generations. Directorate ships tracked down every moth-eaten planet in the whole–'

The vidsender clicked. 'Centaurus II.'

'Information library.'

Norton caught Andrews' arm. 'Please, Captain. Even for *two* kilo positives–'

'I want the following information,' Andrews said into the vid-speaker. 'All facts that are known concerning the planet Earth. Legendary birthplace of the human race.'

'No facts are known,' the detached voice of the library monitor came. 'The subject is classified as metaparticular.'

'What unverified but widely circulated reports have survived?'

'Most legends concerning Earth were lost during the Centauran-Rigan conflict of 4-B33a. What survived is fragmentary. Earth is variously described as a large ringed planet with three moons, as a small, dense planet with a single moon, as the first planet of a ten-planet system located around a dwarf white–'

'What's the most prevalent legend?'

'The Morrison Report of 5-C2 1r analyzed the total ethnic and subliminal accounts of the legendary Earth. The final summation noted that Earth is generally considered to be a small third planet of a nine-planet system, with a single moon. Other than that, no agreement of legends could be constructed.'

'I see. A third planet of a nine-planet system. With a single moon.' Andrews broke the circuit and the screen faded.

'So?' Norton said.

Andrews got quickly to his feet. 'She probably knows every legend about it.' He pointed down–at the passenger quarters below. 'I want to get the accounts straight.'

'Why? What are you going to do?'

Andrews flipped open the master star chart. He ran his fingers down the index and released the scanner. In a moment it turned up a card.

He grabbed the chart and fed it into the robant pilot. 'The Emphor System,' he murmured thoughtfully.

'Emphor? We're going there?'

'According to the chart, there are ninety systems that show a third planet of nine with a single moon. Of the ninety, Emphor is the closest. We're heading there now.'

'I don't get it,' Norton protested. 'Emphor is a routine trading system. Emphor III isn't even a Class D check point.'

Captain Andrews grinned tightly. 'Emphor III has a single moon, and it's the third of nine planets. That's all we want. Does anybody know any more about Earth?' He glanced downwards. 'Does *she* know any more about Earth?'

'I see,' Norton said slowly. 'I'm beginning to get the picture.'

Emphor III turned silently below them. A dull red globe, suspended among sickly clouds, its baked and corroded surface lapped by the congealed remains of ancient seas. Cracked, eroded cliffs jutted starkly up. The flat plains had been dug and stripped bare. Great gouged pits pocketed the surface, endless gaping sores.

Norton's face twisted in revulsion. 'Look at it. Is anything alive down there?'

Captain Andrews frowned. 'I didn't realize it was so gutted.' He crossed abruptly to the robant pilot. 'There's supposed to be an auto-grapple some place down there. I'll try to pick it up.'

'A grapple? You mean that waste is inhabited?'

'A few Emphorites. Degenerate trading colony of some sort.' Andrews consulted the card. 'Commercial ships come here occasionally. Contact with this region has been vague since the Centauran-Rigan War.'

The passage rang with a sudden sound. The gleaming robant and Mrs Gordon emerged through the doorway into the control room. The old woman's face was alive with excitement. 'Captain! Is that–is that Earth down there?'

Andrews nodded. 'Yes.'

The robant led Mrs Gordon over to the big viewscreen. The old woman's face twitched, ripples of emotion stirring her withered features. 'I can hardly believe that's really Earth. It seems impossible.'

Norton glanced sharply at Captain Andrews.

'It's Earth,' Andrews stated, not meeting Norton's glance. 'The moon should be around soon.'

The old woman did not speak. She had turned her back.

Andrews contacted the auto-grapple and hooked the robant pilot on. The transport shuddered and then began to drop, as the beam from Emphor caught it and took over.

'We're landing,' Andrews said to the old woman, touching her on the shoulder.

'She can't hear you, sir,' the robant said.

Andrews grunted. 'Well, she can see.'

Below them the pitted, ruined surface of Emphor III was rising rapidly. The ship entered the cloud belt and emerged, coasting over a barren plain that stretched as far as the eye could see.

'What happened down there?' Norton said to Andrews. 'The war?'

'War. Mining. And it's old. The pits are probably bomb craters. Some of the long trenches may be scoop gouges. Looks like they really exhausted this place.'

A crooked row of broken mountain peaks shot past under them. They were nearing the remains of an ocean. Dark, unhealthy water lapped below, a vast sea, crusted with salt and waste, its edges disappearing into banks of piled debris.

'Why is it that way?' Mrs Gordon said suddenly. Doubt crossed her features. 'Why?'

'What do you mean?' Andrews said.

'I don't understand.' She stared uncertainly down at the surface below. 'It isn't supposed to be this way. Earth is green. Green and alive. Blue water and . . .' Her voice trailed off uneasily. '*Why?*'

Andrews grabbed some paper and wrote:

COMMERCIAL OPERATIONS EXHAUSTED SURFACE

Mrs Gordon studied his words, her lips twitching. A spasm moved through her, shaking the thin, dried-out body. 'Exhausted . . .' Her voice rose in shrill dismay. 'It's not supposed to be this way! I don't *want* it this way!'

The robant took her arm. 'She had better rest. I'll return her to her quarters. Please notify us when the landing has been made.'

'Sure.' Andrews nodded awkwardly as the robant led the old woman from the viewscreen. She clung to the guide rail, face distorted with fear and bewilderment.

'Something's wrong!' she wailed. 'Why is it this way? Why . . .'

The robant led her from the control room. The closing of the hydraulic safety doors cut off her thin cry abruptly.

Andrews relaxed, his body sagging. 'God.' He lit a cigarette shakily. 'What a racket she makes.'

'We're almost down,' Norton said frigidly.

Cold wind lashed at them as they stepped out cautiously. The air smelled bad–sour and acrid. Like rotten eggs. The wind brought salt and sand blowing up against their faces.

A few miles off the thick sea lay. They could hear it swishing faintly, gummily. A few birds passed silently overhead, great wings flapping soundlessly.

'Depressing damn place,' Andrews muttered.

'Yeah. I wonder what the old lady's thinking.'

Down the descent ramp came the glittering robant, helping the little old woman. She moved hesitantly, unsteady, gripping the robant's metal arm. The cold wind whipped around her frail body. For a moment she tottered–and then came on, leaving the ramp and gaining the uneven ground.

Norton shook his head. 'She looks bad. This air. And the wind.'

'I know.' Andrews moved back towards Mrs Gordon and the robant. 'How is she?' he asked.

'She is not well, sir,' the robant answered.

'Captain,' the old woman whispered.

'What is it?'

'You must tell me the truth. Is this–is this really Earth?'

She watched his lips closely. 'You swear it is? You *swear?*' Her voice rose in shrill terror.

'It's Earth!' Andrews snapped irritably. 'I told you before. Of course it's Earth.'

'It doesn't look like Earth.' Mrs Gordon clung to his answer, panic-stricken. 'It doesn't look like Earth, Captain. Is it really Earth?'

'Yes!'

Her gaze wandered towards the ocean. A strange look flickered across her tired face, igniting her faded eyes with sudden hunger. 'Is that water? I want to see.'

Andrews turned to Norton. 'Get the launch out. Drive her where she wants.'

Norton pulled back angrily. 'Me?'

'That's an order.'

'Okay.' Norton returned reluctantly to the ship. Andrews lit a cigarette moodily and waited. Presently the launch slid out of the ship, coasting across the ash towards them.

'You can show her anything she wants,' Andrews said to the robant. 'Norton will drive you.'

'Thank you, sir,' the robant said. 'She will be grateful. She has wanted all her life to stand on Earth. She remembers her grandfather telling her about it. She believes that he came from Earth, a long time ago. She is very old. She is the last living member of her family.'

'But Earth is just a–' Andrews caught himself. 'I mean–'

'Yes, sir. But she is very old. And she has waited many years.' The robant turned to the old woman and led her gently toward the launch. Andrews stared after them sullenly, rubbing his jaw and frowning.

'Okay,' Norton's voice came from the launch. He slid the hatch open and the robant led the old woman carefully inside. The hatch closed after them.

A moment later the launch shot away across the salt flat, towards the ugly, lapping ocean.

*

Norton and Captain Andrews paced restlessly along the shore. The sky was darkening. Sheets of salt blew against them. The mud flats stank in the gathering gloom of night. Dimly, off in the distance, a line of hills faded into the silence and vapors.

'Go on,' Andrews said. 'What then?'

'That's all. She got out of the launch. She and the robant. I stayed inside. They stood looking across the ocean. After a while the old woman sent the robant back to the launch.'

'Why?'

'I don't know. She wanted to be alone, I suppose. She stood for a time by herself. On the shore. Looking over the water. The wind rising. All at once she just sort of settled down. She sank down in a heap, into the salt ash.'

'Then what?'

'While I was pulling myself together, the robant leaped out and ran to her. It picked her up. It stood for a second and then it started for the water. I leaped out of the launch, yelling. It stepped into the water and disappeared. Sank down in the mud and filth. Vanished.' Norton shuddered. 'With her body.'

Andrews tossed his cigarette savagely away. The cigarette rolled off, glowing behind them. 'Anything more?'

'Nothing. It all happened in a second. She was standing there, looking over the water. Suddenly she quivered–like a dead branch. Then she just sort of dwindled away. And the robant was out of the launch and into the water with her before I could figure out what was happening.'

The sky was almost dark. Huge clouds drifted across the faint stars. Clouds of unhealthy night vapors and particles of waste. A flock of immense birds crossed the horizon, flying silently.

Against the broken hills the moon was rising. A diseased, barren globe, tinted faintly yellow. Like old parchment.

'Let's get back in the ship,' Andrews said. 'I don't like this place.'

'I can't figure out why it happened. The old woman.' Norton shook his head.

'The wind. Radio-active toxins. I checked with Centaurus II.

The war devastated the whole system. Left the planet a lethal wreck.'

'Then we won't–'

'No. We won't have to answer for it.' They continued for a time in silence. 'We won't have to explain. It's evident enough. Anybody coming here, especially an old person–'

'Only nobody would come here,' Norton said bitterly. 'Especially an old person.'

Andrews didn't answer. He paced along, head down, hands in pockets. Norton followed silently behind. Above them, the single moon grew brighter as it escaped the mists and entered a patch of clear sky.

'By the way,' Norton said, his voice cold and distant behind Andrews. 'This is the last trip I'll be making with you. While I was in the ship I filed a formal request for new papers.'

'Oh.'

'Thought I'd let you know. And my share of the kilo positives. You can keep it.'

Andrews flushed and increased his pace, leaving Norton behind. The old woman's death had shaken him. He lit another cigarette and then threw it away.

Damn it–the fault wasn't *his*. She had been old. Three hundred and fifty years. Senile and deaf. A faded leaf, carried off by the wind. By the poisonous wind that lashed and twisted endlessly across the ruined face of the planet.

The ruined face. Salt ash and debris. The broken line of crumbling hills. And the silence. The eternal silence. Nothing but the wind and the lapping of the thick stagnant water. And the dark birds overhead.

Something glinted. Something at his feet, in the salt ash. Reflecting the sickly pallor of the moon.

Andrews bent down and groped in the darkness. His fingers closed over something hard. He picked the small disc up and examined it.

'Strange,' he said.

*

It wasn't until they were out in deep space, roaring back towards Fomalhaut, that he remembered the disc.

He slid away from the control panel, searching his pockets for it.

The disc was worn and thin. And terribly old. Andrews rubbed it and spat on it until it was clean enough to make out. A faint impression–nothing more. He turned it over. A token? Washer? Coin?

On the back were a few meaningless letters. Some ancient, forgotten script. He held the disc to the light until he made the letters out.

E PLURIBUS UNUM

He shrugged, tossed the ancient bit of metal into a waste disposal unit beside him, and turned his attention to the star charts, and home . . .

IMPOSTOR

'One of these days I'm going to take time off,' Spence Olham said at first-meal. He looked around at his wife. 'I think I've earned a rest. Ten years is a long time.'

'And the Project?'

'The war will be won without me. This ball of clay of ours isn't really in much danger.' Olham sat down at the table and lit a cigarette. 'The news-machines alter dispatches to make it appear the Outspacers are right on top of us. You know what I'd like to do on my vacation? I'd like to take a camping trip to those mountains outside of town, where we went that time. Remember? I got poison oak and you almost stepped on a gopher snake.'

'Sutton Wood?' Mary began to clear away the food dishes. 'The Wood was burned a few weeks ago. I thought you knew. Some kind of a flash fire.'

Olham sagged. 'Didn't they even try to find the cause?' His lips twisted. 'No one cares anymore. All they can think of is the war.' He clamped his jaws together, the whole picture coming up in his mind, the Outspacers, the war, the needle-ships.

'How can we think about anything else?'

Olham nodded. She was right, of course. The dark little ships out of Alpha Centauri had bypassed the Earth cruisers easily, leaving them like helpless turtles. It had been one-way fights, all the way back to Terra.

All the way, until the protec-bubble was demonstrated by Westinghouse Labs. Thrown around the major Earth cities and finally the planet itself, the bubble was the first real defense, the first legitimate answer to the Outspacers—as the news-machines labeled them.

But to win the war, that was another thing. Every lab, every Project was working night and day, endlessly, to find something more: a weapon for positive combat. His own Project, for example. All day long, year after year.

Olham stood up, putting out his cigarette. 'Like the Sword of Damocles. Always hanging over us. I'm getting tired. All I want to do is take a long rest. But I guess everybody feels that way.'

He got his jacket from the closet and went out on the front porch. The shoot would be along any moment, the fast little bug that would carry him to the Project.

'I hope Nelson isn't late.' He looked at his watch. 'It's almost seven.'

'Here the bug comes,' Mary said, gazing between the rows of houses. The sun glittered behind the roofs, reflecting against the heavy lead plates. The settlement was quiet; only a few people were stirring. 'I'll see you later. Try not to work beyond your shift, Spence.'

Olham opened the car door and slid inside, leaning back against the seat with a sigh. There was an older man with Nelson.

'Well?' Olham said, as the bug shot ahead. 'Heard any interesting news?'

'The usual,' Nelson said. 'A few Outspace ships hit, another asteroid abandoned for strategic reasons.'

'It'll be good when we get the Project into final stage. Maybe it's just the propaganda from the news-machines, but in the last month I've gotten weary of all this. Everything seems so grim and serious, no color to life.'

'Do you think the war is in vain?' the older man said suddenly. 'You are an integral part of it, yourself.'

'This is Major Peters,' Nelson said. Olham and Peters shook hands. Olham studied the older man.

'What brings you along so early?' he said. 'I don't remember seeing you at the Project before.'

'No, I'm not with the Project,' Peters said, 'but I know something about what you're doing. My own work is altogether different.'

A look passed between him and Nelson. Olham noticed it and he frowned. The bug was gaining speed, flashing across the barren, lifeless ground toward the distant rim of the Project building.

'What is your business?' Olham said. 'Or aren't you permitted to talk about it?'

'I'm with the government,' Peters said. 'With FSA, the security organ.'

'Oh?' Olham raised an eyebrow. 'Is there any enemy infiltration in this region?'

'As a matter of fact I'm here to see you, Mr Olham.'

Olham was puzzled. He considered Peters' words, but he could make nothing of them. 'To see me? Why?'

'I'm here to arrest you as an Outspace spy. That's why I'm up so early this morning. *Grab him, Nelson–*'

The gun drove into Olham's ribs. Nelson's hands were shaking, trembling with released emotion, his face pale. He took a deep breath and let it out again.

'Shall we kill him now?' he whispered to Peters. 'I think we should kill him now. We can't wait.'

Olham stared into his friend's face. He opened his mouth to speak, but no words came. Both men were staring at him steadily, rigid and grim with fright. Olham felt dizzy. His head ached and spun.

'I don't understand,' he murmured.

At that moment the shoot car left the ground and rushed up, heading into space. Below them the Project fell away, smaller and smaller, disappearing. Olham shut his mouth.

'We can wait a little,' Peters said. 'I want to ask him some questions first.'

Olham gazed dully ahead as the bug rushed through space.

'The arrest was made all right,' Peters said into the vidscreen. On the screen the features of the security chief showed. 'It should be a load off everyone's mind.'

'Any complications?'

'None. He entered the bug without suspicion. He didn't seem to think my presence was too unusual.'

'Where are you now?'

'On our way out, just inside the protec-bubble. We're moving at a maximum speed. You can assume that the critical period is past. I'm glad the takeoff jets in this craft were in good working order. If there had been any failure at that point–'

'Let me see him,' the security chief said. He gazed directly at Olham where he sat, his hands in his lap, staring ahead.

'So that's the man.' He looked at Olham for a time. Olham said nothing. At last the chief nodded to Peters. 'All right. That's enough.' A faint trace of disgust wrinkled his features. 'I've seen all I want. You've done something that will be remembered for a long time. They're preparing some sort of citation for both of you.'

'That's not necessary,' Peters said.

'How much danger is there now? Is there still much chance that–'

'There is some chance, but not too much. According to my understanding it requires a verbal key phrase. In any case we'll have to take the risk.'

'I'll have the Moon base notified you're coming.'

'No.' Peters shook his head. 'I'll land the ship outside, beyond the base. I don't want it in jeopardy.'

'Just as you like.' The chief's eyes flickered as he glanced again at Olham. Then his image faded. The screen blanked.

Olham shifted his gaze to the window. The ship was already through the protec-bubble, rushing with greater and greater speed all the time. Peters was in a hurry; below him, rumbling under the floor, the jets were wide open. They were afraid, hurrying frantically, because of him.

Next to him on the seat, Nelson shifted uneasily. 'I think we should do it now,' he said. 'I'd give anything if we could get it over with.'

'Take it easy,' Peters said. 'I want you to guide the ship for a while so I can talk to him.'

He slid over beside Olham, looking into his face. Presently he reached out and touched him gingerly, on the arm and then on the cheek.

Olham said nothing. *If I could let Mary know*, he thought again. *If I could find some way of letting her know*. He looked around the ship. How? The vidscreen? Nelson was sitting by the board, holding the gun. There was nothing he could do. He was caught, trapped.

But why?

'Listen,' Peters said, 'I want to ask you some questions. You know where we're going. We're moving Moonward. In an hour we'll land on the far side, on the desolate side. After we land you'll be turned over immediately to a team of men waiting there. Your body will be destroyed at once. Do you understand that?' He looked at his watch. 'Within two hours your parts will be strewn over the landscape. There won't be anything left of you.'

Olham struggled out of his lethargy. 'Can't you tell me–'

'Certainly, I'll tell you.' Peters nodded. 'Two days ago we received a report that an Outspace ship had penetrated the protec-bubble. The ship let off a spy in the form of a humanoid robot. The robot was to destroy a particular human being and take his place.'

Peters looked calmly at Olham.

'Inside the robot was a U-Bomb. Our agent did not know how the bomb was to be detonated, but he conjectured that it might be by a particular spoken phrase, a certain group of words. The robot would live the life of the person he killed, entering into his usual activities, his job, his social life. He had been constructed to resemble that person. No one would know the difference.'

Olham's face went sickly chalk.

'The person whom the robot was to impersonate was Spence Olham, a high-ranking official at one of the research Projects. Because this particular Project was approaching crucial stage, the presence of an animate bomb, moving toward the center of the Project–'

Olham stared down at his hands. *'But I'm Olham!'*

'Once the robot had located and killed Olham it was a simple matter to take over his life. The robot was probably released from the ship eight days ago. The substitution was probably accomplished over the last weekend, when Olham went for a short walk in the hills.'

'But I'm Olham.' He turned to Nelson, sitting at the controls. 'Don't you recognize me? You've known me for twenty years. Don't you remember how we went to college together?' He stood up. 'You and I were at the University. We had the same room.' He went toward Nelson.

'Stay away from me!' Nelson snarled.

'Listen. Remember our second year? Remember that girl? What was her name–' He rubbed his forehead. 'The one with the dark hair. The one we met over at Ted's place.'

'Stop!' Nelson waved the gun frantically. 'I don't want to hear any more. You killed him! You . . . machine.'

Olham looked at Nelson. 'You're wrong. I don't know what happened, but the robot never reached me. Something must have gone wrong. Maybe the ship crashed.' He turned to Peters. 'I'm Olham. I know it. No transfer was made. I'm the same as I've always been.'

He touched himself, running his hands over his body. 'There must be some way to prove it. Take me back to Earth. An X-ray examination, a neurological study, anything like that will show you. Or maybe we can find the crashed ship.'

Neither Peters nor Nelson spoke.

'I am Olham,' he said again. 'I know I am. But I can't prove it.'

'The robot,' Peters said, 'would be unaware that he was not the real Spence Olham. He would become Olham in mind as well as body. He was given an artificial memory system, false recall. He would look like him, have his memories, his thoughts and interests, perform his job.

'But there would be one difference. Inside the robot is a U-Bomb, ready to explode at the trigger phrase.' Peters moved a little away.

'That's the one difference. That's why we're taking you to the Moon. They'll disassemble you and remove the bomb. Maybe it will explode, but it won't matter, not there.'

Olham sat down slowly.

'We'll be there soon,' Nelson said.

He lay back, thinking frantically, as the ship dropped slowly down. Under them was the pitted surface of the Moon, the endless expanse of ruin. What could he do? What would save him?

'Get ready,' Peters said.

In a few minutes he would be dead. Down below he could see a tiny dot, a building of some kind. There were men in the building, the demolition team, waiting to tear him to bits. They would rip him open, pull off his arms and legs, break him apart. When they found no bomb they would be surprised; they would know, but it would be too late.

Olham looked around the small cabin. Nelson was still holding the gun. There was no chance there. If he could get to a doctor, have an examination made–that was the only way. Mary could help him. He thought frantically, his mind racing. Only a few minutes, just a little time left. If he could contact her, get word to her some way.

'Easy,' Peters said. The ship came down slowly, bumping on the rough ground. There was silence.

'Listen,' Olham said thickly. 'I can prove I'm Spence Olham. Get a doctor. Bring him here–'

'There's the squad.' Nelson pointed. 'They're coming.' He glanced nervously at Olham. 'I hope nothing happens.'

'We'll be gone before they start work,' Peters said. 'We'll be out of here in a moment.' He put on his pressure suit. When he had finished he took the gun from Nelson. 'I'll watch him for a moment.'

Nelson put on his pressure suit, hurrying awkwardly. 'How about him?' He indicated Olham. 'Will he need one?'

'No.' Peters shook his head. 'Robots probably don't require oxygen.'

The group of men were almost to the ship. They halted, waiting. Peters signaled to them.

'Come on!' He waved his hand and the men approached warily; stiff, grotesque figures in their inflated suits.

'If you open the door,' Olham said, 'it means my death. It will be murder.'

'Open the door,' Nelson said. He reached for the handle.

Olham watched him. He saw the man's hand tighten around the metal rod. In a moment the door would swing back, the air in the ship would rush out. He would die, and presently they would realize their mistake. Perhaps at some other time, when there was no war, men might not act this way, hurrying an individual to his death because they were afraid. Everyone was frightened, everyone was willing to sacrifice the individual because of the group fear.

He was being killed because they could not wait to be sure of his guilt. There was not enough time.

He looked at Nelson. Nelson had been his friend for years. They had gone to school together. He had been best man at his wedding. Now Nelson was going to kill him. But Nelson was not wicked; it was not his fault. It was the times. Perhaps it had been the same way during the plagues. When men had shown a spot they probably had been killed, too, without a moment's hesitation, without proof, on suspicion alone. In times of danger there was no other way.

He did not blame them. But he had to live. His life was too precious to be sacrificed. Olham thought quickly. What could he do? Was there anything? He looked around.

'Here goes,' Nelson said.

'You're right,' Olham said. The sound of his own voice surprised him. It was the strength of desperation. 'I have no need of air. Open the door.'

They paused, looking at him in curious alarm.

'Go ahead. Open it. It makes no difference.' Olham's hand disappeared inside his jacket. 'I wonder how far you two can run?'

'Run?'

'You have fifteen seconds to live.' Inside his jacket his fingers twisted, his arm suddenly rigid. He relaxed, smiling a little. 'You were wrong about the trigger phrase. In that respect you were mistaken. Fourteen seconds, now.'

Two shocked faces stared at him from the pressure suits. Then they were struggling, running, tearing the door open. The air shrieked out, spilling into the void. Peters and Nelson bolted out of the ship. Olham came after them. He grasped the door and dragged it shut. The automatic pressure system chugged furiously, restoring the air. Olham let his breath out with a shudder.

One more second–

Beyond the window the two men had joined the group. The group scattered, running in all directions. One by one they threw themselves down, prone on the ground. Olham seated himself at the control board. He moved the dials into place. As the ship rose up into the air the men below scrambled to their feet and stared up, their mouths open.

'Sorry,' Olham murmured, 'but I've got to get back to Earth.'

He headed the ship back the way it had come.

It was night. All around the ship crickets chirped, disturbing the chill darkness. Olham bent over the vidscreen. Gradually the image formed; the call had gone through without trouble. He breathed a sigh of relief.

'Mary,' he said. The woman stared at him. She gasped.

'Spence! Where are you? What's happened?'

'I can't tell you. Listen, I have to talk fast. They may break this call off any minute. Go to the Project grounds and get Dr Chamberlain. If he isn't there, get any doctor. Bring him to the house and have him stay there. Have him bring equipment, X-ray, fluoroscope, everything.'

'But–'

'Do as I say. Hurry. Have him get it ready in an hour.' Olham leaned toward the screen. 'Is everything all right? Are you alone?'

'Alone?'

'Is anyone with you? Has . . . has Nelson or anyone contacted you?'

'No. Spence, I don't understand.'

'All right. I'll see you at the house in an hour. And don't tell anyone anything. Get Chamberlain there on any pretext. Say you're very ill.'

He broke the connection and looked at his watch. A moment later he left the ship, stepping down into the darkness. He had a half mile to go.

He began to walk.

One light showed in the window, the study light. He watched it, kneeling against the fence. There was no sound, no movement of any kind. He held his watch up and read it by starlight. Almost an hour had passed.

Along the street a shoot bug came. It went on.

Olham looked toward the house. The doctor should have already come. He should be inside, waiting with Mary. A thought struck him. Had she been able to leave the house? Perhaps they had intercepted her. Maybe he was moving into a trap.

But what else could he do?

With a doctor's records, photographs and reports, there was a chance, a chance of proof. If he could be examined, if he could remain alive long enough for them to study him–

He could prove it that way. It was probably the only way. His one hope lay inside the house. Dr Chamberlain was a respected man. He was the staff doctor for the Project. He would know, his word on the matter would have meaning. He could overcome their hysteria, their madness, with facts.

Madness–That was what it was. If only they would wait, act slowly, take their time. But they could not wait. He had to die, die at once, without proof, without any kind of trial or examination. The simplest test would tell, but they had no time for the simplest test. They could think only of the danger. Danger, and nothing more.

He stood up and moved toward the house. He came up on the porch. At the door he paused, listening. Still no sound. The house was absolutely still.

Too still.

Olham stood on the porch, unmoving. They were trying to be silent inside. Why? It was a small house; only a few feet away, beyond the door, Mary and Dr Chamberlain should be standing. Yet he could hear nothing, no sound of voices, nothing at all. He looked at the door. It was a door he had opened and closed a thousand times, every morning and every night.

He put his hand on the knob. Then, all at once, he reached out and touched the bell instead. The bell pealed, off some place in the back of the house. Olham smiled. He could hear movement.

Mary opened the door. As soon as he saw her face he knew.

He ran, throwing himself into the bushes. A security officer shoved Mary out of the way, firing past her. The bushes burst apart. Olham wriggled around the side of the house. He leaped up and ran, racing frantically into the darkness. A searchlight snapped on, a beam of light circling past him.

He crossed the road and squeezed over a fence. He jumped down and made his way across a backyard. Behind him men were coming, security officers, shouting to each other as they came. Olham gasped for breath, his chest rising and falling.

Her face–He had known at once. The set lips, the terrified, wretched eyes. Suppose he had gone ahead, pushed open the door and entered! They had tapped the call and come at once, as soon as he had broken off. Probably she believed their account. No doubt she thought he was the robot, too.

Olham ran on and on. He was losing the officers, dropping them behind. Apparently they were not much good at running. He climbed a hill and made his way down the other side. In a moment he would be back at the ship. But where to, this time? He slowed down, stopping. He could see the ship already, outlined against the sky, where he had parked it. The settlement was behind him; he was on the outskirts of the wilderness between the inhabited places, where the forests and desolation began. He crossed a barren field and entered the trees.

As he came toward it, the door of the ship opened.

Peters stepped out, framed against the light. In his arms was a heavy Boris gun. Olham stopped, rigid. Peters stared around him, into the darkness. 'I know you're there, some place,' he said. 'Come on up here, Olham. There are security men all around you.'

Olham did not move.

'Listen to me. We will catch you very shortly. Apparently you still do not believe you're the robot. Your call to the woman indicates that you are still under the illusion created by your artificial memories.

'But you *are* the robot. You are the robot, and inside you is the bomb. Any moment the trigger phrase may be spoken, by you, by someone else, by anyone. When that happens the bomb will destroy everything for miles around. The Project, the woman, all of us will be killed. Do you understand?'

Olham said nothing. He was listening. Men were moving toward him, slipping through the woods.

'If you don't come out, we'll catch you. It will be only a matter of time. We no longer plan to remove you to the Moon base. You will be destroyed on sight, and we will have to take the chance that the bomb will detonate. I have ordered every available security officer into the area. The whole county is being searched, inch by inch. There is no place you can go. Around this wood is a cordon of armed men. You have about six hours left before the last inch is covered.'

Olham moved away. Peters went on speaking; he had not seen him at all. It was too dark to see anyone. But Peters was right. There was no place he could go. He was beyond the settlement, on the outskirts where the woods began. He could hide for a time, but eventually they would catch him.

Only a matter of time.

Olham walked quietly through the wood. Mile by mile, each part of the county was being measured off, laid bare, searched, studied, examined. The cordon was coming all the time, squeezing him into a smaller and smaller space.

What was there left? He had lost the ship, the one hope of escape.

They were at his home; his wife was with them, believing, no doubt, that the real Olham had been killed. He clenched his fists. Some place there was a wrecked Outspace needle-ship, and in it the remains of the robot. Somewhere nearby the ship had crashed and broken up.

And the robot lay inside, destroyed.

A faint hope stirred him. What if he could find the remains? If he could show them the wreckage, the remains of the ship, the robot–

But where? Where would he find it?

He walked on, lost in thought. Some place, not too far off, probably. The ship would have landed close to the Project; the robot would have expected to go the rest of the way on foot. He went up the side of a hill and looked around. Crashed and burned. Was there some clue, some hint? Had he read anything, heard anything? Some place close by, within walking distance. Some wild place, a remote spot where there would be no people.

Suddenly Olham smiled. Crashed and burned–

Sutton Wood.

He increased his pace.

It was morning. Sunlight filtered down through the broken trees, onto the man crouching at the edge of the clearing. Olham glanced up from time to time, listening. They were not far off, only a few minutes away. He smiled.

Down below him, strewn across the clearing and into the charred stumps that had been Sutton Wood, lay a tangled mass of wreckage. In the sunlight it glittered a little, gleaming darkly. He had not had too much trouble finding it. Sutton Wood was a place he knew well; he had climbed around it many times in his life, when he was younger. He had known where he would find the remains. There was one peak that jutted up suddenly, without a warning.

A descending ship, unfamiliar with the wood, had little chance of missing it. And now he squatted, looking down at the ship, or what remained of it.

Olham stood up. He could hear them, only a little distance away, coming together, talking in low tones. He tensed himself. Everything depended on who first saw him. If it was Nelson, he had no chance. Nelson would fire at once. He would be dead before they saw the ship. But if he had time to call out, hold them off for a moment–That was all he needed. Once they saw the ship he would be safe.

But if they fired first–

A charred branch cracked. A figure appeared, coming forward uncertainly. Olham took a deep breath. Only a few seconds remained, perhaps the last seconds of his life. He raised his arms, peering intently.

It was Peters.

'Peters!' Olham waved his arms. Peters lifted his gun, aiming. 'Don't fire!' His voice shook. 'Wait a minute. Look past me, across the clearing.'

'I've found him,' Peters shouted. Security men came pouring out of the burned woods around him.

'Don't shoot. Look past me. The ship, the needle-ship. The Outspace ship. Look!'

Peters hesitated. The gun wavered.

'It's down there,' Olham said rapidly. 'I knew I'd find it here. The burned wood. Now you believe me. You'll find the remains of the robot in the ship. Look, will you?'

'There is something down there,' one of the men said nervously.

'Shoot him!' a voice said. It was Nelson.

'Wait.' Peters turned sharply. 'I'm in charge. Don't anyone fire. Maybe he's telling the truth.'

'Shoot him,' Nelson said. 'He killed Olham. Any minute he may kill us all. If the bomb goes off–'

'Shut up.' Peters advanced toward the slope. He stared down. 'Look at that.' He waved two men up to him. 'Go down there and see what that is.'

The men raced down the slope, across the clearing. They bent down, poking in the ruins of the ship.

'Well?' Peters called.

Olham held his breath. He smiled a little. It must be there; he had not had time to look, himself, but it had to be there. Suddenly doubt assailed him. Suppose the robot had lived long enough to wander away? Suppose his body had been completely destroyed, burned to ashes by the fire?

He licked his lips. Perspiration came out on his forehead. Nelson was staring at him, his face still livid. His chest rose and fell.

'Kill him,' Nelson said. 'Before he kills us.'

The two men stood up.

'What have you found?' Peters said. He held the gun steady. 'Is there anything there?'

'Looks like something. It's a needle-ship, all right. There's something beside it.'

'I'll look.' Peters strode past Olham. Olham watched him go down the hill and up to the men. The others were following after him, peering to see.

'It's a body of some sort,' Peters said. 'Look at it!'

Olham came along with them. They stood around in a circle, staring down.

On the ground, bent and twisted in a strange shape, was a grotesque form. It looked human, perhaps; except that it was bent so strangely, the arms and legs flung off in all directions. The mouth was open; the eyes stared glassily.

'Like a machine that's run down,' Peters murmured.

Olham smiled feebly. 'Well?' he said.

Peters looked at him. 'I can't believe it. You were telling the truth all the time.'

'The robot never reached me,' Olham said. He took out a cigarette and lit it. 'It was destroyed when the ship crashed. You were all too busy with the war to wonder why an out-of-the-way woods would suddenly catch fire and burn. Now you know.'

He stood smoking, watching the men. They were dragging the grotesque remains from the ship. The body was stiff, the arms and legs rigid.

'You'll find the bomb now,' Olham said. The men laid the body on the ground. Peters bent down.

'I think I see the corner of it.' He reached out, touching the body.

The chest of the corpse had been laid open. Within the gaping tear something glinted, something metal. The men stared at the metal without speaking.

'That would have destroyed us all, if it had lived,' Peters said. 'That metal box there.'

There was silence.

'I think we owe you something,' Peters said to Olham. 'This must have been a nightmare to you. If you hadn't escaped, we would have–' He broke off.

Olham put out his cigarette. 'I knew, of course, that the robot had never reached me. But I had no way of proving it. Sometimes it isn't possible to prove a thing right away. That was the whole trouble. There wasn't any way I could demonstrate that I was myself.'

'How about a vacation?' Peters said. 'I think we might work out a month's vacation for you. You could take it easy, relax.'

'I think right now I want to go home,' Olham said.

'All right, then,' Peters said. 'Whatever you say.'

Nelson had squatted down on the ground, beside the corpse. He reached out toward the glint of metal visible within the chest.

'Don't touch it,' Olham said. 'It might still go off. We better let the demolition squad take care of it later on.'

Nelson said nothing. Suddenly he grabbed hold of the metal, reaching his hand inside the chest. He pulled.

'What are you doing?' Olham cried.

Nelson stood up. He was holding on to the metal object. His face was blank with terror. It was a metal knife, an Outspace needle-knife, covered with blood.

'This killed him,' Nelson whispered. 'My friend was killed with this.' He looked at Olham. 'You killed him with this and left him beside the ship.'

Olham was trembling. His teeth chattered. He looked from the knife to the body. 'This can't be Olham,' he said. His mind spun, everything was whirling. 'Was I wrong?'

He gaped.

'But if that's Olham, then I must be–'

He did not complete the sentence, only the first phrase. The blast was visible all the way to Alpha Centauri.

JAMES P. CROW

'You're a nasty little—human being,' the newly-formed Z Type robot shrilled peevishly.

Donnie flushed and slunk away. It was true. He was a human being, a human child. And there was nothing science could do. He was stuck with it. A human being in a robot's world.

He wished he were dead. He wished he lay under the grass and the worms were eating him up and crawling through him and devouring his brain, his poor miserable human's brain. The Z-236r, his robot companion, wouldn't have anybody to play with and it would be sorry.

'Where are you going?' Z-236r demanded.

'Home.'

'Sissy.'

Donnie didn't reply. He gathered up his set of fourth-dimensional chess, stuffed it in his pocket, and walked off between the rows of ecarda trees, toward the human quarter. Behind him, Z-236r stood gleaming in the late afternoon sun, a pale tower of metal and plastic.

'See if I care,' Z-236r shouted sullenly. 'Who wants to play with a human being, anyhow? Go on home. You—you smell.'

Donnie said nothing. But he hunched over a little more. And his chin sank lower against his chest.

'Well, it happened,' Edgar Parks said gloomily to his wife, across the kitchen table.

Grace looked quickly up. 'It?'

'Donnie learned his place today. He told me while I was changing my clothes. One of the new robots he was playing with. Called him a human being. Poor kid. Why the hell do they have to rub it in? Why can't they let us alone?'

'So that's why he didn't want any dinner. He's in his room. I knew something had happened.' Grace touched her husband's hand. 'He'll get over it. We all have to learn the hard way. He's strong. He'll snap back.'

Ed Parks got up from the table and moved into the living room of his modest five-room dwelling unit, located in the section of the city set aside for humans. He didn't feel like eating. 'Robots.' He clenched his fists futilely. 'I'd like to get hold of one of them. Just once. Get my hands into their guts. Rip out handfuls of wire and parts. Just once before I die.'

'Maybe you'll get your chance.'

'No. No, it'll never come to that. Anyhow, humans wouldn't be able to run things without robots. It's true, honey. Humans haven't got the integration to maintain a society. The Lists prove that twice a year. Let's face it. Humans are inferior to robots. But it's their damn holding it up to us! Like today with Donnie. Holding it up to our faces. I don't mind being a robot's body servant. It's a good job. Pays well and the work is light. But when my kid gets told he's–'

Ed broke off. Donnie had come out of his room slowly, into the living room. 'Hi, Dad.'

'Hi, son.' Ed thumped the boy gently on the back. 'How you doing? Want to take in a show tonight?'

Humans entertained nightly on the vidscreens. Humans made good entertainers. That was one area the robots couldn't compete in. Human beings painted and wrote and danced and sang and acted for the amusement of robots. They cooked better, too, but robots didn't eat. Human beings had their place. They were understood and wanted: as body servants, entertainers, clerks, gardeners, construction workers, repairmen, odd-jobbers and factory workers.

But when it came to something like civic control coordinator or traffic supervisor for the usone tapes that fed energy into the planet's twelve hydrosystems–

'Dad,' Donnie said, 'can I ask you something?'

'Sure.' Ed sat down on the couch with a sigh. He leaned back and crossed his legs. 'What is it?'

Donnie sat quietly beside him, his little round face serious. 'Dad, I want to ask you about the Lists.'

'Oh, yeah.' Ed rubbed his jaw. 'That's right. Lists in a few weeks. Time to start boning up for your entry. We'll get out some of the sample tests and go over them. Maybe between the two of us we can get you ready for Class Twenty.'

'Listen.' Donnie leaned close to his father, his voice low and intense. 'Dad, how many humans have ever passed their Lists?'

Ed got up abruptly and paced around the room, filling his pipe and frowning. 'Well, son, that's hard to say. I mean, humans don't have access to the C-Bank records. So I can't check to see. The law says any human who gets a score in the top forty per cent is eligible for classification with a gradual upward gradation according to subsequent showing. I don't know how many humans have been able to–'

'Has *any* human ever passed his List?'

Ed swallowed nervously. 'Gosh, kid. I don't know. I mean, I don't honestly know of any, when you put it like that. Maybe not. The Lists have been conducted only three hundred years. Before that the Government was reactionary and forbade humans to compete with robots. Nowadays, we have a liberal Government and we can compete on the Lists and if we get high enough scores . . .' His voice wavered and faded. 'No, kid,' he said miserably. 'No human ever passed a List. We're–just–not–smart enough.'

The room was silent. Donnie nodded faintly, expressionless. Ed didn't look at him. He concentrated on his pipe, hands shaking.

'It's not so bad,' Ed said huskily. 'I have a good job. I'm body servant to a hell of a fine N Type robot. I get big tips at Christmas and Easter. It gives me time off when I'm sick.' He cleared his throat noisily. 'It's not so bad.'

Grace was standing at the door. Now she came into the room, eyes bright. 'No, not bad. Not at all. You open doors for it, bring its instruments to it, make calls for it, run errands for it, oil it, repair it, sing to it, talk to it, scan tapes for it–'

'Shut up,' Ed muttered irritably. 'What the hell should I do? Quit? Maybe I should mow lawns like John Hollister and Pete Klein. At least my robot calls me by name. Like a living thing. It calls me Ed.'

'Will a human ever pass a List?' Donnie asked.

'Yes,' Grace said sharply.

Ed nodded. 'Sure, kid. Of course. Someday maybe humans and robots will live together in equality. There's an Equality Party among the robots. Holds ten seats in the Congress. They think humans should be admitted without Lists. Since it's obvious–' He broke off. 'I mean, since no humans have ever been able to pass their Lists so far–'

'Donnie,' Grace said fiercely, bending down over her son. 'Listen to me. I want you to pay attention. Nobody knows this. The robots don't talk about it. Humans don't know. But it's true.'

'What is it?'

'I know of a human being who–who's classified. He passed his Lists. Ten years ago. And he's gone up. He's up to Class Two. Someday he'll be Class One. Do you hear? A human being. And he's going up.'

Donnie's face showed doubt. 'Really?' The doubt turned to wistful hope. 'Class Two? No kidding?'

'It's just a story,' Ed grunted. 'I've heard that all my life.'

'It's true! I heard two robots talking about it when I was cleaning up one of the Engineering Units. They stopped when they noticed me.'

'What's his name?' Donnie asked, wide-eyed.

'James P. Crow,' Grace said proudly.

'Strange name,' Ed murmured.

'That's his name. I know. It's not a story. It's true! And sometime, someday, he'll be on the top level. On the Supreme Council.'

*

Bob McIntyre lowered his voice. 'Yeah, it's true, all right. James P. Crow is his name.'

'It's not a legend?' Ed demanded eagerly.

'There really is such a human. And he's Class Two. Gone all the way up. Passed his Lists like *that*.' McIntyre snapped his fingers. 'The robs hush it up, but it's a fact. And the news is spreading. More and more humans know.'

The two men had stopped by the service entrance of the enormous Structural Research Building. Robot officials moved busily in and out through the main doors, at the front of the building. Robot planners who guided Terran society with skill and efficiency.

Robots ran Earth. It had always been that way. The history tapes said so. Humans had been invented during the Total War of the Eleventh Millibar. All types of weapons had been tested and used; humans were one of many. The War had utterly wrecked society. For decades after, anarchy and ruin lay everywhere. Only gradually had society reformed under the patient guidance of robots. Humans had been useful in the reconstruction. But why they had originally been made, what they had been used for, how they had served in the War–all knowledge had perished in the hydrogen bomb blasts. The historians had to fill in with conjecture. They did so.

'Why such a strange name?' Ed asked.

McIntyre shrugged. 'All I know is he's sub-Advisor to the Northern Security Conference. And in line for the Council when he makes Class One.'

'What do the robs think?'

'They don't like it. But there's nothing they can do. The law says they have to let a human hold a job if he's qualified. They never thought a human would be qualified, of course. But this Crow passed his Lists.'

'It certainly is strange. A human, smarter than the robs. I wonder why.'

'He was an ordinary repairman. A mechanic, fixing machinery and designing circuits. Unclassified, of course. Then suddenly he passed his first List. Entered Class Twenty. He rose the next bi-annual to Class Nineteen. They had to put him to work.' McIntyre chuckled. 'Too damn bad, isn't it? They have to sit with a human being.'

'How do they react?'

'Some quit. Walk out, rather than sit with a human. But most stay. A lot of robs are decent. They try hard.'

'I'd sure like to meet this fellow Crow.'

McIntyre frowned. 'Well–'

'What is it?'

'I understand he doesn't like to be seen with humans too much.'

'Why not?' Ed bristled. 'What's wrong with humans? Is he too high and mighty, sitting up there with robots–'

'It's not that.' There was a strange look in McIntyre's eyes. A yearning, distant look. 'It's not just that, Ed. He's up to something. Something important. I shouldn't be saying. But it's big. Big as hell.'

'What is it?'

'I can't say. But wait until he gets on the Council. Wait.' McIntyre's eyes were feverish. 'It's so big it'll shake the world. The stars and the sun'll shake.'

'What is it?'

'I don't know. But Crow's got something up his sleeve. Something incredibly big. We're all waiting for it. Waiting for the day . . .'

James P. Crow sat at his polished mahogany desk, thinking. That wasn't his real name, of course. He had taken it after the first experiments, grinning to himself as he did so. Nobody would ever know what it meant; it would remain a private joke, personal and unannounced. But it was a good joke nonetheless. Biting and appropriate.

He was a small man. Irish-German. A little lean light-skinned man with blue eyes and sandy hair that fell down in his face and had to be brushed back. He wore unpressed baggy pants and rolled-up sleeves. He was nervous, high-strung. He smoked all day and drank black coffee and usually couldn't sleep at night. But there was a lot on his mind.

A hell of a lot. Crow got abruptly to his feet and paced over to the vidsender. 'Send in the Commissioner of Colonies,' he ordered.

The Commissioner's metal and plastic body pushed through the door, into the office. An R Type robot, patient and efficient. 'You wished to–' It broke off, seeing a human. For a second its pale eye lens flickered doubtfully. A faint sheen of distaste spread across its features. 'You wished to see me?'

Crow had seen that expression before. Endless times. He was used to it–almost. The surprise, and then the lofty withdrawal, the cold, clipped formality. He was '*Mister* Crow.' Not Jim. The law made them address him as an equal. It hurt some of them more than others. Some showed it without restraint. This one held its feelings back a trifle; Crow was its official superior.

'Yes, I wished to see you,' Crow said calmly. 'I want your report. Why hasn't it come in?'

The robot stalled, still lofty and withdrawn. 'Such a report takes time. We're doing the best we can.'

'I want it within two weeks. No later.'

The robot struggled with itself, life-long prejudices versus the requirements of Governmental codes. 'All right, *sir*. The report will be ready in two weeks.' It moved out of the office. The door formed behind it.

Crow let his breath out with a rush. Doing the best they could? Hardly. Not to please a human being. Even if he was at Advisory Level, Class Two. They all dragged their feet, all the way down the line. Little things here and there.

His door melted and a robot wheeled quickly into the office. 'I say there, Crow. Got a minute?'

'Of course.' Crow grinned. 'Come in and sit down. I'm always glad to talk to you.'

The robot dumped some papers on Crow's desk. 'Tapes and such. Business trifles.' It eyed Crow intently. 'You look upset. Anything happen?'

'A report I want. Overdue. Somebody taking its time.'

L-87t grunted. 'Same old stuff. By the way . . . We're having a meeting tonight. Want to come over and make a speech? Should have a good turn out.'

'Meeting?'

'Party meeting. Equality.' L-87t made a quick sign with its right gripper, a sort of half-arc in the air. The Equality sign. 'We'd be glad to have you, Jim. Want to come?'

'No. I'd like to, but I have things to do.'

'Oh.' The robot moved toward the door. 'All right. Thanks anyhow.' It lingered at the door. 'You'd give us a shot in the arm, you know. Living proof of our contention that a human being is the equal of a robot and should be afforded such recognition.'

Crow smiled faintly. 'But a human isn't the equal of a robot.'

L-87t sputtered indignantly. 'What are you saying? Aren't you the living proof? Look at your List scores. Perfect. Not a mistake. And in a couple of weeks you'll be Class One. Highest there is.'

Crow shook his head. 'Sorry. A human isn't the equal of a robot any more than he's the equal of a stove. Or a diesel motor. Or a snowplow. There are a lot of things a human can't do. Let's face facts.'

L-87t was baffled. 'But–'

'I mean it. You're ignoring reality. Humans and robots are completely different. We humans can sing, act, write plays, stories, operas, paint, design sets, flower gardens, buildings, cook delicious meals, make love, scratch sonnets on menus–and robots can't. But robots can build elaborate cities and machines that function perfectly, work for days without rest, think without emotional interruption, gestalt complex data without a time lag.

'Humans excel in some fields, robots in others. Humans have highly developed emotions and feelings. Esthetic awareness. We're sensitive to colors and sounds and textures and soft music mixed with wine. All very fine things. Worthwhile. But realms totally beyond robots. Robots are purely intellectual. Which is fine, too. Both realms are fine. Emotional humans, sensitive to art and music and drama. Robots who think and plan and design machinery. But that doesn't mean we're both the same.'

L-87t shook its head sadly. 'I don't understand you, Jim. Don't you want to help your race?'

'Of course. But realistically. Not by ignoring facts and making an illusionary assertion that men and robots are interchangeable. Identical elements.'

A curious look slid across L-87t's eye lens. 'What's your solution, then?'

Crow clamped his jaw tight. 'Stick around another few weeks and maybe you'll see.'

Crow headed out of the Terran Security Building and along the street. Around him robots streamed, bright hulls of metal and plastic and d/n fluid. Except for body servants, humans never came to this area. This was the managerial section of the city, the core, the nucleus, where the planning and organization went on. From this area the life of the city was controlled. Robots were everywhere. In the surface cars, on the moving ramps, the balconies, entering buildings, streaming out, standing in pale glowing knots here and there like Roman Senators, talking and discussing business.

A few greeted him, faintly, formally, with a nod of their metal heads. And then turned their backs. Most robots ignored him or pulled aside to avoid contact. Sometimes a clump of talking robots would become abruptly silent, as Crow pushed past. Robot eye lenses fixed on him, solemn and half astonished. They noticed his arm color, Class Two. Surprise and indignation. And after he had passed, a quick angry buzz of resentment. Backward glances at him as he threaded his way toward the human quarter.

A pair of humans stood in front of the Domestic Control Offices, armed with pruning shears and rakes. Gardeners, weeding and watering the lawns of the big public building. They watched Crow pass with excited stares. One waved nervously at him, feverish and hopeful. A menial human waving at the only human ever to reach classification.

Crow waved back briefly.

The two humans' eyes grew wide with awe and reverence. They were still looking after him when he turned the corner at the main intersection and mixed with the business crowds shopping at the trans-planet marts.

Goods from the wealthy colonies of Venus and Mars and Ganymede filled the open-air marts. Robots drifted in swarms, sampling and pricing and discussing and gossiping. A few humans were visible, mostly household servants in charge of maintenance, stocking up on supplies. Crow edged his way through and beyond the marts. He was approaching the human quarter of the city. He could smell it already. The faint pungent scent of humans.

The robots, of course, were odorless. In a world of odorless machines the human scent stood out in bold relief. The human quarter was a section of the city once prosperous. Humans had moved in and property values had dropped. Gradually the houses had been abandoned by robots and now humans exclusively lived there. Crow, in spite of his position, was obliged to live in the human quarter. His house, a uniform five-room dwelling, identical with all the others, was located to the rear of the quarter. One house of many.

He held his hand up to the front door and the door melted. Crow entered quickly and the door reformed. He glanced at his watch. Plenty of time. An hour before he was due back at his desk.

He rubbed his hands. It was always a thrilling moment to come here, to his personal quarters, where he had grown up, lived as an ordinary unclassified human being–before he had come across *it* and begun his meteoric ascent into the upper-class regions.

Crow passed through the small silent house, to the work shed in back. He unlocked the bolted doors and slid them aside. The shed was hot and dry. He clicked off the alarm system. Complex tangles of bells and wires that were really unnecessary: robots never entered the human section, and humans seldom stole from each other.

Locking the doors behind him, Crow seated himself before a bank of machinery assembled in the center of the shed. He snapped on the power and the machinery hummed into life. Dials and meters swung into activity. Lights glowed.

Before him, a square window of gray faded to light pink and shimmered slightly. The Window. Crow's pulse throbbed painfully. He flicked a key. The Window clouded and showed a scene. He slid a tape scanner before the Window and activated it. The scanner clicked as the Window gained shape. Forms moved, dim forms that wavered and hesitated. He steadied the picture.

Two robots were standing behind a table. They moved quickly, jerkily. He slowed them down. The two robots were handling something. Crow increased the power of the image and the objects bloated up, to be caught by the scanning lens and preserved on tape.

The robots were sorting Lists. Class One Lists. Grading and dividing them into groups. Several hundred packets of questions and answers. Before the table a restless crowd waited, eager robots waiting to hear their scores. Crow speeded the image up. The two robots leaped into activity, tossing and arranging Lists in a blur of energy. Then the master Class One List was held up–

The List. Crow caught it in the Window, dropping the velocity to zero. The List was held, fixed tight like a specimen on a slide. The tape scanner hummed away, recording the question and answers.

He felt no guilt. No sting of conscience at using a Time Window to see the results of future Lists. He had been doing it ten years, all the way up from the bottom, from unclassified up to the top List, to Class One. He had never kidded himself. Without advance sight of the answers he could never have passed. He would still be unclassified, at the bottom of the pile, along with the great undifferentiated mass of humans.

The Lists were geared to robot minds. Made up by robots, phased to a robot culture. A culture which was alien to humans, to which humans had to make difficult adjustment. No wonder only robots passed their Lists.

Crow wiped the scene from the Window and threw the scanner aside. He sent the Window back into time, spinning back through the centuries into the past. He never tired of seeing the early days, the days before the Total War wrecked human society and destroyed all human tradition. The days when man lived without robots.

He fiddled with the dials, capturing a moment. The Window showed robots building up their post-war society, swarming over their ruined planet, erecting vast cities and buildings, clearing away the debris. With humans as slaves. Second-class servant citizens.

He saw the Total War, the rain of death from the sky. The blossoming pale funnels of destruction. He saw man's society dissolve into radioactive particles. All human knowledge and culture lost in the chaos.

And once again, he caught his favorite of all scenes. A scene he had examined repeatedly, enjoying with acute satisfaction this unique sight. A scene of human beings in an undersurface lab, in the early days of the War. Designing and building the first robots, the original A Type robots, four centuries before.

Ed Parks walked home slowly, holding his son's hand. Donnie gazed down at the ground. He said nothing. His eyes were red and puffy. He was pale with misery.

'I'm sorry, Dad,' he muttered.

Ed's grip tightened. 'It's okay, kid. You did your best. Don't worry about it. Maybe next time. We'll get started practicing sooner.' He cursed under his breath. 'Those lousy metal tubs. Damn soul-less heaps of tin!'

It was evening. The sun was setting. The two of them climbed the porch steps slowly and entered the house. Grace met them at the door. 'No luck?' She studied their faces. 'I can see. Same old story.'

'Same old story,' Ed said bitterly. 'He didn't have a chance. Hopeless.'

From the dining room came a murmur of sound. Voices, men and women.

'Who's in there?' Ed demanded irritably. 'Do we have to have company? For God's sake, today of all days–'

'Come on.' Grace pulled him toward the kitchen. 'Some news. Maybe it'll make you feel better. Come along, Donnie. This will interest you, too.'

Ed and Donnie entered the kitchen. It was full of people. Bob McIntyre and his wife Pat. John Hollister and his wife Joan and their two daughters. Pete Klein and Rose Klein. Neighbors, Nat Johnson and Tim Davis and Barbara Stanley. An eager murmur buzzed through the room. Everybody was grouped around the table, excited and nervous. Sandwiches and beer bottles were piled up in heaps. The men and women were laughing and grinning happily, eyes bright with agitation.

'What's up?' Ed grumbled. 'Why the party?'

Bob McIntyre clapped him on the shoulder. 'How you doing, Ed? We've got news.' He rattled a public news tape. 'Get ready. Brace yourself.'

'Read it to him,' Pete Klein said excitedly.

'Go on! Read it!' They all grouped around McIntyre. 'Let's hear it again!'

McIntyre's face was alive with emotion. 'Well, Ed. This is it. He made it. He's there.'

'Who? Who made what?'

'Crow. Jim Crow. He made Class One.' The tape spool trembled in McIntyre's hand. 'He's been named to the Supreme Council. Understand? He's in. A human being. A member of the supreme governing body of the planet.'

'Gosh,' Donnie said, awed.

'Now what?' Ed asked. 'What's he going to do?'

McIntyre grinned shakily. 'We'll know, soon. He's got something. We know. We can feel it. And we should start seeing it in action–any time, now.'

Crow strode briskly into the Council Chamber, his portfolio under his arm. He wore a slick new suit. His hair was combed. His shoes were shined. 'Good day,' he said politely.

The five robots regarded him with mixed feelings. They were

old, over a century old. The powerful N Type that had dominated the social scene since its construction. And an incredibly ancient D Type, almost three centuries old. As Crow advanced toward his seat the five robots stepped away, leaving a wide path for him.

'You,' one of the N Types said. 'You are the new Council member?'

'That's right.' Crow took his seat. 'Care to examine my credentials?'

'Please.'

Crow passed over the card plate given him by the Lists Committee. The five robots studied it intently. Finally they passed it back.

'It appears to be in order,' the D admitted reluctantly.

'Of course.' Crow unzippered his portfolio. 'I wish to begin work at once. There's quite a lot of material to cover. I have some reports and tapes you'll find worth your while.'

The robots took their places slowly, eyes still on Jim Crow. 'This is incredible,' the D said. 'Are you serious? Can you really expect to sit with us?'

'Of course,' Crow snapped. 'Let's forgo this and get down to business.'

One of the N Types leaned toward him, massive and contemptuous, its patina-encrusted hull glinting dully. 'Mr Crow,' it said icily. 'You must understand this is utterly impossible. In spite of the legal ruling and your technical right to sit on this–'

Crow smiled calmly back. 'I suggest you check my Listing scoring. You'll discover I've made no errors in all twenty Lists. A perfect score. To my knowledge, none of you has achieved a perfect score. Therefore, according to the Governmental ruling contained in the official Lists Committee decree, I'm your superior.'

The word fell like a bomb shell. The five robots slumped down in their seats, stricken. Their eye lenses flickered uneasily. A worried hum rose in pitch, filling the chamber.

'Let's see,' an N murmured, extending its gripper. Crow tossed his List sheets over and the five robots each scanned them rapidly.

'It's true,' the D stated. 'Incredible. No robot has ever achieved a perfect score. This human outranks us, according to our own laws.'

'Now,' Crow said. 'Let's get down to business.' He spread out his tapes and reports. 'I won't waste any time. I have a proposal to make. An important proposal bearing on the most critical problem of this society.'

'What problem is that?' an N asked apprehensively.

Crow was tense. 'The problem of humans. Humans occupying an inferior position in a robot world. Menials in an alien culture. Servants of robots.'

Silence.

The five robots sat frozen. It had happened. The thing they had feared. Crow sat back in his chair, lighting a cigarette. The robots watched each motion, his hands, the cigarette, the smoke, the match as he ground it out underfoot. The moment had come.

'What do you propose?' the D asked at last, with metallic dignity. 'What is this proposal of yours?'

'I propose you robots evacuate Earth at once. Pack up and leave. Emigrate to the colonies. Ganymede, Mars, Venus. Leave Earth to us humans.'

The robots got instantly up. 'Incredible! We built this world. This is our world! Earth belongs to us. It has always belonged to us.'

'*Has it?*' Crow said grimly.

An uneasy chill moved through the robots. They hesitated, strangely alarmed. 'Of course,' the D murmured.

Crow reached toward his heap of tapes and reports. The robots watched his movement with fear. 'What is that?' an N demanded nervously. 'What do you have there?'

'Tapes,' Crow said.

'What kind of tapes?'

'History tapes.' Crow signalled and a gray-clad human servant hurried into the chamber with a tape scanner. 'Thanks,' Crow said. The human started out. 'Wait. You might like to stay and watch this, my friend.'

The servant's eyes bulged. He found a place in the back and stood trembling and watching.

'Highly irregular,' the D protested. 'What are you doing? What is this?'

'Watch.' Crow snapped on the scanner, feeding the first tape into it. In the air, in the center of the Council table, a three-dimensional image formed. 'Keep your eyes on this. You'll remember this moment for a long time.'

The image hardened. They were looking into the Time Window. A scene from the Total War was in motion. Men, human technicians, working frantically in an undersurface lab. Assembling something. Assembling–

The human servant squawked wildly. 'An A! It's a Type A robot! They're making it!'

The five Council robots buzzed in consternation. 'Get that servant out of here!' the D ordered.

The scene changed. It showed the first robots, the original Type A, rising to the surface to fight the War. Other early robots appeared, snaking through the ruins and ash, approaching warily. The robots clashed. Bursts of white light. Gleaming clouds of particles.

'Robots were originally designed as soldiers,' Crow explained. 'Then more advanced types were produced to act as technicians and lab workers and machinists.'

The scene showed an undersurface factory. Rows of robots worked presses and stampers. The robots worked rapidly, efficiently–supervised by human foremen.

'These tapes are fake!' an N cried angrily. 'Do you expect us to believe this?'

A new scene formed. Robots, more advanced, types more complex and elaborate. Taking over more and more economic and industrial functions as humans were destroyed by the War.

'At first robots were simple,' Crow explained. 'They served simple needs. Then, as the War progressed, more advanced types were created. Finally, humans were making Types D and E. Equal to humans–and in conceptual faculties, superior to humans.'

'This is insane!' an N stated. 'Robots evolved. The early types were simple because they were original stages, primitive forms that gave rise to more complex forms. The laws of evolution fully explain this process.'

A new scene formed. The last stages of the War. Robots fighting men. Robots eventually winning. The complete chaos of the latter years. Endless wastes of rolling ash and radioactive particles. Miles of ruin.

'All cultural records were destroyed,' Crow said. 'Robots emerged masters without knowing how or why, or in what manner they came into being. But now you see the facts. Robots were created as human tools. During the War they got out of hand.'

He snapped off the tape scanner. The image faded. The five robots sat in stunned silence.

Crow folded his arms. 'Well? What do you say?' He jerked his thumb at the human servant crouching in the rear of the chamber, dazed and astonished. 'Now you know and now he knows. What do you imagine he's thinking? I can tell you. He's thinking–'

'How did you get these tapes?' the D demanded. 'They can't be genuine. They must be fakes.'

'Why weren't they found by our archeologists?' an N shouted shrilly.

'I took them personally,' Crow said.

'*You* took them? What do you mean?'

'Through a Time Window.' Crow tossed a thick package onto the table. 'Here are the schematics. You can build a Time Window yourself if you want.'

'A time machine.' The D snatched up the package and leafed through the contents. 'You saw into the past.' Dawning realization showed on its ancient face. 'Then–'

'He saw ahead!' an N searched wildly. 'Into the future! That explains his perfect Lists. He scanned them in advance.'

Crow rattled his papers impatiently. 'You've heard my proposal. You've seen the tapes. If you vote down the proposal I'll release the tapes publicly. And the schematics. Every human in the world will know the true story of his origin, and of yours.'

'So?' an N said nervously. 'We can handle humans. If there's an uprising we'll put it down.'

'Will you?' Crow got suddenly to his feet, his face hard. 'Consider. Civil war raging over the whole planet. Men on one side, centuries of pent-up hatred. On the other side robots suddenly deprived of their myth. Knowing they were originally mechanical tools. Are you sure you'll come out on top this time? Are you positive?'

The robots were silent.

'If you'll evacuate Earth I'll suppress the tapes. The two races can go on, each with its own culture and society. Humans here on Earth. Robots on the colonies. Neither one master. Neither one slave.'

The five robots hesitated, angry and resentful. 'But we worked centuries to build up this planet! It won't make sense. Our leaving. What'll we say? What'll we give as our reason?'

Crow smiled harshly. 'You can say Earth isn't adequate for the great original master race.'

There was silence. The four Type N robots looked at each other nervously, drawing together in a whispered huddle. The massive D sat silent, its archaic brass eye lens fixed intently on Crow, a baffled, defeated expression on its face.

Calmly, Jim Crow waited.

'Can I shake your hand?' L-87t asked timidly. 'I'll be going soon. I'm in one of the first loads.'

Crow stuck out his hand briefly and L-87t shook, a little embarrassed.

'I hope it works out,' L-87t ventured. 'Vid us from time to time. Keep us posted.'

Outside the Council Buildings the blaring voices of the street speakers were beginning to disturb the late afternoon gloom. All up and down the city the speakers roared out their message, the Council Directive.

Men, scurrying home from work, paused to listen. In the uniform houses in the human quarter men and women glanced up, pausing in their routine of living, curious and attentive. Everywhere, in all cities of Earth, robots and human beings ceased their activities and looked up as the Government speakers roared into life.

'This is to announce that the Supreme Council has decreed the rich colony planets Venus, Mars, and Ganymede are to be set aside exclusively for the use of robots. No humans will be permitted outside of Earth. In order to take advantage of the superior resources and living conditions of these colonies, all robots now on Earth are to be transferred to the colony of their choice.

'The Supreme Council has decided that Earth is no fit place for robots. Its wasted and still partly-devastated condition renders it unworthy of the robot race. All robots are to be conveyed to their new homes in the colonies as quickly as adequate transportation can be arranged.

'In no case can humans enter the colony areas. The colonies are exclusively for the use of robots. The human population will be permitted to remain on Earth.

'This is to announce that the Supreme Council has decreed that the rich colony planets of Venus–'

Crow moved away from the window, satisfied.

He returned to his desk and continued assembling papers and reports in neat piles, glancing at them briefly as he classified them and laid them aside.

'I hope you humans will get along all right,' L-87t repeated. Crow continued checking the heaps of top-level reports, marking them with his writing stick. Working rapidly, with absorbed attention, deep in his work. He scarcely noticed the robot lingering at the door. 'Can you give me some idea of the government you'll set up?'

Crow glanced up impatiently. 'What?'

'Your form of government. How will your society be ruled, now that you've maneuvered us off Earth? What sort of government will take the place of our Supreme Council and Congress?'

Crow didn't answer. He had already returned to his work. There was a strange granite cast to his face, a peculiar hardness L-87t had never seen.

'Who'll run things?' L-87t asked. 'Who'll be the Government now that we're gone? You said yourself humans show no ability to manage a complex modern society. Can you find a human capable of keeping the wheels turning? Is there a human being capable of leading mankind?'

Crow smiled thinly. And continued working.

PLANET FOR TRANSIENTS

The late afternoon sun shone down blinding and hot, a great shimmering orb in the sky. Trent halted a moment to get his breath. Inside his lead-lined helmet his face dripped with sweat, drop after drop of sticky moisture that steamed his viewplate and clogged his throat.

He slid his emergency pack over to the other side and hitched up his gun-belt. From his oxygen tank he pulled a couple of exhausted tubes and tossed them away in the brush. The tubes rolled and disappeared, lost in the endless heaps of red-green leaves and vines.

Trent checked his counter, found the reading low enough, slid back his helmet for a precious moment.

Fresh air rushed into his nose and mouth. He took a deep breath, filling his lungs. The air smelled good–thick and moist and rich with the odor of growing plants. He exhaled and took another breath.

To his right a towering column of orange shrubbery rose, wrapped around a sagging concrete pillar. Spread out over the rolling countryside was a vast expanse of grass and trees. In the distance a mass of growth looked like a wall, a jungle of creepers and insects and flowers and underbrush that would have to be blasted as he advanced slowly.

Two immense butterflies danced past him. Great fragile shapes, multicolored, racing erratically around him and then away. Life everywhere–bugs and plants and the rustling small animals in the shrubbery, a buzzing jungle of life in every direction. Trent sighed and snapped his helmet back in place. Two breathfuls was all he dared.

He increased the flow of his oxygen tank and then raised his transmitter to his lips. He clicked it briefly on. 'Trent. Checking with the Mine Monitor. Hear me?'

A moment of static and silence. Then, a faint, ghostly voice. 'Come in, Trent. Where the hell are you?'

'Still going north. Ruins ahead. I may have to bypass. Looks thick.'

'Ruins?'

'New York, probably. I'll check with the map.'

The voice was eager. 'Anything yet?'

'Nothing. Not so far, at least. I'll circle and report in about an hour.' Trent examined his wristwatch. 'It's half-past three. I'll raise you before evening.'

The voice hesitated. 'Good luck. I hope you find something. How's your oxygen holding out?'

'All right.'

'Food?'

'Plenty left. I may find some edible plants.'

'Don't take any chances!'

'I won't.' Trent clicked off the transmitter and returned it to his belt. 'I won't,' he repeated. He gathered up his blast gun and hoisted his pack and started forward, his heavy lead-lined boots sinking deep into the lush foliage and compost underfoot.

It was just past four o'clock when he saw them. They stepped out of the jungle around him. Two of them, young males–tall and thin and horny blue-gray like ashes. One raised his hand in greeting. Six or seven fingers–extra joints. 'Afternoon,' he piped.

Trent stopped instantly. His heart thudded. 'Good afternoon.'

The two youths came slowly around him. One had an axe–a foliage axe. The other carried only his pants and the remains of a canvas shirt. They were nearly eight feet tall. No flesh–bones and hard angles and large, curious eyes, heavily lidded. There were internal changes, radically different metabolism and cell structure, ability to utilize hot salts, altered digestive system. They were both looking at Trent with interest–growing interest.

'Say,' one said. 'You're a human being.'

'That's right,' Trent said.

'My name's Jackson.' The youth extended his thin blue horny hand and Trent shook it awkwardly. The hand was fragile under his lead-lined glove. Its owner added, 'My friend here is Earl Potter.'

Trent shook hands with Potter. 'Greetings,' Potter said. His rough lips twitched. 'Can we have a look at your rig?'

'My rig?' Trent countered.

'Your gun and equipment. What's that on your belt? And that tank?'

'Transmitter–oxygen.' Trent showed them the transmitter. 'Battery operated. Hundred-mile range.'

'You're from a camp?' Jackson asked quickly.

'Yes. Down in Pennsylvania.'

'How many?'

Trent shrugged. 'Couple of dozen.'

The blue-skinned giants were fascinated. 'How have you survived? Penn was hard hit, wasn't it? The pools must be deep around there.'

'Mines,' Trent explained. 'Our ancestors moved down deep in the coal mines when the War began. So the records have it. We're fairly well set up. Grow our own food in tanks. A few machines, pumps and compressors and electrical generators. Some hand lathes. Looms.'

He didn't mention that generators now had to be cranked by hand, that only about half of the tanks were still operative. After three hundred years metal and plastic weren't much good–in spite of endless patching and repairing. Everything was wearing out, breaking down.

'Say,' Potter said. 'This sure makes a fool of Dave Hunter.'

'Dave Hunter?'

'Dave says there aren't any true humans left,' Jackson explained. He poked at Trent's helmet curiously. 'Why don't you come back with us? We've got a settlement near here–only an hour or so away on the tractor–our hunting tractor. Earl and I were out hunting flap-rabbits.'

'Flap-rabbits?'

'Flying rabbits. Good meat but hard to bring down–weigh about thirty pounds.'

'What do you use? Not the axe surely.'

Potter and Jackson laughed. 'Look at this here.' Potter slid a long brass rod from his trousers. It fitted down inside his pants along his pipe-stem leg.

Trent examined the rod. It was tooled by hand. Soft brass, carefully bored and straightened. One end was shaped into a nozzle. He peered down it. A tiny metal pin was lodged in a cake of transparent material. 'How does it work?' he asked.

'Launched by hand–like a blow gun. But once the b-dart is in the air it follows its target forever. The initial thrust has to be provided.' Potter laughed. 'I supply that. A big puff of air.'

'Interesting.' Trent returned the rod. With elaborate casualness, studying the two blue-gray faces, he asked, 'I'm the first human you've seen?'

'That's right,' Jackson said. 'The Old Man will be pleased to welcome you.' There was eagerness in his reedy voice. 'What do you say? We'll take care of you. Feed you, bring you cold plants and animals. For a week, maybe?'

'Sorry,' Trent said. 'Other business. If I come through here on the way back . . .'

The horny faces fell with disappointment. 'Not for a little while? Overnight? We'll pump you plenty of cold food. We have a fine cooler the Old Man fixed up.'

Trent tapped his tank. 'Short on oxygen. You don't have a compressor?'

'No. We don't have any use. But maybe the Old Man could–'

'Sorry.' Trent moved off. 'Have to keep going. You're sure there are no humans in this region?'

'We thought there weren't any left anywhere. A rumor once in a while. But you're the first we've seen.' Potter pointed west. 'There's a tribe of rollers off that way.' He pointed vaguely south. 'A couple of tribes of bugs.'

'And some runners.'

'You've seen them?'

'I came that way.'

'And north there's some of the underground ones–the blind digging kind.' Potter made a face. 'I can't see them and their bores and scoops. But what the hell.' He grinned. 'Everybody has his own way.'

'And to the east,' Jackson added, 'where the ocean begins, there's a lot of the porpoise kind–the undersea type. They swim around–use those big underwater air-domes and tanks–come up sometimes at night. A lot of types come out at night. We're still daylight-oriented.' He rubbed his horny blue-gray skin. 'This cuts radiation fine.'

'I know,' Trent said. 'So long.'

'Good luck.' They watched him go, heavy-lidded eyes still big with astonishment, as the human being pushed slowly off through the lush green jungle, his metal and plastic suit glinting faintly in the afternoon sun.

Earth was alive, thriving with activity. Plants and animals and insects in boundless confusion. Night forms, day forms, land and water types, incredible kinds and numbers that had never been catalogued, probably never would be.

By the end of the War every surface inch was radioactive. A whole planet sprayed and bombarded by hard radiation. All life subjected to beta and gamma rays. Most life died–but not all. Hard radiation brought mutation–at all levels, insect, plant and animal. The normal mutation and selection process was accelerated millions of years in seconds.

These altered progeny littered the Earth. A crawling teeming glowing horde of radiation-saturated beings. In this world, only those forms which could use hot soil and breathe particle-laden air survived. Insects and animals and men who could live in a world with a surface so alive that it glowed at night.

Trent considered this moodily, as he made his way through the steaming jungle, expertly burning creepers and vines with his blaster. Most of the oceans had been vaporized. Water descended still, drenching the land with torrents of hot moisture. This jungle was wet–wet and hot and full of life. Around him creatures scuttled and rustled. He held his blaster tight and pushed on.

The sun was setting. It was getting to be night. A range of ragged hills jutted ahead in the violet gloom. The sunset was going to be beautiful–compounded of particles in suspension, particles that still drifted from the initial blast, centuries ago.

He stopped for a moment to watch. He had come a long way. He was tired–and discouraged.

The horny blue-skinned giants were a typical mutant tribe. *Toads*, they were called. Because of their skin–like desert horned-toads. With their radical internal organs, geared to hot plants and air, they lived easily in a world where he survived only in a lead-lined suit, polarized viewplate, oxygen tank, special cold food pellets grown underground in the Mine.

The Mine–time to call again. Trent lifted his transmitter. 'Trent checking again,' he muttered. He licked his dry lips. He was hungry and thirsty. Maybe he could find some relatively cool spot, free of radiation. Take off his suit for a quarter of an hour and wash himself. Get the sweat and grime off.

Two weeks he had been walking, cooped up in a hot sticky lead-lined suit, like a diver's suit. While all around him countless life-forms scrambled and leaped, unbothered by the lethal pools of radiation.

'Mine,' the faint tinny voice answered.

'I'm about washed up for today. I'm stopping to rest and eat. No more until tomorrow.'

'No luck?' Heavy disappointment.

'None.'

Silence. Then, 'Well, maybe tomorrow.'

'Maybe. Met a tribe of toads. Nice young bucks, eight feet high.' Trent's voice was bitter. 'Wandering around with nothing on but shirts and pants. Bare feet.'

The Mine Monitor was uninterested. 'I know. The lucky stiffs.

Well, get some sleep and raise me tomorrow A.M. A report came in from Lawrence.'

'Where is he?'

'Due west. Near Ohio. Making good progress.'

'Any results?'

'Tribes of rollers, bugs and the digging kind that come up at night–the blind white things.'

'Worms.'

'Yes, worms. Nothing else. When will you report again?'

'Tomorrow,' Trent said. He cut the switch and dropped his transmitter to his belt.

Tomorrow. He peered into the gathering gloom at the distant range of hills. Five years. And always–tomorrow. He was the last of a great procession of men to be sent out. Lugging precious oxygen tanks and food pellets and a blast pistol. Exhausting their last stores in a useless sortie into the jungles.

Tomorrow? Some tomorrow, not far off, there wouldn't be any more oxygen tanks and food pellets. The compressors and pumps would have stopped completely. Broken down for good. The Mine would be dead and silent. Unless they made contact pretty damn soon.

He squatted down and began to pass his counter over the surface, looking for a cool spot to undress. He passed out.

'Look at him,' a faint faraway voice said.

Consciousness returned with a rush. Trent pulled himself violently awake, groping for his blaster. It was morning. Gray sunlight filtered down through the trees. Around him shapes moved.

The blaster . . . gone!

Trent sat up, fully awake. The shapes were vaguely human–but not very. Bugs.

'Where's my gun?' Trent demanded.

'Take it easy.' A bug advanced, the others behind. It was chilly. Trent shivered. He got awkwardly to his feet as the bugs formed a circle around him. 'We'll give it back.'

'Let's have it now.' He was stiff and cold. He snapped his helmet in place and tightened his belt. He was shivering, shaking all over. The leaves and vines dripped wet slimy drops. The ground was soft underfoot.

The bugs conferred. There were ten or twelve of them. Strange creatures, more like insects than men. They were shelled–thick shiny chitin. Multi-lensed eyes. Nervous, vibrating antennae by which they detected radiation.

Their protection wasn't perfect. A strong dose and they were finished. They survived by detection and avoidance and partial immunity. Their food was taken indirectly, first digested by smaller warm-blooded animals and then taken as fecal matter, minus radioactive particles.

'You're a human,' a bug said. Its voice was shrill and metallic. The bugs were asexual–these, at least. Two other types existed, male drones and a Mother. These were neuter warriors, armed with pistols and foliage axes.

'That's right,' Trent said.

'What are you doing here? Are there more of you?'

'Quite a few.'

The bugs conferred again, antennae waving wildly. Trent waited. The jungle was stirring into life. He watched a gelatin-like mass flow up the side of a tree and into the branches, a half-digested mammal visible within. Some drab day moths fluttered past. The leaves stirred as underground creatures burrowed sullenly away from the light.

'Come along with us,' a bug said. It motioned Trent forward. 'Let's get going.'

Trent fell in reluctantly. They marched along a narrow path, cut by axes some time recently. The thick feelers and probes of the jungle were already coming back. 'Where are we going?' Trent demanded.

'To the Hill.'

'Why?'

'Never mind.'

Watching the shiny bugs stride along, Trent had trouble believing they had once been human beings. Their ancestors, at least. In spite of their incredible altered physiology the bugs were mentally about the same as he. Their tribal arrangement approximated the human organic states, communism and fascism.

'May I ask you something?' Trent said.

'What?'

'I'm the first human you've seen? There aren't any more around here?'

'No more.'

'Are there reports of human settlements anywhere?'

'Why?'

'Just curious,' Trent said tightly.

'You're the only one.' The bug was pleased. 'We'll get a bonus for this–for capturing you. There's a standing reward. Nobody's ever claimed it before.'

A human was wanted here too. A human brought with him valuable *gnosis*, odds and ends of tradition the mutants needed to incorporate into their shaky social structures. Mutant cultures were still unsteady. They needed contact with the past. A human being was a shaman, a Wise Man to teach and instruct. To teach the mutants how life had been, how their ancestors had lived and acted and looked.

A valuable possession for any tribe–especially if no other humans existed in the region.

Trent cursed savagely. *None?* No others? There *had* to be other humans–some place. If not north, then east. Europe, Asia, Australia. Some place, somewhere on the globe. Humans with tools and machines and equipment. The Mine couldn't be the only settlement, the last fragment of true man. Prized curiosities–doomed when their compressors burned out and their food tanks dried up.

If he didn't have any luck pretty soon . . .

The bugs halted, listening. Their antennae twitched suspiciously.

'What is it?' Trent asked.

'Nothing.' They started on. 'For a moment–'

A flash. The bugs ahead on the trail winked out of existence. A dull roar of light rolled over them.

Trent sprawled. He struggled, caught in the vines and sappy weeds. Around him bugs twisted and fought wildly. Tangling with small furry creatures that fired rapidly and efficiently with hand weapons and, when they got close, kicked and gouged with immense hind legs.

Runners.

The bugs were losing. They retreated back down the trail, scattering into the jungle. The runners hopped after them, springing on their powerful hind legs like kangaroos. The last bug departed. The noise died down.

'Okay,' a runner ordered. He gasped for breath, straightening up. 'Where's the human?'

Trent got slowly to his feet. 'Here.'

The runners helped him up. They were small, not over four feet high. Fat and round, covered with thick pelts. Little good-natured faces peered up at him with concern. Beady eyes, quivering noses and great kangaroo legs.

'You all right?' one asked. He offered Trent his water canteen.

'I'm all right.' Trent pushed the canteen away. 'They got my blaster.'

The runners searched around. The blaster was nowhere to be seen.

'Let it go.' Trent shook his head dully, trying to collect himself. 'What happened? The light.'

'A grenade.' The runners puffed with pride. 'We stretched a wire across the trail, attached to the pin.'

'The bugs control most of this area,' another said. 'We have to fight our way through.' Around his neck hung a pair of binoculars. The runners were armed with slug-pistols and knives.

'Are you really a human being?' a runner asked. 'The original stock?'

'That's right,' Trent muttered in unsteady tones.

The runners were awed. Their beady eyes grew wide. They touched his metal suit, his viewplate. His oxygen tank and pack. One squatted down and expertly traced the circuit of his transmitter apparatus.

'Where are you from?' the leader asked in his deep purr-like voice. 'You're the first human we've seen in months.'

Trent spun, choking. 'Months? Then . . .'

'None around here. We're from Canada. Up around Montreal. There's a human settlement up there.'

Trent's breath came fast. 'Walking distance?'

'Well, we made it in a couple of days. But we go fairly fast.' The runner eyed Trent's metal-clad legs doubtfully. 'I don't know. For you it would take longer.'

Humans. A human settlement. 'How many? A big settlement? Advanced?'

'It's hard to remember. I saw their settlement once. Down underground–levels, cells. We traded some cold plants for salt. That was a long time ago.'

'They're operating successfully? They have tools–machinery–compressors? Food tanks to keep going?'

The runner twisted uneasily. 'As a matter of fact they may not be there any more.'

Trent froze. Fear cut through him like a knife. 'Not there? What do you mean?'

'They may be gone.'

'Gone where?' Trent's voice was bleak. 'What happened to them?'

'I don't know,' the runner said. 'I don't know what happened to them. Nobody knows.'

He pushed on, hurrying frantically north. The jungle gave way to a bitterly cold fern-like forest. Great silent trees on all sides. The air was thin and brittle.

He was exhausted. And only one tube of oxygen remained in the tank. After that he would have to open his helmet. How long would he last? The first rain cloud would bring lethal particles sweeping into his lungs. Or the first strong wind, blowing from the ocean.

He halted, gasping for breath. He had reached the top of a long slope. At the bottom a plain stretched out–tree-covered–a dark green expanse, almost brown. Here and there a spot of white gleamed. Ruins of some kind. A human city had been here three centuries ago.

Nothing stirred–no sign of life. No sign anywhere.

Trent made his way down the slope. Around him the forest was silent. A dismal oppression hung over everything. Even the usual rustling of small animals was lacking. Animals, insects, men–all were gone. Most of the runners had moved south. The small things probably had died. And the men?

He came out among the ruins. This had been a great city once. Then men had probably gone down in air-raid shelters and mines and subways. Later on they had enlarged their underground chambers. For three centuries men–true men–had held on, living below the surface. Wearing lead-lined suits when they came up, growing food in tanks, filtering their water, compressing particle-free air. Shielding their eyes against the glare of the bright sun.

And now–nothing at all.

He lifted his transmitter. 'Mine,' he snapped. 'This is Trent.'

The transmitter sputtered feebly. It was a long time before it responded. The voice was faint, distant. Almost lost in the static. 'Well? Did you find them?'

'They're gone.'

'But . . .'

'Nothing. No one. Completely abandoned.' Trent sat down on a broken stump of concrete. His body was dead. Drained of life. 'They were here recently. The ruins aren't covered. They must have left in the last few weeks.'

'It doesn't make sense. Mason and Douglas are on their way. Douglas has the tractor car. He should be there in a couple of days. How long will your oxygen last?'

'Twenty-four hours.'

'We'll tell him to make time.'

'I'm sorry I don't have more to report. Something better.' Bitterness welled up in his voice. 'After all these years. They were here all this time. And now that we've finally got to them . . .'

'Any clues? Can you tell what became of them?'

'I'll look.' Trent got heavily to his feet. 'If I find anything I'll report.'

'Good luck.' The faint voice faded off into static. 'We'll be waiting.'

Trent returned the transmitter to his belt. He peered up at the gray sky. Evening–almost night. The forest was bleak and ominous. A faint blanket of snow was falling silently over the brown growth, hiding it under a layer of grimy white. Snow mixed with particles. Lethal dust–still falling, after three hundred years.

He switched on his helmet-beam. The beam cut a pale swath ahead of him through the trees, among the ruined columns of concrete, the occasional heaps of rusted slag. He entered the ruins.

In their center he found the towers and installations. Great pillars laced with mesh scaffolding–still bright. Open tunnels from underground lay like black pools. Silent deserted tunnels. He peered down one, flashing his helmet-beam into it. The tunnel went straight down, deep into the heart of the Earth. But it was empty.

Where had they gone? What had happened to them? Trent wandered around dully. Human beings had lived here, worked here, survived. They had come up to the surface. He could see the bore-nosed cars parked among the towers, now gray with the night snow. They had come up and then–gone.

Where?

He sat down in the shelter of a ruined column and flicked on his heater. His suit warmed up, a slow red glow that made him feel better. He examined his counter. The area was hot. If he intended to eat and drink he'd have to move on.

He was tired. Too damn tired to move on. He sat resting, hunched over in a heap, his helmet-beam lighting up a circle of gray snow ahead of him. Over him the snow fell silently. Presently he was covered, a gray lump sitting among the ruined concrete. As silent and unmoving as the towers and scaffolding around him.

He dozed. His heater hummed gently. Around him a wind came up, swirling the snow, blowing it up against him. He slid forward a little until his metal and plastic helmet came to rest against the concrete.

Towards midnight he woke up. He straightened, suddenly alert. Something–a noise. He listened.

Far off, a dull roaring.

Douglas in the car? No, not yet–not for another two days. He stood up, snow pouring off him. The roar was growing, getting louder. His heart began to hammer wildly. He peered around, his beam flashing through the night.

The ground shook, vibrating through him, rattling his almost empty oxygen tank. He gazed up at the sky–and gasped.

A glowing trail slashed across the sky, igniting the early morning darkness. A deep red, swelling each second. He watched it, open-mouthed.

Something was coming down–landing.

A rocket.

The long metal hull glittered in the morning sun. Men were working busily, loading supplies and equipment. Tunnel cars raced up and down, hauling material from the under-surface levels to the waiting ship. The men worked carefully and efficiently, each in his metal and plastic suit, in his carefully sealed lead-lined protection shield.

'How many back at your Mine?' Norris asked quietly.

'About thirty.' Trent's eyes were on the ship. 'Thirty-three, including all those out.'

'Out?'

'Looking. Like me. A couple are on their way here. They should arrive soon. Late today or tomorrow.'

Norris made some notes on his chart. 'We can handle about

fifteen with this load. We'll catch the rest next time. They can hold out another week?'

'Yes.'

Norris eyed him curiously. 'How did you find us? This is a long way from Pennsylvania. We're making our last stop. If you had come a couple days later . . .'

'Some runners sent me this way. They said you had gone they didn't know where.'

Norris laughed. 'We didn't know where either.'

'You must be taking all this stuff some place. This ship. It's old, isn't it? Fixed up.'

'Originally it was some kind of bomb. We located it and repaired it–worked on it from time to time. We weren't sure what we wanted to do. We're not sure yet. But we know we have to leave.'

'Leave? Leave Earth?'

'Of course.' Norris motioned him towards the ship. They made their way up the ramp to one of the hatches. Norris pointed back down. 'Look down there–at the men loading.'

The men were almost finished. The last cars were half empty, bringing up the final remains from underground. Books, records, pictures, artifacts–the remains of a culture. A multitude of representative objects, shot into the hold of the ship to be carried off, away from Earth.

'Where?' Trent asked.

'To Mars for the time being. But we're not staying there. We'll probably go on out, towards the moons of Jupiter and Saturn. Ganymede may turn out to be something. If not Ganymede, one of the others. If worse comes to worst we can stay on Mars. It's pretty dry and barren but it's not radioactive.'

'There's no chance here–no possibility of reclaiming the radioactive areas? If we could cool off Earth, neutralize the hot clouds and–'

'If we did that,' Norris said, 'they'd all die.'

'They?'

'Rollers, runners, worms, toads, bugs, all the rest. The endless varieties of life. Countless forms adapted to *this* Earth–this hot Earth. These plants and animals use the radioactive metals. Essentially the new basis of life here is an assimilation of hot metallic salts. Salts which are utterly lethal to us.'

'But even so–'

'Even so, it's not really our world.'

'We're the true humans,' Trent said.

'Not any more. Earth is alive, teeming with life. Growing wildly–in all directions. We're one form, an old form. To live here, we'd have to restore the old conditions, the old factors, the balance as it was three hundred and fifty years ago. A colossal job. And if we succeeded, if we managed to cool Earth, none of this would remain.'

Norris pointed at the great brown forests. And beyond it, towards the south, at the beginning of the steaming jungle that continued all the way to the Straits of Magellan.

'In a way it's what we deserve. *We* brought the War. *We* changed Earth. Not destroyed–*changed*. Made it so different we can't live here any longer.'

Norris indicated the lines of helmeted men. Men sheathed in lead, in heavy protection suits, covered with layers of metal and wiring, counters, oxygen tanks, shields, food pellets, filtered water. The men worked, sweated in their heavy suits. 'See them? What do they resemble?'

A worker came up, gasping and panting. For a brief second he lifted his viewplate and took a hasty breath of air. He slammed his plate and nervously locked it in place. 'Ready to go, sir. All loaded.'

'Change of plan,' Norris said. 'We're going to wait until this man's companions get here. Their camp is breaking up. Another day won't make any difference.'

'All right, sir.' The worker pushed off, climbing back down to the surface, a weird figure in his heavy lead-lined suit and bulging helmet and intricate gear.

'We're visitors,' Norris told him.

Trent flinched violently. '*What?*'

'Visitors on a strange planet. Look at us. Shielded suits and helmets, spacesuits–for exploring. We're a rocket-ship stopping at an alien world on which we can't survive. Stopping for a brief period to load up–and then take off again.'

'Closed helmets,' Trent said, in a strange voice.

'Closed helmets. Lead shields. Counters and special food and water. Look over there.'

A small group of runners were standing together, gazing up in awe at the great gleaming ship. Off to the right, visible among the trees, was a runner village. Checker-board crops and animal pens and board houses.

'The natives,' Norris said. 'The inhabitants of the planet. They can breathe the air, drink the water, eat the plant-life. We can't. This is their planet–not ours. They can live here, build up a society.'

'I hope we can come back.'

'Back?'

'To visit–some time.'

Norris smiled ruefully. 'I hope so too. But we'll have to get permission from the inhabitants–permission to land.' His eyes were bright with amusement–and, abruptly, pain. A sudden agony that gleamed out over everything else. 'We'll have to ask them if it's all right. And they may say *no*. They may not want us.'

SMALL TOWN

Verne Haskel crept miserably up the front steps of his house, his overcoat dragging behind him. He was tired. Tired and discouraged. And his feet ached.

'My God,' Madge exclaimed, as he closed the door and peeled off his coat and hat. 'You home already?'

Haskel dumped his briefcase and began untying his shoes. His body sagged. His face was drawn and gray.

'Say something!'

'Dinner ready?'

'No, dinner isn't ready. What's wrong this time? Another fight with Larson?'

Haskel stumped into the kitchen and filled a glass with warm water and soda. 'Let's move,' he said.

'Move?'

'Away from Woodland. To San Francisco. Anywhere.' Haskel drank his soda, his middle-aged flabby body supported by the gleaming sink. 'I feel lousy. Maybe I ought to see Doc Barnes again. I wish this was Friday and tomorrow was Saturday.'

'What do you want for dinner?'

'Nothing. I don't know.' Haskel shook his head wearily. 'Anything.' He sank down at the kitchen table. 'All I want is rest. Open a can of stew. Pork and beans. Anything.'

'I suggest we go out to Don's Steakhouse. On Monday they have good sirloins.'

'No. I've seen enough human faces today.'

'I suppose you're too tired to drive me over to Helen Grant's.'

'The car's in the garage. Busted again.'

'If you took better care of it–'

'What the hell do you want me to do? Carry it around in a cellophane bag?'

'Don't shout at me, Verne Haskell!' Madge flushed with anger. 'Maybe you want to fix your own dinner.'

Haskel got wearily to his feet. He shuffled toward the cellar door. 'I'll see you.'

'Where are you going?'

'Downstairs in the basement.'

'Oh, Lord!' Madge cried wildly. 'Those trains! Those toys! How can a grown man, a middle-aged man–'

Haskel said nothing. He was already half way down the stairs, feeling around for the basement light.

The basement was cool and moist. Haskel took his engineer's cap from the hook and fitted it on his head. Excitement and a faint surge of renewed energy filled his tired body. He approached the great plywood table with eager steps.

Trains ran everywhere. Along the floor, under the coal bin, among the steam pipes of the furnace. The tracks converged at the table, rising up on carefully graded ramps. The table itself was littered with transformers and signals and switches and heaps of equipment and wiring. And–

And the town.

The detailed, painfully accurate model of Woodland. Every tree and house, every store and building and street and fireplug. A minute town, each facet in perfect order. Constructed with elaborate care throughout the years. As long as he could remember. Since he was a kid, building and glueing and working after school.

Haskel turned on the main transformer. All along the track signal lights glowed. He fed power to the heavy Lionel engine parked with its load of freight cars. The engine sped smoothly into life, gliding along the track. A flashing dark projectile of metal that made his breath catch in his throat. He opened an electric switch and the engine headed down the ramp, through a tunnel and off the table. It raced under the workbench.

His trains. And his town. Haskel bent over the miniature houses and streets, his heart glowing with pride. He had built it–himself. Every inch. Every perfect inch. The whole town. He touched the corner of Fred's Grocery Store. Not a detail lacking. Even the windows. The displays of food. The signs. The counters.

The Uptown Hotel. He ran his hand over its flat roof. The sofas and chairs in the lobby. He could see them through the window.

Green's Drugstore. Bunion pad displays. Magazines. Frazier's Auto Parts. Mexico City Dining. Sharpstein's Apparel. Bob's Liquor Store. Ace Billiard Parlor.

The whole town. He ran his hands over it. He had built it; the town was his.

The train came rushing back, out from under the workbench. Its wheels passed over an automatic switch and a drawbridge lowered itself obediently. The train swept over and beyond, dragging its cars behind it.

Haskel turned up the power. The train gained speed. Its whistle sounded. It turned a sharp curve and grated across a cross-track. More speed. Haskel's hands jerked convulsively at the transformer. The train leaped and shot ahead. It swayed and bucked as it shot around a curve. The transformer was turned up to maximum. The train was a clattering blur of speed, rushing along the track, across bridges and switches, behind the big pipes of the floor furnace.

It disappeared into the coal bin. A moment later it swept out the other side, rocking wildly.

Haskel slowed the train down. He was breathing hard, his chest rising painfully. He sat down on the stool by the workbench and lit a cigarette with shaking fingers.

The train, the model town, gave him a strange feeling. It was hard to explain. He had always loved trains, model engines and signals and buildings. Since he was a little kid, maybe six or seven. His father had given him his first train. An engine and a few pieces of track. An old wind-up train. When he was nine he got his first real electric train. And two switches.

He added to it, year after year. Track, engines, switches, cars, signals. More powerful transformers. And the beginnings of the town.

He had built the town up carefully. Piece by piece. First, when he was in junior high, a model of the Southern Pacific Depot. Then the taxi stand next door. The cafe where the drivers ate. Broad Street.

And so on. More and more. Houses, buildings, stores. A whole town, growing under his hands, as the years went by. Every afternoon he came home from school and worked. Glued and cut and painted and sawed.

Now it was virtually complete. Almost done. He was forty-three years old and the town was almost done.

Haskel moved around the big plywood table, his hands extended reverently. He touched a miniature store here and there. The flower shop. The theater. The Telephone Company. Larson's Pump and Valve Works.

That, too. Where he worked. His place of business. A perfect miniature of the plant, down to the last detail.

Haskel scowled. Jim Larson. For twenty years he had worked there, slaved day after day. For what? To see others advanced over him. Younger men. Favorites of the boss. Yes-men with bright ties and pressed pants and wide, stupid grins.

Misery and hatred welled up in Haskel. All his life Woodland had got the better of him. He had never been happy. The town had always been against him. Miss Murphy in high school. The frats in college. Clerks in the snooty department stores. His neighbors. Cops and mailmen and bus drivers and delivery boys. Even his wife. Even Madge.

He had never meshed with the town. The rich, expensive little suburb of San Francisco, down the peninsula beyond the fog belt. Woodland was too damn upper-middle class. Too many big houses and lawns and chrome cars and deck chairs. Too stuffy and sleek. As long as he could remember. In school. His job—

Larson. The Pump and Valve Works. Twenty years of hard work.

Haskel's fingers closed over the tiny building, the model of Larson's Pump and Valve Works. Savagely, he ripped it loose and threw it to the floor. He crushed it underfoot, grinding the bits of glass and metal and cardboard into a shapeless mass.

God, he was shaking all over. He stared down at the remains, his heart pounding wildly. Strange emotions, crazy emotions, twisted through him. Thoughts he never had had before. For a long time he gazed down at the crumpled wad by his hose. What had once been the model of Larson's Pump and Valve Works.

Abruptly he pulled away. In a trance he returned to his workbench and sat stiffly down on the stool. He pulled his tools and materials together, clicking the power drill on.

It took only a few moments. Working rapidly, with quick, expert fingers, Haskel assembled a new model. He painted, glued, fitted pieces together. He lettered a microscopic sign and sprayed a green lawn into place.

Then he carried the new model carefully over to the table and glued it in the correct spot. The place where Larson's Pump and Valve Works had been. The new building gleamed in the overhead light, still moist and shiny.

WOODLAND MORTUARY

Haskel rubbed his hands in an ecstasy of satisfaction. The Valve Works was gone. He had destroyed it. Obliterated it. Removed it from the town. Below him was Woodland–without the Valve Works. A mortuary instead.

His eyes gleamed. His lips twitched. His surging emotions swelled. He had got rid of it. In a brief flurry of action. In a second. The whole thing was simple–amazingly easy.

Odd he hadn't thought of it before.

Sipping a tall glass of ice-cold beer thoughtfully, Madge Haskel said, 'There's something wrong with Verne. I noticed it especially last night. When he came home from work.'

Doctor Paul Tyler grunted absently. 'A highly neurotic type. Sense of inferiority. Withdrawal and introversion.'

'But he's getting worse. Him and his trains. Those damn model trains. My God, Paul! Do you know he has a whole town down there in the basement?'

Tyler was curious. 'Really? I never knew that.'

'All the time I've known him he's had them down there. Started when he was a kid. Imagine a grown man playing with trains! It's–it's disgusting. Every night the same thing.'

'Interesting.' Tyler rubbed his jaw. 'He keeps at them continually? An unvarying pattern?'

'Every night. Last night he didn't even eat dinner. He just came home and went directly down.'

Paul Tyler's polished features twisted into a frown. Across from him Madge sat languidly sipping her beer. It was two in the afternoon. The day was warm and bright. The living room was attractive in a lazy, quiet way. Abruptly Tyler got to his feet. 'Let's take a look at them. The models. I didn't know it had gone so far.'

'Do you really want to?' Madge slid back the sleeve of her green silk lounge pajamas and consulted her wristwatch. 'He won't be home until five.' She jumped to her feet, setting down her glass. 'All right. We have time.'

'Fine. Let's go down.' Tyler caught hold of Madge's arm and they hurried down into the basement, a strange excitement flooding through them. Madge clicked on the basement light and they approached the big plywood table, giggling and nervous, like mischievous children.

'See?' Madge said, squeezing Tyler's arm. 'Look at it. Took years. All his life.'

Tyler nodded slowly. 'Must have.' There was awe in his voice. 'I've never seen anything like it. The detail . . . He has skill.'

'Yes, Verne is good with his hands.' Madge indicated the workbench. 'He buys tools all the time.'

Tyler walked slowly around the big table, bending over and

peering. 'Amazing. Every building. The whole town is here. Look! There's my place.'

He indicated his luxurious apartment building, a few blocks from the Haskel residence.

'I guess it's all there,' Madge said. 'Imagine a grown man coming down here and playing with model trains!'

'Power.' Tyler pushed an engine along a track. 'That's why it appeals to boys. Trains are big things. Huge and noisy. Power-sex symbols. The boy sees the train rushing along the track. It's so huge and ruthless it scares him. Then he gets a toy train. A model, like these. He controls it. Makes it start, stop. Go slow. Fast. He runs it. It responds to him.'

Madge shivered. 'Let's go upstairs where it's warm. It's so cold down here.'

'But as the boy grows up, he gets bigger and stronger. He can shed the model-symbol. Master the real object, the real train. Get genuine control over things. Valid mastery.' Tyler shook his head. 'Not this substitute thing. Unusual, a grown person going to such lengths.' He frowned. 'I never noticed a mortuary on State Street.'

'A mortuary?'

'And this. Steuben Pet Shop. Next door to the radio repair shop. There's no pet shop there.' Tyler cudgeled his brain. 'What *is* there? Next to the radio repair place.'

'Paris Furs.' Madge clasped her arms. 'Brrrrr. Come on, Paul. Let's go upstairs before I freeze.'

Tyler laughed. 'Okay, sissy.' He headed toward the stairs, frowning again. 'I wonder why. Steuben Pets. Never heard of it. Everything is so detailed. He must know the town by heart. To put a shop there that isn't–' He clicked off the basement light. 'And the mortuary. What's supposed to be there? Isn't the–'

'Forget it,' Madge called back, hurrying past him, into the warm living room. 'You're practically as bad as he is. Men are such children.'

Tyler didn't respond. He was deep in thought. His suave confidence was gone; he looked nervous and shaken.

Madge pulled the venetian blinds down. The living room sank into amber gloom. She flopped down on the couch and pulled Tyler down beside her. 'Stop looking like that,' she ordered. 'I've never seen you this way.' Her slim arms circled his neck and her lips brushed close to his ear. 'I wouldn't have let you in if I thought you were going to worry about *him*.'

Tyler grunted, preoccupied. 'Why *did* you let me in?'

The pressure of Madge's arms increased. Her silk pajamas rustled as she moved against him. 'Silly,' she said.

Big red-headed Jim Larson gaped in disbelief. 'What do you mean? What's the matter with you?'

'I'm quitting.' Haskel shoveled the contents of his desk into his briefcase. 'Mail the check to my house.'

'But–'

'Get out of the way.' Haskel pushed past Larson, out into the hall. Larson was stunned with amazement. There was a fixed expression on Haskel's face. A glazed look. A rigid look Larson had never seen before.

'Are you–all right?' Larson asked.

'Sure.' Haskel opened the front door of the plant and disappeared outside. The door slammed after him. 'Sure I'm all right,' he muttered to himself. He made his way through the crowds of late-afternoon shoppers, his lips twitching. 'You're damn right I'm all right.'

'Watch it, buddy,' a laborer muttered ominously, as Haskel shoved past him.

'Sorry.' Haskel hurried on, gripping his briefcase. At the top of the hill he paused a moment to get his breath. Behind him was Larson's Pump and Valve Works. Haskel laughed shrilly. Twenty years–cut short in a second. It was over. No more Larson. No more dull, grinding job, day after day. Without promotion or future. Routine and boredom, months on end. It was over and done for. A new life and beginning.

He hurried on. The sun was setting. Cars streaked by him,

businessmen going home from work. Tomorrow they would be going back–but not him. Not ever again.

He reached his own street. Ed Tildon's house rose up, a great stately structure of concrete and glass. Tildon's dog came rushing out to bark. Haskel hastened past. Tildon's dog. He laughed wildly.

'Better keep away!' he shouted at the dog.

He reached his own house and leaped up the front steps two at a time. He tore the door open. The living room was dark and silent. There was a sudden stir of motion. Shapes untangling themselves, getting quickly up from the couch.

'Verne!' Madge gasped. 'What are you doing home so early?'

Verne Haskel threw his briefcase down and dropped his hat and coat over a chair. His lined face was twisted with emotion, pulled out of shape by violent inner forces.

'What in the world!' Madge fluttered, hurrying toward him nervously, smoothing down her lounge pajamas. 'Has something happened? I didn't expect you so–' She broke off, blushing. 'I mean, I–'

Paul Tyler strolled leisurely toward Haskel. 'Hi there, Verne,' he murmured, embarrassed. 'Dropped by to say hello and return a book to your wife.'

Haskel nodded curtly. 'Afternoon.' He turned and headed toward the basement door, ignoring the two of them. 'I'll be downstairs.'

'But Verne!' Madge protested. 'What's happened?'

Verne halted briefly at the door. 'I quit my job.'

'You *what?*'

'I quit my job. I finished Larson off. There won't be any more of him.' The basement door slammed.

'Good Lord!' Madge shrieked, clutching at Tyler hysterically. 'He's gone out of his mind!'

Down in the basement, Verne Haskel snapped on the light impatiently. He put on his engineer's cap and pulled his stool up beside the great plywood table.

What next?

Morris Home Furnishings. The big plush store. Where the clerks all looked down their noses at him.

He rubbed his hands gleefully. No more of them. No more snooty clerks, lifting their eyebrows when he came in. Only hair and bow ties and folded handkerchiefs.

He removed the model of Morris Home Furnishings and disassembled it. He worked feverishly, with frantic haste. Now that he had really begun he wasted no time. A moment later he was glueing two small buildings in its place. Ritz Shoeshine. Pete's Bowling Alley.

Haskel giggled excitedly. Fitting extinction for the luxurious, exclusive furniture store. A shoeshine parlor and a bowling alley. Just what it deserved.

The California State Bank. He had always hated the Bank. They had once refused him a loan. He pulled the Bank loose.

Ed Tildon's mansion. His damn dog. The dog had bit him on the ankle one afternoon. He ripped the model off. His head spun. He could do anything.

Harrison Appliance. They had sold him a bum radio. Off came Harrison Appliance.

Joe's Cigar and Smoke Shop. Joe had given him a lead quarter in May, 1949. Off came Joe's.

The Ink Works. He loathed the smell of ink. Maybe a bread factory, instead. He loved baking bread. Off came the Ink Works.

Elm Street was too dark at night. A couple of times he had stumbled. A few more streetlights were in order.

Not enough bars along High Street. Too many dress shops and expensive hat and fur shops and ladies' apparel. He ripped a whole handful loose and carried them to the workbench.

At the top of the stairs the door opened slowly. Madge peered down, pale and frightened. 'Verne?'

He scowled up impatiently. 'What do you want?'

Madge came downstairs hesitantly. Behind her Doctor Tyler followed, suave and handsome in his gray suit. 'Verne–is everything all right?'

'Of course.'

'Did–did you really quit your job?'

Haskel nodded. He began to disassemble the Ink Works, ignoring his wife and Doctor Tyler.

'But *why?*'

Haskel grunted impatiently. 'No time.'

Doctor Tyler had begun to look worried. 'Do I understand you're too busy for your job?'

'That's right.'

'Too busy doing *what?*' Tyler's voice rose; he was trembling nervously. 'Working down here on this town of yours? Changing things?'

'Go away,' Haskel muttered. His deft hands were assembling a lovely little Langendorf Bread Factory. He shaped it with loving care, sprayed it with white paint, brushed a gravel walk and shrubs in front of it. He put it aside and began on a park. A big green park. Woodland had always needed a park. It would go in place of State Street Hotel.

Tyler pulled Madge away from the table, off in a corner of the basement. 'Good God.' He lit a cigarette shakily. The cigarette flipped out of his hands and rolled away. He ignored it and fumbled for another. 'You see? You see what he's doing?'

Madge shook her head mutely. 'What is it? I don't–'

'How long has he been working on this? All his life?'

Madge nodded, white-faced. 'Yes, all his life.'

Tyler's features twisted. 'My God, Madge. It's enough to drive you out of your mind. I can hardly believe it. We've got to do something.'

'What's happening?' Madge moaned. 'What–'

'He's losing himself into it.' Tyler's face was a mask of incredulous disbelief. 'Faster and faster.'

'He's always come down here,' Madge faltered. 'It's nothing new. He's always wanted to get away.'

'Yes. Get away.' Tyler shuddered, clenched his fists and pulled himself together. He advanced across the basement and stopped by Verne Haskel.

'What do you want?' Haskel muttered, noticing him.

Tyler licked his lips. 'You're adding some things, aren't you? New buildings.'

Haskel nodded.

Tyler touched the little bread factory with shaking fingers. 'What's this? Bread? Where does it go?' He moved around the table. 'I don't remember any bread factory in Woodland.' He whirled. 'You aren't by any chance *improving* on the town? Fixing it up here and there?'

'Get the hell out of here,' Haskel said, with ominous calm. 'Both of you.'

'Verne!' Madge squeaked.

'I've got a lot to do. You can bring sandwiches down about eleven. I hope to finish sometime tonight.'

'Finish?' Tyler asked.

'Finish,' Haskel answered, returning to his work.

'Come on, Madge.' Tyler grabbed her and pulled her to the stairs. 'Let's get out of here.' He strode ahead of her, up the stairs and into the hall. 'Come on!' As soon as she was up he closed the door tightly after them.

Madge dabbed at her eyes hysterically. 'He's gone crazy, Paul! What'll we do?'

Tyler was deep in thought. 'Be quiet. I have to think this out.' He paced back and forth, a hard scowl on his features. 'It'll come soon. It won't be long, not at this rate. Sometime tonight.'

'*What?* What do you mean?'

'His withdrawal. Into his substitute world. The improved model he controls. Where he can get away.'

'Isn't there something we can do?'

'Do?' Tyler smiled faintly. 'Do we want to do something?'

Madge gasped. 'But we can't just–'

'Maybe this will solve our problem. This may be what we've been looking for.' Tyler eyed Mrs Haskel thoughtfully. 'This may be just the thing.'

It was after midnight, almost two o'clock in the morning, when he began to get things into final shape. He was tired–but alert. Things were happening fast. The job was almost done.

Virtually perfect.

He halted work a moment, surveying what he had accomplished. The town had been radically changed. About ten o'clock he had begun basic structural alterations in the lay-out of the streets. He had removed most of the public buildings, the civic center and the sprawling business district around it.

He had erected a new city hall, police station, and an immense park with fountains and indirect lighting. He had cleared the slum area, the old rundown stores and houses and streets. The streets were wider and well-lit. The houses were now small and clean. The stores modern and attractive–without being ostentatious.

All advertising signs had been removed. Most of the filling stations were gone. The immense factory area was gone, too. Rolling countryside took its place. Trees and hills and green grass.

The wealthy district had been altered. There were now only a few of the mansions left–belonging to persons he looked favorably on. The rest had been cut down, turned into uniform two-bedroom dwellings, one story, with a single garage each.

The city hall was no longer an elaborate, rococo structure. Now it was low and simple, modeled after the Parthenon, a favorite of his.

There were ten or twelve persons who had done him special harm. He had altered their houses considerably. Given them wartime housing unit apartments, six to a building, at the far edge of town. Where the wind came off the bay, carrying the smell of decaying mud-flats.

Jim Larson's house was completely gone. He had erased Larson utterly. He no longer existed, not in this new Woodland–which was now almost complete.

Almost. Haskel studied his work intently. All the changes had to be made *now*. Not later. This was the time of creation. Later, when it had been finished, it could not be altered. He had to catch all the necessary changes now–or forget them.

The new Woodland looked pretty good. Clean and neat–and simple. The rich district had been toned down. The poor district had been improved. Glaring ads, signs, displays, had all been changed or removed. The business community was smaller. Parks and countryside took the place of factories. The civic center was lovely.

He added a couple of playgrounds for smaller kids. A small theater instead of the enormous Uptown with its flashing neon sign. After some consideration he removed most of the bars he had previously constructed. The new Woodland was going to be moral. Extremely moral. Few bars, no billiards, no red light district. And there was an especially fine jail for undesirables.

The most difficult part had been the microscopic lettering on the main office door of the city hall. He had left it until last, and then painted the words with agonizing care:

MAYOR VERNON R. HASKEL

A few last changes. He gave the Edwardses a '39 Plymouth instead of a new Cadillac. He added more trees in the downtown district. One more fire department. One less dress shop. He had never liked taxis. On impulse, he removed the taxi stand and put in a flower shop.

Haskel rubbed his hands. Anything more? Or was it complete . . . Perfect . . . He studied each part intently. What had he overlooked?

The high school. He removed it and put in two smaller high schools, one at each end of town. Another hospital. That took almost half an hour. He was getting tired. His hands were less swift. He mopped his forehead shakily. Anything else? He sat down on his stool wearily, to rest and think.

All done. It was complete. Joy welled up in him. A bursting cry of happiness. His work was over.

'Finished!' Verne Haskel shouted.

He got unsteadily to his feet. He closed his eyes, held his arms out, and advanced toward the plywood table. Reaching, grasping, fingers extended, Haskel headed toward it, a look of radiant exaltation on his seamed, middle-aged face.

Upstairs, Tyler and Madge heard the shout. A distant booming that rolled through the house in waves. Madge winced in terror. 'What was that?'

Tyler listened intently. He heard Haskel moving below them, in the basement. Abruptly, he stubbed out his cigarette. 'I think it's happened. Sooner than I expected.'

'It? You mean he's–'

Tyler got quickly to his feet. 'He's gone, Madge. Into his other world. We're finally free.'

Madge caught his arm. 'Maybe we're making a mistake. It's so terrible. Shouldn't we–try to do something? Bring him out of it–try to pull him back.'

'Bring him back?' Tyler laughed nervously. 'I don't think we could, now. Even if we wanted to. It's too late.' He hurried toward the basement door. 'Come on.'

'It's horrible.' Madge shuddered and followed reluctantly. 'I wish we had never got started.'

Tyler halted briefly at the door. 'Horrible? He's happier, where he is, now. And you're happier. The way it was, nobody was happy. This is the best thing.'

He opened the basement door. Madge followed him. They moved cautiously down the stairs, into the dark, silent basement, damp with the faint night mists.

The basement was empty.

Tyler relaxed. He was overcome with dazed relief. 'He's gone. Everything's okay. It worked out exactly right.'

'But I don't understand,' Madge repeated hopelessly, as Tyler's Buick purred along the dark, deserted streets. 'Where did he go?'

'You know where he went,' Tyler answered. 'Into his substitute world, of course.' He screeched around a corner on two wheels. 'The rest should be fairly simple. A few routine forms. There really isn't much left, now.'

The night was frigid and bleak. No lights showed, except an occasional lonely streetlamp. Far off, a train whistle sounded mournfully, a dismal echo. Rows of silent houses flickered by on both sides of them.

'Where are we going?' Madge asked. She sat huddled against the door, face pale with shock and terror, shivering under her coat.

'To the police station.'

'Why?'

'To report him, naturally. So they'll know he's gone. We'll have to wait; it'll be several years before he'll be declared legally dead.' Tyler reached over and hugged her briefly. 'We'll make out in the meantime, I'm sure.'

'What if–they find him?'

Tyler shook his head angrily. He was still tense, on edge. 'Don't you understand? They'll never find him–he doesn't exist. At least, not in our world. He's in his own world. You saw it. The model. The improved substitute.'

'He's there?'

'All his life he's worked on it. Built it up. Made it real. He brought that world into being–and now he's in it. That's what he wanted. That's why he built it. He didn't merely dream about an escape world. He actually constructed it–every bit and piece. Now he's warped himself right out of our world, into it. Out of our lives.'

Madge finally began to understand. 'Then he really *did* lose himself in his substitute world. You meant that, what you said about him–getting away.'

'It took me a while to realize it. The mind constructs reality. Frames it. Creates it. We all have a common reality, a common dream. But Haskel turned his back on our common reality and created his own. And he had a unique capacity–far beyond the ordinary. He devoted his whole life, his whole skill to building it. He's there now.'

Tyler hesitated and frowned. He gripped the wheel tightly and increased speed. The Buick hissed along the dark street, through the silent, unmoving bleakness that was the town.

'There's only one thing,' he continued presently. 'One thing I don't understand.'

'What is it?'

'The model. It was also gone. I assumed he'd—shrink, I suppose. Merge with it. But the model's gone, too.' Tyler shrugged. 'It doesn't matter.' He peered into the darkness. 'We're almost there. This is Elm.'

It was then Madge screamed. '*Look!*'

To the right of the car was a small, neat building. And a sign. The sign was easily visible in the darkness.

WOODLAND MORTUARY

Madge was sobbing in horror. The car roared forward, automatically guided by Tyler's numb hands. Another sign flashed by briefly, as they coasted up before the city hall.

STEUBEN PET SHOP

The city hall was lit by recessed, hidden illumination. A low, simple building, a square of glowing white. Like a marble Greek temple.

Tyler pulled the car to a halt. Then suddenly shrieked and started up again. But not soon enough.

The two shiny-black police cars came silently up around the Buick, one on each side. The four stern cops already had their hands on the door. Stepping out and coming toward him, grim and efficient.

SOUVENIR

'Here we go, sir,' the robot pilot said. The words startled Rogers and made him look up sharply. He tensed his body and adjusted the trace web inside his coat as the bubble ship started dropping, swiftly and silently, toward the planet's surface.

This–his heart caught–was Williamson's World. The legendary lost planet–found, after three centuries. By accident, of course. This blue and green planet, the holy grail of the Galactic System, had been almost miraculously discovered by a routine charting mission.

Frank Williamson had been the first Terran to develop an outer-space drive–the first to hop off from the Solar System toward the universe beyond. He had never come back. He–his world, his colony–had never been found. There had been endless rumors, false leads, fake legends–and nothing more.

'I'm receiving field clearance.' The robot pilot raised the gain on the control speaker, and clicked to attention.

'Field ready,' came a ghostly voice from below. 'Remember, your drive mechanism is unfamiliar to us. How much run is required? Emergency brake-walls are up.'

Rogers smiled. He could hear the pilot telling them that no run would be required. Not with this ship. The brake-walls could be lowered with perfect safety.

Three hundred years! It had taken a long time to find Williamson's World. Many authorities had given him up. Some believed he had never landed, had died out in space. Perhaps there was *no* Williamson's World. Certainly there had been no real clues, nothing tangible to go on. Frank Williamson and three families had utterly disappeared in the trackless void, never to be heard from again.

Until now . . .

The young man met him at the field. He was thin and red-haired and dressed in a colorful suit of bright material. 'You're from the Galactic Relay Center?' he asked.

'That's right,' Rogers said huskily. 'I'm Edward Rogers.'

The young man held out his hand. Rogers shook it awkwardly. 'My name is Williamson,' the young man said. 'Gene Williamson.'

The name thundered in Rogers' ears. 'Are you–'

The young man nodded, his gaze enigmatical. 'I'm his great-great-great-great-grandson. His tomb is here. You may see it, if you wish.'

'I almost expected to see him. He's–well, almost a god-figure to us. The first man to break out of the Solar System.'

'He means a lot to us, too,' the young man said. 'He brought us here. They searched a long time before they found a planet that was habitable.' Williamson waved at the city stretched out beyond the field. 'This one proved satisfactory. It's the System's tenth planet.'

Rogers' eyes began to shine. Williamson's World. Under his feet. He stamped hard as they walked down the ramp together, away from the field. How many men in the Galaxy had dreamed of striding down a landing ramp onto Williamson's World with a young descendant of Frank Williamson beside them?

'They'll all want to come here,' Williamson said, as if aware of his thoughts. 'Throw rubbish around and break off the flowers. Pick up handfuls of dirt to take back.' He laughed a little nervously. 'The Relay will control them, of course.'

'Of course,' Rogers assured him.

At the ramp-end Rogers stopped short. For the first time he saw the city.

'What's wrong?' Gene Williamson asked, with a faint trace of amusement.

They had been cut off, of course. Isolated–so perhaps it wasn't so surprising. It was a wonder they weren't living in caves, eating raw meat. But Williamson had always symbolized progress–development. He had been a man *ahead* of other men.

True, his space-drive by modern standards had been primitive, a curiosity. But the concept remained unaltered; Williamson the pioneer, and inventor. The man who built.

Yet the city was nothing more than a village, with a few dozen houses, and some public buildings and industrial units at its perimeter. Beyond the city stretched green fields, hills, and broad prairies. Surface vehicles crawled leisurely along the narrow streets and most of the citizens walked on foot. An incredible anachronism it seemed, dragged up from the past.

'I'm accustomed to the uniform Galactic culture,' Rogers said. 'Relay keeps the technocratic and ideological level constant throughout. It's hard to adjust to such a radically different social stage. But you've been cut off.'

'Cut off?' asked Williamson.

'From Relay. You've had to develop without help.'

In front of them a surface vehicle crept to a halt. The driver opened the doors manually.

'Now that I recall these factors, I can adjust,' Rogers assured him.

'On the contrary,' Williamson said, entering the vehicle. 'We've been receiving your Relay coordinates for over a century.' He motioned Rogers to get in beside him.

Rogers was puzzled. 'I don't understand. You mean you hooked onto the web and yet made no attempt to–'

'We receive your coordinates,' Gene Williamson said, 'but our citizens are not interested in using them.'

The surface vehicle hurried along the highway, past the rim of an immense red hill. Soon the city lay behind them–a faintly glowing place reflecting the rays of the sun. Bushes and plants appeared along the highway. The sheer side of the cliff rose, a towering wall of deep red sandstone; ragged, untouched.

'Nice evening,' Williamson said.

Rogers nodded in disturbed agreement.

Williamson rolled down the window. Cool air blew into the car. A few gnatlike insects followed. Far off, two tiny figures were plowing a field—a man and a huge lumbering beast.

'When will we be there?' Rogers asked.

'Soon. Most of us live away from the cities. We live in the country—in isolated self-sufficient farm units. They're modeled on the manors of the Middle Ages.'

'Then you maintain only the most rudimentary subsistence level. How many people live on each farm?'

'Perhaps a hundred men and women.'

'A hundred people can't manage anything more complex than weaving and dyeing and paper pressing.'

'We have special industrial units—manufacturing systems. This vehicle is a good example of what we can turn out. We have communication and sewage and medical agencies. We have technological advantages equal to Terra's.'

'Terra of the twenty-first century,' Rogers protested. 'But that was three hundred years ago. You're purposely maintaining an archaic culture in the face of the Relay coordinates. It doesn't make any sense.'

'Maybe we prefer it.'

'But you're not free to prefer an inferior cultural stage. Every culture has to keep pace with the general trend. Relay makes actual a uniformity of development. It integrates the valid factors and rejects the rest.'

They were approaching the farm, Gene Williamson's 'manor.' It consisted of a few simple buildings clustered together in a valley, to the side of the highway, surrounded by fields and pastures. The surface vehicle turned down a narrow side road and spiralled cautiously toward the floor of the valley. The air became darker. Cold wind blew into the car, and the driver clicked his headlights on.

'No robots?' Rogers asked.

'No,' Williamson replied. 'We do all our own work.'

'You're making a purely arbitrary distinction,' Rogers pointed out. 'A robot is a machine. You don't dispense with machines as such. This car is a machine.'

'True,' Williamson acknowledged.

'The machine is a development of the tool,' Rogers went on. 'The axe is a simple machine. A stick becomes a tool, a simple machine, in the hands of a man reaching for something. A machine is merely a multi-element tool that increases the power ratio. Man is the tool-making animal. The history of man is the history of tools into machines, greater and more efficient functioning elements. If you reject machinery you reject man's essential key.'

'Here we are,' Williamson said. The vehicle came to a halt and the driver opened the doors for them.

Three or four huge wooden buildings loomed up in the darkness. A few dim shapes moved around–human shapes.

'Dinner's ready,' Williamson said, sniffing. 'I can smell it.'

They entered the main building. Several men and women were sitting at a long rough table. Plates and dishes had been set in front of them. They were waiting for Williamson.

'This is Edward Rogers,' Williamson announced. The people studied Rogers curiously, then turned back to their food.

'Sit down,' a dark-eyed girl urged. 'By me.'

They made a place for him near the end of the table. Rogers started forward, but Williamson restrained him. 'Not there. You're *my* guest. You're expected to sit with me.'

The girl and her companions laughed. Rogers sat down awkwardly by Williamson. The bench was rough and hard under him. He examined a hand-made wooden drinking cup. The food was piled in huge wooden bowls. There was a stew and a salad and great loaves of bread.

'We could be back in the fourteenth century,' Rogers said.

'Yes,' Williamson agreed. 'Manor life goes back to Roman times and to the classical world. The Gauls. Britons.'

'These people here. Are they–'

Williamson nodded. 'My family. We're divided up into small units arranged according to the traditional patriarch basis. I'm the oldest male and titular head.'

The people were eating rapidly, intent on their food–boiled meat, vegetables, scooped up with hunks of bread and butter and washed down with milk. The room was lit by fluorescent lighting.

'Incredible,' Rogers murmured. 'You're still using electric power.'

'Oh, yes. There are plenty of waterfalls on this planet. The vehicle was electric. It was run by a storage battery.'

'Why are there no older men?' Rogers saw several dried-up old women, but Williamson was the oldest man. And he couldn't have been over thirty.

'The fighting,' Williamson replied, with an expressive gesture.

'Fighting?'

'Clan wars between families are a major part of our culture.' Williamson nodded toward the long table. 'We don't live long.'

Rogers was stunned. 'Clan wars? But–'

'We have pennants, and emblems–like the old Scottish tribes.'

He touched a bright ribbon on his sleeve, the representation of a bird. 'There are emblems and colors for each family and we fight over them. The Williamson family no longer controls this planet. There is no central agency, now. For a major issue we have the plebiscite–a vote by all the clans. Each family on the planet has a vote.'

'Like the American Indians.'

Williamson nodded. 'It's a tribal system. In time we'll be distinct tribes, I suppose. We still retain a common language, but we're breaking up–decentralizing. And each family to its own ways, its own customs and manners.'

'Just what do you fight for?'

Williamson shrugged. 'Some real things like land and women. Some imaginary. Prestige for instance. When honor is at stake we have an official semi-annual public battle. A man from each family takes part. The best warrior and his weapons.'

'Like the medieval joust.'

'We've drawn from all traditions. Human tradition as a whole.'

'Does each family have its separate deity?'

Williamson laughed. 'No. We worship in common a vague

animism. A sense of the general positive vitality of the universal process.' He held up a loaf of bread. 'Thanks for all this.'

'Which you grew yourselves.'

'On a planet provided for us.' Williamson ate his bread thoughtfully. 'The old records say the ship was almost finished. Fuel just about gone–one dead, arid waste after another. If this planet hadn't turned up, the whole expedition would have perished.'

'Cigar?' Williamson said, when the empty bowls had been pushed back.

'Thanks.' Rogers accepted a cigar noncommittally. Williamson lit his own, and settled back against the wall.

'How long are you staying?' he asked presently.

'Not long,' Rogers answered.

'There's a bed fixed up for you,' Williamson said. 'We retire early, but there'll be some kind of dancing, also singing and dramatic acts. We devote a lot of time to staging and producing drama.'

'You place an emphasis on psychological release?'

'We enjoy making and doing things, if that's what you mean.'

Rogers stared about him. The walls were covered with murals painted directly on the rough wood. 'So I see,' he said. 'You grind your own colors from clay and berries?'

'Not quite,' Williamson replied. 'We have a big pigment industry. Tomorrow I'll show you our kiln where we fire our own things. Some of our best work is with fabrics and screen processes.'

'Interesting. A decentralized society, moving gradually back into primitive tribalism. A society that voluntarily rejects the advanced technocratic and cultural products of the Galaxy, and thus deliberately withdraws from contact with the rest of mankind.'

'From the uniform Relay-controlled society only,' Williamson insisted.

'Do you know why Relay maintains a uniform level for all worlds?' Rogers asked. 'I'll tell you. There are two reasons. First, the body of knowledge which men have amassed doesn't permit duplication of experiment. There's no time.

'When a discovery has been made it's absurd to repeat it on countless planets throughout the universe. Information gained on any of the thousand worlds is flashed to Relay Center and then out again to the whole Galaxy. Relay studies and selects experiences and co-ordinates them into a rational, functional system without contradictions. Relay orders the total experience of mankind into a coherent structure.'

'And the second reason?'

'If uniform culture is maintained, controlled from a central source, there won't be war.'

'True,' Williamson admitted.

'We've abolished war. It's as simple as that. We have a homogeneous culture like that of ancient Rome–a common culture for all mankind which we maintain throughout the Galaxy. Each planet is as involved in it as any other. There are no backwaters of culture to breed envy and hatred.'

'Such as this.'

Rogers let out his breath slowly. 'Yes–you've confronted us with a strange situation. We've searched for Williamson's World for three centuries. We've wanted it, dreamed of finding it. It has seemed like Prester John's Empire–a fabulous world, cut off from the rest of humanity. Maybe not real at all. Frank Williamson might have crashed.'

'But he didn't.'

'He didn't, and Williamson's World is alive with a culture of its own. Deliberately set apart, with its own way of life, its own standards. Now contact has been made, and our dream has come true. The people of the Galaxy will soon be informed that Williamson's World has been found. We can now restore the first colony outside the Solar System to its rightful place in the Galactic culture.'

Rogers reached into his coat, and brought out a metal packet. He unfastened the packet and laid a clean, crisp document on the table.

'What's this?' Williamson asked.

'The Articles of Incorporation. For you to sign, so that Williamson's World can become a part of the Galactic culture.'

Williamson and the rest of the people in the room fell silent. They gazed down at the document, none of them speaking.

'Well?' Rogers said. He was tense. He pushed the document toward Williamson. 'Here it is.'

Williamson shook his head. 'Sorry.' He pushed the document firmly back toward Rogers. 'We've already taken a plebiscite. I hate to disappoint you, but we've already decided not to join. That's our *final* decision.'

The Class-One battleship assumed an orbit outside the gravity belt of Williamson's World.

Commander Ferris contacted the Relay Center. 'We're here. What next?'

'Send down a wiring team. Report back to me as soon as it has made surface contact.'

Ten minutes later Corporal Pete Matson was dropped overboard in a pressurized gravity suit. He drifted slowly toward the blue and green globe beneath, turning and twisting as he neared the surface of the planet.

Matson landed and bounced a couple of times. He got shakily to his feet. He seemed to be at the edge of a forest. In the shadow of the huge trees he removed his crash helmet. Holding his blast rifle tightly he made his way forward, cautiously advancing among the trees.

His earphones clicked. 'Any sign of activity?'

'None, Commander,' he signaled back.

'There's what appears to be a village to your right. You may run into someone. Keep moving, and watch out. The rest of the team is dropping, now. Instructions will follow from your Relay web.'

'I'll watch out,' Matson promised, cradling his blast rifle. He sighted it experimentally at a distant hill and squeezed the trigger. The hill disintegrated into dust, a rising column of waste particles.

Matson climbed a long ridge and shielded his eyes to peer around him.

He could see the village. It was small, like a country town on Terra. It looked interesting. For a moment he hesitated. Then he stepped quickly down from the ridge and headed toward the village, moving rapidly, his supple body alert.

Above him, from the Class-One battleship, three more of the team were already falling, clutching their guns and tumbling gently toward the surface of the planet . . .

Rogers folded up the Incorporation papers and returned them slowly to his coat. 'You understand what you're doing?' he asked.

The room was deathly silent. Williamson nodded. 'Of course. We're refusing to join your Relay system.'

Rogers' fingers touched the trace web. The web warmed into life. 'I'm sorry to hear that,' he said.

'Does it surprise you?'

'Not exactly. Relay submitted our scout's report to the computers. There was always the possibility you'd refuse. I was given instructions in case of such an event.'

'What are your instructions?'

Rogers examined his wristwatch. 'To inform you that you have six hours to join us–or be blasted out of the universe.' He got abruptly to his feet. 'I'm sorry this had to happen. Williamson's World is one of our most precious legends. But nothing must destroy the unity of the Galaxy.'

Williamson had risen. His face was ash white, the color of death. They faced each other defiantly.

'We'll fight,' Williamson said quietly. His fingers knotted together violently, clenching and unclenching.

'That's unimportant. You've received Relay coordinates on weapons development. You know what our war fleet has.'

The other people sat quietly at their places, staring rigidly down at their empty plates. No one moved.

'Is it necessary?' Williamson said harshly.

'Cultural variation must be avoided if the Galaxy is to have peace,' Rogers replied firmly.

'You'd destroy us to avoid war?'

'We'd destroy anything to avoid war. We can't permit our society to degenerate into bickering provinces, forever quarreling and fighting–like your clans. We're stable because we lack the very concept of variation. Uniformity must be preserved and separation must be discouraged. The idea itself must remain unknown.'

Williamson was thoughtful. 'Do you think you can keep the idea unknown? There are so many semantic correlatives, hints, verbal leads. Even if you blast us, it may arise somewhere else.'

'We'll take that chance.' Rogers moved toward the door. 'I'll return to my ship and wait there. I suggest you take another vote. Maybe knowing how far we're prepared to go will change the results.'

'I doubt it.'

Rogers' web whispered suddenly. 'This is North at Relay.'

Rogers fingered the web in acknowledgment.

'A Class-One battleship is in your area. A team has already been landed. Keep your ship grounded until it can fall back. I've ordered the team to lay out its fission-mine terminals.'

Rogers said nothing. His fingers tightened around the web convulsively.

'What's wrong?' Williamson asked.

'Nothing.' Rogers pushed the door open. 'I'm in a hurry to return to my ship. Let's go.'

Commander Ferris contacted Rogers as soon as his ship had left Williamson's World.

'North tells me you've already informed them,' Ferris said.

'That's right. He also contacted your team directly. Had it prepare to attack.'

'So I'm informed. How much time did you offer them?'

'Six hours.'

'Do you think they'll give in?'

'I don't know,' Rogers said. 'I hope so. But I doubt it.'

Williamson's World turned slowly in the viewscreen with its green and blue forest, rivers and oceans. Terra might have looked that way, once. He could see the Class-One battleship, a great silvery globe moving slowly in its orbit around the planet.

The legendary world had been found and contacted. Now it would be destroyed. He had tried to prevent it, but without success. He couldn't prevent the inevitable.

If Williamson's World refused to join the Galactic culture its destruction became a necessity–grim, axiomatic. It was either Williamson's World or the Galaxy. To preserve the greater, the lesser had to be sacrificed.

He made himself as comfortable as possible by the viewscreen, and waited.

At the end of six hours a line of black dots rose from the planet and headed slowly toward the Class-One battleship. He recognized them for what they were–old-fashioned jet-driven rocket ships. A formation of antiquated war vessels, rising up to give battle.

The planet had not changed its mind. It was going to fight. It was willing to be destroyed, rather than give up its way of life.

The black dots grew swiftly larger, became roaring blazing metal disks puffing awkwardly along. A pathetic sight. Rogers felt strangely moved, watching the jet-driven ships divide up for the contact. The Class-One battleship had secured its orbit, and was swinging in a lazy, efficient arc. Its banks of energy tubes were slowly rising, lining up to meet the attack.

Suddenly the formation of the ancient rocket ships dived. They rumbled over the Class-One, firing jerkily. The Class-One's tubes followed their path. They began to reform clumsily, gaining distance for a second try, and another run.

A tongue of colorless energy flicked out. The attackers vanished.

Commander Ferris contacted Rogers. 'The poor tragic fools.' His heavy face was gray. 'Attacking us with those things.'

'Any damage?'

'None whatever.' Ferris wiped his forehead shakily. 'No damage to me at all.'

'What next?' Rogers asked stonily.

'I've declined the mine operation and passed it back to Relay. They'll have to do it. The impulse should already be–'

Below them, the green and blue globe shuddered convulsively. Soundlessly, effortlessly, it flew apart. Fragments rose, bits of debris and the planet dissolved in a cloud of white flame, a blazing mass of incandescent fire. For an instant it remained a miniature sun, lighting up the void. Then it faded into ash.

The screens of Rogers' ship hummed into life, as the debris struck. Particles rained against them, and were instantly disintegrated.

'Well,' Ferris said. 'It's over. North will report the original scout mistaken. Williamson's World wasn't found. The legend will remain a legend.'

Rogers continued to watch until the last bits of debris had ceased flying, and only a vague, discolored shadow remained. The screens clicked off automatically. To his right, the Class-One battleship picked up speed and headed toward the Riga System.

Williamson's World was gone. The Galactic Relay culture had been preserved. The idea, the concept of a separate culture with its own ways, its own customs, had been disposed of in the most effective possible way.

'Good job,' the Relay trace web whispered. North was pleased. 'The fission mines were perfectly placed. Nothing remains.'

'No,' Rogers agreed. 'Nothing remains.'

Corporal Pete Matson pushed the front door open, grinning from ear to ear. 'Hi, honey! Surprise!'

'Pete!' Gloria Matson came running, throwing her arms around her husband. 'What are you doing home? Pete–'

'Special leave. Forty-eight hours.' Pete tossed down his suitcase triumphantly. 'Hi there, kid.'

His son greeted him shyly. 'Hello.'

Pete squatted down and opened his suitcase. 'How have things been going? How's school?'

'He's had another cold,' Gloria said. 'He's almost over it. But what happened? Why did they–'

'Military secret.' Pete fumbled in his suitcase. 'Here.' He held something out to his son. 'I brought you something. A souvenir.'

He handed his son a hand-made wooden drinking cup. The boy took it shyly and turned it around, curious and puzzled. 'What's a–a *souvenir?*'

Matson struggled to express the difficult concept. 'Well, it's something that reminds you of a different place. Something you don't have, where you are. You know.' Matson tapped the cup. 'That's to drink out of. It's sure not like our plastic cups, is it?'

'No,' the child said.

'Look at this, Gloria.' Pete shook out a great folded cloth from his suitcase, printed with multi-colored designs. 'Picked this up cheap. You can make a skirt out of it. What do you say? Ever seen anything like it?'

'No,' Gloria said, awed. 'I haven't.' She took the cloth and fingered it reverently.

Pete Matson beamed, as his wife and child stood clutching the souvenirs he had brought them, reminders of his excursions to distant places. Foreign lands.

'Gee,' his son whispered, turning the cup around and around. A strange light glowed in his eyes. 'Thanks a lot, Dad. For the–*souvenir.*'

The strange light grew.

SURVEY TEAM

Halloway came up through six miles of ash to see how the rocket looked in landing. He emerged from the lead-shielded bore and joined Young, crouching down with a small knot of surface troops.

The surface of the planet was dark and silent. The air stung his nose. It smelled foul. Halloway shivered uneasily. 'Where the hell are we?'

A soldier pointed into the blackness. 'The mountains are over there. See them? The Rockies, and this is Colorado.'

Colorado . . . The old name awakened vague emotion in Halloway. He fingered his blast rifle. 'When will it get here?' he asked. Far off, against the horizon, he could see the Enemy's green and yellow signal flares. And an occasional flash of fission white.

'Any time now. It's mechanically controlled all the way, piloted by robot. When it comes it really comes.'

An Enemy mine burst a few dozen miles away. For a brief instant the landscape was outlined in jagged lightning. Halloway and the troops dropped to the ground automatically. He caught the dead burned smell of the surface of Earth as it was now, thirty years after the war began.

It was a lot different from the way he remembered it when he was a kid in California. He could remember the valley country, grape orchards and walnuts and lemons. Smudge pots under the orange trees. Green mountains and sky the color of a woman's eyes. And the fresh smell of the soil . . .

That was all gone now. Nothing remained but gray ash pulverized with the white stones of buildings. Once a city had been in this spot. He could see the yawning cavities of cellars, filled now with slag, dried rivers of rust that had once been buildings. Rubble strewn everywhere, aimlessly . . .

The mine flare faded out and the blackness settled back. They got cautiously to their feet. 'Quite a sight,' a soldier murmured.

'It was a lot different before,' Halloway said.

'Was it? I was born undersurface.'

'In those days we grew our food right in the ground, on the surface. In the soil. Not in underground tanks. We–'

Halloway broke off. A great rushing sound filled the air suddenly, cutting off his words. An immense shape roared past them in the blackness, struck someplace close, and shook the earth.

'The rocket!' a soldier shouted. They all began running, Halloway lumbering awkwardly along.

'Good news, I hope,' Young said, close by him.

'I hope, too,' Halloway gasped. 'Mars is our last chance. If this doesn't work we're finished. The report on Venus was negative; nothing there but lava and steam.'

Later they examined the rocket from Mars.

'It'll do,' Young murmured.

'You're sure?' Director Davidson asked tensely. 'Once we get there we can't come running back.'

'We're sure.' Halloway tossed the spools across the desk to Davidson. 'Examine them yourself. The air on Mars will be thin, and dry. The gravity is much weaker than ours. But we'll be able to live there, which is more than you can say for this God-forsaken Earth.'

Davidson picked up the spools. The unblinking recessed lights gleamed down on the metal desk, the metal walls and floor of the office. Hidden machinery wheezed in the walls, maintaining the air and temperature. 'I'll have to rely on you experts, of course. If some vital factor is not taken into account–'

'Naturally, it's a gamble,' Young said. 'We can't be sure of all factors at this distance.' He tapped the spools. 'Mechanical samples and photos. Robots creeping around, doing the best they can. We're lucky to have *anything* to go on.'

'There's no radiation at least,' Halloway said. 'We can count on that. But Mars will be dry and dusty and cold. It's a long way out. Weak sun. Deserts and wrinkled hills.'

'Mars is old,' Young agreed.

'It was cooled a long time ago. Look at it this way: We have eight planets, excluding Earth. Pluto to Jupiter is *out*. No chance of survival there. Mercury is nothing but liquid metal. Venus is still volcano and steam–pre-Cambrian. That's seven of the eight. Mars is the only possibility *a priori*.'

'In other words,' Davidson said slowly, 'Mars *has* to be okay because there's nothing else for us to try.'

'We could stay here. Live on here in the undersurface systems like gophers.'

'We could not last more than another year. You've seen the recent psych graphs.'

They had. The tension index was up. Men weren't made to live in metal tunnels, living on tank-grown food, working and sleeping and dying without seeing the sun.

It was the children they were really thinking about. Kids that had never been up to the surface. Wan-faced pseudo mutants with eyes like blind fish. A generation born in the subterranean world. The tension index was up because men were seeing their children alter and meld in with a world of tunnels and slimy darkness and dripping luminous rocks.

'Then it's agreed?' Young said.

Davidson searched the faces of the two technicians. 'Maybe we could reclaim the surface, revive Earth again, renew its soil. It hasn't really gone that far, has it?'

'No chance,' Young said flatly. 'Even if we could work an arrangement with the Enemy there'll be particles in suspension for another fifty years. Earth will be too hot for life the rest of this century. *And we can't wait*.'

'All right,' Davidson said. 'I'll authorize the survey team. We'll risk that, at least. You want to go? Be the first humans to land on Mars?'

'You bet,' Halloway said grimly. 'It's in our contract that I go.'

The red globe that was Mars grew steadily larger. In the control room Young and van Ecker, the navigator, watched it intently.

'We'll have to bail,' van Ecker said. 'No chance of landing at this velocity.'

Young was nervous. 'That's all right for us, but how about the first load of settlers? We can't expect women and children to jump.'

'By then we'll know more.' Van Ecker nodded and Captain Mason sounded the emergency alarm. Throughout the ship relay bells clanged ominously. The ship throbbed with scampering feet as crew members grabbed their jump-suits and hurried to the hatches.

'Mars,' Captain Mason murmured, still at the viewscreen. 'Not like Luna. This is the real thing.'

Young and Halloway moved toward the hatch. 'We better get going.'

Mars was swelling rapidly. An ugly bleak globe, dull red. Halloway fitted on his jump helmet. Van Ecker came behind him.

Mason remained in the control cabin. 'I'll follow,' he said, 'after the crew's out.'

The hatch slid back and they moved out onto the jump shelf. The crew were already beginning to leap.

'Too bad to waste a ship,' Young said.

'Can't be helped.' Van Ecker clamped his helmet on and jumped. His brake-units sent him spinning upward, rising like a balloon into the blackness above them. Young and Halloway followed. Below them the ship plunged on, downward toward the surface of Mars. In the sky tiny luminous dots drifted–the crew members.

'I've been thinking,' Halloway said into his helmet speaker.

'What about?' Young's voice came in his earphones.

'Davidson was talking about overlooking some vital factor. There is one we haven't considered.'

'What's that?'

'The Martians.'

'Good God!' van Ecker chimed in. Halloway could see him drifting off to his right, settling slowly toward the planet below. 'You think there *are* Martians?'

'It's possible. Mars will sustain life. If we can live there other complex forms could exist, too.'

'We'll know soon enough,' Young said.

Van Ecker laughed. 'Maybe they trapped one of our robot rockets. Maybe they're expecting us.'

Halloway was silent. It was too close to be funny. The red planet was growing rapidly. He could see white spots at the poles. A few hazy blue-green ribbons that had once been called *canals*. Was there a civilization down there, an organized culture waiting for them, as they drifted slowly down? He groped at his pack until his fingers closed over the butt of his pistol.

'Better get your guns out,' he said.

'If there's a Martian defense system waiting for us we won't have a chance,' Young said. 'Mars cooled millions of years ahead of Earth. It's a cinch they'll be so advanced we won't even be–'

'Too late now,' Mason's voice came faintly. 'You experts should have thought of that before.'

'Where are you?' Halloway demanded.

'Drifting below you. The ship is empty. Should strike any moment. I got all the equipment out, attached it to automatic jump units.'

A faint flash of light exploded briefly below, winked out. The ship, striking the surface . . .

'I'm almost down,' Mason said nervously. 'I'll be the first . . .'

Mars had ceased to be a globe. Now it was a great red dish, a vast plain of dull rust spread out beneath them. They fell slowly, silently, toward it. Mountains became visible. Narrow trickles of water that were rivers. A vague checker-board pattern that might have been fields and pastures . . .

Halloway gripped his pistol tightly. His brake-units shrieked as the air thickened. He was almost down. A muffled *crunch* sounded abruptly in his earphones.

'Mason!' Young shouted.

'I'm down,' Mason's voice came faintly.

'You all right?'

'Knocked the wind out of me. But I'm all right.'

'How does it look?' Halloway demanded.

For a moment there was silence. Then: 'Good God!' Mason gasped. 'A *city*!'

'A city?' Young yelled. 'What kind? What's it like?'

'Can you see them?' van Ecker shouted. 'What are they like? Are there a lot of them?'

They could hear Mason breathing. His breath rasped hoarsely in their phones. 'No,' he gasped at last. 'No sign of life. No activity. The city is–it looks deserted.'

'Deserted?'

'Ruins. Nothing but ruins. Miles of wrecked columns and walls and rusting scaffolding.'

'Thank God,' Young breathed. 'They must have died out. We're safe. They must have evolved and finished their cycle a long time ago.'

'Did they leave us anything?' Fear clutched at Halloway. 'Is there anything left for *us*?' He clawed wildly at his brake-units, struggling frantically to hurry his descent. 'Is it all gone?'

'You think they used up everything?' Young said. 'You think they exhausted all the–'

'I can't tell,' Mason's weak voice came, tinged with uneasiness. 'It looks bad. Big pits. Mining pits. I can't tell, but it looks bad . . .'

Halloway struggled desperately with his brake-units.

The planet was a shambles.

'Good God,' Young mumbled. He sat down on a broken column and wiped his face. 'Not a damn thing left. Nothing.'

*

Around them the crew were setting up emergency defense units. The communications team was assembling a battery-driven transmitter. A bore team was drilling for water. Other teams were scouting around, looking for food.

'There won't be any signs of life,' Halloway said. He waved at the endless expanse of debris and rust. 'They're gone, finished a long time ago.'

'I don't understand,' Mason muttered. 'How could they wreck a whole planet?'

'We wrecked Earth in thirty years.'

'Not this way. They've *used* Mars up. Used up everything. Nothing left. Nothing at all. It's one vast scrap-heap.'

Shakily Halloway tried to light a cigarette. The match burned feebly, then sputtered out. He felt light and dopey. His heart throbbed heavily. The distant sun beat down, pale and small. Mars was a cold, a lonely dead world.

Halloway said, 'They must have had a hell of a time, watching their cities rot away. No water or minerals, finally no soil.' He picked up a handful of dry sand, let it trickle through his fingers.

'Transmitter working,' a crew member said.

Mason got to his feet and lumbered awkwardly over to the transmitter. 'I'll tell Davidson what we've found.' He bent over the microphone.

Young looked across at Halloway. 'Well, I guess we're stuck. How long will our supplies carry us?'

'Couple of months.'

'And then–' Young snapped his fingers. 'Like the Martians.' He squinted at the long corroded wall of a ruined house. 'I wonder what they were like.'

'A semantics team is probing the ruins. Maybe they'll turn up something.'

Beyond the ruined city stretched out what had once been an industrial area. Fields of twisted installations, towers and pipes and machinery. Sand-covered and partly rusted. The surface of the land was pocked with great gaping sores. Yawning pits where scoops had once dredged. Entrances of underground mines. Mars was honeycombed. Termite-ridden. A whole race had burrowed and dug in trying to stay alive. The Martians had sucked Mars dry, then fled it.

'A graveyard,' Young said. 'Well, they got what they deserved.'

'You blame them? What should they have done? Perished a few thousand years sooner and left their planet in better shape?'

'They could have left us *something*,' Young said stubbornly. 'Maybe we can dig up their bones and boil them. I'd like to get my hands on one of them long enough to–'

A pair of crewmen came hurrying across the sand. 'Look at these!' They carried armloads of metal tubes, glittering cylinders heaped up in piles. 'Look what we found buried!'

Halloway roused himself. 'What is it?'

'Records. Written documents. Get these to the semantics team!' Carmichael spilled his armload at Halloway's feet. 'And this isn't all. We found something else–installations.'

'Installations? What kind?'

'Rocket launchers. Old towers, rusty as hell. There are fields of them on the other side of the town.' Carmichael wiped perspiration from his red face. 'They didn't die, Halloway. They took off. They used up this place, then left.'

Doctor Judde and Young pored over the gleaming tubes. 'It's coming,' Judde murmured, absorbed in the shifting pattern undulating across the scanner.

'Can you make anything out?' Halloway asked tensely.

'They left, all right. Took off. The whole lot of them.'

Young turned to Halloway. 'What do you think of that? So they didn't die out.'

'Can't you tell where they went?'

Judde shook his head. 'Some planet their scout ships located. Ideal climate and temperature.' He pushed the scanner aside. 'In their last period the whole Martian civilization was oriented around this escape planet. Big project, moving a society lock, stock and barrel. It took them three or four hundred years to get everything of value off Mars and on its way to the other planet.'

'How did the operation come out?'

'Not so good. The planet was beautiful. But they had to adapt. Apparently they didn't anticipate all the problems arising from colonization on a strange planet.' Judde indicated a cylinder. 'The colonies deteriorated rapidly. Couldn't keep the traditions and techniques going. The society broke apart. Then came war, barbarism.'

'Then their migration was a failure.' Halloway pondered. 'Maybe it can't be done. Maybe it's impossible.'

'Not a failure,' Judde corrected. 'They lived, at least. This place was no good any more. Better to live as savages on a strange world than stay here and die. So they say, on these cylinders.'

'Come along,' Young said to Halloway. The two men stepped outside the semantics hut. It was night. The sky was littered with glowing stars. The two moons had risen. They glimmered coldly, two dead eyes in the chilly sky.

'This place won't do,' Young stated. 'We can't migrate here. That's settled.'

Halloway eyed him. 'What's on your mind?'

'This was the last of the nine planets. We tested every one of them.' Young's face was alive with emotion. 'None of them will support life. All of them are lethal or useless, like this rubbish heap. The whole damn solar system is out.'

'So?'

'We'll have to leave the solar system.'

'And go where? *How?*'

Young pointed toward the Martian ruins, to the city and the rusted, bent rows of towers. 'Where *they* went. They found a place to go. An untouched world outside the solar system. And they developed some kind of outer-space drive to get them there.'

'You mean–'

'Follow them. This solar system is dead. But outside, someplace in some other system, they found an escape world. And they were able to get there.'

'We'd have to fight with them if we land on their planet. They won't want to share it.'

Young spat angrily on the sand. 'Their colonies deteriorated. Remember? Broke down into barbarism. We can handle them. We've got everything in the way of war weapons–weapons that can wipe a planet clean.'

'We don't want to do that.'

'What *do* we want to do? Tell Davidson we're stuck on Terra? Let the human race turn into underground moles? Blind crawling things . . .'

'If we follow the Martians we'll be competing for their world. They found it; the damn thing belongs to them, not us. And maybe we can't work out their drive. Maybe the schematics are lost.'

Judde emerged from the semantics hut. 'I've some more information. The whole story is here. Details on the escape planet. Fauna and flora. Studies of its gravity, air density, mineral possessions, soil layer, climate, temperature–everything.'

'How about their drive?'

'Breakdown on that, too. Everything.' Judde was shaking with excitement. 'I have an idea. Let's get the designs team on these drive schematics and see if they can duplicate it. If they can, we could follow the Martians. We could sort of *share* their planet with them.'

'See?' Young said to Halloway. 'Davidson will say the same thing. It's obvious.'

Halloway turned and walked off.

'What's wrong with him?' Judde asked.

'Nothing. He'll get over it.' Young scratched out a quick message on a piece of paper. 'Have this transmitted to Davidson back on Terra.'

Judde peered at the message. He whistled. 'You're telling him about the Martian migration. And about the escape planet.'

'We want to get started. It'll take a long time to get things under way.'

'Will Halloway come around?'

'He'll come around,' Young said. 'Don't worry about him.'

*

Halloway gazed up at the towers. The leaning, sagging towers from which the Martian transports had been launched thousands of years before.

Nothing stirred. No sign of life. The whole dried-up planet was dead.

Halloway wandered among the towers. The beam from his helmet cut a white path in front of him. Ruins, heaps of rusting metal. Bales of wire and building material. Parts of uncompleted equipment. Half-buried construction sections sticking up from the sand.

He came to a raised platform and mounted the ladder cautiously. He found himself in an observation mount, surrounded by the remains of dials and meters. A telescopic sight stuck up, rusted in place, frozen tight.

'Hey,' a voice came from below. 'Who's up there?'

'Halloway.'

'God, you scared me.' Carmichael slid his blast rifle away and climbed the ladder. 'What are you doing?'

'Looking around.'

Carmichael appeared beside him, puffing and red-faced. 'Interesting, these towers. This was an automatic sighting station. Fixed the take-off for supply transports. The population was already gone.' Carmichael slapped at the ruined control board. 'These supply ships continued to take off, loaded by machines and dispatched by machines, after all the Martians were gone.'

'Lucky for them they had a place to go.'

'Sure was. The minerals team says there's not a damn thing left here. Nothing but dead sand and rock and debris. Even the water's no good. They took everything of value.'

'Judde says their escape world is pretty nice.'

'Virgin.' Carmichael smacked his fat lips. 'Never touched. Trees and meadows and blue oceans. He showed me a scanner translation of a cylinder.'

'Too bad we don't have a place like that to go. A virgin world for ourselves.'

Carmichael was bent over the telescope. 'This here sighted for them. When the escape planet swam into view a relay delivered a trigger charge to the control tower. The tower launched the ships. When the ships were gone a new flock came up into position.' Carmichael began to polish the encrusted lenses of the telescope, wiping the accumulated rust and debris away. 'Maybe we'll see their planet.'

In the ancient lenses a vague luminous globe was swimming. Halloway could make it out, obscured by the filth of centuries, hidden behind a curtain of metallic particles and dirt.

Carmichael was down on his hands and knees, working with the focus mechanism. 'See anything?' he demanded.

Halloway nodded. 'Yeah.'

Carmichael pushed him away. 'Let me look.' He squinted into the lens. 'Aw, for God's sake!'

'What's wrong? Can't you see it?'

'I see it,' Carmichael said, getting down on his hands and knees again. 'The thing must have slipped. Or the time shift is too great. But this is supposed to adjust automatically. Of course, the gear box has been frozen for–'

'What's wrong?' Halloway demanded.

'That's Earth. Don't you recognize it?'

'Earth!'

Carmichael sneered with disgust. 'This fool thing must be busted. I wanted to get a look at their dream planet. That's just old Terra, where we came from. All my work trying to fix this wreck up, and what do we see?'

'*Earth!*' Halloway murmured. He had just finished telling Young about the telescope.

'I can't believe it,' Young said. 'But the description fitted Earth thousands of years ago . . .'

'How long ago did they take off?' Halloway asked.

'About six hundred thousand years ago,' Judde said.

'And their colonies descended into barbarism on the new planet.'

The four men were silent. They looked at each other, tight-lipped.

'We've destroyed two worlds,' Halloway said at last. 'Not one. Mars first. We finished up here, then we moved to Terra. And we destroyed Terra as systematically as we did Mars.'

'A closed circle,' Mason said. 'We're back where we started. Back to reap the crop our ancestors sowed. They left Mars this way. Useless. And now we're back here poking around the ruins like ghouls.'

'Shut up,' Young snapped. He paced angrily back and forth. 'I can't believe it.'

'We're Martians. Descendants of the original stock that left here. We're back from the colonies. Back home.' Mason's voice rose hysterically. 'We're home again, where we belong!'

Judde pushed aside the scanner and got to his feet. 'No doubt about it. I checked their analysis with our own archeological records. It fits. Their escape world was Terra, six hundred thousand years ago.'

'What'll we tell Davidson?' Mason demanded. He giggled wildly. 'We've found a perfect place. A world untouched by human hands. Still in the original cellophane wrapper.'

Halloway moved to the door of the hut, stood gazing silently out. Judde joined him. 'This is catastrophic. We're really stuck. What the hell are you looking at?'

Above them, the cold sky glittered. In the bleak light the barren plains of Mars stretched out, mile after mile of empty, wasted ruin.

'At that,' Halloway said. 'You know what it reminds me of?'

'A picnic site.'

'Broken bottles and tin cans and wadded-up plates. After the picnickers have left. Only, the picnickers are back. They're back–and they have to live in the mess they made.'

'What'll we tell Davidson?' Mason demanded.

'I've already called him,' Young said wearily. 'I told him there was a planet, out of the solar system. Someplace we could go. The Martians had a drive.'

'A drive.' Judde pondered. 'Those towers.' His lips twisted. 'Maybe they did have an outer-space drive. Maybe it's worth going on with the translation.'

They looked at each other.

'Tell Davidson we're going on,' Halloway ordered. 'We'll keep on until we find it. We're not staying on this God-forsaken junkyard.' His gray eyes glowed. 'We'll find it, yet. A virgin world. A world that's unspoiled.'

'*Unspoiled*,' Young echoed. 'Nobody there ahead of us.'

'We'll be the first,' Judde muttered avidly.

'It's wrong!' Mason shouted. 'Two are enough! Let's not destroy a third world!'

Nobody listened to him. Judde and Young and Halloway gazed up, faces eager, hands clenching and unclenching. As if they were already there. As if they were already holding onto the new world, clutching it with all their strength. Tearing it apart, atom by atom . . .

PROMINENT AUTHOR

'My husband,' said Mary Ellis, 'although he is a very prompt man, and hasn't been late to work in twenty-five years, is actually still some place around the house.' She sipped at her faintly scented hormone and carbohydrate drink. 'As a matter of fact, he won't be leaving for another ten minutes.'

'Incredible,' said Dorothy Lawrence, who had finished *her* drink, and now basked in the dermalmist spray that descended over her virtually unclad body from an automatic jet above the couch. 'What they won't think of next!'

Mrs Ellis beamed proudly, as if she personally were an employee of Terran Development. 'Yes, it is incredible. According to somebody down at the office, the whole history of civilization can be explained in terms of transportation techniques. Of course, I don't know anything about history. That's for Government research people. But from what this man told Henry–'

'Where's my briefcase?' came a fussy voice from the bedroom. 'Good Lord, Mary. I know I left it on the clothes-cleaner last night.'

'You left it upstairs,' Mary replied, raising her voice slightly. 'Look in the closet.'

'Why would it be in the closet?' Sounds of angry stirring-arounds. 'You'd think a man's own briefcase would be safe.' Henry Ellis stuck his head into the living room briefly. 'I found it. Hello, Mrs Lawrence.'

'Good morning,' Dorothy Lawrence replied. 'Mary was explaining that you're still here.'

'Yes, I'm still here.' Ellis straightened his tie, as the mirror revolved slowly around him. 'Anything you want me to pick up downtown, honey?'

'No,' Mary replied. 'Nothing I can think of. I'll vid you at the office if I remember something.'

'Is it true,' Mrs Lawrence asked, 'that *as soon as you step into it* you're all the way downtown?'

'Well, almost all the way.'

'A hundred and sixty miles! It's beyond belief. Why, it takes my husband two and a half hours to get his monojet through the commercial lanes and down at the parking lot then walk all the way up to his office.'

'I know,' Ellis muttered, grabbing his hat and coat. 'Used to take me about that long. But no more.' He kissed his wife good-bye. 'So long. See you tonight. Nice to have seen you again, Mrs Lawrence.'

'Can I–watch?' Mrs Lawrence asked hopefully.

'Watch? Of course, of course.' Ellis hurried through the house, out the back door and down the steps into the yard. 'Come along!' he shouted impatiently. 'I don't want to be late. It's nine fifty-nine and I have to be at my desk by ten.'

Mrs Lawrence hurried eagerly after Ellis. In the back yard stood a big circular hoop that gleamed brightly in the mid-morning sun. Ellis turned some controls at the base. The hoop changed color, from silver to a shimmering red.

'Here I go!' Ellis shouted. He stepped briskly into the hoop. The hoop fluttered about him. There was a faint *pop*. The glow died.

'Good heavens!' Mrs Lawrence gasped. 'He's gone!'

'He's in downtown N'York,' Mary Ellis corrected.

'I wish *my* husband had a Jiffi-scuttler. When they show up on the market commercially maybe I can afford to get him one.'

'Oh, they're very handy,' Mary Ellis agreed. 'He's probably saying hello to the boys right this minute.'

Henry Ellis was in a sort of tunnel. All around him a gray, formless tube stretched out in both directions, a sort of hazy sewer-pipe.

Framed in the opening behind him, he could see the faint outline of his own house. His back porch and yard, Mary standing on the steps in her red bra and slacks. Mrs Lawrence beside her in green-checkered shorts. The cedar tree and rows of petunias. A hill. The neat little houses of Cedar Groves, Pennsylvania. And in front of him–

New York City. A wavering glimpse of the busy street-corner in front of his office. The great building itself, a section of concrete and glass and steel. People moving. Skyscrapers. Monojets landing in swarms. Aerial signs. Endless white-collar workers hurrying everywhere, rushing to their offices.

Ellis moved leisurely toward the New York end. He had taken the Jiffi-scuttler often enough to know just exactly how many steps it was. Five steps. Five steps along the wavery gray tunnel and he had gone a hundred and sixty miles. He halted, glancing back. So far he had gone three steps. Ninety-six miles. More than half way.

The fourth dimension was a wonderful thing.

Ellis lit his pipe, leaning his briefcase against his trouser-leg and groping in his coat pocket for his tobacco. He still had thirty seconds to get to work. Plenty of time. The pipe-lighter flared and he sucked in expertly. He snapped the lighter shut and restored it to his pocket.

A wonderful thing, all right. The Jiffi-scuttler had already revolutionized society. It was now possible to go anywhere in the world *instantly*, with no time lapse. And without wading through endless lanes of other monojets, also going places. The transportation problem had been a major headache since the middle of the twentieth century. Every year more families moved from the cities out into the country, adding numbers to the already swollen swarms that choked the roads and jetlanes.

But it was all solved now. An *infinite* number of Jiffi-scuttlers could be set up; there was no interference between them. The Jiffi-scuttler bridged distances non-spacially, through another dimension of some kind (they hadn't explained that part too clearly to him). For a flat thousand credits any Terran family could have Jiffi-scuttler hoops set up, one in the back yard–the other in Berlin, or Bermuda, or San Francisco, or Port Said. Anywhere in the world. Of course, there was one drawback. The hoop had to be anchored in one specific spot. You picked your destination and that was that.

But for an office worker, it was perfect. Step in one end, step out the other. Five steps—a hundred and sixty miles. A hundred and sixty miles that had been a two-hour nightmare of grinding gears and sudden jolts, monojets cutting in and out, speeders, reckless flyers, alert cops waiting to pounce, ulcers and bad tempers. It was all over now. All over for him, at least, as an employee of Terran Development, the manufacturer of the Jiffi-scuttler. And soon for everybody, when they were commercially on the market.

Ellis sighed. Time for work. He could see Ed Hall racing up the steps of the TD building two at a time. Tony Franklin hurrying after him. Time to get moving. He bent down and reached for his briefcase—

It was then he saw them.

The wavery gray haze was thin there. A sort of thin spot where the shimmer wasn't so strong. Just a bit beyond his foot and past the corner of his briefcase.

Beyond the thin spot were three tiny figures. Just beyond the gray waver. Incredibly small men, no larger than insects. Watching him with incredulous astonishment.

Ellis gazed down intently, his briefcase forgotten. The three tiny men were equally dumbfounded. None of them stirred, the three tiny figures, rigid with awe, Henry Ellis bent over, his mouth open, eyes wide.

A fourth little figure joined the others. They all stood rooted to the spot, eyes bulging. They had on some kind of robes. Brown robes and sandals. Strange, unTerran costumes. Everything about them was unTerran. Their size, their oddly colored dark faces, their clothing—and their voices.

Suddenly the tiny figures were shouting shrilly at each other, squeaking a strange gibberish. They had broken out of their freeze and now ran about in queer, frantic circles. They raced with incredible speed, scampering like ants on a hot griddle. They raced jerkily, their arms and legs pumping wildly. And all the time they squeaked in their shrill high-pitched voices.

Ellis found his briefcase. He picked it up slowly. The figures watched in mixed wonder and terror as the huge bag rose, only a short distance from them. An idea drifted through Ellis's brain. Good Lord–could they come into the Jiffi-scuttler, through the gray haze?

But he had no time to find out. He was already late as it was. He pulled away and hurried towards the New York end of the tunnel. A second later he stepped out in the blinding sunlight, abruptly finding himself on the busy street-corner in front of his office.

'Hey, there, Hank!' Donald Potter shouted, as he raced through the doors into the TD building. 'Get with it!'

'Sure, sure.' Ellis followed after him automatically. Behind the entrance to the Jiffi-scuttler was a vague circle above the pavement, like the ghost of a soap-bubble.

He hurried up the steps and inside the offices of Terran Development, his mind already on the hard day ahead.

As they were locking up the office and getting ready to go home, Ellis stopped Coordinator Patrick Miller in his office. 'Say, Mr Miller. You're also in charge of the research end, aren't you?'

'Yeah. So?'

'Let me ask you something. Just where does the Jiffi-scuttler go? It must go somewhere.'

'It goes out of this continuum completely.' Miller was impatient to get home. 'Into another dimension.'

'I know that. But–*where?*'

Miller unfolded his breast-pocket handkerchief rapidly and spread it out on his desk. 'Maybe I can explain it to you this way. Suppose you're a two-dimensional creature and this handkerchief represents your–'

'I've seen that a million times,' Ellis said, disappointed. 'That's merely an analogy, and I'm not interested in an analogy. I want a factual answer. Where does my Jiffi-scuttler go, between here and Cedar Groves?'

Miller laughed. 'What the hell do you care?'

Ellis became abruptly guarded. He shrugged indifferently. 'Just curious. It certainly must go *some place*.'

Miller put his hand on Ellis's shoulder in a friendly big-brother fashion. 'Henry, old man, you just leave that up to us. Okay? We're the designers, you're the consumer. Your job is to use the 'scuttler, try it out for us, report any defects or failure so when we put it on the market next year we'll be sure there's nothing wrong with it.'

'As a matter of fact–' Ellis began.

'What is it?'

Ellis clamped his sentence off. 'Nothing.' He picked up his brief-case. 'Nothing at all. I'll see you tomorrow. Thanks, Mr Miller. Goodnight.'

He hurried downstairs and out of the TD building. The faint outline of his Jiffi-scuttler was visible in the fading late-afternoon sunlight. The sky was already full of monojets taking off. Weary workers beginning their long trip back to their homes in the country. The endless commute. Ellis made his way to the hoop and stepped into it. Abruptly the bright sunlight dimmed and faded.

Again he was in the wavery gray tunnel. At the far end flashed a circle of green and white. Rolling green hills and his own house. His back yard. The cedar tree and flower beds. The town of Cedar Groves.

Two steps down the tunnel. Ellis halted, bending over. He studied the floor of the tunnel intently. He studied the misty gray wall, where it rose and flickered–and the thin place. The place he had noticed.

They were still there. *Still?* It was a different bunch. This time ten or eleven of them. Men and women and children. Standing together, gazing up at him with awe and wonder. No more than a half-inch high, each. Tiny distorted figures, shifting and changing shape oddly. Altering colors and hues.

Ellis hurried on. The tiny figures watched him go. A brief glimpse of their microscopic astonishment–and then he was stepping out into his back yard.

He clicked off the Jiffi-scuttler and mounted the back steps. He entered his house, deep in thought.

'Hi,' Mary cried, from the kitchen. She rustled towards him in her hip-length mesh shirt, her arms out. 'How was work today?'

'Fine.'

'Is anything wrong? You look–strange.'

'No. No, nothing's wrong.' Ellis kissed his wife absently on the forehead. 'What's for dinner?'

'Something choice. Siriusian mole steak. One of your favorites. Is that all right?'

'Sure.' Ellis tossed his hat and coat down on the chair. The chair folded them up and put them away. His thoughtful, preoccupied look still remained. 'Fine, honey.'

'Are you *sure* there's nothing wrong? You didn't get into another argument with Pete Taylor, did you?'

'No. Of course not.' Ellis shook his head in annoyance. 'Everything's all right, honey. Stop needling me.'

'Well, I *hope* so,' Mary said, with a sigh.

The next morning they were waiting for him.

He saw them the first step into the Jiffi-scuttler. A small group waiting within the wavering gray, like bugs caught in a block of jello. They moved jerkily, rapidly, arms and legs pumping in a blur of motion. Trying to attract his attention. Piping wildly in their pathetically faint voices.

Ellis stopped and squatted down. They were putting something through the wall of the tunnel, through the thin place in the gray. It was small, so incredibly small he could scarcely see it. A square of white at the end of a microscopic pole. They were watching him eagerly, faces alive with fear and hope. Desperate, pleading hope.

Ellis took the tiny square. It came loose like some fragile rose petal from its stalk. Clumsily, he let it drop and had to hunt all around for it. The little figures watched in an agony of dismay as his huge hands moved blindly around the floor of the tunnel. At last he found it and gingerly lifted it up.

It was too small to make out. *Writing?* Some tiny lines–but he couldn't read them. Much too small to read. He got out his wallet and carefully placed the square between two cards. He restored his wallet to his pocket.

'I'll look at it later,' he said.

His voice boomed and echoed up and down the tunnel. At the sound the tiny creatures scattered. They all fled, shrieking in their shrill, piping voices, away from the gray shimmer, into the dimness beyond. In a flash they were gone. Like startled mice. He was alone.

Ellis knelt down and put his eye against the gray shimmer, where it was thin. Where they had stood waiting. He could see something dim and distorted, lost in a vague haze. A landscape of some sort. Indistinct. Hard to make out.

Hills. Trees and crops. But so tiny. And dim . . .

He glanced at his watch. God, it was ten! Hastily he scrambled to his feet and hurried out of the tunnel, on to the blazing New York pavement.

Late. He raced up the stairs of the Terran Development building and down the long corridor to his office.

At lunchtime he stopped in at the Research Labs. 'Hey,' he called, as Jim Andrews brushed past, loaded down with reports and equipment. 'Got a second?'

'What do you want, Henry?'

'I'd like to borrow something. A magnifying glass.' He considered. 'Maybe a photon-microscope would be better. One- or two-hundred power.'

'Kids' stuff.' Jim found him a small microscope. 'Slides?'

'Yeah, a couple of blank slides.'

He carried the microscope back to his office. He set it up on his desk, clearing away his paper. As a precaution he sent Miss Nelson, his secretary, out of the room and off to lunch. Then carefully, cautiously, he got the tiny wisp from his wallet and slipped it between two slides.

It was writing, all right. But nothing he could read. Utterly unfamiliar. Complex, interlaced little characters.

For a time he sat thinking. Then he dialed his inter-department vidphone. 'Give me the Linguistics Department.'

After a moment Earl Peterson's good-natured face appeared. 'Hi there, Ellis. What can I do for you?'

Ellis hesitated. He had to do this right. 'Say, Earl, old man. Got a little favor to ask you.'

'Like what? Anything to oblige an old pal.'

'You, uh–you have that Machine down there, don't you? That translating business you use for working over documents from non-Terran cultures?'

'Sure. So?'

'Think I could use it?' He talked fast. 'It's a screwy sort of a deal, Earl. I got this pal living on–uh–Centaurus VI, and he writes me in–uh–you know, the Centauran native semantic system, and I–'

'You want the Machine to translate a letter? Sure, I think we could manage it. This once, at least. Bring it down.'

He brought it down. He got Earl to show him how the intake feed worked, and as soon as Earl had turned his back he fed in the tiny square of material. The Linguistics Machine clicked and whirred. Ellis prayed silently that the paper wasn't too small. Wouldn't fall out between the relay-probes of the Machine.

But sure enough, after a couple of seconds, a tape unreeled from the output slot. The tape cut itself off and dropped into a basket. The Linguistics Machine turned promptly to other stuff, more vital material from TD's various export branches.

With trembling fingers Ellis spread out the tape. The words danced before his eyes.

Questions. They were asking him questions. God, it was getting complicated. He read the questions intently, his lips moving. What was he getting himself into? They were expecting answers. He had taken their paper, gone off with it. Probably they would be waiting for him, on his way home.

He returned to his office and dialed his vidphone. 'Give me outside,' he ordered.

The regular vid monitor appeared. 'Yes, sir?'

'I want the Federal Library of Information,' Ellis said. 'Cultural Research Division.'

That night they were waiting, all right. But not the same ones. It was odd–each time a different group. Their clothing was slightly different, too. A new hue. And in the background the landscape had also altered slightly. The trees he had seen were gone. The hills were still there, but a different shade. A hazy gray-white. Snow?

He squatted down. He had worked it out with care. The answers from the Federal Library of Information had gone back to the Linguistics Machine for re-translation. The answers were now in the original tongue of the questions–but on a trifle larger piece of paper.

Ellis made like a marble game and flicked the wad of paper through the gray shimmer. It bowled over six or seven of the watching figures and rolled down the side of the hill on which they were standing. After a moment of terrified immobility the figures scampered frantically after it. They disappeared into the vague and invisible depths of their world and Ellis got stiffly to his feet again.

'Well,' he muttered to himself, 'that's that.'

But it wasn't. The next morning there was a new group–and a new list of questions. The tiny figures pushed their microscopic square of paper through the thin spot in the wall of the tunnel and stood waiting and trembling as Ellis bent over and felt around for it.

He found it–finally. He put it in his wallet and continued on his way, stepping out at New York, frowning. This was getting serious. Was this going to be a full-time job?

But then he grinned. It was the damn oddest thing he had ever heard of. The little rascals were cute, in their own way. Tiny intent faces, screwed up with serious concern. And terror. They were scared of him, really scared. And why not? Compared to them he was a giant.

He conjectured about their world. What kind of planet was theirs? Odd to be so small. But size was a relative matter. Small, though, compared to him. Small and reverent. He could read fear and yearning, gnawing hope, as they pushed up their papers. They were depending on him. Praying he'd give them answers.

Ellis grinned. 'Damn unusual job,' he said to himself.

'What's this?' Peterson said, when he showed up in the Linguistics Lab at noontime.

'Well, you see, I got another letter from my friend on Centaurus VI.'

'Yeah?' A certain suspicion flickered across Peterson's face. 'You're not ribbing me, are you, Henry? This Machine has a lot to do, you know. Stuff's coming in all the time. We can't afford to waste any time with–'

'This is really serious stuff, Earl.' Ellis patted his wallet. 'Very important business. Not just gossip.'

'Okay. If you say so.' Peterson gave the nod to the team operating the Machine. 'Let this guy use the Translator, Tommie.'

'Thanks,' Ellis murmured.

He went through the routine, getting a translation and then carrying the questions up to his vidphone and passing them over to the Library research staff. By nightfall the answers were back in the original tongue and, with them carefully in his wallet, Ellis headed out of the Terran Development building and into his Jiffi-scuttler.

As usual, a new group was waiting.

'Here you are, boys,' Ellis boomed, flicking the wad through the thin place in the shimmer. The wad rolled down the microscopic countryside, bouncing from hill to hill, the little people tumbling jerkily after it in their funny stiff-legged fashion. Ellis watched them go, grinning with interest–and pride.

They really hurried; no doubt about that. He could make them out only vaguely, now. They had raced wildly off away from the shimmer. Only a small portion of their world was tangent to the Jiffi-scuttler, apparently. Only the one spot, where the shimmer was thin. He peered intently through.

They were getting the wad open, now. Three or four of them, unprying the paper and examining the answers.

Ellis swelled with pride as he continued along the tunnel and out into his own back yard. He couldn't read their questions–and when translated, he couldn't answer them. The Linguistics Department did the first part, the Library research staff the rest. Nevertheless, Ellis felt pride. A deep, glowing spot of warmth far down inside him. The expression on their faces. The look they gave him when they saw the answer-wad in his hand. When they realized he was going to answer their questions. And the way they scampered after it. It was sort of–satisfying. It made him feel damn good.

'Not bad,' he murmured, opening the back door and entering the house. 'Not bad at all.'

'What's not bad, dear?' Mary asked, looking quickly up from the table. She laid down her magazine and got to her feet. 'Why, you look so *happy*! What is it?'

'Nothing. Nothing at all!' He kissed her warmly on the mouth. 'You're looking pretty good tonight yourself, kid.'

'Oh, Henry!' Much of Mary blushed prettily. 'How sweet.'

He surveyed his wife in her two-piece wraparound of clear plastic with appreciation. 'Nice-looking fragments you have on.'

'Why, Henry! What's come over you? You seem so–so *spirited*!'

Ellis grinned. 'Oh, I guess I enjoy my job. You know, there's nothing like taking pride in your work. A job well done, as they say. Work you can be proud of.'

'I thought you always said you were nothing but a cog in a great impersonal machine. Just a sort of cipher.'

'Things are different,' Ellis said firmly. 'I'm doing a–uh–a new project. A new assignment.'

'A new assignment?'

'Gathering information. A sort of–creative business. So to speak.'

By the end of the week he had turned over quite a body of information to them.

He began starting for work about nine-thirty. That gave him a whole thirty minutes to spend squatting down on his hands and knees, peering through the thin place in the shimmer. He got so he was pretty good at seeing them and what they were doing in their microscopic world.

Their civilization was somewhat primitive. No doubt of that. By Terran standards it was scarcely a civilization at all. As near as he could tell, they were virtually without scientific techniques; a kind of agrarian culture, rural communism, a monolithic tribal-based organization apparently without too many members.

At least, not at one time. That was the part he didn't understand. Every time he came past there was a different group of them. No familiar faces. And their world changed, too. The trees, the crops, fauna. The weather, apparently.

Was their time rate different? They moved rapidly, jerkily. Like a vidtape speeded up. And their shrill voices. Maybe that was it. A totally different universe in which the whole time structure was radically different.

As to their attitude towards him, there was no mistaking it. After the first couple of times they began assembling offerings, unbelievably small bits of smoking food, prepared in ovens and on open brick hearths. If he got down with his nose against the gray shimmer he could get a faint whiff of the food. It smelled good. Strong and pungent. Highly spiced. Meat, probably.

On Friday he brought a magnifying glass along and watched them through it. It was meat, all right. They were bringing ant-sized animals to be killed and cooked, leading them up to the ovens. With the magnifying glass he could see more of their faces. They had strange faces. Strong and dark, with a peculiar firm look.

Of course, there was only one look *he* got from them. A combination of fear, reverence, and hope. The look made him feel good. It was a look for him, only. Between themselves they shouted and argued—and sometimes stabbed and fought each other furiously, rolling in their brown robes in a wild tangle. They were a passionate and strong species. He got so he admired them.

Which was good—because it made him feel better. To have the reverent awe of such a proud, sturdy race was really something. There was nothing craven about them.

About the fifth time he came there was a rather attractive structure built. Some kind of temple. A place of religious worship.

To him! They were developing a real religion about him. No doubt of it. He began going to work at nine o'clock, to give himself a full hour with them. They had, by the middle of the second week, a full-sized ritual evolved. Processions, lighted tapers, what seemed to be songs or chants. Priests in long robes. And the spiced offerings.

No idols, though. Apparently he was so big they couldn't make out his appearance. He tried to imagine what it looked like to be on their side of the shimmer. An immense shape looming up above them, beyond a wall of gray haze. An indistinct being, something like themselves, yet not like them at all. A different kind of being, obviously. Larger–but different in other ways. And when he spoke–booming echoes up and down the Jiffi-scuttler. Which still sent them fleeing in panic.

An evolving religion. He was changing them. Through his actual presence and through his answers, the precise, correct responses he obtained from the Federal Library of Information and had the Linguistics Machine translate into their language. Of course, by *their* time rate they had to wait generations for the answers. But they had become accustomed to it, by now. They waited. They expected. They passed up questions and after a couple centuries he passed down answers, answers which they no doubt put to good use.

'What in the world?' Mary demanded, as he got home from work an hour late one night. 'Where have you been?'

'Working,' Ellis said carelessly, removing his hat and coat. He threw himself down on the couch. 'I'm tired. Really tired.' He sighed with relief and motioned for the couch-arm to bring him a whiskey sour.

Mary came over by the couch. 'Henry, I'm a little worried.'

'Worried?'

'You shouldn't work so hard. You ought to take it easy, more. How long since you've had a real vacation? A trip off Terra. Out of the System. You know, I'd just like to call that fellow Miller and ask him why it's necessary a man your age put in so much–'

'A man my age!' Ellis bristled indignantly. 'I'm not so old.'

'Of course not.' Mary sat down beside him and put her arms around him affectionately. 'But you shouldn't have to do so much. You deserve a rest. Don't you think?'

'This is different. You don't understand. This isn't the same old stuff. Reports and statistics and the damn filing. This is–'

'What is it?'

'This is *different*. I'm not a cog. This gives me something. I can't explain it to you, I guess. But it's something I have to do.'

'If you could tell me more about it–'

'I can't tell you any more about it,' Ellis said. 'But there's nothing in the world like it. I've worked twenty-five years for Terran Development. Twenty-five years at the same reports, again and again. Twenty-five years–and I never felt this way.'

'Oh, yeah?' Miller roared. 'Don't give me that! Come clean, Ellis!'

Ellis opened and closed his mouth. 'What are you talking about?' Horror rolled through him. 'What's happened?'

'Don't try to give *me* the runaround.' On the vidscreen Miller's face was purple. 'Come into my office.'

The screen went dead.

Ellis sat stunned at his desk. Gradually, he collected himself and got shakily to his feet. 'Good Lord.' Weakly, he wiped cold sweat from his forehead. All at once. Everything in ruins. He was dazed with the shock.

'Anything wrong?' Miss Nelson asked sympathetically.

'No.' Ellis moved numbly towards the door. He was shattered. What had Miller found out? Good God! Was it possible he had–

'Mr Miller looked angry.'

'Yeah.' Ellis moved blindly down the hall, his mind reeling. Miller looked angry all right. Somehow he had found out. But why was he mad? Why did he care? A cold chill settled over Ellis. It looked bad. Miller was his superior–with hiring and firing powers. Maybe he'd done something wrong. Maybe he had somehow broken a law. Committed a crime. But what?

What did Miller care about *them*? What concern was it of Terran Development?

He opened the door to Miller's office. 'Here I am, Mr Miller,' he muttered. 'What's the trouble?'

Miller glowered at him in rage. 'All this goofy stuff about your cousin on Proxima.'

'It's–uh–you mean a business friend on Centaurus VI.'

'You–you swindler!' Miller leaped up. 'And after all the Company's done for you.'

'I don't understand,' Ellis muttered. 'What have–'

'Why do you think we gave you the Jiffi-scuttler in the first place?'

'Why?'

'To *test*! To try out, you wall-eyed Venusian stink-cricket! The Company magnanimously consented to allow you to operate a Jiffi-scuttler in advance of market presentation, and what do you do? Why, you–'

Ellis started to get indignant. After all, he had been with TD twenty-five years. 'You don't have to be so offensive. I plunked down my thousand gold credits for it.'

'Well, you can just mosey down to the accountant's office and get your money back. I've already sent out a directive for a construction team to crate up your Jiffi-scuttler and bring it back to receiving.'

Ellis was dumbfounded. 'But *why*?'

'Why indeed! Because it's defective. Because it doesn't work. That's why.' Miller's eyes blazed with technological outrage. 'The inspection crew found a leak a mile wide in it.' His lip curled. 'As if you didn't know.'

Ellis's heart sank. 'Leak?' he croaked apprehensively.

'Leak. It's a damn good thing I authorized a periodic inspection. If we depended on people like you to–'

'Are you *sure*? It seemed all right to me. That is, it got me here without any trouble,' Ellis floundered. 'Certainly no complaints from my end.'

'No. No complaints from your end. That's exactly why you're not getting another one. That's why you're taking the monojet transport back home tonight. Because you didn't report the leak! And if you ever try to put something over on this office again–'

'How do you know I was aware of the–defect?'

Miller sank down in his chair, overcome with fury. 'Because,' he said carefully, 'of your daily pilgrimage to the Linguistics Machine. With your alleged letter from your grandmother on Betelgeuse II. Which wasn't any such thing. Which was an utter fraud. Which you got through the leak in the Jiffi-scuttler!'

'How do you know?' Ellis squeaked boldly, driven to the wall. 'So maybe there was a defect. But you can't prove there's any connection between your badly constructed Jiffi-scuttler and my–'

'Your missive,' Miller stated, 'which you foisted on our Linguistics Machine, was not a non-Terran script. It was not from Centaurus VI. It was not from any non-Terran system. It was ancient Hebrew. And there's only one place you could have got it, Ellis. So don't try to kid me.'

'Hebrew!' Ellis exclaimed, startled. He turned white as a sheet. 'Good Lord. The other continuum–the fourth dimension. Time, of course.' He trembled. 'And the expanding universe. That would explain their size. And it explains why a new group, a new generation–'

'We're taking enough of a chance as it is, with these Jiffi-scuttlers. Warping a tunnel through other space-time continua.' Miller shook his head wearily. 'You meddler. You *knew* you were supposed to report any defect.'

'I don't think I did any harm, did I?' Ellis was suddenly terribly nervous. 'They seemed pleased, even grateful. Gosh, I'm sure I didn't cause any trouble.'

Miller shrieked in insane rage. For a time he danced around the room. Finally he threw something down on his desk, directly in front of Ellis. 'No trouble. No, none. Look at this. I got this from the Ancient Artifacts Archives.'

'What is it?'

'Look at it! I compared one of your question sheets to this. The same. *Exactly* the same. All your sheets, questions and answers, every one of them's in here. You multi-legged Ganymedean mange beetle!'

Ellis picked up the book and opened it. As he read the pages a strange look came slowly over his face. 'Good heavens. So they kept a record of what I gave them. They put it all together in a book. Every word of it. And some commentaries, too. It's all here–Every single word. It *did* have an effect, then. They passed it on. Wrote all of it down.'

'Go back to your office. I'm through looking at you for today. I'm through looking at you forever. Your severance check will come through regular channels.'

In a trance, his face flushed with a strange excitement, Ellis gripped the book and moved dazedly towards the door. 'Say, Mr Miller. Can I have this? Can I take it along?'

'Sure,' Miller said wearily. 'Sure, you can take it. You can read it on your way home tonight. On the public monojet transport.'

'Henry has something to show you,' Mary Ellis whispered excitedly, gripping Mrs Lawrence's arm. 'Make sure you say the right thing.'

'The right thing?' Mrs Lawrence faltered nervously, a trifle uneasy. 'What is it? Nothing alive, I hope.'

'No, no.' Mary pushed her towards the study door. 'Just smile.' She raised her voice. 'Henry, Dorothy Lawrence is here.'

Henry Ellis appeared at the door of his study. He bowed slightly, a dignified figure in silk dressing gown, pipe in his mouth, fountain pen in one hand. 'Good evening, Dorothy,' he said in a low, well-modulated voice. 'Care to step into my study a moment?'

'Study?' Mrs Lawrence came hesitantly in. 'What do you study? I mean, Mary says you've been doing something very interesting recently, now that you're not with–I mean, now that you're home more. She didn't give me any idea what it was, though.'

Mrs Lawrence's eyes roved curiously around the study. The study was full of reference volumes, charts, a huge mahogany desk, an atlas, globe, leather chairs, an unbelievably ancient electric typewriter.

'Good heavens!' she exclaimed. 'How odd. All these old things.'

Ellis lifted something carefully from the bookcase and held it out to her casually. 'By the way—you might glance at this.'

'What is it? A book?' Mrs Lawrence took the book and examined it eagerly. 'My goodness. Heavy, isn't it?' She read the back, her lips moving. 'What does it mean? It looks old. What strange letters! I've never seen anything like it. *Holy Bible.*' She glanced up brightly. 'What is this?'

Ellis smiled faintly. 'Well—'

A light dawned. Mrs Lawrence gasped in revelation. 'Good heavens! You didn't *write* this, did you?'

Ellis's smile broadened into a deprecating blush. A dignified hue of modesty. 'Just a little thing I threw together,' he murmured indifferently. 'My first, as a matter of fact.' Thoughtfully, he fingered his fountain pen. 'And now, if you'll excuse me, I really should be getting back to my work . . .'

FAIR GAME

Professor Anthony Douglas lowered gratefully into his red-leather easy chair and sighed. A long sigh, accompanied by labored removal of his shoes and numerous grunts as he kicked them into the corner. He folded his hands across his ample middle and lay back, eyes closed.

'Tired?' Laura Douglas asked, turning from the kitchen stove a moment, her dark eyes sympathetic.

'You're darn right.' Douglas surveyed the evening paper across from him on the couch. Was it worth it? No, not really. He felt around in his coat pocket for his cigarettes and lit up slowly, leisurely. 'Yeah, I'm tired, all right. We're starting a whole new line of research. Whole flock of bright young men in from Washington today. Briefcases and slide rules.'

'Not–'

'Oh, I'm still in charge.' Professor Douglas grinned expansively. 'Perish the thought.' Pale gray cigarette smoke billowed around him. 'It'll be another few years before they're ahead of me. They'll have to sharpen up their slide rules just a little bit more . . .'

His wife smiled and continued preparing dinner. Maybe it was the atmosphere of the little Colorado town. The sturdy, impassive mountain peaks around them. The thin, chill air. The quiet citizens. In any case, her husband seemed utterly unbothered by the tensions and doubts that pressured other members of his profession. A lot of aggressive newcomers were swelling the ranks of nuclear physics these days. Old-timers were tottering in their positions, abruptly insecure. Every college, every physics department and lab was being invaded by the new horde of skilled young men. Even here at Bryant College, so far off the beaten track.

But if Anthony Douglas worried, he never let it show. He rested happily in his easy chair, eyes shut, a blissful smile on his face. He was tired–but at peace. He sighed again, this time more from pleasure than fatigue.

'It's true,' he murmured lazily. 'I may be old enough to be their father, but I'm still a few jumps ahead of them. Of course, I know the ropes better. And–'

'And the wires. The ones worth pulling.'

'Those, too. In any case, I think I'll come off from this new line we're doing just about . . .'

His voice trailed off.

'What's the matter?' Laura asked.

Douglas half rose from his chair. His face had gone suddenly white. He stared in horror, gripping the arms of his chair, his mouth opening and closing.

At the window was a great eye. An immense eye that gazed into the room intently, studying him. The eye filled the whole window.

'Good God!' Douglas cried.

The eye withdrew. Outside there was only the evening gloom, the dark hills and trees, the street. Douglas sank down slowly in his chair.

'What was it?' Laura demanded sharply. 'What did you see? Was somebody out there?'

Douglas clasped and unclasped his hands. His lips twitched violently. 'I'm telling you the truth, Bill. I saw it myself. It was real. I wouldn't say so, otherwise. You know that. Don't you believe me?'

'Did anybody else see it?' Professor William Henderson asked, chewing his pencil thoughtfully. He had cleared a place on the dinner table, pushed back his plate and silver and laid out his notebook. 'Did Laura see it?'

'No. Laura had her back turned.'

'What time was it?'

'Half an hour ago. I had just got home. About six-thirty. I had my shoes off, taking it easy.' Douglas wiped his forehead with a shaking hand.

'You say it was unattached? There was nothing else? Just the–eye?'

'Just the eye. One huge eye looking in at me. Taking in everything. As if–'

'As if what?'

'As if it was looking down a microscope.'

Silence.

From across the table, Henderson's red-haired wife spoke up. 'You always were a strict empiricist, Doug. You never went in for any nonsense before. But this . . . It's too bad nobody else saw it.'

'Of course nobody else saw it!'

'What do you mean?'

'The damn thing was looking at *me*. It was *me* it was studying.' Douglas's voice rose hysterically. 'How do you think I feel–scrutinized by an eye as big as a piano! My God, if I weren't so well integrated, I'd be out of my mind!'

Henderson and his wife exchanged glances. Bill, dark-haired and handsome, ten years Douglas's junior. Vivacious Jean Henderson, lecturer in child psychology, lithe and full-bosomed in her nylon blouse and slacks.

'What do you make of this?' Bill asked her. 'This is more along your line.'

'It's in *your* line,' Douglas snapped. 'Don't try to pass this off as a morbid projection. I came to you because you're head of the Biology Department.'

'You think it's an animal? A giant sloth or something?'

'It must be an animal.'

'Maybe it's a joke,' Jean suggested. 'Or an advertising sign. An oculist's display. Somebody may have been carrying it past the window.'

Douglas took a firm grip on himself. 'The eye was alive. It looked at me. It considered me. Then it withdrew. As if it had moved away from the lens.' He shuddered. 'I tell you it was *studying* me!'

'You only?'

'Me. Nobody else.'

'You seem curiously convinced it was looking down from above,' Jean said.

'Yes, down. Down at me. That's right.' An odd expression flickered across Douglas's face. 'You have it, Jean. As if it came from up there.' He jerked his hand upward.

'Maybe it was God,' Bill said thoughtfully.

Douglas said nothing. His face turned ash white and his teeth chattered.

'Nonsense,' Jean said. 'God is a psychological transcendent symbol expressing unconscious forces.'

'Did it look at you accusingly?' asked Bill. 'As if you'd done something wrong?'

'No. With interest. With considerable interest.' Douglas raised himself. 'I have to get back. Laura thinks I'm having some kind of fit. I haven't told her, of course. She's not scientifically disciplined. She wouldn't be able to handle such a concept.'

'It's a little tough even for us,' Bill said.

Douglas moved nervously toward the door. 'You can't think of any explanation? Something thought extinct that might still be roaming around these mountains?'

'None that we know of. If I should hear of any–'

'You said it looked down,' Jean said. 'Not bending down to peer in at you. Then it couldn't have been an animal or terrestrial being.' She was deep in thought. 'Maybe we're being observed.'

'Not you,' Douglas said miserably. 'Just me.'

'By another race,' Bill put in. 'You think–'

'Maybe it's an eye from Mars.'

Douglas opened the front door carefully and peered out. The night was black. A faint wind moved through the trees and along the highway. His car was dimly visible, a black square against the hills. 'If you think of anything, call me.'

'Take a couple of phenobarbitals before you hit the sack,' Jean suggested. 'Calm your nerves.'

Douglas was out on the porch. 'Good idea. Thanks.' He shook his head. 'Maybe I'm out of my mind. Good Lord. Well, I'll see you later.'

He walked down the steps, gripping the rail tightly. 'Good night!' Bill called. The door closed and the porch light clicked off.

Douglas went cautiously toward his car. He reached out into the darkness, feeling for the door handle. One step. Two steps. It was silly. A grown man–practically middle-aged–in the twentieth century. Three steps.

He found the door and opened it, sliding quickly inside and locking it after him. He breathed a silent prayer of thanks as he snapped on the motor and the headlights. Silly as hell. A giant eye. A stunt of some sort.

He turned the thoughts over in his mind. Students? Jokesters? Communists? A plot to drive him out of his mind? He was important. Probably the most important nuclear physicist in the country. And this new project . . .

He drove the car slowly forward, onto the silent highway. He watched each bush and tree as the car gained speed.

A Communist plot. Some of the students were in a left-wing club. Some sort of Marxist study group. Maybe they had rigged up–

In the glare of the headlights something glittered. Something at the edge of the highway.

Douglas gazed at it, transfixed. Something square, a long block in the weeds at the side of the highway, where the great dark trees began. It glittered and shimmered. He slowed down, almost to a stop.

A bar of gold, lying at the edge of the road.

It was incredible. Slowly, Professor Douglas rolled down the window and peered out. Was it really gold? He laughed nervously. Probably not. He had often seen gold, of course. This *looked* like gold. But maybe it was lead, an ingot of lead with a gilt coating.

But–why?

A joke. A prank. College kids. They must have seen his car go past toward the Hendersons' and knew he'd soon be driving back.

Or—or it really *was* gold. Maybe an armored car had gone past. Turned the corner too swiftly. The ingot had slid out and fallen into the weeds. In that case there was a little fortune lying there, in the darkness at the edge of the highway.

But it was illegal to possess gold. He'd have to return it to the Government. But couldn't he saw off just a little piece? And if he did return it there was no doubt a reward of some kind. Probably several thousand dollars.

A mad scheme flashed briefly through his mind. Get the ingot, crate it up, fly it to Mexico, out of the country. Eric Barnes owned a Piper Cub. He could easily get it into Mexico. Sell it. Retire. Live in comfort the rest of his life.

Professor Douglas snorted angrily. It was his duty to return it. Call the Denver Mint, tell them about it. Or the police department. He reversed his car and backed up until he was even with the metal bar. He turned off the motor and slid out onto the dark highway. He had a job to do. As a loyal citizen—and, God knew, fifty tests had shown he *was* loyal—there was a job for him here. He leaned into the car and fumbled in the dashboard for the flashlight. If somebody had lost a bar of gold, it was up to him . . .

A bar of gold. Impossible. A slow, cold chill settled over him, numbing his heart. A tiny voice in the back of his mind spoke clearly and rationally to him: *Who would walk off and leave an ingot of gold?*

Something was going on.

Fear gripped him. He stood frozen, trembling with terror. The dark, deserted highway. The silent mountains. He was alone. A perfect spot. If they wanted to get him—

They?

Who?

He looked quickly around. Hiding in the trees, most likely. Waiting for him. Waiting for him to cross the highway, leave the road and enter the woods. Bend down and try to pick up the ingot. One quick blow as he bent over; that would be it.

Douglas scrambled back into his car and snapped on the motor.

He raced the motor and released the brake. The car jerked forward and gained speed. His hands shaking, Douglas bore down desperately on the wheel. He had to get out. Get away before—whoever they were got him.

As he shifted into high he took one last look back, peering around through the open window. The ingot was still there, still glowing among the dark weeds at the edge of the highway. But there was a strange vagueness about it, an uncertain waver in the nearby atmosphere.

Abruptly the ingot faded and disappeared. Its glow receded into darkness.

Douglas glanced up, and gasped in horror.

In the sky above him, something blotted out the stars. A great shape, so huge it staggered him. The shape moved, a disembodied circle of living presence, directly over his head.

A face. A gigantic, cosmic face peering down. Like some great moon, blotting out everything else. The face hung for an instant, intent on him—on the spot he had just vacated. Then the face, like the ingot, faded and sank into darkness.

The stars returned. He was alone.

Douglas sank back against the seat. The car veered crazily and roared down the highway. His hands slid from the wheel and dropped at his sides. He caught the wheel again, just in time.

There was no doubt about it. Somebody was after him. Trying to get him. But no Communists or student practical jokers. Or any beast, lingering from the dim past.

Whatever it was, whoever they were, had nothing to do with Earth. It—they—were from some other world. They were out to get him.

Him.

But—why?

Pete Berg listened closely. 'Go on,' he said when Douglas halted.

'That's all.' Douglas turned to Bill Henderson. 'Don't try to tell me I'm out of my mind. I really saw it. It was looking down at me. The whole face this time, not just the eye.'

'You think this was the face that the eye belonged to?' Jean Henderson asked.

'I know it. The face had the same expression as the eye. Studying me.'

'We've got to call the police,' Laura Douglas said in a thin, clipped voice. 'This can't go on. If somebody's out to get him–'

'The police won't do any good.' Bill Henderson paced back and forth. It was late, after midnight. All the lights in the Douglas house were on. In one corner old Milton Erick, head of the Math Department, sat curled up, taking everything in, his wrinkled face expressionless.

'We can assume,' Professor Erick said calmly, removing his pipe from between his yellow teeth, 'they're a nonterrestrial race. Their size and their position indicate they're not Earthbound in any sense.'

'But they can't just *stand* in the sky!' Jean exploded. 'There's nothing up there!'

'There may be other configurations of matter not normally connected or related to our own. An endless or multiple coexistence of universe systems, lying along a plane of coordinates totally unexplainable in present terms. Due to some singular juxtaposition of tangents, we are, at this moment, in contact with one of these other configurations.'

'He means,' Bill Henderson explained, 'that these people after Doug don't belong to our universe. They come from a different dimension entirely.'

'The face wavered,' Douglas murmured. 'The gold and the face both wavered and faded out.'

'Withdrew,' Erick stated. 'Returned to their own universe. They have entry into ours at will, it would seem, a hole, so to speak, that they can enter through and return again.'

'It's a pity,' Jean said, 'they're so damn big. If they were smaller–'

'Size is in their favor,' Erick admitted. 'An unfortunate circumstance.'

'All this academic wrangling!' Laura cried wildly. 'We sit here working out theories and meanwhile they are after him!'

'This might explain gods,' Bill said suddenly.

'Gods?'

Bill nodded. 'Don't you see? In the past these beings looked across the nexus at us, into our universe. Maybe even stepped down. Primitive people saw them and weren't able to explain them. They built religions around them. Worshipped them.'

'Mount Olympus,' Jean said. 'Of course. And Moses met God at the top of Mount Sinai. We're high up in the Rockies. Maybe contact only comes at high places. In the mountains, like this.'

'And the Tibetan monks are situated in the highest land mass in the world,' Bill added. 'That whole area. The highest and the oldest part of the world. All the great religions have been revealed in the mountains. Brought down by people who saw God and carried the word back.'

'What I can't understand,' Laura said, 'is why they want *him*.' She spread her hands helplessly. 'Why not somebody else? Why do they have to single him out?'

Bill's face was hard. 'I think that's pretty clear.'

'Explain,' Erick rumbled.

'What is Doug? About the best nuclear physicist in the world. Working on top-secret projects in nuclear fission. Advanced research. The Government is underwriting everything Bryant College is doing–because Douglas is here.'

'So?'

'They want him because of his ability. Because he *knows* things. Because of their size-relationship to this universe, they can subject our lives to as careful a scrutiny as we maintain in the biology labs of–well, of a culture of Sarcina Pulmonum. But that doesn't mean they're culturally advanced over us.'

'Of course!' Pete Berg exclaimed. 'They want Doug for his knowledge. They want to pirate him off and make use of his mind for their own cultures.'

'Parasites!' Jean gasped. 'They must have always depended on us. Don't you see? Men in the past who have disappeared, spirited off by these creatures.' She shivered. 'They probably regard us as some sort of testing ground, where techniques and knowledge are painfully developed–for their benefit.'

Douglas started to answer, but the words never escaped his mouth. He sat rigid in his chair, his head turned to one side.

Outside, in the darkness beyond the house, someone was calling his name.

He got up and moved toward the door. They were all staring at him in amazement.

'What is it?' Bill demanded. 'What's the matter, Doug?'

Laura caught his arm. 'What's wrong? Are you sick? Say something! *Doug!*'

Professor Douglas jerked free and pulled open the front door. He stepped out onto the porch. There was a faint moon. A soft light hovered over everything.

'Professor Douglas!' The voice again, sweet and fresh–a girl's voice.

Outlined by the moonlight, at the foot of the porch steps, stood a girl. Blonde-haired, perhaps twenty years old. In a checkered skirt, pale Angora sweater, a silk kerchief around her neck. She was waving at him anxiously, her small face pleading.

'Professor, do you have a minute? Something terrible has gone wrong with . . .' Her voice trailed off as she moved nervously away from the house, into the darkness.

'What's the matter?' he shouted.

He could hear her voice faintly. She was moving off.

Douglas was torn with indecision. He hesitated, then hurried impatiently down the stairs after her. The girl retreated from him, wringing her hands together, her full lips twisting wildly with despair. Under her sweater, her breasts rose and fell in an agony of terror, each quiver sharply etched by the moonlight.

'What is it?' Douglas cried. 'What's wrong?' He hurried angrily after her. 'For God's sake, stand still!'

The girl was still moving away, drawing him farther and farther away from the house, toward the great green expanse of lawn, the beginning of the campus. Douglas was overcome with annoyance. Damn the girl! Why couldn't she wait for him?

'Hold on a minute!' he said, hurrying after her. He started out onto the dark lawn, puffing with exertion. 'Who are you? What the hell do you–'

There was a flash. A bolt of blinding light crashed past him and seared a smoking pit in the lawn a few feet away.

Douglas halted, dumbfounded. A second bolt came, this one just ahead of him. The wave of heat threw him back. He stumbled and half fell. The girl had abruptly stopped. She stood silent and unmoving, her face expressionless. There was a peculiar waxy quality to her. She had become, all at once, utterly inanimate.

But he had no time to think about that. Douglas turned and lumbered back toward the house. A third bolt came, striking just ahead of him. He veered to the right and threw himself into the shrubs growing near the wall. Rolling and gasping, he pressed against the concrete side of the house, squeezing next to it as hard as he could.

There was a sudden shimmer in the star-studded sky above him. A faint motion. Then nothing. He was alone. The bolts ceased. And–

The girl was gone, also.

A decoy. A clever imitation to lure him away from the house, so he'd move out into the open where they could take a shot at him.

He got shakily to his feet and edged around the side of the house. Bill Henderson and Laura and Berg were on the porch, talking nervously and looking around for him. There was his car, parked in the driveway. Maybe, if he could reach it–

He peered up at the sky. Only stars. No hint of them. If he could get in his car and drive off, down the highway, away from the mountains, toward Denver, where it was lower, maybe he'd be safe.

He took a deep, shuddering breath. Only ten yards to the car. Thirty feet. If he could once get in it–

He ran. Fast. Down the path and along the driveway. He grabbed open the car door and leaped inside. With one quick motion he threw the switch and released the brake.

The car glided forward. The motor came on with a sputter. Douglas bore down desperately on the gas. The car leaped forward. On the porch, Laura shrieked and started down the stairs. Her cry and Bill's startled shout were lost in the roar of the engine.

A moment later he was on the highway, racing away from town, down the long, curving road toward Denver.

He could call Laura from Denver. She could join him. They could take the train east. The hell with Bryant College. His life was at stake. He drove for hours without stopping, through the night. The sun came up and rose slowly in the sky. More cars were on the road now. He passed a couple of diesel trucks rumbling slowly and cumbersomely along.

He was beginning to feel a little better. The mountains were behind. More distance between him and them . . .

His spirits rose as the day warmed. There were hundreds of universities and laboratories scattered around the country. He could easily continue with his work someplace else. They'd never get him, once he was out of the mountains.

He slowed his car down. The gas gauge was near empty.

To the right of the road was a filling station and a small roadside cafe. The sight of the cafe reminded him he hadn't eaten breakfast. His stomach was beginning to protest. There were a couple of cars pulled up in front of the cafe. A few people were sitting inside at the counter.

He turned off the highway and coasted into the gas station.

'Fill her up!' he called to the attendant. He got out on the hot gravel, leaving the car in gear. His mouth watered. A plateful of hotcakes, side order of ham, steaming black coffee . . . 'Can I leave her here?'

'The car?' The white-clad attendant unscrewed the cap and began filling the tank. 'What do you mean?'

'Fill her up and park her for me. I'll be out in a few minutes. I want to catch some breakfast.'

'Breakfast?'

Douglas was annoyed. What was the matter with the man? He indicated the cafe. A truck driver had pushed the screen door open and was standing on the step, picking his teeth thoughtfully. Inside, the waitress hustled back and forth. He could already smell the coffee, the bacon frying on the griddle. A faint tinny sound of a jukebox drifted out. A warm, friendly sound. 'The cafe.'

The attendant stopped pumping gas. He put down the hose slowly and turned toward Douglas, a strange expression on his face. 'What cafe?' he said.

The cafe wavered and abruptly winked out. Douglas fought down a scream of terror. Where the cafe had been there was only an open field.

Greenish brown grass. A few rusty tin cans. Bottles. Debris. A leaning fence. Off in the distance, the outline of the mountains.

Douglas tried to get hold of himself. 'I'm a little tired,' he muttered. He climbed unsteadily back into the car. 'How much?'

'I just hardly began to fill the–'

'Here.' Douglas pushed a bill at him. 'Get out of the way.' He turned on the motor and raced out onto the highway, leaving the astonished attendant staring after him.

That had been close. Damn close. A trap. And he had almost stepped inside.

But the thing that really terrified him wasn't the closeness. *He was out of the mountains and they had still been ahead of him.*

It hadn't done any good. He wasn't any safer than last night. They were everywhere.

The car sped along the highway. He was getting near Denver–but so what? It wouldn't make any difference. He could dig a hole in Death Valley and still not be safe. They were after him and they weren't going to give up. That much was clear.

He racked his mind desperately. He had to think of something, some way to get loose.

A parasitic culture. A race that preyed on humans, utilized human knowledge and discoveries. Wasn't that what Bill had said? They were after his know-how, his unique ability and knowledge of nuclear physics. He had been singled out, separated from the pack because of his superior ability and training. They would keep after him until they got him. And then—what?

Horror gripped him. The gold ingot. The decoy. The girl had *looked* perfectly real. The cafe full of people. Even the smells of food. Bacon frying. Steaming coffee.

God, if only he were just an ordinary person, without skill, without special ability. If only—

A sudden flapping sound. The car lurched. Douglas cursed wildly. A flat. Of all times . . .

Of all times.

Douglas brought the car to a halt at the side of the road. He switched off the motor and put on the brake. For a while he sat in silence. Finally he fumbled in his coat and got out a mashed package of cigarettes. He lit up slowly and then rolled the window down to let in some air.

He was trapped, of course. There was nothing he could do. The flat had obviously been arranged. Something on the road, sprinkled down from above. Tacks, probably.

The highway was deserted. No cars in sight. He was utterly alone, between towns. Denver was thirty miles ahead. No chance of getting there. Nothing around him but terribly level fields, desolated plains.

Nothing but level ground—and the blue sky above.

Douglas peered up. He couldn't see them, but they were there, waiting for him to get out of his car. His knowledge, his ability, would be utilized by an alien culture. He would become an instrument in their hands. All his learning would be theirs. He would be a slave and nothing more.

Yet, in a way, it was a compliment. From a whole society, he alone had been selected. His skill and knowledge, over everything else. A faint glow rose in his cheeks. Probably they had been studying him for some time. The great eye had no doubt often peered down through its telescope, or microscope, or whatever it was, peered down and seen him. Seen his ability and realized what that would be worth to its own culture.

Douglas opened the car door. He stepped out onto the hot pavement. He dropped his cigarette and calmly stubbed it out. He took a deep breath, stretching and yawning. He could see the tacks now, bright bits of light on the surface of the pavement. Both front tires were flat.

Something shimmered above him. Douglas waited quietly. Now that it had finally come, he was no longer afraid. He watched with a kind of detached curiosity. The something grew. It fanned out over him, swelling and expanding. For a moment it hesitated. Then it descended.

Douglas stood still as the enormous cosmic net closed over him. The strands pressed against him as the net rose. He was going up, heading toward the sky. But he was relaxed, at peace, no longer afraid.

Why be afraid? He would be doing much the same work as always. He would miss Laura and the college, of course, the intellectual companionship of the faculty, the bright faces of the students. But no doubt he would find companionship up above. Persons to work with. Trained minds with which to communicate.

The net was lifting him faster and faster. The ground fell rapidly away. The Earth dwindled from a flat surface to a globe. Douglas watched with professional interest. Above him, beyond the intricate strands of the net, he could see the outline of the other universe, the new world toward which he was heading.

Shapes. Two enormous shapes squatting down. Two incredibly huge figures bending over. One was drawing in the net. The other watched, holding something in its hand. A landscape. Dim forms too vast for Douglas to comprehend.

At last, a thought came. *What a struggle.*

It was worth it, thought the other creature.

Their thoughts roared through him. Powerful thoughts, from immense minds.

I was right. The biggest yet. What a catch!

Must weigh all of twenty-four ragets!

At last!

Suddenly Douglas's composure left him. A chill of horror flashed through his mind. What were they talking about? What did they mean?

But then he was being dumped from the net. He was falling. Something was coming up at him. A flat, shiny surface. What was it?

Oddly, it looked almost like a frying pan.

THE HANGING STRANGER

At five o'clock Ed Loyce washed up, tossed on his hat and coat, got his car out and headed across town toward his TV sales store. He was tired. His back and shoulders ached from digging dirt out of the basement and wheeling it into the back yard. But for a forty-year-old man he had done okay. Janet could get a new vase with the money he had saved; and he liked the idea of repairing the foundations himself.

It was getting dark. The setting sun cast long rays over the scurrying commuters, tired and grim-faced, women loaded down with bundles and packages, students swarming home from the university, mixing with clerks and businessmen and drab secretaries. He stopped his Packard for a red light and then started it up again. The store had been open without him; he'd arrive just in time to spell the help for dinner, go over the records of the day, maybe even close a couple of sales himself. He drove slowly past the small square of green in the center of the street, the town park. There were no parking places in front of LOYCE TV SALES AND SERVICE. He cursed under his breath and swung the car in a U-turn. Again he passed the little square of green with its lonely drinking fountain and bench and single lamppost.

From the lamppost something was hanging. A shapeless dark bundle, swinging a little with the wind. Like a dummy of some sort. Loyce rolled down his window and peered out. What the hell was it? A display of some kind? Sometimes the Chamber of Commerce put up displays in the square.

Again he made a U-turn and brought his car around. He passed the park and concentrated on the dark bundle. It wasn't a dummy. And if it was a display it was a strange kind. The hackles on his neck rose and he swallowed uneasily. Sweat slid out on his face and hands.

It was a body. A human body.

'Look at it!' Loyce snapped. 'Come on out here!'

Don Fergusson came slowly out of the store, buttoning his pin-stripe coat with dignity. 'This is a big deal, Ed. I can't just leave the guy standing there.'

'See it?' Ed pointed into the gathering gloom. The lamppost jutted up against the sky–the post and the bundle swinging from it. 'There it is. How the hell long has it been there?' His voice rose excitedly. 'What's wrong with everybody? They just walk on past!'

Don Fergusson lit a cigarette slowly. 'Take it easy, old man. There must be a good reason, or it wouldn't be there.'

'A reason! What kind of a reason?'

Fergusson shrugged. 'Like the time the Traffic Safety Council put that wrecked Buick there. Some sort of civic thing. How would I know?'

Jack Potter from the shoe shop joined them. 'What's up, boys?'

'There's a body hanging from the lamppost,' Loyce said. 'I'm going to call the cops.'

'They must know about it,' Potter said. 'Or otherwise it wouldn't be there.'

'I got to get back in.' Fergusson headed back into the store. 'Business before pleasure.'

Loyce began to get hysterical. 'You see it? You see it hanging there? A man's body! A dead man!'

'Sure, Ed. I saw it this afternoon when I went out for coffee.'

'You mean it's been there all afternoon?'

'Sure. What's the matter?' Potter glanced at his watch. 'Have to run. See you later, Ed.'

Potter hurried off, joining the flow of people moving along the sidewalk. Men and women, passing by the park. A few glanced up curiously at the dark bundle–and then went on. Nobody stopped. Nobody paid any attention.

'I'm going nuts,' Loyce whispered. He made his way to the curb and crossed out into traffic, among the cars. Horns honked angrily at him. He gained the curb and stepped up onto the little square of green.

The man had been middle-aged. His clothing was ripped and torn, a gray suit, splashed and caked with dried mud. A stranger. Loyce had never seen him before. Not a local man. His face was partly turned away, and in the evening wind he spun a little, turning gently, silently. His skin was gouged and cut. Red gashes, deep scratches of congealed blood. A pair of steel-rimmed glasses hung from one ear, dangling foolishly. His eyes bulged. His mouth was open, tongue thick and ugly blue.

'For Heaven's sake,' Loyce muttered, sickened. He pushed down his nausea and made his way back to the sidewalk. He was shaking all over, with revulsion–and fear.

Why? Who was the man? Why was he hanging there? What did it mean?

And–why didn't anybody notice?

He bumped into a small man hurrying along the sidewalk. 'Watch it!' the man grated. 'Oh, it's you, Ed.'

Ed nodded dazedly. 'Hello, Jenkins.'

'What's the matter?' The stationery clerk caught Ed's arm. 'You look sick.'

'The body. There in the park.'

'Sure, Ed.' Jenkins led him into the alcove of LOYCE TV SALES AND SERVICE. 'Take it easy.'

Margaret Henderson from the jewelry store joined them. 'Something wrong?'

'Ed's not feeling well.'

Loyce yanked himself free. 'How can you stand here? Don't you see it? For God's sake–'

'What's he talking about?' Margaret asked nervously.

'The body!' Ed shouted. 'The body hanging there!'

More people collected. 'Is he sick? It's Ed Loyce. You okay, Ed?'

'The body!' Loyce screamed, struggling to get past them. Hands caught at him. He tore loose. 'Let me go! The police! Get the police!'

'Ed–'

'Better get a doctor!'

'He must be sick.'

'Or drunk.'

Loyce fought his way through the people. He stumbled and half fell. Through a blur he saw rows of faces, curious, concerned, anxious. Men and women halting to see what the disturbance was. He fought past them toward his store. He could see Fergusson inside talking to a man, showing him an Emerson TV set. Pete Foley in the back at the service counter, setting up a new Philco. Loyce shouted at them frantically. His voice was lost in the roar of traffic and the murmuring around him.

'Do something!' he screamed. 'Don't stand there! Do something! Something's wrong! Something's happened! Things are going on!'

The crowd melted respectfully for the two heavy-set cops moving efficiently toward Loyce.

'Name?' the cop with the notebook murmured.

'Loyce.' He mopped his forehead wearily. 'Edward C. Loyce. Listen to me. Back there–'

'Address?' the cop demanded. The police car moved swiftly through traffic, shooting among the cars and buses. Loyce sagged against the seat, exhausted and confused. He took a deep shuddering breath.

'1368 Hurst Road.'

'That's here in Pikeville?'

'That's right.' Loyce pulled himself up with a violent effort. 'Listen to me. Back there. In the square. Hanging from the lamppost–'

'Where were you today?' the cop behind the wheel demanded.

'Where?' Loyce echoed.

'You weren't in your shop, were you?'

'No.' He shook his head. 'No, I was home. Down in the basement.'

'In the *basement*?'

'Digging. A new foundation. Getting out the dirt to pour a cement frame. Why? What has that to do with–'

'Was anybody else down there with you?'

'No. My wife was downtown. My kids were at school.' Loyce looked from one heavy-set cop to the other. Hope flickered across his face, wild hope. 'You mean because I was down there I missed–the explanation? I didn't get in on it? Like everybody else?'

After a pause the cop with the notebook said: 'That's right. You missed the explanation.'

'Then it's official? The body–it's *supposed* to be hanging there?'

'It's supposed to be hanging there. For everybody to see.'

Ed Loyce grinned weakly. 'Good Lord. I guess I sort of went off the deep end. I thought maybe something had happened. You know, something like the Ku Klux Klan. Some kind of violence. Communists or Fascists taking over.' He wiped his face with his breast-pocket handkerchief, his hands shaking. 'I'm glad to know it's on the level.'

'It's on the level.' The police car was getting near the Hall of Justice. The sun had set. The streets were gloomy and dark. The lights had not yet come on.

'I feel better,' Loyce said. 'I was pretty excited there, for a minute. I guess I got all stirred up. Now that I understand, there's no need to take me in, is there?'

The two cops said nothing.

'I should be back at my store. The boys haven't had dinner. I'm all right, now. No more trouble. Is there any need of–'

'This won't take long,' the cop behind the wheel interrupted. 'A short process. Only a few minutes.'

'I hope it's short,' Loyce muttered. The car slowed down for a stoplight. 'I guess I sort of disturbed the peace. Funny, getting excited like that and–'

Loyce yanked the door open. He sprawled out into the street and rolled to his feet. Cars were moving all around him, gaining speed as the light changed. Loyce leaped onto the curb and raced among the people, burrowing into the swarming crowds. Behind him he heard sounds, shouts, people running.

They weren't cops. He had realized that right away. He knew every cop in Pikeville. A man couldn't own a store, operate a business in a small town for twenty-five years without getting to know all the cops.

They weren't cops–and there hadn't been any explanation. Potter, Fergusson, Jenkins, none of them knew why it was there. They didn't know–and they didn't care. *That* was the strange part.

Loyce ducked into a hardware store. He raced toward the back, past the startled clerks and customers, into the shipping room and through the back door. He tripped over a garbage can and ran up a flight of concrete steps. He climbed over a fence and jumped down on the other side, gasping and panting.

There was no sound behind him. He had got away.

He was at the entrance of an alley, dark and strewn with boards and ruined boxes and tires. He could see the street at the far end. A street light wavered and came on. Men and women. Stores. Neon signs. Cars.

And to his right–the police station.

He was close, terribly close. Past the loading platform of a grocery store rose the white concrete side of the Hall of Justice. Barred windows. The police antenna. A great concrete wall rising up in the darkness. A bad place for him to be near. He was too close. He had to keep moving, get farther away from them.

Them?

Loyce moved cautiously down the alley. Beyond the police station was the City Hall, the old-fashioned yellow structure of wood and gilded brass and broad cement steps. He could see the endless rows of offices, dark windows, the cedars and beds of flowers on each side of the entrance.

And–something else.

Above the City Hall was a patch of darkness, a cone of gloom denser than the surrounding night. A prism of black that spread out and was lost into the sky.

He listened. Good God, he could hear something. Something

that made him struggle frantically to close his ears, his mind, to shut out the sound. A buzzing. A distant, muted hum like a great swarm of bees.

Loyce gazed up, rigid with horror. The splotch of darkness, hanging over the City Hall. Darkness so thick it seemed almost solid. *In the vortex something moved.* Flickering shapes. Things, descending from the sky, pausing momentarily above the City Hall, fluttering over it in a dense swarm and then dropping silently onto the roof.

Shapes. Fluttering shapes from the sky. From the crack of darkness that hung above him.

He was seeing–them.

For a long time Loyce watched, crouched behind a sagging fence in a pool of scummy water.

They were landing. Coming down in groups, landing on the roof of the City Hall and disappearing inside. They had wings. Like giant insects of some kind. They flew and fluttered and came to rest–and then crawled crab-fashion, sideways, across the roof and into the building.

He was sickened. And fascinated. Cold night wind blew around him and he shuddered. He was tired, dazed with shock. On the front steps of the City Hall were men, standing here and there. Groups of men coming out of the building and halting for a moment before going on.

Were there more of them?

It didn't seem possible. What he saw descending from the black chasm weren't men. They were alien–from some other world, some other dimension. Sliding through this slit, this break in the shell of the universe. Entering through this gap, winged insects from another realm of being.

On the steps of the City Hall a group of men broke up. A few moved toward a waiting car. One of the remaining shapes started to re-enter the City Hall. It changed its mind and turned to follow the others.

Loyce closed his eyes in horror. His senses reeled. He hung on tight, clutching at the sagging fence. The shape, the man-shape, had abruptly fluttered up and flapped after the others. It flew to the sidewalk and came to rest among them.

Pseudo-men. Imitation men. Insects with ability to disguise themselves as men. Like other insects familiar to Earth. Protective coloration. Mimicry.

Loyce pulled himself away. He got slowly to his feet. It was night. The alley was totally dark. But maybe they could see in the dark. Maybe darkness made no difference to them.

He left the alley cautiously and moved out onto the street. Men and women flowed past, but not so many, now. At the bus stops stood waiting groups. A huge bus lumbered along the street, its lights flashing in the evening gloom.

Loyce moved forward. He pushed his way among those waiting and when the bus halted he boarded it and took a seat in the rear, by the door. A moment later the bus moved into life and rumbled down the street.

Loyce relaxed a little. He studied the people around him. Dulled, tired faces. People going home from work. Quite ordinary faces. None of them paid any attention to him. All sat quietly, sunk down in their seats, jiggling with the motion of the bus.

The man sitting next to him unfolded a newspaper. He began to read the sports section, his lips moving. An ordinary man. Blue suit. Tie. A businessman, or a salesman. On his way home to his wife and family.

Across the aisle a young woman, perhaps twenty. Dark eyes and hair, a package on her lap. Nylons and heels. Red coat and white Angora sweater. Gazing absently ahead of her.

A high school boy in jeans and black jacket.

A great triple-chinned woman with an immense shopping bag loaded with packages and parcels. Her thick face dim with weariness.

Ordinary people. The kind that rode the bus every evening. Going home to their families. To dinner.

Going home—with their minds dead. Controlled, filmed over

with the mask of an alien being that had appeared and taken possession of them, their town, their lives. Himself, too. Except that he happened to be deep in his cellar instead of in the store. Somehow, he had been overlooked. They had missed him. Their control wasn't perfect, foolproof.

Maybe there were others.

Hope flickered in Loyce. They weren't omnipotent. They had made a mistake, not got control of him. Their net, their field of control, had passed over him. He had emerged from his cellar as he had gone down. Apparently their power-zone was limited.

A few seats down the aisle a man was watching him. Loyce broke off his chain of thought. A slender man, with dark hair and a small mustache. Well-dressed, brown suit and shiny shoes. A book between his small hands. He was watching Loyce, studying him intently. He turned quickly away.

Loyce tensed. One of *them*? Or–another they had missed?

The man was watching him again. Small dark eyes, alive and clever. Shrewd. A man too shrewd for them–or one of the things itself, an alien insect from beyond.

The bus halted. An elderly man got on slowly and dropped his token into the box. He moved down the aisle and took a seat opposite Loyce.

The elderly man caught the sharp-eyed man's gaze. For a split second something passed between them.

A look rich with meaning.

Loyce got to his feet. The bus was moving. He ran to the door. One step down into the well. He yanked the emergency door release. The rubber door swung open.

'Hey!' the driver shouted, jamming on the brakes. 'What the hell–?'

Loyce squirmed through. The bus was slowing down. Houses on all sides. A residential district, lawns and tall apartment buildings. Behind him, the bright-eyed man had leaped up. The elderly man was also on his feet. They were coming after him.

Loyce leaped. He hit the pavement with terrific force and rolled against the curb. Pain lapped over him. Pain and a vast tide of blackness. Desperately, he fought it off. He struggled to his knees and then slid down again. The bus had stopped. People were getting off.

Loyce groped around. His fingers closed over something. A rock, lying in the gutter. He crawled to his feet, grunting with pain. A shape loomed before him. A man, the bright-eyed man with the book.

Loyce kicked. The man gasped and fell. Loyce brought the rock down. The man screamed and tried to roll away. '*Stop!* For God's sake listen–'

He struck again. A hideous crunching sound. The man's voice cut off and dissolved in a bubbling wail. Loyce scrambled up and back. The others were there, now. All around him. He ran, awkwardly, down the sidewalk, up a driveway. None of them followed him. They had stopped and were bending over the inert body of the man with the book, the bright-eyed man who had come after him.

Had he made a mistake?

But it was too late to worry about that. He had to get out–away from them. Out of Pikeville, beyond the crack of darkness, the rent between their world and his.

'Ed!' Janet Loyce backed away nervously. 'What is it? What–'

Ed Loyce slammed the door behind him and came into the living room. 'Pull down the shades. Quick.'

Janet moved toward the window. 'But–'

'Do as I say. Who else is here besides you?'

'Nobody. Just the twins. They're upstairs in their room. What's happened? You look so strange. Why are you home?'

Ed locked the front door. He prowled around the house, into the kitchen. From the drawer under the sink he slid out the big butcher knife and ran his finger along it. Sharp. Plenty sharp. He returned to the living room.

'Listen to me,' he said. 'I don't have much time. They know I escaped and they'll be looking for me.'

'Escaped?' Janet's face twisted with bewilderment and fear. 'Who?'

'The town has been taken over. They're in control. I've got it pretty well figured out. They started at the top, at the City Hall and police department. What they did with the *real* humans they–'

'What are you talking about?'

'We've been invaded. From some other universe, some other dimension. They're insects. Mimicry. And more. Power to control minds. Your mind.'

'My mind?'

'Their entrance is *here*, in Pikeville. They've taken over all of you. The whole town–except me. We're up against an incredibly powerful enemy, but they have their limitations. That's our hope. They're limited! They can make mistakes!'

Janet shook her head. 'I don't understand, Ed. You must be insane.'

'Insane? No. Just lucky. If I hadn't been down in the basement I'd be like all the rest of you.' Loyce peered out the window. 'But I can't stand here talking. Get your coat.'

'My coat?'

'We're getting out of here. Out of Pikeville. We've got to get help. Fight this thing. They *can* be beaten. They're not infallible. It's going to be close–but we may make it if we hurry. Come on!' He grabbed her arm roughly. 'Get your coat and call the twins. We're all leaving. Don't stop to pack. There's no time for that.'

White-faced, his wife moved toward the closet and got down her coat. 'Where are we going?'

Ed pulled open the desk drawer and spilled the contents out onto the floor. He grabbed up a road map and spread it open. 'They'll have the highway covered, of course. But there's a back road. To Oak Grove. I got onto it once. It's practically abandoned. Maybe they'll forget about it.'

'The old Ranch Road? Good Lord–it's completely closed. Nobody's supposed to drive over it.'

'I know.' Ed thrust the map grimly into his coat. 'That's our best chance. Now call down the twins and let's get going. Your car is full of gas, isn't it?'

Janet was dazed.

'The Chevy? I had it filled up yesterday afternoon.' Janet moved toward the stairs. 'Ed, I–'

'Call the twins!' Ed unlocked the front door and peered out. Nothing stirred. No sign of life. All right so far.

'Come on downstairs,' Janet called in a wavering voice. 'We're–going out for a while.'

'Now?' Tommy's voice came.

'Hurry up,' Ed barked. 'Get down here, both of you.'

Tommy appeared at the top of the stairs. 'I was doing my homework. We're starting fractions. Miss Parker says if we don't get this done–'

'You can forget about fractions.' Ed grabbed his son as he came down the stairs and propelled him toward the door. 'Where's Jim?'

'He's coming.'

Jim started slowly down the stairs. 'What's up, Dad?'

'We're going for a ride.'

'A ride? Where?'

Ed turned to Janet. 'We'll leave the lights on. And the TV set. Go turn it on.' He pushed her toward the set. 'So they'll think we're still–'

He heard the buzz. And dropped instantly, the long butcher knife out. Sickened, he saw it coming down the stairs at him, wings a blur of motion as it aimed itself. It still bore a vague resemblance to Jimmy. It was small, a baby one. A brief glimpse–the thing hurtling at him, cold, multi-lensed inhuman eyes. Wings, body still clothed in yellow T-shirt and jeans, the mimic outline still stamped on it. A strange half-turn of its body as it reached him. What was it doing?

A stinger.

Loyce stabbed wildly at it. It retreated, buzzing frantically. Loyce rolled and crawled toward the door. Tommy and Janet stood still as statues, faces blank. Watching without expression. Loyce stabbed again. This time the knife connected. The thing shrieked and faltered. It bounced against the wall and fluttered down.

Something lapped through his mind. A wall of force, energy, an alien mind probing into him. He was suddenly paralyzed. The mind entered his own, touched against him briefly, shockingly. An utter alien presence, settling over him—and then it flickered out as the thing collapsed in a broken heap on the rug.

It was dead. He turned it over with his foot. It was an insect, a fly of some kind. Yellow T-shirt, jeans. His son Jimmy . . . He closed his mind tight. It was too late to think about that. Savagely he scooped up his knife and headed toward the door. Janet and Tommy stood stone-still, neither of them moving.

The car was out. He'd never get through. They'd be waiting for him. It was ten miles on foot. Ten long miles over rough ground, gulleys and open fields and hills of uncut forest. He'd have to go alone.

Loyce opened the door. For a brief second he looked back at his wife and son. Then he slammed the door behind him and raced down the porch steps.

A moment later he was on his way, hurrying swiftly through the darkness toward the edge of town.

The early morning sunlight was blinding. Loyce halted, gasping for breath, swaying back and forth. Sweat ran down in his eyes. His clothing was torn, shredded by the brush and thorns through which he had crawled. Ten miles—on his hands and knees. Crawling, creeping through the night. His shoes were mud-caked. He was scratched and limping, utterly exhausted.

But ahead of him lay Oak Grove.

He took a deep breath and started down the hill. Twice he stumbled and fell, picking himself up and trudging on. His ears rang. Everything receded and wavered. But he was there. He had got out, away from Pikeville.

A farmer in a field gaped at him. From a house a young woman watched in wonder. Loyce reached the road and turned onto it.

Ahead of him was a gasoline station and a drive-in. A couple of trucks, some chickens pecking in the dirt, a dog tied with a string.

The white-clad attendant watched suspiciously as he dragged himself up to the station. 'Thank God.' He caught hold of the wall. 'I didn't think I was going to make it. They followed me most of the way. I could hear them buzzing. Buzzing and flitting around behind me.'

'What happened?' the attendant demanded. 'You in a wreck? A hold-up?'

Loyce shook his head wearily. 'They have the whole town. The City Hall and the police station. They hung a man from the lamp-post. That was the first thing I saw. They've got all the roads blocked. I saw them hovering over the cars coming in. About four this morning I got beyond them. I knew it right away. I could feel them leave. And then the sun came up.'

The attendant licked his lip nervously. 'You're out of your head. I better get a doctor.'

'Get me into Oak Grove,' Loyce gasped. He sank down on the gravel. 'We've got to get started–cleaning them out. Got to get started right away.'

They kept a tape recorder going all the time he talked. When he had finished the Commissioner snapped off the recorder and got to his feet. He stood for a moment, deep in thought. Finally he got out his cigarettes and lit up slowly, a frown on his beefy face.

'You don't believe me,' Loyce said.

The Commissioner offered him a cigarette. Loyce pushed it impatiently away. 'Suit yourself.' The Commissioner moved over to the window and stood for a time looking out at the town of Oak Grove. 'I believe you,' he said abruptly.

Loyce sagged. 'Thank God.'

'So you got away.' The Commissioner shook his head. 'You were down in your cellar instead of at work. A freak chance. One in a million.'

Loyce sipped some of the black coffee they had brought him. 'I have a theory,' he murmured.

'What is it?'

'About them. Who they are. They take over one area at a time. Starting at the top—the highest level of authority. Working down from there in a widening circle. When they're firmly in control they go on to the next town. They spread, slowly, very gradually. I think it's been going on for a long time.'

'A long time?'

'Thousands of years. I don't think it's new.'

'Why do you say that?'

'When I was a kid . . . A picture they showed us in Bible League. A religious picture—an old print. The enemy gods, defeated by Jehovah. Moloch, Beelzebub, Moab, Baalin, Ashtaroth—'

'So?'

'They were all represented by figures.' Loyce looked up at the Commissioner. 'Beelzebub was represented as—a giant fly.'

The Commissioner grunted. 'An old struggle.'

'They've been defeated. The Bible is an account of their defeats. They make gains—but finally they're defeated.'

'Why defeated?'

'They can't get everyone. They didn't get me. And they never got the Hebrews. The Hebrews carried the message to the whole world. The realization of the danger. The two men on the bus. I think they understood. Had escaped, like I did.' He clenched his fists. 'I killed one of them. I made a mistake. I was afraid to take a chance.'

The Commissioner nodded. 'Yes, they undoubtedly had escaped, as you did. Freak accidents. But the rest of the town was firmly in control.' He turned from the window. 'Well, Mr Loyce. You seem to have figured everything out.'

'Not everything. The hanging man. The dead man hanging from the lamppost. I don't understand that. *Why?* Why did they deliberately hang him there?'

'That would seem simple.' The Commissioner smiled faintly. '*Bait*.'

Loyce stiffened. His heart stopped beating. 'Bait? What do you mean?'

'To draw you out. Make you declare yourself. So they'd know who was under control–and who had escaped.'

Loyce recoiled with horror. 'Then they *expected* failures! They anticipated–' He broke off. 'They were ready with a trap.'

'And you showed yourself. You reacted. You made yourself known.' The Commissioner abruptly moved toward the door. 'Come along, Loyce. There's a lot to do. We must get moving. There's no time to waste.'

Loyce started slowly to his feet, numbed. 'And the man. *Who was the man?* I never saw him before. He wasn't a local man. He was a stranger. All muddy and dirty, his face cut, slashed–'

There was a strange look on the Commissioner's face as he answered. 'Maybe,' he said softly, 'you'll understand that, too. Come along with me, Mr Loyce.' He held the door open, his eyes gleaming. Loyce caught a glimpse of the street in front of the police station. Policemen, a platform of some sort. A telephone pole–and a rope! 'Right this way,' the Commissioner said, smiling coldly.

As the sun set, the vice-president of the Oak Grove Merchants' Bank came up out of the vault, threw the heavy time locks, put on his hat and coat, and hurried outside onto the sidewalk. Only a few people were there, hurrying home to dinner.

'Good night,' the guard said, locking the door after him.

'Good night,' Clarence Mason murmured. He started along the street toward his car. He was tired. He had been working all day down in the vault, examining the lay-out of the safety deposit boxes to see if there was room for another tier. He was glad to be finished.

At the corner he halted. The street lights had not yet come on. The street was dim. Everything was vague. He looked around–and froze.

From the telephone pole in front of the police station, something large and shapeless hung. It moved a little with the wind.

What the hell was it?

Mason approached it warily. He wanted to get home. He was tired and hungry. He thought of his wife, his kids, a hot meal on the dinner table. But there was something about the dark bundle, something ominous and ugly. The light was bad; he couldn't tell what it was. Yet it drew him on, made him move closer for a better look. The shapeless thing made him uneasy. He was frightened by it. Frightened–and fascinated.

And the strange part was that nobody else seemed to notice it.

THE EYES HAVE IT

It was quite by accident I discovered this incredible invasion of Earth by lifeforms from another planet. As yet, I haven't done anything about it; I can't think of anything to do. I wrote to the Government, and they sent back a pamphlet on the repair and maintenance of frame houses. Anyhow, the whole thing is known; I'm not the first to discover it. Maybe it's even under control.

I was sitting in my easy-chair, idly turning the pages of a paperbacked book someone had left on the bus, when I came across the reference that first put me on the trail. For a moment I didn't respond. It took some time for the full import to sink in. After I'd comprehended, it seemed odd I hadn't noticed it right away.

The reference was clearly to a nonhuman species of incredible properties, not indigenous to Earth. A species, I hasten to point out, customarily masquerading as ordinary human beings. Their disguise, however, became transparent in the face of the following observations by the author. It was at once obvious the author knew everything. Knew everything–and was taking it in his stride. The line (and I tremble remembering it even now) read:

. . . his eyes slowly roved about the room.

Vague chills assailed me. I tried to picture the eyes. Did they roll like dimes? The passage indicated not; they seemed to move through the air, not over the surface. Rather rapidly, apparently. No one in the story was surprised. That's what tipped me off. No sign of amazement at such an outrageous thing. Later the matter was amplified.

. . . his eyes moved from person to person.

There it was in a nutshell. The eyes had clearly come apart from the rest of him and were on their own. My heart pounded and my breath choked in my windpipe. I had stumbled on an accidental mention of a totally unfamiliar race. Obviously non-Terrestrial. Yet, to the characters in the book, it was perfectly natural–which suggested they belonged to the same species.

And the author? A slow suspicion burned in my mind. The author was taking it rather *too easily* in his stride. Evidently, he felt this was quite a usual thing. He made absolutely no attempt to conceal this knowledge. The story continued:

. . . presently his eyes fastened on Julia.

Julia, being a lady, had at least the breeding to feel indignant. She is described as blushing and knitting her brows angrily. At this, I sighed with relief. They weren't *all* non-Terrestrials. The narrative continues:

. . . slowly, calmly, his eyes examined every inch of her.

Great Scott! But here the girl turned and stomped off and the matter ended. I lay back in my chair gasping with horror. My wife and family regarded me in wonder.

'What's wrong, dear?' my wife asked.

I couldn't tell her. Knowledge like this was too much for the ordinary run-of-the-mill person. I had to keep it to myself. 'Nothing,' I gasped. I leaped up, snatched the book, and hurried out of the room.

In the garage, I continued reading. There was more. Trembling, I read the next revealing passage:

. . . he put his arm around Julia. Presently she asked him if he would remove his arm. He immediately did so, with a smile.

It's not said what was done with the arm after the fellow had removed it. Maybe it was left standing upright in the corner. Maybe it was thrown away. I don't care. In any case, the full meaning was there, staring me right in the face.

Here was a race of creatures capable of removing portions of their anatomy at will. Eyes, arms—and maybe more. Without batting an eyelash. My knowledge of biology came in handy, at this point. Obviously they were simple beings, uni-cellular, some sort of primitive single-celled things. Beings no more developed than starfish. Starfish can do the same thing, you know.

I read on. And came to this incredible revelation, tossed off coolly by the author without the faintest tremor:

... outside the movie theater we split up. Part of us went inside, part over to the cafe for dinner.

Binary fission, obviously. Splitting in half and forming two entities. Probably each lower half went to the cafe, it being farther, and the upper halves to the movies. I read on, hands shaking. I had really stumbled onto something here. My mind reeled as I made out this passage:

... I'm afraid there's no doubt about it. Poor Bibney has lost his head again.

Which was followed by:

... and Bob says he has utterly no guts.

Yet Bibney got around as well as the next person. The next person, however, was just as strange. He was soon described as:

... totally lacking in brains.

There was no doubt of the thing in the next passage. Julia, whom I had thought to be the one normal person, reveals herself as also being an alien lifeform, similar to the rest:

... quite deliberately, Julia had given her heart to the young man.

It didn't relate what the final disposition of the organ was, but I didn't really care. It was evident Julia had gone right on living in her usual manner, like all the others in the book. Without heart, arms, eyes, brains, viscera, dividing up in two when the occasion demanded. Without a qualm.

... thereupon she gave him her hand.

I sickened. The rascal now had her hand, as well as her heart. I shudder to think what he's done with them, by this time.

... he took her arm.

Not content to wait, he had to start dismantling her on his own. Flushing crimson, I slammed the book shut and leaped to my feet. But not in time to escape one last reference to those carefree bits of anatomy whose travels had originally thrown me on the track:

. . . *her eyes followed him all the way down the road and across the meadow.*

I rushed from the garage and back inside the warm house, as if the accursed things were following *me*. My wife and children were playing Monopoly in the kitchen. I joined them and played with frantic fervor, brow feverish, teeth chattering.

I had had enough of the thing. I want to hear no more about it. Let them come on. Let them invade Earth. I don't want to get mixed up in it.

I have absolutely no stomach for it.

THE GOLDEN MAN

'Is it always hot like this?' the salesman demanded. He addressed everybody at the lunch counter and in the shabby booths against the wall. A middle-aged fat man with a good-natured smile, rumpled gray suit, sweat-stained white shirt, a drooping bowtie, and a Panama hat.

'Only in the summer,' the waitress answered.

None of the others stirred. The teenage boy and girl in one of the booths, eyes fixed intently on each other. Two workmen, sleeves rolled up, arms dark and hairy, eating bean soup and rolls. A lean, weathered farmer. An elderly businessman in a blue-serge suit, vest and pocket watch. A dark rat-faced cab driver drinking coffee. A tired woman who had come in to get off her feet and put down her bundles.

The salesman got out a package of cigarettes. He glanced curiously around the dingy cafe, lit up, leaned his arms on the counter, and said to the man next to him: 'What's the name of this town?'

The man grunted. 'Walnut Creek.'

The salesman sipped at his Coke for a while, cigarette held loosely between plump white fingers. Presently he reached in his coat and brought out a leather wallet. For a long time he leafed thoughtfully through cards and papers, bits of notes, ticket stubs, endless odds and ends, soiled fragments–and finally a photograph.

He grinned at the photograph, and then began to chuckle, a low moist rasp. 'Look at this,' he said to the man beside him.

The man went on reading his newspaper.

'Hey, look at this.' The salesman nudged him with his elbow and pushed the photograph at him. 'How's that strike you?'

Annoyed, the man glanced briefly at the photograph. It showed a nude woman, from the waist up. Perhaps thirty-five years old. Face turned away. Body white and flabby. With eight breasts.

'Ever seen anything like that?' the salesman chuckled, his little red eyes dancing. His face broke into lewd smiles and again he nudged the man.

'I've seen that before.' Disgusted, the man resumed reading his newspaper.

The salesman noticed the lean old farmer was looking at the picture. He passed it genially over to him. 'How's that strike you, pop? Pretty good stuff, eh?'

The farmer examined the picture solemnly. He turned it over, studied the creased back, took a second look at the front, then tossed it to the salesman. It slid from the counter, turned over a couple of times, and fell to the floor face up.

The salesman picked it up and brushed it off. Carefully, almost tenderly, he restored it to his wallet. The waitress's eyes flickered as she caught a glimpse of it.

'Damn nice,' the salesman observed, with a wink. 'Wouldn't you say so?'

The waitress shrugged indifferently. 'I don't know. I saw a lot of them around Denver. A whole colony.'

'That's where this was taken. Denver DCA Camp.'

'Any still alive?' the farmer asked.

The salesman laughed harshly. 'You kidding?' He made a short, sharp swipe with his hand. 'Not any more.'

They were all listening. Even the high school kids in the booth had stopped holding hands and were sitting up straight, eyes wide with fascination.

'Saw a funny kind down near San Diego,' the farmer said. 'Last year, some time. Had wings like a bat. Skin, not feathers. Skin and bone wings.'

The rat-eyed taxi driver chimed in. 'That's nothing. There was a two-headed one in Detroit. I saw it on exhibit.'

'Was it alive?' the waitress asked.

'No. They'd already euthed it.'

'In sociology,' the high school boy spoke up, 'we saw tapes of a whole lot of them. The winged kind from down south, the big-headed one they found in Germany, an awful-looking one with sort of cones, like an insect. And–'

'The worst of all,' the elderly businessman stated, 'are those English ones. That hid out in the coal mines. The ones they didn't find until last year.' He shook his head. 'Forty years, down there in the mines, breeding and developing. Almost a hundred of them. Survivors from a group that went underground during the War.'

'They just found a new kind in Sweden,' the waitress said. 'I was reading about it. Controls minds at a distance, they said. Only a couple of them. The DCA got there plenty fast.'

'That's a variation of the New Zealand type,' one of the workmen said. 'It read minds.'

'Reading and controlling are two different things,' the businessman said. 'When I hear something like that I'm plenty glad there's the DCA.'

'There was a type they found right after the War,' the farmer said. 'In Siberia. Had the ability to control objects. Psychokinetic ability. The Soviet DCA got it right away. Nobody remembers that any more.'

'I remember that,' the businessman said. 'I was just a kid, then. I remember because that was the first deeve I ever heard of. My father called me into the living room and told me and my brothers and sisters. We were still building the house. That was in the days when the DCA inspected everyone and stamped their arms.' He held up his thin, gnarled wrist. 'I was stamped there, sixty years ago.'

'Now they just have the birth inspection,' the waitress said. She shivered. 'There was one in San Francisco this month. First in over a year. They thought it was over, around here.'

'It's been dwindling,' the taxi driver said. 'Frisco wasn't too bad hit. Not like some. Not like Detroit.'

'They still get ten or fifteen a year in Detroit,' the high school boy said. 'All around there. Lots of pools still left. People go into them, in spite of the robot signs.'

'What kind was this one?' the salesman asked. 'The one they found in San Francisco.'

The waitress gestured. 'Common type. The kind with no toes. Bent-over. Big eyes.'

'The nocturnal type,' the salesman said.

'The mother had hid it. They say it was three years old. She got the doctor to forge the DCA chit. Old friend of the family.'

The salesman had finished his Coke. He sat playing idly with his cigarettes, listening to the hum of talk he had set into motion. The high school boy was leaning excitedly toward the girl across from him, impressing her with his fund of knowledge. The lean farmer and the businessman were huddled together, remembering the old days, the last years of the War, before the first Ten-Year Reconstruction Plan. The taxi driver and the two workmen were swapping yarns about their own experiences.

The salesman caught the waitress's attention. 'I guess,' he said thoughtfully, 'that one in Frisco caused quite a stir. Something like that happening so close.'

'Yeah,' the waitress murmured.

'This side of the Bay wasn't really hit,' the salesman continued. 'You never get any of them over here.'

'No.' The waitress moved abruptly. 'None in this area. Ever.' She scooped up dirty dishes from the counter and headed toward the back.

'Never?' the salesman asked, surprised. 'You've never had any deeves on this side of the Bay?'

'No. None.' She disappeared into the back, where the fry cook stood by his burners, white apron and tattooed wrists. Her voice was a little too loud, a little too harsh and strained. It made the farmer pause suddenly and glance up.

Silence dropped like a curtain. All sound cut off instantly. They were all gazing down at their food, suddenly tense and ominous.

'None around here,' the taxi driver said, loudly and clearly, to no one in particular. 'None ever.'

'Sure,' the salesman agreed genially. 'I was only–'

'Make sure you get that straight,' one of the workmen said.

The salesman blinked. 'Sure, buddy. Sure.' He fumbled nervously in his pocket. A quarter and a dime jangled to the floor and he hurriedly scooped them up. 'No offense.'

For a moment there was silence. Then the high school boy spoke up, aware for the first time that nobody was saying anything. 'I heard something,' he began eagerly, voice full of importance. 'Somebody said they saw something up by the Johnson farm that looked like it was one of those–'

'*Shut up*,' the businessman said, without turning his head.

Scarlet-faced, the boy sagged in his seat. His voice wavered and broke off. He peered hastily down at his hands and swallowed unhappily.

The salesman paid the waitress for his coke. 'What's the quickest road to Frisco?' he began. But the waitress had already turned her back.

The people at the counter were immersed in their food. None of them looked up. They ate in frozen silence. Hostile, unfriendly faces, intent on their food.

The salesman picked up his bulging briefcase, pushed open the screen door, and stepped out into the blazing sunlight. He moved toward his battered 1978 Buick, parked a few meters up. A blue-shirted traffic cop was standing in the shade of an awning, talking languidly to a young woman in a yellow silk dress that clung moistly to her slim body.

The salesman paused a moment before he got into his car. He waved his hand and hailed the policeman. 'Say, you know this town pretty good?'

The policeman eyed the salesman's rumpled gray suit, bowtie, his sweat-stained shirt. The out-of-state license. 'What do you want?'

'I'm looking for the Johnson farm,' the salesman said. 'Here to see him about some litigation.' He moved toward the policeman, a small white card between his fingers. 'I'm his attorney–from the New York Guild. Can you tell me how to get out there? I haven't been through here in a couple of years.'

*

Nat Johnson gazed up at the noonday sun and saw that it was good. He sat sprawled out on the bottom step of the porch, a pipe between his yellowed teeth, a lithe, wiry man in red-checkered shirt and canvas jeans, powerful hands, iron-gray hair that was still thick despite sixty-five years of active life.

He was watching the children play. Jean rushed laughing in front of him, bosom heaving under her sweatshirt, black hair streaming behind her. She was sixteen, bright-eyed, legs strong and straight, slim young body bent slightly forward with the weight of the two horseshoes. After her scampered Dave, fourteen, white teeth and black hair, a handsome boy, a son to be proud of. Dave caught up with his sister, passed her, and reached the far peg. He stood waiting, legs apart, hands on his hips, his two horseshoes gripped easily. Gasping, Jean hurried toward him.

'Go ahead!' Dave shouted. 'You shoot first. I'm waiting for you.'

'So you can knock them away?'

'So I can knock them closer.'

Jean tossed down one horseshoe and gripped the other with both hands, eyes on the distant peg. Her lithe body bent, one leg slid back, her spine arched. She took careful aim, closed one eye, and then expertly tossed the shoe. With a clang the shoe struck the distant peg, circled briefly around it, then bounced off again and rolled to one side. A cloud of dust rolled up.

'Not bad,' Nat Johnson admitted, from his step. 'Too hard, though. Take it easy.' His chest swelled with pride as the girl's glistening body took aim and again threw. Two powerful, handsome children, almost ripe, on the verge of adulthood. Playing together in the hot sun.

And there was Cris.

Cris stood by the porch, arms folded. He wasn't playing. He was watching. He had stood there since Dave and Jean had begun playing, the same half-intent, half-remote expression on his finely-cut face. As if he were seeing past them, beyond the two of them. Beyond the field, the barn, the creek bed, the rows of cedars.

'Come on, Cris!' Jean called, as she and Dave moved across the field to collect their horseshoes. 'Don't you want to play?'

No, Cris didn't want to play. He never played. He was off in a world of his own, a world into which none of them could come. He never joined in anything, games or chores or family activities. He was by himself always. Remote, detached, aloof. Seeing past everyone and everything–that is, until all at once something clicked and he momentarily rephased, reentered their world briefly.

Nat Johnson reached out and knocked his pipe against the step. He refilled it from his leather tobacco pouch, his eyes on his eldest son. Cris was now moving into life. Heading out onto the field. He walked slowly, arms folded calmly, as if he had, for the moment, descended from his own world into theirs. Jean didn't see him; she had turned her back and was getting ready to pitch.

'Hey,' Dave said, startled. 'Here's Cris.'

Cris reached his sister, stopped, and held out his hand. A great dignified figure, calm and impassive. Uncertainly, Jean gave him one of the horseshoes. 'You want this? You want to play?'

Cris said nothing. He bent slightly, a supple arc of his incredibly graceful body, then moved his arm in a blur of speed. The shoe sailed, struck the far peg, and dizzily spun around it. Ringer.

The corners of Dave's mouth turned down. 'What a lousy darn thing.'

'Cris,' Jean reproved. 'You don't play fair.'

No, Cris didn't play fair. He had watched half an hour–then come out and thrown once. One perfect toss, one dead ringer.

'He never makes a mistake,' Dave complained.

Cris stood, face blank. A golden statue in the mid-day sun. Golden hair, skin, a light down of gold fuzz on his bare arms and legs–

Abruptly he stiffened. Nat sat up, startled. 'What is it?' he barked.

Cris turned in a quick circle, magnificent body alert. 'Cris!' Jean demanded. 'What–'

Cris shot forward. Like a released energy beam he bounded across the field, over the fence, into the barn and out the other side. His flying figure seemed to skim over the dry grass as he descended into the barren creek bed, between the cedars. A momentary flash of gold–and he was gone. Vanished. There was no sound. No motion. He had utterly melted into the scenery.

'What was it this time?' Jean asked wearily. She came over to her father and threw herself down in the shade. Sweat glowed on her smooth neck and upper lip; her sweatshirt was streaked and damp. 'What did he see?'

'He was after something,' Dave stated, coming up.

Nat grunted. 'Maybe. There's no telling.'

'I guess I better tell Mom not to set a place for him,' Jean said. 'He probably won't be back.'

Anger and futility descended over Nat Johnson. No, he wouldn't be back. Not for dinner and probably not the next day–or the one after that. He'd be gone God only knew how long. Or where. Or why. Off by himself, alone some place. 'If I thought there was any use,' Nat began, 'I'd send you two after him. But there's no–'

He broke off. A car was coming up the dirt road toward the farmhouse. A dusty, battered old Buick. Behind the wheel sat a plump red-faced man in a gray suit, who waved cheerfully at them as the car sputtered to a stop and the motor died into silence.

'Afternoon,' the man nodded, as he climbed out the car. He tipped his hat pleasantly. He was middle-aged, genial-looking, perspiring freely as he crossed the dry ground toward the porch. 'Maybe you folks can help me.'

'What do you want?' Nat Johnson demanded hoarsely. He was frightened. He watched the creek bed out of the corner of his eye, praying silently. God, if only he *stayed* away. Jean was breathing quickly, sharp little gasps. She was terrified. Dave's face was expressionless, but all color had drained from it. 'Who are you?' Nat demanded.

'Name's Baines. George Baines.' The man held out his hand but Johnson ignored it. 'Maybe you've heard of me. I own the Pacifica Development Corporation. We built all those little bomb-proof houses just outside town. Those little round ones you see as you come up the main highway from Lafayette.'

'What do you want?' Johnson held his hands steady with an

effort. He'd never heard of the man, although he'd noticed the housing tract. It couldn't be missed–a great ant-heap of ugly pill-boxes straddling the highway. Baines looked like the kind of man who'd own them. But what did he want here?

'I've bought some land up this way,' Baines was explaining. He rattled a sheaf of crisp papers. 'This is the deed, but I'll be damned if I can find it.' He grinned good-naturedly. 'I know it's around this way, some place, this side of the State road. According to the clerk at the County Recorder's Office, a mile or so this side of that hill over there. But I'm no damn good at reading maps.'

'It isn't around here,' Dave broke in. 'There's only farms around here. Nothing for sale.'

'This is a farm, son,' Baines said genially. 'I bought it for myself and my missus. So we could settle down.' He wrinkled his pug nose. 'Don't get the wrong idea–I'm not putting up any tracts around here. This is strictly for myself. An old farmhouse, twenty acres, a pump and a few oak trees–'

'Let me see the deed.' Johnson grabbed the sheaf of papers, and while Baines blinked in astonishment, he leafed rapidly through them. His face hardened and he handed them back. 'What are you up to? This deed is for a parcel fifty miles from here.'

'Fifty miles!' Baines was dumbfounded. 'No kidding? But the clerk told me–'

Johnson was on his feet. He towered over the fat man. He was in top-notch physical shape–and he was plenty damn suspicious. 'Clerk, hell. You get back into your car and drive out of here. I don't know what you're after, or what you're here for, but I want you off my land.'

In Johnson's massive fist something sparkled. A metal tube that gleamed ominously in the mid-day sunlight. Baines saw it–and gulped. 'No offense, mister.' He backed nervously away. 'You folks sure are touchy. Take it easy, will you?'

Johnson said nothing. He gripped the lash-tube tighter and waited for the fat man to leave.

But Baines lingered. 'Look, buddy. I've been driving around this furnace five hours, looking for my damn place. Any objection to my using your–facilities?'

Johnson eyed him with suspicion. Gradually the suspicion turned to disgust. He shrugged. 'Dave, show him where the bathroom is.'

'Thanks.' Baines grinned thankfully. 'And if it wouldn't be too much trouble, maybe a glass of water. I'd be glad to pay you for it.' He chuckled knowingly. 'Never let the city people get away with anything, eh?'

'Christ.' Johnson turned away in revulsion as the fat man lumbered after his son, into the house.

'Dad,' Jean whispered. As soon as Baines was inside she hurried up onto the porch, eyes wide with fear. 'Dad, do you think he–'

Johnson put his arm around her. 'Just hold on tight. He'll be gone, soon.'

The girl's dark eyes flashed with mute terror. 'Every time the man from the water company, or the tax collector, some tramp, children, *anybody* come around, I get a terrible stab of pain–here.' She clutched at her heart, hand against her breasts. 'It's been that way thirteen years. How much longer can we keep it going? *How long?*'

The man named Baines emerged gratefully from the bathroom. Dave Johnson stood silently by the door, body rigid, youthful face stony.

'Thanks, son,' Baines sighed. 'Now where can I get a glass of cold water?' He smacked his thick lips in anticipation. 'After you've been driving around the sticks looking for a dump some red-hot real estate agent stuck you with–'

Dave headed into the kitchen. 'Mom, this man wants a drink of water. Dad said he could have it.'

Dave had turned his back. Baines caught a brief glimpse of the mother, gray-haired, small, moving toward the sink with a glass, face withered and drawn, without expression.

Then Baines hurried from the room down a hall. He passed through a bedroom, pulled a door open, found himself facing a closet. He turned and raced back, through the living room, into a dining room, then another bedroom. In a brief instant he had gone through the whole house.

He peered out a window. The back yard. Remains of a rusting truck. Entrance of an underground bomb shelter. Tin cans. Chickens scratching around. A dog, asleep under a shed. A couple of old auto tires.

He found a door leading out. Soundlessly, he tore the door open and stepped outside. No one was in sight. There was the barn, a leaning, ancient wood structure. Cedar trees beyond, a creek of some kind. What had once been an outhouse.

Baines moved cautiously around the side of the house. He had perhaps thirty seconds. He had left the door of the bathroom closed; the boy would think he had gone back in there. Baines looked into the house through a window. A large closet, filled with old clothing, boxes and bundles of magazines.

He turned and started back. He reached the corner of the house and started around it.

Nat Johnson's gaunt shape loomed up and blocked his way. 'All right, Baines. You asked for it.'

A pink flash blossomed. It shut out the sunlight in a single blinding burst. Baines leaped back and clawed at his coat pocket. The edge of the flash caught him and he half-fell, stunned by the force. His suit-shield sucked in the energy and discharged it, but the power rattled his teeth and for a moment he jerked like a puppet on a string. Darkness ebbed around him. He could feel the mesh of the shield glow white, as it absorbed the energy and fought to control it.

His own tube came out–and Johnson had no shield. 'You're under arrest,' Baines muttered grimly. 'Put down your tube and your hands up. And call your family.' He made a motion with the tube. 'Come on, Johnson. Make it snappy.'

The lash-tube wavered and then slipped from Johnson's fingers. 'You're still alive.' Dawning horror crept across his face. 'Then you must be–'

Dave and Jean appeared. '*Dad!*'

'Come over here,' Baines ordered. 'Where's your mother?'

Dave jerked his head numbly. 'Inside.'

'Get her and bring her here.'

'You're DCA,' Nat Johnson whispered.

Baines didn't answer. He was doing something with his neck, pulling at the flabby flesh. The wiring of a contact mike glittered as he slipped it from a fold between two chins and into his pocket. From the dirt road came the sound of motors, sleek purrs that rapidly grew louder. Two teardrops of black metal came gliding up and parked beside the house. Men swarmed out, in the dark gray-green of the Government Civil Police. In the sky swarms of black dots were descending, clouds of ugly flies that darkened the sun as they spilled out men and equipment. The men drifted slowly down.

'He's not here,' Baines said, as the first man reached him. 'He got away. Inform Wisdom back at the lab.'

'We've got this section blocked off.'

Baines turned to Nat Johnson, who stood in dazed silence, uncomprehending, his son and daughter beside him. 'How did he know we were coming?' Baines demanded.

'I don't know,' Johnson muttered. 'He just–knew.'

'A telepath?'

'I don't know.'

Baines shrugged. 'We'll know, soon. A clamp is out, all around here. He can't get past, no matter what the hell he can do. Unless he can dematerialize himself.'

'What'll you do with him when you–if you catch him?' Jean asked huskily.

'Study him.'

'And then kill him?'

'That depends on the lab evaluation. If you could give me more to work on, I could predict better.'

'We can't tell you anything. We don't know anything more.' The girl's voice rose with desperation. 'He doesn't talk.'

Baines jumped. '*What?*'

'He doesn't talk. He never talked to us. Ever.'

'How old is he?'

'Eighteen.'

'No communication.' Baines was sweating. 'In eighteen years there hasn't been any semantic bridge between you? Does he have *any* contact? Signs? Codes?'

'He–ignores us. He eats here, stays with us. Sometimes he plays when we play. Or sits with us. He's gone days on end. We've never been able to find out what he's doing–or where. He sleeps in the barn–by himself.'

'Is he really gold-colored?'

'Yes. Skin, eyes, hair, nails. Everything.'

'And he's large? Well-formed?'

It was a moment before the girl answered. A strange emotion stirred her drawn features, a momentary glow. 'He's incredibly beautiful. A god come down to earth.' Her lips twisted. 'You won't find him. He can do things. Things you have no comprehension of. Powers so far beyond your limited–'

'You don't think we'll get him?' Baines frowned. 'More teams are landing all the time. You've never seen an Agency clamp in operation. We've had sixty years to work out all the bugs. If he gets away it'll be the first time–'

Baines broke off abruptly. Three men were quickly approaching the porch. Two green-clad Civil Police. And a third man between them. A man who moved silently, lithely, a faintly luminous shape that towered above them.

'*Cris!*' Jean screamed.

'We got him,' one of the police said.

Baines fingered his lash-tube uneasily. 'Where? How?'

'He gave himself up,' the policeman answered, voice full of awe. 'He came to us voluntarily. Look at him. He's like a metal statue. Like some sort of–god.'

The golden figure halted for a moment beside Jean. Then it turned slowly, calmly, to face Baines.

'Cris!' Jean shrieked. '*Why did you come back?*'

The same thought was eating at Baines, too. He shoved it aside–for the time being. 'Is the jet out front?' he demanded quickly.

'Ready to go,' one of the CP answered.

'Fine.' Baines strode past them, down the steps and onto the dirt field. 'Let's go. I want him taken directly to the lab.' For a moment he studied the massive figure who stood calmly between the two Civil Policemen. Beside him, they seemed to have shrunk, become ungainly and repellent. Like dwarves . . . What had Jean said? *A god come to earth*. Baines broke angrily away. 'Come on,' he muttered brusquely. 'This one may be tough; we've never run up against one like it before. We don't know what the hell it can do.'

The chamber was empty, except for the seated figure. Four bare walls, floor and ceiling. A steady glare of white light relentlessly etched every corner of the chamber. Near the top of the far wall ran a narrow slot, the view windows through which the interior of the chamber was scanned.

The seated figure was quiet. He hadn't moved since the chamber locks had slid into place, since the heavy bolts had fallen from outside and the rows of bright-faced technicians had taken their places at the view windows. He gazed down at the floor, bent forward, hands clasped together, face calm, almost expressionless. In four hours he hadn't moved a muscle.

'Well?' Baines said. 'What have you learned?'

Wisdom grunted sourly. 'Not much. If we don't have him doped out in forty-eight hours we'll go ahead with the euth. We can't take any chances.'

'You're thinking about the Tunis type,' Baines said. He was, too. They had found ten of them, living in the ruins of the abandoned North African town. Their survival method was simple. They killed and absorbed other life forms, then imitated them and took their places. *Chameleons*, they were called. It had cost sixty lives, before the last one was destroyed. Sixty top-level experts, highly trained DCA men.

'Any clues?' Baines asked.

'He's different as hell. This is going to be tough.' Wisdom thumbed a pile of tape-spools. 'This is the complete report, all the material we got from Johnson and his family. We pumped them with the psych-wash, then let them go home. Eighteen years–and no semantic bridge. Yet, he looks fully developed. Mature at thirteen–a shorter, faster life-cycle than ours. But why the mane? All the gold fuzz? Like a Roman monument that's been gilded.'

'Has the report come in from the analysis room? You had a wave-shot taken, of course.'

'His brain pattern has been fully scanned. But it takes time for them to plot it out. We're all running around like lunatics while he just sits there!' Wisdom poked a stubby finger at the window. 'We caught him easily enough. He can't have *much*, can he? But I'd like to know what it is. Before we euth him.'

'Maybe we should keep him alive until we know.'

'Euth in forty-eight hours,' Wisdom repeated stubbornly. 'Whether we know or not. I don't like him. He gives me the creeps.'

Wisdom stood chewing nervously on his cigar, a red-haired, beefy-faced man, thick and heavy-set, with a barrel chest and cold, shrewd eyes deep-set in his hard face. Ed Wisdom was Director of DCA's North American Branch. But right now he was worried. His tiny eyes darted back and forth, alarmed flickers of gray in his brutal, massive face.

'You think,' Baines said slowly, 'this is *it*?'

'I always think so,' Wisdom snapped. 'I have to think so.'

'I mean–'

'I know what you mean.' Wisdom paced back and forth, among the study tables, technicians at their benches, equipment and humming computers. Buzzing tape-slots and research hook-ups. 'This thing lived eighteen years with his family and *they* don't understand it. *They* don't know what it has. They know what it does, but not how.'

'What does it do?'

'It knows things.'

'What kind of things?'

Wisdom grabbed his lash-tube from his belt and tossed it on a table. 'Here.'

'What?'

'Here.' Wisdom signalled, and a view window was slid back an inch. 'Shoot him.'

Baines blinked. 'You said forty-eight hours.'

With a curse, Wisdom snatched up the tube, aimed it through the window directly at the seated figure's back, and squeezed the trigger.

A blinding flash of pink. A cloud of energy blossomed in the center of the chamber. It sparkled, then died into dark ash.

'Good God!' Baines gasped. 'You–'

He broke off. The figure was no longer sitting. As Wisdom fired, it had moved in a blur of speed, away from the blast, to the corner of the chamber. Now it was slowly coming back, face blank, still absorbed in thought.

'Fifth time,' Wisdom said, as he put his tube away. 'Last time Jamison and I fired together. Missed. He knew exactly when the bolts would hit. And where.'

Baines and Wisdom looked at each other. Both of them were thinking the same thing. 'But even reading minds wouldn't tell him where they were going to hit,' Baines said. 'When, maybe. But not where. Could you have called your own shots?'

'Not mine,' Wisdom answered flatly. 'I fired fast, damn near at random.' He frowned. '*Random*. We'll have to make a test of this.' He waved a group of technicians over. 'Get a construction team up here. On the double.' He grabbed paper and pen and began sketching.

While construction was going on, Baines met his fiancée in the lobby outside the lab, the great central lounge of the DCA Building.

'How's it coming?' she asked. Anita Ferris was tall and blonde, blue eyes and a mature, carefully cultivated figure. An attractive, competent-looking woman in her late twenties. She wore a metal foil dress and cape–with a red and black stripe on the sleeve, the emblem of the A-Class. Anita was Director of the Semantics Agency, a top-level Government Coordinator. 'Anything of interest, this time?'

'Plenty.' Baines guided her from the lobby into the dim recess of the bar. Music played softly in the background, a shifting variety of patterns formed mathematically. Dim shapes moved expertly through the gloom, from table to table. Silent, efficient robot waiters.

As Anita sipped her Tom Collins, Baines outlined what they had found.

'What are the chances,' Anita asked slowly, 'that he's built up some kind of deflection-cone? There was one kind that warped their environment by direct mental effort. No tools. Direct mind to matter.'

'Psychokinetics?' Baines drummed restlessly on the table top. 'I doubt it. The thing has ability to predict, not to control. He can't stop the beams, but he can sure as hell get out of the way.'

'Does he jump between the molecules?'

Baines wasn't amused. 'This is serious. We've handled these things sixty years–longer than you and I have been around added together. Eighty-seven types of deviants have shown up, real mutants that could reproduce themselves, not mere freaks. This is the eighty-eighth. We've been able to handle each of them in turn. But this–'

'Why are you so worried about this one?'

'First, it's eighteen years old. That in itself is incredible. Its family managed to hide it that long.'

'Those women around Denver were older than that. Those ones with–'

'They were in a Government camp. Somebody high up was toying with the idea of allowing them to breed. Some sort of industrial use. We withheld euth for years. But Cris Johnson stayed alive *outside our control.* Those things at Denver were under constant scrutiny.'

'Maybe he's harmless. You always assume a deeve is a menace. He might even be beneficial. Somebody thought those women might work in. Maybe this thing has something that would advance the race.'

'*Which* race? Not the human race. It's the old "the operation was a success but the patient died" routine. If we introduce a mutant to keep us going it'll be mutants, not us, who'll inherit the earth. It'll be mutants surviving for their own sake. Don't think for a moment we can put padlocks on them and expect them to serve us. If they're really superior to homo sapiens, they'll win out in even competition. To survive, we've got to cold-deck them right from the start.'

'In other words, we'll know homo superior when he comes–by definition. He'll be the one we won't be able to euth.'

'That's about it,' Baines answered. 'Assuming there *is* a homo superior. Maybe there's just homo peculiar. Homo with an improved line.'

'The Neanderthal probably thought the Cro-Magnon man had merely an improved line. A little more advanced ability to conjure up symbols and shape flint. From your description, this thing is more radical than a mere improvement.'

'This thing,' Baines said slowly, 'has an ability to predict. So far, it's been able to stay alive. It's been able to cope with situations better than you or I could. How long do you think we'd stay alive in that chamber, with energy beams blazing down at us? In a sense it's got the ultimate survival ability. If it can always be accurate–'

A wall-speaker sounded. 'Baines, you're wanted in the lab. Get the hell out of the bar and upramp.'

Baines pushed back his chair and got to his feet. 'Come along. You may be interested in seeing what Wisdom has got dreamed up.'

A tight group of top-level DCA officials stood around in a circle, middle-aged, gray-haired, listening to a skinny youth in a white shirt and rolled-up sleeves explaining an elaborate cube of metal and plastic that filled the center of the view-platform. From it jutted an ugly array of tube snouts, gleaming muzzles that disappeared into an intricate maze of wiring.

'This,' the youth was saying briskly, 'is the first real test. It fires at random–as nearly random as we can make it, at least. Weighted balls are thrown up in an air stream, then dropped free to fall back and cut relays. They can fall in almost any pattern. The thing fires according to their pattern. Each drop produces a new configuration of timing and position. Ten tubes, in all. Each will be in constant motion.'

'And *nobody* knows how they'll fire?' Anita asked.

'Nobody.' Wisdom rubbed his thick hands together. 'Mind reading won't help him, not with this thing.'

Anita moved over to the view windows, as the cube was rolled into place. She gasped. 'Is that him?'

'What's wrong?' Baines asked.

Anita's cheeks were flushed. 'Why, I expected a–a *thing*. My God, he's beautiful! Like a golden statue. Like a deity!'

Baines laughed. 'He's eighteen years old, Anita. Too young for you.'

The woman was still peering through the view window. 'Look at him. Eighteen? I don't believe it.'

Cris Johnson sat in the center of the chamber, on the floor. A posture of contemplation, head bowed, arms folded, legs tucked under him. In the stark glare of the overhead lights his powerful body glowed and rippled, a shimmering figure of downy gold.

'Pretty, isn't he?' Wisdom muttered. 'All right. Start it going.'

'You're going to *kill* him?' Anita demanded.

'We're going to try.'

'But he's–' She broke off uncertainly. 'He's not a monster. He's not like those others, those hideous things with two heads, or those insects. Or those awful things from Tunis.'

'What is he, then?' Baines asked.

'I don't know. But you can't just *kill* him. It's terrible!'

The cube clicked into life. The muzzles jerked, silently altered position. Three retracted, disappeared into the body of the cube. Others came out. Quickly, efficiently, they moved into position–and abruptly, without warning, opened fire.

A staggering burst of energy fanned out, a complex pattern that altered each moment, different angles, different velocities, a bewildering blur that cracked from the windows down into the chamber.

The golden figure moved. He dodged back and forth, expertly avoiding the bursts of energy that seared around him on all sides. Rolling clouds of ash obscured him; he was lost in a mist of crackling fire and ash.

'Stop it!' Anita shouted. 'For God's sake, you'll destroy him!'

The chamber was an inferno of energy. The figure had completely disappeared. Wisdom waited a moment, then nodded to the technicians operating the cube. They touched guide buttons and the muzzles slowed and died. Some sank back into the cube. All became silent. The works of the cube ceased humming.

Cris Johnson was still alive. He emerged from the settling clouds of ash, blackened and singed. But unhurt. He had avoided each beam. He had weaved between them and among them as they came, a dancer leaping over glittering sword-points of pink fire. He had survived.

'No,' Wisdom murmured, shaken and grim. 'Not a telepath. Those were at random. No prearranged pattern.'

The three of them looked at each other, dazed and frightened. Anita was trembling. Her face was pale and her blue eyes were wide. 'What, then?' she whispered. 'What is it? What does he have?'

'He's a good guesser,' Wisdom suggested.

'He's not guessing,' Baines answered. 'Don't kid yourself. That's the whole point.'

'No, he's not guessing.' Wisdom nodded slowly. 'He *knew*. He predicted each strike. I wonder . . . *Can* he err? *Can* he make a mistake?'

'We caught him,' Baines pointed out.

'You said he came back voluntarily.' There was a strange look on Wisdom's face. 'Did he come back *after* the clamp was up?'

Baines jumped. 'Yes, after.'

'He couldn't have got through the clamp. So he came back.' Wisdom grinned wryly. 'The clamp must actually have been perfect. It was supposed to be.'

'If there had been a single hole,' Baines murmured, 'he would have known it–gone through.'

Wisdom ordered a group of armed guards over. 'Get him out of there. To the euth stage.'

Anita shrieked. 'Wisdom, you can't–'

'He's too far ahead of us. We can't compete with him.' Wisdom's eyes were bleak. 'We can only guess what's going to happen. *He knows*. For him, it's a sure thing. I don't think it'll help him at euth, though. The whole stage is flooded simultaneously. Instantaneous gas, released throughout.' He signalled impatiently to the guards. 'Get going. Take him down right away. Don't waste any time.'

'Can we?' Baines murmured thoughtfully.

The guards took up positions by one of the chamber locks. Cautiously, the tower control slid the lock back. The first two guards stepped cautiously in, lash-tubes ready.

Cris stood in the center of the chamber. His back was to them as they crept toward him. For a moment he was silent, utterly unmoving. The guards fanned out, as more of them entered the chamber. Then–

Anita screamed. Wisdom cursed. The golden figure spun and leaped forward, in a flashing blur of speed. Past the triple line of guards, through the lock and into the corridor.

'Get him!' Baines shouted.

Guards milled everywhere. Flashes of energy lit up the corridor, as the figure raced among them up the ramp.

'No use,' Wisdom said calmly. 'We can't hit him.' He touched a button, then another. 'But maybe this will help.'

'What–' Baines began. But the leaping figure shot abruptly at him, straight at him, and he dropped to one side. The figure flashed past. It ran effortlessly, face without expression, dodging and jumping as the energy beams seared around it.

For an instant the golden face loomed up before Baines. It passed and disappeared down a side corridor. Guards rushed after it, kneeling and firing, shouting orders excitedly. In the bowels of the building, heavy guns were rumbling up. Locks slid into place as escape corridors were systematically sealed off.

'Good God,' Baines gasped, as he got to his feet. 'Can't he do anything but run?'

'I gave orders,' Wisdom said, 'to have the building isolated. There's no way out. Nobody comes and nobody goes. He's loose here in the building–but he won't get out.'

'If there's one exit overlooked, he'll know it,' Anita pointed out shakily.

'We won't overlook any exit. We got him once; we'll get him again.'

A messenger robot had come in. Now it presented its message respectfully to Wisdom. 'From analysis, sir.'

Wisdom tore the tape open. 'Now we'll know how it thinks.' His hands were shaking. 'Maybe we can figure out its blind spot. It may be able to out-think us, but that doesn't mean it's invulnerable. It only predicts the future–it can't change it. If there's only death ahead, its ability won't . . .'

Wisdom's voice faded into silence. After a moment he passed the tape to Baines.

'I'll be down in the bar,' Wisdom said. 'Getting a good stiff drink.' His face had turned lead-gray. 'All I can say is *I hope to hell this isn't the race to come.*'

'What's the analysis?' Anita demanded impatiently, peering over Baines' shoulder. 'How does it think?'

'It doesn't,' Baines said, as he handed the tape back to his boss. 'It doesn't think at all. Virtually no frontal lobe. It's not a human being–it doesn't use symbols. It's nothing but an animal.'

'An animal,' Wisdom said. 'With a single highly-developed faculty. Not a superior man. Not a man at all.'

Up and down the corridors of the DCA Building, guards and equipment clanged. Loads of Civil Police were pouring into the building and taking up positions beside the guards. One by one, the corridors and rooms were being inspected and sealed off. Sooner or later the golden figure of Cris Johnson would be located and cornered.

'We were always afraid a mutant with superior intellectual

powers would come along,' Baines said reflectively. 'A deeve who would be to us what we are to the great apes. Something with a bulging cranium, telepathic ability, a perfect semantic system, ultimate powers of symbolization and calculation. A development along our own path. A better human being.'

'He acts by reflex,' Anita said wonderingly. She had the analysis and was sitting at one of the desks studying it intently. 'Reflex–like a lion. A golden lion.' She pushed the tape aside, a strange expression on her face. 'The lion god.'

'Beast,' Wisdom corrected tartly. 'Blond beast, you mean.'

'He runs fast,' Baines said, 'and that's all. No tools. He doesn't build anything or utilize anything outside himself. He just stands and waits for the right opportunity and then he runs like hell.'

'This is worse than anything we've anticipated,' Wisdom said. His beefy face was lead-gray. He sagged like an old man, his blunt hands trembling and uncertain. 'To be replaced by an animal! Something that runs and hides. Something without a language!' He spat savagely. 'That's why they weren't able to communicate with it. We wondered what kind of semantic system it had. It hasn't got any! No more ability to talk and think than a–dog.'

'That means intelligence has failed,' Baines went on huskily. 'We're the last of our line–like the dinosaur. We've carried intelligence as far as it'll go. Too far, maybe. We've already got to the point where we know so much–think so much–we can't act.'

'Men of thought,' Anita said. 'Not men of action. It's begun to have a paralyzing effect. But this thing–'

'This thing's faculty works better than ours ever did. We can recall past experiences, keep them in mind, learn from them. At best, we can make shrewd guesses about the future, from our memory of what's happened in the past. But we can't be certain. We have to speak of probabilities. Grays. Not blacks and whites. We're only guessing.'

'Cris Johnson isn't guessing,' Anita added.

'He can look ahead. See what's coming. He can–prethink. Let's call it that. He can see into the future. Probably he doesn't perceive it as the future.'

'No,' Anita said thoughtfully. 'It would seem like the present. He has a broader present. But his present lies ahead, not back. Our present is related to the past. Only the past is certain, to us. To him, the future is certain. And he probably doesn't remember the past, any more than any animal remembers what happened.'

'As he develops,' Baines said, 'as his race evolves, it'll probably expand its ability to prethink. Instead of ten minutes, thirty minutes. Then an hour. A day. A year. Eventually they'll be able to keep ahead a whole lifetime. Each one of them will live in a solid, unchanging world. There'll be no variables, no uncertainty. No motion! They won't have anything to fear. Their world will be perfectly static, a solid block of matter.'

'And when death comes,' Anita said, 'they'll accept it. There won't be any struggle; to them, it'll already have happened.'

'*Already have happened*,' Baines repeated. 'To Cris, our shots had already been fired.' He laughed harshly. 'Superior survival doesn't mean superior man. If there were another world-wide flood, only fish would survive. If there were another ice age, maybe nothing but polar bears would be left. When we opened the lock, he had already seen the men, seen exactly where they were standing and what they'd do. A neat faculty–but not a development of mind. A pure physical *sense*.'

'But if every exit is covered,' Wisdom repeated, 'he'll see he can't get out. He gave himself up before–he'll give himself up again.' He shook his head. 'An animal. Without language. Without tools.'

'With his new sense,' Baines said, 'he doesn't need anything else.' He examined his watch. 'It's after two. Is the building completely sealed off?'

'You can't leave,' Wisdom stated. 'You'll have to stay here all night–or until we catch the bastard.'

'I meant her.' Baines indicated Anita. 'She's supposed to be back at Semantics by seven in the morning.'

Wisdom shrugged. 'I have no control over her. If she wants, she can check out.'

'I'll stay,' Anita decided. 'I want to be here when he–when he's destroyed. I'll sleep here.' She hesitated. 'Wisdom, isn't there some other way? If he's just an animal couldn't we–'

'A zoo?' Wisdom's voice rose in a frenzy of hysteria. 'Keep it penned up in the zoo? Christ no! It's got to be killed!'

For a long time the great gleaming shape crouched in the darkness. He was in a store room. Boxes and cartons stretched out on all sides, heaped up in orderly rows, all neatly counted and marked. Silent and deserted.

But in a few moments people burst in and searched the room. He could see this. He saw them in all parts of the room, clear and distinct, men with lash-tubes, grim-faced, stalking with murder in their eyes.

The sight was one of many. One of a multitude of clearly-etched scenes lying tangent to his own. And to each was attached a further multitude of interlocking scenes, that finally grew hazier and dwindled away. A progressive vagueness, each syndrome less distinct.

But the immediate one, the scene that lay closest to him, was clearly visible. He could easily make out the sight of the armed men. Therefore it was necessary to be out of the room before they appeared.

The golden figure got calmly to its feet and moved to the door. The corridor was empty; he could see himself already outside, in the vacant, drumming hall of metal and recessed lights. He pushed the door boldly open and stepped out.

A lift blinked across the hall. He walked to the lift and entered it. In five minutes a group of guards would come running along and leap into the lift. By that time he would have left it and sent it back down. Now he pressed a button and rose to the next floor.

He stepped out into a deserted passage. No one was in sight. That didn't surprise him. He couldn't be surprised. The element didn't exist for him. The positions of things, the space relationships of all matter in the immediate future, were as certain for him as his own body. The only thing that was unknown was that which had already passed out of being. In a vague, dim fashion, he had occasionally wondered where things went after he had passed them.

He came to a small supply closet. It had just been searched. It would be a half hour before anyone opened it again. He had that long; he could see that far ahead. And then–

And then he would be able to see another area, a region farther beyond. He was always moving, advancing into new regions he had never seen before. A constantly unfolding panorama of sights and scenes, frozen landscapes spread out ahead. All objects were fixed. Pieces on a vast chess board through which he moved, arms folded, face calm. A detached observer who saw objects that lay ahead of him as clearly as those under foot.

Right now, as he crouched in the small supply closet, he saw an unusually varied multitude of scenes for the next half hour. Much lay ahead. The half hour was divided into an incredibly complex pattern of separate configurations. He had reached a critical region; he was about to move through worlds of intricate complexity.

He concentrated on a scene ten minutes away. It showed, like a three-dimensional still, a heavy gun at the end of the corridor, trained all the way to the far end. Men moved cautiously from door to door, checking each room again, as they had done repeatedly. At the end of the half hour they had reached the supply closet. A scene showed them looking inside. By that time he was gone, of course. He wasn't in that scene. He had passed on to another.

The next scene showed an exit. Guards stood in a solid line. No way out. He was in that scene. Off to one side, in a niche just inside the door. The street outside was visible, stars, lights, outlines of passing cars and people.

In the next tableau he had gone back, away from the exit. There was no way out. In another tableau he saw himself at other exits, a legion of golden figures, duplicated again and again, as he explored regions ahead, one after another. But each exit was covered.

In one dim scene he saw himself lying charred and dead; he had tried to run through the line, out the exit.

But that scene was vague. One wavering, indistinct still out of many. The inflexible path along which he moved would not deviate in that direction. It would not turn him that way. The golden figure in that scene, the miniature doll in that room, was only distantly related to him. It was himself, but a far-away self. A self he would never meet. He forgot it and went on to examine the other tableaux.

The myriad of tableaux that surrounded him were an elaborate maze, a web which he now considered bit by bit. He was looking down into a doll's house of infinite rooms, rooms without number, each with its furniture, its dolls, all rigid and unmoving. The same dolls and furniture were repeated in many. He, himself, appeared often. The two men on the platform. The woman. Again and again the same combinations turned up; the play was redone frequently, the same actors and props moved around in all possible ways.

Before it was time to leave the supply closet, Cris Johnson had examined each of the rooms tangent to the one he now occupied. He had consulted each, considered its contents thoroughly.

He pushed the door open and stepped calmly out into the hall. He knew exactly where he was going. And what he had to do. Crouched in the stuffy closet, he had quietly and expertly examined each miniature of himself, observed which clearly-etched configuration lay along his inflexible path, the one room of the doll's house, the one set out of legions, toward which he was moving.

Anita slipped out of her metal foil dress, hung it over a hanger, then unfastened her shoes and kicked them under the bed. She was just starting to unclip her bra when the door opened.

She gasped. Soundlessly, calmly, the great golden shape closed the door and bolted it after him.

Anita snatched up her lash-tube from the dressing table. Her hand shook; her whole body was trembling. 'What do you want?' she demanded. Her fingers tightened convulsively around the tube. 'I'll kill you.'

The figure regarded her silently, arms folded. It was the first time she had seen Cris Johnson closely. The great dignified face, handsome and impassive. Broad shoulders. The golden mane of hair, golden skin, pelt of radiant fuzz–

'Why?' she demanded breathlessly. Her heart was pounding wildly. 'What do you want?'

She could kill him easily. But the lash-tube wavered. Cris Johnson stood without fear; he wasn't at all afraid. Why not? Didn't he understand what it was? What the small metal tube could do to him?

'Of course,' she said suddenly, in a choked whisper. 'You can see ahead. You know I'm not going to kill you. Or you wouldn't have come here.'

She flushed, terrified–and embarrassed. He knew exactly what she was going to do; he could see it as easily as she saw the walls of the room, the wall-bed with its covers folded neatly back, her clothes hanging in the closet, her purse and small things on the dressing table.

'All right.' Anita backed away, then abruptly put the tube down on the dressing table. 'I won't kill you. Why should I?' She fumbled in her purse and got out her cigarettes. Shakily, she lit up, her pulse racing. She was scared. And strangely fascinated. 'Do you expect to stay here? It won't do any good. They've come through the dorm twice, already. They'll be back.'

Could he understand her? She saw nothing on his face, only blank dignity. God, he was huge! It wasn't possible he was only eighteen, a boy, a child. He looked more like some great golden god, come down to earth.

She shook the thought off savagely. He wasn't a god. He was a beast. *The blond beast*, come to take the place of man. To drive man from the earth.

Anita snatched up the lash-tube. 'Get out of here! You're an animal! A big stupid animal! You can't even understand what I'm saying–you don't even have a language. You're not human.'

Cris Johnson remained silent. As if he were waiting. Waiting for what? He showed no sign of fear or impatience, even though the corridor outside rang with the sound of men searching, metal against metal, guns and energy tubes being dragged around, shouts and dim rumbles as section after section of the building was searched and sealed off.

'They'll get you,' Anita said. 'You'll be trapped here. They'll be searching this wing any moment.' She savagely stubbed out her cigarette. 'For God's sake, what do you expect *me* to do?'

Cris moved toward her. Anita shrank back. His powerful hands caught hold of her and she gasped in sudden terror. For a moment she struggled blindly, desperately.

'Let go!' She broke away and leaped back from him. His face was expressionless. Calmly, he came toward her, an impassive god advancing to take her. 'Get away!' She groped for the lash-tube, trying to get up. But the tube slipped from her fingers and rolled onto the floor.

Cris bent down and picked it up. He held it out to her, in the open palm of his hand.

'Good God,' Anita whispered. Shakily, she accepted the tube, gripped it hesitantly, then put it down again on the dressing table.

In the half-light of the room, the great golden figure seemed to glow and shimmer, outlined against the darkness. A god–no, not a god. An animal. A great golden beast, without a soul. She was confused. Which was he–or was he both? She shook her head, bewildered. It was late, almost four. She was exhausted and confused.

Cris took her in his arms. Gently, kindly, he lifted her face and kissed her. His powerful hands held her tight. She couldn't breathe. Darkness, mixed with the shimmering golden haze, swept around her. Around and around it spiralled, carrying her senses away. She sank down into it gratefully. The darkness covered her and dissolved her in a swelling torrent of sheer force that mounted in intensity each moment, until the roar of it beat against her and at last blotted out everything.

Anita blinked. She sat up and automatically pushed her hair into place. Cris was standing before the closet. He was reaching up, getting something down.

He turned toward her and tossed something on the bed. Her heavy metal foil traveling cape.

Anita gazed down at the cape without comprehension. 'What do you want?'

Cris stood by the bed, waiting.

She picked up the cape uncertainly. Cold creepers of fear plucked at her. 'You want me to get you out of here,' she said softly. 'Past the guards and the CP.'

Cris said nothing.

'They'll kill you instantly.' She got unsteadily to her feet. 'You can't run past them. Good God, don't you do anything but run? There must be a better way. Maybe I can appeal to Wisdom. I'm Class A–Director Class. I can go directly to the Full Directorate. I ought to be able to hold them off, keep back the euth indefinitely. The odds are a billion to one against us if we try to break past–'

She broke off.

'But you don't gamble,' she continued slowly. 'You don't go by odds. You *know* what's coming. You've seen the cards already.' She studied his face intently. 'No, you can't be cold-decked. It wouldn't be possible.'

For a moment she stood deep in thought. Then with a quick, decisive motion, she snatched up the cloak and slipped it around her bare shoulders. She fastened the heavy belt, bent down and got her shoes from under the bed, snatched up her purse, and hurried to the door.

'Come on,' she said. She was breathing quickly, cheeks flushed. 'Let's go. While there are still a number of exits to choose from. My car is parked outside, in the lot at the side of the building. We can get to my place in an hour. I have a winter home in Argentina. If worst comes to worst we can fly there. It's in the back country, away from the cities. Jungle and swamps. Cut off from almost everything.' Eagerly she started to open the door.

Cris reached out and stopped her. Gently, patiently, he moved in front of her.

He waited a long time, body rigid. Then he turned the knob and stepped boldly out into the corridor.

The corridor was empty. No one was in sight. Anita caught a faint glimpse, the back of a guard hurrying off. If they had come out a second earlier–

Cris started down the corridor. She ran after him. He moved rapidly, effortlessly. The girl had trouble keeping up with him. He seemed to know exactly where to go. Off to the right, down a side hall, a supply passage. Onto an ascent freight-lift. They rose, then abruptly halted.

Cris waited again. Presently he slid the door back and moved out of the lift. Anita followed nervously. She could hear sounds: guns and men, very close.

They were near an exit. A double line of guards stood directly ahead. Twenty men, a solid wall–and a massive heavy-duty robot gun in the center. The men were alert, faces strained and tense. Watching wide-eyed, guns gripped tight. A Civil Police officer was in charge.

'We'll never get past,' Anita gasped. 'We wouldn't get ten feet.' She pulled back. 'They'll–'

Cris took her by the arm and continued calmly forward. Blind terror leaped inside her. She fought wildly to get away, but his fingers were like steel. She couldn't pry them loose. Quietly, irresistibly, the great golden creature drew her along beside him toward the double line of guards.

'*There he is!*' Guns went up. Men leaped into action. The barrel of the robot cannon swung around. '*Get him!*'

Anita was paralyzed. She sagged against the powerful body beside her, tugged along helplessly by his inflexible grasp. The lines of guards came nearer, a sheer wall of guns. Anita fought to control her terror. She stumbled, half-fell. Cris supported her effortlessly. She scratched, fought at him, struggled to get loose–

'Don't shoot!' she screamed.

Guns wavered uncertainly. 'Who is she?' The guards were moving around, trying to get a sight on Cris without including her. 'Who's he got there?'

One of them saw the stripe on her sleeve. Red and black. Director Class. Top-level.

'She's Class A.' Shocked, the guards retreated. 'Miss, get out of the way!'

Anita found her voice. 'Don't shoot. He's–in my custody. You understand? I'm taking him out.'

The wall of guards moved back nervously. 'No one's supposed to pass. Director Wisdom gave orders–'

'I'm not subject to Wisdom's authority.' She managed to edge her voice with a harsh crispness. 'Get out of the way. I'm taking him to the Semantics Agency.'

For a moment nothing happened. There was no reaction. Then slowly, uncertainly, one guard stepped aside.

Cris moved. A blur of speed, away from Anita, past the confused guards, through the breach in the line, out the exit, and onto the street. Bursts of energy flashed wildly after him. Shouting guards milled out. Anita was left behind, forgotten. The guards, the heavy-duty gun, were pouring out into the early morning darkness. Sirens wailed. Patrol cars roared into life.

Anita stood dazed, confused, leaning against the wall, trying to get her breath.

He was gone. He had left her. Good God–what had she done? She shook her head, bewildered, her face buried in her hands. She had been hypnotized. She had lost her will, her common sense. Her reason! The animal, the great golden beast, had tricked her. Taken advantage of her. And now he was gone, escaped into the night.

Miserable, agonized tears trickled through her clenched fingers. She rubbed at them futilely; but they kept on coming.

'He's gone,' Baines said. 'We'll never get him, now. He's probably a million miles from here.'

Anita sat huddled in the corner, her face to the wall. A little bent heap, broken and wretched.

Wisdom paced back and forth. 'But where can he go? Where can he hide? Nobody'll hide him! Everybody knows the law about deeves!'

'He's lived out in the woods most of his life. He'll hunt–that's what he's always done. They wondered what he was up to, off by himself. He was catching game and sleeping under trees.' Baines laughed harshly. 'And the first woman he meets will be glad to hide him–as *she* was.' He indicated Anita with a jerk of his thumb.

'So all that gold, that mane, that god-like stance, was *for* something. Not just ornament.' Wisdom's thick lips twisted. 'He doesn't have just one faculty–he has two. One is new, the newest thing in survival method. The other is old as life.' He stopped pacing to glare at the huddled shape in the corner. 'Plumage. Bright feathers, combs for the rooster, swans, birds, bright scales for the fish. Gleaming pelts and manes for the animals. An animal isn't necessarily *bestial.* Lions aren't bestial. Or tigers. Or any of the big cats. They're anything but bestial.'

'He'll never have to worry,' Baines said. 'He'll get by–as long as human women exist to take care of him. And since he can see ahead, into the future, he already knows he's sexually irresistible to human females.'

'We'll get him,' Wisdom muttered. 'I've had the Government declare an emergency. Military and Civil Police will be looking for him. Armies of men–a whole planet of experts, the most advanced machines and equipment. We'll flush him, sooner or later.'

'By that time it won't make any difference,' Baines said. He put his hand on Anita's shoulder and patted her ironically. 'You'll have company, sweetheart. You won't be the only one. You're just the first of a long procession.'

'Thanks,' Anita grated.

'The oldest survival method and the newest. Combined to form one perfectly adapted animal. How the hell are we going to stop him? We can put *you* through a sterilization tank–but we can't pick them all up, all the women he meets along the way. And if we miss one we're finished.'

'We'll have to keep trying,' Wisdom said. 'Round up as many as we can. Before they can spawn.' Faint hope glinted in his tired, sagging face. 'Maybe his characteristics are recessive. Maybe ours will cancel his out.'

'I wouldn't lay any money on that,' Baines said. 'I think I know already which of the two strains is going to turn up dominant.' He grinned wryly. 'I mean, I'm making a good *guess*. It won't be us.'

THE TURNING WHEEL

Bard Chai said thoughtfully, 'Cults.' He examined a tape-report grinding from the receptor. The receptor was rusty and unoiled; it whined piercingly and sent up an acrid wisp of smoke. Chai shut it off as its pitted surface began to heat ugly red. Presently he finished with the tape and tossed it with a heap of refuse jamming the mouth of a disposal slot.

'What about cults?' Bard Sung-wu asked faintly. He brought himself back with an effort, and forced a smile of interest on his plump olive-yellow face. 'You were saying?'

'Any stable society is menaced by cults; our society is no exception.' Chai rubbed his finely-tapered fingers together reflectively. 'Certain lower strata are axiomatically dissatisfied. Their hearts burn with envy of those the wheel has placed above them; in secret they form fanatic, rebellious bands. They meet in the dark of night; they insidiously express inversions of accepted norms; they delight in flouting basic mores and customs.'

'Ugh,' Sung-wu agreed. 'I mean,' he explained quickly, 'it seems incredible people could practice such fanatic and disgusting rites.' He got nervously to his feet. 'I must go, if it's permitted.'

'Wait,' snapped Chai. 'You are familiar with the Detroit area?'

Uneasily, Sung-wu nodded. 'Very slightly.'

With characteristic vigor, Chai made his decision. 'I'm sending you; investigate and make a blue-slip report. If this group is dangerous, the Holy Arm should know. It's of the worst elements–the Techno class.' He made a wry face. 'Caucasians, hulking, hairy things. We'll give you six months in Spain, on your return; you can poke over ruins of abandoned cities.'

'Caucasians!' Sung-wu exclaimed, his face turning green. 'But I haven't been well; please, if somebody else could go–'

'You, perhaps, hold to the Broken Feather theory?' Chai raised an eyebrow. 'An amazing philologist, Broken Feather; I took partial instruction from him. He held, you know, the Caucasian to be descended of Neanderthal stock. Their extreme size, thick body hair, their general brutish cast, reveal an innate inability to comprehend anything but a purely animalistic horizontal; proselytism is a waste of time.'

He affixed the younger man with a stern eye. 'I wouldn't send you, if I didn't have unusual faith in your devotion.'

Sung-wu fingered his beads miserably. 'Elron be praised,' he muttered; 'you are too kind.'

Sung-wu slid into a lift and was raised, amid great groans and whirrings and false stops, to the top level of the Central Chamber building. He hurried down a corridor dimly lit by occasional yellow bulbs. A moment later he approached the doors of the scanning offices and flashed his identification at the robot guard. 'Is Bard Fei-p'ang within?' he inquired.

'Verily,' the robot answered, stepping aside.

Sung-wu entered the offices, bypassed the rows of rusted, discarded machines, and entered the still-functioning wing. He located his brother-in-law, hunched over some graphs at one of the desks, laboriously copying material by hand. 'Clearness be with you,' Sung-wu murmured.

Fei-p'ang glanced up in annoyance. 'I told you not to come again; if the Arm finds out I'm letting you use the scanner for a personal plot, they'll stretch me on the rack.'

'Gently,' Sung-wu murmured, his hand on his relation's shoulder. 'This is the last time. I'm going away; one more look, a final look.' His olive face took on a pleading, piteous cast. 'The turn comes for me very soon; this will be our last conversation.'

Sung-wu's piteous look hardened into cunning. 'You wouldn't

want it on your soul; no restitution will be possible at this late date.'

Fei-p'ang snorted. 'All right; but for Elron's sake, do it quickly.'

Sung-wu hurried to the mother-scanner and seated himself in the rickety basket. He snapped on the controls, clamped his forehead to the viewpiece, inserted his identity tab, and set the space-time finger into motion. Slowly, reluctantly, the ancient mechanism coughed into life and began tracing his personal tab along the future track.

Sung-wu's hands shook; his body trembled; sweat dripped from his neck, as he saw himself scampering in miniature. *Poor Sung-wu*, he thought wretchedly. The mite of a thing hurried about its duties; this was but eight months hence. Harried and beset, it performed its tasks–and then, in a subsequent continuum, fell down and died.

Sung-wu removed his eyes from the viewpiece and waited for his pulse to slow. He could stand that part, watching the moment of death; it was what came next that was too jangling for him.

He breathed a silent prayer. Had he fasted enough? In the four-day purge and self-flagellation, he had used the whip with metal points, the heaviest possible. He had given away all his money; he had smashed a lovely vase his mother had left him, a treasured heirloom; he had rolled in the filth and mud in the center of town. Hundreds had seen him. Now, surely, all this was enough. But time was so short!

Faint courage stirring, he sat up and again put his eyes to the viewpiece. He was shaking with terror. What if it hadn't changed? What if his mortification weren't enough? He spun the controls, sending the finger tracing his time-track past the moment of death.

Sung-wu shrieked and scrambled back in horror. His future was the same, exactly the same; there had been no change at all. His guilt had been too great to be washed away in such short a time; it would take ages–and he didn't have ages.

He left the scanner and passed by his brother-in-law. 'Thanks,' he muttered shakily.

For once, a measure of compassion touched Fei-p'ang's efficient brown features. 'Bad news? The next turn brings an unfortunate manifestation?'

'Bad scarcely describes it.'

Fei-p'ang's pity turned to righteous rebuke. 'Who do you have to blame but yourself?' he demanded sternly. 'You know your conduct in this manifestation determines the next; if you look forward to a future life as a lower animal, it should make you glance over your behavior and repent your wrongs. The cosmic law that governs us is impartial. It is true justice: cause and effect; what you do determines what you next become–there can be no blame and no sorrow. There can be only understanding and repentance.' His curiosity overcame him. 'What is it? A snake? A squirrel?'

'It's no affair of yours,' Sung-wu said, as he moved unhappily toward the exit doors.

'I'll look myself.'

'Go ahead.' Sung-wu pushed moodily out into the hall. He was dazed with despair: it hadn't changed; it was still the same.

In eight months he would die, stricken by one of the numerous plagues that swept over the inhabited parts of the world. He would become feverish, break out with red spots, turn and twist in an anguish of delirium. His bowels would drop out; his flesh would waste away; his eyes would roll up; and after an interminable time of suffering, he would die. His body would lie in a mass heap, with hundreds of others–a whole streetful of dead, to be carted away by one of the robot sweepers, happily immune. His mortal remains would be burned in a common rubbish incinerator at the outskirts of the city.

Meanwhile, the eternal spark, Sung-wu's divine soul, would hurry from this space-time manifestation to the next in order. But it would not rise; it would sink; he had watched its descent on the scanner many times. There was always the same hideous picture–a sight beyond endurance–of his soul, as it plummeted down like a stone, into one of the lowest continua, a sinkhole of a manifestation at the very bottom of the ladder.

He had sinned. In his youth, Sung-wu had got mixed up with a black-eyed wench with long flowing hair, a glittering waterfall down her back and shoulders. Inviting red lips, plump breasts, hips that undulated and beckoned unmistakably. She was the wife of a friend, from the Warrior class, but he had taken her as his mistress; he had been *certain* time remained to rectify his venality.

But he was wrong: the wheel was soon to turn for him. The plague–not enough time to fast and pray and do good works. He was determined to go down, straight down to a wallowing, foul-aired planet in a stinking red-sun system, an ancient pit of filth and decay and unending slime–a jungle world of the lowest type.

In it, he would be a shiny-winged fly, a great blue-bottomed, buzzing carrion-eater that hummed and guzzled and crawled through the rotting carcasses of great lizards, slain in combat.

From this swamp, this pest-ridden planet in a diseased, contaminated system, he would have to rise painfully up the endless rungs of the cosmic ladder he had already climbed. It had taken eons to climb this far, to the level of a human being on the planet Earth, in the bright yellow Sol system; now he would have to do it all over again.

Chai beamed, 'Elron be with you,' as the corroded observation ship was checked by the robot crew, and finally okayed for limited flight. Sung-wu slowly entered the ship and seated himself at what remained of the controls. He waved listlessly, then slammed the lock and bolted it by hand.

As the ship limped into the late afternoon sky, he reluctantly consulted the reports and records Chai had transferred to him.

The Tinkerists were a small cult; they claimed only a few hundred members, all drawn from the Techno class, which was the most despised of the social castes. The Bards, of course, were at the top; they were the teachers of society, the holy men who guided man to clearness. Then the Poets; they turned into saga the great legends of Elron Hu, who lived (according to legend) in the hideous days of the Time of Madness. Below the Poets were the Artists; then the

Musicians; then the Workers, who supervised the robot crews. After them the Businessmen, the Warriors, the Farmers, and finally, at the bottom, the Technos.

Most of the Technos were Caucasians—immense white-skinned things, incredibly hairy, like apes; their resemblance to the great apes was striking. Perhaps Broken Feather was right; perhaps they did have Neanderthal blood and were outside the possibility of clearness. Sung-wu had always considered himself an anti-racist; he disliked those who maintained the Caucasians were a race apart. Extremists believed eternal damage would result to the species if the Caucasians were allowed to intermarry.

In any case, the problem was academic; no decent, self-respecting woman of the higher classes—of Indian or Mongolian, or Bantu stock—would allow herself to be approached by a *Cauc*.

Below his ship, the barren countryside spread out, ugly and bleak. Great red spots that hadn't yet been overgrown, and slag surfaces were still visible—but by this time most ruins were covered by soil and crabgrass. He could see men and robots farming; villages, countless tiny brown circles in the green fields; occasional ruins of ancient cities—gaping sores like blind mouths, eternally open to the sky. They would never close, not now.

Ahead was the Detroit area, named, so it ran, for some now-forgotten spiritual leader. There were more villages, here. Off to his left, the leaden surface of a body of water, a lake of some kind. Beyond that—only Elron knew. No one went that far; there was no human life there, only wild animals and deformed things spawned from radiation infestation still lying heavy in the north.

He dropped his ship down. An open field lay to his right; a robot farmer was plowing with a metal hook welded to its waist, a section torn off some discarded machine. It stopped dragging the hook and gazed up in amazement, as Sung-wu landed the ship awkwardly and bumped to a halt.

'Clearness be with you,' the robot rasped obediently, as Sung-wu climbed out.

Sung-wu gathered up his bundle of reports and papers and

stuffed them in a briefcase. He snapped the ship's lock and hurried off toward the ruins of the city. The robot went back to dragging the rusty metal hook through the hard ground, its pitted body bent double with the strain, working slowly, silently, uncomplaining.

The little boy piped, 'Whither, Bard?' as Sung-wu pushed wearily through the tangled debris and slag. He was a little black-faced Bantu, in red rags sewed and patched together. He ran alongside Sung-wu like a puppy, leaping and bounding and grinning white-teethed.

Sung-wu became immediately crafty; his intrigue with the black-haired girl had taught him elemental dodges and evasions. 'My ship broke down,' he answered cautiously; it was certainly common enough. 'It was the last ship still in operation at our field.'

The boy skipped and laughed and broke off bits of green weeds that grew along the trail. 'I know somebody who can fix it,' he cried carelessly.

Sung-wu's pulse-rate changed. 'Oh?' he murmured, as if uninterested. 'There are those around here who practice the questionable art of repairing?'

The boy nodded solemnly.

'Technos?' Sung-wu pursued. 'Are there many of them here, around these old ruins?'

More black-faced boys, and some little dark-eyed Bantu girls, came scampering through the slag and ruins. 'What's the matter with your ship?' one hollered at Sung-wu. 'Won't it run?'

They all ran and shouted around him, as he advanced slowly—an unusually wild bunch, completely undisciplined. They rolled and fought and tumbled and chased each other around madly.

'How many of you,' Sung-wu demanded, 'have taken your first instruction?'

There was a sudden uneasy silence. The children looked at each other guiltily; none of them answered.

'Good Elron!' Sung-wu exclaimed in horror. 'Are you all untaught?'

Heads hung guiltily.

'How do you expect to phase yourselves with the cosmic will?

How can you expect to know the divine plan? This is really too much!'

He pointed a plump finger at one of the boys. 'Are you constantly preparing yourself for the life to come? Are you constantly purging and purifying yourself? Do you deny yourself meat, sex, entertainment, financial gain, education, leisure?'

But it was obvious; their unrestrained laughter and play proved they were still jangled, far from clear–And clearness is the only road by which a person can gain understanding of the eternal plan, the cosmic wheel which turns endlessly, for all living things.

'Butterflies!' Sung-wu snorted with disgust. 'You are no better than the beasts and birds of the field, who take no heed of the morrow. You play and game for today, thinking tomorrow won't come. Like insects–'

But the thought of insects reminded him of the shiny-winged blue-rumped fly, creeping over a rotting lizard carcass, and Sung-wu's stomach did a flip-flop; he forced it back in place and strode on, toward the line of villages emerging ahead.

Farmers were working the barren fields on all sides. A thin layer of soil over slag; a few limp wheat stalks waved, thin and emaciated. The ground was terrible, the worst he had seen. He could feel the metal under his feet; it was almost to the surface. Bent men and women watered their sickly crops with tin cans, old metal containers picked from the ruins. An ox was pulling a crude cart.

In another field, women were weeding by hand; all moved slowly, stupidly, victims of hookworms, from the soil. They were all barefoot. The children hadn't picked it up yet, but they soon would.

Sung-wu gazed up at the sky and gave thanks to Elron; here, suffering was unusually severe; trials of exceptional vividness lay on every hand. These men and women were being tempered in a hot crucible; their souls were probably purified to an astonishing degree. A baby lay in the shade, beside a half-dozing mother. Flies crawled over its eyes; its mother breathed heavily, hoarsely, her mouth open. An unhealthy flush discolored her brown cheeks.

Her belly bulged; she was already pregnant again. Another eternal soul to be raised from a lower level. Her great breasts sagged and wobbled as she stirred in her sleep, spilling out over her dirty wraparound.

'Come here,' Sung-wu called sharply to the gang of black-faced children who followed along after him. 'I'm going to talk to you.'

The children approached, eyes on the ground, and assembled in a silent circle around him. Sung-wu sat down, placed his briefcase beside him and folded his legs expertly under him in the traditional posture outlined by Elron in his seventh book of teaching.

'I will ask and you will answer,' Sung-wu stated. 'You know the basic catechisms?' He peered sharply around. 'Who knows the basic catechisms?'

One or two hands went up. Most of the children looked away unhappily.

'First!' snapped Sung-wu. '*Who are you?* You are a minute fragment of the cosmic plan.

'Second! *What are you?* A mere speck in a system so vast as to be beyond comprehension.

'Third! *What is the way of life?* To fulfill what is required by the cosmic forces.

'Fourth! *Where are you?* On one step of the cosmic ladder.

'Fifth! *Where have you been?* Through endless steps; each turn of the wheel advances or depresses you.

'Sixth! *What determines your direction at the next turn?* Your conduct in this manifestation.

'Seventh! *What is right conduct?* Submitting yourself to the eternal forces, the cosmic elements that make up the divine plan.

'Eighth! *What is the significance of suffering?* To purify the soul.

'Ninth! *What is the significance of death?* To release the person from this manifestation, so he may rise to a new rung of the ladder.

'Tenth–'

But at that moment Sung-wu broke off. Two quasi-human shapes were approaching him. Immense white-skinned figures striding across the baked fields, between the sickly rows of wheat.

Technos–coming to meet him; his flesh crawled. Caucs. Their skin glittered pale and unhealthy, like nocturnal insects, dug from under rocks.

He rose to his feet, conquered his disgust, and prepared to greet them.

Sung-wu said, 'Clearness!' He could smell them, a musky sheep smell, as they came to a halt in front of him. Two bucks, two immense sweating males, skin damp and sticky, with beards, and long disorderly hair. They wore sailcloth trousers and boots. With horror Sung-wu perceived a thick body-hair, on their chests, like woven mats–tufts in their armpits, on their arms, wrists, even the backs of their hands. Maybe Broken Feather was right; perhaps, in these great lumbering blond-haired beasts, the archaic Neanderthal stock–the false men–still survived. He could almost see the ape, peering from behind their blue eyes.

'Hi,' the first Cauc said. After a moment he added reflectively, 'My name's Jamison.'

'Pete Ferris,' the other grunted. Neither of them observed the customary deferences; Sung-wu winced but managed not to show it. Was it deliberate, a veiled insult, or perhaps mere ignorance? This was hard to tell; in lower classes there was, as Chai said, an ugly undercurrent of resentment and envy, and hostility.

'I'm making a routine survey,' Sung-wu explained, 'on birth and death rates in rural areas. I'll be here a few days. Is there some place I can stay? Some public inn or hostel?'

The two Cauc bucks were silent. 'Why?' one of them demanded bluntly.

Sung-wu blinked. 'Why? Why what?'

'Why are you making a survey? If you want any information we'll supply it.'

Sung-wu was incredulous. 'Do you know to whom you're talking? I'm a Bard! Why, you're ten classes down; how dare you–' He choked with rage. In these rural areas the Technos had utterly forgotten their place. What was ailing the local Bards? Were they letting the system break apart?

He shuddered violently at the thought of what it would mean if Technos and Farmers and Businessmen were allowed to intermingle—even intermarry, and eat, and drink, in the same places. The whole structure of society would collapse. If all were to ride the same carts, use the same outhouses; it passed belief. A sudden nightmare picture loomed up before Sung-wu, of Technos living and mating with women of the Bard and Poet classes. He visioned a horizontally-oriented society, all persons on the same level, with horror. It went against the very grain of the cosmos, against the divine plan; it was the Time of Madness all over again. He shuddered.

'Where is the Manager of this area?' he demanded. 'Take me to him; I'll deal directly with him.'

The two Caucs turned and headed back the way they had come, without a word. After a moment of fury, Sung-wu followed behind them.

They led him through withered fields and over barren, eroded hills on which nothing grew; the ruins increased. At the edge of the city, a line of meager villages had been set up; he saw leaning, rickety wood huts, and mud streets. From the villages a thick stench rose, the smell of offal and death.

Dogs lay sleeping under the huts; children poked and played in the filth and rotting debris. A few old people sat on porches, vacant-faced, eyes glazed and dull. Chickens pecked around, and he saw pigs and skinny cats—and the eternal rusting piles of metal, sometimes thirty feet high. Great towers of red slag were heaped up everywhere.

Beyond the villages were the ruins proper—endless miles of abandoned wreckage; skeletons of buildings; concrete walls; bathtubs and pipe; overturned wrecks that had been cars. All these were from the Time of Madness, the decade that had finally rung the curtain down on the sorriest interval in man's history. The five centuries of madness and jangledness were now known as the Age of Heresy, when man had gone against the divine plan and taken his destiny in his own hands.

They came to a larger hut, a two-story wood structure. The Caucs climbed a decaying flight of steps; boards creaked and gave ominously under their heavy boots. Sung-wu followed them nervously; they came out on a porch, a kind of open balcony.

On the balcony sat a man, an obese copper-skinned official in unbuttoned breeches, his shiny black hair pulled back and tied with a bone against his bulging red neck. His nose was large and prominent, his face flat and wide, with many chins. He was drinking lime juice from a tin cup and gazing down at the mud street below. As the two Caucs appeared he rose slightly, a prodigious effort.

'This man,' the Cauc named Jamison said, indicating Sung-wu, 'wants to see you.'

Sung-wu pushed angrily forward. 'I am a Bard, from the Central Chamber; do you people recognize *this*?' He tore open his robe and flashed the symbol of the Holy Arm, gold worked to form a swathe of flaming red. 'I insist you accord me proper treatment! I'm not here to be pushed around by any–'

He had said too much; Sung-wu forced his anger down and gripped his briefcase. The fat Indian was studying him calmly; the two Caucs had wandered to the far end of the balcony and were squatting down in the shade. They lit crude cigarettes and turned their backs.

'Do you permit this?' Sung-wu demanded, incredulous. 'This–mingling?'

The Indian shrugged and sagged down even more in his chair. 'Clearness be with you,' he murmured; 'will you join me?' His calm expression remained unchanged; he seemed not to have noticed. 'Some lime juice? Or perhaps coffee? Lime juice is good for these.' He tapped his mouth; his soft gums were lined with caked sores.

'Nothing for me,' Sung-wu muttered grumpily, as he took a seat opposite the Indian; 'I'm here on an official survey.'

The Indian nodded faintly. 'Oh?'

'Birth and death rates.' Sung-wu hesitated, then leaned toward the Indian. 'I insist you send those two Caucs away; what I have to say to you is private.'

The Indian showed no change of expression; his broad face was utterly impassive. After a time he turned slightly. 'Please go down to the street level,' he ordered. 'As you will.'

The two Caucs got to their feet, grumbling, and pushed past the table, scowling and daring resentful glances at Sung-wu. One of them hawked and elaborately spat over the railing, an obvious insult.

'Insolence!' Sung-wu choked. 'How can you allow it? Did you see them? By Elron, it's beyond belief!'

The Indian shrugged indifferently–and belched. 'All men are brothers on the wheel. Didn't Elron Himself teach that, when He was on Earth?'

'Of course. But–'

'Are not even these men our brothers?'

'Naturally,' Sung-wu answered haughtily, 'but they must know their place; they're an insignificant class. In the rare event some object wants fixing, they're called; but in the last year I do not recall a single incident when it was deemed advisable to repair anything. The need of such a class diminishes yearly; eventually such a class and the elements composing it–'

'You perhaps advocate sterilization?' the Indian inquired, heavy-lidded and sly.

'I advocate *something*. The lower classes reproduce like rabbits; spawning all the time–much faster than we Bards. I always see some swollen-up Cauc woman, but hardly a single Bard is born these days; the lower classes must fornicate constantly.'

'That's about all that's left them,' the Indian murmured mildly. He sipped a little lime juice. 'You should try to be more tolerant.'

'Tolerant? I have nothing against them, as long as they–'

'It is said,' the Indian continued softly, 'that Elron Hu, Himself, was a Cauc.'

Sung-wu spluttered indignantly and started to rejoin, but the hot words stuck fast in his mouth; down in the mud street something was coming.

Sung-wu demanded, 'What is it?' He leaped up excitedly and hurried to the railing.

A slow procession was advancing with solemn step. As if at a signal, men and women poured from their rickety huts and excitedly lined the street to watch. Sung-wu was transfixed, as the procession neared; his senses reeled. More and more men and women were collecting each moment; there seemed to be hundreds of them. They were a dense, murmuring mob, packed tight, swaying back and forth, faces avid. An hysterical moan passed through them, a great wind that stirred them like leaves of a tree. They were a single collective whole, a vast primitive organism, held ecstatic and hypnotized by the approaching column.

The marchers wore a strange costume: white shirts, with the sleeves rolled up; dark gray trousers of an incredibly archaic design, and black shoes. All were dressed exactly alike. They formed a dazzling double line of white shirts, gray trousers, marching calmly and solemnly, faces up, nostrils flared, jaws stern. A glazed fanaticism stamped each man and woman, such a ruthless expression that Sung-wu shrank back in terror. On and on they came, figures of grim stone in their primordial white shirts and gray trousers, a frightening breath from the past. Their heels struck the ground in a dull, harsh beat that reverberated among the rickety huts. The dogs woke; the children began to wail. The chickens flew squawking.

'Elron!' Sung-wu cried. 'What's happening?'

The marchers carried strange symbolic implements, ritualistic images with esoteric meaning that of necessity escaped Sung-wu. There were tubes and poles, and shiny webs of what looked like metal. *Metal!* But it was not rusty; it was shiny and bright. He was stunned; they looked–new.

The procession passed directly below. After the marchers came a huge rumbling cart. On it was mounted an obvious fertility symbol, a corkscrew-bore as long as a tree; it jutted from a square cube of gleaming steel; as the cart moved forward the bore lifted and fell.

After the cart came more marchers, also grim-faced, eyes glassy, loaded down with pipes and tubes and armfuls of glittering equipment. They passed on, and then the street was filled by surging throngs of awed men and women, who followed after them, utterly dazed. And then came children and barking dogs.

The last marcher carried a pennant that fluttered above her as she strode along, a tall pole hugged tight to her chest. At the top, the bright pennant fluttered boldly. Sung-wu made its marking out, and for a moment consciousness left him. There it was, directly below; it had passed under his very nose, out in the open for all to see–unconcealed. The pennant had a great T emblazoned on it.

'They–' he began, but the obese Indian cut him off.

'The Tinkerists,' he rumbled, and sipped his lime juice.

Sung-wu grabbed up his briefcase and scrambled toward the stairs. At the bottom, the two hulking Caucs were already moving into motion. The Indian signaled quickly to them. 'Here!' They started grimly up, little blue eyes mean, red-rimmed and cold as stone; under their pelts their bulging muscles rippled.

Sung-wu fumbled in his cloak. His shiver-gun came out; he squeezed the release and directed it toward the two Caucs. But nothing happened; the gun had stopped functioning. He shook it wildly; flakes of rust and dried insulation fluttered from it. It was useless, worn out; he tossed it away and then, with the resolve of desperation, jumped through the railing.

He, and a torrent of rotten wood, cascaded to the street. He hit, rolled, struck his head against the corner of a hut, and shakily pulled himself to his feet.

He ran. Behind him, the two Caucs pushed after him through the throngs of men and women milling aimlessly along. Occasionally he glimpsed their white, perspiring faces. He turned a corner, raced between shabby huts, leaped over a sewage ditch, climbed heaps of sagging debris, slipped and rolled and at last lay gasping behind a tree, his briefcase still clutched.

The Caucs were nowhere in sight. He had evaded them; for the moment, he was safe.

He peered around. Which way was his ship? He shielded his

eyes against the late afternoon sun until he managed to make out its bent, tubular outline. It was far off to his right, barely visible in the dying glare that hung gloomily across the sky. Sung-wu got unsteadily to his feet and began walking cautiously in that direction.

He was in a terrible spot; the whole region was pro-Tinkerist—even the Chamber-appointed Manager. And it wasn't along class lines; the cult had knifed to the top level. And it wasn't just Caucs, anymore; he couldn't count on Bantu or Mongolian or Indian, not in this area. An entire countryside was hostile, and lying in wait for him.

Elron, it was worse than the Arm had thought! No wonder they wanted a report. A whole area had swung over to a fanatic cult, a violent extremist group of heretics, teaching a most diabolical doctrine. He shuddered—and kept on, avoiding contact with the farmers in their fields, both human and robot. He increased his pace, as alarm and horror pushed him suddenly faster.

If the thing were to spread, if it were to hit a sizable portion of mankind, it might bring back the Time of Madness.

The ship was taken. Three or four immense Caucs stood lounging around it, cigarettes dangling from their slack mouths, white-faced and hairy. Stunned, Sung-wu moved back down the hillside, prickles of despair numbing him. The ship was lost; they had got there ahead of him. What was he supposed to do now?

It was almost evening. He'd have to walk fifty miles through the darkness, over unfamiliar, hostile ground, to reach the next inhabited area. The sun was already beginning to set, the air turning cool; and in addition, he was sopping wet with filth and slimy water. He had slipped in the gloom and fallen in a sewage ditch.

He retraced his steps, mind blank. What could he do? He was helpless; his shiver-gun had been useless. He was alone, and there was no contact with the Arm. Tinkerists swarming on all sides; they'd probably gut him and sprinkle his blood over the crops—or worse.

He skirted a farm. In the fading twilight, a dim figure was working, a young woman. He eyed her cautiously, as he passed; she had her back to him. She was bending over, between rows of corn. What was she doing? Was she–good Elron!

He stumbled blindly across the field toward her, caution forgotten. 'Young woman! *Stop!* In the name of Elron, stop at once!'

The girl straightened up. 'Who are you?'

Breathless, Sung-wu arrived in front of her, gripping his battered briefcase and gasping. 'Those are our *brothers*! How can you destroy them? They may be close relatives, recently deceased.' He struck and knocked the jar from her hand; it hit the ground and the imprisoned beetles scurried off in all directions.

The girl's cheeks flushed with anger. 'It took me an hour to collect those!'

'You were killing them! Crushing them!' He was speechless with horror. 'I saw you!'

'Of course.' The girl raised her black eyebrows. 'They gnaw the corn.'

'They're our brothers!' Sung-wu repeated wildly. 'Of course they gnaw the corn; because of certain sins committed, the cosmic forces have–' He broke off, appalled. 'Don't you *know*? You've never been told?'

The girl was perhaps sixteen. In the fading light she was a small, slender figure, the empty jar in one hand, a rock in the other. A tide of black hair tumbled down her neck. Her eyes were large and luminous; her lips full and deep red; her skin a smooth copper-brown–Polynesian, probably. He caught a glimpse of firm brown breasts as she bent to grab a beetle that had landed on its back. The sight made his pulse race; in a flash he was back three years.

'What's your name?' he asked, more kindly.

'Frija.'

'How old are you?'

'Seventeen.'

'I am a Bard; have you ever spoken to a Bard before?'

'No,' the girl murmured. 'I don't think so.'

She was almost invisible in the darkness. Sung-wu could scarcely see her, but what he saw sent his heart into an agony of paroxysms; the same cloud of black hair, the same deep red lips. This girl was younger, of course–a mere child, and from the Farmer class, at that. But she had Liu's figure, and in time she'd ripen–probably in a matter of months.

Ageless, honeyed craft worked his vocal cords. 'I have landed in this area to make a survey. Something has gone wrong with my ship and I must remain the night. I know no one here, however. My plight is such that–'

'Oh,' Frija said, immediately sympathetic. 'Why don't you stay with us, tonight? We have an extra room, now that my brother's away.'

'Delighted,' Sung-wu answered instantly. 'Will you lead the way? I'll gladly repay you for your kindness.' The girl moved off toward a vague shape looming up in the darkness. Sung-wu hurried quickly after her. 'I find it incredible you haven't been instructed. This whole area has deteriorated beyond belief. What ways have you fallen in? We'll have to spend much time together; I can see that already. Not one of you even approaches clearness–you're jangled, every one of you.'

'What does that mean?' Frija asked, as she stepped up on the porch and opened the door.

'Jangled?' Sung-wu blinked in amazement. 'We *will* have to study much together.' In his eagerness, he tripped on the top step, and barely managed to catch himself. 'Perhaps you need complete instruction; it may be necessary to start from the very bottom. I can arrange a stay at the Holy Arm for you–under my protection, of course. Jangled means out of harmony with the cosmic elements. How can you live this way? My dear, you'll have to be brought back in line with the divine plan!'

'What plan is that?' She led him into a warm living room; a crackling fire burned in the grate. Two or three men sat around a rough wood table, an old man with long white hair and two younger men. A frail, withered old woman sat dozing in a rocker in the corner. In the kitchen, a buxom young woman was fixing the evening meal.

'Why, *the* plan!' Sung-wu answered, astounded. His eyes darted around. Suddenly his briefcase fell to the floor. 'Caucs,' he said.

They were all Caucasians, even Frija. She was deeply tanned; her skin was almost black; but she was a Cauc, nonetheless. He recalled: Caucs, in the sun, turned dark, sometimes even darker than Mongolians. The girl had tossed her work robe over a door hook; in her household shorts her thighs were as white as milk. And the old man and woman–

'This is my grandfather,' Frija said, indicating the old man. 'Benjamin Tinker.'

Under the watchful eyes of the two younger Tinkers, Sung-wu was washed and scrubbed, given clean clothes, and then fed. He ate only a little; he didn't feel very well.

'I can't understand it,' he muttered, as he listlessly pushed his plate away. 'The scanner at the Central Chamber said I had eight months left. The plague will–' He considered. 'But it can always change. The scanner goes on prediction, not certainty; multiple possibilities; free will . . . Any overt act of sufficient significance–'

Ben Tinker laughed. 'You want to stay alive?'

'Of course!' Sung-wu muttered indignantly.

They all laughed–even Frija, and the old woman in her shawl, snow-white hair and mild blue eyes. They were the first Cauc women he had ever seen. They weren't big and lumbering like the male Caucs; they didn't seem to have the same bestial characteristics. The two young Cauc bucks looked plenty tough, though; they and their father were poring over an elaborate series of papers and reports, spread out on the dinner table, among the empty plates.

'This area,' Ben Tinker murmured. 'Pipes should go here. And here. Water's the main need. Before the next crop goes in, we'll dump a few hundred pounds of artificial fertilizers and plow it in. The power plows should be ready, then.'

'After that?' one of the tow-headed sons asked.

'Then spraying. If we don't have the nicotine sprays, we'll have to try the copper dusting again. I prefer the spray, but we're still behind on production. The bore has dug us up some good storage caverns, though. It ought to start picking up.'

'And here,' a son said, 'there's going to be need of draining. A lot of mosquito breeding going on. We can try the oil, as we did over here. But I suggest the whole thing be filled in. We can use the dredge and scoop, if they're not tied up.'

Sung-wu had taken this all in. Now he rose unsteadily to his feet, trembling with wrath. He pointed a shaking finger at the elder Tinker.

'You're–meddling!' he gasped.

They looked up. 'Meddling?'

'With the plan! With the cosmic plan! Good Elron–you're interfering with the divine processes. Why–' He was staggered by a realization so alien it convulsed the very core of his being. 'You're actually going to set back turns of the wheel.'

'That,' said old Ben Tinker, 'is right.'

Sung-wu sat down again, stunned. His mind refused to take it all in. 'I don't understand; what'll happen? If you slow the wheel, if you disrupt the divine plan–'

'He's going to be a problem,' Ben Tinker murmured thoughtfully. 'If we kill him, the Arm will merely send another; they have hundreds like him. And if we don't kill him, if we send him back, he'll raise a hue and cry that'll bring the whole Chamber down here. It's too soon for this to happen. We're gaining support fast, but we need another few months.'

Sweat stood out on Sung-wu's plump forehead. He wiped it away shakily. 'If you kill me,' he muttered, 'you will sink down many rungs of the cosmic ladder. You have risen this far; why undo the work accomplished in endless ages past?'

Ben Tinker fixed one powerful blue eye on him. 'My friend,' he said slowly, 'isn't it true one's next manifestation is determined by one's moral conduct in this?'

Sung-wu nodded. 'Such is well-known.'

'And what is right conduct?'

'Fulfilling the divine plan,' Sung-wu responded immediately.

'Maybe our whole Movement is part of the plan,' Ben Tinker said thoughtfully. 'Maybe the cosmic forces *want* us to drain the swamps and kill the grasshoppers and inoculate the children; after all, the cosmic forces put us all here.'

'If you kill me,' Sung-wu wailed, 'I'll be a carrion-eating fly. I *saw* it, a shiny-winged blue-rumped fly crawling over the carcass of a dead lizard–In a rotting, steaming jungle in a filthy cesspool of a planet.' Tears came; he dabbed at them futilely. 'In an out-of-the-way system, at the bottom of the ladder!'

Tinker was amused. 'Why this?'

'I've sinned.' Sung-wu sniffed and flushed. 'I committed adultery.'

'Can't you purge yourself?'

'There's no time!' His misery rose to wild despair. 'My mind is *still* impure!' He indicated Frija, standing in the bedroom doorway, a supple white and tan shape in her household shorts. 'I continue to think carnal thoughts; I can't rid myself. In eight months the plague will turn the wheel on me–and it'll be done! If I lived to be an old man, withered and toothless–no more appetite–' His plump body quivered in a frenzied convulsion. 'There's no *time* to purge and atone. According to the scanner, I'm going to die a young man!'

After this torrent of words, Tinker was silent, deep in thought. 'The plague,' he said, at last. 'What, exactly, are the symptoms?'

Sung-wu described them, his olive face turning to a sickly green. When he had finished, the three men looked significantly at each other.

Ben Tinker got to his feet. 'Come along,' he commanded briskly, taking the Bard by the arm. 'I have something to show you. It is left from the old days. Sooner or later we'll advance enough to turn out our own, but right now we have only these remaining few. We have to keep them guarded and sealed.'

'This is for a good cause,' one of the sons said. 'It's worth it.' He caught his brother's eye and grinned.

*

Bard Chai finished reading Sung-wu's blue-slip report; he tossed it suspiciously down and eyed the younger Bard. 'You're sure? There's no further need of investigation?'

'The cult will wither away,' Sung-wu murmured indifferently. 'It lacks any real support; it's merely an escape valve, without intrinsic validity.'

Chai wasn't convinced. He reread parts of the report again. 'I suppose you're right; but we've heard so many–'

'Lies,' Sung-wu said vaguely. 'Rumors. Gossip. May I go?' He moved toward the door.

'Eager for your vacation?' Chai smiled understandingly. 'I know how you feel. This report must have exhausted you. Rural areas, stagnant backwaters. We must prepare a better program of rural education. I'm convinced whole regions are in a jangled state. We've got to bring clearness to these people. It's our historic role; our class function.'

'Verily,' Sung-wu murmured, as he bowed his way out of the office and down the hall.

As he walked he fingered his beads thankfully. He breathed a silent prayer as his fingers moved over the surface of the little red pellets, shiny spheres that glowed freshly in place of the faded old–the gift of the Tinkerists. The beads would come in handy; he kept his hand on them tightly. Nothing must happen to them, in the next eight months. He had to watch them carefully, while he poked around the ruined cities of Spain–and finally came down with the plague.

He was the first Bard to wear a rosary of penicillin capsules.

THE LAST OF THE MASTERS

Consciousness collected around him. He returned with reluctance; the weight of centuries, an unbearable fatigue, lay over him. The ascent was painful. He would have shrieked if there were anything to shriek with. And anyhow, he was beginning to feel glad.

Eight thousand times he had crept back thus, with ever-increasing difficulty. Someday he wouldn't make it. Someday the black pool would remain. But not this day. He was still alive; above the aching pain and reluctance came joyful triumph.

'Good morning,' a bright voice said. 'Isn't it a nice day? I'll pull the curtains and you can look out.'

He could see and hear. But he couldn't move. He lay quietly and allowed the various sensations of the room to pour in on him. Carpets, wallpaper, tables, lamps, pictures. Desk and vidscreen. Gleaming yellow sunlight streamed through the window. Blue sky. Distant hills. Fields, buildings, roads, factories. Workers and machines.

Peter Green was busily straightening things, his young face wreathed with smiles. 'Lots to do today. Lots of people to see you. Bills to sign. Decisions to make. This is Saturday. There will be people coming in from the remote sectors. I hope the maintenance crew has done a good job.' He added quickly, 'They have, of course. I talked to Fowler on my way over here. Everything's fixed up fine.'

The youth's pleasant tenor mixed with the bright sunlight. Sounds and sights, but nothing else. He could feel nothing. He tried to move his arm but nothing happened.

'Don't worry,' Green said, catching his terror. 'They'll soon be along with the rest. You'll be all right. You *have* to be. How could we survive without you?'

He relaxed. God knew, it had happened often enough before. Anger surged dully. Why couldn't they coordinate? Get it up all at once, not piecemeal. He'd have to change their schedule. Make them organize better.

Past the bright window a squat metal car chugged to a halt. Uniformed men piled out, gathered up heavy armloads of equipment, and hurried toward the main entrance of the building.

'Here they come,' Green exclaimed with relief. 'A little late, eh?'

'Another traffic tie-up,' Fowler snorted, as he entered. 'Something wrong with the signal system again. Outside flow got mixed up with the urban stuff; tied up on all sides. I wish you'd change the law.'

Now there was motion all around him. The shapes of Fowler and McLean loomed, two giant moons abruptly ascendant. Professional faces that peered down at him anxiously. He was turned over on his side. Muffled conferences. Urgent whispers. The clank of tools.

'Here,' Fowler muttered. 'Now here. No, that's later. Be careful. Now run it up through here.'

The work continued in taut silence. He was aware of their closeness. Dim outlines occasionally cut off his light. He was turned this way and that, thrown around like a sack of meal.

'Okay,' Fowler said. 'Tape it.'

A long silence. He gazed dully at the wall, at the slightly-faded blue and pink wallpaper. An old design that showed a woman in hoopskirts, with a little parasol over her dainty shoulder. A frilly white blouse, tiny tips of shoes. An astoundingly clean puppy at her side.

Then he was turned back, to face upward. Five shapes groaned and strained over him. Their fingers flew, their muscles rippled under their shirts. At last they straightened up and retreated. Fowler wiped sweat from his face; they were all tense and bleary-eyed.

'Go ahead,' Fowler rasped. 'Throw it.'

Shock hit him. He gasped. His body arched, then settled slowly down.

His body. He could feel. He moved his arms experimentally. He touched his face, his shoulder, the wall. The wall was real and hard. All at once the world had become three-dimensional again.

Relief showed on Fowler's face. 'Thank–God.' He sagged wearily. 'How do you feel?'

After a moment he answered, 'All right.'

Fowler sent the rest of the crew out. Green began dusting again, off in the corner. Fowler sat down on the edge of the bed and lit his pipe. 'Now listen to me,' he said. 'I've got bad news. I'll give it to you the way you always want it, straight from the shoulder.'

'What is it?' he demanded. He examined his fingers. He already knew.

There were dark circles under Fowler's eyes. He hadn't shaved. His square-jawed face was drawn and unhealthy. 'We were up all night. Working on your motor system. We've got it jury-rigged, but it won't hold. Not more than another few months. The thing's climbing. The basic units can't be replaced. When they wear out they're gone. We can weld in relays and wiring, but we can't fix the five synapsis-coils. There were only a few men who could make those, and they've been dead two centuries. If the coils burn out–'

'Is there any deterioration in the synapsis-coils?' he interrupted.

'Not yet. Just motor areas. Arms, in particular. What's happening to your legs will happen to your arms and finally all your motor system. You'll be paralyzed by the end of the year. You'll be able to see, hear, and think. And broadcast. But that's all.' He added, 'Sorry, Bors. We're doing all we can.'

'All right,' Bors said. 'You're excused. Thanks for telling me straight. I–guessed.'

'Ready to go down? A lot of people with problems, today. They're stuck until you get there.'

'Let's go.' He focused his mind with an effort and turned his attention to the details of the day. 'I want the heavy metals research program speeded. It's lagging, as usual. I may have to pull a number of men from related work and shift them to the generators. The water level will be dropping soon. I want to start feeding power along the lines while there's still power to feed. As soon as I turn my back everything starts falling apart.'

Fowler signalled Green and he came quickly over. The two of them bent over Bors and, grunting, hoisted him up and carried him to the door. Down the corridor and outside.

They deposited him in the squat metal car, the new little service truck. Its polished surface was a startling contrast to his pitted, corroded hull, bent and splotched and eaten away. A dull, patina-covered machine of archaic steel and plastic that hummed faintly, rustily, as the men leaped in the front seat and raced the car out onto the main highway.

Edward Tolby perspired, pushed his pack up higher, hunched over, tightened his gun belt, and cursed.

'Daddy,' Silvia reproved. 'Cut that.'

Tolby spat furiously in the grass at the side of the road. He put his arm around his slim daughter. 'Sorry, Silv. Nothing personal. The damn heat.'

Mid-morning sun shimmered down on the dusty road. Clouds of dust rose and billowed around the three as they pushed slowly along. They were dead tired. Tolby's heavy face was flushed and sullen. An unlit cigarette dangled between his lips. His big, powerfully built body was hunched resentfully forward. His daughter's canvas shirt clung moistly to her arms and breasts. Moons of sweat darkened her back. Under her jeans her thigh muscles rippled wearily.

Robert Penn walked a little behind the two Tolbys, hands deep in his pockets, eyes on the road ahead. His mind was blank; he was half asleep from the double shot of hexobarb he had swallowed at the last League camp. And the heat lulled him. On each side of the road fields stretched out, pastures of grass and weeds, a few trees here and there. A tumbled-down farmhouse. The ancient rusting remains of a bomb shelter, two centuries old. Once, some dirty sheep.

'Sheep,' Penn said. 'They eat the grass too far down. It won't grow back.'

'Now he's a farmer,' Tolby said to his daughter.

'Daddy,' Silvia snapped. 'Stop being nasty.'

'It's this heat. This damn heat.' Tolby cursed again, loudly and futilely. 'It's not worth it. For ten pinks I'd go back and tell them it was a lot of pig swill.'

'Maybe it is, at that,' Penn said mildly.

'All right, you go back,' Tolby grunted. 'You go back and tell them it's a lot of pig swill. They'll pin a medal on you. Maybe raise you up a grade.'

Penn laughed. 'Both of you shut up. There's some kind of town ahead.'

Tolby's massive body straightened eagerly. 'Where?' He shielded his eyes. 'By God, he's right. A village. And it isn't a mirage. You see it, don't you?' His good humor returned and he rubbed his big hands together. 'What say, Penn. A couple of beers, a few games of throw with some of the local peasants–maybe we can stay overnight.' He licked his thick lips with anticipation. 'Some of those village wenches, the kind that hang around the grog shops–'

'I know the kind you mean,' Penn broke in. 'The kind that are tired of doing nothing. Want to see the big commercial centers. Want to meet some guy that'll buy them mecho-stuff and take them places.'

At the side of the road a farmer was watching them curiously. He had halted his horse and stood leaning on his crude plow, hat pushed back on his head.

'What's the name of this town?' Tolby yelled.

The farmer was silent a moment. He was an old man, thin and weathered. 'This town?' he repeated.

'Yeah, the one ahead.'

'That's a nice town.' The farmer eyed the three of them. 'You been through here before?'

'No, sir,' Tolby said. 'Never.'

'Team break down?'

'No, we're on foot.'

'How far you come?'

'About a hundred and fifty miles.'

The farmer considered the heavy packs strapped on their backs. Their cleated hiking shoes. Dusty clothing and weary, sweat-streaked faces. Jeans and canvas shirts. Ironite walking staffs. 'That's a long way,' he said. 'How far you going?'

'As far as we feel like it,' Tolby answered. 'Is there a place ahead we can stay? Hotel? Inn?'

'That town,' the farmer said, 'is Fairfax. It has a lumber mill, one of the best in the world. A couple of pottery works. A place where you can get clothes put together by machines. Regular mecho-clothing. A gun shop where they pour the best shot this side of the Rockies. And a bakery. Also there's an old doctor living there, and a lawyer. And some people with books to teach the kids. They came with t.b. They made a school house out of an old barn.'

'How large a town?' Penn asked.

'Lot of people. More born all the time. Old folks die. Kids die. We had a fever last year. About a hundred kids died. Doctor said it came from the water hole. We shut the water hole down. Kids died anyhow. Doctor said it was the milk. Drove off half the cows. Not mine. I stood out there with my gun and I shot the first of them came to drive off my cow. Kids stopped dying as soon as fall came. I think it was the heat.'

'Sure is hot,' Tolby agreed.

'Yes, it gets hot around here. Water's pretty scarce.' A crafty look slid across his old face. 'You folks want a drink? The young lady looks pretty tired. Got some bottles of water down under the house. In the mud. Nice and cold.' He hesitated. 'Pink a glass.'

Tolby laughed. 'No, thanks.'

'Two glasses a pink,' the farmer said.

'Not interested,' Penn said. He thumped his canteen and the three of them started on. 'So long.'

The farmer's face hardened. 'Damn foreigners,' he muttered. He turned angrily back to his plowing.

The town baked in silence. Flies buzzed and settled on the backs of stupefied horses, tied up at posts. A few cars were parked here and there. People moved listlessly along the sidewalks. Elderly lean-bodied men dozed on porches. Dogs and chickens slept in the shade under houses. The houses were small, wooden, chipped and peeling boards, leaning and angular–and old. Warped and split by age and heat. Dust lay over everything. A thick blanket of dry dust over the cracking houses and the dull-faced men and animals.

Two lank men approached them from an open doorway. 'Who are you? What do you want?'

They stopped and got out their identification. The men examined the sealed-plastic cards. Photographs, fingerprints, data. Finally they handed them back.

'AL,' one said. 'You really from the Anarchist League?'

'That's right,' Tolby said.

'Even the girl?' The men eyed Silvia with languid greed. 'Tell you what. Let us have the girl a while and we'll skip the head tax.'

'Don't kid me,' Tolby grunted. 'Since when does the League pay head tax or any other tax?' He pushed past them impatiently. 'Where's the grog shop? I'm dying!'

A two-story white building was on their left. Men lounged on the porch, watching them vacantly. Penn headed toward it and the Tolbys followed. A faded, peeling sign lettered across the front read: *Beer, Wine on Tap.*

'This is it,' Penn said. He guided Silvia up the sagging steps, past the men, and inside. Tolby followed; he unstrapped his pack gratefully as he came.

The place was cool and dark. A few men and women were at the bar; the rest sat around tables. Some youths were playing throw in the back. A mechanical tune-maker wheezed and composed in the corner, a shabby, half-ruined machine only partially functioning. Behind the bar a primitive scene-shifter created and destroyed vague phantasmagoria: seascapes, mountain peaks, snowy valleys, great rolling hills, a nude woman that lingered and then dissolved into one vast breast. Dim, uncertain processions that no one noticed or looked at. The bar itself was an incredibly ancient sheet of transparent plastic, stained and chipped and yellow with age. Its n-grav coat had faded from one end; bricks now propped it up. The drink mixer had long since fallen apart. Only wine and beer were served. No living man knew how to mix the simplest drink.

Tolby moved up to the bar. 'Beer,' he said. 'Three beers.' Penn and Silvia sank down at a table and removed their packs, as the bartender served Tolby three mugs of thick, dark beer. He showed his card and carried the mugs over to the table.

The youths in the back had stopped playing. They were watching the three as they sipped their beer and unlaced their hiking boots. After a while one of them came slowly over.

'Say,' he said. 'You're from the League.'

'That's right,' Tolby murmured sleepily.

Everyone in the place was watching and listening. The youth sat down across from the three; his companions flocked excitedly around and took seats on all sides. The juveniles of the town. Bored, restless, dissatisfied. Their eyes took in the ironite staffs, the guns, the heavy metal-cleated boots. A murmured whisper rustled through them. They were about eighteen. Tanned, rangy.

'How do you get in?' one demanded bluntly.

'The League?' Tolby leaned back in his chair, found a match, and lit his cigarette. He unfastened his belt, belched loudly, and settled back contentedly. 'You get in by examination.'

'What do you have to know?'

Tolby shrugged. 'About everything.' He belched again and scratched thoughtfully at his chest, between two buttons. He was conscious of the ring of people around on all sides. A little old man with a beard and horn-rimmed glasses. At another table, a great tub of a man in a red shirt and blue-striped trousers, with a bulging stomach.

Youths. Farmers. A Negro in a dirty white shirt and trousers, a book under his arm. A hard-jawed blonde, hair in a net, red nails and high heels, tight yellow dress. Sitting with a gray-haired businessman in a dark brown suit. A tall young man holding hands with a young black-haired girl, huge eyes, in a soft white blouse and skirt, little slippers kicked under the table. Under the table her bare, tanned feet twisted; her slim body was bent forward with interest.

'You have to know,' Tolby said, 'how the League was formed. You have to know how we pulled down the governments that day. Pulled them down and destroyed them. Burned all the buildings. And all the records. Billions of microfilms and papers. Great bonfires that burned for weeks. And the swarms of little white things that poured out when we knocked the buildings over.'

'You killed them?' the great tub of a man asked, lips twitching avidly.

'We let them go. They were harmless. They ran and hid. Under rocks.' Tolby laughed. 'Funny little scurrying things. Insects. Then we went in and gathered up all the records and equipment for making records. By God, we burned everything.'

'And the robots,' a youth said.

'Yeah, we smashed all the government robots. There weren't many of them. They were used only at high levels. When a lot of facts had to be integrated.'

The youth's eyes bulged. 'You saw them? You were there when they smashed the robots?'

Penn laughed. 'Tolby means the League. That was two hundred years ago.'

The youth grinned nervously. 'Yeah. Tell us about the marches.'

Tolby drained his mug and pushed it away. 'I'm out of beer.'

The mug was quickly refilled. He grunted his thanks and continued, voice deep and furry, dulled with fatigue. 'The marches. That was really something, they say. All over the world, people getting up, throwing down what they were doing–'

'It started in East Germany,' the hard-jawed blonde said. 'The riots.'

'Then it spread to Poland,' the Negro put in shyly. 'My grandfather used to tell me how everybody sat and listened to the television. His grandfather used to tell him. It spread to Czechoslovakia and then Austria and Roumania and Bulgaria. Then France. And Italy.'

'France was first!' the little old man with beard and glasses cried violently. 'They were without a government a whole month. The people saw they could live without a government!'

'The marches started it,' the black-haired girl corrected. 'That was the first time they started pulling down the government buildings. In East Germany and Poland. Big mobs of unorganized workers.'

'Russia and America were the last,' Tolby said. 'When the march on Washington came there was close to twenty million of us. We were big in those days! They couldn't stop us when we finally moved.'

'They shot a lot,' the hard-faced blonde said.

'Sure. But the people kept coming. And yelling to the soldiers. "Hey, Bill! Don't shoot!" "Hey, Jack! It's me, Joe." "Don't shoot–we're your friends!" "Don't kill us, join us!" And by God, after a while they did. They couldn't keep shooting their own people. They finally threw down their guns and got out of the way.'

'And then you found the place,' the little black-haired girl said breathlessly.

'Yeah. We found the place. *Six* places. Three in America. One in Britain. Two in Russia. It took us ten years to find the last place–and make sure it was the last place.'

'What then?' the youth asked, bug-eyed.

'Then we busted every one of them.' Tolby raised himself up, a massive man, beer mug clutched, heavy face flushed dark red. 'Every damn A-bomb in the whole world.'

There was an uneasy silence.

'Yeah,' the youth murmured. 'You sure took care of those war people.'

'Won't be any more of them,' the great tub of a man said. 'They're gone for good.'

Tolby fingered his ironite staff. 'Maybe so. And maybe not. There just might be a few of them left.'

'What do you mean?' the tub of a man demanded.

Tolby raised his hard gray eyes. 'It's time you people stopped kidding us. You know damn well what I mean. We've heard rumors. Someplace around this area there's a bunch of them. Hiding out.'

Shocked disbelief, then anger hummed to a roar. 'That's a lie!' the tub of a man shouted.

'Is it?'

The little man with beard and glasses leaped up. 'There's nobody here has anything to do with governments! We're all good people!'

'You better watch your step,' one of the youths said softly to Tolby. 'People around here don't like to be accused.'

Tolby got unsteadily to his feet, his ironite staff gripped. Penn got up beside him and they stood together. 'If any of you knows something,' Tolby said, 'you better tell it. Right now.'

'Nobody knows anything,' the hard-faced blonde said. 'You're talking to honest folks.'

'That's so,' the Negro said, nodding his head. 'Nobody here's doing anything wrong.'

'You saved our lives,' the black-haired girl said. 'If you hadn't pulled down the governments we'd all be dead in the war. Why should we hold back something?'

'That's true,' the great tub of a man grumbled. 'We wouldn't be alive if it wasn't for the League. You think we'd do anything against the League?'

'Come on,' Silvia said to her father. 'Let's go.' She got to her feet and tossed Penn his pack.

Tolby grunted belligerently. Finally he took his own pack and hoisted it to his shoulder. The room was deathly silent. Everyone stood frozen, as the three gathered their things and moved toward the door.

The little dark-haired girl stopped them. 'The next town is thirty miles from here,' she said.

'The road's blocked,' her tall companion explained. 'Slides closed it years ago.'

'Why don't you stay with us tonight? There's plenty of room at our place. You can rest up and get an early start tomorrow.'

'We don't want to impose,' Silvia murmured.

Tolby and Penn glanced at each other, then at the girl. 'If you're sure you have plenty of room–'

The great tub of a man approached them. 'Listen. I have ten yellow slips. I want to give them to the League. I sold my farm last year. I don't need any more slips; I'm living with my brother and his family.' He pushed the slips at Tolby. 'Here.'

Tolby pushed them back. 'Keep them.'

'This way,' the tall young man said, as they clattered down the sagging steps, into a sudden blinding curtain of heat and dust. 'We have a car. Over this way. An old gasoline car. My dad fixed it so it burns oil.'

'You should have taken the slips,' Penn said to Tolby, as they got into the ancient, battered car. Flies buzzed around them. They could hardly breathe; the car was a furnace. Silvia fanned herself with a rolled-up paper. The black-haired girl unbuttoned her blouse.

'What do we need money for?' Tolby laughed good-naturedly. 'I haven't paid for anything in my life. Neither have you.'

The car sputtered and moved slowly forward, onto the road. It began to gain speed. Its motor banged and roared. Soon it was moving surprisingly fast.

'You saw them,' Silvia said, over the racket. 'They'd give us anything they had. We saved their lives.' She waved at the fields, the farmers and their crude teams, the withered crops, the sagging old farmhouses. 'They'd all be dead, if it hadn't been for the League.' She smashed a fly peevishly. 'They depend on us.'

The black-haired girl turned toward them, as the car rushed along the decaying road. Sweat streaked her tanned skin. Her half-covered breasts trembled with the motion of the car. 'I'm Laura Davis. Pete and I have an old farmhouse his dad gave us when we got married.'

'You can have the whole downstairs,' Pete said.

'There's no electricity, but we've got a big fireplace. It gets cold at night. It's hot in the day, but when the sun sets it gets terribly cold.'

'We'll be all right,' Penn murmured. The vibration of the car made him a little sick.

'Yes,' the girl said, her black eyes flashing. Her crimson lips twisted. She leaned toward Penn intently, her small face strangely alight. 'Yes, we'll take good care of you.'

At that moment the car left the road.

Silvia shrieked. Tolby threw himself down, head between his knees, doubled up in a ball. A sudden curtain of green burst around Penn. Then a sickening emptiness, as the car plunged down. It struck with a roaring crash that blotted out everything. A single titanic cataclysm of fury that picked Penn up and flung his remains in every direction.

'Put me down,' Bors ordered. 'On this railing for a moment before I go inside.'

The crew lowered him onto the concrete surface and fastened magnetic grapples into place. Men and women hurried up the wide steps, in and out of the massive building that was Bors' main offices.

The sight from these steps pleased him. He liked to stop here and look around at his world. At the civilization he had carefully constructed. Each piece added painstakingly, scrupulously, with infinite care, throughout the years.

It wasn't big. The mountains ringed it on all sides. The valley was a level bowl, surrounded by dark violet hills. Outside, beyond the hills, the regular world began. Parched fields. Blasted, poverty-stricken towns. Decayed roads. The remains of houses, tumbled-down farm buildings. Ruined cars and machinery. Dust-covered people creeping listlessly around in hand-made clothing, dull rags and tatters.

He had seen the outside. He knew what it was like. At the mountains the blank faces, the disease, the withered crops, the crude plows and ancient tools all ended here. Here, within the ring of hills, Bors had constructed an accurate and detailed reproduction of a society two centuries gone. The world as it had been in the old days. The time of governments. The time that had been pulled down by the Anarchist League.

Within his five synapsis-coils the plans, knowledge, information, blueprints of a whole world existed. In the two centuries he had carefully recreated that world, had made this miniature society that glittered and hummed on all sides of him. The roads, buildings, houses, industries of a dead world, all a fragment of the past, built with his hands, his own metal fingers and brain.

'Fowler,' Bors said.

Fowler came over. He looked haggard. His eyes were red-rimmed and swollen. 'What is it? You want to go inside?'

Overhead, the morning patrol thundered past. A string of black dots against the sunny, cloudless sky. Bors watched with satisfaction. 'Quite a sight.'

'Right on the nose,' Fowler agreed, examining his wristwatch. To their right, a column of heavy tanks snaked along a highway between green fields. Their gun-snouts glittered. Behind them a column of foot soldiers marched, faces hidden behind bacteria masks.

'I'm thinking,' Bors said, 'that it may be unwise to trust Green any longer.'

'Why the hell do you say that?'

'Every ten days I'm inactivated. So your crew can see what repairs are needed.' Bors twisted restlessly. 'For twelve hours I'm completely helpless. Green takes care of me. Sees nothing happens. But–'

'But what?'

'It occurs to me perhaps there'd be more safety in a squad of troops. It's too much of a temptation for one man, alone.'

Fowler scowled. 'I don't see that. How about me? I have charge of inspecting you. I could switch a few leads around. Send a load through your synapsis-coils. Blow them out.'

Bors whirred wildly, then subsided. 'True. You could do that.' After a moment he demanded, 'But what would you gain? You know I'm the only one who can keep all this together. I'm the only one who knows how to maintain a planned society, not a disorderly chaos! If it weren't for me, all this would collapse, and you'd have dust and ruins and weeds. The whole outside would come rushing in to take over!'

'Of course. So why worry about Green?'

Trucks of workers rumbled past. Loads of men in blue-green, sleeves rolled up, armloads of tools. A mining team, heading for the mountains.

'Take me inside,' Bors said abruptly.

Fowler called McLean. They hoisted Bors and carried him past the throngs of people, into the building, down the corridor and to his office. Officials and technicians moved respectfully out of the way as the great pitted, corroded tank was carried past.

'All right,' Bors said impatiently. 'That's all. You can go.'

Fowler and McLean left the luxurious office, with its lush carpets, furniture, drapes and rows of books. Bors was already bent over his desk, sorting through heaps of reports and papers.

Fowler shook his head, as they walked down the hall. 'He won't last much longer.'

'The motor system? Can't we reinforce the–'

'I don't mean that. He's breaking up mentally. He can't take the strain any longer.'

'None of us can,' McLean muttered.

'Running this thing is too much for him. Knowing it's all dependent on him. Knowing as soon as he turns his back or lets down it'll begin to come apart at the seams. A hell of a job, trying to shut out the real world. Keeping his model universe running.'

'He's gone on a long time,' McLean said.

Fowler brooded. 'Sooner or later we're going to have to face the situation.' Gloomily, he ran his fingers along the blade of a large screwdriver. 'He's wearing out. Sooner or later somebody's going to have to step in. As he continues to decay . . .' He stuck the screwdriver back in his belt, with his pliers and hammer and soldering iron. 'One crossed wire.'

'What's that?'

Fowler laughed. 'Now he's got me doing it. One crossed wire and–*poof*. But what then? That's the big question.'

'Maybe,' McLean said softly, 'you and I can then get off this rat race. You and I and all the rest of us. And live like human beings.'

'*Rat race*,' Fowler murmured. 'Rats in a maze. Doing tricks. Performing chores thought up by somebody else.'

McLean caught Fowler's eye. 'By somebody of another species.'

Tolby struggled vaguely. Silence. A faint dripping close by. A beam pinned his body down. He was caught on all sides by the twisted wreck of the car. He was head down. The car was turned on its side. Off the road in a gully, wedged between two huge trees. Bent struts and smashed metal all around him. And bodies.

He pushed up with all his strength. The beam gave, and he managed to get to a sitting position. A tree branch had burst in the windshield. The black-haired girl, still turned toward the back seat, was impaled on it. The branch had driven through her spine, out her chest, and into the seat; she clutched at it with both hands, head limp, mouth half open. The man beside her was also dead. His hands were gone; the windshield had burst around him. He lay in a heap among the remains of the dashboard and the bloody shine of his own internal organs.

Penn was dead. Neck snapped like a rotten broom handle. Tolby pushed his corpse aside and examined his daughter. Silvia didn't stir. He put his ear to her shirt and listened. She was alive. Her heart beat faintly. Her bosom rose and fell against his ear.

He wound a handkerchief around her arm, where the flesh was ripped open and oozing blood. She was badly cut and scratched; one leg was doubled under her, obviously broken. Her clothes were ripped, her hair matted with blood. But she was alive. He pushed the twisted door open and stumbled out. A fiery tongue of afternoon sunlight struck him and he winced. He began to ease her limp body out of the car, past the twisted door-frame.

A sound.

Tolby glanced up, rigid. Something was coming. A whirring insect that rapidly descended. He let go of Silvia, crouched, glanced around, then lumbered awkwardly down the gully. He slid and fell and rolled among the green vines and jagged gray boulders. His gun gripped, he lay gasping in the moist shadows, peering upward.

The insect landed. A small air-ship, jet-driven. The sight stunned him. He had heard about jets, seen photographs of them. Been briefed and lectured in the history-indoctrination courses at the League camps. But to *see* a jet!

Men swarmed out. Uniformed men who started from the road, down the side of the gully, bodies crouched warily as they approached the wrecked car. They lugged heavy rifles. They looked grim and experienced, as they tore the car doors open and scrambled in.

'One's gone,' a voice drifted to him.

'Must be around somewhere.'

'Look, this one's alive! This woman. Started to crawl out. The rest all dead.'

Furious cursing. 'Damn Laura! She should have leaped! The fanatic little fool!'

'Maybe she didn't have time. God's sake, the thing's all the way through her.' Horror and shocked dismay. 'We won't hardly be able to get her loose.'

'Leave her.' The officer directing things waved the men back out of the car. 'Leave them all.'

'How about this wounded one?'

The leader hesitated. 'Kill her,' he said finally. He snatched a rifle and raised the butt. 'The rest of you fan out and try to get the other one. He's probably–'

Tolby fired, and the leader's body broke in half. The lower part sank down slowly; the upper dissolved in ashy fragments. Tolby turned and began to move in a slow circle, firing as he crawled. He got two more of them before the rest retreated in panic to their jet-powered insect and slammed the lock.

He had the element of surprise. Now that was gone. They had strength and numbers. He was doomed. Already, the insect was rising. They'd be able to spot him easily from above. But he had saved Silvia. That was something.

He stumbled down a dried-up creek bed. He ran aimlessly; he had no place to go. He didn't know the countryside, and he was on foot. He slipped on a stone and fell headlong. Pain and billowing darkness beat at him as he got unsteadily to his knees. His gun was gone, lost in the shrubbery. He spat broken teeth and blood. He peered wildly up at the blazing afternoon sky.

The insect was leaving. It hummed off toward the distant hills. It dwindled, became a black ball, a fly-speck, then disappeared.

Tolby waited a moment. Then he struggled up the side of the ravine to the wrecked car. They had gone to get help. They'd be back. Now was his only chance. If he could get Silvia out and down the road, into hiding. Maybe to a farmhouse. Back to town.

He reached the car and stood, dazed and stupefied. Three bodies remained, the two in the front seat, Penn in the back. But Silvia was gone.

They had taken her with them. Back where they came from. She had been dragged to the jet-driven insect; a trail of blood led from the car up the side of the gully to the highway.

With a violent shudder Tolby pulled himself together. He climbed into the car and pried loose Penn's gun from his belt. Silvia's ironite staff rested on the seat; he took that, too. Then he started off down the road, walking without haste, carefully, slowly.

An ironic thought plucked at his mind. He had found what they were after. The men in uniform. They were organized, responsible to a central authority. In a newly-assembled jet.

Beyond the hills was a government.

'Sir,' Green said. He smoothed his short blond hair anxiously, his young face twisting.

Technicians and experts and ordinary people in droves were everywhere. The offices buzzed and echoed with the business of the day. Green pushed through the crowd and to the desk where Bors sat, propped up by two magnetic frames.

'Sir,' Green said. 'Something's happened.'

Bors looked up. He pushed a metal-foil slate away and laid down his stylus. His eye cells clicked and flickered; deep inside his battered trunk motor gears whined. 'What is it?'

Green came close. There was something in his face, an expression Bors had never seen before. A look of fear and glassy determination. A glazed, fanatic cast, as if his flesh had hardened to rock. 'Sir, scouts contacted a League team moving North. They met the team outside Fairfax. The incident took place directly beyond the first road block.'

Bors said nothing. On all sides, officials, experts, farmers, workmen, industrial managers, soldiers, people of all kinds buzzed and murmured and pushed forward impatiently. Trying to get to Bors' desk. Loaded down with problems to be solved, situations to be explained. The pressing business of the day. Roads, factories, disease control. Repairs. Construction. Manufacture. Design. Planning. Urgent problems for Bors to consider and deal with. Problems that couldn't wait.

'Was the League team destroyed?' Bors said.

'One was killed. One was wounded and brought here.' Green hesitated. 'One escaped.'

For a long time Bors was silent. Around him the people murmured and shuffled; he ignored them. All at once he pulled the vidscanner to him and snapped the circuit open. 'One escaped? I don't like the sound of that.'

'He shot three members of our scout unit. Including the leader. The others got frightened. They grabbed the injured girl and returned here.'

Bors' massive head lifted. 'They made a mistake. They should have located the one who escaped.'

'This was the first time the situation–'

'I know,' Bors said. 'But it was an error. Better not to have touched them at all, than to have taken two and allowed the third to get away.' He turned to the vidscanner. 'Sound an emergency alert. Close down the factories. Arm the work crews and any male farmers capable of using weapons. Close every road. Remove the women and children to the undersurface shelters. Bring up the heavy guns and supplies. Suspend all non-military production and–'

He considered. 'Arrest everyone we're not sure of. On the C sheet. Have them shot.' He snapped the scanner off.

'What'll happen?' Green demanded, shaken.

'The thing we've prepared for. Total war.'

'We have weapons!' Green shouted excitedly. 'In an hour there'll be ten thousand men ready to fight. We have jet-driven ships. Heavy artillery. Bombs. Bacteria pellets. What's the League? A lot of people with packs on their backs!'

'Yes,' Bors said. 'A lot of people with packs on their backs.'

'How can they do anything? How can a bunch of anarchists organize? They have no structure, no control, no central power.'

'They have the whole world. A billion people.'

'*Individuals!* A club, not subject to law. Voluntary membership. We have disciplined organization. Every aspect of our economic life operates at maximum efficiency. We–you–have your thumb on everything. All you have to do is give the order. Set the machine in motion.'

Bors nodded slowly. 'It's true the anarchist can't coordinate. The League can't organize. It's a paradox. Government by anarchists . . . Anti-government, actually. Instead of governing the world they tramp around to make sure no one else does.'

'Dog in the manger.'

'As you say, they're actually a voluntary club of totally unorganized individuals. Without law or central authority. They maintain no society–they can't govern. All they can do is interfere with anyone else who tries. Troublemakers. But–'

'But what?'

'It was this way before. Two centuries ago. They were unorganized. Unarmed. Vast mobs, without discipline or authority. Yet they pulled down all the governments. All over the world.'

'We've got a whole army. All the roads are mined. Heavy guns. Bombs. Pellets. Every one of us is a soldier. We're an armed camp!'

Bors was deep in thought. 'You say one of them is here? One of the League agents?'

'A young woman.'

Bors signalled the nearby maintenance crew. 'Take me to her. I want to talk to her in the time remaining.'

Silvia watched silently, as the uniformed men pushed and grunted their way into the room. They staggered over to the bed, pulled two chairs together, and carefully laid down their massive armload.

Quickly they snapped protective struts into place, locked the chairs together, threw magnetic grapples into operation, and then warily retreated.

'All right,' the robot said. 'You can go.' The men left. Bors turned to face the woman on the bed.

'A machine,' Silvia whispered, white-faced. 'You're a machine.'

Bors nodded slightly without speaking.

Silvia shifted uneasily on the bed. She was weak. One leg was in a transparent plastic cast. Her face was bandaged and her right arm ached and throbbed. Outside the window, the late afternoon sun sprinkled through the drapes. Flowers bloomed. Grass. Hedges. And beyond the hedges, buildings and factories.

For the last hour the sky had been filled with jet-driven ships. Great flocks that raced excitedly across the sky toward distant hills. Along the highway cars hurtled, dragging guns and heavy military equipment. Men were marching in close rank, rows of gray-clad soldiers, guns and helmets and bacteria masks. Endless lines of figures, identical in their uniforms, stamped from the same matrix.

'There are a lot of them,' Bors said, indicating the marching men.

'Yes.' Silvia watched a couple of soldiers hurry by the window. Youths with worried expressions on their smooth faces. Helmets bobbing at their waists. Long rifles. Canteens. Counters. Radiation shields. Bacteria masks wound awkwardly around their necks, ready to go into place. They were scared. Hardly more than kids. Others followed. A truck roared into life. The soldiers were swept off to join the others.

'They're going to fight,' Bors said, 'to defend their homes and factories.'

'All this equipment. You manufacture it, don't you?'

'That's right. Our industrial organization is perfect. We're totally productive. Our society here is operated rationally. Scientifically. We're fully prepared to meet this emergency.'

Suddenly Silvia realized what the emergency was. 'The League! One of us must have got away.' She pulled herself up. 'Which of them? Penn or my father?'

'I don't know,' the robot murmured indifferently.

Horror and disgust choked Silvia. 'My God,' she said softly. 'You have no understanding of us. You run all this, and you're incapable of empathy. You're nothing but a mechanical computer. One of the old government integration robots.'

'That's right. Two centuries old.'

She was appalled. 'And you've been alive all this time. We thought we destroyed all of you!'

'I was missed. I had been damaged. I wasn't in my place. I was in a truck, on my way out of Washington. I saw the mobs and escaped.'

'Two hundred years ago. Legendary times. You actually saw the events they tell us about. The old days. The great marches. The day the governments fell.'

'Yes. I saw it all. A group of us formed in Virginia. Experts, officials, skilled workmen. Later we came here. It was remote enough, off the beaten path.'

'We heard rumors. A fragment . . . Still maintaining itself. But we didn't know where or how.'

'I was fortunate,' Bors said. 'I escaped by a fluke. All the others were destroyed. It's taken a long time to organize what you see here. Fifteen miles from here is a ring of hills. This valley is a bowl–mountains on all sides. We've set up road blocks in the form of natural slides. Nobody comes here. Even in Fairfax, thirty miles off, they know nothing.'

'That girl. Laura.'

'Scouts. We keep scout teams in all inhabited regions within a hundred-mile radius. As soon as you entered Fairfax, word was relayed to us. An air unit was dispatched. To avoid questions, we arranged to have you killed in an auto wreck. But one of you escaped.'

Silvia shook her head, bewildered. 'How?' she demanded. 'How do you keep going? Don't the people revolt?' She struggled to a sitting position. 'They must know what's happened everywhere else. How do you control them? They're going out now, in their uniforms. But–*will they fight? Can you count on them?*'

Bors answered slowly. 'They trust me,' he said. 'I brought with me a vast amount of knowledge. Information and techniques lost to the rest of the world. Are jet-ships and vidscanners and power cables made anywhere else in the world? I retain all that knowledge. I have memory units, synapsis-coils. Because of me they have these things. Things you know only as dim memories, vague legends.'

'What happens when you die?'

'I won't die! I'm eternal!'

'You're wearing out. You have to be carried around. And your right arm. You can hardly move it!' Silvia's voice was harsh, ruthless. 'Your whole tank is pitted and rusty.'

The robot whirred; for a moment he seemed unable to speak. 'My knowledge remains,' he grated finally. 'I'll always be able to communicate. Fowler has arranged a broadcast system. Even when I talk–' He broke off. 'Even then. Everything is under control. I've organized every aspect of the situation. I've maintained this system for two centuries. It's got to be kept going!'

Silvia lashed out. It happened in a split second. The boot of her cast caught the chairs on which the robot rested. She thrust violently with her foot and hands; the chairs teetered, hesitated–

'Fowler!' the robot screamed.

Silvia pushed with all her strength. Blinding agony seared through her leg; she bit her lip and threw her shoulder against the robot's pitted hulk. He waved his arms, whirred wildly, and then the two chairs slowly collapsed. The robot slid quietly from them, over on his back, his arms still waving helplessly.

Silvia dragged herself from the bed. She managed to pull herself to the window; her broken leg hung uselessly, a dead weight in its transparent plastic cast. The robot lay like some futile bug, arms waving, eye lens clicking, its rusty works whirring in fear and rage.

'Fowler!' it screamed again. 'Help me!'

Silvia reached the window. She tugged at the locks; they were sealed. She grabbed up a lamp from the table and threw it against the glass. The glass burst around her, a shower of lethal fragments. She stumbled forward–and then the repair crew was pouring into the room.

Fowler gasped at the sight of the robot on its back. A strange expression crossed his face. 'Look at him!'

'Help me!' the robot shrilled. 'Help me!'

One of the men grabbed Silvia around the waist and lugged her back to the bed. She kicked and bit, sunk her nails into the man's cheek. He threw her on the bed, face down, and drew his pistol. 'Stay there,' he gasped.

The others were bent over the robot, getting him to an upright position.

'What happened?' Fowler said. He came over to the bed, his face twisting. 'Did he fall?'

Silvia's eyes glowed with hatred and despair. 'I pushed him over. I almost got there.' Her chest heaved. 'The window. But my leg–'

'Get me back to my quarters!' Bors cried.

The crew gathered him up and carried him down the hall, to his private office. A few moments later he was sitting shakily at his desk, his mechanism pounding wildly, surrounded by his papers and memoranda.

He forced down his panic and tried to resume his work. He had to keep going. His vidscreen was alive with activity. The whole system was in motion. He blankly watched a subcommander sending up a cloud of black dots, jet bombers that shot up like flies and headed quickly off.

The system had to be preserved. He repeated it again and again. He had to save it. Had to organize the people and make *them* save it. If the people didn't fight, wasn't everything doomed?

Fury and desperation overwhelmed him. The system couldn't preserve itself; it wasn't a thing apart, something that could be separated from the people who lived it. Actually it *was* the people. They were identical; when the people fought to preserve the system they were fighting to preserve nothing less than themselves.

They existed only as long as the system existed.

He caught sight of a marching column of white-faced troops, moving toward the hills. His ancient synapsis-coils radiated and shuddered uncertainly, then fell back into pattern. He was two centuries old. He had come into existence a long time ago, in a different world. That world had created him; through him that world still lived. As long as he existed, that world existed. In miniature, it still functioned. His model universe, his recreation. His rational, controlled world, in which each aspect was fully organized, fully analyzed and integrated.

He kept a rational, progressive world alive. A humming oasis of productivity on a dusty, parched planet of decay and silence.

Bors spread out his papers and went to work on the most pressing problem. The transformation from a peace-time economy to full military mobilization. Total military organization of every man, woman, child, piece of equipment and dyne of energy under his direction.

Edward Tolby emerged cautiously. His clothes were torn and ragged. He had lost his pack, crawling through the brambles and vines. His face and hands were bleeding. He was utterly exhausted.

Below him lay a valley. A vast bowl. Fields, houses, highways. Factories. Equipment. Men.

He had been watching the men three hours. Endless streams of them, pouring from the valley into the hills, along the roads and paths. On foot, in trucks, in cars, armored tanks, weapons carriers. Overhead, in fast little jet-fighters and great lumbering bombers. Gleaming ships that took up positions above the troops and prepared for battle.

Battle in the grand style. The two-centuries-old full-scale war that was supposed to have disappeared. But here it was, a vision from the past. He had seen this in the old tapes and records, used in the camp orientation courses. A ghost army resurrected to fight again. A vast host of men and guns, prepared to fight and die.

Tolby climbed down cautiously. At the foot of a slope of boulders a soldier had halted his motorcycle and was setting up a communications antenna and transmitter. Tolby circled, crouched, expertly approached him. A blond-haired youth, fumbling nervously with the wires and relays, licking his lips uneasily, glancing up and grabbing for his rifle at every sound.

Tolby took a deep breath. The youth had turned his back; he was tracing a power circuit. It was now or never. With one stride Tolby stepped out, raised his pistol and fired. The clump of equipment and the soldier's rifle vanished.

'Don't make a sound,' Tolby said. He peered around. No one had seen; the main line was half a mile to his right. The sun was setting. Great shadows were falling over the hills. The fields were rapidly fading from brown-green to a deep violet. 'Put your hands up over your head, clasp them, and get down on your knees.'

The youth tumbled down in a frightened heap. 'What are you going to do?' He saw the ironite staff, and the color left his face. 'You're a League agent!'

'Shut up,' Tolby ordered. 'First, outline your system of responsibility. *Who's your superior?*'

The youth stuttered forth what he knew. Tolby listened intently. He was satisfied. The usual monolithic structure. Exactly what he wanted.

'At the top,' he broke in. 'At the top of the pillar. Who has ultimate responsibility?'

'Bors.'

'Bors!' Tolby scowled. 'That doesn't sound like a name. Sounds like–' He broke off, staggered. 'We should have guessed! An old government robot. Still functioning.'

The youth saw his chance. He leaped up and darted frantically away.

Tolby shot him above the left ear. The youth pitched over on his face and lay still. Tolby hurried to him and quickly pulled off his dark gray uniform. It was too small for him of course. But the motorcycle was just right. He'd seen tapes of them; he'd wanted one since he was a child. A fast little motorcycle to propel his weight around. Now he had it.

Half an hour later he was roaring down a smooth, broad highway toward the center of the valley and the buildings that rose against the dark sky. His headlights cut into the blackness; he still wobbled from side to side, but for all practical purposes he had the hang of it. He increased speed; the road shot by, trees and fields, haystacks, stalled farm equipment. All traffic was going against him, troops hurrying to the front.

The front. Lemmings going out into the ocean to drown. A thousand, ten thousand, metal-clad figures, armed and alert. Weighted down with guns and bombs and flame throwers and bacteria pellets.

There was only one hitch. No army opposed them. A mistake had been made. It took two sides to make a war, and only one had been resurrected.

A mile outside the concentration of buildings he pulled his motorcycle off the road and carefully hid it in a haystack. For a moment he considered leaving his ironite staff. Then he shrugged and grabbed it up, along with his pistol. He always carried his staff, it was the League symbol. It represented the walking Anarchists who patrolled the world on foot, the world's protection agency.

He loped through the darkness toward the outline ahead. There were fewer men here. He saw no women or children. Ahead, charged wire was set up. Troops crouched behind it, armed to the teeth. A searchlight moved back and forth across the road. Behind it, radar vanes loomed and behind them an ugly square of concrete. The great offices from which the government was run.

For a time he watched the searchlight. Finally he had its motion plotted. In its glare, the faces of the troops stood out, pale and drawn.

Youths. They had never fought. This was their first encounter. They were terrified.

When the light was off him, he stood up and advanced toward the wire. Automatically, a breach was slid back for him. Two guards raised up and awkwardly crossed bayonets ahead of him.

'Show your papers!' one demanded. Young lieutenants. Boys, white-lipped, nervous. Playing soldier.

Pity and contempt made Tolby laugh harshly and push forward. 'Get out of my way.'

One anxiously flashed a pocket light. 'Halt! What's the code-key for this watch?' He blocked Tolby's way with his bayonet, hands twisting convulsively.

Tolby reached in his pocket, pulled out his pistol, and as the searchlight started to swerve back, blasted the two guards. The bayonets clattered down and he dived forward. Yells and shapes rose on all sides. Anguished, terrified shouts. Random firing. The night was lit up, as he dashed and crouched, turned a corner past a supply warehouse, raced up a flight of stairs and into the massive building ahead.

He had to work fast. Gripping his ironite staff, he plunged down a gloomy corridor. His boots echoed. Men poured into the building behind him. Bolts of energy thundered past him; a whole section of the ceiling burst into ash and collapsed behind him.

He reached stairs and climbed rapidly. He came to the next floor and groped for the door handle. Something flickered behind him. He half-turned, his gun quickly up–

A stunning blow sent him sprawling. He crashed against the wall; his gun flew from his fingers. A shape bent over him, rifle gripped. 'Who are you? What are you doing here?'

Not a soldier. A stubble-chinned man in stained shirt and rumpled trousers. Eyes puffy and red. A belt of tools, hammer, pliers, screwdriver, a soldering iron, around his waist.

Tolby raised himself up painfully. 'If you didn't have that rifle–'

Fowler backed warily away. 'Who are you? This floor is forbidden to troops of the line. You know this–' Then he saw the ironite staff.

'By God,' he said softly. 'You're the one they didn't get.' He laughed shakily. 'You're the one who got away.'

Tolby's fingers tightened around the staff, but Fowler reacted instantly. The snout of the rifle jerked up, on a line with Tolby's face.

'Be careful,' Fowler warned. He turned slightly; soldiers were hurrying up the stairs, boots drumming, echoing shouts ringing. For a moment he hesitated, then waved his rifle toward the stairs ahead. 'Up. Get going.'

Toby blinked. 'What–'

'Up!' The rifle snout jabbed into Tolby. 'Hurry!'

Bewildered, Tolby hurried up the stairs, Fowler close behind him. At the third floor Fowler pushed him roughly through the doorway, the snout of his rifle digging urgently into his back. He found himself in a corridor of doors. Endless offices.

'Keep going,' Fowler snarled. 'Down the hall. Hurry!'

Tolby hurried, his mind spinning. 'What the hell are you–'

'I could never do it,' Fowler gasped, close to his ear. 'Not in a million years. But it's got to be done.'

Tolby halted. 'What is this?'

They faced each other defiantly, faces contorted, eyes blazing. 'He's in there,' Fowler snapped, indicating a door with his rifle. 'You have one chance. Take it.'

For a fraction of a second Tolby hesitated. Then he broke away. 'Okay. I'll take it.'

Fowler followed after him. 'Be careful. Watch your step. There's a series of check points. Keep going straight, in all the way. As far as you can go. And for God's sake, hurry!'

His voice faded, as Tolby gained speed. He reached the door and tore it open.

Soldiers and officials ballooned. He threw himself against them; they sprawled and scattered. He scrambled on, as they struggled up and stupidly fumbled for their guns. Through another door, into an inner office, past a desk where a frightened girl sat, eyes wide, mouth open. Then a third door, into an alcove.

A wild-faced youth leaped up and snatched frantically for his pistol. Tolby was unarmed, trapped in the alcove. Figures already pushed against the door behind him. He gripped his ironite staff and backed away as the blond-haired fanatic fired blindly. The bolt burst a foot away; it flicked him with a tongue of heat.

'You dirty anarchist!' Green screamed. His face distorted, he fired again and again. 'You murdering anarchist spy!'

Tolby hurled his ironite staff. He put all his strength in it; the staff leaped through the air in a whistling arc, straight at the youth's head. Green saw it coming and ducked. Agile and quick, he jumped away, grinning humorlessly. The staff crashed against the wall and rolled clanging to the floor.

'Your walking staff!' Green gasped and fired.

The bolt missed him on purpose. Green was playing games with him. Tolby bent down and groped frantically for the staff. He picked it up. Green watched, face rigid, eyes glittering. 'Throw it again!' he snarled.

Tolby leaped. He took the youth by surprise. Green grunted, stumbled back from the impact, then suddenly fought with maniacal fury.

Tolby was heavier. But he was exhausted. He had crawled hours, beat his way through the mountains, walked endlessly. He was at the end of his strength. The car wreck, the days of walking. Green was in perfect shape. His wiry, agile body twisted away. His hands came up. Fingers dug into Tolby's windpipe; he kicked the youth in the groin. Green staggered back, convulsed and bent over with pain.

'All right,' Green gasped, face ugly and dark. His hand fumbled with his pistol. The barrel came up.

Half of Green's head dissolved. His hands opened and his gun fell to the floor. His body stood for a moment, then settled down in a heap, like an empty suit of clothes.

Tolby caught a glimpse of a rifle snout pushed past him–and the man with the tool belt. The man waved him on frantically. 'Hurry!'

Tolby raced down a carpeted hall, between two great flickering yellow lamps. A crowd of officials and soldiers stumbled uncertainly after him, shouting and firing at random. He tore open a thick oak door and halted.

He was in a luxurious chamber. Drapes, rich wallpaper. Lamps. Bookcases. A glimpse of the finery of the past. The wealth of the old days. Thick carpets. Warm radiant heat. A vidscreen. At the far end, a huge mahogany desk.

At the desk a figure sat. Working on heaps of papers and reports, piled masses of material. The figure contrasted starkly with the lushness of the furnishings. It was a great pitted, corroded tank of metal. Bent and greenish, patched and repaired. An ancient machine.

'Is that you, Fowler?' the robot demanded.

Tolby advanced, his ironite staff gripped.

The robot turned angrily. 'Who is it? Get Green and carry me down into the shelter. One of the road blocks has reported a League agent already–' The robot broke off. Its cold, mechanical eye lens bored up at the man. It clicked and whirred in uneasy astonishment. 'I don't know you.'

It saw the ironite staff.

'League agent,' the robot said. 'You're the one who got through.' Comprehension came. '*The third one*. You came here. You didn't go back.' Its metal fingers fumbled clumsily at the objects on the desk, then in the drawer. It found a gun and raised it awkwardly.

Tolby knocked the gun away; it clattered to the floor. 'Run!' he shouted at the robot. 'Start running!'

It remained. Tolby's staff came down. The fragile, complex brain-unit of the robot burst apart. Coils, wiring, relay fluid, spattered over his arms and hands. The robot shuddered. Its machinery thrashed. It half-rose from its chair, then swayed and toppled. It crashed full length on the floor, parts and gears rolling in all directions.

'Good God,' Tolby said, suddenly seeing it for the first time. Shakily, he bent over its remains. 'It was crippled.'

Men were all around him. 'He's killed Bors!' Shocked, dazed faces. 'Bors is dead!'

Fowler came up slowly. 'You got him, all right. There's nothing left now.'

Tolby stood holding his ironite staff in his hands. 'The poor blasted thing,' he said softly. 'Completely helpless. Sitting there and I came and killed him. He didn't have a chance.'

The building was bedlam. Soldiers and officials scurried crazily about, grief-stricken, hysterical. They bumped into each other, gathered in knots, shouted and gave meaningless orders.

Tolby pushed past them; nobody paid any attention to him. Fowler was gathering up the remains of the robot. Collecting the smashed pieces and bits. Tolby stopped beside him. Like Humpty-Dumpty, pulled down off his wall, he'd never be back together, not now.

'Where's the woman?' he asked Fowler. 'The League agent they brought in.'

Fowler straightened up slowly. 'I'll take you.' He led Tolby down the packed, surging hall, to the hospital wing of the building.

Silvia sat up apprehensively as the two men entered the room. 'What's going on?' She recognized her father. 'Dad! Thank God! It was you who got out.'

Tolby slammed the door against the chaos of sound hammering up and down the corridor. 'How are you? How's your leg?'

'Mending. What happened?'

'I got him. The robot. He's dead.'

For a moment the three of them were silent. Outside, in the halls, men ran frantically back and forth. Word had already leaked out. Troops gathered in huddled knots outside the building. Lost men, wandering away from their posts. Uncertain. Aimless.

'It's over,' Fowler said.

Tolby nodded. 'I know.'

'They'll get tired of crouching in their foxholes,' Fowler said. 'They'll come filtering back. As soon as the news reaches them, they'll desert and throw away their equipment.'

'Good,' Tolby grunted. 'The sooner the better.' He touched Fowler's rifle. 'You, too, I hope.'

Silvia hesitated. 'Do you think–'

'Think what?'

'Did we make a mistake?'

Tolby grinned wearily. 'Hell of a time to think about that.'

'He was doing what he thought was right. They built up their homes and factories. This whole area . . . They turn out a lot of goods. I've been watching through the window. It's made me think. They've done so much. Made so much.'

'Made a lot of guns,' Tolby said.

'We have guns, too. We kill and destroy. We have all the disadvantages and none of the advantages.'

'We don't have war,' Tolby answered quietly. 'To defend this neat little organization there are ten thousand men up there in those hills. All waiting to fight. Waiting to drop their bombs and bacteria pellets, to keep this place running. But they won't. Pretty soon they'll give up and start to trickle back.'

'This whole system will decay rapidly,' Fowler said. 'He was already losing his control. He couldn't keep the clock back much longer.'

'Anyhow, it's done,' Silvia murmured. 'We did our job.' She smiled a little. 'Bors did his job and we did ours. But the times were against him and with us.'

'That's right,' Tolby agreed. 'We did our job. And we'll never be sorry.'

Fowler said nothing. He stood with his hands in his pockets, gazing silently out the window. His fingers were touching something. Three undamaged synapsis-coils. Intact memory elements from the dead robot, snatched from the scattered remains.

Just in case, he said to himself. *Just in case the times change.*

THE FATHER-THING

'Dinner's ready,' commanded Mrs Walton. 'Go get your father and tell him to wash his hands. The same applies to you, young man.' She carried a steaming casserole to the neatly set table. 'You'll find him out in the garage.'

Charles hesitated. He was only eight years old, and the problem bothering him would have confounded Hillel. 'I–' he began uncertainly.

'What's wrong?' June Walton caught the uneasy tone in her son's voice and her matronly bosom fluttered with sudden alarm. 'Isn't Ted out in the garage? For heaven's sake, he was sharpening the hedge shears a minute ago. He didn't go over to the Andersons', did he? I told him dinner was practically on the table.'

'He's in the garage,' Charles said. 'But he's–talking to himself.'

'Talking to himself!' Mrs Walton removed her bright plastic apron and hung it over the doorknob. 'Ted? Why, he never talks to himself. Go tell him to come in here.' She poured boiling black coffee in the little blue-and-white china cups and began ladling out creamed corn. 'What's wrong with you? Go tell him!'

'I don't know which of them to tell,' Charles blurted out desperately. 'They both look alike.'

June Walton's fingers lost their hold on the aluminum pan; for a moment the creamed corn slushed dangerously. 'Young man–' she began angrily, but at that moment Ted Walton came striding into the kitchen, inhaling and sniffing and rubbing his hands together.

'Ah,' he cried happily. 'Lamb stew.'

'Beef stew,' June murmured. 'Ted, what were you doing out there?'

Ted threw himself down at his place and unfolded his napkin. 'I got the shears sharpened like a razor. Oiled and sharpened. Better not touch them–they'll cut your hand off.' He was a good-looking man in his early thirties; thick blond hair, strong arms, competent hands, square face and flashing brown eyes. 'Man, this stew looks good. Hard day at the office–Friday, you know. Stuff piles up and we have to get all the accounts out by five. Al McKinley claims the department could handle 20 per cent more stuff if we organized our lunch hours; staggered them so somebody was there all the time.' He beckoned Charles over. 'Sit down and let's go.'

Mrs Walton served the frozen peas. 'Ted,' she said, as she slowly took her seat, 'is there anything on your mind?'

'On my mind?' He blinked. 'No, nothing unusual. Just the regular stuff. Why?'

Uneasily, June Walton glanced over at her son. Charles was sitting bolt-upright at his place, face expressionless, white as chalk. He hadn't moved, hadn't unfolded his napkin or even touched his milk. A tension was in the air; she could feel it. Charles had pulled his chair away from his father's; he was huddled in a tense little bundle as far from his father as possible. His lips were moving, but she couldn't catch what he was saying.

'What is it?' she demanded, leaning toward him.

'*The other one*,' Charles was muttering under his breath. 'The other one came in.'

'What do you mean, dear?' June Walton asked out loud. 'What other one?'

Ted jerked. A strange expression flitted across his face. It vanished at once; but in the brief instant Ted Walton's face lost all familiarity. Something alien and cold gleamed out, a twisting, wriggling mass. The eyes blurred and receded, as an archaic sheen filmed over them. The ordinary look of a tired, middle-aged husband was gone.

And then it was back–or nearly back. Ted grinned and began to wolf down his stew and frozen peas and creamed corn. He laughed, stirred his coffee, kidded and ate. But something terrible was wrong.

'The other one,' Charles muttered, face white, hands beginning to tremble. Suddenly he leaped up and backed away from the table. 'Get away!' he shouted. 'Get out of here!'

'Hey,' Ted rumbled ominously. 'What's got into you?' He pointed sternly at the boy's chair. 'You sit down there and eat your dinner, young man. Your mother didn't fix it for nothing.'

Charles turned and ran out of the kitchen, upstairs to his room. June Walton gasped and fluttered in dismay. 'What in the world–'

Ted went on eating. His face was grim; his eyes were hard and dark. 'That kid,' he grated, 'is going to have to learn a few things. Maybe he and I need to have a little private conference together.'

Charles crouched and listened.

The father-thing was coming up the stairs, nearer and nearer. 'Charles!' it shouted angrily. 'Are you up there?'

He didn't answer. Soundlessly, he moved back into his room and pulled the door shut. His heart was pounding heavily. The father-thing had reached the landing; in a moment it would come in his room.

He hurried to the window. He was terrified; it was already fumbling in the dark hall for the knob. He lifted the window and climbed out on the roof. With a grunt he dropped into the flower garden that ran by the front door, staggered and gasped, then leaped to his feet and ran from the light that streamed out the window, a patch of yellow in the evening darkness.

He found the garage; it loomed up ahead, a black square against the skyline. Breathing quickly, he fumbled in his pocket for his flashlight, then cautiously slid the door up and entered.

The garage was empty. The car was parked out front. To the left was his father's workbench. Hammers and saws on the wooden walls. In the back were the lawnmower, rake, shovel, hoe. A drum of kerosene. License plates nailed up everywhere. Floor was concrete and dirt; a great oil slick stained the center, tufts of weeds greasy and black in the flickering beam of the flashlight.

Just inside the door was a big trash barrel. On top of the barrel were stacks of soggy newspapers and magazines, moldy and damp. A thick stench of decay issued from them as Charles began to move them around. Spiders dropped to the cement and scampered off; he crushed them with his foot and went on looking.

The sight made him shriek. He dropped the flashlight and leaped wildly back. The garage was plunged into instant gloom. He forced himself to kneel down, and for an ageless moment, he groped in the darkness for the light, among the spiders and greasy weeds. Finally he had it again. He managed to turn the beam down into the barrel, down the well he had made by pushing back the piles of magazines.

The father-thing had stuffed it down in the very bottom of the barrel. Among the old leaves and torn-up cardboard, the rotting remains of magazines and curtains, rubbish from the attic his mother had lugged down here with the idea of burning someday. It still looked a little like his father, enough for him to recognize. He had found it–and the sight made him sick at his stomach. He hung onto the barrel and shut his eyes until finally he was able to look again. In the barrel were the remains of his father, his real father. Bits the father-thing had no use for. Bits it had discarded.

He got the rake and pushed it down to stir the remains. They were dry. They cracked and broke at the touch of the rake. They were like a discarded snake skin, flaky and crumbling, rustling at the touch. *An empty skin.* The insides were gone. The important part. This was all that remained, just the brittle, cracking skin, wadded down at the bottom of the trash barrel in a little heap. This was all the father-thing had left; it had eaten the rest. Taken the insides–and his father's place.

A sound.

He dropped the rake and hurried to the door. The father-thing was coming down the path, toward the garage. Its shoes crushed the gravel; it felt its way along uncertainly. 'Charles!' it called angrily. 'Are you in there? Wait'll I get my hands on you, young man!'

His mother's ample, nervous shape was outlined in the bright doorway of the house. 'Ted, please don't hurt him. He's all upset about something.'

'I'm not going to hurt him,' the father-thing rasped; it halted to strike a match. 'I'm just going to have a little talk with him. He needs to learn better manners. Leaving the table like that and running out at night, climbing down the roof–'

Charles slipped from the garage; the glare of the match caught his moving shape, and with a bellow the father-thing lunged forward.

'*Come here!*'

Charles ran. He knew the ground better than the father-thing; it knew a lot, had taken a lot when it got his father's insides, but nobody knew the way like *he* did. He reached the fence, climbed it, leaped into the Andersons' yard, raced past their clothesline, down the path around the side of their house, and out on Maple Street.

He listened, crouched down and not breathing. The father-thing hadn't come after him. It had gone back. Or it was coming around the sidewalk.

He took a deep, shuddering breath. He had to keep moving. Sooner or later it would find him. He glanced right and left, made sure it wasn't watching, and then started off at a rapid dog-trot.

'What do you want?' Tony Peretti demanded belligerently. Tony was fourteen. He was sitting at the table in the oak-panelled Peretti dining room, books and pencils scattered around him, half a ham-and-peanut-butter sandwich and a Coke beside him. 'You're Walton, aren't you?'

Tony Peretti had a job uncrating stoves and refrigerators after school at Johnson's Appliance Shop, downtown. He was big and blunt-faced. Black hair, olive skin, white teeth. A couple of times he had beaten up Charles; he had beaten up every kid in the neighborhood.

Charles twisted. 'Say, Peretti. Do me a favor?'

'What do you want?' Peretti was annoyed. 'You looking for a bruise?'

Gazing unhappily down, his fists clenched, Charles explained what had happened in short, mumbled words.

When he had finished, Peretti let out a low whistle. 'No kidding.'

'It's true.' He nodded quickly. 'I'll show you. Come on and I'll show you.'

Peretti got slowly to his feet. 'Yeah, show me. I want to see.'

He got his b.b. gun from his room, and the two of them walked silently up the dark street, toward Charles' house. Neither of them said much. Peretti was deep in thought, serious and solemn-faced. Charles was still dazed; his mind was completely blank.

They turned down the Anderson driveway, cut through the back yard, climbed the fence, and lowered themselves cautiously into Charles' back yard. There was no movement. The yard was silent. The front door of the house was closed.

They peered through the living room window. The shades were down, but a narrow crack of yellow streamed out. Sitting on the couch was Mrs Walton, sewing a cotton T-shirt. There was a sad, troubled look on her large face. She worked listlessly, without interest. Opposite her was the father-thing. Leaning back in his father's easy chair, its shoes off, reading the evening newspaper. The TV was on, playing to itself in the corner. A can of beer rested on the arm of the easy chair. The father-thing sat exactly as his own father had sat; it had learned a lot.

'Looks just like him,' Peretti whispered suspiciously. 'You sure you're not bulling me?'

Charles led him to the garage and showed him the trash barrel. Peretti reached his long tanned arms down and carefully pulled up the dry, flaking remains. They spread out, unfolded, until the whole figure of his father was outlined. Peretti laid the remains on the floor and pieced broken parts back into place. The remains were colorless. Almost transparent. An amber yellow, thin as paper. Dry and utterly lifeless.

'That's all,' Charles said. Tears welled up in his eyes. 'That's all that's left of him. The thing has the insides.'

Peretti had turned pale. Shakily, he crammed the remains back in the trash barrel. 'This is really something,' he muttered. 'You say you saw the two of them together?'

'Talking. They looked exactly alike. I ran inside.' Charles wiped the tears away and sniveled; he couldn't hold it back any longer. 'It ate him while I was inside. Then it came in the house. It pretended it was him. But it isn't. It killed him and ate his insides.'

For a moment Peretti was silent. 'I'll tell you something,' he said suddenly. 'I've heard about this sort of thing. It's a bad business. You have to use your head and not get scared. You're not scared, are you?'

'No,' Charles managed to mutter.

'The first thing we have to do is figure out how to kill it.' He rattled his b.b. gun. 'I don't know if this'll work. It must be plenty tough to get hold of your father. He was a big man.' Peretti considered. 'Let's get out of here. It might come back. They say that's what a murderer does.'

They left the garage. Peretti crouched down and peeked through the window again. Mrs Walton had got to her feet. She was talking anxiously. Vague sounds filtered out. The father-thing threw down its newspaper. They were arguing.

'For God's sake!' the father-thing shouted. 'Don't do anything stupid like that.'

'Something's wrong,' Mrs Walton moaned. 'Something terrible. Just let me call the hospital and see.'

'Don't call anybody. He's all right. Probably up the street playing.'

'He's never out this late. He never disobeys. He was terribly upset—afraid of you! I don't blame him.' Her voice broke with misery. 'What's wrong with you? You're so strange.' She moved out of the room, into the hall. 'I'm going to call some of the neighbors.'

The father-thing glared after her until she had disappeared. Then a terrifying thing happened. Charles gasped; even Peretti grunted under his breath.

'Look,' Charles muttered. 'What—'

'Golly,' Peretti said, black eyes wide.

As soon as Mrs Walton was gone from the room, the father-thing sagged in its chair. It became limp. Its mouth fell open. Its eyes peered vacantly. Its head fell forward, like a discarded rag doll.

Peretti moved away from the window. 'That's it,' he whispered. 'That's the whole thing.'

'What is it?' Charles demanded. He was shocked and bewildered. 'It looked like somebody turned off its power.'

'Exactly.' Peretti nodded slowly, grim and shaken. 'It's controlled from outside.'

Horror settled over Charles. 'You mean, something outside our world?'

Peretti shook his head with disgust. 'Outside the house! In the yard. You know how to find?'

'Not very well.' Charles pulled his mind together. 'But I know somebody who's good at finding.' He forced his mind to summon the name. 'Bobby Daniels.'

'That little black kid? Is he good at finding?'

'The best.'

'All right,' Peretti said. 'Let's go get him. We have to find the thing that's outside. That made *it* in there, and keeps it going . . .'

'It's near the garage,' Peretti said to the small, thin-faced Negro boy who crouched beside them in the darkness. 'When it got him, he was in the garage. So look there.'

'In the garage?' Daniels asked.

'*Around* the garage. Walton's already gone over the garage, inside. Look around outside. Nearby.'

There was a small bed of flowers growing by the garage, and a great tangle of bamboo and discarded debris between the garage and the back of the house. The moon had come out; a cold, misty light filtered down over everything. 'If we don't find it pretty soon,' Daniels said, 'I got to go back home. I can't stay up much later.' He wasn't any older than Charles. Perhaps nine.

'All right,' Peretti agreed. 'Then get looking.'

The three of them spread out and began to go over the ground with care. Daniels worked with incredible speed; his thin little body moved in a blur of motion as he crawled among the flowers, turned over rocks, peered under the house, separated stalks of plants, ran his expert hands over leaves and stems, in tangles of compost and weeds. No inch was missed.

Peretti halted after a short time. 'I'll guard. It might be dangerous. The father-thing might come and try to stop us.' He posted himself on the back step with his b.b. gun while Charles and Bobby Daniels searched. Charles worked slowly. He was tired, and his body was cold and numb. It seemed impossible, the father-thing and what had happened to his own father, his real father. But terror spurred him on; what if it happened to his mother, or to him? Or to everyone? Maybe the whole world.

'I found it!' Daniels called in a thin, high voice. 'You all come around here quick!'

Peretti raised his gun and got up cautiously. Charles hurried over; he turned the flickering yellow beam of his flashlight where Daniels stood.

The Negro boy had raised a concrete stone. In the moist, rotting soil the light gleamed on a metallic body. A thin, jointed thing with endless crooked legs was digging frantically. Plated, like an ant; a red-brown bug that rapidly disappeared before their eyes. Its rows of legs scrabbled and clutched. The ground gave rapidly under it. Its wicked-looking tail twisted furiously as it struggled down the tunnel it had made.

Peretti ran into the garage and grabbed up the rake. He pinned down the tail of the bug with it. 'Quick! Shoot it with the b.b. gun!'

Daniels snatched the gun and took aim. The first shot tore the tail of the bug loose. It writhed and twisted frantically; its tail dragged uselessly and some of its legs broke off. It was a foot long, like a great millipede. It struggled desperately to escape down its hole.

'Shoot again,' Peretti ordered.

Daniels fumbled with the gun. The bug slithered and hissed. Its head jerked back and forth; it twisted and bit at the rake holding it down. Its wicked specks of eyes gleamed with hatred. For a moment it struck futilely at the rake; then abruptly, without warning, it thrashed in a frantic convulsion that made them all draw away in fear.

Something buzzed through Charles' brain. A loud humming, metallic and harsh, a billion metal wires dancing and vibrating at once. He was tossed about violently by the force; the banging crash of metal made him deaf and confused. He stumbled to his feet and backed off; the others were doing the same, white-faced and shaken.

'If we can't kill it with the gun,' Peretti gasped, 'we can drown it. Or burn it. Or stick a pin through its brain.' He fought to hold onto the rake, to keep the bug pinned down.

'I have a jar of formaldehyde,' Daniels muttered. His fingers fumbled nervously with the b.b. gun. 'How do this thing work? I can't seem to–'

Charles grabbed the gun from him. 'I'll kill it.' He squatted down, one eye to the sight, and gripped the trigger. The bug lashed and struggled. Its force-field hammered in his ears, but he hung onto the gun. His finger tightened . . .

'All right, Charles,' the father-thing said. Powerful fingers gripped him, a paralyzing pressure around his wrists. The gun fell to the ground as he struggled futilely. The father-thing shoved against Peretti. The boy leaped away and the bug, free of the rake, slithered triumphantly down its tunnel.

'You have a spanking coming, Charles,' the father-thing droned on. 'What got into you? Your poor mother's out of her mind with worry.'

It had been there, hiding in the shadows. Crouched in the darkness watching them. Its calm, emotionless voice, a dreadful parody of his father's, rumbled close to his ear as it pulled him relentlessly toward the garage. Its cold breath blew in his face, an icy-sweet odor, like decaying soil. Its strength was immense; there was nothing he could do.

'Don't fight me,' it said calmly. 'Come along, into the garage. This is for your own good. I know best, Charles.'

'Did you find him?' his mother called anxiously, opening the back door.

'Yes, I found him.'

'What are you going to do?'

'A little spanking.' The father-thing pushed up the garage door. 'In the garage.' In the half-light a faint smile, humorless and utterly without emotion, touched its lips. 'You go back in the living room, June. I'll take care of this. It's more in my line. You never did like punishing him.'

The back door reluctantly closed. As the light cut off, Peretti bent down and groped for the b.b. gun. The father-thing instantly froze.

'Go on home, boys,' it rasped.

Peretti stood undecided, gripping the b.b. gun.

'Get going,' the father-thing repeated. 'Put down that toy and get out of here.' It moved slowly toward Peretti, gripping Charles with one hand, reaching toward Peretti with the other. 'No b.b. guns allowed in town, sonny. Your father know you have that? There's a city ordinance. I think you better give me that before–'

Peretti shot it in the eye.

The father-thing grunted and pawed at its ruined eye. Abruptly it slashed out at Peretti. Peretti moved down the driveway, trying to cock the gun. The father-thing lunged. Its powerful fingers snatched the gun from Peretti's hands. Silently, the father-thing mashed the gun against the wall of the house.

Charles broke away and ran numbly off. Where could he hide? It was between him and the house. Already, it was coming back toward him, a black shape creeping carefully, peering into the darkness, trying to make him out. Charles retreated. If there were only some place he could hide . . .

The bamboo.

He crept quickly into the bamboo. The stalks were huge and old. They closed after him with a faint rustle. The father-thing was fumbling in its pocket; it lit a match, then the whole pack flared up. 'Charles,' it said. 'I know you're here, some place. There's no use hiding. You're only making it more difficult.'

His heart hammering, Charles crouched among the bamboo. Here, debris and filth rotted. Weeds, garbage, papers, boxes, old clothing, boards, tin cans, bottles. Spiders and salamanders squirmed around him. The bamboo swayed with the night wind. Insects and filth.

And something else.

A shape, a silent, unmoving shape that grew up from the mound of filth like some nocturnal mushroom. A white column, a pulpy mass that glistened moistly in the moonlight. Webs covered it, a moldy cocoon. It had vague arms and legs. An indistinct half-shaped head. As yet, the features hadn't formed. But he could tell what it was.

A mother-thing. Growing here in the filth and dampness, between the garage and the house. Behind the towering bamboo.

It was almost ready. Another few days and it would reach maturity. It was still a larva, white and soft and pulpy. But the sun would dry and warm it. Harden its shell. Turn it dark and strong. It would emerge from its cocoon, and one day when his mother came by the garage . . . Behind the mother-thing were other pulpy white larvae, recently laid by the bug. Small. Just coming into existence. He could see where the father-thing had broken off; the place where it had grown. It had matured here. And in the garage, his father had met it.

Charles began to move numbly away, past the rotting boards, the filth and debris, the pulpy mushroom larvae. Weakly, he reached out to take hold of the fence—and scrambled back.

Another one. Another larva. He hadn't seen this one, at first. It wasn't white. It had already turned dark. The web, the pulpy softness, the moistness, were gone. It was ready. It stirred a little, moved its arm feebly.

The Charles-thing.

The bamboo separated, and the father-thing's hand clamped

firmly around the boy's wrist. 'You stay right here,' it said. 'This is exactly the place for you. Don't move.' With its other hand it tore at the remains of the cocoon binding the Charles-thing. 'I'll help it out–it's still a little weak.'

The last shred of moist gray was stripped back, and the Charles-thing tottered out. It floundered uncertainly, as the father-thing cleared a path for it toward Charles.

'This way,' the father-thing grunted. 'I'll hold him for you. When you've fed you'll be stronger.'

The Charles-thing's mouth opened and closed. It reached greedily toward Charles. The boy struggled wildly, but the father-thing's immense hand held him down.

'Stop that, young man,' the father-thing commanded. 'It'll be a lot easier for you if you–'

It screamed and convulsed. It let go of Charles and staggered back. Its body twitched violently. It crashed against the garage, limbs jerking. For a time it rolled and flopped in a dance of agony. It whimpered, moaned, tried to crawl away. Gradually it became quiet. The Charles-thing settled down in a silent heap. It lay stupidly among the bamboo and rotting debris, body slack, face empty and blank.

At last the father-thing ceased to stir. There was only the faint rustle of the bamboo in the night wind.

Charles got up awkwardly. He stepped down onto the cement driveway. Peretti and Daniels approached, wide-eyed and cautious. 'Don't go near it,' Daniels ordered sharply. 'It ain't dead yet. Takes a little while.'

'What did you do?' Charles muttered.

Daniels set down the drum of kerosene with a gasp of relief. 'Found this in the garage. We Daniels always used kerosene on our mosquitoes, back in Virginia.'

'Daniels poured the kerosene down the bug's tunnel,' Peretti explained, still awed. 'It was his idea.'

Daniels kicked cautiously at the contorted body of the father-thing. 'It's dead, now. Died as soon as the bug died.'

'I guess the other'll die, too,' Peretti said. He pushed aside the bamboo to examine the larvae growing here and there among the debris. The Charles-thing didn't move at all, as Peretti jabbed the end of a stick into its chest. 'This one's dead.'

'We better make sure,' Daniels said grimly. He picked up the heavy drum of kerosene and lugged it to the edge of the bamboo. 'It dropped some matches in the driveway. You get them, Peretti.'

They looked at each other.

'Sure,' Peretti said softly.

'We better turn on the hose,' Charles said. 'To make sure it doesn't spread.'

'Let's get going,' Peretti said impatiently. He was already moving off. Charles quickly followed him and they began searching for the matches, in the moonlit darkness.

STRANGE EDEN

Captain Johnson was the first man out of the ship. He scanned the planet's great rolling forests, its miles of green that made your eyes ache. The sky overhead that was pure blue. Off beyond the trees lapped the edges of an ocean, about the same color as the sky, except for a bubbling surface of incredibly bright seaweed that darkened the blue almost to purple.

He had only four feet to go from the control board to the automatic hatch, and from there down the ramp to the soft black soil dug up by the jet blast and strewn everywhere, still steaming. He shaded his eyes against the golden sun, and then, after a moment, removed his glasses and polished them on his sleeve. He was a small man, thin and sallow-faced. He blinked nervously without his glasses and quickly fitted them back in place. He took a deep breath of the warm air, held it in his lungs, let it roll through his system, then reluctantly let it escape.

'Not bad,' Brent rumbled, from the open hatch.

'If this place were closer to Terra there'd be empty beer cans and plastic plates strewn around. The trees would be gone. There'd be old jet motors in the water. The beaches would stink to high heaven. Terran Development would have a couple of million little plastic houses set up everywhere.'

Brent grunted indifferently. He jumped down, a huge barrel-chested man, sleeves rolled up, arms dark and hairy.

'What's that over there? Some kind of trail?'

Captain Johnson uneasily got out a star chart and studied it. 'No ship ever reported this area, before us. According to this chart the whole system's uninhabited.'

Brent laughed. 'Ever occur to you there might already be culture here? Non-Terran?'

Captain Johnson fingered his gun. He had never used it; this was the first time he had been assigned to an exploring survey outside the patrolled area of the galaxy. 'Maybe we ought to take off. Actually, we don't have to map this place. We've mapped the three bigger planets, and this one isn't really required.'

Brent strode across the damp ground, toward the trail. He squatted down and ran his hands over the broken grass. 'Something comes along here. There's a rut worn in the soil.' He gave a startled exclamation. 'Footprints!'

'People?'

'Looks like some kind of animal. Large–maybe a big cat.' Brent straightened up, his heavy face thoughtful. 'Maybe we could get ourselves some fresh game. And if not, maybe a little sport.'

Captain Johnson fluttered nervously. 'How do we know what sort of defenses these animals have? Let's play it safe and stay in the ship. We can make the survey by air; the usual processes ought to be enough for a little place like this. I hate to stick around here.' He shivered. 'It gives me the creeps.'

'The creeps?' Brent yawned and stretched, then started along the trail, toward the rolling miles of green forest. 'I like it. A regular national park–complete with wildlife. You stay in the ship. I'll have a little fun.'

Brent moved cautiously through the dark woods, one hand on his gun. He was an old-time surveyor; he had wandered around plenty of remote places in his time, enough to know what he was doing. He halted from time to time, examining the trail and feeling the soil. The large prints continued and were joined by others. A whole group of animals had come along this way, several species, all large. Probably flocking to a water source. A stream or pool of some kind.

He climbed a rise—then abruptly crouched. Ahead of him an animal was curled up on a flat stone, eyes shut, obviously sleeping. Brent moved around in a wide circle, carefully keeping his face to the animal. It was a cat, all right. But not the kind of cat he had ever seen before. Something like a lion—but larger. As large as a Terran rhino. Long tawny fur, great pads, a tail like a twisted spare-rope. A few flies crawled over its flanks; muscles rippled and the flies darted off. Its mouth was slightly open; he could see gleaming white fangs that sparkled moistly in the sun. A vast pink tongue. It breathed heavily, slowly, snoring in its slumber.

Brent toyed with his r-pistol. As a sportsman he couldn't shoot it sleeping: he'd have to chuck a rock at it and wake it up. But as a man looking at a beast twice his weight, he was tempted to blast its heart out and lug the remains back to the ship. The head would look fine; the whole damn pelt would look fine. He could make up a nice story to go along with it—the thing dropping on him from a branch, or maybe springing out of a thicket, roaring and snarling.

He knelt down, rested his right elbow on his right knee, clasped the butt of his pistol with his left hand, closed one eye, and carefully aimed. He took a deep breath, steadied the gun, and released the safety catch.

As he began squeezing the trigger, two more of the great cats sauntered past him along the trail, nosed briefly at their sleeping relation, and continued on into the brush.

Feeling foolish, Brent lowered his gun. The two beasts had paid no attention to him. One had glanced his way slightly, but neither had paused or taken any notice. He got unsteadily to his feet, cold sweat breaking out on his forehead. Good God, if they had wanted they could have torn him apart. Crouching there with his back turned—

He'd have to be more careful. Not stop and stay in one place. Keep moving, or go back to the ship. No, he wouldn't go back to the ship. He still needed something to show pipsqueak Johnson. The little Captain was probably sitting nervously at the controls, wondering what had happened to him. Brent pushed carefully through the shrubs and regained the trail on the far side of the sleeping cat.

He'd explore some more, find something worth bringing back, maybe camp the night in a sheltered spot. He had a pack of hard rations, and in an emergency he could raise Johnson with his throat transmitter.

He came out on a flat meadow. Flowers grew everywhere, yellow and red and violet blossoms; he strode rapidly through them. The planet was virgin—still in its primitive stage. No humans had come here; as Johnson said, in a while there'd be plastic plates and beer cans and rotting debris. Maybe he could take out a lease. Form a corporation and claim the whole damn thing. Then slowly subdivide, only to the best people. Promise them no commercialization; only the most exclusive homes. A garden retreat for wealthy Terrans who had plenty of leisure. Fishing and hunting: all the game they wanted. Completely tame, too. Unfamiliar with humans.

His scheme pleased him. As he came out of the meadow and plunged into dense trees, he considered how he'd raise the initial investment. He might have to cut others in on it; get somebody with plenty of loot to back him. They'd need good promotion and advertising; really push the thing good. Untouched planets were getting scarce; this might well be the last. If he missed this, it might be a long time before he had another chance to . . .

His thoughts died. His scheme collapsed. Dull resentment choked him and he came to an abrupt halt.

Ahead the trail broadened. The trees were farther apart; bright sunlight sifted down into the silent darkness of the ferns and bushes and flowers. On a little rise was a building. A stone house, with steps, a front porch, solid white walls like marble. A garden grew around it. Windows. A path. Smaller buildings in the back. All neat and pretty—and extremely modern-looking. A small fountain sprinkled blue water into a basin. A few birds moved around the gravel paths, pecking and scratching.

The planet was inhabited.

Brent approached warily. A wisp of gray smoke trailed out of the stone chimney. Behind the house were chicken pens, a cow-like thing dozing in the shade by its water trough. Other animals, some dog-like, and a group that might have been sheep. A regular little farm–but not like any farm he had seen. The buildings were of marble, or what looked like marble. And the animals were penned in by some kind of force-field. Everything was clean; in one corner a disposal tube sucked exhausted water and refuse into a half-buried tank.

He came to steps leading up to a back porch and, after a moment of thought, climbed them. He wasn't especially frightened. There was a serenity about the place, an orderly calm. It was hard to imagine any harm coming from it. He reached the door, hesitated, and then began looking for a knob.

There wasn't any knob. At his touch the door swung open. Feeling foolish, Brent entered. He found himself in a luxurious hall; recessed lights flickered on at the pressure of his boots on the thick carpets. Long glowing drapes hid the windows. Massive furniture–he peered into a room. Strange machines and objects. Pictures on the walls. Statues in the corners. He turned a corner and emerged into a large foyer. And still no one.

A huge animal, as large as a pony, moved out of a doorway, sniffed at him curiously, licked his wrist, and wandered off. He watched it go, heart in his mouth.

Tame. All the animals were tame. What kind of people had built this place? Panic stabbed at him. Maybe not people. Maybe some other race. Something alien, from beyond the galaxy. Maybe this was the frontier of an alien empire, some kind of advanced station.

While he was thinking about it, wondering if he should try to get out, run back to the ship, vid the cruiser station at Orion IX, there was a faint rustle behind him. He turned quickly, hand on his gun.

'Who–' he gasped. And froze.

A girl stood there, face calm, eyes large and dark, a cloudy black. She was tall, almost as tall as he, a little under six feet. Cascades of black hair spilled down her shoulders, down to her waist. She wore a glistening robe of some oddly-metallic material; countless facets glittered and sparkled and reflected the overhead lights. Her lips were deep red and full. Her arms were folded beneath her breasts;

they stirred faintly as she breathed. Beside her stood the pony-like animal that had nosed him and gone on.

'Welcome, Mr Brent,' the girl said. She smiled at him; he caught a flash of her tiny white teeth. Her voice was gentle and lilting, remarkably pure. Abruptly she turned; her robe fluttered behind her as she passed through the doorway and into the room beyond. 'Come along. I've been expecting you.'

Brent entered cautiously. A man stood at the end of the long table, watching him with obvious dislike. He was huge, over six feet, broad shoulders and arms that rippled as he buttoned his cloak and moved toward the door. The table was covered with dishes and bowls of food; robot servants were clearing away the things silently. Obviously, the girl and man had been eating.

'This is my brother,' the girl said, indicating the dark-faced giant. He bowed slightly to Brent, exchanged a few words with the girl in an unfamiliar, liquid tongue, and then abruptly departed. His footsteps died down the hall.

'I'm sorry,' Brent muttered. 'I didn't mean to bust in here and break up anything.'

'Don't worry. He was going. Actually, we don't get along very well.' The girl drew the drapes aside to reveal a wide window overlooking the forest. 'You can watch him go. His ship is parked out there. See it?'

It took a moment for Brent to make out the ship. It blended into the scenery perfectly. Only when it abruptly shot upward at a ninety-degree angle did he realize it had been there all the time. He had walked within yards of it.

'He's quite a person,' the girl said, letting the drapes fall back in place. 'Are you hungry? Here, sit down and eat with me. Now that Aeetes is gone and I'm all alone.'

Brent sat down cautiously. The food looked good. The dishes were some kind of semi-transparent metal. A robot set places in front of him, knives, forks, spoons, then waited to be instructed. The girl gave it orders in her strange liquid tongue. It promptly served Brent and retired.

He and the girl were alone. Brent began to eat greedily, the food was delicious. He tore the wings from a chicken-like fowl and gnawed at it expertly. He gulped down a tumbler of dark red wine, wiped his mouth on his sleeve, and attacked a bowl of ripe fruit. Vegetables, spiced meats, seafood, warm bread–he gobbled down everything with pleasure. The girl ate a few dainty bites; she watched him curiously, until finally he was finished and had pushed his empty dishes away.

'Where's your captain?' she asked. 'Didn't he come?'

'Johnson? He's back at the ship.' Brent belched noisily. 'How come you speak Terran? It's not your natural language. And how did you know there's somebody with me?'

The girl laughed, a tinkling musical peal. She wiped her slim hands on a napkin and drank from a dark red glass. 'We watched you on the scanner. We were curious. This is the first time one of your ships has penetrated this far. We wondered what your intentions were.'

'You didn't learn Terran by watching our ship on a scanner.'

'No. I learned your language from people of your race. That was a long time ago. I've spoken your language as long as I can remember.'

Brent was baffled. 'But you said our ship was the first to come here.'

The girl laughed. 'True. But we've often visited your little world. We know all about it. It's a stop-over point when we travel in that direction. I've been there many times–not for a while, but in the old days when I traveled more.'

A strange chill settled over Brent. 'Who are you people? Where are you from?'

'I don't know where we're from originally,' the girl answered. 'Our civilization is all over the universe, by now. It probably started from one place, back in legendary times. By now it's practically everywhere.'

'Why haven't we run into your people before?'

The girl smiled and continued eating. 'Didn't you hear what I said? You *have* met us. Often. We've even brought Terrans here. I remember one time very clearly, a few thousand years ago–'

'How long are your years?' Brent demanded.

'We don't have years.' The girl's dark eyes bored into him, luminous with amusement. 'I mean *Terran* years.'

It took a minute for the full impact to hit him. 'Thousand years,' he murmured. 'You've been alive a thousand years?'

'Eleven thousand,' the girl answered simply. She nodded, and a robot cleared away the dishes. She leaned back in her chair, yawned, stretched like a small, lithe cat, then abruptly sprang to her feet. 'Come on. We've finished eating. I'll show you my house.'

Brent scrambled up and hurried after her, his confidence shattered. 'You're immortal, aren't you?' He moved between her and the door, breathing rapidly, heavy face flushed. 'You don't age.'

'Age? No, of course not.'

Brent managed to find words. 'You're gods.'

The girl smiled up at him, dark eyes flashing merrily. 'Not really. You have just about everything we have–almost as much knowledge, science, culture. Eventually you'll catch up with us. We're an old race. Millions of years ago our scientists succeeded in slowing down the processes of decay; since then we've ceased to die.'

'Then your race stays constant. None die, none are born.'

The girl pushed past him, through the doorway and down the hall. 'Oh, people are born all the time. Our race grows and expands.' She halted at a doorway. 'We haven't given up any of our pleasures.' She eyed Brent thoughtfully, his shoulders, arms, his dark hair, heavy face. 'We're about like you, except that we're eternal. You'll probably solve that, too, sometime.'

'You've moved among us?' Brent demanded. He was beginning to understand. 'Then all those old religions and myths were true. Gods. Miracles. You've had contact with us, given us things. Done things for us.' He followed her wonderingly into the room.

'Yes. I suppose we've done things for you. As we pass through.' The girl moved about the room, letting down massive drapes. Soft darkness fell over the couches and bookcases and statues. 'Do you play chess?'

'CHESS?'

'It's our national game. We introduced it to some of your Brahmin ancestors.' Disappointment showed on her sharp little face. 'You don't play? Too bad. What do you do? What about your companion? He looked as if his intellectual capacity was greater than yours. Does he play chess? Maybe you ought to go back and get him.'

'I don't think so,' Brent said. He moved toward her. 'As far as I know he doesn't do anything.' He reached out and caught her by the arm. The girl pulled away, astonished. Brent gathered her up in his big arms and drew her tight against him. 'I don't think we need him,' he said.

He kissed her on the mouth. Her red lips were warm and sweet; she gasped and fought wildly. He could feel her slim body struggling against him. A cloud of fragrant scent billowed from her dark hair. She tore at him with her sharp nails, breasts heaving violently. He let go and she slid away, wary and bright-eyed, breathing quickly, body tense, drawing her luminous robe about her.

'I could kill you,' she whispered. She touched her jeweled belt. 'You don't understand, do you?'

Brent came forward. 'You probably can. But I bet you won't.'

She backed away from him. 'Don't be a fool.' Her red lips twisted and a smile flickered briefly. 'You're brave. But not very smart. Still, that's not such a bad combination in a man. Stupid and brave.' Agilely, she avoided his grasp and slipped out of his reach. 'You're in good physical shape, too. How do you manage it aboard that little ship?'

'Quarterly fitness courses,' Brent answered. He moved between her and the door. 'You must get pretty damn bored here, all by yourself. After the first few thousand years it must get trying.'

'I find things to do,' she said. 'Don't come any closer to me. As much as I admire your daring, it's only fair to warn you that–'

Brent grabbed her. She fought wildly; he pinned her hands together behind her back with one paw, arched her body taut, and kissed her half-parted lips. She sank her tiny white teeth into him;

he grunted and jerked away. She was laughing, black eyes dancing, as she struggled. Her breath came rapidly, cheeks flushed, half-covered breasts quivering, body twisting like a trapped animal. He caught her around the waist and grabbed her up in his arms.

A wave of force hit him.

He dropped her; she landed easily on her feet and danced back. Brent was doubled up, face gray with agony. Cold sweat stood out on his neck and hands. He sank down on a couch and closed his eyes, muscles knotted, body writhing with pain.

'Sorry,' the girl said. She moved around the room, ignoring him, 'It's your own fault–I told you to be careful. Maybe you better get out of here. Back to your little ship. I don't want anything to happen to you. It's against our policy to kill Terrans.'

'What–was that?'

'Nothing much. A form of repulsion, I suppose. This belt was constructed on one of our industrial planets; it protects me but I don't know the operational principle.'

Brent managed to get to his feet. 'You're pretty tough for a little girl.'

'A little girl? I'm pretty *old* for a little girl. I was old before you were born. I was old before your people had rocket ships. I was old before you knew how to weave clothing and write your thoughts down with symbols. I've watched your race advance and fall back into barbarism and advance again. Endless nations and empires. I was alive when the Egyptians first began spreading out into Asia Minor. I saw the city builders of the Tigris Valley begin putting up their brick houses. I saw the Assyrian war chariots roll out to fight. I and my friends visited Greece and Rome and Minos and Lydia and the great kingdoms of the red-skinned Indians. We were gods to the ancients, saints to the Christians. We come and go. As your people advanced we came less often. We have other way-stations; yours isn't the only stop-over point.'

Brent was silent. Color was beginning to come back to his face. The girl had thrown herself down on one of the soft couches; she leaned back against a pillow and gazed up at him calmly, one arm outstretched, the other across her lap. Her long legs were tucked under her, tiny feet pressed together. She looked like a small, contented kitten resting after a game. It was hard for him to believe what she had told him. But his body still ached; he had felt a minute portion of her power-field, and it had almost killed him. That was something to think about.

'Well?' the girl asked, presently. 'What are you going to do? It's getting late. I think you ought to go back to your ship. Your captain will be wondering what happened to you.'

Brent moved over to the window and drew aside the heavy drapes. The sun had set. Darkness was settling over the forests outside. Stars had already begun to come out, tiny dots of white in the thickening violet. A distant line of hills jutted up black and ominous.

'I can contact him,' Brent said. He tapped at his neck. 'In case of emergency. Tell him I'm all right.'

'*Are you all right?* You shouldn't be here. You think you know what you're doing? You think you can handle me.' She raised herself up slightly and tossed her black hair back over her shoulders. 'I can see what's going on in your mind. I'm so much like a girl you had an affair with, a young brunette you used to wrap around your finger–and boast about to your companions.'

Brent flushed. 'You're a telepath. You should have told me.'

'A partial telepath. All I need. Toss me your cigarettes. We don't have such things.'

Brent fumbled in his pocket, got his pack out and tossed it to her. She lit up and inhaled gratefully. A cloud of gray smoke drifted around her; it mixed with the darkening shadows of the room. The corners dissolved into gloom. She became an indistinct shape, curled up on the couch, the glowing cigarette between her dark red lips.

'I'm not afraid,' Brent said.

'No, you're not. You're not a coward. If you were as smart as you are brave–but then I guess you wouldn't be brave. I admire your bravery, stupid as it is. Man has a lot of courage. Even though it's based on ignorance, it's impressive.' After a moment, she said, 'Come over here and sit with me.'

*

'What do I have to be worried about?' Brent asked after a while. 'If you don't turn on that damn belt, I'll be all right.'

In the darkness, the girl stirred. 'There's more than that.' She sat up a little, arranged her hair, pulled a pillow behind her head. 'You see, we're of totally different races. My race is millions of years advanced over yours. Contact with us–close contact–is lethal. Not to us, of course. To you. You can't be with me and remain a human being.'

'What do you mean?'

'You'll undergo changes. Evolutionary changes. There's pull which we exert. We're fully charged; close contact with us will exert influence on the cells of your body. Those animals outside. They've evolved slightly; they're no longer wild beasts. They're able to understand simple commands and follow basic routines. As yet, they have no language. With such low animals it's a long process; and my contact with them hasn't really been close. But with you–'

'I see.'

'We're not supposed to let humans near us. Aeetes cleared out of here. I'm too lazy to go–I don't especially care. I'm not mature and responsible, I suppose.' She smiled slightly. 'And my kind of close contact is a little closer than most.'

Brent could barely make out her slim form in the darkness. She lay back against the pillows, lips parted, arms folded beneath her breasts, head tilted back. She was lovely. The most beautiful woman he had ever seen. After a moment he leaned toward her. This time she didn't move away. He kissed her gently. Then he put his arms around her slender body and drew her tight against him. Her robe rustled. Her soft hair brushed against him, warm and fragrant.

'It's worth it,' he said.

'You're sure? You can't turn back, once it's begun. Do you understand? You won't be human any more. You'll have evolved. Along lines your race will take millions of years from now. You'll be an outcast, a forerunner of things to come. Without companions.'

'I'll stay.' He caressed her cheek, her hair, her neck. He could feel the blood pulsing beneath the downy skin; a rapid pounding in the hollow of her throat. She was breathing rapidly; her breasts rose and fell against him. 'If you'll let me.'

'Yes,' she murmured. 'I'll let you. If it's what you really want. But don't blame me.' A half-sad, half-mischievous smile flitted across her sharp features; her dark eyes sparkled. 'Promise you won't blame me? It's happened before–I hate people to reproach me. I always say never again. No matter what.'

'Has it happened before?'

The girl laughed, softly and close to his ear. She kissed him warmly and hugged him hard against her. 'In eleven thousand years,' she whispered, 'it's happened quite often.'

Captain Johnson had a bad night. He tried to raise Brent on the emergency com, but there was no response. Only faint static and a distant echo of a vid program from Orion X. Jazz music and sugary commercials.

The sounds of civilization reminded him that they had to keep moving. Twenty-four hours was all the time allotted to this planet, smallest of its system.

'Damn,' he muttered. He fixed a pot of coffee and checked his wristwatch. Then he got out of the ship and wandered around in the early-morning sunlight. The sun was beginning to come up. The air turned from dark violet to gray. It was cold as hell. He shivered and stamped his feet and watched some small bird-like things fly down to peck around the bushes.

He was just beginning to think of notifying Orion XI when he saw her.

She walked quickly toward the ship. Tall and slim in a heavy fur jacket, her arms buried in the deep pelt. Johnson stood rooted to the spot, dumbfounded. He was too astonished even to touch his gun. His mouth fell open as the girl halted a little way off, tossed her dark hair back, blew a cloud of silvery breath at him and then said, 'I'm sorry you had a bad night. It's my fault. I should have sent him right back.'

Captain Johnson's mouth opened and shut. 'Who are you?' he managed finally. Fear seized him. 'Where's Brent? What happened?'

'He'll be along.' She turned back toward the forest and made a sign. 'I think you'd better leave, now. He wants to stay here and that is best–for he's changed. He'll be happy in my forest with the other–men. It's strange how all you humans come out exactly alike. Your race is moving along an unusual path. It might be worth our while to study you, sometime. It must have something to do with your low esthetic plateau. You seem to have an innate vulgarity, which eventually will dominate you.'

From out of the woods came a strange shape. For a moment, Captain Johnson thought his eyes were playing tricks on him. He blinked, squinted, then grunted in disbelief. Here, on this remote planet–but there was no mistake. It was definitely an immense cat-like beast that came slowly and miserably out of the woods after the girl.

The girl moved away, then halted to wave to the beast, who whined wretchedly around the ship.

Johnson stared at the animal and felt a sudden fear. Instinctively he knew that Brent was not coming back to the ship. Something had happened on this strange planet–that girl . . .

Johnson slammed the airlock shut and hurried to the control panel. He had to get back to the nearest base and make a report. This called for an elaborate investigation.

As the rockets blasted Johnson glanced through the viewplate. He saw the animal shaking a huge paw futilely in the air after the departing ship.

Johnson shuddered. That was too much like a man's angry gesture . . .

TONY AND THE BEETLES

Reddish-yellow sunlight filtered through the thick quartz windows into the sleep-compartment. Tony Rossi yawned, stirred a little, then opened his black eyes and sat up quickly. With one motion he tossed the covers back and slid to the warm metal floor. He clicked off his alarm clock and hurried to the closet.

It looked like a nice day. The landscape outside was motionless, undisturbed by winds or dust-shift. The boy's heart pounded excitedly. He pulled his trousers on, zipped up the reinforced mesh, struggled into his heavy canvas shirt, and then sat down onto the edge of the cot to tug on his boots. He closed the seams around their tops and then did the same with his gloves. Next he adjusted the pressure on his pump unit and strapped it between his shoulder blades. He grabbed his helmet from the dresser, and he was ready for the day.

In the dining-compartment his mother and father had finished breakfast. Their voices drifted to him as he clattered down the ramp. A disturbed murmur; he paused to listen. What were they talking about? Had he done something wrong, again?

And then he caught it. Behind their voices was another voice. Static and crackling pops. The all-system audio signal from Rigel IV. They had it turned up full blast; the dull thunder of the monitor's voice boomed loudly. The war. Always the war. He sighed, and stepped out into the dining-compartment.

'Morning,' his father muttered.

'Good morning, dear,' his mother said absently. She sat with her head turned to one side, wrinkles of concentration webbing her forehead. Her thin lips were drawn together in a tight line of concern. His father had pushed his dirty dishes back and was smoking, elbows on the table, dark hairy arms bare and muscular. He was scowling, intent on the jumbled roar from the speaker above the sink.

'How's it going?' Tony asked. He slid into his chair and reached automatically for the ersatz grapefruit. 'Any news from Orion?'

Neither of them answered. They didn't hear him. He began to eat his grapefruit. Outside, beyond the little metal and plastic housing unit, sounds of activity grew. Shouts and muffled crashes, as rural merchants and their trucks rumbled along the highway toward Karnet. The reddish daylight swelled; Betelgeuse was rising quietly and majestically.

'Nice day,' Tony said. 'No flux wind. I think I'll go down to the n-quarter awhile. We're building a neat spaceport, a model, of course, but we've been able to get enough materials to lay out strips for–'

With a savage snarl his father reached out and struck. The audio roar immediately died. 'I knew it!' He got up and moved angrily away from the table. 'I told them it would happen. They shouldn't have moved so soon. Should have built up Class A supply bases, first.'

'Isn't our main fleet moving in from Bellatrix?' Tony's mother fluttered anxiously. 'According to last night's summary the worst that can happen is Orion IX and X will be dumped.'

Joseph Rossi laughed harshly. 'The hell with last night's summary. They know as well as I do what's happening.'

'What's happening?' Tony echoed, as he pushed aside his grapefruit and began to ladle out dry cereal. 'Are we losing the battle?'

'Yes!' His father's lips twisted. 'Earthmen, losing to–to *beetles*. I told them. But they couldn't wait. My God, there's ten good years left in this system. Why'd they have to push on? Everybody knew Orion would be tough. The whole damn beetle fleet's strung out around there. Waiting for us. And we have to barge right in.'

'But nobody ever thought beetles would fight,' Leah Rossi

protested mildly. 'Everybody thought they'd just fire a few blasts and then–'

'They *have* to fight! Orion's the last jump-off. If they don't fight here, where the hell can they fight?' Rossi swore savagely. 'Of course they're fighting. We have all their planets except the inner Orion string–not that they're worth much, but it's the principle of the thing. If we'd built up strong supply bases, we could have broken up the beetle fleet and really clobbered it.'

'Don't say "beetle",' Tony murmured, as he finished his cereal. 'They're Pas-udeti, same as here. The word "beetle" comes from Betelgeuse. An Arabian word we invented ourselves.'

Joe Rossi's mouth opened and closed. 'What are you, a goddamn beetle-lover?'

'Joe,' Leah snapped. 'For heaven's sake.'

Rossi moved toward the door. 'If I was ten years younger I'd be out there. I'd really show those shiny-shelled insects what the hell they're up against. Them and their junky beat-up old hulks. Converted freighters!' His eyes blazed. 'When I think of them shooting down Terran cruisers with *our* boys in them–'

'Orion's their system,' Tony murmured.

'*Their* system! When the hell did you get to be an authority on space law? Why, I ought to–' He broke off, choked with rage. 'My own kid,' he muttered. 'One more crack out of you today and I'll hang one on you you'll feel the rest of the week.'

Tony pushed his chair back. 'I won't be around today. I'm going into Karnet, with my EEP.'

'Yeah, to play with beetles!'

Tony said nothing. He was already sliding his helmet in place and snapping the clamps tight. As he pushed through the back door, into the lock membrane, he unscrewed his oxygen tap and set the tank filter into action. An automatic response, conditioned by a lifetime spent on a colony planet in an alien system.

A faint flux wind caught at him and swept yellow-red dust around his boots. Sunlight glittered from the metal roof of his family's housing unit, one of endless rows of squat boxes set in the sandy slope, protected by the line of ore-refining installations against the horizon. He made an impatient signal, and from the storage shed his EEP came gliding out, catching the sunlight on its chrome trim.

'We're going down into Karnet,' Tony said, unconsciously slipping into the Pas dialect. 'Hurry up!'

The EEP took up its position behind him, and he started briskly down the slope, over the shifting sand, toward the road. There were quite a few traders out, today. It was a good day for the market; only a fourth of the year was fit for travel. Betelgeuse was an erratic and undependable sun, not at all like Sol (according to the edutapes fed to Tony four hours a day, six days a week–he had never seen Sol himself).

He reached the noisy road. Pas-udeti were everywhere. Whole groups of them, with their primitive combustion-driven trucks, battered and filthy, motors grinding protestingly. He waved at the trucks as they pushed past him. After a moment one slowed down. It was piled with *tis*, bundled heaps of gray vegetables, dried and prepared for the table. A staple of the Pas-udeti diet. Behind the wheel lounged a dark-faced elderly Pas, one arm over the open window, a rolled leaf between his lips. He was like all other Pas-udeti: lank and hard-shelled, encased in a brittle sheath in which he lived and died.

'You want a ride?' the Pas murmured–required protocol when an Earthman on foot was encountered.

'Is there room for my EEP?'

The Pas made a careless motion with his claw. 'It can run behind.' Sardonic amusement touched his ugly old face. 'If it gets to Karnet we'll sell it for scrap. We can use a few condensers and relay tubing. We're short of electronic maintenance stuff.'

'I know,' Tony said solemnly, as he climbed into the cabin of the truck. 'It's all been sent to the big repair base at Orion I. For your warfleet.'

Amusement vanished from the leathery face. 'Yes, the warfleet.'

He turned away and started up the truck again. In the back, Tony's EEP had scrambled up on the load of *tis* and was gripping precariously with its magnetic lines.

Tony noticed the Pas-udeti's sudden change of expression, and he was puzzled. He started to speak to him–but now he noticed unusual quietness among the other Pas, in the other trucks, behind and in front of his own. The war, of course. It had swept through this system a century ago; these people had been left behind. Now all eyes were on Orion, on the battle between the Terran warfleet and the Pas-udeti collection of armed freighters.

'Is it true,' Tony asked carefully, 'that you're winning?'

The elderly Pas grunted. 'We hear rumors.'

Tony considered. 'My father says Terra went ahead too fast. He says we should have consolidated. We didn't assemble adequate supply bases. He used to be an officer, when he was younger. He was with the fleet for two years.'

The Pas was silent a moment. 'It's true,' he said at last, 'that when you're so far from home, supply is a great problem. We, on the other hand, don't have that. We have no distances to cover.'

'Do you know anybody fighting?'

'I have distant relatives.' The answer was vague; the Pas obviously didn't want to talk about it.

'Have you ever seen your warfleet?'

'Not as it exists now. When this system was defeated most of our units were wiped out. Remnants limped to Orion and joined the Orion fleet.'

'Your relatives were with the remnants?'

'That's right.'

'Then you were alive when this planet was taken?'

'Why do you ask?' The old Pas quivered violently. 'What business is it of yours?'

Tony leaned out and watched the walls and buildings of Karnet grow ahead of them. Karnet was an old city. It had stood thousands of years. The Pas-udeti civilization was stable; it had reached a certain point of technocratic development and then leveled off.

The Pas had intersystem ships that had carried people and freight between planets in the days before the Terran Confederation. They had combustion-driven cars, audiophones, a power network of a magnetic type. Their plumbing was satisfactory and their medicine was highly advanced. They had art forms, emotional and exciting. They had a vague religion.

'Who do you think will win the battle?' Tony asked.

'I don't know.' With a sudden jerk the old Pas brought the truck to a crashing halt. 'This is as far as I go. Please get out and take your EEP with you.'

Tony faltered in surprise. 'But aren't you going–?'

'No farther!'

Tony pushed the door open. He was vaguely uneasy; there was a hard, fixed expression on the leathery face, and the old creature's voice had a sharp edge he had never heard before. 'Thanks,' he murmured. He hopped down into the red dust and signaled his EEP. It released its magnetic lines, and instantly the truck started up with a roar, passing on inside the city.

Tony watched it go, still dazed. The hot dust lapped at his ankles; he automatically moved his feet and slapped at his trousers. A truck honked, and his EEP quickly moved him from the road, up to the level pedestrian ramp. Pas-udeti in swarms moved by, endless lines of rural people hurrying into Karnet on their daily business. A massive public bus had stopped by the gate and was letting off passengers. Male and female Pas. And children. They laughed and shouted; the sounds of their voices blended with the low hum of the city.

'Going in?' a sharp Pas-udeti voice sounded close behind him. 'Keep moving–you're blocking the ramp.'

It was a young female, with a heavy armload clutched in her claws. Tony felt embarrassed; female Pas had a certain telepathic ability, part of their sexual makeup. It was effective on Earthmen at close range.

'Here,' she said. 'Give me a hand.'

Tony nodded his head, and the EEP accepted the female's heavy armload. 'I'm visiting the city,' Tony said, as they moved with the crowd toward the gates. 'I got a ride most of the way, but the driver let me off out here.'

'You're from the settlement?'

'Yes.'

She eyed him critically. 'You've always lived here, haven't you?'

'I was born here. My family came here from Earth four years before I was born. My father was an officer in the fleet. He earned an Emigration Priority.'

'So you've never seen your own planet. How old are you?'

'Ten years. Terran.'

'You shouldn't have asked the driver so many questions.'

They passed through the decontamination shield and into the city. An information square loomed ahead; Pas men and women were packed around it. Moving chutes and transport cars rumbled everywhere. Buildings and ramps and open-air machinery; the city was sealed in a protective dust-proof envelope. Tony unfastened his helmet and clipped it to his belt. The air was stale-smelling, artificial, but usable.

'Let me tell you something,' the young female said carefully, as she strode along the foot-ramp beside Tony. 'I wonder if this is a good day for you to come to Karnet. I know you've been coming here regularly to play with your friends. But perhaps today you ought to stay home, in your settlement.'

'Why?'

'Because today everybody is upset.'

'I know,' Tony said. 'My mother and father were upset. They were listening to the news from our base in the Rigel system.'

'I don't mean your family. Other people are listening, too. These people here. My race.'

'They're upset, all right,' Tony admitted. 'But I come here all the time. There's nobody to play with at the settlement, and anyhow we're working on a project.'

'A model spaceport.'

'That's right.' Tony was envious. 'I sure wish I was a telepath. It must be fun.'

The female Pas-udeti was silent. She was deep in thought. 'What would happen,' she asked, 'if your family left here and returned to Earth?'

'That couldn't happen. There's no room for us on Earth. C-bombs destroyed most of Asia and North America back in the twentieth century.'

'Suppose you *had* to go back?'

Tony did not understand. 'But we can't. Habitable portions of Earth are overcrowded. Our main problem is finding places for Terrans to live, in other systems.' He added, 'And anyhow, I don't particularly want to go to Terra. I'm used to it here. All my friends are here.'

'I'll take my packages,' the female said. 'I go this other way, down this third-level ramp.'

Tony nodded to his EEP and it lowered the bundles into the female's claws. She lingered a moment, trying to find the right words.

'Good luck,' she said.

'With what?'

She smiled faintly, ironically. 'With your model spaceport. I hope you and your friends get to finish it.'

'Of course we'll finish it,' Tony said, surprised. 'It's almost done.' What did she mean?

The Pas-udeti woman hurried off before he could ask her. Tony was troubled and uncertain; more doubts filled him. After a moment he headed slowly into the lane that took him toward the residential section of the city. Past the stores and factories, to the place where his friends lived.

The group of Pas-udeti children eyed him silently as he approached. They had been playing in the shade of an immense *bengelo*, whose ancient branches drooped and swayed with the air currents pumped through the city. Now they sat unmoving.

'I didn't expect you today,' B'prith said, in an expressionless voice.

Tony halted awkwardly, and his EEP did the same. 'How are things?' he murmured.

'Fine.'

'I got a ride part way.'

'Fine.'

Tony squatted down in the shade. None of the Pas children stirred. They were small, not as large as Terran children. Their shells had not hardened, had not turned dark and opaque, like horn. It gave them a soft, unformed appearance, but at the same time it lightened their load. They moved more easily than their elders: they could hop and skip around, still. But they were not skipping right now.

'What's the matter?' Tony demanded. 'What's wrong with everybody?'

No one answered.

'Where's the model?' he asked. 'Have you fellows been working on it?'

After a moment Llyre nodded slightly.

Tony felt dull anger rise up inside him. 'Say something! What's the matter? What're you all mad about?'

'Mad?' B'prith echoed. 'We're not mad.'

Tony scratched aimlessly in the dust. He knew what it was. The war, again. The battle going on near Orion. His anger burst up wildly. 'Forget the war. Everything was fine yesterday, before the battle.'

'Sure,' Llyre said. 'It was fine.'

Tony caught the edge to his voice. 'It happened a hundred years ago. It's not my fault.'

'Sure,' B'prith said.

'This is my home. Isn't it? Haven't I got as much right here as anybody else? I was born here.'

'Sure,' Llyre said, tonelessly.

Tony appealed to them helplessly. 'Do you have to act this way? You didn't act this way yesterday. I was here yesterday–all of us were here yesterday. What's happened since yesterday?'

'The battle,' B'prith said.

'What difference does *that* make? Why does that change everything? There's always war. There've been battles all the time, as long as I can remember. What's different about this?'

B'prith broke apart a clump of dirt with his strong claws. After a moment he tossed it away and got slowly to his feet. 'Well,' he said thoughtfully, 'according to our audio relay, it looks as if our fleet is going to win, this time.'

'Yes,' Tony agreed, not understanding. 'My father says we didn't build up adequate supply bases. We'll probably have to fall back to . . .' And then the impact hit him. 'You mean, for the first time in a hundred years–'

'Yes,' Llyre said, also getting up. The others got up, too. They moved away from Tony, toward the nearby house. 'We're winning. The Terran flank was turned, half an hour ago. Your right wing has folded completely.'

Tony was stunned. 'And it matters. It matters to all of you.'

'Matters!' B'prith halted, suddenly blazing out in fury. 'Sure it matters! For the first time–in a century. The first time in our lives we're beating you. We have you on the run, you–' He choked out the word, almost spat it out. 'You white-grubs!'

They disappeared into the house. Tony sat gazing stupidly down at the ground, his hands still moving aimlessly. He had heard the word before, seen it scrawled on walls and in the dust near the settlement. *White-grubs*. The Pas term of derision for Terrans. Because of their softness, their whiteness. Lack of hard shells. Pulpy, doughy skin. But they had never dared say it out loud, before. To an Earthman's face.

Beside him, his EEP stirred restlessly. Its intricate radio mechanism sensed the hostile atmosphere. Automatic relays were sliding into place; circuits were opening and closing.

'It's all right,' Tony murmured, getting slowly up. 'Maybe we'd better go back.'

He moved unsteadily toward the ramp, completely shaken. The EEP walked calmly ahead, its metal face blank and confident, feeling nothing, saying nothing. Tony's thoughts were a wild turmoil; he shook his head, but the crazy spinning kept up. He couldn't make his mind slow down, lock in place.

'Wait a minute,' a voice said. B'prith's voice, from the open doorway. Cold and withdrawn, almost unfamiliar.

'What do you want?'

B'prith came toward him, claws behind his back in the formal Pas-udeti posture, used between total strangers. 'You shouldn't have come here, today.'

'I know,' Tony said.

B'prith got out a bit of *tis* stalk and began to roll it into a tube. He pretended to concentrate on it. 'Look,' he said. 'You said you have a right here. But you don't.'

'I–' Tony murmured.

'Do you understand why not? You said it isn't your fault. I guess not. But it's not my fault, either. Maybe it's nobody's fault. I've known you a long time.'

'Five years. Terran.'

B'prith twisted the stalk up and tossed it away. 'Yesterday we played together. We worked on the spaceport. But we can't play today. My family said to tell you not to come here any more.' He hesitated, and did not look Tony in the face. 'I was going to tell you, anyhow. Before they said anything.'

'Oh,' Tony said.

'Everything that's happened today–the battle, our fleet's stand. We didn't know. We didn't dare hope. You see? A century of running. First this system. Then the Rigel system, all the planets. Then the other Orion stars. We fought here and there–scattered fights. Those that got away joined up. We supplied the base at Orion–you people didn't know. But there was no hope; at least, nobody thought there was.' He was silent a moment. 'Funny,' he said, 'what happens when your back's to the wall, and there isn't any further place to go. Then you have to fight.'

'If our supply bases–' Tony began thickly, but B'prith cut him off savagely.

'Your supply bases! Don't you understand? We're beating you! Now you'll have to get out! All you white-grubs. Out of our system!'

Tony's EEP moved forward ominously. B'prith saw it. He bent down, snatched up a rock, and hurled it straight at the EEP. The rock clanged off the metal hull and bounced harmlessly away. B'prith snatched up another rock. Llyre and the others came quickly out of the house. An adult Pas loomed up behind them. Everything was happening too fast. More rocks crashed against the EEP. One struck Tony on the arm.

'Get out!' B'prith screamed. 'Don't come back! This is our planet!' His claws snatched at Tony. 'We'll tear you to pieces if you–'

Tony smashed him in the chest. The soft shell gave like rubber, and the Pas stumbled back. He wobbled and fell over, gasping and screeching.

'*Beetle*,' Tony breathed hoarsely. Suddenly he was terrified. A crowd of Pas-udeti was forming rapidly. They surged on all sides, hostile faces, dark and angry, a rising thunder of rage.

More stones showered. Some struck the EEP, others fell around Tony, near his boots. One whizzed past his face. Quickly he slid his helmet in place. He was scared. He knew his EEP's E-signal had already gone out, but it would be minutes before a ship could come. Besides, there were other Earthmen in the city to be taken care of; there were Earthmen all over the planet. In all the cities. On all the twenty-three Betelgeuse planets. On the fourteen Rigel planets. On the other Orion planets.

'We have to get out of here,' he muttered to the EEP. 'Do something!'

A stone hit him on the helmet. The plastic cracked; air leaked out, and then the autoseal filmed over. More stones were falling. The Pas swarmed close, a yelling, seething mass of black-sheathed creatures. He could smell them, the acrid body-odor of insects, hear their claws snap, feel their weight.

The EEP threw its heat beam on. The beam shifted in a wide band toward the crowd of Pas-udeti. Crude hand weapons appeared. A clatter of bullets burst around Tony; they were firing at the EEP.

He was dimly aware of the metal body beside him. A shuddering crash–the EEP was toppled over. The crowd poured over it; the metal hull was lost from sight.

Like a demented animal, the crowd tore at the struggling EEP. A few of them smashed in its head; others tore off struts and shiny arm-sections. The EEP ceased struggling. The crowd moved away, panting and clutching jagged remains. They saw Tony.

As the first line of them reached for him, the protective envelope high above them shattered. A Terran scout ship thundered down, heat beam screaming. The crowd scattered in confusion, some firing, some throwing stones, others leaping for safety.

Tony picked himself up and made his way unsteadily toward the spot where the scout was landing.

'I'm sorry,' Joe Rossi said gently. He touched his son on the shoulder. 'I shouldn't have let you go down there today. I should have known.'

Tony sat hunched over in the big plastic easychair. He rocked back and forth, face pale with shock. The scout ship which had rescued him had immediately headed back toward Karnet; there were other Earthmen to bring out, besides this first load. The boy said nothing. His mind was blank. He still heard the roar of the crowd, felt its hate–a century of pent-up fury and resentment. The memory drove out everything else; it was all around him, even now. And the sight of the floundering EEP, the metallic ripping sound, as its arms and legs were torn off and carried away.

His mother dabbed at his cuts and scratches with antiseptic. Joe Rossi shakily lit a cigarette and said, 'If your EEP hadn't been along they'd have killed you. Beetles.' He shuddered. 'I never should have let you go down there. All this time . . . They might have done it any time, any day. Knifed you. Cut you open with their filthy goddamn claws.'

Below the settlement the reddish-yellow sunlight glinted on gunbarrels. Already, dull booms echoed against the crumbling hills. The defense ring was going into action. Black shapes darted and scurried up the side of the slope. Black patches moved out from

Karnet, toward the Terran settlement, across the dividing line the Confederation surveyors had set up a century ago. Karnet was a bubbling pot of activity. The whole city rumbled with feverish excitement.

Tony raised his head. 'They–they turned our flank.'

'Yeah.' Joe Rossi stubbed out his cigarette. 'They sure did. That was at one o'clock. At two they drove a wedge right through the center of our line. Split the fleet in half. Broke it up–sent it running. Picked us off one by one as we fell back. Christ, they're like maniacs. Now that they've got the scent, the taste of our blood.'

'But it's getting better,' Leah fluttered. 'Our main fleet units are beginning to appear.'

'We'll get them,' Joe muttered. 'It'll take a while. But by God we'll wipe them out. Every last one of them. If it takes a thousand years. We'll follow every last ship down–we'll get them all.' His voice rose in frenzy. 'Beetles! Goddamn insects! When I think of them, trying to hurt my kid, with their filthy black claws–'

'If you were younger, you'd be in the line,' Leah said. 'It's not your fault you're too old. The heart strain's too great. You did your job. They can't let an older person take chances. It's not your fault.'

Joe clenched his fists. 'I feel so–futile. If there was only something I could do.'

'The fleet will take care of them,' Leah said soothingly. 'You said so yourself. They'll hunt every one of them down. Destroy them all. There's nothing to worry about.'

Joe sagged miserably. 'It's no use. Let's cut it out. Let's stop kidding ourselves.'

'What do you mean?'

'Face it! We're not going to win, not this time. We went too far. Our time's come.'

There was silence.

Tony sat up a little. 'When did you know?'

'I've known a long time.'

'I found out today. I didn't understand, at first. This is–stolen ground. I was born here, but it's stolen ground.'

'Yes. It's stolen. It doesn't belong to us.'

'We're here because we're stronger. But now we're not stronger. We're being beaten.'

'They know Terrans can be licked. Like anybody else.' Joe Rossi's face was gray and flabby. 'We took their planets away from them. Now they're taking them back. It'll be a while, of course. We'll retreat slowly. It'll be another five centuries going back. There're a lot of systems between here and Sol.'

Tony shook his head, still uncomprehending. 'Even Llyre and B'prith. All of them. Waiting for their time to come. For us to lose and go away again. Where we came from.'

Joe Rossi paced back and forth. 'Yeah, we'll be retreating from now on. Giving ground, instead of taking it. It'll be like this today–losing fights, draws. Stalemates and worse.'

He raised his feverish eyes toward the ceiling of the little metal housing unit, face wild with passion and misery.

'But, by God, we'll give them a run for their money. All the way back! Every inch!'

NULL-O

Lemuel clung to the wall of his dark bedroom, tense, listening. A faint breeze stirred the lace curtains. Yellow street-light filtered over the bed, the dresser, the books and toys and clothes.

In the next room, two voices were murmuring together. 'Jean, we've got to do something,' the man's voice said.

A strangled gasp. 'Ralph, please don't hurt him. You must control yourself. I won't let you hurt him.'

'I'm not going to hurt him.' There was brute anguish in the man's whisper. 'Why does he do these things? Why doesn't he play baseball and tag like normal boys? Why does he have to burn down stores and torture helpless animals? *Why?*'

'He's different, Ralph. We must try to understand.'

'Maybe we better take him to the doctor,' his father said. 'Maybe he's got some kind of glandular disease.'

'You mean old Doc Grady? But you said he couldn't find–'

'Not Doc Grady. He quit after Lemuel destroyed his X-ray equipment and smashed all the furniture in his office. No, this is bigger than that.' A tense pause. 'Jean, I'm taking him up to the Hill.'

'Oh, Ralph! Please–'

'I mean it.' Grim determination, the harsh growl of a trapped animal. 'Those psychologists may be able to do something. Maybe they can help him. Maybe not.'

'But they might not let us have him back. And oh, Ralph, he's all we've got!'

'Sure,' Ralph muttered hoarsely. 'I know he is. But I've made up my mind. That day he slashed his teacher with a knife and leaped out the window. That day I made up my mind. Lemuel is going up to the Hill . . .'

The day was warm and bright. Between the swaying trees the huge white hospital sparkled, all concrete and steel and plastic. Ralph Jorgenson peered about uncertainly, hat twisted between his fingers, subdued by the immensity of the place.

Lemuel listened intently. Straining his big, mobile ears, he could hear many voices, a shifting sea of voices that surged around him. The voices came from all the rooms and offices, on all the levels. They excited him.

Dr James North came toward them, holding out his hand. He was tall and handsome, perhaps thirty, with brown hair and black horn-rimmed glasses. His stride was firm, his grip, when he shook hands with Lemuel, brief and confident. 'Come in here,' he boomed. Ralph moved toward the office, but Dr North shook his head. 'Not you. The boy. Lemuel and I are going to have a talk alone.'

Excited, Lemuel followed Dr North into his office. North quickly secured the door with triple magnetic locks. 'You can call me James,' he said, smiling warmly at the boy. 'And I'll call you Lem, right?'

'Sure,' Lemuel said guardedly. He felt no hostility emanating from the man, but he had learned to keep his guard up. He had to be careful, even with this friendly, good-looking doctor, a man of obvious intellectual ability.

North lit a cigarette and studied the boy. 'When you tied up and dissected those old derelicts,' he said thoughtfully, 'you were scientifically curious, weren't you? You wanted to *know*–facts, not opinions. You wanted to find out for yourself how human beings were constructed.'

Lemuel's excitement grew. 'But no one understood.'

'No.' North shook his head. 'No, they wouldn't. Do you know why?'

'I think so.'

North paced back and forth. 'I'll give you a few tests. To find out things. You don't mind, do you? We'll both learn more about you.

I've been studying you, Lem. I've examined the police records and the newspaper files.' Abruptly, he opened the drawer of his desk and got out the Minnesota Multi-phasic, the Rorschach blots, the Bender Gestalt, the Rhine deck of ESP cards, an ouija board, a pair of dice, a magic writing tablet, a wax doll with fingernail parings and bits of hair, and a small piece of lead to be turned into gold.

'What do you want me to do?' Lemuel asked.

'I'm going to ask you a few questions, and give you a few objects to play with. I'll watch your reactions, note down a few things. How's that sound?'

Lemuel hesitated. He needed a friend so badly–but he was afraid. 'I–'

Dr North put his hand on the boy's shoulder. 'You can trust me. I'm not like those kids that beat you up, that morning.'

Lemuel glanced up gratefully. 'You know about that? I discovered the rules of their game were purely arbitrary. Therefore I naturally oriented myself to the basic reality of the situation, and when I came up at bat I hit the pitcher and the catcher over the head. Later I discovered that all human ethics and morals are exactly the same sort of–' He broke off, suddenly afraid. 'Maybe I–'

Dr North sat down behind his desk and began shuffling the Rhine ESP deck. 'Don't worry, Lem,' he said softly. 'Everything will be all right. I understand.'

After the tests, the two of them sat in silence. It was six o'clock, and the sun was beginning to set outside. At last Dr North spoke.

'Incredible. I can scarcely believe it, myself. You're utterly logical. You've completely cast off all thalamic emotion. Your mind is totally free of moral and cultural bias. You're a perfect paranoid, without any empathic ability whatever. You're utterly incapable of feeling sorrow or pity or compassion, or *any* of the normal human emotions.'

Lemuel nodded. 'True.'

Dr North leaned back, dazed. 'It's hard even for me to grasp this. It's overwhelming. You possess super-logic, completely free of value-orientation bias. And you conceive of the entire world as organized against you.'

'Yes.'

'Of course. You've analyzed the structure of human activity and seen that as soon as they find out, they'll pounce on you and try to destroy you.'

'Because I'm different.'

North was overcome. 'They've always classed paranoia as a mental illness. But it isn't! There's no lack of contact with reality– on the contrary, the paranoid is *directly* related to reality. He's a perfect empiricist. Not cluttered with ethical and moral-cultural inhibitions. The paranoid sees things as they really are; he's actually the only sane man.'

'I've been reading *Mein Kampf*,' Lemuel said. 'It shows me I'm not alone.' And in his mind he breathed the silent prayer of thanks: *Not alone*. Us. There are more of us.

Dr North caught his expression. 'The wave of the future,' he said. 'I'm not a part of it, but I can try to understand. I can appreciate I'm just a human being, limited by my thalamic emotional and cultural bias. I can't be one of you, but I can sympathize . . .' He looked up, face alight with enthusiasm. 'And I can help!'

The next few days were filled with excitement for Lemuel. Dr North arranged for custody of him, and the boy took up residence at the doctor's uptown apartment. Here, he was no longer under pressure from his family; he could do as he pleased. Dr North began at once to aid Lemuel in locating other mutant paranoids.

One evening after dinner, Dr North asked, 'Lemuel, do you think you could explain your theory of Null-O to me? It's hard to grasp the principle of non-object orientation.'

Lemuel indicated the apartment with a wave of his hand. 'All these apparent objects–each has a name. Book, chair, couch, rug, lamp, drapes, window, door, wall, and so on. But this division into objects is purely artificial. Based on an antiquated system of thought. In reality there are no objects. The universe is actually a unity. We have been taught to think in terms of objects. This *thing*, that *thing*. When Null-O is realized, this purely verbal division will cease. It has long since outlived its usefulness.'

'Can you give me an example, a demonstration?'

Lemuel hesitated. 'It's hard to do alone. Later on, when we've contacted others . . . I can do it crudely, on a small scale.'

As Dr North watched intently, Lemuel rushed about the apartment gathering everything together in a heap. Then, when all the books, pictures, rugs, drapes, furniture and bric-a-brac had been collected, he systematically smashed everything into a shapeless mass.

'You see,' he said, exhausted and pale from the violent effort, 'the distinction into arbitrary objects is now gone. This unification of things into their basic homogeneity can be applied to the universe as a whole. The universe is a gestalt, a unified substance, without division into living and non-living, being and non-being. A vast vortex of energy, not discrete particles! Underlying the purely artificial appearance of material objects lies the world of reality: a vast undifferentiated realm of pure energy. Remember: the object is not the reality. First law of Null-O thought!'

Dr North was solemn, deeply impressed. He kicked at a bit of broken chair, part of the shapeless heap of wood and cloth and paper and shattered glass. 'Do you think this restoration to reality can be accomplished?'

'I don't know,' Lemuel said simply. 'There will be opposition, of course. Human beings will fight us; they're incapable of rising above their monkey-like preoccupation with *things*–bright objects they can touch and possess. It will all depend on how well we can co-ordinate with each other.'

Dr North unfolded a slip of paper from his pocket. 'I have a lead,' he said quietly. 'The name of a man I think is one of you. We'll visit him tomorrow–then we'll see.'

Dr Jacob Weller greeted them with brisk efficiency at the entrance of his well-guarded lab overlooking Palo Alto. Rows of uniformed government guards protected the vital work he was doing, the immense system of labs and research offices. Men and women in white robes were working day and night.

'My work,' he explained, as he signaled for the heavy-duty entrance locks to be closed behind them, 'was basic in the development of the C-bomb, the cobalt case for the H-bomb. You will find that many top nuclear physicists are Null-O.'

Lemuel's breath caught. 'Then–'

'Of course.' Weller wasted no words. 'We've been working for years. Rockets at Peenemunde, the A-bomb at Los Alamos, the hydrogen bomb, and now this, the C-bomb. There are, of course, many scientists who are not Null-O, regular human beings with thalamic bias. Einstein, for example. But we're well on the way; unless too much opposition is encountered we'll be able to go into action very shortly.'

The rear door of the laboratory slid aside, and a group of white-clad men and women filed solemnly in. Lemuel's heart gave a jump. Here they were, full-fledged adult Null-Os! Men and women both, *and they had been working for years*! He recognized them easily; all had the elongated and mobile ears, by which the mutant Null-O picked up minute air vibrations over great distances. It enabled them to communicate, wherever they were, throughout the world.

'Explain our program,' Weller said to a small blond man who stood beside him, calm and collected, face stern with the importance of the moment.

'The C-bomb is almost ready,' the man said quietly, with a slight German accent. 'But it is not the final step in our plans. There is also the E-bomb, which is the ultimate of this initial phase. We have never made the E-bomb public. If human beings should find out about it, we should have to cope with serious emotional opposition.'

'What is the E-bomb?' Lemuel asked, glowing with excitement.

'The phrase, "the E-bomb,"' said the small blond man, 'describes the process by which the Earth itself becomes a pile, is brought up to critical mass, and then allowed to detonate.'

Lemuel was overcome. 'I had no idea you had developed the plan this far!'

The blond man smiled faintly. 'Yes, we have done a lot, since the early days. Under Dr Rust, I was able to work out the basic ideological concepts of our program. Ultimately, we will unify the entire universe into a homogeneous mass. Right now, however, our concern is with the Earth. But once we have been successful here, there's no reason why we can't continue our work indefinitely.'

'Transportation,' Weller explained, 'has been arranged to other planets. Dr Frisch here–'

'A modification of the guided missiles we developed at Peenemunde,' the blond man continued. 'We have constructed a ship which will take us to Venus. There, we will initiate the second phase of our work. A V-bomb will be developed, which will restore Venus to its primordial state of homogeneous energy. And then–' He smiled faintly. 'And then an S-bomb. The Sol bomb. Which will, if we are successful, unify this whole system of planets and moons into a vast gestalt.'

By June 25, 1969, Null-O personnel had gained virtual control of all major world governments. The process, begun in the middle thirties, was for all practical purposes complete. The United States and Soviet Russia were firmly in the hands of Null-O individuals. Null-O men controlled all policy-level positions, and hence, could speed up the program of Null-O. The time had come. Secrecy was no longer necessary.

Lemuel and Dr North watched from a circling rocket as the first H-bombs were detonated. By careful arrangement, both nations began H-bomb attacks simultaneously. Within an hour, class-one results were obtained; most of North America and Eastern Europe were gone. Vast clouds of radioactive particles drifted and billowed. Fused pits of metal bubbled and sputtered as far as the eye could see. In Africa, Asia, on endless islands and out-of-the-way places, surviving human beings cowered in terror.

'Perfect,' came Dr Weller's voice in Lemuel's ears. He was somewhere below the surface, down in the carefully protected headquarters where the Venus ship was in its last stages of assembly.

Lemuel agreed. 'Great work. We've managed to unify at least a fifth of the world's land surface!'

'But there's more to come. Next the C-bombs are to be released. This will prevent human beings from interfering with our final work, the E-bomb installations. The terminals must still be erected. That can't be done as long as humans remain to interfere.'

Within a week, the first C-bomb was set off. More followed, hurtled up from carefully concealed launchers in Russia and America.

By August 5, 1969, the human population of the world had been diminished to three thousand. The Null-Os, in their subsurface offices, glowed with satisfaction. Unification was proceeding exactly as planned. The dream was coming true.

'Now,' said Dr Weller, 'we can begin erection of the E-bomb terminals.'

One terminal was begun at Arequipa, Peru. The other, at the opposite side of the globe, at Bandoeng, Java. Within a month the two immense towers rose high against the dust-swept sky. In heavy protective suits and helmets, the two colonies of Null-Os worked day and night to complete the program.

Dr Weller flew Lemuel to the Peruvian installation. All the way from San Francisco to Lima there was nothing but rolling ash and still-burning metallic fires. No sign of life or separate entities: everything had been fused into a single mass of heaving slag. The oceans themselves were steam and boiling water. All distinction between land and sea had been lost. The surface of the Earth was a single expanse of dull gray and white, where blue oceans and green forests, roads and cities and fields had once been.

'There,' Dr Weller said. 'See it?'

Lemuel saw it, all right. His breath caught in his throat at its sheer beauty. The Null-Os had erected a vast bubble-shield, a sphere of transparent plastic amidst the rolling sea of liquid slag. Within the bubble the terminal itself could be seen, an intricate web of flashing metal and wires that made both Dr Weller and Lemuel fall silent.

'You see,' Weller explained, as he dropped the rocket through the locks of the shield, 'we have only unified the surface of the Earth and perhaps a mile of rock beneath. The vast mass of the planet, however, is unchanged. But the E-bomb will handle that. The still-liquid core of the planet will erupt; the whole sphere will become a new sun. And when the S-bomb goes off, the entire system will become a unified mass of fiery gas.'

Lemuel nodded. 'Logical. And then–'

'The G-bomb. The galaxy itself is next. The final stages of the plan . . . So vast, so awesome, we scarcely dare think of them. The G-bomb, and finally–' Weller smiled slightly, his eyes bright. 'Then the U-bomb.'

They landed, and were met by Dr Frisch, full of nervous excitement. 'Dr Weller!' he gasped. 'Something has gone wrong!'

'What is it?'

Frisch's face was contorted with dismay. By a violent Null-O leap he managed to integrate his mental faculties and throw off thalamic impulses. 'A number of human beings have survived!'

Weller was incredulous. 'What do you mean? How–'

'I picked up the sound of their voices. I was rotating my ears, enjoying the roar and lap of the slag outside the bubble, when I picked up the noise of ordinary human beings.'

'But where?'

'Below the surface. Certain wealthy industrialists had secretly transferred their factories below ground, in violation of their governments' absolute orders to the contrary.'

'Yes, we had an explicit policy to prevent that.'

'These industrialists acted with typical thalamic greed. They transferred whole labor forces below, to work as slaves when war began. At least ten thousand humans were spared. They are still alive. And–'

'And what?'

'They have improvised huge bores, are now moving this way as quickly as possible. We're going to have a fight on our hands. I've already notified the Venus ship. It's being brought up to the surface at once.'

Lemuel and Dr Weller glanced at each other in horror. There were only a thousand Null-Os; they'd be outnumbered ten to one. 'This is terrible,' Weller said thickly. 'Just when everything seemed near completion. How long before the power towers are ready?'

'It will be another six days before the Earth can be brought up to critical mass,' Frisch muttered. 'And the bores are virtually here. Rotate your ears. You'll hear them.'

Lemuel and Dr Weller did so. At once, a confusing babble of human voices came to them. A chaotic clang of sound, from a number of bores converging on the two terminal bubbles.

'Perfectly ordinary humans!' Lemuel gasped. 'I can tell by the sound!'

'We're trapped!' Weller grabbed up a blaster, and Frisch did so, too. All the Null-Os were arming themselves. Work was forgotten. With a shattering roar the snout of a bore burst through the ground and aimed itself directly at them. The Null-Os fired wildly; they scattered and fell back toward the tower.

A second bore appeared, and then a third. The air was alive with blazing beams of energy, as the Null-Os fired and the humans fired back. The humans were the most common possible, a variety of laborers taken subsurface by their employers. The lower forms of human life: clerks, bus drivers, day-laborers, typists, janitors, tailors, bakers, turret lathe operators, shipping clerks, baseball players, radio announcers, garage mechanics, policemen, necktie peddlers, ice-cream vendors, door-to-door salesmen, bill collectors, receptionists, welders, carpenters, construction laborers, farmers, politicians, merchants–the men and women whose very existence terrified the Null-Os to their core.

The emotional masses of ordinary people who resented the Great Work, the bombs and bacteria and guided missiles, were coming to the surface. They were rising up–finally. Putting an end to super-logic: rationality without responsibility.

'We haven't a chance,' Weller gasped. 'Forget the towers. Get the ship to the surface.'

A salesman and two plumbers were setting fire to the terminal. A group of men in overalls and canvas shirts were ripping down the wiring. Others just as ordinary were turning their heat guns on the intricate controls. Flames licked up. The terminal tower swayed ominously.

The Venus ship appeared, lifted to the surface by an intricate stage-system. At once the Null-Os poured into it, in two efficient lines, all of them controlled and integrated as the crazed human beings decimated their ranks.

'Animals,' Weller said sadly. 'The mass of men. Mindless animals, dominated by their emotions. Beasts, unable to see things logically.'

A heat beam finished him off, and the man behind moved forward. Finally the last remaining Null-O was aboard, and the great hatches slammed shut. With a thunderous roar the jets of the ship opened, and it shot through the bubble into the sky.

Lemuel lay where he had fallen, when a heat beam, wielded by a crazed electrician, had touched his left leg. Sadly, he saw the ship rise, hesitate, then crash through and dwindle into the flaming sky. Human beings were all around him, repairing the damaged protection bubble, shouting orders and yelling excitedly. The babble of their voices beat against his sensitive ears; feebly, he put his hands up and covered them.

The ship was gone. He had been left behind. But the plan would continue without him.

A distant voice came to him. It was Dr Frisch aboard the Venus ship, yelling down with cupped hands. The voice was faint, lost in the trackless miles of space, but Lemuel managed to make it out above the noise and hubbub around him.

'Goodbye . . . We'll remember you . . .'

'Work hard!' the boy shouted back. 'Don't give up until the plan is complete!'

'We'll work . . .' The voice grew more faint. 'We'll keep on . . .' It died out, then returned for a brief instant. 'We'll succeed . . .' And then there was only silence.

With a peaceful smile on his face, a smile of happiness and contentment, satisfaction at a job well done, Lemuel lay back and waited for the pack of irrational human animals to finish him.

TO SERVE THE MASTER

Applequist was cutting across a deserted field, up a narrow path beside the yawning crack of a ravine, when he heard the voice.

He stopped frozen, hand on his S-pistol. For a long time he listened, but there was only the distant lap of the wind among the broken trees along the ridge, a hollow murmuring that mixed with the rustle of the dry grass beside him. The sound had come from the ravine. Its bottom was snarled and debris-filled. He crouched down at the lip and tried to locate the voice.

There was no motion. Nothing to give away the place. His legs began to ache. Flies buzzed at him, settled on his sweating forehead. The sun made his head ache; the dust clouds had been thin the last few months.

His radiation-proof watch told him it was three o'clock. Finally he shrugged and got stiffly to his feet. The hell with it. Let them send out an armed team. It wasn't his business; he was a letter carrier grade four, and a civilian.

As he climbed the hill toward the road, the sound came again. And this time, standing high above the ravine, he caught a flash of motion. Fear and puzzled disbelief touched him. It couldn't be—but he had seen it with his own eyes. It wasn't a newscircular rumor.

What was a robot doing down in the deserted ravine? All robots had been destroyed years ago. But there it lay, among the debris and weeds. A rusted, half-corroded wreck. Calling feebly up at him as he passed along the trail.

*

The Company defense ring admitted him through the three-stage lock into the tunnel area. He descended slowly, deep in thought all the way down to the organizational level. As he slid off his letter pack Assistant Supervisor Jenkins hurried over.

'Where the hell have you been? It's almost four.'

'Sorry.' Applequist turned his S-pistol over to a nearby guard. 'What are the chances of a five-hour pass? There's something I want to look into.'

'Not a chance. You know they're scrapping the whole right-wing setup. They need everybody on strict twenty-four-hour alert.'

Applequist began sorting letters. Most were personals between big-shot supervisors of the North American Companies. Letters to entertainment women beyond the Company peripheries. Letters to families and petitions from minor officials. 'In that case,' he said thoughtfully, 'I'll have to go anyhow.'

Jenkins eyed the young man suspiciously. 'What's going on? Maybe you found some undamaged equipment left over from the war. An intact cache, buried someplace? Is that it?'

Applequist almost told him, at that point. But he didn't. 'Maybe,' he answered indifferently. 'It's possible.'

Jenkins shot him a grimace of hate and stalked off to roll aside the doors of the observation chamber. At the big wall map officials were examining the day's activities. Half a dozen middle-aged men, most of them bald, collars dirty and stained, lounged around in chairs. In the corner Supervisor Rudde was sound asleep, fat legs stuck out in front of him, hairy chest visible under his open shirt. These were the men who ran the Detroit Company. Ten thousand families, the whole subsurface living-shelter, depended on them.

'What's on your mind?' a voice rumbled in Applequist's ear. Director Laws had come into the chamber and, as usual, taken him unawares.

'Nothing, sir,' Applequist answered. But the keen eyes, blue as china, bored through and beneath. 'The usual fatigue. My tension index is up. I've been meaning to take some of my leave, but with all the work . . .'

'Don't try to fool me. A fourth-class letter carrier isn't needed. What are you really getting at?'

'Sir,' Applequist said bluntly, 'why were the robots destroyed?'

There was silence. Laws' heavy face registered surprise, then hostility. Before he could speak Applequist hurried on: 'I know my class is forbidden to make theoretical inquiries. But it's very important I find out.'

'The subject is closed,' Laws rumbled ominously. 'Even to top-level personnel.'

'What did the robots have to do with the war? Why was the war fought? What was life like before the war?'

'The subject,' Laws repeated, 'is closed.' He moved slowly toward the wall map and Applequist was left standing alone, in the middle of the clicking machines, among the murmuring officials and bureaucrats.

Automatically, he resumed sorting letters. There had been the war, and robots were involved in it. That much he knew. A few had survived; when he was a child his father had taken him to an industrial center and he had seen them at their machines. Once, there had been more complex types. Those were all gone; even the simple ones would soon be scrapped. Absolutely no more were manufactured.

'*What happened?*' he had asked, as his father dragged him away. 'Where did all the robots go?'

No answer then either. That was sixteen years ago, and now the last had been scrapped. Even the memory of robots was disappearing; in a few years the word itself would cease. *Robots.* What had happened?

He finished with the letters and moved out of the chamber. None of the supervisors noticed; they were arguing some erudite point of strategy. Maneuvering and countermaneuvering among the Companies. Tension and exchanged insults. He found a crushed cigarette in his pocket and inexpertly lit up.

'Dinner call,' the passage speaker announced tinnily. 'One-hour break for top-class personnel.'

A few supervisors filed noisily past him. Applequist crushed out his cigarette and moved toward his station. He worked until six. Then his dinner hour came up. No other break until Saturday. But if he went without dinner . . .

The robot was probably a low-order type, scrapped with the final group. The inferior kind he had seen as a child. It couldn't be one of the elaborate war-time robots. To have survived in the ravine, rusting and rotting through the years since the war . . .

His mind skirted the hope. Heart pounding, he entered a lift and touched the stud. By nightfall he'd know.

The robot lay among heaps of metal slag and weeds. Jagged, rusted fragments barred Applequist's way as he moved cautiously down the side of the ravine, S-gun in one hand, radiation mask pulled tight over his face.

His counter clicked loudly: the floor of the ravine was hot. Pools of contamination, over the reddish metal fragments, the piles and masses of fused steel and plastic and gutted equipment. He kicked webs of blackened wiring aside and gingerly stepped past the yawning fuel-tank of some ancient machine, now overgrown with vines. A rat scuttled off. It was almost sunset. Dark shadows lay over everything.

The robot was watching him silently. Half of it was gone; only the head, arms, and upper trunk remained. The lower waist ended in shapeless struts, abruptly sliced off. It was clearly immobile. Its whole surface was pitted and corroded. One eye-lens was missing. Some of its metal fingers were bent grotesquely. It lay on its back facing the sky.

It was a war-time robot, all right. In the one remaining eye glinted archaic consciousness. This was not the simple worker he had glimpsed as a child. Applequist's breath hammered in his throat. This was the real thing. It was following his movements intently. It was alive.

All this time, Applequist thought. *All these years*. The hackles of his neck rose. Everything was silent, the hills and trees and masses of ruin. Nothing stirred; he and the ancient robot were the only living things. *Down here in this crack waiting for somebody to come along.*

A cold wind rustled at him and he automatically pulled his overcoat together. Some leaves blew over the inert face of the robot. Vines had crept along its trunk, twisted into its works. It had been rained on; the sun had shone on it. In winter the snow had covered it. Rats and animals had sniffed at it. Insects had crawled through it. And it was still alive.

'I heard you,' Applequist muttered. 'I was walking along the path.'

Presently the robot said, 'I know. I saw you stop.' Its voice was faint and dry. Like ashes rubbing together. Without quality or pitch. 'Would you make the date known to me? I suffered a power failure for an indefinite period. Wiring terminals shorted temporarily.'

'It's June 11,' Applequist said. '2136,' he added.

The robot was obviously hoarding its meager strength. It moved one arm slightly, then let it fall back. Its one good eye blurred over, and deep within, gears whirred rustily. Realization came to Applequist: the robot might expire any moment. It was a miracle it had survived this long. Snails clung to its body. It was criss-crossed with slimy trails. A century . . .

'How long have you been here?' he demanded. 'Since the war?'

'Yes.'

Applequist grinned nervously. 'That's a long time. Over a hundred years.'

'That's so.'

It was getting dark fast. Automatically, Applequist fumbled for his flashlight. He could hardly make out the sides of the ravine. Someplace a long way off a bird croaked dismally in the darkness. The bushes rustled.

'I need help,' the robot said. 'Most of my motor equipment was destroyed. I can't move from here.'

'In what condition is the rest of you? Your energy supply. How long can–'

'There's been considerable cell destruction. Only a limited number of relay circuits still function. And those are overloaded.' The robot's one good eye was on him again. 'What is the technological situation? I have seen airborne ships fly overhead. You still manufacture and maintain electronic equipment?'

'We operate an industrial unit near Pittsburgh.'

'If I describe basic electronic units will you understand?' the robot asked.

'I'm not trained in mechanical work. I'm classed as a fourth-grade letter carrier. But I have contacts in the repair department. We keep our own machines functioning.' He licked his lips tensely. 'It's risky, of course. There are laws.'

'Laws?'

'All robots were destroyed. You are the only one left. The rest were liquidated years ago.'

No expression showed in the robot's eye. 'Why did you come down here?' it demanded. Its eye moved to the S-gun in Applequist's hand. 'You are a minor official in some hierarchy. Acting on orders from above. A mechanically-operating integer in a larger system.'

Applequist laughed. 'I suppose so.' Then he stopped laughing. 'Why was the war fought? What was life like before?'

'Don't you know?'

'Of course not. No theoretical knowledge is permitted, except to top-level personnel. And even the supervisors don't know about the war.' Applequist squatted down and shone the beam of his flashlight into the darkening face of the robot. 'Things were different before, weren't they? We didn't always live in subsurface shelters. The world wasn't always a scrap heap. People didn't always slave for their Companies.'

'Before the war there were no Companies.'

Applequist grunted with triumph. 'I knew it.'

'Men lived in cities, which were demolished in the war. Companies, which were protected, survived. Officials of these Companies became the government. The war lasted a long time. Everything of value was destroyed. What you have left is a burned-out shell.'

The robot was silent a moment and then continued, 'The first robot was built in 1979. By 2000 all routine work was done by robots. Human beings were free to do what they wanted. Art, science, entertainment, whatever they liked.'

'What is art?' Applequist asked.

'Creative work, directed toward realization of an internal standard. The whole population of the earth was free to expand culturally. Robots maintained the world; man enjoyed it.'

'What were cities like?'

'Robots rebuilt and reconstructed new cities according to plans drawn up by human artists. Clean, sanitary, attractive. They were the cities of gods.'

'Why was the war fought?'

The robot's single eye flickered. 'I've already talked too much. My power supply is dangerously low.'

Applequist trembled. 'What do you need? I'll get it.'

'Immediately, I need an atomic A pack. Capable of putting out ten thousand f-units.'

'Yes.'

'After that, I'll need tools and aluminum sections. Low resistance wiring. Bring pen and paper—I'll give you a list. You won't understand it, but someone in electronic maintenance will. A power supply is the first need.'

'And you'll tell me about the war?'

'Of course.' The robot's dry rasp faded into silence. Shadows flickered around it; cold evening air stirred the dark weeds and bushes. 'Kindly hurry. Tomorrow, if possible.'

'I ought to turn you in,' Assistant Supervisor Jenkins snapped. 'Half an hour late, and now this business. What are you doing? You want to get fired out of the Company?'

Applequist pushed close to the man. 'I have to get this stuff. The—cache is below surface. I have to construct a secure passage. Otherwise the whole thing will be buried by falling debris.'

'How large a cache is it?' Greed edged suspicion off Jenkins' gnarled face. He was already spending the Company reward. 'Have you been able to see in? Are there unknown machines?'

'I didn't recognize any,' Applequist said impatiently. 'Don't waste time. The whole mass of debris is apt to collapse. I have to work fast.'

'Where is it? I want to see it!'

'I'm doing this alone. You supply the material and cover for my absence. That's your part.'

Jenkins twisted uncertainly. 'If you're lying to me, Applequist–'

'I'm not lying,' Applequist answered angrily. 'When can I expect the power unit?'

'Tomorrow morning. I'll have to fill out a bushel of forms. Are you sure you can operate it? I better send a repair team along with you. To be sure–'

'I can handle it,' Applequist interrupted. 'Just get me the stuff. I'll take care of the rest.'

Morning sunlight filtered over the rubble and trash. Applequist nervously fitted the new power pack in place, screwed the leads tight, clamped the corroded shield over it, and then got shakily to his feet. He tossed away the old pack and waited.

The robot stirred. Its eye gained life and awareness. Presently it moved its arm in exploratory motions, over its damaged trunk and shoulders.

'All right?' Applequist demanded huskily.

'Apparently.' The robot's voice was stronger; full and more confident. 'The old power pack was virtually exhausted. It was fortunate you came along when you did.'

'You say men lived in cities,' Applequist plunged in eagerly. 'Robots did the work?'

'Robots did the routine labor needed to maintain the industrial system. Humans had leisure to enjoy whatever they wanted. We were glad to do their work for them. It was our job.'

'What happened? What went wrong?'

The robot accepted the pencil and paper; as it talked it carefully wrote down figures. 'There was a fanatic group of humans. A religious organization. They claimed that God intended man to work by the sweat of his brow. They wanted robots scrapped and men put back in the factories to slave away at routine tasks.'

'But why?'

'They claimed work was spiritually ennobling.' The robot tossed the paper back. 'Here's the list of what I want. I'll need those materials and tools to restore my damaged system.'

Applequist fingered the paper. 'This religious group–'

'Men separated in two factions. The Moralists and the Leisurists. They fought each other for years, while we stood on the sidelines waiting to know our fate. I couldn't believe the Moralists would win out over reason and common sense. But they did.'

'Do you think–' Applequist began, and then broke off. He could hardly give voice to the thought that was struggling inside him. 'Is there a chance robots might be brought back?'

'Your meaning is obscure.' The robot abruptly snapped the pencil in half and threw it away. 'What are you driving at?'

'Life isn't pleasant in the Companies. Death and hard work. Forms and shifts and work periods and orders.'

'It's your system. I'm not responsible.'

'How much do you recall about robot construction? What were you, before the war?'

'I was a unit controller. I was on my way to an emergency unit-factory, when my ship was shot down.' The robot indicated the debris around it. 'That was my ship and cargo.'

'What is a unit controller?'

'I was in charge of robot manufacture. I designed and put into production basic robot types.'

Applequist's head spun dizzily. 'Then you do know robot construction.'

'Yes.' The robot gestured urgently at the paper in Applequist's hand. 'Kindly get those tools and materials as soon as possible. I'm completely helpless this way. I want my mobility back. If a rocketship should fly overhead . . .'

'Communication between Companies is bad. I deliver my letters on foot. Most of the country is in ruins. You could work undetected. What about your emergency unit-factory? Maybe it wasn't destroyed.'

The robot nodded slowly. 'It was carefully concealed. There is the bare possibility. It was small, but completely outfitted. Self-sufficient.'

'If I get repair parts, can you–'

'We'll discuss this later.' The robot sank back down. 'When you return, we'll talk further.'

He got the material from Jenkins, and a twenty-four-hour pass. Fascinated, he crouched against the wall of the ravine as the robot systematically pulled apart its own body and replaced the damaged elements. In a few hours a new motor system had been installed. Basic leg cells were welded into position. By noon the robot was experimenting with its pedal extremities.

'During the night,' the robot said, 'I was able to make weak radio contact with the emergency unit-factory. It exists intact, according to the robot monitor.'

'Robot? You mean–'

'An automatic machine for relaying transmission. Not alive, as I am. Strictly speaking, I'm not a robot.' Its voice swelled. 'I'm an android.'

The fine distinction was lost on Applequist. His mind was racing excitedly over the possibilities. 'Then we can go ahead. With your knowledge, and the materials available at the–'

'You didn't see the terror and destruction. The Moralists systematically demolished us. Each town they seized was cleared of androids. Those of my race were brutally wiped out, as the Leisurists retreated. We were torn from our machines and destroyed.'

'But that was a century ago! Nobody wants to destroy robots any more. We need robots to rebuild the world. The Moralists won the war and left the world in ruins.'

The robot adjusted its motor system until its legs were coordinated. 'Their victory was a tragedy, but I understand the situation better than you. We must advance cautiously. If we are wiped out this time, it may be for good.'

Applequist followed after the robot as it moved hesitantly through the debris toward the wall of the ravine. 'We're crushed by work. Slaves in underground shelters. We can't go on this way. People will welcome robots. We need you. When I think how it must have been in the Golden Age, the foundations and flowers, the beautiful cities above ground . . . Now there's nothing but ruin and misery. The Moralists won, but nobody's happy. We'd gladly–'

'Where are we? What is the location here?'

'Slightly west of the Mississippi, a few miles or so. We must have freedom. We can't live this way, toiling underground. If we had free time we could investigate the mysteries of the whole universe. I found some old scientific tapes. Theoretical work in biology. Those men spent years working on abstract topics. They had the time. They were free. While robots maintained the economic system those men could go out and–'

'During the war,' the robot said thoughtfully, 'the Moralists rigged up detection screens over hundreds of square miles. Are those screens still functioning?'

'I don't know. I doubt it. Nothing outside of the immediate Company shelters still works.'

The robot was deep in thought. It had replaced its ruined eye with a new cell; both eyes flickered with concentration. 'Tonight we'll make plans concerning your Company. I'll let you know my decision then. Meanwhile, don't bring this situation up with anyone. You understand? Right now I'm concerned with the road system.'

'Most roads are in ruins.' Applequist tried hard to hold back his excitement. 'I'm convinced most in my Company are–Leisurists. Maybe a few at the top are Moralists. Some of the supervisors, perhaps. But the lower classes and families–'

'All right,' the robot interrupted. 'We'll see about that later.' It glanced around. 'I can use some of that damaged equipment. Part of it will function. For the moment, at least.'

*

Applequist managed to avoid Jenkins, as he hurriedly made his way across the organizational level to his work station. His mind was in a turmoil. Everything around him seemed vague and unconvincing. The quarreling supervisors. The clattering, humming machines. Clerks and minor bureaucrats hurrying back and forth with messages and memoranda. He grabbed a mass of letters and mechanically began sorting them into their slots.

'You've been outside,' Director Laws observed sourly. 'What is it, a girl? If you marry outside the Company you lose the little rating you have.'

Applequist pushed aside his letters. 'Director, I want to talk to you.'

Director Laws shook his head. 'Be careful. You know the ordinances governing fourth-class personnel. Better not ask any more questions. Keep your mind on your work and leave the theoretical issues to us.'

'Director,' Applequist asked, 'which side was our Company, Moralist or Leisurist?'

Laws didn't seem to understand the question. 'What do you mean?' He shook his head. 'I don't know those words.'

'In the war. Which side of the war were we on?'

'Good God,' Laws said. 'The human side, of course.' An expression like a curtain dropped over his heavy face. 'What do you mean, *Moralist*? What are you talking about?'

Suddenly Applequist was sweating. His voice would hardly come. 'Director, something's wrong. The war was between the two groups of humans. The Moralists destroyed the robots because they disapproved of humans living in leisure.'

'The war was fought between men and robots,' Laws said harshly. 'We won. We destroyed the robots.'

'But they worked for us!'

'They were built as workers, but they revolted. They had a philosophy. Superior beings–androids. They considered us nothing but cattle.'

Applequist was shaking all over. 'But it told me–'

'They slaughtered us. Millions of humans died, before we got the upper hand. They murdered, lied, hid, stole, did everything to survive. It was them or us–no quarter.' Laws grabbed Applequist by the collar. 'You damn fool! What the hell have you done? Answer me! What have you done?'

The sun was setting, as the armored twin-track roared up to the edge of the ravine. Troops leaped out and poured down the sides, S-rifles clattering. Laws emerged quickly, Applequist beside him.

'This is the place?' Laws demanded.

'Yes.' Applequist sagged. 'But it's gone.'

'Naturally. It was fully repaired. There was nothing to keep it here.' Laws signalled his men. 'No use looking. Plant a tactical A-bomb and let's get out of here. The air fleet may be able to catch it. We'll spray this area with radioactive gas.'

Applequist wandered numbly to the edge of the ravine. Below, in the darkening shadows, were the weeds and tumbled debris. There was no sign of the robot, of course. A place where it had been, bits of wire and discarded body sections. The old power pack where he had thrown it. A few tools. Nothing else.

'Come on,' Laws ordered his men. 'Let's get moving. We have a lot to do. Get the general alarm system going.'

The troops began climbing the sides of the ravine. Applequist started after them, toward the twin-track.

'No,' Laws said quickly. 'You're not coming with us.'

Applequist saw the look on their faces. The pent-up fear, the frantic terror and hate. He tried to run, but they were on him almost at once. They worked grimly and silently. When they were through they kicked aside his still-living remains and climbed into the twin-track. They slammed the locks and the motor thundered up. The track rumbled down the trail to the road. In a few moments it dwindled and was gone.

He was alone, with the half-buried bomb and the settling shadows. And the vast empty darkness that was collecting everywhere.

EXHIBIT PIECE

'That's a strange suit you have on,' the robot pubtrans driver observed. It slid back its door and came to rest at the curb. 'What are the little round things?'

'Those are buttons,' George Miller explained. 'They are partly functional, partly ornamental. This is an archaic suit of the twentieth century. I wear it because of the nature of my employment.'

He paid the robot, grabbed up his briefcase, and hurried along the ramp to the History Agency. The main building was already open for the day; robed men and women wandered everywhere. Miller entered a PRIVATE lift, squeezed between two immense controllers from the pre-Christian division, and in a moment was on his way to his own level, the Middle Twentieth Century.

'Gorning,' he murmured, as Controller Fleming met him at the atomic engine exhibit.

'Gorning,' Fleming responded brusquely. 'Look here, Miller. Let's have this out once and for all. What if everyone dressed like you? The Government sets up strict rules for dress. Can't you forget your damn anachronisms once in a while? What in God's name is that thing in your hand? It looks like a squashed Jurassic lizard.'

'This is an alligator hide briefcase,' Miller explained. 'I carry my study spools in it. The briefcase was an authority symbol of the managerial class of the later twentieth century.' He unzipped the briefcase. 'Try to understand, Fleming. By accustoming myself to everyday objects of my research period I transform my relation from mere intellectual curiosity to genuine empathy. You have frequently noticed I pronounce certain words oddly. The accent is that of an American businessman of the Eisenhower administration. Dig me?'

'Eh?' Fleming muttered.

'*Dig me* was a twentieth-century expression.' Miller laid out his study spools on his desk. 'Was there anything you wanted? If not I'll begin today's work. I've uncovered fascinating evidence to indicate that although twentieth-century Americans laid their own floor tiles, they did not weave their own clothing. I wish to alter my exhibits on this matter.'

'There's no fanatic like an academician,' Fleming grated. 'You're two hundred years behind times. Immersed in your relics and artifacts. Your damn authentic replicas of discarded trivia.'

'I love my work,' Miller answered mildly.

'Nobody complains about your work. But there are other things than work. You're a political-social unit here in this society. Take warning, Miller! The Board has reports on your eccentricities. They approve devotion to work . . .' His eyes narrowed significantly. 'But you go too far.'

'My first loyalty is to my art,' Miller said.

'Your what? What does that mean?'

'A twentieth-century term.' There was undisguised superiority on Miller's face. 'You're nothing but a minor bureaucrat in a vast machine. You're a function of an impersonal cultural totality. You have no standards of your own. In the twentieth century men had personal standards of workmanship. Artistic craft. Pride of accomplishment. These words mean nothing to you. You have no soul–another concept from the golden days of the twentieth century when men were free and could speak their minds.'

'Beware, Miller!' Fleming blanched nervously and lowered his voice. 'You damn scholars. Come up out of your tapes and face reality. You'll get us all in trouble, talking this way. Idolize the past, if you want. But remember–it's gone and buried. Times change. Society progresses.' He gestured impatiently at the exhibits that occupied the level. 'That's only an imperfect replica.'

‘You impugn my research?’ Miller was seething. ‘This exhibit is absolutely accurate! I correct it to all new data. There isn’t anything I don’t know about the twentieth century.’

Fleming shook his head. ‘It’s no use.’ He turned and stalked wearily off the level, on to the descent ramp.

Miller straightened his collar and bright hand-painted necktie. He smoothed down his blue pinstripe coat, expertly lit a pipeful of two-century-old tobacco, and returned to his spools.

Why didn’t Fleming leave him alone? Fleming, the officious representative of the great hierarchy that spread like a sticky gray web over the whole planet. Into each industrial, professional, and residential unit. Ah, the freedom of the twentieth century! He slowed his tape scanner a moment, and a dreamy look slid over his features. The exciting age of virility and individuality, when men were men . . .

It was just about then, just as he was settling deep in the beauty of his research, that he heard the inexplicable sounds. They came from the center of his exhibit, from within the intricate, carefully regulated interior.

Somebody was in his exhibit.

He could hear them back there, back in the depths. Somebody or something had gone past the safety barrier set up to keep the public out. Miller snapped off his tape scanner and got slowly to his feet. He was shaking all over as he moved cautiously toward the exhibit. He killed the barrier and climbed the railing on to a concrete pavement. A few curious visitors blinked, as the small, oddly dressed man crept among the authentic replicas of the twentieth century that made up the exhibit and disappeared within.

Breathing hard, Miller advanced up the pavement and on to a carefully tended gravel path. Maybe it was one of the other theorists, a minion of the Board, snooping around looking for something with which to discredit him. An inaccuracy here–a trifling error of no consequence there. Sweat came out on his forehead; anger became terror. To his right was a flower bed. Paul Scarlet roses and low-growing pansies. Then the moist green lawn. The gleaming white garage, with its door half up. The sleek rear of a 1954 Buick—and then the house itself.

He'd have to be careful. If it *was* somebody from the Board he'd be up against official hierarchy. Maybe it was somebody big. Maybe even Edwin Carnap, President of the Board, the highest ranking official in the N'York branch of the World Directorate. Shakily, Miller climbed the three cement steps. Now he was on the porch of the twentieth-century house that made up the center of the exhibit.

It was a nice little house; if he had lived back in those days he would have wanted one of his own. Three bedrooms, a ranch-style California bungalow. He pushed open the front door and entered the living room. Fireplace at one end. Dark wine-colored carpets. Modern couch and easy chair. Low hardwood glass-topped coffee table. Copper ashtrays. A cigarette lighter and a stack of magazines. Sleek plastic and steel floor lamps. A bookcase. Television set. Picture window overlooking the front garden. He crossed the room to the hall.

The house was amazingly complete. Below his feet the floor furnace radiated a faint aura of warmth. He peered into the first bedroom. A woman's boudoir. Silk bedcover. White starched sheets. Heavy drapes. A vanity table. Bottles and jars. Huge round mirror. Clothes visible within the closet. A dressing gown thrown over the back of a chair. Slippers. Nylon hose carefully placed at the foot of the bed.

Miller moved down the hall and peered into the next room. Brightly painted wallpaper: clowns and elephants and tight-rope walkers. The children's room. Two little beds for the two boys. Model airplanes. A dresser with a radio on it, pair of combs, school books, pennants, a No Parking sign, snapshots stuck in the mirror. A postage stamp album.

Nobody there, either.

Miller peered in the modern bathroom, even in the yellow-tiled shower. He passed through the dining room, glanced down the basement stairs where the washing machine and dryer were. Then he opened the back door and examined the back yard. A lawn, and the incinerator. A couple of small trees and then the three-dimensional projected backdrop of other houses receding off into incredibly convincing blue hills. And still no one. The yard was empty–deserted. He closed the door and started back.

From the kitchen came laughter.

A woman's laugh. The clink of spoons and dishes. And smells. It took him a moment to identify them, scholar that he was. Bacon and coffee. And hot cakes. Somebody was eating breakfast. A twentieth-century breakfast.

He made his way down the hall, past a man's bedroom, shoes and clothing strewn about, to the entrance of the kitchen.

A handsome late-thirtyish woman and two teenage boys were sitting around the little chrome and plastic breakfast table. They had finished eating; the two boys were fidgeting impatiently. Sunlight filtered through the window over the sink. The electric clock read half past eight. The radio was chirping merrily in the corner. A big pot of black coffee rested in the center of the table, surrounded by empty plates and milk glasses and silverware.

The woman had on a white blouse and checkered tweed skirt. Both boys wore faded blue jeans, sweatshirts, and tennis shoes. As yet they hadn't noticed him. Miller stood frozen at the doorway, while laughter and small talk bubbled around him.

'You'll have to ask your father,' the woman was saying, with mock sternness. 'Wait until he comes back.'

'He already said we could,' one of the boys protested.

'Well, ask him again.'

'He's always grouchy in the morning.'

'Not today. He had a good night's sleep. His hay fever didn't bother him. The new anti-hist the doctor gave him.' She glanced up at the clock. 'Go see what's keeping him, Don. He'll be late for work.'

'He was looking for the newspaper.' One of the boys pushed back his chair and got up. 'It missed the porch again and fell in the flowers.' He turned towards the door, and Miller found himself confronting him face to face. Briefly, the observation flashed through his mind that the boy looked familiar. Damn familiar–like somebody he knew, only younger. He tensed himself for the impact, as the boy abruptly halted.

'Gee,' the boy said. 'You scared me.'

The woman glanced quickly up at Miller. 'What are you doing out there, George?' she demanded. 'Come on back in here and finish your coffee.'

Miller came slowly into the kitchen. The woman was finishing her coffee; both boys were on their feet and beginning to press around him.

'Didn't you tell me I could go camping over the weekend up at Russian River with the group from school?' Don demanded. 'You said I could borrow a sleeping bag from the gym because the one I had you gave to the Salvation Army because you were allergic to the kapok in it.'

'Yeah,' Miller muttered uncertainly. Don. That was the boy's name. And his brother, Ted. But how did he know that? At the table the woman had got up and was collecting the dirty dishes to carry over to the sink. 'They said you already promised them,' she said over her shoulder. The dishes clattered into the sink and she began sprinkling soap flakes over them. 'But you remember that time they wanted to drive the car and the way they said it, you'd think they had got your okay. And they hadn't, of course.'

Miller sank weakly down at the table. Aimlessly, he fooled with his pipe. He set it down in the copper ashtray and examined the cuff of his coat. What was happening? His head spun. He got up abruptly and hurried to the window, over the sink.

Houses, streets. The distant hills beyond the town. The sights and sounds of people. The three-dimensional projected backdrop was utterly convincing; or was it the projected backdrop? How could he be sure. *What was happening?*

'George, what's the matter?' Marjorie asked, as she tied a pink plastic apron around her waist and began running hot water in the sink. 'You better get the car out and get started to work. Weren't you saying last night old man Davidson was shouting about employees being late for work and standing around the water cooler talking and having a good time on company time?'

Davidson. The word stuck in Miller's mind. He knew it, of course. A clear picture leaped up; a tall, white-haired old man, thin and stern. Vest and pocket watch. And the whole office, United Electronic Supply. The twelve-story building in downtown San Francisco. The newspaper and cigar stand in the lobby. The honking cars. Jammed parking lots. The elevator, packed with bright-eyed secretaries, tight sweaters and perfume.

He wandered out of the kitchen, through the hall, past his own bedroom, his wife's, and into the living room. The front door was open and he stepped out on to the porch.

The air was cool and sweet. It was a bright April morning. The lawns were still wet. Cars moved down Virginia Street, towards Shattuck Avenue. Early morning commuting traffic, businessmen on their way to work. Across the street Earl Kelly cheerfully waved his *Oakland Tribune* as he hurried down the pavement towards the bus stop.

A long way off Miller could see the Bay Bridge, Yerba Buena Island, and Treasure Island. Beyond that was San Francisco itself. In a few minutes he'd be shooting across the bridge in his Buick, on his way to the office. Along with thousands of other businessmen in blue pinstripe suits.

Ted pushed past him and out on the porch. 'Then it's okay? You don't care if we go camping?'

Miller licked his dry lips. 'Ted, listen to me. There's something strange.'

'Like what?'

'I don't know.' Miller wandered nervously around on the porch. 'This is Friday, isn't it?'

'Sure.'

'I thought it was.' But how did he know it was Friday? How did he know anything? But of course it was Friday. A long hard week–old man Davidson breathing down his neck. Wednesday, especially, when the General Electric order was slowed down because of a strike.

'Let me ask you something,' Miller said to his son. 'This morning–I left the kitchen to get the newspaper.'

Ted nodded. 'Yeah. So?'

'I got up and went out of the room. *How long was I gone?* Not long, was I?' He searched for words, but his mind was a maze of disjointed thoughts. 'I was sitting at the breakfast table with you all, and then I got up and went to look for the paper. Right? And then I came back in. Right?' His voice rose desperately. 'I got up and shaved and dressed this morning. I ate breakfast. Hot cakes and coffee. Bacon. *Right?*'

'Right,' Ted agreed. 'So?'

'Like I always do.'

'We only have hot cakes on Friday.'

Miller nodded slowly. 'That's right. Hot cakes on Friday. Because your uncle Frank eats with us Saturday and Sunday and he can't stand hot cakes, so we stopped having them on weekends. Frank is Marjorie's brother. He was in the Marines in the First World War. He was a corporal.'

'Good-bye,' Ted said, as Don came out to join him. 'We'll see you this evening.'

School books clutched, the boys sauntered off towards the big modern high school in the center of Berkeley.

Miller re-entered the house and automatically began searching the closet for his briefcase. Where was it? Damn it, he needed it. The whole Throckmorton account was in it; Davidson would be yelling his head off if he left it anywhere, like in the True Blue Cafeteria that time they were all celebrating the Yankees' winning the series. Where the hell was it?

He straightened up slowly, as memory came. Of course. He had left it by his work desk, where he had tossed it after taking out the research tapes. While Fleming was talking to him. Back at the History Agency.

He joined his wife in the kitchen. 'Look,' he said huskily. 'Marjorie, I think maybe I won't go down to the office this morning.'

Marjorie spun in alarm. 'George, is anything wrong?'

'I'm–completely confused.'

'Your hay fever again?'

'No. My mind. What's the name of that psychiatrist the PTA recommended when Mrs Bentley's kid had that fit?' He searched his disorganized brain. 'Grunberg, I think. In the Medical-Dental building.' He moved towards the door. 'I'll drop by and see him. Something's wrong–really wrong. And I don't know what it is.'

Adam Grunberg was a large heavy-set man in his late forties, with curly brown hair and horn-rimmed glasses. After Miller had finished, Grunberg cleared his throat, brushed at the sleeve of his Brooks Bros. suit, and asked thoughtfully, 'Did anything happen while you were out looking for the newspaper? Any sort of accident? You might try going over that part in detail. You got up from the breakfast table, went out on the porch, and started looking around in the bushes. And then what?'

Miller rubbed his forehead vaguely. 'I don't know. It's all confused. I don't remember looking for any newspaper. I remember coming back in the house. Then it gets clear. But before that it's all tied up with the History Agency and my quarrel with Fleming.'

'What was that again about your briefcase? Go over that.'

'Fleming said it looked like a squashed Jurassic lizard. And I said–'

'No. I mean, about looking for it in the closet and not finding it.'

'I looked in the closet and it wasn't there, of course. It's sitting beside my desk at the History Agency. On the Twentieth Century level. By my exhibits.' A strange expression crossed Miller's face. 'Good God, Grunberg. You realize this may be nothing but an *exhibit*? You and everybody else–maybe you're not real. Just pieces of this exhibit.'

'That wouldn't be very pleasant for us, would it?' Grunberg said, with a faint smile.

'People in dreams are always secure until the dreamer wakes up,' Miller retorted.

'So you're dreaming me,' Grunberg laughed tolerantly. 'I suppose I should thank you.'

'I'm not here because I especially like you. I'm here because I can't stand Fleming and the whole History Agency.'

Grunberg protested. 'This Fleming. Are you aware of thinking about him before you went out looking for the newspaper?'

Miller got to his feet and paced around the luxurious office, between the leather-covered chairs and the huge mahogany desk. 'I want to face this thing. I'm an exhibit. An artificial replica of the past. Fleming said something like this would happen to me.'

'Sit down, Mr Miller,' Grunberg said, in a gentle but commanding voice. When Miller had taken his chair again, Grunberg continued, 'I understand what you say. You have a general feeling that everything around you is unreal. A sort of stage.'

'An exhibit.'

'Yes, an exhibit in a museum.'

'In the N'York History Agency. Level R, the Twentieth Century level.'

'And in addition to this general feeling of–insubstantiality, there are specific projected memories of persons and places beyond this world. Another realm in which this one is contained. Perhaps I should say, the reality within which this is only a sort of shadow world.'

'This world doesn't look shadowy to me.' Miller struck the leather arm of the chair savagely. 'This world is completely real. That's what's wrong. I came in to investigate the noises and now I can't get back out. Good God, do I have to wander around this replica the rest of my life?'

'You know, of course, that your feeling is common to most of mankind. Especially during periods of great tension. Where–by the way–was the newspaper? Did you find it?'

'As far as I'm concerned–'

'Is that a source of irritation with you? I see you react strongly to a mention of the newspaper.'

Miller shook his head wearily. 'Forget it.'

'Yes, a trifle. The paperboy carelessly throws the newspaper in the bushes, not on the porch. It makes you angry. It happens again and again. Early in the day, just as you're starting to work. It seems to symbolize in a small way the whole petty frustrations and defeats of your job. Your whole life.'

'Personally, I don't give a damn about the newspaper.' Miller examined his wristwatch. 'I'm going–it's almost noon. Old man Davidson will be yelling his head off if I'm not at the office by–' He broke off. 'There it is again.'

'There what is?'

'All this!' Miller gestured impatiently out the window. 'This whole place. This damn world. This *exhibition*.'

'I have a thought,' Doctor Grunberg said slowly. 'I'll put it to you for what it's worth. Feel free to reject it if it doesn't fit.' He raised his shrewd, professional eyes. 'Ever see kids playing with rocket ships?'

'Lord,' Miller said wretchedly. 'I've seen commercial rocket freighters hauling cargo between Earth and Jupiter, landing at La Guardia Spaceport.'

Grunberg smiled slightly. 'Follow me through on this. A question. Is it job tension?'

'What do you mean?'

'It would be nice,' Grunberg said blandly, 'to live in the world of tomorrow. With robots and rocket ships to do all the work. You could just sit back and take it easy. No worries, no cares. No frustrations.'

'My position in the History Agency has plenty of cares and frustrations.' Miller rose abruptly. 'Look, Grunberg. Either this is an exhibit on R level of the History Agency, or I'm a middle-class businessman with an escape fantasy. Right now I can't decide which. One minute I think this is real, and the next minute–'

'We can decide easily,' Grunberg said.

'How?'

'You were looking for the newspaper. Down the path, on to the lawn. *Where did it happen?* Was it on the path? On the porch? Try to remember.'

'I don't have to try. I was still on the pavement. I had just jumped over the rail past the safety screens.'

'On the pavement. Then go back there. Find the exact place.'

'Why?'

'So you can prove to yourself there's nothing on the other side.'

Miller took a deep slow breath. 'Suppose there is?'

'There can't be. You said yourself: only one of the worlds can be real. This world is real–' Grunberg thumped his massive mahogany desk. 'Ergo, you won't find anything on the other side.'

'Yes,' Miller said, after a moment's silence. A peculiar expression cut across his face and stayed there. 'You've found the mistake.'

'What mistake?' Grunberg was puzzled. 'What–'

Miller moved towards the door of the office. 'I'm beginning to get it. I've been putting up a false question. Trying to decide which world is real.' He grinned humorlessly back at Doctor Grunberg. 'They're both real, of course.'

He grabbed a taxi and headed back to the house. No one was home. The boys were in school and Marjorie had gone downtown to shop. He waited indoors until he was sure nobody was watching along the street, and then started down the path to the pavement.

He found the spot without any trouble. There was a faint shimmer in the air, a weak place just at the edge of the parking strip. Through it he could see faint shapes.

He was right. There it was–complete and real. As real as the pavement under him.

A long metallic bar was cut off by the edges of the circle. He recognized it; the safety railing he had leaped over to enter the exhibit. Beyond it was the safety screen system. Turned off, of course. And beyond that, the rest of the level and the far walls of the History building.

He took a cautious step into the weak haze. It shimmered around him, misty and oblique. The shapes beyond became clearer. A moving figure in a dark blue robe. Some curious person examining the exhibits. The figure moved on and was lost. He could see his own work desk now. His tape scanner and heaps of study spools. Beside the desk was his briefcase, exactly where he had expected it.

While he was considering stepping over the railing to get the briefcase, Fleming appeared.

Some inner instinct made Miller step back through the weak spot, as Fleming approached. Maybe it was the expression on Fleming's face. In any case, Miller was back and standing firmly on the concrete pavement, when Fleming halted just beyond the juncture, face red, lips twisted with indignation.

'Miller,' he said thickly. 'Come out of there.'

Miller laughed. 'Be a good fellow, Fleming. Toss me my briefcase. It's that strange-looking thing over by the desk. I showed it to you–remember?'

'Stop playing games and listen to me!' Fleming snapped. 'This is serious. *Carnap knows*. I had to inform him.'

'Good for you. The loyal bureaucrat.'

Miller bent over to light his pipe. He inhaled and puffed a great cloud of gray tobacco smoke through the weak spot, out into the R level. Fleming coughed and retreated.

'What's that stuff?' he demanded.

'Tobacco. One of the things they have around here. Very common substance in the twentieth century. You wouldn't know about that–your period is the second century, BC. The Hellenistic world. I don't know how well you'd like that. They didn't have very good plumbing back there. Life expectancy was damn short.'

'What are you talking about?'

'In comparison, the life expectancy of *my* research period is quite high. And you should see the bathroom I've got. Yellow tile. And a shower. We don't have anything like that at the Agency leisure-quarters.'

Fleming grunted sourly. 'In other words, you're going to stay in there.'

'It's a pleasant place,' Miller said easily. 'Of course, my position is better than average. Let me describe it for you. I have an attractive wife: marriage is permitted, even sanctioned, in this era. I have two fine kids–both boys–who are going up to the Russian River this weekend. They live with me and my wife–we have complete custody of them. The State has no power of that, yet. I have a brand-new Buick–'

'Illusions,' Fleming spat. 'Psychotic delusions.'

'Are you sure?'

'You damn fool! I always knew you were too ego-recessive to face reality. You and your anachronistic retreats. Sometimes I'm ashamed I'm a theoretician. I wish I had gone into engineering.' Fleming's lips twitched. 'You're insane, you know. You're standing in the middle of an artificial exhibit, which is owned by the History Agency, a bundle of plastic and wire and struts. A replica of a past age. An imitation. And you'd rather be there than in the real world.'

'Strange,' Miller said thoughtfully. 'Seems to me I've heard the same thing very recently. You don't know a Doctor Grunberg, do you? A psychiatrist.'

Without formality, Director Carnap arrived with his company of assistants and experts. Fleming quickly retreated. Miller found himself facing one of the most powerful figures of the twenty-second century. He grinned and held out his hand.

'You insane imbecile,' Carnap rumbled. 'Get out of there before we drag you out. If we have to do that, you're through. You know what they do with advanced psychotics. It'll be euthanasia for you. I'll give you one last chance to come out of that fake exhibit–'

'Sorry,' Miller said. 'It's not an exhibit.'

Carnap's heavy face registered sudden surprise. For a brief instant his massive poise vanished. 'You still try to maintain–'

'This is a time gate,' Miller said quietly. 'You can't get me out, Carnap. You can't reach me. I'm in the past, two hundred years back. I've crossed back to a previous existence-coordinate. I found a bridge and escaped from your continuum to this. And there's nothing you can do about it.'

Carnap and his experts huddled together in a quick technical conference. Miller waited patiently. He had plenty of time; he had decided not to show up at the office until Monday.

After a while Carnap approached the juncture again, being

careful not to step over the safety rail. 'An interesting theory, Miller. That's the strange part about psychotics. They rationalize their delusions into a logical system. *A priori*, your concept stands up well. It's internally consistent. Only–'

'Only what?'

'Only it doesn't happen to be true.' Carnap had regained his confidence; he seemed to be enjoying the interchange. 'You think you're really back in the past. Yes, this exhibit is extremely accurate. Your work has always been good. The authenticity of detail is unequalled by any of the other exhibits.'

'I tried to do my work well,' Miller murmured.

'You wore archaic clothing and affected archaic speech mannerisms. You did everything possible to throw yourself back. You devoted yourself to your work.' Carnap tapped the safety railing with his fingernail. 'It would be a shame, Miller. A terrible shame to demolish such an authentic replica.'

'I see your point,' Miller said, after a time. 'I agree with you, certainly. I've been very proud of my work–I'd hate to see it all torn down. But that really won't do you any good. All you'll succeed in doing is closing the time gate.'

'You're sure?'

'Of course. The exhibit is only a bridge, a link with the past. I passed *through* the exhibit, but I'm not there now. I'm beyond the exhibit.' He grinned tightly. 'Your demolition can't reach me. But seal me off, if you want. I don't think I'll be wanting to come back. I wish you could see this side, Carnap. It's a nice place here. Freedom, opportunity. Limited government, responsible to the people. If you don't like a job here you quit. There's no euthanasia, here. Come on over. I'll introduce you to my wife.'

'We'll get you,' Carnap said. 'And all your psychotic figments along with you.'

'I doubt if any of my "psychotic figments" are worried. Grunberg wasn't. I don't think Marjorie is–'

'We've already begun demolition preparations,' Carnap said calmly. 'We'll do it piece by piece, not all at once. So you may have the opportunity to appreciate the scientific and–*artistic* way we take your imaginary world apart.'

'You're wasting your time,' Miller said. He turned and walked off, down the pavement, to the gravel path and up on to the front porch of the house.

In the living room he threw himself down in the easy chair and snapped on the television set. Then he went to the kitchen and got a can of ice-cold beer. He carried it happily back into the safe, comfortable living room.

As he was seating himself in front of the television set he noticed something rolled up on the low coffee table.

He grinned wryly. It was the morning newspaper, which he had looked so hard for. Marjorie had brought it in with the milk, as usual. And of course forgotten to tell him. He yawned contentedly and reached over to pick it up. Confidently, he unfolded it–and read the big black headlines.

RUSSIA REVEALS COBALT BOMB

TOTAL WORLD DESTRUCTION AHEAD

NOTES

All notes in italics are by Philip K. Dick. The year when the note was written appears in parentheses following the note. Most of these notes were written as story notes for the collections *The Best of Philip K. Dick* (published 1977) and *The Golden Man* (published 1980). A few were written at the request of editors publishing or reprinting a PKD story in a book or magazine.

When there is a date following the name of a story, it is the date the manuscript of that story was first received by Dick's agent, per the records of the Scott Meredith Literary Agency. Absence of a date means no record is available. The name of a magazine followed by a month and year indicates the first published appearance of a story. An alternate name following a story indicates Dick's original name for the story, as shown in the agency records.

These four volumes include all of Philip K. Dick's short fiction, with the exception of short novels later published as or included in novels, childhood writings, and unpublished writings for which manuscripts have not been found. The stories are arranged as closely as possible in chronological order of composition; research for this chronology was done by Gregg Rickman and Paul Williams.

THE COSMIC POACHERS ('BURGLAR')
Oct. 22, 1952. *Imagination*, July 1953.

PROGENY
Nov. 3, 1952. *If*, Nov. 1954.

SOME KINDS OF LIFE ('THE BELEAGUERED')
Nov. 3, 1952. *Fantastic Universe*, Oct.-Nov. 1953 [under the pseudonym Richard Phillips].

MARTIANS COME IN CLOUDS ('THE BUGGIES')
Nov. 5, 1952. *Fantastic Universe*, June-July 1954.

THE COMMUTER
Nov. 19, 1952. *Amazing*, Aug.-Sept. 1953.

THE WORLD SHE WANTED
Nov. 24, 1952. *Science Fiction Quarterly*, May 1953.

A SURFACE RAID
Dec. 2, 1952. *Fantastic Universe*, July 1955.

PROJECT: EARTH ('ONE WHO STOLE')
Jan. 6, 1953. *Imagination*, Dec. 1953.

THE TROUBLE WITH BUBBLES ('PLAYTHING')
Jan. 13, 1953. *If*, Sept. 1953.

BREAKFAST AT TWILIGHT
Jan. 17, 1953. *Amazing*, July 1954.

There you are in your home, and the soldiers smash down the door and tell you you're in the middle of World War III. Something's gone wrong with time. I like to fiddle with the idea of basic categories of reality, such as space and time, breaking down. It's my love of chaos, I suppose. (1976)

A PRESENT FOR PAT
Jan. 17, 1953. *Startling Stories*, Jan. 1954.

THE HOOD MAKER ('IMMUNITY')
Jan. 26, 1953. *Imagination*, June 1955.

OF WITHERED APPLES
Jan. 26, 1953. *Cosmos Science Fiction and Fantasy*, July 1954.

HUMAN IS
Feb. 2, 1953. *Startling Stories*, Winter 1955.

To me, this story states my early conclusions as to what is human. I have not really changed my view since I wrote this story, back in the Fifties. It's not what you look like, or what planet you were born on. It's how kind you are. The quality of kindness, to me, distinguishes us from rocks and sticks and metal, and will forever, whatever shape we take, wherever we go, whatever we become. For me, 'Human Is' is my credo. May it be yours. (1976)

ADJUSTMENT TEAM

Feb. 11, 1953. *Orbit Science Fiction*, Sept.-Oct. 1954.

THE IMPOSSIBLE PLANET ('LEGEND')

Feb. 11, 1953. *Imagination*, Oct. 1953.

IMPOSTOR

Feb. 24, 1953. *Astounding*, June 1953.

Here was my first story on the topic of: Am I a human? Or am I just programmed to believe I am human? When you consider that I wrote this back in 1953, it was, if I may say so, a pretty damn good new idea in sf. Of course, by now I've done it to death. But the theme still preoccupies me. It's an important theme because it forces us to ask: What is a human? And–what isn't? (1976)

JAMES P. CROW

Mar. 17, 1953. *Planet Stories*, May 1954.

PLANET FOR TRANSIENTS ('THE ITINERANTS')

Mar. 23, 1953. *Fantastic Universe*, Oct.-Nov. 1953. [Parts of this story were adapted for the novel *Deus Irae*.]

SMALL TOWN ('ENGINEER')

Mar. 23, 1953. *Amazing*, May 1954.

Here the frustrations of a defeated small person–small in terms of power, in particular power over others–gradually become transformed into something sinister: the force of death. In rereading this story (which is of course a fantasy, not science fiction) I am impressed by the subtle change which takes place in the protagonist from Trod-Upon to Treader. Verne Haskel initially appears as the prototype of the impotent human being, but this conceals a drive at his core self which is anything but weak. It is as if I am saying, The put-upon person may be very dangerous. Be careful as to how you misuse him; he may be a mask for thanatos: the antagonist of life; he may not secretly wish to rule; he may wish to destroy. (1979)

SOUVENIR

Mar. 26, 1953. *Fantastic Universe*, Oct. 1954.

SURVEY TEAM
Apr. 3, 1953. *Fantastic Universe*, May 1954.

PROMINENT AUTHOR
Apr. 20, 1953. *If*, May 1954.

FAIR GAME
Apr. 21, 1953. *If*, Sept. 1959.

THE HANGING STRANGER
May 4, 1953. *Science Fiction Adventures*, Dec. 1953.

THE EYES HAVE IT
May 13, 1953. *Science Fiction Stories*, no. 1, 1953.

THE GOLDEN MAN ('THE GOD WHO RUNS')
June 24, 1953. *If*, Apr. 1954.

In the early Fifties much American science fiction dealt with human mutants and their glorious super-powers and super-faculties by which they would presently lead mankind to a higher state of existence, a sort of Promised Land. John W. Campbell, Jr, editor of Analog, *demanded that the stories he bought deal with such wonderful mutants, and he also insisted that the mutants always be shown as (1) good; and (2) firmly in charge. When I wrote 'The Golden Man' I intended to show that (1) the mutant might not be good, at least good for the rest of mankind, for us ordinaries; and (2) not in charge but sniping at us as a bandit would, a feral mutant who potentially would do us more harm than good. This was specifically the view of psionic mutants that Campbell loathed, and the theme in fiction that he refused to publish . . . so my story appeared in* If.

We sf writers of the Fifties liked If *because it had high-quality paper and illustrations; it was a classy magazine. And, more important, it would take a chance with unknown authors. A fairly large number of my early stories appeared in* If*; for me it was a major market. The editor of* If *at the beginning was Paul W. Fairman. He would take a badly-written story by you and rework it until it was okay–which I appreciated. Later James L. Quinn the publisher became himself the editor, and then Frederik Pohl. I sold to all three of them.*

In the issue of If *that followed the publishing of 'The Golden Man' appeared a two-page editorial consisting of a letter by a lady school teacher complaining about 'The Golden Man.' Her complaints consisted of John W. Campbell, Jr's complaint: she upbraided me for presenting mutants in a negative light and she offered the notion that certainly we could expect mutants to be (1) good; and (2) firmly in charge. So I was back to square one.*

My theory as to why people took this view is: I think these people secretly imagined they were themselves early manifestations of these kindly, wise, super-intelligent Übermenschen *who would guide the stupid–i.e. the rest of us–to the Promised Land. A power phantasy was involved here, in my opinion. The idea of the psionic superman taking over was a role that appeared originally in Stapleton's* Odd John *and A. E. van Vogt's* Slan. *'We are persecuted now,' the message ran, 'and despised and rejected. But later on, boy oh boy, will we show them!'*

As far as I was concerned, for psionic mutants to rule us would be to put the fox in charge of the hen house. I was reacting to what I considered a dangerous hunger for power on the part of neurotic people, a hunger which I felt John W. Campbell, Jr was pandering to–and deliberately so. If, *on the other hand, was not committed to selling any one particular idea; it was a magazine devoted to genuinely new ideas, willing to take any side of an issue. Its several editors should be commended, inasmuch as they understood the real task of science fiction: to look in* all *directions without restraint.* (1979)

Here I am also saying that mutants are dangerous to us ordinaries, a view which John W. Campbell, Jr. deplored. We were supposed to view them as our leaders. But I always felt uneasy as to how they would view us. I mean, maybe they wouldn't want *to lead us. Maybe from their superevolved lofty level we wouldn't seem worth leading. Anyhow, even if they agreed to lead us, I felt uneasy as to where we would wind up going. It might have something to do with buildings marked* Showers *but which really weren't.* (1978)

THE TURNING WHEEL

July 8, 1953. *Science Fiction Stories*, no. 2, 1954.

THE LAST OF THE MASTERS ('PROTECTION AGENCY')

July 15, 1953. *Orbit Science Fiction*, Nov.-Dec. 1954.

Now I show trust of robot as leader, a robot who is the suffering servant, which is to say a form of Christ. Leader as servant of man: leader who should be dispensed with–perhaps. An ambiguity hangs over the morality of this story. Should we have a leader or should we think for ourselves? Obviously the latter, in principle. But–sometimes there lies a gulf between what is theoretically right and that which is practical. It's interesting that I would trust a robot and not an android. Perhaps it's because a robot does not try to deceive you as to what it is. (1978)

THE FATHER-THING

July 21, 1953. *Fantasy & Science Fiction*, Dec. 1954.

I always had the impression, when I was very small, that my father was two people, one good, one bad. The good father goes away and the bad father replaces him. I guess many kids have this feeling. What if it were so? This story is another instance of a normal feeling, which is in fact incorrect, somehow becoming correct... with the added misery that one cannot communicate it to others. Fortunately, there are other kids to tell it to. Kids understand: they are wiser than adults–hmmm, I almost said, 'Wiser than humans.' (1976)

STRANGE EDEN ('IMMOLATION')
Aug. 4, 1953. *Imagination*, Dec. 1954.

TONY AND THE BEETLES
Aug. 31, 1953. *Orbit Science Fiction*, no. 2, 1953.

NULL-O ('LOONY LEMUEL')
Aug. 31, 1953. *If*, Dec. 1958.

TO SERVE THE MASTER ('BE AS GODS!')
Oct. 21, 1953. *Imagination*, Feb. 1956.

EXHIBIT PIECE
Oct. 21, 1953. *If*, Aug. 1954.